Rain, Steam and Speed

Allissa Oldenberg

Grosvenor House
Publishing Limited

This book is published by
Grosvenor House Publishing Ltd
Link House
140 The Broadway, Tolworth, Surrey, KT6 7HT.
www.grosvenorhousepublishing.co.uk

A CIP record for this book
is available from the British Library

ISBN 978-1-80381-939-6
eBook ISBN 978-1-80381-940-2

For my brother

Having ridden his 250cc Honda up the scaffolding plank, used as a ramp across the two steps from path to road, Owen Linton-House set the bike on its stand under the overhanging branches of a large cherry tree. In the time it took him to carry the plank and lay it down against the bottom of the wall, at the side of the house, the dripping branches had made his saddle wet. After closing the gate, he rubbed off the worst, with the sleeve of his jacket, acknowledged his sister, who was watching through the living room window, and rode off, in the direction of Wateringbury. If he was lucky, he would arrive in Caterham, before the next weather front closed in, although as he was driving towards the darkening horizon, a dry outcome was unlikely. Helen went into the kitchen to make some cheese on toast.

Glancing at the calendar, hanging on the back of the kitchen door, which Owen had given their mother, last Christmas, Helen noticed two things. Firstly, that the picture for the month was Joseph Mallord William Turner's *Rain, Steam and Speed*. Although Helen was a huge fan of Monet, she appreciated Turner's paintings as much, if not more. Secondly, 19th June 1979 was a due date for the cats' worming tablets. Cadbury, the chocolate-point Burmese, was a sucker for cheese, and never noticed his pill, when disguised as a lump of cheddar. Joey, on the other hand, a rather fetching ginger shorthair, was less inclined to take his medicine. He generally needed four hands, two to hold him with two more to prize open his jaws and push the tablet down his throat, close his mouth, and rub his chin until he swallowed. Despite this palaver, he regularly outwitted his owners, if only a partial victory, which lasted until the tablet was swept up from under the table or cupboard, the next morning, and the process repeated.

Tomorrow would be Owen's eighteenth birthday. What Helen could not have appreciated at the time, was that 19th June 1979 would be the last time she saw her brother, for twelve years. Had she known, it is hard to imagine how she might have felt, or what she might have done. The last few months had been difficult. After all the sacrifices the family had made, Owen had been expelled from school. Perhaps the outcome was more lenient than it could have been. Although he was expelled, they allowed him to take his 'A' levels, and they made a point of not informing the university. Beyond exam trips to Tonbridge, Owen had spent the last few weeks in his room, revising, avoiding his parents. He had no intention of spending the summer at home. He wanted to go and build his life, somewhere other than in the shadow of his parents' pagoda.

The image was an interesting reflection on his life. After eighteen months, without any word from Owen, Gail and Ben Linton-House had decided to clear Owen's belongings and turn his room into a guest bedroom. Before all Owen's stuff was boxed up or discarded, Helen had sneaked into his desk, a rather fetching, although second hand, walnut-veneered bureau, with the key still in the lock, and discovered an exercise book, containing Owen's poetry. That is where Helen read the words, 'Why must you build your life in the shadow of your parents' pagoda?'.

When finally, his search to cast his own shadow came to an end, Helen received the first of two phone calls in her life, she would never forget. It was twelve years, since Helen had heard Owen's voice, since any of the family had contact from him. Around ten o'clock, one evening in May 1991, the home phone rang.

"There's someone here who wants to speak to you," Ben informed his daughter.

The deep, ex-patriot voice Helen heard next was unfamiliar to her.

"Hello, Sweetheart. How are you?"

For a split second, she did not know what to think or say, which caused her to ask a somewhat daft question.

"Are you in the UK?"

"Yes, I'm at Mummy and Daddy's. We've already started the bottle of cognac I bought."

"Stay up. I'm leaving now. I should get to you by one-thirty, two o'clock."

"See you soon."

Helen grabbed some clothes and her wallet. The journey from Nottingham to Kent, at that time of night, was clear, although when she reached the M25, the surface water suggested some quite heavy rain. Three and a half hours later she pulled up next to the back-garden gate and went into the Linton-Houses' living room for a long overdue family reunion. Owen, Ben, and Gail had already polished off most of the bottle of cognac. Helen was not the slightest bit offended as she did not much like cognac, other than as flavouring in brandy sauce, or flaming a Christmas pudding. She hugged Owen, hardly able to believe her eyes.

Over the next few weeks and months, Owen visited Helen, in Nottingham, on several occasions, hitching a lift north, and being collected from the hotel at Junction 25 or similar destination if he could not get a ride into Nottingham. She helped him create a curriculum vitae which encapsulated the skills and experience he had gained over the last decade, without revealing secrets, official or unofficial. He shared with Helen, his adventures, since he rode off on his Honda 250, the day before his eighteenth birthday.

The second phone call came almost exactly a year later, at the end of May. Helen was heavily pregnant, when the phone rang, shortly after eight o'clock in the morning. This time it was her mother.

"Sit down."

Helen did not argue, but she knew in her stomach that something was wrong. She sat down.

"Owen crashed his motorcycle last night and died."

Helen was stunned.

"He was on his way home. He hit a gate post. The police came here and asked if we could go and identify him, at the scene, as it was only a mile up the road. The ambulanceman said he would have died instantly. There was no other vehicle involved."

"But he only came home a year ago."

"I know. There will have to be an inquest, so we won't be able to plan a funeral."

"Oh. OK."

The inquest concluded that it was an accidental death, Owen having four times the legal limit of alcohol in his blood. When the arrangements were made, Gail would not allow Helen to attend the funeral, because she was so close to her due date, and travelling for such an emotionally difficult event was unwise. Apparently, it rained all day. In the end, the baby was ten days overdue. Helen's contractions started the day before what would have been Owen's birthday, and to Helen's relief, after thirty-six hours in labour, Emily was born at one-thirty in the morning, the day after Owen should have turned thirty-one.

On several occasions, in the years before those two phone calls, during Owen's self-imposed exile, Helen chose the unadventurous course of action. She told herself this was out of a sense of not wanting to heap further disappointment on her parents, but maybe it was just fear. Owen was either foolhardy or courageous. It turned out he was both, in equal measure, which is why Helen decided to write his story. This would be her third novel, since becoming Helen Painter, and starting her new life in France. She wanted her brother to be remembered for all he had accomplished, and not simply for the mistakes he had made. After all, they had both grown up during the intervening years.

The more of Owen's poetry Helen read, the more she gained perspective on the brother she hardly knew. He had a tremendous grasp of the English language, rich creativity, and had been badly hurt by a girl. Most significant, though, was his perspective on his own life. He had felt under so much pressure, to live his parents' dreams and ambitions. At the age of nine, they had entered him, on the primary school's recommendation, in a countywide competition for a scholarship. The prizes were two fully paid places as Yardley Court Preparatory School, followed by fifty percent of the fees for Tonbridge School. Owen had been successful, to his parents' immense pride. They would cross the bridge of the other half of the Tonbridge School fees when they came to it, when Owen turned thirteen.

For the years he was at Yardley Court, Owen got up Monday to Saturday at six o'clock each morning, cycled two and a half miles to Marden train station, the nearest station to Collier Street, in all weathers, and home again each evening, arriving shortly after six o'clock. When the family moved to Yalding, the nearest station was Wateringbury, only a mile away, although up and down a steep hill. Although the cycle ride was shorter, the school day was longer, and since Owen had become involved with amateur dramatics and the Combined Cadet Force, three evenings a week he did not arrive home until a little after eight o'clock, which meant a very long day. As soon as Owen had eaten his tea, he would go to his room to do homework, after which, it was bath time and bedtime. The television, an unreliable black and white unit, which regularly required a bang of encouragement on the side, was only watched on Sundays. Occasionally, Owen would spend the weekend at the home of one or other of his two closest friends, Mason Somersby and Caleb Harris, even holidayed with Mason's family, but neither of them ever came to stay. Caleb visited once, the previous year, as a seventeen-year-old, with a Suzuki motorbike, and Helen developed a crush on him, much to Owen's annoyance.

It was hard to say, if the burden of his parents' educational aspirations for Owen justified the effort. He was a bright boy, which is why he had won a scholarship, and no doubt, he benefitted from smaller class sizes than his sister's secondary school. Would the connections he made, help him up the career ladder? Would attending a private school increase his chances of a place at Oxbridge? Owen had grown up in poverty, with Ben's illness rendering him unable to work, living in rented accommodation, not owning a car. Would social mobility be possible? How Ben and Gail had managed to pay the other half of the fees for Tonbridge School, Helen never knew, other than money always being short. When he was fifteen, Owen even went on a school trip to Russia. Helen remembered him being bought a new suitcase, as well as a smart jacket and trousers. Helen's trip to Beauvais, a couple of years later, involved the same suitcase, and no new clothes.

Ben never attended parents' evenings, but Gail would make the twice-yearly trip to Tonbridge. She also went along to all of Owen's school plays, often, just making the last train back. With her received pronunciation and general knowledge, Gail could carry off the social chit-chat with teachers and other parents, so long as the subjects of careers and acquisitions were avoided. Ben would have found it harder, although, he was uncomfortable in most social situations. It was clear from Owen's poetry, that he felt he belonged in the context, a lot less than Gail.

Owen took fourth term Oxbridge entrance exams, unsuccessfully, and went on to achieve 'A' levels in French, Russian, History and General Studies, with high enough grades to secure his place at the School of Slavonic and Eastern European Studies (SSEES). Too embarrassed and ashamed to live at home, until the start of the university term, he had made the decision, to sleep at friends' houses, over the summer. His overnight bag, stuffed in the top-box of his motorbike, gave no indication that he would not be coming home. In his mind, it was better this way.

Helen and Owen were born twenty months apart. Up until
Owen started at Tonbridge School, they wavered between
fighting tooth and nail or playing nicely together, although it
was never long before the playing gave way to squabbling.
They shared a bedroom until Helen was eight, and Gail
decorated half the attic, the half that was a room with a door.
Helen's new quarters gave her space and independence, and
more importantly, a sense of equality. Owen was older, and
he was a boy. The reality was that Helen felt she was treated
as second-best. Once Owen started at Tonbridge School,
they mostly kept out of each other's way.

The irony, concerning Helen's feelings about favouritism,
was that Owen was neither sporty nor practical, two things
which their father was. It was Helen who played for the
school, and later, Kent-county hockey team. It was Helen
who was Daddy's little helper, on Ben's do-it-yourself
projects, and as she grew up and gained skills and strength,

it was Helen who helped in the garden or with decorating tasks, in ways that Owen simply could not. Ben once went along as a spectator to a Kent Under 18 hockey match against Hampshire, bizarrely, on the pitches of Tonbridge School, and watched Helen score an amazing goal. So, once Owen had left home for good, Helen came to feel her role was to make up for Owen's failure.

Unlike Owen, she navigated the state system of education and came away with some 'O' levels, 'A' levels, and a place at Nottingham University. Would having similar opportunities to Owen have made any difference to her grades? Unlike Owen, Helen never touched drugs. Even before he had left home for Caterham and university, Owen had dabbled in cannabis and magic mushrooms.

One brief moment of adolescent solidarity shared by Owen and Helen was the day Ben discovered a tiny ball of resin in Owen's room. Helen knew he had placed it in one of the pair of candlesticks on the mantlepiece, and she had swapped it for an equally sized rabbit dropping, returning the cannabis to her brother, much to his appreciation. Psychologists may differ in their opinions on whether cannabis and magic mushrooms can lead to heroin, as the family would one day learn was Owen's case. After he left home, he became a heroin addict. So it was, in the summer of 1979, that whilst Helen settled into an extended summer vacation of picking strawberries, cherries and runner beans, enough to by her own 50cc Honda, before embarking on sixth form, Owen finished sixth form, tried to numb his pain with drugs, and began to chart his own course in life.

As anticipated, Owen rode into oncoming rain, just past Wrotham, heading along the A25, and arrived at the party soaked. Padlocking his motorcycle in the driveway, he grabbed his overnight bag from the top-box, replaced it with his helmet and rang the bell.

"Yikes, Owen, you look like a drowned rat," Francis greeted him.

"Thank you. I don't suppose I could use your shower."

"Of course. Make yourself at home."

Owen went in, removing his boots in the doorway. Francis picked up Owen's boots and started to walk towards the kitchen.

"I'll put these in the garage, out of everyone's way."

"Thanks."

"Shower's upstairs, second door on the left. First door on the left is the airing cupboard, where you'll find the towels. We can put your wet clothes in the washing machine. You're staying over for a few nights, anyway."

"I am. Thanks a bunch. See you shortly."

Owen ran up the stairs, chose a towel from the airing cupboard and went for a quick shower. When he came downstairs, he stuck his head round the sitting-room door to find the party in full swing. Santana, *Abraxas*, was playing, loudly, and some individuals he did not know were smoking a joint. Owen went into the kitchen and poured half a glass of vodka, topped up with orange juice.

"Owen, for God's sake, what did you get caught for?" asked Dominic, ironically.

Dominic Andrews was one of the Whitworth house prefects, at Tonbridge School, and would be heading off to Oxford in September.

"It is what it is. Still think I was providing a useful service in an all-boys school. I probably got off lightly."

"You're still going to SSEES then?"

"Yep. They didn't inform the university."

"How lucky are you."

"I know. Do you know if anyone else from our year is coming, tonight?"

"No idea. Francis seems to have various different circles of friends. It's early yet."

"OK. Catch up later."

Owen disappeared into the sitting room and sat down on the floor, leaning against the wall. One of the strangers offered him the joint, which he accepted, taking a short, sharp drag, and handing it back. Just then, there was an almighty crash, in the hallway. Owen got up from his perch on the floor and went over to the door. A sixth former he recognised from school, although did not know his name, was lying in a heap on the floor, with a girl leaning over the banister looking down on him. Owen knelt on the floor, next to the sixth former.

"You OK, mate?"

There was no response. Owen put his cheek near his mouth.

"He said he could fly," explained the girl.

"You mean he fell over the banister?"

"Yes."

"He's breathing. I don't want to move him, because he might have broken his back, or worse, his neck."

By now Francis had arrived in the hallway, and Dominic was standing in the kitchen doorway.

"Christ!" he exclaimed.

"Phone for an ambulance Francis," insisted Owen. "I'll stay here with him."

"Have you and Richard been taking mushrooms, Mandy?" Francis asked the girl.

She nodded, sheepishly. Francis went into the sitting-room and turned off the music.

"Guys. Get rid of the evidence. I'm phoning for an ambulance. Open the windows. Make sure there are no roaches, lying on the floor. If you need to scram, scram. They're bound to ask questions and might call the police. Actually, I think you should all leave. Apologies. We've got less than ten minutes, probably eight."

He went back into the hallway and dialled 999. Owen could hear one side of the conversation. Francis managed to avoid the subject of drugs for now. He simply offered falling from the stairs as an explanation. When he got off the phone, Francis looked up at Mandy, who was sitting on the top stair, hugging her knees, shivering and crying.

"Is there any evidence of the mushrooms? Never mind. Just go and check there's no evidence. Flush anything down the toilet. Go into Richard's room, put yourself to bed, and sleep it off. I'll bring you some sugary tea in a bit, just in case you're still awake."

Mandy nodded, again, stood up, and went along the landing.

Owen could hear the toilet flush upstairs, followed by a door closing. Richard was still breathing, but unconscious. Francis checked the other bedrooms and flushed the toilet a second time. He hoped Richard did not have a secret hiding place somewhere in his room in case the police came with a warrant. Back downstairs, he went into the sitting room. The others had heeded his instructions and left. Francis did a quick check, under the furniture. The smell of cannabis still hung in the air. He lit a patchouli oil dispenser on the mantlepiece. Dominic, who had gone back into the kitchen, came out carrying two mugs of tea. He handed one to Owen and the other to Francis, who had come back out into the hallway. Francis took the tea upstairs and put it on the bedside table, next to Mandy.

"What do you want me to do? Should I stay or leave?" asked Dominic, when Francis reached the bottom of the stairs.

"Are you sober? No drugs in your system?"

"Yes, I'm sober. No, I haven't touched any drugs."

"It's up to you. If you stay, we need to get our stories straight?"

"They're bound to find out, at the hospital."

"I know. By the time the police get involved, I'm hoping we'll be in the clear. There's nothing else in the house. At least I can't find anything obvious. I'll just say I don't know what Richard and Mandy were doing upstairs. Which is true, mostly. I mean, I didn't know they had mushrooms. Owen, can you start tidying away the glasses and bottles, too, please?"

"Sure."

Francis followed Dominic into the kitchen and helped with the drying up. Just then, they heard the siren. A blue flashing light pulled up in front of the house. Francis went to the door, opened it, and stood waiting.

"Good evening. We haven't moved him. We think he fell over the banister. He's unconscious but breathing."

"Does he have a name?"

"Richard Lovatt."

"What time did this happen?"

"About ten minutes ago, maybe fifteen. I mean, we were checking him over before we phoned for the ambulance."

"And you are?"

"Francis Grey. This is my house. Well, it's not my house, as such, it's a rented, shared house. I was the one who phoned for an ambulance. He lives here, too."

By now, one of the two paramedics had started to check over Richard Lovatt and carefully fixed a neck brace, before the two of them gently manoeuvred him onto a stretcher.

"Is he going to be alright?" asked Owen.

"Let's hope so. It's way too early to tell. It will be helpful to saving your friend's life if you are honest with us. Have you been taking drugs?"

"I think he may have taken some mushrooms, but we were downstairs at the time and only heard the crash. Two of us had a joint, for personal use only."

"Thank you. We have no interest in whether you were breaking the law or not. Just in the contents of your friend's bloodstream. Being under the influence, when falling over the banister, may have saved him from more serious harm, because the chances are, he would have been relaxed."

"Oh. Good. I mean, let's hope he's OK," stuttered Owen.

The paramedics lifted the stretcher, carried Richard Lovatt to the ambulance, and sped off with their blue lights flashing and sirens whining.

"I'm going to have to tell any latecomers that the party's off," reflected Francis, with a certain frustration. "Better go and check on Mandy, upstairs."

Owen poured himself a double shot of vodka, topped it up with orange juice, downed it in one go, said goodbye to Dominic, assuming he would be gone, in the morning, and went to bed. The alcohol took effect, and he drifted off to sleep but woke at just gone two o'clock. Having crept to the bathroom, not flushed the toilet, and crept back to bed, he lay there, unable to sleep. His head was whirring with what had happened, the decision he had made, his lack of means, what it would be like at SSEES, with the third year spent somewhere in Russia, whether he even wanted to go to university. It was another of those things his parents had aspired to. No one ever asked him if he wanted to go. It was just assumed he would go to university. Not that he was sure what he could do instead. It would have been nice to make himself a mug of tea, but he was in someone else's house, and did not want to wake anyone else up. There was not much he could do to change his current situation, not until his grant cheque came through, at the start of term. Although Francis had said he was welcome to stay, he did not want to overstay his welcome.

For several months now, Owen's room at Commonwealth Hall had been reserved. All that was required for confirmation, was his results, securing his place on the course. Owen realised he would have to go to Tonbridge to find out his 'A' level results. He certainly did not want them posting to his parents' house, even though he was unsure if he would be welcome at the school. He would turn up on the morning of the results day, as soon as the doors opened, and hopefully, no one would question his being there. Owen's mind turned to more practical things, like his lack of clothes. He had only two pairs of jeans, two T-shirts, two pairs of pairs of underpants and two pairs of socks. It would mean daily washing of underwear and weekly washing of T-shirts and jeans. At least he had antiperspirant in his bag. Toothpaste and soap he would have to borrow, until he went shopping, which he would do today.

At some point, he must have fallen back to sleep, because he was woken up by an alarm in the adjacent bedroom. Who sets their alarm for seven o'clock, on the weekend? That was when Owen remembered it had been a mid-week party, to celebrate the end of exams, and today was Wednesday. It was also his eighteenth birthday, and a wave of depression washed over him. When he got up at seven-fifteen, Mandy was in the kitchen, making toast.

"How are you?" he enquired.

"Alright. Do you know where Richard is?"

"You mean you can't remember what happened?"

"I know he fell from the stairs, and I went to bed."

"He was taken off in an ambulance. I don't know which hospital. Maybe Francis will know, but I'm guessing he's still asleep."

"Is Richard OK?" she persisted.

"I have no idea. Can you stick a couple of slices under the grill, for me, please?"

Mandy replaced her toast with two slices of bread, for Owen.

"Do you want a coffee?" he asked, topping up the kettle and switching it on.

"Please."

Owen grabbed two mugs from the mug tree. The coffee, tea and sugar were in matching containers, next to the kettle.

"Sugar?"

"Two, thanks."

When the kettle boiled, he made them each a coffee and buttered his toast.

"I'm going to take a ride into the Big Smoke today. It's my eighteenth, and I feel like I should do something to celebrate. The National Gallery is free, as are the Science and Natural History museums. I might take a detour and go see where my hall of residence will be."

"Happy birthday."

"Thanks. It doesn't feel like it, just at this moment."

"You not celebrating with your family?"

The direct, but perfectly reasonable question, caused Owen to feel sick, in the pit of his stomach.

"It's complicated."

Mandy was about to say something, when the toilet flushed, upstairs.

"Francis must be up. You can ask him about the hospital.

A sleepy Francis appeared in the kitchen doorway.

"Morning."

"Good morning, Francis. Did you know it's Owen's eighteenth birthday, today?"

"I didn't. Happy birthday, mate."

"Owen says you might know where Richard is."

"You can phone the hospital. If he's not local, they might be able to tell you where he's gone. What are you going to do to celebrate your eighteenth, Owen?"

"I'm going to go into London and visit a museum or a gallery. They're free. Then, I'm going to check out Commonwealth Hall. And I'm going to buy some toiletries. Is there anything else I should buy?"

"No, thanks. Unless you want a cake. You're welcome to eat the food in my fridge and cupboards, but I'm not making you a cake!"

They all laughed. Owen finished his toast and coffee.

"I'm used to finding my way round London with the Underground map. I don't suppose you have a street-map?"

"Wait up."

Francis rummaged in a drawer and pulled out an A to Z of London.

"There you go."

"Thanks. Are my boots in the garage, still?"

"Yes. Hopefully they've dried out," replied Francis, pointing at the door out into the garage. Shall I do a wash-load for you?

"Oh, right. Yes, thanks. Wait. No, just show me how to use the machine, now, before I head off?"

"Of course."

The machine was in the garage, where Owen's boots were. The lining felt dry, but the leather was still damp. He did not have proper motorcycle boots, just a tired pair of leather jack boots. Francis showed him where the washing powder was, and which setting to put it on.

"Honestly, I'm happy to hang it out for you, when your washing's finished."

"Cheers."

Owen followed Francis back in from the garage, carried his boots to the front door, and took his jacket from the coat hooks.

"Where's your helmet?" asked Mandy.

"Hopefully, still in my top-box."

"See you later," said Francis.

"Yeah. See you later. Bye."

Owen rode through the commuter traffic, weaving in and out of the cars. Central London could be a bit scary for a motorcycle rider and Owen had only attempted the journey once before. He rode along by Trafalgar Square and parked his Honda next to St Martin-in-the-Fields church, figuring it would be safe there. Crossing the road, he entered the National Gallery and stood looking at the floor plan. He particularly wanted to see the paintings by Turner, Van Gogh and Monet, and paid little attention to all the other paintings he walked past. As he passed the various paintings it occurred to Owen that the last time he had visited an art gallery was the Hermitage in St Petersburg, or Leningrad as it was called, when he visited the city. If he was not feeling bad enough already, he remembered the sacrifices his family had made for him to go on the school trip to Russia.

Owen came to the Turner paintings and stood for a while in front of *The Fighting Temeraire*, and *Rain, Steam and*

Speed. He remembered something his General Studies teacher had said about Turner being ahead of his time, in terms of recognising technology as a legitimate subject for painting. Owen knew very little about art, but he could tell that Turner's skill enabled his industrial subjects to come alive. Although he had seen pictures of *Rain, Steam and Speed*, previously, including on the calendar in his parents' kitchen, Owen had never noticed the rabbits before. Or were they hares? It would make sense for them to be hares. Hares are speedy creatures. On closer inspection, Owen realised he had not noticed the boat before, either. The quality of light, the colours, the textures, and the atmosphere, of dirty rain and smog, were superb. In that moment, Owen told himself, he would one day visit the Louvre in Paris and the Rijksmuseum in Amsterdam.

Having satisfied his present hunger for art, Owen left the gallery, got back on his motorcycle, and rode to Cartwright Gardens, to investigate Commonwealth Hall. According to the information he had received, all his meals would be provided. It did not look so bad, although he had not seen inside a room. He wondered if he should go in and ask, although he knew that the building was used for conferences in the holidays. June 20th was not yet the end of term, so maybe he could see inside a room. He rested his Honda on its stand, removed his helmet, and went into the building. There was no one around who looked official enough to ask, so he turned and left. As he sat back on his motorcycle, he thought he would visit the Science Museum, in South Kensington.

A rumbling in his stomach indicated he was hungry, so he considered buying chips, if he passed a fish and chip shop, which he did. The great thing about a motorcycle was you could wheel it onto the pavement and park it on its stand, long enough to nip into any shop. He bought a portion of chips, with lashings of salt and vinegar, and a can of cola. Sitting astride his motorcycle, he ate his lunch, getting off again, to place the wrapper and empty can in a bin. Next stop, South Kensington. Inspired by the Turner paintings, Owen was fascinated to see some of the machinery from the industrial revolution, and wondered how it was, that his strengths lay in modern languages, rather than science.

After an enjoyable couple of hours wandering around the exhibits, Owen used the facilities, and got back on his motorcycle. Getting out the A to Z, he plotted a route back to Caterham, the first phase of which waffled through Chelsea and over the Battersea Bridge. Curious to see up close, the famous power station, made familiar to Owen by the cover sleeve to Pink Floyd's Animals album, with its inflatable pink pig, he took a short detour. No 'pigs on the wing' today. He smiled to himself. The only things he knew about Battersea were the dogs' home and the power station. Heading south, he rode past several boarded-up properties, and an idea started to crystalize in Owen's head. Why spend £300 a term on accommodation, when he could live in a squat for free? Even with gas, electric and water bills, it would be vastly cheaper, and he still was not sure that he was going to see his university course through to the end. For now, he would not say anything to Francis, but this week or next, he would return to Battersea, and find himself a squat.

When Owen returned to Battersea, he rode round the area several times, taking in the geography, looking at the environment, the litter, the condition of the houses, trying to identify where might be the safest area to live in, always assuming a squat was available. In the end, he settled on a property on John Parker Square, just off the Thomas Baines Road. His plan was to gain access, to remove the boards and have the locks changed, to get gas and electricity re-connected and register to pay his water rates. The more 'normal' his existence, the less attention he would attract. Pretty certain the property belonged to Wandsworth Borough Council, he was sure they would not notice for a while. If they were to discover someone was living in their property, rent-free, he would try to convince them it was an administrative oversight, and if that failed, he had squatters' rights on his side.

He would stick it out at university for at least the first term so that he could bank the grant cheque. This would give him a cushion, whilst he worked on ways of generating income. Between now and September, he would do odd jobs. The New Covent Garden Market was just up the road, and he could lift and carry, or he could deliver takeaways, or work as a waiter in a local restaurant. He had a balance of £207.36 in his bank account, which would cover gas, electricity, and food until the start of the university term. He would buy a suit, shirt, tie, and smart shoes, in one of the many charity shops, and he would approach a local charity supporting homeless people, in order to acquire some furniture, a fridge and a cooker, even a few pots and pans.

There was no time like the present, so he parked his motorcycle and scoured the charity shops for his suit, shirt, tie, and shoes. With his purchases made, he got changed in the public toilets, packing his T-shirt and jeans into the top-box. At a local hardware store, he bought both flathead and Phillips screwdrivers and returned to John Parker Square. Looking as official as he felt he could, he removed the boards covering the windows of a first-floor flat and forced the lock. Once inside, he had a brief look round, realised there was no gas, only electric storage heaters and cooker connection, noted down the electricity meter reading, and left, closing the door behind him.

Immediately, he went to a key-cutting shop and enquired about a locksmith, explaining his dilemma as losing his keys and arriving home drunk, the night before. If the shopkeeper had any suspicions, he kept them to himself, disappeared into the back room, and was followed out by a man who introduced himself as a locksmith. Owen paid £12.50 cash, and within three quarters of an hour, was the proud keyholder of a first-floor flat on John Parker Square. He would return to Caterham, borrow a sleeping bag from Francis, thank him for his hospitality, and move into his squat. After going down to his motorbike for his clothes, Owen changed back into his jeans and T-shirt, locked the door, and returned to where he had parked his Honda. Removing helmet, boots, and jacket from the top-box, he replaced them with his smart clothes, and set off for Caterham.

Francis was cooking potatoes, when he arrived, to go with some chicken and ham pies.

"Hi. Have you heard how Richard is?"

"As far as I know, he's been transferred to Stoke Mandeville."

"That is not good news, if my understanding of their expertise in orthopaedics is correct."

"No. It's very bad news, although not without some long-term hope of rehabilitation. So, if you want to move in, officially, you're welcome."

"Actually, there's something I need to talk to you about. I've been working on future plans, and I've got myself a squat in Battersea. It's a nice, dry, first floor flat, and I've already had the locks changed. I was wondering if you had a sleeping bag I could borrow, until I get some furniture and things."

"You're full of surprises. You can borrow a sleeping bag and blanket, and I reckon I can spare a towel. What are you going to do about utilities?"

"There's no gas. I just need to set up the electricity in my name. They don't ask for proof of tenancy. I'll get a job, as a waiter or something, until term starts. It's summer, so I'm not expecting it to be cold. I can eat sandwiches, until I get a cooker. There's lots of local charity shops."

Francis thought for a moment or two.

"Would you like a mug, a plate, a dish and a knife, fork and spoon, for your first few days?"

"Thank you. Really appreciate your giving me a roof over my head and helping me get settled under a roof of my own."

"You're welcome. I'll come and visit when you're sorted."

"Be my guest."

"You're surely not going back there this evening?"

"Not if I can stay here tonight. I'll leave first thing, which will give me the whole day to sort out electricity and anything else I need."

"Would you like to make the phone call from here, before you go?"

"That would be helpful. Thank you. How's Mandy coping, by the way?"

"I haven't seen her. When she left, I told her to get in touch if she needed any help. She hasn't got in touch."

When he got up, the following morning, Owen made the call to the London Electricity Board, and succeeded in getting the account transferred to his name. Francis had already left for work, so Owen made sure the back door was locked, and exited by the front door, dropping it on the Yale latch. He had to attach the sleeping bag and blanket, which were in plastic bags, to the pillion seat, with bungee cords. Parking right next to the stairs up to his flat, he carried in his stuff, and having checked that the lights were working, locked the door and went in search of charity shops in and around Wandsworth.

"Is this a church charity?" asked Owen, entering his third charity shop of the day.

"Yes, but you don't have to be a churchgoer to receive care. How can we help? Are you looking for anything in particular?"

"I've just moved into my first flat, and to be honest, apart from a sleeping bag and something to eat and drink from, I've got nothing."

"No bed? No cooker? No fridge?"

"Nothing."

"Have you been homeless?"

"Friends' sofas. I can't live at home anymore."

"Then we'd better see if we can turn your house into a home. Are you living in the area?"

"Yes. John Parker Square. It's a one-bedroom flat, with a bathroom, living room and kitchen."

"I'll just call my colleague from out the back, and he can take you to the store, where you'll be able to select some furniture. We'll probably be able to deliver it for you as well, hopefully later this afternoon."

"Thank you so much."

"Jim! Can you come up front for a moment, please," she called.

A man, in his fifties, appeared through the plastic curtain.

"Jim, this gentleman has just moved into a flat, with nothing. Can you take him to the store and get him sorted out, please?"

"Hi, I'm Jim," the man said, extending his hand towards Owen.

"Owen House. Pleased to meet you," responded Owen, dropping the double-barrelled surname, and shaking Jim's hand.

"Come with me."

Jim led Owen through the plastic curtain, between shelves stacked with household items, out through the back door, to a van.

"Whatever household items we can't find at the store, we can pick up here," explained Jim as they climbed in.

"Great. Thanks."

Five minutes later, the van pulled into a yard where two men were loading a single bed onto the roof-rack of an estate car. Jim acknowledged them and parked the van to allow the car space to get by. Inside the store was an Aladdin's cave of second-hand furniture.

"We'll start at the beds and work our way round. Just tell me if I point to something that you don't need. Are you able to help lift, by the way?"

"Sure."

"In that case, we'll load up and take it straight round to your flat. What floor is it on?"

"First."

"Reckon you can help lift and carry up to the first floor?"

"Of course."

After three quarters of an hour, the van was packed with a single bed and mattress, a fridge, a cooker, a two-person table and two chairs, a two-seater settee, and a chest of drawers. They also loaded an electric kettle, a set of three saucepans, cooking utensils and cutlery, four plates, bowls and mugs, a frying pan, containers for tea, coffee and sugar, and two pillows. Jim checked the drawer at the bottom of the cooker to make sure there was a grill pan.

"We'll go back to the shop and pick up sheets and pillowcases, a couple of towels and tea towels, and some curtains.

"Thank you. This is so helpful."

"You're welcome."

Back at the shop, Jim led Owen into the storeroom and picked out the bed linen, towels, and curtains. He spotted a stereo cassette player.

"Would you like this?" he asked, kindly.

"Excellent, thank you," replied Owen, thinking he would get some cassettes when he could afford, having left his record collection at his parents' house.

"Did you walk here?" asked Jim.

"Yes."

"Well then, you can ride with me."

"I really am very grateful," responded Owen, climbing back into the passenger seat.

They drove the short distance to Owen's flat. Piece of furniture by piece of furniture, they unloaded the van, and carried the items up the stairs.

"Let us know if you need anything else, or if any of this stuff breaks. It's all been checked, but you never know."

"I will. Thank you, again."

Jim held out his hand again, and Owen shook it gratefully.

The van drove off, and Owen set about arranging his furniture and putting up the curtains, which was when he discovered there were no curtain hooks. The fridge was working, but Owen was not sure what to do about the cooker. There were two wires in the cable which hung from the back of the cooker, and two poles on the cooker point. He knew enough about electricity to switch off the power at the fuse box. What damage could he cause if he got the wires the wrong way round? Surely, there would simply be no circuit. Taking his Phillips screwdriver in hand, he attached the wires, switched the electricity back on and turned on one of the rings. Nothing. Owen repeated the process but fixed the wires the opposite way round. This time, the ring glowed red. Filling one of the saucepans with water, Owen set it on the hob to boil. He could not smell any burning rubber or plastic, so gave himself a pat on the back, for successfully installing his cooker. Having compiled a short shopping list, including curtain hooks, Owen made sure everything was turned off, and went out.

He bought the curtain hooks at the same store he had purchased his screwdrivers.

"Have you just moved house?" asked the man behind the counter.

Owen thought it was a little nosy, but he was probably just being friendly.

"Yes. Might be round for some paint, at some point."

At the supermarket, Owen bought coffee, tea, milk and sugar, bread, baked beans, eggs, butter, cheese, marmalade, orange juice, and a bottle of vodka. For the next few weeks, his diet would be simple. Back at the flat, he made a mug of coffee and set about hanging the curtains. Longer than the windows, the key thing was the curtains were wide enough. He now had some privacy in the bedroom and living room. The final thing to do was make the bed.

Owen sank back into his settee and wondered if he could afford to treat himself to just one cassette. It occurred to him that he might be able to get something agreeable at one of the charity shops he had visited earlier in the day. He would do the washing up and go out once more. No washing up liquid. Stupidly, he had forgotten to buy cleaning materials, so would have to go and get some. Another list was required because he really did not want to have to go out again, today. Washing up liquid, bleach, multi-surface cleaner, washing powder, scouring pads and cloths. Laughing at himself, he added 'cassette' at the bottom.

That evening, he cooked beans on toast, drank a glass of vodka and orange to celebrate, did the washing up, and listened to a Led Zeppelin cassette. He fell asleep on the settee, and chided himself, when he woke in the small hours, because the light was still on, and now, he had to pay for his electricity. He went to the toilet and got into bed, falling asleep to the thought that it was not much, but it was his first independent home, even if he was not paying rent. In the morning, he would tackle income generation, along with trying to source some cannabis, for personal use.

Owen got up at eight o'clock and made himself some toast. He put his suit, shirt, tie, and smart shoes on, and set off to find work. If he could not find work in Battersea, he would go further afield on his motorcycle, but he wanted to try and find something he could walk to. He noticed a couple of other motorcycles parked outside, and thought his motorcycle could be left safely, with its steering lock, chained to the structure or a metal fence post. No one else seemed to have bothered to attach their ride to anything, though.

Owen was not getting a lot of joy in the centre of Battersea, so he widened his search. When he walked into The Prince Albert, a man he guessed was the landlord, was stacking the glasses.

"Hi. I don't suppose you have any shifts I could cover. I'm new to the area and looking for work."

"Have you worked in a pub before?"

"I haven't worked anywhere before. Other than a few weeks fruit-picking, that is. Left school, a few weeks ago. I'm a quick learner and willing to work hard."

"Come in at six o'clock this evening, and you can do a trial shift."

"Wow, thanks. Should I wear suit, shirt and tie or jeans and T-shirt?"

"Smart-casual. Jeans are OK, but no trainers, and no T-shirts. Needs to be a shirt you can button up."

"Thanks. See you later."

Owen turned and walked out of the pub, feeling chuffed and relieved. Whatever misgivings he might have had, and been denying, about his project to move to Battersea, Owen seemed to have fallen on his feet. The flat was in good condition, he had been given all the furniture and household goods he needed, and now, he had the chance at a part time job. When he got back to the flat, he changed back into his jeans, washed his dirty shirts and underwear, and started to clean the kitchen and bathroom. Perhaps he should have cleaned the flat before moving all his stuff in, but he was not really the master of his own circumstances and was just happy to have found the furniture so quickly.

At five minutes to six he was back at The Prince Albert.

"Fill in this form, will you, please?" instructed the landlord, handing Owen a printed sheet of paper and a pen.

Writing down his address, he felt pride, even though he knew the council might discover his residency one day. Later rather than sooner, he hoped. When he got to the part where he needed a reference, he put, 'First job' and hoped they would not ask for the school contact details. Apart from thinking they would refuse a reference, due to his expulsion, he did not want anyone from his recent past knowing where he was living, now. He also did not know what his National Insurance number was. He would have to find a telephone directory, to know where the tax office was located.

"I hope that's OK. I will need a few days to get a National Insurance number, and I don't have a reference."

"Hmm. OK. I'll pay you cash in hand for tonight, and if I keep you on, cash in hand for the first few weeks until we can sort tax for you. As for the reference, we'll have to make do with what we see for ourselves."

"Thank you," replied Owen, feeling hopeful. "What would you like me to do first?"

The landlord pointed at the upside-down spirit bottles.

"Let's begin with the optics. See, this is how you dispense a measure," said the landlord, demonstrating with the gin. "That's fairly straightforward. Anything that doesn't have an optic, you need the measure, here. Make sure you rinse it out after you've used it, and check it is clean before you use it. What we need to work on, now, is pulling a pint. Watch!"

Owen watched while the landlord pulled the hand-pump into a slanting glass, slowly righting the glass as it filled up.

"We're aiming for a full glass, with the top half inch, frothy. It's the same thing with these pumps, but you lower the lever, rather than pull a pump. OK?"

Owen nodded.

"Now, you try."

Owen took an empty pint glass and pulled a perfect pint of bitter. The landlord smiled.

"If you hadn't told me you'd not done this before, I'd have said you'd done this before," he laughed.

Owen laughed too.

"Collect the glasses when there's a lull at the bar. You'll be on with someone else. Tonight, it's Vince. Here's the bottle opener," he added, pointing at the equipment attached to the side of the bar. Empty the beer troughs in the sink when they're full. Empty bottles go in this bin."

He was just about to show Owen the ice and the lemons, when Vince walked through the door.

"Vinnie, my mate. You've got a new bartender with you, tonight. Owen. He's new to bar work, but I already think he'll pick it up quickly. I'll leave him in your capable hands."

"OK, Mr Longstaff."

The landlord went into the back office. Vince was wearing black trousers and a black shirt, with the pub name embroidered over his left pectoral muscle.

"I'm Vince."

"I'm Owen. Pleased to meet you."

"I take it the boss has shown you the basics?"

"Yes."

"Any questions, just ask."

"I think Mr Longstaff was just about to say something about ice and lemons."

"Right. Chopping board and knife here. Lemons in the fridge. Ice in those two buckets. There's a freezer in the cellar. Maybe after closing, I'll show you the cellar. Did the boss show you how to work the till?"

"No."

"Fairly straightforward. We don't give receipts. This till-roll records the sales, so the boss can check we're not misbehaving. Press the exact amount for each drink and this is the total button. If the till-roll runs out, you can watch me change it. I reckon we've got two minutes until we open. Do you need to use the facilities or to get a drink of water?"

Not knowing if or when, he might get a break, Owen went to the toilet. When he came back, the landlord was unlocking the front door.

Owen soon realised that Vince knew most of the customers by name. It was not until the fifth customer, that Owen got a chance to put into practice his new skills.

"Keep one eye on the tables. If the customer leaves, go and grab the glasses. If the customer stays, you can go over and pass the time of day, as you collect the empties."

"Are most of the customers regulars?"

"In the week, yes. Fridays and Saturdays, there are loads of people I don't recognise."

Vince seemed nice enough. He introduced Owen to a couple of the regulars. As the pub became busier, both bartenders were serving, at the same time. They had to wait for each other to use the pumps on a few occasions. Halfway through the evening the bitter pump started to splutter.

"I'll go change the barrel," explained Vince. "Hold the fort! Tell anyone who asks for bitter, that it'll be back on, in two ticks."

As Vince went off to the cellar, Owen realised he was momentarily, in charge. It felt good. No one came to the bar, though, and Owen looked round the room. He saw a man hand something to another man and take a banknote from him. Was a drugs trade taking place? Did Mr Longstaff know this was happening? Owen resolved to say nothing but kept an eye on the men. Vince came back in and ran off a pint.

"Whenever you change the barrel, you always run off at least the first pint," he explained, pouring the pint down the sink.

Vince looked up and saw the man who had handed something over.

"Have you seen that bloke do anything suspicious?"

"Suspicious, as in hand something over and take some money for it?"

"Yes."

"He's been coming in here for the last three weeks, but it's impossible to catch him. I think he's dealing, but the last thing Mr Longstaff wants is a scene. Cocky bastard. The man, not Mr Longstaff. You'd think he'd have the decency to do it outside, or in the toilet, not in front of us. Hey! Do you smoke cannabis?"

The direct question threw Owen.

"I have done. You?"

"Want to know where to get it locally?"

"Maybe."

After a quarter of an hour or so, Vince handed a small, folded piece of paper to Owen.

"Stick that in your pocket," he whispered, winking.

"Thanks," Owen whispered back, slipping the paper in his back pocket.

For the rest of the evening, the man at the table entertained three different individuals, each time, exchanging something with them.

"Does Mr Longstaff know about him?"

"Yes, I think so."

"But he doesn't say anything?"

"He doesn't want the police in here, and if he challenged the bloke, it might cause a scene. There's some nasty incidents happen after dark round these parts. Organised crime, gangs, turf wars."

"Right. I grew up in a village. Never come across that sort of thing before."

"Watch your back, and if you can't be good, be safe!"

"I'll try."

"It's ten to eleven. Do you want to shout, 'Last orders' or shall I?"

"You can."

"Gentlemen and ladies, last orders, please," Vince spoke out over the chit-chat."

There was a last rush, at the bar, whilst most of the customers topped up their glasses.

"Time, ladies and gentlemen, please," called Vince at eleven o'clock.

"They've now got ten minutes to drink up before we throw them out."

One by one, the regular customers brought their empty glasses to the bar and bade Vince and Owen a good night.

Mr Longstaff came out of the back office and beckoned to Owen.

"How was that?"

"Great. And Vince was really helpful."

"I'm glad to hear it. Now you wash the glasses, clean up the bar, empty beer troughs and the like, take the bottle bin out back, wipe down tables and generally make the place ship-shape. I'll pay you from six till twelve. Do you want the job?"

"Thanks. Yes. I accept."

"We probably need to work out how many shifts you want to do, but I could use you for four lunchtimes and four evenings. That's something like forty hours, at £2.05 per hour. No tax, for the moment. Don't forget to sort out your National Insurance number. How does that sound?"

"Works for me," replied Owen, not even thinking what starting at university might mean.

"Come at eleven o'clock in the morning."

"Thanks."

Mr Longstaff returned to the back office and Owen and Vince cleared away all evidence of the evening's drinking. They finished at five to midnight.

"You on tomorrow?" asked Vince.

"I am."

"See you tomorrow. Then."

"Thanks. Bye."

Owen left the pub. As he was walking home he retrieved the folded piece of paper from his pocket. There was a name, Steve, and an address on Balfern Street. Presumably, he would have to knock on the door, or put a note through the letter box. Still, he trusted Vince, even though he had only just met him. It took half an hour to walk home. Owen wondered if he could leave his motorcycle in the back yard of the pub, next to the bins. He would ask Mr Longstaff, tomorrow. In the meantime, he thought another trip to the charity shops might be useful, to find a couple more shirts.

At nine-thirty in the morning, Owen was parking his motorcycle outside one of the charity shops. He went in and looked on the rails for shirts. The price labels indicated they were 20p each, and he selected a grey one and a pale blue one with fine red stripes. They smelt like they had been laundered, so when he got home, he put the blue stripy one on. It was too early to make lunch, but he had noticed a corner shop on his way home the night before and hoped it would be open when he walked past, today. Not sure of the eating arrangements when on shift, he bought a Mars bar, which he ate during the second half of his journey.

When he arrived, Mr Longstaff greeted him. Owen went into the toilet. Catching his reflection in the mirror, he winked at himself, or at least, he winked at the imaginary girl standing behind the mirror. Owen thought he should get some shoe polish and brushes, next time he went shopping. Also, his unruly brown curls were letting him know he was in serious need of a haircut. Vince walked in.

"Hey, Owen. Alright?" he asked, from the cubicle.

"Yes, thanks. You OK?"

"Yes, I am. There's a different crowd in here at lunchtime, mostly. More people, but less drink per customer."

"OK."

"I never got round to showing you how to change a barrel, last night. Maybe later."

"Whenever suits. Thanks. See you out there," he called over his shoulder.

Mr Longstaff was behind the bar, stocking up the crisps.

"It took me half an hour to walk home last night. I was wondering if I would be able to lock my motorcycle in the back yard, while I'm at work?"

"Of course. The gate bolts from the inside. It should be safe."

"Thanks. I'll come on it, this evening."

The landlord disappeared into the back office as Vince crossed the room.

"Does Mr Longstaff ever work behind the bar?"

"Yes. He does the shifts when you, me or Wendy aren't working in pairs. He's probably working on a new rota, as we speak. You've yet to meet Wendy."

"What's she like?"

"I'll leave you to find that out for yourself," he laughed, checking the ice buckets. "Follow me down to the cellar. We've got time to fetch ice from the freezer. No time to show you the barrels though."

Owen followed Vince down to the cellar and took a bag of ice out of the freezer. Vince turned off the light and followed Owen back up the stairs.

"Split the bag between the two ice buckets."

"OK."

Owen slit the plastic with the lemon knife and poured half the ice cubes into one plastic bucket and half into the other.

Mr Longstaff came into the bar, opened the till, poured in a bag of ten pence pieces, closed the till and went over to unlock the door. Instead of going back into the back office, he carried on out through the open front door. Halfway through the shift, the landlord came back through the front door, his face drained of colour. Going behind the bar, he poured himself at least two shots of single malt, without using the measure, and took the glass into the back office. He had plucked up the courage to go and sort out the drug-dealer. Not knowing who the man was, or where to find him, but he had put the word out, and was now confident that the matter was in hand. Owen noticed that the customer who had been exchanging things previously, did not come in for a drink today.

At the end of the shift, after they had cleared up, Vince showed Owen how to change a barrel. The lager had run out, fortuitously, just as last orders were called.

"Now go and draw off a pint and chuck it down the sink."

The two bartenders went back up to the bar, and Owen did as Vince had instructed him. Mr Longstaff appeared behind the bar.

"Gentlemen. We won't be seeing our dodgy customer with the drugs anymore. I've sorted it."

"Good on you, Mr Longstaff," Vince encouraged him.

"Yes. Well done," added Owen, with no inkling that the process might well have involved actual bodily harm.

"He knows that if he comes back, he'll be paying accident and emergency a visit."

The man who had been exchanging things was not seen in The Prince Albert, for the rest of the summer.

In the evening, Owen met Wendy. As Vince had suggested, Wendy was indescribable. Her personality was as voluminous as her chest, and her laugh even louder. She took to Owen, almost to the extent of mothering him, and she was old enough to be his mother, certainly. By the end of the shift, Owen felt exhausted, mainly because he had spent the evening trying not to be pinched in the cheek, affectionately, by this matronly woman, who he had only just met. How old did she think he was? Sixteen?

Wendy Mallone had worked behind the bar of The Prince Albert for the best part of twenty years. She had watched many of the current clientele grow up, and there were few secrets they could hide from her. A pillar, in the local community, she was respected by many, and loved by more. When she was not behind the bar, she made pies for the homeless, volunteered at the dogs' home, and offered her sofa to many a troubled teenager, after a row with their parents, more often than not, going round to the house and sorting the problem out. If she had a weakness, it was her refusal to recognise personal space. That and gin, which her crackling voice told Owen, she had probably been drinking since she was six.

Over the next few weeks, Owen came to feel safe with Wendy, although he was not yet ready to tell her his own story of family breakdown. The last thing he wanted was for her to go and sort it out for him. Nevertheless, nothing seemed to shock her, and her heart was in the right place. She invited him round for a Sunday lunch, where he met her husband, Greg, a scaffolder, built like a brick outhouse, with a heart to match, and their slightly hapless teenage son, who may well have been less hapless, had Wendy not mothered him so much. His ambition in life was to join the RAF, but, as Mr Mallone pointed out, he could not even tie his own tie.

It was over roast beef, that Owen and Wendy got to talking about the dogs' home.

"How long have you volunteered there?"

"Almost as long as I've worked at The Prince Albert."

"You don't have a dog?"

"No. Mr Mallone knows I'd have a house full of them if I persuaded him to let me adopt the first one. I don't really need a pet, though, do I, when I get to walk them and play with them, every week. Are you a dog person, Owen?"

"To tell you the truth, I've never really thought about it. We always had cats at home."

"You can't beat a dog. Don't get me wrong. I love cats, but a dog is different. They depend on you. Anyone who says animals don't have feelings has never worked with dogs. I've seen the dirtiest, most neglected, terrified creature come to rest his head on my lap. All it takes is patience and love. Patience and love."

"Maybe, I could visit the dogs' home one day?"

"I'll show you round myself. You just tell me when you want to go. It'll be my pleasure."

"Thank you."

Wendy cleared away the plates and went into the kitchen. Denis picked up the gravy jug and followed her out. When he reappeared, the jug was filled with custard and Wendy was carrying a large rhubarb crumble. She certainly knew how to cook. It was a long time since Owen had eaten a full Sunday roast, and he was stuffed.

"Can I help with the washing up?"

"No, you can't. You can go home and get some rest. I believe you're on the rota this evening with the boss."

Owen got up, put on his jacket.

"Thank you so much for having me round. Great lunch. See you, Mr Mallone, Denis. Tuesday lunchtime, I believe, Wendy. We're on together again."

"Probably. Take care, Owen."

She pinched his cheek as he went out through the door. He did not even have the heart to resent it after a meal like that.

Good to her word, two weekends later, she showed Owen round the dogs' home. As they walked along the cages, Owen stopped to interact with a rather fetching red Afghan Hound.

"That's Kochai. I think it means 'nomad' in Pashto. He's six years old. He was found in a shed, a week after his owner died. As far as we can tell, he was so well-behaved, he didn't even bark when the police came to break down the door to the house. It had taken a week before one of the neighbours put two and two together, when they didn't see him out walking the dog, and raised the alarm. Other than that, he's healthy."

"I think I've just become a dog person."

"Seriously?"

"After I came round for lunch, I've thought more and more about getting a dog. I just didn't know which sort of dog I wanted. Because I work shifts, there should be no problem leaving him alone, while I'm at work, and I can take him for walks in the park and along the river. He's beautiful. Can I adopt him?"

"They'll do a home-check and it'll cost you a donation. Also, because you've not had a dog before, they'll probably want to see you with him. He's been neutered. It's policy. So as long as you have a home for him, you can afford to feed him and take him to the vets if needed, you should be fine."

"Wow. I'm surprised no one's adopted him, yet."

"Maybe he was waiting for you, before he showed his true colours," replied Wendy, oozing kindness and encouragement.

"How do I go about adopting him?"

"Come to the office, fill out a form, and they'll take it from there."

Wendy led Owen to the office and introduced him to a colleague.

"Matt, here, is one of our adoption handlers."

"Hi. I was wondering if I could adopt Kochai."

"You'll need to fill out this form."

Owen completed the application form and booked a home-visit, for the Tuesday afternoon after his shift at the pub.

"Can I see him now? I mean, can he come out of his cage?"

"Wait a minute, and I'll see if the yard is empty," replied Matt.

He went out of the room and came back five minutes later.

"Yes, if you'd like to follow me, we'll bring Kochai out to meet you. Are you coming too, Wendy?"

She looked at Owen, who nodded. All three of them went to the yard and Matt went to fetch Kochai. As soon as Matt let go of his lead he ran to Owen and sat down in front of him.

"Hey Kochai. Do you want to come and live with me?" he asked the dog, rubbing his ears and cupping his chin in both hands.

Kochai lifted a paw, which Owen shook.

"He really seems to like you," said Wendy.

"I agree," added Matt. "I think Kochai's found his owner. Of course, we can't make a final decision until after the home-visit, but I'm really hoping that will go smoothly."

"Me too," smiled Owen.

"Me three," Wendy laughed loudly.

Matt led Kochai away to his cage and met Wendy and Owen in the front office.

"See you on Tuesday then."

"Definitely. Thanks. Bye."

"Bye, Matt. See you when I'm next in."

"Bye," replied Matt.

"I can't believe you're about to adopt a dog," reflected Wendy as she and Owen left the dogs' home.

"Me neither. I'm so excited."

"Any time you need someone to look after him when you're on holiday, or if you're poorly, and can't walk him, just let me know."

"Thank you. I can see Kochai is going to be your secret weapon, for getting a dog past Mr Mallone!" laughed Owen.

Wendy laughed even louder.

On Tuesday, Matt knocked on Owen's door.

"Welcome. Come in," Owen greeted him, nervously.

"Hi. Tell me. What made you decide to adopt a dog?"

"This is my first independent home, and I've never been able to before. He'll be my companion and he'll make sure I don't hide from the world. I'm looking forward to walking him, even in the rain!"

"Well, it all looks fine to me. When would you like to pick him up?"

"Really! I'll go and get a bed, some food and a chew toy when you leave, and come to the dogs' home."

"Any chance you could make it first thing in the morning, only I have two other visits to do, and I'll need to file the paperwork?"

"Of course. No problem. What time does the office open?"

"Ten o'clock."

"Ok. See you at ten o'clock, tomorrow."

"Great stuff. Bye."

"Bye."

No sooner had Matt left, than Owen locked up and went in search of a pet shop. He bought a dog blanket, a collar and lead, a grooming brush, a ball, a rubber bone, two different sorts of dog food, dried and tinned, and two plastic bowls.

In his head, Owen envisaged Kochai sleeping on the blanket in a cut-down cardboard box for his bed. He could bring one home from the pub after this evening's shift. A dog basket was a luxury he would buy in a few weeks.

Owen walked into the dogs' home carrying Kochai's new lead and collar. Matt was in the office and came out when he heard Owen mention the name 'Kochai.'

"Good morning. Big day."

"Yes. I've brought his lead and collar with me."

"I just need a signature from you, and then, we'll bring Kochai out to you. He will have a small bag of food. I'll write the brand down for you. Don't forget you'll need to get a dog licence. From the post office."

Owen was realising how stupid he had been to buy any old food, not knowing what Kochai was accustomed to eating.

"Right, yes."

Matt handed him the form and a pen, and Owen signed. Matt put the paperwork back in the office and went to fetch Kochai, who was very excited to see Owen when he was brought back through the door. Owen crouched down and cupped Kochai's face in his hands.

"Hey Kochai. You're coming home with me, today. We're going to have so much fun together."

He took the collar and replaced the dogs' home one, attaching his new lead.

"Do you have any dog tags?" asked Matt. "You'll need his name and address or phone number if you have one. Most key-cut places can engrave it for you."

Owen shook his head. There were so many things he had not considered.

"You can buy one here, or at the local hardware store."

"I'll buy one from here," replied Owen.

Matt went and picked one off the stand and handed it to Owen.

"How much?"

"50p."

Owen felt in his pocket and took out some notes.

"There. That should cover the donation and the dog tag."

"Thank you. Don't be afraid to get in touch if you have any questions. Wait, you know Wendy, don't you? Or you can just ask her."

"Thanks, I will. Bye. Say 'Goodbye,' Kochai."

"See you, mate. Good luck," Matt addressed the Afghan Hound, ruffling Kochai's head, and handing Owen the bag of food.

"Bye."

"Bye. Good luck to you, as well."

Owen led Kochai out of the dogs' home and walked back to his flat via the park. He was already a well-trained, obedient dog, which made things easier for Owen, especially as a first-time dog owner. They met three other dog owners and their dogs, an old man with a Jack Russell, a middle-aged couple with a Labrador, and man, probably in his forties, with a greyhound. Kochai pulled at the lead, wanting to socialise with them.

"I'm not letting you off the lead, yet, mate," Owen explained to Kochai, "Not until you're sure who's your owner, and you know my voice. I can see we're going to have to get you some treats."

It was hard to put into words just what he was feeling. The flat was already a major step towards Owen's independence and charting his own course in life. Owning a dog, was like a confirmation, an affirmation even, of who Owen Linton-House now was. Kochai decided to do his business, at the side of the path, and Owen realised he had nothing to clear it away with. Feeling in his pocket, he had a used tissue. There was a bin about fifty yards along the path so he carefully picked up the dog pooh and deposited it in the bin, making a mental note to get treats and bags, at the next opportunity.

When they arrived back at the flat, Owen let Kochai off his lead to explore, filled one of the plastic bowls with water, and poured the bag of food into the other. Kochai barked a single joyful bark. It was the first time Owen recalled hearing him bark and he was suddenly worried that the neighbours might complain and report him to the council. One of the good things about Kochai was how he had not barked even when left in the shed by accident.

"Please don't bark, mate. What is it you want? Come."

Kochai stopped barking and approached Owen, who cupped his face in his hands.

"You're a good boy. Are you just excited?"

Kochai started eating the food, and Owen noticed a spider in the corner of the room. He went into the bathroom, tore off some toilet roll, picked up the spider, and dropped it out of the window.

Owen was due on shift that evening, so he took Kochai for another walk, fifty minutes or so, before making sure he had food, water, and his blanket, and locking him in the flat. To Owen's relief, Kochai did not bark. Hopefully, he would curl up and go to sleep after his exercise. When he got to The Prince Albert, Wendy was full of questions.

"Have you got Kochai yet?"

"Yes, this morning."

"Has he settled in?"

"I took him straight to the park, and then we had another longish walk, this evening, before I left to come here. I'm hoping he'll sleep on his new blanket. He has food and water."

"I'm sure he'll be fine. Can I see him?"

"You don't think it'll confuse him? I mean of course, but won't he think he's going back to the dogs' home?"

"Don't be daft! Bring him round on Sunday. You can stay for a roast again, if you want, and afterwards, we can take Kochai for a walk."

"Deal."

At the end of his shift Owen sorted out a large cardboard box, which had been collapsed and stacked behind the bins. Thankfully, it had not rained. Owen was not quite sure how to attach it to his Honda, and in the end, he positioned it so one end was just across the part of the seat where he sat and rested it against the top-box. He sat on the end of the box to anchor it, and rode the short journey home, as fast as he could. Kochai was waiting the other side of the door.

"Hey, Kochai. I missed you. Have you been a good boy?"

Kochai stayed by the door, pawing at the handle.

"Ah. You need to go out, don't you?"

Owen got his lead and took him along the street. They were hardly down the stairs when Kochai relieved himself against the corner of the building.

"Good boy," Owen encouraged him. "I'm not working tomorrow, so we can go for a nice long walk."

Once back indoors, Owen re-constructed the cardboard box and cut it down to about six inches in height, folded the blanket, and laid it in the bottom. Kochai came to investigate, and curled up on the blanket in his cardboard basket.

"There's a good boy."

He poured some food into the bowl, topped up the water bowl and went to bed. Kochai got out of the cardboard basket and jumped on the bed.

"Basket. Go in your basket," commanded Owen, firmly, but calmly.

Kochai got off the bed and returned to his blanket.

"Good boy. Good night."

When Owen woke up, Kochai was lying on the bed next to his feet.

"You're hilarious!"

Owen and Kochai soon got into a routine, of walks and feeding and shifts. Owen began to recognise triggers, gestures, and behaviours. He had been using treats as rewards, and after a few weeks, felt he understood what Kochai wanted or needed and communicated with him. Kochai, for his part, slept each night on Owen's bed, did not bark, as far as Owen knew, or at least, the neighbours said nothing, and appeared to be a happy dog. Wendy took Kochai for a walk once a week, so that Kochai got used to her, if Owen needed to go away, ever. Owen did not believe a word of it, and ribbed Wendy that she was trying to convince Mr Mallone to let her have a dog.

Summer passed quickly, and the first day of the university term arrived. Owen had every intention of keeping his job at The Prince Albert and had asked Mr Longstaff if he could work evenings only, during the week, and lunchtimes, at the weekend. To his great relief, Mr Longstaff had agreed. He hoped the university days would be short, once he knew what his timetable looked like. After taking Kochai for an early walk, he got on his motorcycle and headed for the School of Slavonic and Eastern European Studies.

There was a welcome lecture and timetables were handed out, followed by a tour of the department. In the afternoon, the freshers went to the students' union and Owen was able to collect his grant cheque. As soon as he could escape, he went to the nearest branch of his bank, paid in the cheque, and went back to Battersea, impatient to see Kochai. They went straight out for a walk. Owen's head was buzzing. Part of him wanted to explore the course, but the other part of him just was not sure if he could stick it through to the end. Maybe he would try one term at a time. He suddenly realised that, since acquiring Kochai, he had not even thought about getting cannabis. In fact, he could not even remember what he had done with the folded piece of paper Vince had given him.

After feeding Kochai and throwing some toast down his own throat, he rushed off to work. He really hoped it was an exception, that he was out all day at university and out all evening at work. Even so, he could always ask for Wendy's help, if it turned out he had to spend all day at university. Not only that, with his motorcycle, if needs be, he could always pop home at lunchtime. There was going to be a whole new routine to find, and Owen was grateful that Kochai was such a good-natured dog.

As usual, when Owen came back from his evening shift, he took Kochai for a short walk. Unusually, they took a slightly different route, and to Owen's consternation, he witnessed, albeit at a distance, what he thought might be a drug deal, gone bad. A black BMW pulled up alongside a man standing on the corner of the street, a shot was fired, the BMW sped off, and the man was left in a crumpled heap, on the pavement. Owen was terrified, too terrified to go and check on the victim. If he had been on his own, he would not have been so concerned, for his own safety, but with a rather distinct dog, he would be instantly recognisable, and if the shooter in the BMW had seen him, his life would be in danger. Part of him hoped a resident had heard the shot and would call the police, and part of him felt guilty. Knowing there was a phone box on the next street, Owen jogged to it and called 999, described what happened, said he was terrified, and hung up.

As he walked the rest of the way home, he just about succeeded in convincing himself that he had been too far away for the shooter, or driver, to recognise what kind of dog it was. In any case, the number plate was unreadable, and he was way too far away to see any faces, and hopefully, that is what the shooter would also realise. Nevertheless, Owen decided to walk Kochai somewhere completely different from the local park, for the next couple of weeks. After all, there were lots of dog-walkers around, and any one of them could have been out that evening and witnessed the incident.

In the morning, woken by his alarm at six-thirty, Owen took Kochai under the railway line, in the direction of

Wandsworth Common, which was a bit further to walk before arriving in an open green space. Throughout the area, it was easy to find small patches of grass, enough for a dog to do its business, but if it was wide open spaces, you were looking for, enough to throw a ball, these were fewer and further between. They played 'fetch' for around twenty minutes and headed back to the flat. After filling both food and water bowls, Owen set off for SSEES.

His timetable was looking hopeful, with two mornings of lectures and tutorials on three afternoons, only one of which coincided with a morning of lectures. With some judicious use of the library, along with purchasing a handful of books, Owen felt he would hardly ever have to leave Kochai on his own for the whole day. Having bought a coffee, he went to his first proper lecture.

Up to now, Owen had read only six set texts in Russian, two for 'O' level and four for 'A' Level. He had also played a minor part in a school performance of Chekov's *The Cherry Orchard*. Now he was going to be studying modules in Old Russian Literature, The Nineteenth Century Novel, Writers of the Silver Age, Soviet Era Writers and Émigré Writers, each involving at least eight primary texts, not to mention the history and language modules.

Owen found himself impatient, to hear this morning's lecture on Vladimir Vladimirovich Mayakovsky, 1983 to 1930. Owen was immediately struck by how young Mayakovsky was when he died. As a teenager, he had been forced to leave grammar school because his recently widowed mother could not afford the school fees. Heavily influenced by the writings of Karl Marx, Mayakovsky became a Bolshevik activist, and served an eleven-month prison sentence for his revolutionary activities. Whilst in prison he began writing, and on release, gave up being a revolutionary and focused on academia. Owen would have been lying if he said he did not feel a tremendous affinity with Mayakovsky.

The recommended texts were *The Bedbug, Mystery Bouffe* and *The Bathhouse*. The lecturer gave scant background, saying the students would hear more on the history module, and could discover more by engaging with the reading list, but he did give a brief overview and commentary on each of the three works. Owen could not help being distracted by the attractive blonde student, who had taken the next but one seat, from him. At the end of the lecture, the lecturer reminded the students, that their first assignment was on the role played by bathhouses in *The Bathhouse*. Owen turned to the attractive, blonde student and introduced himself.

"Hi. I'm Owen."

"Hello. My name is Katya."

Her accent was not British.

"You're not from round here, are you?"

"I live in London, but I am Russian. You can speak Russian if you are taking this course?"

"Yes. I speak Russian badly. You speak English well. I am always insanely jealous of people who are fluent in a language, studying that language for a qualification. It hardly seems fair."

"Thank you," laughed Katya. "Do you understand about bathhouses?"

"I'm not sure I understand the assignment title. Surely, a play called *The Bathhouse* must be about a bathhouse. Or am I missing something?"

"Perhaps you would like me to tell you, over a cup of coffee?"

Owen looked at his watch and thought it would do no harm to spend another hour at the university.

"That would be brilliant."

They made their way to the cafeteria, where Owen bought two coffees, and sat down at a vacant table.

"You were going to tell me about bathhouses, were you not?"

"Ah, yes. The 'banya'. Let me ask you a question. What does it mean to be clean?"

"Is that a rhetorical question?"

"Perhaps you think of a bath or a shower. For Russians, it is as important, if not more important, to cleanse the souls. Think about that as a symbol of the Revolution, of cleansing society. But first, let me tell you a bit about the 'banya'."

"Please do."

"The 'banya' is the community space where Russians find their place in the world. But, back in the Middle Ages, there were some doctors who suggested that it was unhealthy to take baths."

"Unhealthy?"

"Yes. It was the Church which was against it. We, Russians were looked down on, because we loved to take baths. But our 'banya' are like steam baths. Our 'banya' are great levellers of social class, where all bathers become equal. Mayakovsky had something important to say. Although his play is mostly about a time machine, and looking at the future of Soviet society, after the Revolution, he was saying that society needed to be purged of those who would not accept the new era, and that it had to be thoroughly cleansed of the old, tsarist way of life. Yes, *The Bathhouse* is a satire of Stalin's opportunistic stupidity, but it is also a metaphor for the cleansing of soviet society."

"I have to say, that is fascinating."

"Would you like to experience the 'banya'?"

"What? Are you telling me there are 'banya' in London?"

"I know of a secret 'banya' which I can take you to. We live in the middle of the Cold War, where the Secret Service follows us, the Russians, who are living in London. The 'banya' is a community space where stories are told, messages are passed on and secrets are shared. So, would you like to come to the secret 'banya' one day?"

"Er, yes, thank you. I would. Listen, I really need to be somewhere else. Are you going to be coming to the lectures next week?"

"Yes, I am."

"Then, please, let's sit together again. I would like to get to know you."

"I look forward to spending some more time with you, Owen. Goodbye."

She stood up to leave.

"Bye. Take care."

Kochai had been perfectly fine, when Owen had left him during his first half day of lectures, the day he met Katya. It was a weight off his mind. Over the last week, Owen had started to experience thoughts he had not thought for a while, thoughts of an imagined future relationship, rather than regrets of a remembered past relationship. So, when Owen entered the lecture theatre, he was nervously pleased to see Katya sitting there, with her bag claiming the adjacent seat. He sat down next to her.

"Hi. How's your week been?"

"Good. Yours?"

"Good. I have a dog, Kochai, and I was worried that he might not settle when I was here during the day, because I also have a part-time job and that's a long time to be left on his own."

"You have a dog?"

"He's an Afghan Hound. A rescue from Battersea Dogs' Home."

"I would love to meet this Kochai, one day."

"I'm sure we can make that happen."

The lecturer started to draw the students' attention to him.

"Good morning. This morning, our subject is Maxim Gorky, 1868 to 1936. We often think of the Russian Revolution as one, smooth homogenous event, but I can assure you, it wasn't. Our writer, this week, was a Bolshevik, yes, but he all too often disagreed with Lenin….."

By the end of the lecture, Owen found himself to be even more acquainted with the Russian working classes.

"Picasso had a 'blue' period, but Gorky had a 'tramp' period," laughed Katya.

"Yes, he did."

"Do you want to come to the 'banya' with me this weekend?"

Owen was distracted, momentarily, by the intense blue of her eyes.

"Yes. I am working lunchtime and evening on Saturday and then, evening again on Sunday. As long as I am home by four-thirty, we could go on Sunday afternoon."

"Meet me outside Euston Station, at one o'clock."

"Looking forward to it. See you."

"Bye, Owen."

He went to the library for some books about the writers of the Silver Age, along with six of the primary texts. Unable to find a couple of the prescribed texts, he went to the bookshop and bought two paperbacks. Realising he did not have a dictionary, at least, not a sufficiently detailed one, the sort you can play a party game with, along the lines of, 'I use my Russian dictionary to stand on when I'm cleaning the cobwebs on my ceiling' or 'I use my Russian dictionary to prop up the three-legged armchair', a bit like 'I went shopping and I bought …'. Of course, the drunker you were, the more ridiculous the uses of the Russian dictionary.

The great thing about studying one of the humanities at university, was that there were few classes, but lots of books to read at home. Even by adding a morning a week in the library to his sparse lecture timetable, to make use of the short-loan collection, or to photocopy short articles, he still would not have to leave Kochai on his own for too long. That said, even short periods could be unpredictable, as Owen was about to discover. When he arrived back at his flat Kochai greeted him with a half-chewed brown envelope.

"Oh no! You've not done that before, Kochai. Am I going to have to make some sort of a cage or box, to catch the letters?"

It suddenly occurred to Owen, that this was only his second letter, since adopting Kochai, so how could he have known that Kochai had acquired a taste for manila paper? Assuming, from the small window on the front, that it was some sort of bill, he threw it onto the kitchen table.

"We'll deal with that later, mate," he informed Kochai. "Let's go for a walk."

Kochai was sitting at the door, impatiently, and hardly let Owen attach the lead, straining to get out of the door. Pulling Owen to the trees in the middle of the square, he released a soft, almost runny stool.

"What a good boy. Did I leave you too long? I'm sorry. No, wait! That's the envelope you ate. Serves you right, you rascal."

Owen pulled a plastic bag from his pocket and cleared up the dog muck, as best he could. There was a bin just along the street. He thought they might explore a narrow strip of grass running alongside the railway. Halfway along, Kochai started sniffing, animatedly, at a plastic carrier bag, at the base of the metal fence.

"What is it? What've you got there?"

Owen bent down and pulled open the bag. At first, he thought it might be mud, or worse, another dog's business, but it was a sizeable lump, even for a large breed. Also, dogs don't usually deposit bricks, and this substance was the size of a small packet of flour. He poked at it from the outside of the bag. It was resistant, but not rock hard. Putting his face closer to the opening, he sniffed, but it did not smell like dog pooh. It had an unmistakable aroma. Owen could hardly believe it. He was holding a block of cannabis resin. Goodness only knows what the street value was. Where had it come from? Was it thrown there, in panic, or left there, on purpose? Surely, no one would leave that much cannabis unattended, deliberately. He took the bag handles, and folded the bag around the block, sticking it inside his jacket. As they continued on their walk, Owen's mind started to weigh up the pros and cons of keeping it.

Back at the flat, he put the entire package, bag and cannabis, under the clothes in his top drawer and settled onto the settee to read one of the novels he had just bought. At five o'clock, he put down the book and went to the kitchen to make some scrambled eggs on toast. The letter was still on the table, so he opened it. It was from Post Office Telecommunications, and not actually addressed to him. Apparently, the process of introducing STD codes was now complete. Owen had not thought about a telephone, up until that moment, and wondered how much it would cost. There was just time for a short toilet excursion with Kochai, before getting changed into a buttoned shirt and leaving for work. This evening, he was on the rota with Vince and could not make up his mind whether to tell him about the cannabis find.

By the middle of their shift, he had decided not to tell Vince, but wanted to pick his brains. He was curious to know how Vince had made contact with the dealer whose address he had given Owen. The more Owen had thought about his find, the more he was starting to entertain the possibility of selling the cannabis. He just was not at all sure where to start.

"Steve, the dealer you gave me the contact for, how did you find out about him, in the first place?"

"Word of mouth. Friend of a friend."

"And how did the friend of a friend find out about him?"

"No idea. Why are you asking?"

"Worried about something I saw. Made me start worrying about how anonymous it all is."

Vince went to serve a customer, and nothing else was said. It occurred to Owen that, despite owning a fortune in cannabis resin, he might need to buy some, if only so he could communicate with Steve, and realised how ridiculous his idea was. A dealer is hardly going to give away details, or chat with a customer. Perhaps he could build a customer base through the university. It might take a few months to get it off the ground, and he would have to get himself invited to parties, but it just might work.

After his shift, he took Kochai out for a short walk and checked on the package, before going to bed. The temptation to smoke some himself was strong. Tomorrow, he would get some tobacco and Rizlas. He would be quite limited for opportunities to smoke because he was either at work or at university. It might not be wise to smoke in the flat, because there was no guarantee he could keep the smell within the four walls. Maybe, Kochai's final walk before bed, some evenings. He certainly could not make it a regular habit, otherwise he had never be able to concentrate on his studies, and he had reading to do and assignments to write. He fell asleep wondering if Katya smoked cannabis.

The weekend came around quickly. Owen was thinking about his impending trip to the 'banya' and realised he did not have any trunks. Even though he could afford a new pair, he still went to the local charity shops. Unable to find anything suitable, he had to buy some at a sports store. As it was not really swimming, he opted for a pair of shorts.

On the Sunday morning, he took Kochai for a walk and afterwards packed up a towel and his new shorts. Having thrown a couple of slices of cheese on toast down his throat, he got on his Honda and went to Euston Station. At first, he could not decide whether to park up and meet Katya on foot or stay with the motorcycle. By the time he arrived, he had made up his mind. Parking up, he took his towel and shorts out of the top-box and put his helmet in. Making his way to the main entrance, he could see Katya, standing there, although she was looking in the opposite direction. He was only a few paces from her when she turned towards him. Owen's nerves were set at ease by her involuntary smile.

"Hi," she greeted him.

"Hi back!"

"The 'banya' are a ten-minute walk from here."

"I've brought swim-shorts. I wasn't sure."

"Swim-shorts are good."

"And a towel."

"They lend us a bathrobe."

"That's good."

Nothing else was said, until they reached the door of an unassuming building just off Gower Street. Katya rang the doorbell, and a middle-aged woman, who obviously knew Katya, opened it. The two women spoke in Russian, and Owen understood enough to know he was being introduced as a friend of a member. It turned out, the 'banya' were a private club. The middle-aged woman ushered them in, leading them down to the basement, where Owen could already feel some steam in the atmosphere. Muffled laughter could be heard beyond a door. The middle-aged woman handed them each a bathrobe and opened the door, which Owen followed Katya through.

"You have to go in there to get changed and take a shower, but I will meet you in the steam room."

"OK."

He was nervous, partly because he was stepping into the unknown, and partly because Katya was about to see him in swim-shorts, not to mention his being about to see her in a swimsuit. Taking a towel and bar of soap from the shelf, he removed his watch, took the fastest shower he could, put his clothes in his bag and put on the bathrobe. He noticed the towel went in a large basket and followed the signs to the steam room. Katya was waiting outside, in her bathrobe.

"Put one of these towels round you, like this," she directed him, taking two towels from the dresser and handing one to him. "Hang the bathrobe and your bag here, make sure you're not wearing anything metal, and come on in."

"OK. I didn't put my watch back on, after the shower."

He hung up his things and Katya hung her bathrobe on top of Owen's. He followed her into the steam room, where they sat down on one of the slatted wooden benches. It was hot. There were four other people already seated, a woman in her forties and three men in their late fifties or early sixties. Katya greeted them in Russian, although Owen did not get the impression that she knew them, personally. He was starting to sweat.

They sat for thirty minutes, without saying a word. Katya was either shy or did not want anyone overhearing what she had to say. Owen was listening to the two conversations which were going on, trying to get the gist of them, struggling a little. His Russian was solid, but it was always easier to speak than to listen, because he had no control over the speed with which people responded. The woman and one of the men left, bidding the others goodbye and opening and closing the door as quickly as possible. Owen felt the cold draft across his bare leg.

"Five more minutes," announced Katya, quietly to Owen.

She got up and Owen followed suit, feeling confident enough to say goodbye, in Russian. Once through the door, Katya took her bathrobe and put it on.

"Now for the worst part. Put your bathrobe back on and follow me."

"The worst part?"

"Yes. Now we must take a cold shower."

She opened a door which led into a communal shower room.

"If we were in Russia, now, we would just jump in the snow!" she laughed.

"No kidding?"

She pushed the button and pulled Owen under a burst of cold water.

"Aaghh!" he let out his sense of shock.

"We must stay just as long as the automatic tap allows us. It's good for your skin. It closes the pores which the steam opened up. Afterwards, we rub ourselves dry with a towel, to get the blood flowing again. It's not so bad!"

"No, it's not," Owen forced himself to concur.

The water stopped falling on them, and Katya walked across to the shelves, taking a towel and passing it to Owen, and another one for herself. She rubbed her arms and legs vigorously, threw the towel in the basket, and put on her bathrobe. Owen did the same.

"Now, we go and get changed."

"Great!" Owen responded.

"I'll meet you back in reception.

"OK."

They each went into their respective changing rooms, and Owen found himself arriving in reception first. The middle-aged woman asked him, in Russian, if he had found the 'banya' pleasant, to which he replied, in Russian, that it was a wonderful experience, just as Katya re-appeared.

"Did you enjoy that?" asked Katya, as she came up the stairs.

"Yes, thank you."

"So, you would like to come back again?"

"Absolutely!"

"Next time, we should stay a little longer, or perhaps spend less time in the steam room. There are treatments, here, we can take."

"I'm looking forward to it already.

They said goodbye to the middle-aged woman and walked back to Euston Station.

"I have my motorcycle here," Owen pointed.

"If I had a helmet, you could give me a lift," reflected Katya.

"Then I must get a second helmet," Owen replied, affirmingly. "See you in class."

"Yes, see you on Tuesday. Bye."

"Bye."

She had disappeared round the corner, by the time Owen had sorted his top-box out, put his helmet on and kickstarted the Honda. Kochai was pleased to see him, when he arrived home, and sniffed at his hands.

"Do you like the soap, mate? It's a shame they don't do 'banyas' for dogs. Let's take you for a walk."

By the time Owen visited the 'banya' a second time, he had managed to submit two assignments, and to his credit, had attended all the lectures, but he was struggling to balance work, study, dog-walking and the amount of time he now seemed to be thinking about Katya, instead of concentrating on his reading. Katya had suggested that they meet at Euston Station again, because it was safer for Owen to park his motorcycle, and he could not leave it on the pavement outside the 'banya'. In any case, he was not sure he could remember the exact route they had walked or the number of the building. Since he would need to be invited in by a member, he could not just turn up. So, Euston Station it was.

Owen was there waiting at one o'clock when he saw Katya crossing the road.

"Hi."

"Hello. Today we will spend less time in the steam room, and we will have massages. Would you like that?"

"Definitely. How come you are a member of an exclusive club?"

"That's easy. My father works with the diplomatic service."

"What does he do?"

"I don't really know. He attends a lot of dinners with my mother and a lot of meetings without her. She's French-Canadian."

"So, you speak French, as well?"

"Oui, bien sûr."

"Any other benefits to your being the daughter of someone who works with the diplomatic service?"

"No more clubs, you mean to say. No. There is a downside. We can be sent to a different country just like that."

"How long have you lived in London?"

"Three years."

"It must be tough, making new friends all the time."

"I like my own company. I choose my friends carefully. Are you my friend, Owen?"

"If you'd like me to be."

"I would like that."

They arrived at the 'banya' club and went in. The same middle-aged woman was in reception. She greeted Owen like he was a long-lost son. This time Owen knew the routine, up until they came out of the steam room.

"We don't need to take a cold shower today. We go straight to the massage, while our muscles are relaxed."

"OK."

"Come this way."

Katya led them up to the first floor, in their bathrobes, where they went into a room with two massage couches.

A lady in her twenties or thirties came in and greeted Katya with a kiss on each cheek. She was wearing a white tunic.

"This is Yelena. I have known her for three years. She is the daughter of a friend of my father's."

Just as Katya was introducing Yelena, an older woman came in.

"And this is Yelena's mother, Irina.

Irina also greeted Katya with a kiss on each cheek and a hug.

"So, this is your young man?" she teased Katya, in Russian.

Katya blushed.

"This is Owen. Be careful what you say," laughed Katya, also speaking Russian, "He understands Russian."

"Please lie face down on the couch," she invited Owen, in her mother tongue.

Owen and Katya each lay face down on a couch. Irina slipped Owen's arms out of his bathrobe and folded it down, to just above his bottom. She spread a clean towel out and slid it over his bottom as she lowered the bath robe. Yelena did the same with Katya, and Owen could not help noting the smooth side of her breast pressed flat against the leather of the couch. He turned his head away, not because he did not want to watch, but because he did not want the embarrassment of an erection. The room was filled with the aroma of eucalyptus oil. Irina moved her hands in rhythmical circles across Owen's back. He found himself on the verge of falling asleep. This was quite the most sensuous experience he remembered ever having had. He wondered whether he should buy some massage oil for when Katya might come to his flat.

The pleasure was over all too quickly. Irina and Yelena spread the bathrobes over Owen and Katya, so that they could slip their arms back into the sleeves.

"Do you want a warm shower, before you get dressed?" asked Katya.

"No, I'm good. What about you?"

"No, I'm fine too. I like the smell of the oil."

"Kochai was interested in the smell of soap on my hands, last time. He's going to go mad when he smells me, this time."

They were just approaching the station when Owen plucked up the courage to invite Katya to his flat.

"Would you like to come to my flat next weekend, and meet Kochai?"

"Yes. Thank you. Bye. See you in class."

"Thank you for the experience. See you in class. Bye."

Katya was not in the same tutorial group as Owen. He only saw her at lectures, but they always sat together. He was encouraged by her saying that she chose her friends carefully and wanted him to be her friend. He was also painfully aware of her revelation that her father could be moved to a different country, at the drop of a hat, and Owen did not want to get his heart broken again. Broken heart or not, relationship or no relationship, Katya was gorgeous and sexy, and he really wanted to sleep with her. Would this weekend be too soon?

Before going to his tutorial, Owen went to check the departmental pigeon-holes. There was a large brown envelope with his name scrawled on the front. He opened it, to find one of his recently submitted essays with a marking sheet attached. The score was low, only fifty percent, and the comment indicated he had not used enough references. He was disappointed but not surprised as he had only read one critique to write the essay. Owen wondered whether the other assignment would be returned in the tutorial he was about to attend.

Standing outside the room, Owen pushed the envelope into his bag and thought about Katya on the massage couch. The tutor opened his door and the students filed in. Owen was on automatic pilot. His wandering thoughts were interrupted by the tutor handing him back his essay.

"That's a good start, Owen, but if you had just made more of the metaphor of the 'banya' I could have given it a two-one."

"Thank you," responded Owen, taking the paper from him.

Owen did not know what to think. He had enjoyed writing the essay, but he simply did not have the time he needed to give to his studies. He only contributed to the tutorial discussion when asked a question, directly, because he did not feel he knew enough.

At the end of the tutorial, he went to the library to exchange his books, and rode home. Unusually, he had to work the whole week. Wendy was on holiday, and Mr Longstaff had asked him to cover two of her shifts.

"Sorry, mate. Got to be a shorter walk than normal."

Kochai looked at Owen, almost as if he understood. He attached the lead and took Kochai to the nearby park, passing a woman, with a child in a pushchair, on the way.

"Doggy!" exclaimed the child.

Owen looked at the mother and stopped to let the child touch Kochai's coat.

"He's beautiful," said the mother.

"Thank you."

They went their separate ways.

Owen was certain that Katya would fall in love with Kochai, and once she was hooked, surely, she would fall in love with him too. He still had not done anything with his massive stash of cannabis, and with the news of his essays and a late finish, after today's midweek shift, the thought again crossed Owen's mind about selling the drugs. Then, he would be able to give up his job at The Prince Albert. Or should he just knock the degree on the head? That was becoming a less attractive option, since he had met Katya. It was nearly one o'clock in the morning, when Owen took Kochai out for his bedtime toilet walk.

"You're such a good boy, Kochai. And there's a beautiful girl I want you to meet. I'm sorry, by the way, that you'll never now be able to meet a Mrs Kochai."

Kochai did not say anything, but he lapped up the water in his bowl and lay down on the settee. Owen replenished the bowl, went to the loo, and fell into bed. His last thought before falling asleep, was that Kochai needed a good brushing, before he met Katya.

Katya was there, keeping Owen's seat for him, again, in the lecture theatre.

"Are you still coming to meet Kochai, on Saturday?"

"Of course, I am."

"How will you get there. I live very close to Clapham Junction railway station, or I can give you a lift on my motorcycle, if you tell me where to pick you up."

"Have you bought a second helmet?"

"Not yet, but if you want to come on the Honda, I will get one for you."

"No need. I will catch the train. Meet me at the station at three o'clock."

"You realise I am working at the pub both evenings, this weekend?"

"Yes. I won't stay the night."

Owen kicked himself. How was he ever going to sleep with Katya when he worked evening shifts at The Prince

Albert? At which point he thought, he would not have to sleep. He could give her an afternoon massage and make love to her there and then, if everything went to plan. Although, on reflection, a walk with Kochai would probably be all there was time for this weekend. Perhaps next time, but what if she did not want to come back to his flat again, having met Kochai? But if she really liked him, then she would want to spend time with him. You just cannot rush these things.

The lecturer began his lecture.

"This morning, we are thinking about Dmitry Merezhkovsky, who, you may be surprised to know, was a very religious man. He wrote historical fiction as a way of searching for a new future. He considered himself as a philosopher and a prophet, who saw the Revolution as a transcendental tragedy, and who wrote against both the Bolsheviks and the fascists….."

Owen was busy making notes. Katya had her copy of *Symbols* open and was flicking through the poems.

"You're not making any notes," observed Owen, in a whisper.

"I have studied this before."

"Do you wing it, all the time?" he whispered, up close to her ear.

Almost as if she was flirting with him, she put her mouth right next to Owen's ear, and whispered, "Well, it's true I don't need to work very hard at the language side of things, but I still have to read the literature. I just don't really like Merezhkovsky, and I think I know just enough to get by."

Nothing else was said, until the end of the lecture.

"Your English is really very good."

"Thank you. I have to rush off, today."

"I'll see you on Saturday, at three o'clock, outside Clapham Junction station."

"I am looking forward to meeting Kochai."

"Bye."

"Bye."

Katya had flirted with him, Owen was sure. This was promising. On his way home, he called in at the supermarket and bought some provisions. He wanted to get something special, for when Katya came, but he realised he still knew virtually nothing about her. Did she eat chocolate? Did she drink alcohol? He enjoyed vodka, but would she? What about a cake or some fancy biscuits? Alcohol was a bad idea, because he would be going on shift afterwards, and the staff were not supposed to drink at work, which probably included just before work. In the end, he opted for a small box of Black Magic chocolates, after all, 'Who knows the secret of the Black Magic box?' as the advert said. He was just about to queue at the check-out when it occurred to him Katya might not like dark chocolate. Instead, he picked up a box of Terry's All Gold. Once home, he put the perishables straight in the fridge, in the plastic carrier bag, and took Kochai out for his walk.

Back from the walk, he sorted the fridge out and then got Kochai's brush to groom him. Kochai lay down on the ground, inviting Owen to brush him.

"You like this, don't you, mate?"

Kochai lifted his legs into the air.

"That's so not helpful. I need you to stand up, with your coat hanging downwards, if I'm going to brush you without it pulling. Come on. Stand up, mate."

Owen gestured with his hands and Kochai stood up. Owen continued brushing.

"You look like David Gilmour, with your long hair!"

Kochai ran off and jumped on the settee. Owen picked up lumps of hair that he had pulled out of the brush several times.

"There's enough here to stuff a cushion."

Kochai sat with his front pours crossed over the edge of the settee and said nothing. Having thrown the hair in the bin, Owen set about cleaning the flat. When the kitchen and bathroom were pristine, he read. After beans on toast, he read some more, and following Kochai's evening walk, he continued to read. Having returned from Kochai's late night toilet excursion, he read until he fell asleep.

On Saturday, Owen took Kochai to the park, and walked him back via Clapham Junction, arriving at five minutes to three.

"Now we have to sit and wait, for a bit. There's someone who's impatient to meet you. Be on your best behaviour, OK, mate."

Kochai sat beside Owen, panting.

"Sorry, no water. When we get home. At least it's not hot."

It was, in fact, quite chilly, standing around. A train pulled into the station, and presently, Katya appeared through the door. Kochai, sensing his moment, stood up and barked, once.

"He's saying 'Hello' to you."

"Hello, Kochai," Katya greeted him, crouching down. "Pleased to meet you. Can you give me your paw?"

She held out her hand, and to Owen's delight, Kochai lifted his paw, which Katya shook, and stood up.

"How are you?" she asked Owen.

"All good, here. You?"

"Well."

"Would you like to hold the lead?"

"Can I? He won't pull or run off, will he?"

"Well, if he does, it'll be the first time, ever," replied Owen, handing Katya the lead.

They continued walking, with a beautifully behaved Kochai walking to heel, between them. Owen might have preferred it if Kochai had walked on the other side of Katya, giving him the excuse to get close to her, but he settled for walking to heel and being well-behaved.

"Welcome to my humble abode."

Owen opened the door and stood aside to allow Katya to go in first. He followed her in with Kochai, whose lead he removed, hanging it on the hook by the door.

"I can offer you tea, coffee, cola or vodka."

"A cup of tea would be nice, thank you."

"Have a seat," responded Owen, switching on the kettle.

Katya sat on the settee and Kochai joined her.

"Is he allowed on the furniture?"

"Sorry, yes."

"No need to apologise."

"It was never my original intention, but because I leave him, I didn't want to miss anything that could help him stay calm. So, he gets to lie on the settee. He's really very good. Do you want milk and sugar?"

"No milk, just sugar please. One."

Owen put a teaspoonful of sugar in Katya's black tea and some milk in his own and carried the mugs into the living room. He went back into the kitchen, retrieved the Terry's

88

All Gold from the fridge, and offered Katya the open box. To his amusement, she took a dark chocolate one, so he needn't have worried about the Black Magic. A pang of embarrassment shot through him.

"It's basic, here, but it's my own home."

"How long have you been here?"

"Start of the summer."

"You don't live with your parents, then?"

"Complicated. No. I left in the summer. On my own now. I assume you live with parents, here, in London?"

"Until I leave home, I will continue to move around with them wherever we go. Sometimes, I wish I had more independence. I can't just have a party or take a guy back to my room, but I don't have to pay anything."

"And would you want to take a guy back to your room?"

"Interesting question. If I found the right guy, maybe I would."

Owen had been standing, because he only had the settee, by way of a comfortable seat, and Kochai had taken the other half.

"Kochai, would you like to give me some space? Come on. Shove up!" he laughed, squeezing in between Katya and the dog, so that Kochai had to move towards the arm of the settee.

"Can I kiss you?" asked Owen, uncertain about where the audacity had come from.

"Yes."

The answer took him even more by surprise. He moved his face towards Katya's, until his lips were about half an inch from hers and looked into her piercing blue eyes. As he leant in to make contact, Kochai whined, jealously, and the two students burst into laughter. Owen felt the moment was spoiled and was no longer quite sure how to retrieve it, but he needn't have worried, because Katya took his head in her hands, and kissed him longingly on the mouth. He put his arms round her, and developed the kiss into French kissing, which seemed to last around five minutes.

"I have some massage oil. Would you like a massage?"

They say that fortune favours the brave, and Owen was fully aware that this might be the last time he ever sat next to Katya.

"Where shall we go? Here, or in the bedroom?"

Owen was annoyed with himself for not having replaced the sheets, but they were only three days into their week on the bed, and he had not done anything apart from sleeping in them. He took Katya's hand and pulled her up.

"May I use your bathroom?"

"Of course," replied Owen, pointing at the door.

"Kochai, mate. I know you can't have any fun yourself, but please, please, please, be a good boy, and let me have mine," he whispered in Kochai's ear.

"I need the bathroom too. Would you like to go and get ready, in the bedroom? Here's a towel. I'll be two minutes."

In his two-minute window, Owen peed, brushed his teeth, washed his hands and took the oil from the shelf. By the time he went into the bedroom, Kochai was lying next to Katya on the bed. They laughed.

"In your basket, Kochai," commanded Owen, pointing at Kochai's bed.

Reluctantly, the Afghan Hound jumped off the bed and lay in his basket.

"Good boy!"

Owen sat straddled across Katya's bottom, his knees on the bedspread. She had removed her shirt and her bra and was lying face down, her chin leaning on her folded arms across the pillow. Owen squeezed some oil onto his hand, closed the bottle, rubbed both hands together, and started to make firm circular movements on Katya's back. She moaned with pleasure. After a few moments, he made the movements larger, more elongated, running his hands down the sides of her torso. She continued to moan, each time he moved forwards with pressure. He ran his hands back, stroking the sides of her breasts. She did not protest, so he stopped massaging her and started to kiss her back and shoulders and neck. As he kissed her neck, she turned towards him, her breasts in full view.

"Are we going all the way?" he ventured.

"If you want to."

If he wanted to? Who wouldn't? She was beautiful, sexy and naked down to her waist. He pulled off his shirt and continued to kiss her. He reached to undo her belt, and she reciprocated, by unbuckling his and releasing his jeans button and zip. She let go of Owen and pulled off her jeans and briefs. He did the same. Owen broke off the French kissing to ask a question.

"Are you on the pill?" he whispered in Katya's ear.

"Yes."

Owen was so relieved to hear her affirmation because he did not want to have to stop, and he did not feel confident about withdrawing at the last moment. He made love to her, something he had only ever done once before, to the girl who broke his heart. She helped him with her own rhythmic body movements, and they peaked together, not that Owen would have known if she were faking it. He kissed her gently and rolled off her.

"That was amazing. Thank you," he declared, between breaths.

They lay there, relaxing on the bedspread, waiting for their energy to return. Kochai decided he had been good long enough and jumped up next to them. His body warmth was welcome.

"Hey Kochai. Thank you for being patient," Katya encouraged him.

After twenty minutes or so, Owen got up and put his clothes back on.

"Coffee?"

"Yes please," replied Katya, getting dressed again.

Owen made two mugs of coffee.

"Do you want this black, too?"

"Yes. And one sugar, thank you."

He brought in the mugs and handed one to Katya, who was now sitting back on the settee.

"Are we going to the 'banya' again, next Sunday?"

"Would love to. I'm going to find it hard to look at you and not think about today, though."

Katya laughed. As soon as she finished her coffee, she got up to leave.

"You probably need a shower, before you go to work."

"I don't have a shower. It'll have to be a bath, but nothing like a 'banya'!"

"Bye Kochai. See you soon," Katya said, rubbing his head.

"See you in class. Thank you for today."

"See you in class, Owen. I can find my own way back to the station," she laughed. "Bye."

"Bye," said Owen, opening the door and closing it behind her.

He ran a two-inch bath and jumped in. There was just time for a short toilet walk for Kochai, before he had to go to work. After filling Kochai's water bowl and food bowl, Owen grabbed five chocolates and left for The Prince Albert. Eating chocolates behind a full-face motorcycle helmet was an interesting experience. He could not wait to see Katya again.

Katya and Owen had arranged to meet at Euston Station again, for what had become their regular trip to the 'banya'. The last time found them both enjoying a massage. Katya had an even more pleasurable surprise for Owen on this occasion. The middle-aged woman in reception greeted them in her usual way, said something in Russian to Katya that Owen did not quite understand, and they headed for the showers. The steam room was followed by a cold shower, like the first time, and after getting changed, Katya led Owen into a room on the second floor.

Yelena was there, lying on some giant floor cushions, with a man who Owen assumed was her boyfriend. The atmosphere smelt of vanilla. Yelana jumped up and greeted Katya with a kiss on each cheek.

"Hello Owen," she greeted Owen, in Russian. "This is Vasily, my handsome Cossack boyfriend."

Vasily stood up and extended his hand to Owen.

"Hi. I'm Owen," he introduced himself, in Russian.

"Hello, Owen. Before you ask, I can't dance," came the reply.

They all laughed. Owen noticed that Vasily had been holding a strange looking pipe, which was now sitting on a stand over a candle.

"Come. Sit," Vasily beckoned Owen, as he sat back on the cushion.

Yelena and Katya joined them on the cushions. Yelena draped herself over Vasily. Katya lent her head on Owen's shoulder. Vasily took the pipe, drew in a mouthful of vapour, laid back, inhaling with an exaggerated breath, and handed the pipe to Owen. Not wanting to offend, but not quite sure what was in the pipe, Owen took his first mouthful of opium vapour. The others were watching, so he inhaled. Yelena took the pipe, drew in a mouthful of vapour, and handed the pipe to Katya. Owen was watching Katya, so did not see Yelena release the vapour without inhaling. Katya drew in a mouthful, passed the pipe back to Vasily, lent towards Owen, affectionately and whispered in his ear, releasing the vapour, beyond his field of vision.

"I told you I had a surprise for you," she whispered, placing her hand on his chest, evocatively.

After the third time the pipe was passed round, endorphins in Owen's brain were beginning to party. The pleasure he felt was intense in ways that smoking cannabis had not afforded him, not that the highs from cannabis were not enjoyable. The sensation Owen felt was on a par with sexual release. Vasily passed him the pipe once more, and then blew out the vanilla candle. Yelena nodded to Katya, and took Vasily's hand, pulling him up from the cushion and out of the room, shutting the door behind them. Owen had a sudden panic, knowing he was on shift later, realising he had to ride his motorcycle home, not to mention Kochai needing his walk, but all he felt like doing was lying back and sleeping.

"If you like this, you can buy more from the 'banya', whispered Katya, kissing Owen on the mouth.

"I don't think I'm up to sex," confessed Owen, "and I need to get home. I'm not sure I can ride my bike. I have to take Kochai for his walk. I have to work."

"I'll get you some coffee. Maybe the fresh air will help."

Katya left the room and returned with a small cup of strong, sweet, black coffee, which Owen drank. He collected his thoughts and stood up, feeling a little wobbly. When they left the building, Katya put her arm round him, until they reached Euston Station.

"Do you think you can ride your bike?"

"I don't have a choice. I have to get back for Kochai."

"Maybe I can bring a pipe round one evening when you're not working?"

"Maybe. See you in class. Thank you."

Katya let him kiss her, clumsily on the mouth, and watched while he put on his helmet. He revved the bike and rode off. Thankfully, there was very little traffic, and he made it home, without incident.

The walk with Kochai was kept short, and Owen made a cheese sandwich and more coffee. He had just under an hour to get his act together. Up to now, he had never taken time off sick. He would have to use the phone box at the end of the next street if he was not clear-headed enough to do his shift, but he did not want to leave Mr Longstaff in the lurch. Setting his alarm for fifty minutes later, he lay down on his bed and closed his eyes. The opium high was amazing, but just not a good idea on a day when he had work to do. Maybe he would take up Katya's suggestion of bringing a pipe round. The 'banya' was a veritable house of fun. No doubt its exclusive membership, and the fact that it was Russian, probably under the cover of the diplomatic service, meant it was free to operate outside the law.

That was Owen's last thought before he was rudely awakened by his alarm. He jumped up, boiled the kettle, fed Kochai, and made a cup of strong coffee, with enough milk added to lower the temperature sufficiently to gulp it down.

"See you, mate. Long walk tomorrow. Promise."

Owen just made it to work on time, kept himself to himself, got on with his work, and spoke as little as possible. Halfway through the shift, he started to feel more normal, but Wendy noticed something had not been right. At the end of the shift, she came up close to him and quietly asked, "Everything OK?"

"Yes. Well, I think I might be going down with something," he lied, reluctantly.

"Let me know if you need me to walk Kochai."

"Thank you."

"Go on. Take yourself home. I'll take out the empties and close up."

"Thank you. I owe you one. Bye."

"Bye."

Owen got his jacket and left The Prince Albert. He took Kochai for a short toilet walk and went to bed. Unfortunately, he had drunk so much coffee to wake himself up enough to ride his motorcycle home and work a shift at the pub, that he was now wide awake. He picked up his copy of *The Idiot* and read until twenty-past three, when he went to the bathroom. Kochai was confused and was sitting by the door when Owen came out.

"It's too early, mate. I'm going to try and sleep now, if I can. You're a good boy, aren't you? I've probably been a bit of an idiot myself," he added, tearing off a strip of file paper to mark the page in his book.

Katya was there in their usual place, saving Owen's seat in the lecture theatre.

"How are you feeling? I trust you arrived home safely. Did you go to work?"

"Fine and yes, thank you. I'm not going to make the same mistake again, taking drugs on a day when I have to work."

"Shall I come round on Thursday evening, if you're not working?"

"Can you stay the night?"

"I'm not sure. I'll bring something to give us a rush."

"Great!"

Their conversation was interrupted by the voice of the lecturer.

"Good morning. Our first subject this morning is Fyodor Dostoevsky's *The Idiot*. Let's think about the ideal human being for a moment. What happens when the ideal human being comes into contact with the real world? And what does redemption look like, in Dostoevsky?....."

By the end of the lecture, they had sped through *The Idiot*, *The Brothers Karamazov* and *Crime and Punishment*.

"So far, I have read *The Idiot*. What about you? Or is this something else you've studied before?" joked Owen.

"Actually, two of them. I have to read *Crime and Punishment*."

"How have your assignments gone, so far?"

"I get mostly two-ones."

"I'm impressed. Mine are only just above fifty percent. Struggling for time, between work and Kochai. To be honest, I'm not even sure why I'm here. I kind of just ended up here. It was expected of me. Russian was my favourite subject."

"I'm very pleased to hear that Russian is your favourite subject," laughed Katya.

"And you are my favourite Russian subject. Did that sound too corny?"

"No. I quite like it. What time shall I come round on Thursday?"

"Seven."

"OK. See you then. Bye."

"See you. Bye."

Owen did not go straight home. He rode all the way to Caterham and rang Francis' doorbell. He heard footsteps in the hall. The door opened and a face Owen thought he recognised, from the fateful party, when Richard Lovatt thought he could fly, appeared between door and door jamb.

"Can I help you?"

"Hi. I was looking for Francis."

"He's not back from work. It's Owen, isn't it? Do you want to come in?"

"Thanks. I think I remember you from the party, when Richard had his accident, but I'm sorry, I don't remember your name."

"Not sure we were ever formally introduced. George Marsh."

Owen went into the hall.

"What time is Francis due back?"

"Maybe five-ish. Want a coffee or something?"

"I can't. I have a dog, and he's been in my flat all morning, while I was at the university. I should really go and let him out. Can you tell Francis that Owen dropped by? And can you give me the phone number for here, please?"

George got a pen and paper and jotted down the number which was written on a label stuck to the phone.

"There you go."

"Thanks. By the way, I've got a good supply chain of cannabis, if you're interested. Put the word out, will you?"

"How can you be contacted?"

"I can't. I'll call you at the end of next week."

"Alright. Cheers."

"Gotta go. Bye."

"Bye."

Most of the traffic was now heading out of London, so it did not take long for Owen to arrive back in Battersea. Kochai greeted him enthusiastically. Owen went to the bathroom, attached Kochai's lead, and took him to the park. Due to the incident with the car that he witnessed, Owen had avoided this park for a while, so it was quite nice to see the old man with the Jack Russell, the middle-aged couple with the Labrador, and the man with a greyhound. There was also a newcomer to the park, a lady in her thirties, with a three-to-four-month-old German Shepherd. Kochai was exceedingly interested in the German Shepherd puppy.

"How old is he?"

"Sixteen weeks."

"He's adorable."

"Thank you."

"I never knew this one as a puppy. He's a rescue. Love him to bits."

"He's handsome."

"Thank you. Come on, mate. Let's be going," Owen cajoled Kochai, walking off.

Back home, he did some more reading and made fish fingers and beans for tea. Afterwards, he sat at the table making notes for an assignment on Dostoevsky. He also made up his mind to get a telephone. If he was going to establish a network of customers, it would probably be necessary.

On Thursday evening Owen had walked Kochai, eaten tea, and showered when there was a knock at the door.

"Hello. How are you?"

"Good. You?"

Owen kissed her and beckoned her in.

"Tea, coffee or vodka?"

"Vodka."

"Neat, orange or coke?"

"Neat, please."

Owen poured two vodkas and topped his own up with orange juice. Katya was sitting on the settee, chatting to Kochai.

"I was thinking," hesitated Owen. "Even with staying over, tonight, I won't be much use if I'm asleep. How about we make love before getting high?"

"A man who knows what he wants," laughed Katya.

"Well, yes. I do want you. I like you very much. And you are, very sexy."

Owen put down his glass and started to kiss Katya, who did not resist. They ended up with their clothes in the living room and their naked, satisfied bodies in the bedroom.

"Let's get dressed and partake of the pipe."

"I didn't bring a pipe. I brought something else."

"Oh yes?"

Katya sat at the table and beckoned Owen to sit down opposite her. She took an envelope out of her bag. Inside, was a drinking straw, a small piece of folded baking foil and a strip of cardboard. Owen watched as she unfolded the aluminium foil to reveal some white powder, which she tipped out onto the table.

"I hope your table is clean," she laughed. "Do you have some scissors?"

Owen reached in the drawer and handed Katya a pair of kitchen scissors. She divided up the powder into four two-inch lines and cut the drinking straw in half.

"Now watch."

Placing one end of her half of the straw in her nostril, she passed the other end along one of the lines, inhaling the cocaine through the straw.

"Now you try," she invited Owen, handing him the other half of the straw.

He did what Katya had done. It felt weird and he wanted to choke. He coughed instead.

"Never done this before?"

"No."

"Try again."

Owen snorted another line and Katya the fourth. The narcotic started to take effect, and Owen grinned at Katya.

They went into the living room and relaxed into the cushions on the sofa. Owen put his arm round her and they sat for a while.

"Which did you prefer? The opium pipe or the coke?"

"Not sure. Possibly the pipe."

"There are other ways to enjoy heroin, you know?"

"The thought of sticking a needle in my arm scares me to death," laughed Owen.

"It's OK, if you know how to do it properly."

"Where do you get this stuff from?"

"Where do you think?"

"The 'banya'?"

"Of course."

"And where does the 'banya' get it from?"

"You ask a lot of questions Owen."

"Just curious."

"Isn't it true that curiosity killed the cat?"

They both laughed, but Katya still did not say where the drugs came from.

"Are you coming with me to walk Kochai? He always has a short walk before bed."

"Of course."

Owen attached Kochai's lead and they walked half a mile down the road, and back again. Owen was feeding Kochai, when his stomach notified him that he was also feeling hungry.

"Would you like some toast?"

"Yes please."

He put four slices of bread under the grill.

"Butter, marmalade, jam or cheese?"

"Jam, please."

When the toast was done, they sat at the table, scrunching away, without a word. Katya washed up and they went to bed. When Owen's alarm went off, Katya was up and dressed before he had fully woken up.

"I have to get back, before my parents miss me."

"See you in class."

"Yes. Bye. Thank you."

"Bye."

She slipped out of the flat and Owen threw on some clothes to take Kochai out for his morning walk. He had to knuckle down and study, for the rest of the day, and he was working in the evening. As he read about the Russian working classes, he wondered how much heroin cost on the streets.

The next time Owen visited the 'banya' Katya dropped a bombshell on him. They were sitting in the smoke room, with Yelena, Vasily, and another young man, named Rudi, enjoying an opium pipe, when Katya laid her head on Owen's shoulder.

"I am sorry, but my father is being sent to Canada. This is the last time I will bring you to the 'banya'. It's actually the last time I will see you, as there is no time to pack, if I attend classes this week, and to be honest, no point, as I am leaving the course."

The 'no point' stung a little. Owen felt that if roles were reversed, he would want to attend, just to see Katya once more. Perhaps she was being more realistic. Firm to be kind.

"Oh no. I will really miss you."

"I have enjoyed spending time with you, Owen. I am going to ask them to make you a member here, so you can come and use the steam room," Katya reassured him, adding, in Russian, so the others could hear, "and you will be able to buy anything you use in this room. Vasily, here, will look after you."

"Vasily nodded in acknowledgement.

"But I'm not sure I will want to come here without you," replied Owen, in English.

"It will be good for your Russian, to speak with our friends here. Where else will you get what you need?" she asked, winking at him.

The pipe came round again, and Owen took a deep drag.

"You must write to me."

"I think it is better you heal your heart and find someone else. Maybe she will be Russian too."

Owen was not even thinking about the future possibility of another girlfriend. He was starting to question his luck when it came to women. In his naivety, it had not once occurred to him that Katya might never have been interested in him as a boyfriend, that she might have simply been wooing him as a customer.

Just like his last visit to the smoke room, Owen had work in the evening. He was feeling physically wobbly and emotionally stunned.

"Can we just leave now?" he asked Katya in English.

"If that is what you want."

"Your news has hit me hard."

"Come on, then," replied Katya, standing up.

"Please come again," Vasily insisted. "You have friends here. We know how to have a good time."

"Thank you."

In reception, Katya asked the middle-aged woman to fill out a membership card, which she did, without any questions.

"You will be able to use the steam room for free, but anything you use in the smoke room must be paid for. When you have been a member for six months, you will be able to bring a guest with you," she explained, in Russian, handing Owen the card. "And remember, these are secret 'banya' for a reason!"

"Not a problem. I won't tell a soul," responded Owen, wondering what the consequences might be for any transgression.

Katya walked him to Euston Station. Owen took her in his arms.

"One last kiss?"

Katya allowed herself to be kissed.

"Goodbye, Owen."

"Goodbye, Katya."

Owen stood watching her walk back across the road and went into the concourse to buy a strong coffee, before getting on his motorcycle. Perhaps she was right. A clean break was for the best. The coffee made him feel more in control of his senses, so he rode back to Battersea, where Kochai was waiting patiently.

"Walk?"

Owen got the lead, attached it to Kochai's collar, went to the bathroom, and took the dog for a walk. While they were walking, he thought it was time to phone Francis. On the way back to the flat, he stopped at the phone box. The number was in his wallet. After five rings, someone picked up, the beeps sounded, and Owen slotted in his ten pence piece.

"Is that Francis?"

"Owen?"

"Yes."

"Long time, no speak."

"Sorry. Didn't have the number. Can I pop over, this week?"

"Sure. End of the day on Wednesday?"

"Great. Look forward to it. Bye."

"Bye."

Owen replaced the receiver. He hoped George might also be there, with some news of potential customers.

Wednesday came round soon enough, and having spent the day studying, apart from two walks with Kochai, Owen made himself some scrambled eggs on toast, fed Kochai, and set off for Caterham. He rang the doorbell and, to Owen's relief, George opened it.

"Hey George. How are you?"

"Good thanks."

"Any interest?"

"Yes, how will they contact you?"

"I should be getting a phone after Christmas. For now, tell them I will be outside the train station, here, on Saturday morning from ten until eleven. Ask for the 'Nomad'."

"The Nomad. Right."

Francis appeared at the top of the stairs, and Owen could hear the toilet flush.

"Hi Francis."

"Hello, Owen. How's uni?"

"So-so. Still not sure if I'll stick it out."

"Why not?"

"Not really enjoying it and I have a job and a dog, so don't have a lot of free time."

"A dog?"

"Yes. An Afghan Hound, from the dogs' home. He's called Kochai. He's brilliant."

"Well, I never. I always had you down as a cat person."

"How's your job?"

"So-so. Enjoying it as much as it sounds like you're enjoying uni," replied Francis, laughing.

"Have you heard how Richard is, these days?"

"As far as I know, he's still at Stoke Mandeville."

"Does Mandy still live here?"

"No. She broke up with Richard and moved out. No idea where she is and not sure I care much."

"That's sad for Richard."

"Not really. If she wouldn't stick by him, what would the future be like?"

"Is he going to recover?"

"I believe he will walk again, but not play rugby or run."

"That's bad news. I mean, it's good that he'll walk."

"Small mercies. It's his own silly fault for taking mushrooms, isn't it? I've done drugs myself, but never hallucinogenic drugs. They really are bad news."

"True," responded Owen, thinking about the various drugs he had now tried, none of which were hallucinogenic.

"Are you sticking around long enough for food?"

"I ate before I came, but I wouldn't say 'no' to a mug of coffee."

"Right you are."

Francis put the kettle on and got three mugs from the mug tree.

"Apart from the study, tell me about your job. Wait. Have you got yourself a girlfriend?"

"I thought I had. I met this beautiful Russian student, but her father has something to do with the embassy and she's moving to Canada, this week."

"That's a pain."

"My job is in a pub. Been there pretty much since I left here. They've been great, giving me shifts to fit round my classes."

"Does it pay well?"

"Well enough. With my grant cheque I manage."

"So how did you end up with an Afghan Hound?"

"There's a woman, who works at the pub. She's taken me under her wing. Had meals with her family. Anyway, she volunteers at Battersea Dogs' Home. She showed me round, one day, and I fell in love with Kochai. I'm still a little surprised they let me adopt him, but they seemed happy with my flat. Obviously, I didn't tell them it's a squat. He's extremely well behaved. Apparently, he was really faithful to his owner, an old man, and when he died, it took several days for them to discover Kochai in the shed, because he hadn't barked. We go for lots of nice walks, and he's great on his own during classes or shifts. His name means 'nomad'. It's Pashto."

"I'd like to meet him, one day. Come to think of it, I'd like to see your flat."

"You're more than welcome."

The kettle boiled and Francis made the coffees.

"George. Your coffee's here," he called.

There were running steps on the stairs and George appeared in the doorway.

"Cheers."

"Owen's got an Afghan Hound."

"Really. I love dogs."

He took his coffee and went back upstairs.

"Where were we? The Russian girl. Did you sleep with her?"

"To the point, as ever. As a matter of fact, yes."

"Good for you."

"She never seemed to do any work. Spoke really good English. Hardly seems fair that she was bi-lingual."

"It is what it is."

"Have you kept in touch with any of the others?"

"Not really. Most of them went off to university. Doubt we'll ever meet up again. I for one, won't be going to some school reunion, in ten years' time."

"Pretty sure I won't be either," laughed Owen, finishing his coffee. "OK. I'll ring you when I get my phone installed and you can come round. Have a good Christmas."

"You, too. It's only a couple of weeks away, isn't it?"

"Bye. Thanks for the coffee."

"Yes. See you. Ride safely."

"Cheers."

Owen left and rode home. He was encouraged by George's networking abilities.

That Friday afternoon, before going to work, Owen took his stash of cannabis resin and cut off about a third of the block, which he divided into smaller lumps, about the size of a half-pence piece. He rolled the lumps into balls and wrapped them individually in aluminium foil. They looked like sweets, the kind of mints you sometimes find in baskets on the counters in hotel receptions. He placed the foil-covered resin sweets in a bowl on the top shelf of one of his eye-level kitchen cabinets, away from Kochai's reach.

The following morning, after a nice, long, early-morning walk with Kochai, as soon as it got light at around eight o'clock, he put the drugs in the outside pocket of his holdall and set off Caterham. It was chilly, hanging around outside the station. Shortly after ten o'clock, a student-aged man approached him.

"Excuse me. Do you, by any chance, know who the nomad is?"

"Yes."

Owen reached inside the holdall pocket and brought out one of the foil-wrapped balls of cannabis resin.

"It's thirty quid."

The man got out three £10 notes from his back pocket and exchanged them with Owen.

"Same time, same place, two weeks' time."

Owen pocketed the money and the man walked off, almost running. It was another fifteen minutes, before a woman, in her forties, approached Owen.

"Are you the Nomad?"

Owen reached into the holdall pocket and brought out another measure of cannabis resin.

"How much?"

"Thirty."

She reached into her coat pocket and pulled out some screwed-up banknotes.

"There you are."

Owen handed her the drugs.

"Cheers."

"Fortnight. Same time, same place."

She disappeared into the station.

The next two customers arrived almost simultaneously and performed a slightly awkward dance, unsure of letting the other one see that they were trying to buy cannabis. Eventually, one of them walked away, whilst the other carried out their transaction.

"Thirty," said Owen, getting out a ball of cannabis resin.

The man, or rather teenager, handed him a twenty and a tenner.

"Same time, two weeks' time."

The other dancer returned when the coast was clear.

"What you got?"

Owen showed him one of the wrapped balls.

"Thirty quid's worth."

"Can you change a fifty?"

Owen nodded, and pulled two notes from his pocket, one at a time, so as not to reveal how much he was holding.

"When you next here?"

He was the first customer to ask.

"Same time, in a fortnight. Tell your mates."

"Thanks."

By eleven o'clock, Owen was £210 richer. He realised that he might have been better to make the window two hours, rather than one, but it all depended on how many customers there were. If George had only networked with eight people, one hour was enough for seven of them to make their purchases. All he could do now, was hope that some of today's customers would return, and they would have done their own networking for him. It was a good start, and as far as he was aware, no passers-by had been suspicious, and no police had been visible, not that he would have known if a plain-clothes officer had showed up.

Owen had not anticipated how depressing Christmas would be. The Mallones had gone to Wendy's mother's house otherwise she would have invited Owen. He had no tree or decorations, no turkey and trimmings, and no presents, other than the secret Santa gift, from the pub. His was a pack of playing cards. It was Vince who received the box of chocolates he contributed. He poured himself a vodka and dealt out the cards for solitaire. He had wrapped a bone-chew up for Kochai.

"Come here, mate. Try getting into this parcel. I bought it specially for you."

He put the parcel on the floor and Kochai sniffed at it. After a few moments of chewing the bone with the paper on, Owen unwrapped it for him.

"There you go." Happy Christmas.

Owen had Christmas Day off and was back on shift on Boxing Day. Wendy was on good form and was wearing tinsel round her head. She gave Owen a huge kiss on the cheek.

"Happy Christmas!"

"You too, Wendy. Did you have a good day, yesterday, with the family?"

"I did, thank you. What did you do?"

"It was a very quiet Christmas. Just Kochai and me."

"Oh, Owen. If we hadn't been at my mum's."

"Don't worry. You do so much for me."

"Can you go and change the barrel on the lager, please? They're drinking like fish today!"

"Of course."

Owen disappeared to the cellar. The Prince Albert was busy. It was as if the regulars had missed being there on Christmas Day and were wanting to make up for it. It was gone four o'clock, when the pair of them finished clearing away the lunchtime shift.

When Owen arrived back at the flat, poor Kochai was desperate and only just made it to the bottom of the steps, before relieving himself. They went as far as the park but did not stay. Owen needed to get some food before going back for the evening shift, which he was sharing with Mr Longstaff. He also washed in the bathroom basin and put on fresh antiperspirant.

It was several months now, that Owen had been working at The Prince Albert. He was confident, with every task he had to accomplish, but for some reason, when he had to work alongside Mr Longstaff, the landlord, he was nervous.

"I just wanted to let you know that it's been great having you on staff, Owen," declared Mr Longstaff, a third of the way through the shift. "I wasn't a hundred percent sure, but I'm really glad I offered you the job. I'm going to increase your wages by twenty pence an hour. That's my way of giving you a Christmas bonus, by the way."

"Thank you very much, Mr Longstaff. I enjoy it here. I like the sense of family, amongst the regulars."

"That's true. It is like an extended family. And a pretty dysfunctional one, at that, I have no doubt," he laughed. "Did you spend Christmas Day with your family?"

"No, Mr Longstaff. Pretty dysfunctional. I'm in Battersea because I kind of left home."

"It's none of my business, Owen, but whatever you said or did, or whatever they said or did, it's family. One day, you should aim to go back. That's all I'm going to say about it."

"That's good advice, Mr Longstaff, Thank you."

Mr Longstaff said nothing else to Owen, all shift. It was cause for Owen to ponder. One day, he might return. Maybe, when he reached the ripe old age of thirty, he would consider it. Even after the worst Christmas Day he had ever experienced, Owen had no regrets about his decision to leave the shadow of his parents' pagoda.

The following day, after his morning constitutional with Kochai, Owen went to the newsagents, where he had a regular order for Pravda. His Russian language tutor insisted that every week, his students found an article in an up-to-date Russian newspaper, about something that could only be local to Russia, about two to three hundred words long, and to translate it into English. The reason for the emphasis on local news was so that the students could not simply cross-reference the text with an English newspaper.

It was not until Owen sat at the kitchen table, and unfolded the newspaper, that he read the headline. The Russians had intervened in Afghanistan to support the communist government against anti-communist insurgents, rising up against social and land reforms. He switched on the radio, which was tuned into Radio Four. The news came on, with the headline that the Soviet Union had invaded Afghanistan. Two opposing perspectives on the same event. Owen wondered where the truth lay. He would buy an English newspaper, next time he went out.

Leaving the international headlines and editorial behind, Owen sought out two more insignificant articles to translate. He was two pieces of work behind schedule, but the tutor had given him the Christmas holidays to catch up, for which he was grateful, even though he was increasingly persuaded to give up. There was a story about plunging in the snow, after visiting the 'banya', which Owen thought he could translate, with confidence. The other story he selected was about an unusual friendship between a tortoise and a domesticated hare. Assisted by his dictionary, Owen finished his translations after an hour and a half. He was supposed to hand them in on the first day of term, or he would be marked 'zero' for both pieces of work.

During the Christmas holidays, Owen made his first trip to the 'banya' without Katya. It felt weird, but the middle-aged woman on reception greeted him in her usual way. As soon as he disappeared through the door, she made a phone call. While he was sweating in the steam room, Vasily entered and sat down next to him.

"Hello, my friend. It's good to see you."

"Hello. It feels strange without Katya."

"I'm sure it does. Are you coming to the smoke room afterwards? I can get you what you need."

"Thank you, yes."

It was the longest conversation Owen had actually held in Russian, with a Russian, since the school trip. He was pleased with himself.

"We'll stay ten more minutes and then take our showers, yes?"

"Yes."

Vasily was quiet for those ten minutes, but Owen could pick up some of the conversation between two middle-aged men on the opposite bench. They were talking about Afghanistan, and the impact of the war on supply chains. They did not mention what was being supplied. Owen tried not to stare, but at one point, he looked up and caught the gaze of one of the men. His eyes were blue-grey and menacingly piercing. The man nodded, and Owen looked down at the floor, tensing with an uneasy embarrassment. After ten minutes, Vasily stood up, and Owen followed him out of the steam room to the cold showers.

Up in the smoke room, Yelena was waiting for Vasily.

"Hello, Owen. Good to see you again."

"Hi. Good to be here again."

"Today, I will show you how to get an even better rush," explained Vasily.

He went over to a dresser on the other side of the room to the floor cushions and took out what looked like individually wrapped drinking straws, from where Owen was sitting. He also took hold of a length of rubber tubing. Instead of the usual opium pipe, on the stand over the candle, which today smelt of spices, there was a small container with liquid in.

"I will show you this way," indicated Vasily, pointing at the container, "but you can also use spring water to dissolve it. I will demonstrate on myself. Then you can do it, and if you have trouble finding a vein, I will help you. Watch carefully."

Owen realised the drinking straws were in fact syringes. He watched as Vasily tore the paper off one and drew some of the liquid from the container into the barrel of the syringe.

He took the rubber tubing and wound it round his left biceps and identified a vein. He expelled some of the liquid, to make sure there were no air bubbles, and inserted the needle into his vein, injecting the heroin. He released the tourniquet and relaxed.

"Now you try."

He handed the tubing to Owen. Owen removed the paper from his syringe and drew in some of the liquid.

"Only go to the first gradation!" Laughed Vasily, although he was serious about not wanting Owen to overdose. "That's right. Now put the tourniquet on."

Owen wound the rubber tubing round his right bicep, as he was left-handed. He was nervous about injecting himself.

"What happens if I hit an artery, not a vein?"

"You will know, because the pressure will send some blood into the syringe. Then. You just withdraw the needle and try again."

Owen chose a prominent vein, squirted out some liquid from the syringe and stuck the needle in. He pushed on the plunger, his hand shaking, and pulled out the needle.

"There you go. Now take off the tourniquet and relax."

Owen removed the rubber tubing and lay back on the cushions. A few moments later, he experienced the best rush of his life.

"Was that good?" asked Vasily.

"Amazing."

"Good. But that is the last time we can give you the drugs for free. Next time you pay. I can also sell you some to take home. And a couple of syringes."

"How much?"

"£80 for a gram."

"How much did I just use?"

"That was probably only about a tenth to a fifth of a gram," replied Vasily, looking at how much liquid was still in the container.

"I will buy some next time I come."

"Alright, my friend."

"Have you heard anything from Katya?"

"No, my friend."

Owen waited around half an hour and got up to leave. As before, he bought a coffee at Euston Station, to drink before attempting his ride back to Battersea. He also bought a copy of the Guardian newspaper. Kochai, greeted him, sniffing his clothes. Owen went to the toilet and drank a glass of water. He wondered what he should do if he used the other method that Vasily had mentioned, dissolving the heroin in water. He would ask him, next time he went to the 'banya'.

"Let's take you for your walk, mate."

He attached Kochai's lead to his collar and took him to the park.

Owen had spent the holidays working out what to do about his future. He was hoping to establish a network of customers for the cannabis, out of Caterham railway station, in the first instance, which would pay for his own heroin use. He would continue working at The Prince Albert, but he would give up his university course. Even though he felt, guilty, Owen decided to cash his second term's grant cheque and slowly stop attending classes. At some point in the last two weeks of term, he would tell his personal tutor that it was all too much, not what he had expected, and that he was giving up. Apart from any other consideration, Owen could not see how he would be able to spend his third year in Russia, now that he owned Kochai. He might be prepared to give up his beloved Afghan Hound for a couple of weeks to take a holiday, especially as he knew how much Wendy wanted to look after Kochai, but never for nine months to live abroad.

It was coming up to his second outing to Caterham train station, so he prepared some more cannabis resin wraps. He had no idea how many customers there would be, but he prepared for twelve. It was just as cold, when he got up, as it had been the first time, and he had been chilled to the marrow, so he put a second pair of socks on, and wore a scarf, making a mental note to get a hat. Wearing his helmet, most of the time, when he was outdoors, he had not felt the need for one up to then.

His first customer was there wandering around the car park when Owen arrived, and he kicked himself, for not parking somewhere else. Next time, he would leave his motorcycle a short walk away. The customer was not familiar to him.

"Are you the Nomad?" asked the man, approaching Owen, once he was parked, had removed his helmet and standing by the entrance.

"Yes. It's thirty."

He got out a measure of cannabis, and the man gave him some ten-pound notes.

"Same time, two weeks' time. Tell your friends. I'll be here for an hour."

"Thanks," replied the man, rushing off.

By the end of the morning, Owen had sold ten lots of cannabis.

The following lunchtime, he took himself off to the 'banya', with eighty pounds in his wallet. As he got changed into his bath robe, he had a sudden concern that someone might try to rob him. It had never occurred to him before, but he had never been going to buy drugs there before, and he knew that Vasily knew that he wanted to buy some. How was he going to keep his money in sight, when he was in the steam room? Foolish or resourceful, he was not yet sure, but Owen wrapped the wallet against his lower back, tightly, with the towel, hoping it would not fall out, or the bank notes would not get damp. His plan was successful, and the wallet survived.

When he went through to the smoke room, Vasily was there with Yelena and the two men he had heard discussing supply chains, on his previous visit to the steam room.

"My name is Nikolai," the man with the blue-grey eyes introduced himself. "This is Mikhail. Welcome to our 'banya'. I understand you speak Russian?"

"Yes, I do."

"And I also understand that you like our heroin?" added Nikolai, his gaze penetrating Owen's soul.

"That is correct."

Owen was starting to feel very uneasy. He wished Katya was there.

"I have a proposition for you. How would you like never to have to pay for your heroin?"

"That is interesting. What would I have to do?"

"We have a shipment arriving in Amsterdam in two weeks and we need someone to go and pick it up. We will pay for your train ticket to Harwich, your crossing, your train ticket from Hook of Holland to Amsterdam, and your return. When you get to Amsterdam, you will be met by a friend, stay overnight at their house, and return the next day with the shipment."

"How do I get the shipment through customs?"

"That is a very good question. It will be disguised in a Delft tea service. Please try not to break it! The whole thing will weigh around three kilograms, and you will be able to carry it in your rucksack or holdall."

"And then I get free heroin?"

"Yes. You will be able to come here every two weeks for a year, and get your rush at no cost, here in the smoke room."

Owen sensed he had just been made a proposition that he would be unable to decline. His head was racing, thinking about Kochai, and missing his shifts.

"I have to go midweek, because of my shifts at the pub. I don't want to raise suspicions, by asking for a whole weekend off."

"That is a reasonable request. I have one more question for you. Is your passport up to date?"

"Just about. I got it when I was fifteen and I have to change my first passport after five years, but I won't be twenty until next year."

"Good. That is settled, then. As a gesture of goodwill, you can have today's measure for free."

Nikolai held out his hand and Owen shook it.

"Do we have a deal, Owen?"

"We have a deal."

He needn't have worried about being robbed. Vasily had got out two syringes, and the rubber tubing. He handed a syringe to Owen.

"After you, Vasily."

Vasily smiled and injected himself. Owen took the rubber tubing and followed suit.

When he got back home, and took Kochai for his walk, Owen started to reflect on what had just happened. Suddenly, the supply chains made sense. If he had not suspected it before, Owen was pretty sure that the 'banya' was a cover for the drug trade, and worse, possibly even the Russian Mafia.

He wondered how involved Katya had been. It certainly accounted for why she was cagy when he asked where the drugs came from. At that point, his stomach knotted, and he felt sick to the core of his being. Had Katya really been interested in him, or was she just trying to get him hooked on drugs? Did her father even work with the diplomatic service?

The next day, a large brown envelope dropped through Owen's letterbox, into the wire anti-Kochai cage he had made. It bore no stamp and the address was hand-written. Perhaps it was from the charity where he got the furniture or from The Prince Albert? He was racking his brains trying to think who knew his address, as he pulled open the flap. Inside was a cardboard ticket folder and a piece of paper.

"Shit!!!" he exclaimed.

Nikolai knew where he lived. Of course, he did. Katya had been to his flat. The outward ticket was dated for the Tuesday night crossing of next week. The return was dated for the Thursday evening, arriving in the UK on Friday morning. Both times he would be in a cabin. There was also a return train ticket from Liverpool Street to Harwich. Why had they given him an extra day? Possibly to make it look more like a business trip than drugs trafficking. Hopefully, he might be able to do some sight-seeing during the day on the Thursday or Friday. He had promised himself a visit to the Rijksmuseum. Owen glanced over the letter. It was written in Russian. 'Dear Owen. Please wear a suit for your business trip. Your host is Anton Alexeyev. 179 Korte Spinhuisseteeg. He is expecting you. Enjoy your day of sightseeing. See you on the Sunday. Please ask Anton if his dog has had her puppies yet. All good wishes.' All good wishes? Owen was now terrified. Had they been watching him? Did they know he sold cannabis in Caterham? Was the shooting he witnessed Nikolai? Did his stash of cannabis belong to Nikolai?

Wednesday was the start of the spring term. Owen collected and banked his grant cheque and handed in his translations, as stipulated, even though it no longer mattered if they were marked or not, as he had made up his mind to drop out. At the end of classes, he called round Wendy's house.

"You alright, Owen?" asked Wendy, surprised to see him.

"Can I come in for a moment?"

"Of course. It's not Kochai, is it?"

"No. I think I'm just tired. I've not been sleeping much."

"As long as you're alright."

"Actually, I need to ask a favour. I have to go and sort something out. Is there any chance you could look after Kochai next Tuesday night, Wednesday, Thursday and Friday? I'll be back early afternoon on the Friday."

"You know I will. What time will you drop him off, on Tuesday?"

"Five. Thank you so much."

"No problem."

She pinched his cheek, but did not pry, to Owen's relief.

Tuesday came round all too quickly. Owen could not remember the last time he was this nervous. If he was feeling nervous for the outward journey, what would he be like for the return? The return journey mattered far more, and he could not risk acting suspiciously. Packing was easy. As he was wearing his suit for both journeys, he only needed T-shirt and jeans and some clean underwear, for the days in between. He packed his jack boots into the holdall, which weighed a ton. Not only were they heavy, but he remembered he needed to leave room for the Delft tea service, on the return journey. Perhaps he would leave them behind and wear his smart shoes with his jeans. He also packed an English translation of Tolstoy's *Anna Karenina*, for the journey.

He made some baked beans on toast for his tea and took Kochai for a walk. When they got back, he allowed Kochai long enough to lap up half a bowl of water and put the two bowls and some food into a plastic carrier bag.

"You're going to have a short holiday, with Wendy, mate. I've got to go away for a few days, on business, you understand. I'll miss you."

Re-attaching his lead, Owen walked Kochai round to Wendy's house and rang the doorbell.

"Hi," she greeted Owen, almost without looking at him, crouching down to give Kochai attention. "Hello gorgeous. Who's coming to stay with Wendy. I've got so much fun planned for you."

"Bye, mate," said Owen, cupping Kochai's face in his hands. "See you soon."

"Don't worry. He'll be fine," Wendy comforted him.

"Thank you again. Oh, here's his food and bowls," he added, handing over the bag.

Owen regularly left Kochai at home in the daytime, but this was the first time he had left him overnight, and he felt sad and a little bit guilty.

Once back at his flat, he went to the toilet, checked the lights were off, grabbed his holdall and went out. He was able to fit the holdall in his top-box but wondered if there would be room on the return journey. He would cross that bridge when he came to it. In Central London, he almost went into automatic pilot, heading for Euston Station and realised he was not sure how to get to Liverpool Street Station. He kept an A to Z in the top-box, so pulled up, set the Honda on its stand, and got off to check the route. It also occurred to him that he knew what parking was like at Euston but what about Liverpool Street? And would it be alright to leave his bike for three days? It was too late to do anything about it now.

When he reached the station, he looked for where the motorcycles were parked and slotted his into a gap between

650cc Kawasaki and a 100cc Yamaha, wondering if he would ever get round to buying a more powerful motorcycle than his 250cc Honda. Having checked the departures, he bought a copy of the *Times* newspaper, from the kiosk, and walked to the platform, where the Harwich train was waiting. Getting into the first carriage, he walked through until he found an empty seat, beyond first class, beyond the buffet car, and sat down. Owen had no real preference between *Times* and *Guardian*. He only read them to keep up with current affairs, and hardly bothered to analyse the editorials.

He opened his newspaper and began to flick through the pages. His interest was engaged by an article about the international response to Brezhnev sending the 40th Army over the border, on Christmas Eve, staging a coup and killing Hafizullah Amin. President Jimmy Carter immediately withdrew the US ambassador. Apparently, the administration had not expected an invasion, and were caught on the hop. The invasion was unacceptable and threatened global security and the supply of oil. There was concern that Pakistan and Iran might be next. The United Nations Security Council met to discuss the invasion but could not achieve agreement between the permanent members. Resolution 462 called for an emergency special session of the General Assembly, and predictably, the Russians and East Germans voting against it. During the emergency special session, Russia insisted their intervention was legitimate, having been invited by the Afghans to have a role in their civil war. In the end, the legitimacy of the Russian invasion was not recognised, and a further resolution passed, calling for the immediate withdrawal of foreign armed forces, and an end to interference in internal Afghan political and economic affairs. As expected, the Russians went on to ignore the resolution.

It felt like an odd time to be studying Russian at university. Even with the status quo, this seemed like a new departure from the Cold War. Owen almost stopped himself from swapping the newspaper for his copy of *Anna Karenina*, for fear of what the passengers sitting opposite might think. Although he knew it was unwise to judge by appearances, a swift appraisal of the older woman and wannabee punk rocker facing him, encouraged Owen that they were unlikely to be well-informed about the situation in Afghanistan, and if they were, reading a copy of *Anna Karenina*, in English, hardly constituted Russian sympathies. He took the novel from his holdall and started reading, glancing towards the man and woman, to look for any reaction.

A guard was making his way along the aisle. Owen got out his ticket.

"Change at Manningtree. Thank you, sir," grunted the guard, handing back his ticket.

"Thank you, madam. Change at Manningtree."

The punk rocker was having difficulty locating his ticket.

"Sorry. Just a moment."

The guard turned to the passengers across the aisle and turned back to the punk rocker, who handed him a ticket.

"Thank you, sir. Change at Manningtree."

Owen wondered if they were all heading for the ferry. It was dark outside, and he had no idea where they were. He looked at his watch. There was about twenty minutes still to travel. Having read two chapters, Owen put both newspaper and novel in his holdall, and peered out through the window. An illuminated station rushed past, too fast for Owen to read the name. The black countryside, punctuated by a few lights, gave way to the streetlamps of

Manningtree, and the train decelerated. He got off with the older woman and punk rocker but sat apart from them on the connecting train, finding himself in their company once more, when they queued to board the ship.

Owen was glad to be in his cabin. Lying on the bunk, his thoughts turned to Kochai. Would he be sleeping peacefully? There was an information leaflet on the bedside table. The bar was still open, so he made his way there and bought a vodka and orange. He had no idea if removing his glass from the bar was permitted, but he returned to his cabin, removed his suit, shirt and tie, discovered he had forgotten to pack pyjamas, downed the vodka and orange, and read *Anna Karenina*, until he fell asleep. He was rudely awakened by the public address system announcing the ship's impending arrival in the Netherlands, whereupon he washed his face, got dressed and went up to the deck where he had boarded. He could see the older woman and the punk rocker, across the floor, engaged in conversation.

After a lot of bumps and bangs and metallic grinding noises, the doors opened, and the passengers started moving. Half an hour later, Owen had passed through passport control and was sitting on a train bound for Amsterdam, curious to know what Anton Alexeyev would be like. The address was on a piece of paper in his inside jacket pocket, which was also where his train ticket was. Relieved that no one had sat next to him, he leant across and glanced along the train to see a man carrying a coffee cup, unsteadily walking along the aisle. Once the man had passed, Owen got up, leaving his holdall on his seat, and went in search of the restaurant car. He bought a coffee, disappointed with himself for not being able to speak Dutch and returned to his seat.

When the train arrived at Amsterdam Central station, Owen alighted and stood in the concourse, trying to get his bearings. There was a tourist information kiosk, so he approached.

"I'm sorry. I don't speak Dutch."

"Not a problem, sir. How can I help you," came the reply in fluent English.

"I need a map of the city, please."

The man behind the counter took a folding map from a holder on the wall and handed it to Owen.

"Do you have accommodation?"

"Yes, thank you."

"Enjoy your stay, sir."

"Thank you."

Owen unfolded the map and looked down the index to find Korte Spinhuisseteeg. It was within easy walking distance of the Dam, the main square, which was less than a mile from the station. He set off, following several rucksack-bedecked pedestrians. From the Dam, he headed east, crossing over a couple of canals, turning south and making his way to Korte Spinhuisseteeg, where he knocked on the door of Number 179.

A gaunt man, who looked older than he probably was, opened the door a few inches and muttered something in Dutch, but with a distinctly Russian accent. Owen was sure this must be Anton Alexeyev. Smiling, he drew in his breath and replied in Russian.

"Hello. Has your dog had her puppies?"

"Owen?"

Owen nodded and the man pulled open the door to allow him room to cross the threshold.

"I am Anton," he introduced himself, now speaking Russian, as soon as the door was shut, again. "Pleasant journey?"

"Thank you."

"Are you hungry?"

"Yes, I am. I had no breakfast."

"Then we shall eat. Come. Let me show you to your room."

He led Owen to a bedroom and left him there to go and put the kettle on. Owen went in and dumped his holdall.

"May I use your bathroom, please?"

"Of course. It is the room next to yours."

"Thanks."

Owen disappeared again and returned to the kitchen to find the table set with hot coffee, bread and cheese.

"How is Nikolai?"

"He's fine."

"You are here until tomorrow evening, yes?"

"Yes."

"Then you have this afternoon and all day tomorrow to explore this beautiful city."

"I want to visit the Rijksmuseum."

"Why the Rijksmuseum?"

"I like the paintings of Van Gogh."

"Then, my friend, it is the Van Gogh Museum you must visit. True, you will see Rembrandt works in the Rijksmuseum, but Van Gogh has his own special place."

"Thank you. I will remember that. What else do you recommend?"

"Apart from the red-light district, you mean?" he laughed.

Owen laughed but had no intention of visiting the infamous area.

"You could see a diamond-cutting demonstration. Or there are cafés, ones where you can eat cannabis cake. Of course, there are the canals to see."

"Thank you," replied Owen, tucking into some bread and cheese. "This cheese is good. So is the coffee."

"I will tell my wife. She is not here, just now. She will be home in a couple of hours. You can meet her later. By the way, in case you haven't noticed, I don't actually have a dog."

They both laughed.

After eating, Owen took himself off into the centre of Amsterdam. First things first, he needed to exchange some money. This might be an all-expenses-paid trip, but spending-money was his responsibility. He decided to go into a bank. He had no idea if it was a good exchange rate, but it seemed to be the most straightforward option.

When he got to the museum, he discovered it was only a stone's throw from the Rijksmuseum. On entering the Van Gogh Museum, Owen read that the Van Gogh collection was in the Rietveld Building. There was another building, the Kurokawa Building, but that was of no interest to Owen. He spent the next hour, wandering through Van Gogh's career. So many of the paintings were unfamiliar to Owen. He was hoping to see *Starry Night*, but it was not in the collection.

Walking along the side of one of the many canals, he came to a café and went in. He sat down at a vacant table and waited to be served. The waiter acknowledged him but took a few moments to approach as the place was busy.

"Good afternoon, sir. What can I get you?"

"Is it that obvious I'm English?" laughed Owen.

"Would you like to try some of our cannabis cake?"

"Yes, please. And a milky coffee."

"It'll be with you immediately, sir. Thank you."

The waiter went behind the counter, steamed some milk, made the coffee, and transferred a piece of cake from the servery to a plate, with a pair of stainless-steel tongs.

"Forgive me for asking, but have you tried this kind of cake before?" he asked, placing the mug and plate on the table in front of Owen.

"Err, no. But I have smoked cannabis," added Owen, sheepishly.

"I must advise you that you may feel dizzy or sleepy. Some people feel sick."

"No problem. Thank you."

The waiter went about his business and Owen tucked into his snack. A few minutes later, on his way to serve another customer, the waiter passed a copy of the Guardian to Owen.

"Thanks."

After about half an hour of reading and munching, Owen washed his cake down with the last of the coffee and indicated to the waiter that he wanted to pay. It was not until he had left the café and was walking back towards the Dam that Owen started to feel the effect, and it was a much stronger feeling than when he had smoked the drug, although nothing like the rush of heroin. He warned himself not to step too close to the edge of the canal but thought he would try and walk it off. Without realising quite where he was going, he found himself walking in the red-light district. Had he not been feeling the effects of his cannabis cake, he might have been tempted, just to have experienced sex, here, in Amsterdam, but he was not accustomed to frequenting sex workers, so he smiled and shook his head at two scantily dressed women, looking out of their windows. Owen arrived back at the train station, which was slightly frustrating, but at least he knew where he was.

Back at Anton's house, he met Kristina.

"What have you done today?"

"I went to the Van Gogh Museum and I ate some cake, in a café."

He was not sure what the Russian for 'cannabis' was.

"You mean cannabis cake?" she replied.

Owen nodded and smiled. The word was the same.

"What did you think of the museum?"

"I really like Van Gogh's paintings."

"What else did you do?"

"I got lost and found myself walking through the red-light area."

"You were tempted, of course?" laughed Anton.

"No," replied Owen, going red.

"Don't tease our guest, Anton. Are you hungry?"

"Is it mealtime?"

"If you would like it to be mealtime."

"Then yes, thank you. Let me just use the bathroom."

Kristina brought in a large plate of what looked like burgers.

"Have you eaten cutlets?" she asked.

"I don't think so."

"Serve yourself, while I get the potato."

As Kristina went back into the kitchen to fetch the mashed potato, Anton grabbed the serving spoon and piled three of the meaty burgers onto Owen's plate. When the mashed potato arrived, he served his own. Anton opened some bottles of beer.

"You drink beer?"

"Thank you."

Owen was glad to have some food in his stomach. He took a mouthful of beer, but did not drink again, until he had eaten most of his main course. For dessert, Kristina opened a packet of chocolate-covered apricots.

"I ate these in Russia."

"When did you go to Russia?" asked Anton.

"When I was fifteen. On a school trip. To Leningrad and Moscow."

"Kristina is from Moscow."

"Really! How did you start living in Amsterdam?"

"How do most people start living in Amsterdam? The lifestyle is so free."

"What jobs do you do?"

"I am a wood-turner, in a factory."

"I am a hairdresser. What about you, Owen?" inquired Kristina.

"I am a student and I work in a pub."

"Did you like it in Russia?" asked Anton.

"I was a tourist on a school trip. I don't think I experienced the real Russia. I liked the museums and sight-seeing."

"Perhaps you would not enjoy the real Russia, although we try not to talk about these things."

"How long have you lived here?"

"Five years in Amsterdam and two years in this apartment."

"Now, no more questions," Anton interjected. "Let's play chess."

"I don't play chess. I never learnt."

"Oh dear. Then we must play Durak. I will show you how. Kristina will bring us the vodka and play as well, won't you, my angel?"

The game, Durak, was not overly complicated, but Owen was tired, and a little woozy. After the third game, he made his excuses and went to bed.

Breakfast was a veritable feast of pancakes and coffee. Anton had already left for work when Owen got up. Kristina sat with him and drank a mug of coffee.

"What will you do today?"

"Maybe go to the Rijksmuseum. I like walking back and forth across the canals."

"You can go on a boat trip."

"Can you?"

"Yes. Will you go back for more cannabis cake?"

"I might," laughed Owen.

He wondered how much Kristina knew about the reason for his visit.

"I know why you are here, Owen. Be careful," she declared, to Owen's surprise.

He nodded.

"Thank you for breakfast. Delicious."

"You're welcome. I'm serious, Owen. Get out, if you still can."

Owen could see the fear in her eyes. The problem was, he could not see how to get out. They clearly knew where he lived. If he was useful to them, he would be alright. Surely?

Today, Owen visited the Rijksmuseum. He was not sure if he had ever seen quite so many religious paintings in one place before. He wished he had artistic talent, and had a momentary crisis of confidence, because he could not put his finger on just what his own talents were. He felt pretty average at most things and had no idea what he really wanted to do with his life. It was true, he picked up languages fairly easily, but what practical skills did he have?

Having left the museum, he went in search of a boat trip. It was not quite lunchtime yet. At least, Owen was still feeling stuffed from his pancakes. As he stood on one of the canal bridges, staring out along the water, a man, probably in his early thirties, approached Owen.

"Hi. Are you English?"

"Yes. You're the second person in Amsterdam who has asked me that, in two days, even before I've opened my mouth."

"I'm Floyd," the man introduced himself.

"I'm Owen."

"How long are you here for?"

"Just until this evening. I am catching the overnight ferry from Hook of Holland."

"My wife and I have a house-boat, just behind the train station. Would you like to come and have a cup of tea, or something? I'm afraid we can't offer you any cake like they might offer you in some of the cafés here, but Sally, my wife, does a mean carrot cake."

"Sounds good," replied Owen, wondering why he was so polite and amiable.

"Great. Come this way."

Owen walked alongside Floyd.

"What do you do in England?"

"I am a student, for a while, anyway. I'm not really enjoying the course, and I work some shifts in a pub."

"What are you studying?"

"Russian."

"Wow. That's amazing. I bet there are comparatively few people who speak Russian in England. Most people study French or German, possibly even Spanish."

"That may well be true. It's just not what I thought. I'm not sure what I did think, but I really don't enjoy half the literature."

"What do you enjoy?"

"The so-called 'Silver Age' of writers, who interpreted the Revolution."

"Ah. You are a dreamer who wants to change the world."

"I've never really looked at it like that before."

They arrived at the houseboat.

The windows were steamed up, and Owen could smell coffee and baking. A student aged woman came out and ran up the gangplank, just as Floyd was about to descend.

"Hi, Esme."

"Hi Floyd. See you later."

"She's one of our volunteers, here. Follow me. Welcome to our houseboat."

Owen followed Floyd down the gangplank. Floyd walked over to a woman and kissed her on the cheek.

"I'd like to introduce you to my gorgeous wife, Sally. Sally, this is Owen."

"Hello, Owen. Would you like tea or coffee? Maybe a cold drink?"

"Coffee would be great. Thank you."

"Have a seat, Owen," Floyd ushered him to a bench. "We see a lot of students here, in Amsterdam. Many are searching for themselves. Many are just lost. We like to offer a listening ear and a hot drink."

"Would you like some carrot cake, Owen?" Sally interrupted them.

"Please," replied Owen, and turning back to Floyd, "How long have you been in Amsterdam?"

"Since about 1973, I think. I lose track of time. Before that, we were in Afghanistan."

"Really! I have an Afghan Hound, called Kochai."

"Nomad."

"You speak Pashto?"

"Yes."

"What do you think about the Russian intervention?"

"The Russian invasion? I try not to be political, although I am pretty sure that they shouldn't be there. I understand, the UN has told them to withdraw their troops. As you can tell, we're American, and I think President Carter needs to find non-military ways of addressing the issue."

"Such as?"

"Who knows. Perhaps boycotting the Olympics, later this year."

Sally cut the carrot cake and handed Owen a plate and a coffee.

"What brings you to Amsterdam?"

"Honestly? I got involved with some people doing some stuff I probably shouldn't have done, and now they have asked me to come to Amsterdam to fetch something and take it back to the United Kingdom for them."

"I think I understand, Owen. Just be careful. And if you need a place to come and relax, or you want someone to talk to, we're here."

"Thanks."

Owen was struck by the way they welcomed him without any hint of judging him for what he had done or was doing now. They genuinely seemed interested in his wellbeing. Another student came through the door.

"Excuse me, Owen. I need to turn my back on you for a moment."

"It's OK."

Owen finished his coffee and cake, whilst Sally was making a coffee for the newcomer and Floyd was chatting to him. When he finished, Owen quietly put his jacket back on and left, acknowledging Sally and Floyd with a silently mouthed, "Thank you."

That was not how Owen had thought he would spend a couple of hours in Amsterdam, but it was actually quite enjoyable. Sally and Floyd seemed like genuine people.

He still had not been on a boat trip along the canals, so looked for a mooring, with a board offering canal tours. They were not too expensive, so he waited in line. There was a choice between a one hour or a half hour trip. The hour trip went right out beyond the station, where he had just been, whilst the half hour tour kept to the canals closest to the centre. He opted for the half hour trip.

The difference in perspective surprised Owen. Not only was the view of the canals, from below street level, an interesting one, but the slow speed also gave the impression of being suspended in time. Owen told himself he would definitely return to Amsterdam, one day. The half hour passed, and the boat docked at its mooring again. Owen climbed back up to street level. There was one thing he had meant to ask, the day before, and had not taken the opportunity, so he went looking for the café where he had eaten cannabis cake. As he entered, the waiter recognised him.

"Back for some more cake?"

"Not today, thank you. Just a coffee. I have to be somewhere."

When the waiter brought Owen his coffee, Owen plucked up the courage to ask his question.

"Can I ask you something?" he inquired in a low voice.

"Yes, you can," replied the waiter, leaning closer, to hear Owen.

"I have noticed that Amsterdam is a free place to live. Cannabis cake is readily available, in cafés, for example. How easy is it to buy drugs here?"

"Very easy. Are you looking for some?"

"Not this time. However, I have decided I would very much like to come back again. That's when I might be seriously interested."

"Come here, when you are ready, and I will put you in contact with someone."

"Thank you."

"You're welcome."

Owen drank his coffee and returned to Anton and Kristina's apartment. They were both there.

"So, Owen, what did you do today?" inquired Kristina.

"I went to the Rijksmuseum. Interesting, but not as enjoyable as the Van Gogh Museum. I got invited to go and have some coffee and cake on a houseboat behind the train station and I went on a short boat trip along the canals. That was awesome."

"I know about that houseboat. I think the owners are Christians. Some sort of mission to prostitutes and drug addicts."

"And students," added Anton.

"They seemed genuine."

"We will feed you some soup and bread, and then you have a train to catch. This is the shipment. The Delft tea service. Be careful with it, Owen. We don't want it smashing in front of the customs officers."

Owen started to feel apprehensive, again. He forced his soup and bread down. The Delft tea service box fitted easily into his holdall. Owen put his suit back on and packed his jeans and T-shirt.

After double-checking that he had not left anything behind, he went to the toilet, picked up his holdall and stood by the door.

"Thank you for your hospitality."

"Good luck," responded Anton, holding out his hand.

Owen shook it.

"Nice to meet you, Owen," added Kristina. "Remember, be careful!"

Anton looked across at her but said nothing. Owen left for the train station where he sat for ten minutes on the platform, waiting. As the train pulled out of Amsterdam Central Station, Owen reflected on how great his time in the city had been. He would return, definitely. In fact, he was already thinking about how he might be able to replenish his stash, once the block of cannabis he had found ran out.

At the ferry terminal, Owen tried hard to relax, and not drawer attention to himself. He handed over his passport, was not asked about his luggage, and was soon in his cabin on the ship. He did not bother with a drink from the bar, this time. After walking around the city for two days, he was tired. Removing his suit, shirt and tie, he lay down on his bunk and drifted off to sleep.

In the morning, after washing his face, he put his suit on again. This last leg of the journey required even sterner metal than leaving the Netherlands, because he now had to pass through the 'Nothing to Declare' line, in customs. Should he look the official in the eye or avoid eye contact? Was it obvious he was sweating? In his head, he tried to remember a line from *The Cherry Orchard*, from the school production he had taken part in. The focus, and mundane nature of his thoughts, enabled him to pass through customs without acting suspiciously. Twenty minutes later, Owen was sitting on a train, heading for Liverpool Street Station, via Manningtree. He did not put the holdall in a luggage rack but sat with it across his lap. Once past Manningtree, and a change of trains, he allowed himself to fall asleep, one arm through the handle of the holdall. Soon enough, the train slowed down into Liverpool Street Station and came to a standstill.

As he walked across the concourse, for the first time since leaving London, Owen wondered if his motorcycle was still in one piece, where he had parked it. The Kawasaki and Yamaha had been replaced by a Honda Goldwing and a 500cc Suzuki, but to his relief, his Honda was still where he had left it. After attaching the holdall to the pillion seat with bungee cords, Owen fastened his helmet, and set off for Battersea. His intention was to dump the holdall in his flat, use the toilet, get changed into his jeans, and go straight round to Wendy's to pick up Kochai. There would be time for a decent walk, and then he had to work, for which he felt slightly guilty, having to leave Kochai again, when he had only just picked him up. Kochai would understand, he was sure.

As he walked round to Wendy's house, he really wanted to tell her about his trip to Amsterdam, but there was no easy way to do so and avoid further questions, so he would just have to keep it a secret. He would tell Kochai, his trusty confidant, all about it, instead. He rang the doorbell. Wendy opened wide the door, and Kochai practically knocked him off his feet.

"Good boy. I missed you. Have you had fun? Good Kochai."

"Did you get sorted what you needed to get sorted?" asked Wendy.

"Yes. Thank you. And thank you again for looking after Kochai."

"No problem. He's had a ball."

"I'm sure he has. Are you on tonight or is it Vince?"

"I think it's Vince. I'll see you tomorrow lunchtime."

"Great. Bye. Thanks again."

He attached Kochai's lead, took the plastic bag with the food bowls, which Wendy had now fetched from the kitchen, and set off home, via the local park. He was relieved to be home safe, without any glitches, and even happier to be reunited with Kochai, but the trickier part of the road ahead was yet to be navigated.

At midday, on Sunday, Owen placed the Delft tea service in his top-box and rode into Central London, parking in his usual place outside Euston Station. It was hard to know what kind of reception to expect at the 'banya'. Would Nikolai be happy, grateful even? Would Owen suddenly become surplus to requirements, in spite of the promise? The middle-aged woman at the reception desk greeted him in her usual way, and he carried his holdall through to the changing room and showers. Hardly had he put down the holdall, when Nikolai came in.

"How were the puppies, my friend?"

"I believe the puppies have made it to the UK," responded Owen, glancing at the holdall.

"Well, what are you waiting for?"

"Ah, yes. Sorry," stuttered Owen, unzipping the holdall and getting out the Delft tea service. "There you are. All in one piece, I hope."

"I hope it has three pieces," joked Nikolai. "Teapot, sugar bowl and jug. Have you not looked inside?"

"No. I haven't opened the box at all."

Nikolai took out a penknife, which made Owen feel nervous, and slit the tape holding the lid fast. He carefully opened the box, lifted out the teapot and removed the lid. The smile on his face turned into a broad grin, as he held the lidless teapot towards Owen.

"Take a look."

Owen peered inside to see it was packed with what he assumed must be heroin.

"Welcome to the family, Owen. Join me in the smoke room when you are done here."

"Yes."

"And thank you, Owen."

It dawned on Owen that he had just trafficked two to three kilos of heroin into the country. What did Nikolai mean by 'Welcome to the family'? Was this a good sign. He showered and went into the steam room, where Vasily was waiting. He stood and gave Owen a bear hug.

"Welcome back, my friend."

They sat in silence. Owen was beginning to feel more confident. His status seemed to have gone from guest to winning goal scorer over the last few days, although he was getting a niggling feeling that it was not the last trip he would have to make.

After their cold showers, Vasily and Owen went up to the smoke room where Nikolai was waiting. A metal dish was sitting in the stand over a candle, and the atmosphere smelt spicy. The syringes and rubber tubing were on the floor. At least the syringes were still individually wrapped. Vasily picked them up and handed one to Owen. As long as a went first, Owen knew the heroin would be alright.

"After you," he encouraged Vasily, passing him the rubber tubing.

"Our hero should go first," insisted Nikolai.

Now Owen was petrified. It occurred to him, if they were going to kill him, they were going to kill him, whether by causing him to overdose or shooting him in the street. He had no choice and no possibility of escape. He went through the process of drawing some heroin into the syringe, attaching the tourniquet and expelling some of the liquid in the syringe to remove any air bubbles. Finding a vein was harder than usual and he was relieved when he removed the rubber tubing and started to feel the rush. Vasily followed suit. Nikolai did not partake of the heroin.

"Remember Owen, we look after our own. You are welcome to come here once a week for your fix. The 'banya' you can use anytime, for free," remarked Nikolai, as he stood up to leave.

Owen was working a shift later that day. He left it as late as possible, to leave the 'banya' and was feeling a lot better about his situation than when he entered the building. He sorted himself out, with his usual strong coffee, bought in Euston Station, before riding home. Kochai was waiting by the door, and they went to the park as soon as Owen had used the toilet and gulped down a glass of water.

That evening, without thinking, he rolled up his sleeves to wash the glasses.

"You been giving blood?" asked Vince.

"It's a very good thing to do," responded Owen, neither admitting nor denying the cause of the needle marks.

He wondered whether Vince had guessed he was using, and he made up his mind to investigate veins that were not visible, especially as he was going from fortnightly to weekly needles. Hopefully, the puncture wounds on his arm would heal sooner rather than later, as they had not yet developed into full track-marks.

For the next few weeks, Owen got into a routine of weekly visits to the 'banya'. He stopped going at the weekend, preferring a day when he was unlikely to be working an evening shift. Having missed a day of lectures for his trip to Amsterdam, Owen decided to give up one of the modules, although not tell anyone yet, and spend an hour each week in the language laboratory learning Dutch. For his other modules, he continued to attend lectures, but only concentrated on the reading for half of them, knowing this would have a detrimental effect on his overall marks. If the lecturers asked him, he had resolved to explain he was finding it a struggle, to read everything he had to read, in Russian.

His weekly trips to the 'banya' passed uneventfully. Vasily was always present, but he did not see Nikolai again, until the middle of March. It was clear to Owen, that he was developing an addiction, although he was sure that if he kept the craving to a weekly dose, the habit was manageable, both from the point of view of lifestyle, he could keep all his regular commitments, and financially, he did not have to pay.

His own network of customers was expanding, and there were now around twenty-five of them, sixteen to eighteen of whom came on any given visit to Caterham. He was running low on his stash, though, and was already thinking about a trip to Amsterdam, for his own purposes, during the university vacation, when Nikolai approached him in the smoke room.

"Owen, my friend. I would very much appreciate it if you could collect another shipment for me. I will pay you, this time, of course. How does a hundred sound?"

"I'm sure it sounds perfectly OK," replied Owen, knowing he had just been made another offer he could not refuse.

"Excellent. It will be just like the first time. You will stay with Anton and bring back a Delft tea service. No need to ask about the puppies this time, though," he added, laughing.

"Will it be Tuesday to Friday again?"

"Quite possibly. And thank you."

Owen felt rather pleased that he would not have to fund his own trip. He did, however, need to give some thought to how he might conceal a block of cannabis resin, and at present, was not even sure how much he would be able to buy, in Amsterdam, and at what cost. The exchange rate was around four guilders to the pound, so he decided to change two hundred pounds, next time he went shopping, and take another one hundred in sterling with him.

On his next trip to SSEES, Owen went to the bookstore and bought a Dutch dictionary, a small, pocket-sized one, not a volume like his Russian dictionary. His Dutch language skills were coming along nicely, and he was keen to practise them for real. When he arrived home, there was another large brown envelope that had been put through his letter box. The envelope contained early morning train tickets from Charing Cross to Dover on the Wednesday of next week, morning ferry ticket to Ostend, and train ticket from Ostend to Amsterdam. The return journey was another early start on the Friday morning, arriving back in London in the evening. Owen knew this meant crossing one extra border, between Belgium and the Netherlands, but, presumably, Nikolai did not want to generate suspicion with a regular trip via Harwich. Would that mean an extra lot of customs, getting off and on the train again, or would it simply be a case of a border guard checking passports on the train? Probably, the latter, as he could not imagine Nikolai risking three kilograms of heroin being seized. Owen's more immediate problem was the Friday evening shift. Neither was he certain that Wendy would be available to take care of Kochai, again. On checking the rota, he thought it might be possible to swap the Friday evening with Vince.

Next time they shared a shift, he sidled up to Wendy, behind the bar.

"Favourite dog-sitter, can I ask another favour, on behalf of a certain Afghan Hound?"

"Are you off again?"

"Any chance of Wednesday until Friday evening?"

"What time Wednesday?"

"About 5.30 in the morning."

"Why don't you bring him round on Tuesday evening?"

"Thanks. Before your shift?"

"Yes. And I want to meet this mystery woman, Owen!" she joked.

"Haha."

After Owen dropped Kochai at Wendy's house, on the Tuesday evening, he was unable to sleep. It was more than nerves. He had not slept on his own in the flat since the day he adopted Kochai. The place felt empty, and worse, lonely. Owen got up several times in the night to go to the toilet and make a cup of tea. In the end, he turned off his alarm, and got up, washed and dressed, three quarters of an hour before it was due to go off. He made a mug of strong coffee, and added two teaspoonfuls of sugar, because he did not feel like breakfast.

Having checked he had his passport, tickets and money, he went to leave, and realised he had put his toothbrush and toothpaste back on the shelf, on autopilot, instead of in the holdall. The matter rectified, he set off for Charing Cross. Although he considered walking there, he decided his motorcycle was probably safer outside the station than it was left unattended outside the flats, so he rode. No sooner had he arrived at the station, than he realised how hard parking was to find. With only about fifteen minutes to play with, his rudimentary knowledge of Central London told him that St Martin-in-the-Fields was just over the road, so he parked where he had done when he visited the National Gallery. The train was sitting at the platform, when he got back to Charing Cross.

A garbled voice over the public address system seemed to suggest that the train would split at Tonbridge, with the front four carriages going non-stop to Ashford. He counted off the carriages and sat down in the third one from the front. Two hours later, he found himself waiting to board the ferry. This was a much smaller ship than the crossings to and from Harwich. In fact, once they had left the shelter of the port, Owen started to feel increasingly nauseous. He went up on deck, hoping the fresh air would improve things, but it was unbelievably windy and freezing, so he returned to the lounge area, found an empty seat, sat down and closed his eyes.

At Ostend, he walked gingerly off the ship, and had just about started to feel normal, when he reached customs.

"Are you OK, sir?" asked a man in uniform, speaking English with an accent.

"Fine. Thank you. Sea-sick."

Owen wondered how he would have reacted if the man in uniform were to approach him on his return journey. Once through customs, he boarded the train for Amsterdam. The border came just after Antwerp, and as predicted, a guard passed along the train asking to see passports. There was no guarantee it would be as smooth an operation on the return journey, as surely, Amsterdam to a seaport was a likely drugs trafficking route. On reflection, there was little Owen could do about it.

For the second time in his life, Owen alighted at Amsterdam Central Station and made his way to Anton Alexeyev's house, who greeted him like a long-lost brother.

"Come in, come in. I did not think we would meet again so soon."

"Me neither."

"How are you?"

"Good. How are you? How's Kristina?"

"She's expecting!"

"Wow! Congratulations. When?"

"November."

"Your first, yes?"

"First of many, I hope. We should celebrate."

"Shouldn't we wait for Kristina to come home."

"No," laughed Anton, grabbing two beers from the fridge and levering off the tops.

"To family," Owen toasted.

"To family. Hey, Owen. Do you have a family?"

"Do you mean, do I have kids? No. As for my family, I don't see them anymore."

"That is very sad, but it is none of my business. Tell me, which way did you come?"

"Ostend."

"And what tourism will you do this time?"

"Not sure but I'm open to suggestions."

Why don't you hire a bicycle?"

"Interesting idea."

"Go to see the Anne Frank House and visit the Jewish Quarter."

"I'm not religious."

"That's not religion, that's history, my friend."

"I'll think about it. Thanks."

Just then, Kristina came through the door.

"Owen. So good to see you."

"You, too. Anton tells me you are expecting."

Kristina looked at Anton with an 'I'm going to throttle you later' look.

"Congratulations. How are you feeling."

"Still a little sick. Shall we eat?"

It was too late for lunch and too early for the evening meal.

"Why not. I haven't eaten all day. I felt sick on the ship."

"It's cold food. It's been waiting for your arrival, in the fridge."

She brought out herrings and cheese, bread and pickles. Anton opened two more bottles of beer. He poured a glass of orange juice for Kristina.

"We could drive you to Haalem tomorrow, couldn't we, Anton. To see the windmills."

"That would be awesome. But you don't have to."

"Of course, we don't have to. We want to, though, don't we, Anton?"

"Yes. It would be our pleasure, added Anton.

"That settles it," continued Kristina. "We will go tomorrow morning. Now, enjoy your meal."

That was going to be quite a challenge as Owen did not much care for fish, but he did not wish to offend his host, so chewed and drank beer and chewed and drank beer some more. He was relieved to be able to eat some cheese.

When the savouries had been consumed, Kristina produced a plate of cake, cut into squares, which looked remarkably similar to the cannabis cake he had bought on his last trip.

"It's not what you're thinking, Owen. We don't go anywhere near these drugs."

Owen was confused. At first, he thought Anton was joking. What if Kristina knew the reason for his visits, but Anton did not? What if Anton thought the shipment was actually the Delft tea service? What if they were involved with hard drugs, but did not go near cannabis? What if they were caught up in something they did not wish to be involved with?

"You don't eat cannabis cake, you mean?"

"We don't do drugs. Anyway, I'm pregnant, as you well know."

"They were chocolate brownies, and delicious. Do people 'squat' in Amsterdam?"

Anton and Kristina looked blankly at Owen. He was having difficulty explaining in Russian.

"Do people live in empty houses without paying rent?"

"Do people live for free in other people's houses without the owners knowing?" responded Kristina.

"Yes. I live in a council flat, but the council doesn't know I'm there and I pay no rent."

"I don't know of this, but there are lots of empty buildings. Are you thinking of moving to Amsterdam?"

"Just wondering," Owen laughed it off.

"Sometimes people live on houseboats, on one of the canals," suggested Anton.

"Now that would be fun!" responded Owen. "Guys, I'm really tired. I didn't sleep last night. I think I will go to bed. Thank you for a lovely meal."

"Goodnight, Owen," they greeted him in unison.

"Goodnight."

As Owen got into bed, he realised how much he liked Anton and Kristina, and how sad it would be if he were to move to Amsterdam and not see them. He knew that if he moved to Amsterdam, he would have to deal drugs to survive, and if they had links to the 'banya' in London, he would never escape the reach of the people who had made him an offer he could not refuse. However, Owen was seriously considering moving to Amsterdam, if he could find a way of bringing Kochai with him. He fell asleep wondering if the suppliers of cannabis in Amsterdam were linked to the Russians, also.

Kristina was up preparing breakfast when Owen came out of his room.

"Good morning. Did you sleep?"

"Thank you. I did."

Anton came out of the bathroom.

"Are you not going to work, today?"

"I asked for some holiday because I wanted to spend some time with you. I am working this afternoon."

"Well, I am honoured. Thank you."

They ate bread and cheese and left for Haalem.

The only other time Owen remembered seeing a windmill was when he was a child, and he and Helen played visual treasure-hunting in the car on the journey to stay with their grandparents. There was a windmill that they passed. Here in Haalem, there were several.

"They are really pretty. Are they just for tourists or are they for making flour to sell?"

"I doubt if the business is commercial, but they do sell the flour they make, usually to the tourists," laughed Anton.

"May I buy you both a coffee somewhere?"

"Thank you, Owen. Let's find a café."

As they were looking for a café, they passed a gift-shop, with rows of wooden models of windmills stacked outside. Owen had a sudden brainwave, to buy a windmill and hide the cannabis he was hoping to buy later this afternoon, inside the windmill.

"Wait. I want to buy a windmill."

"Do you need help to speak in Dutch?"

"I want to try in Dutch."

"You speak Dutch now?"

"I have tried to learn a little."

They went into the shop, and Owen asked in his best Dutch, "Hello. I want to buy a windmill, please."

"Yes, sir. Would you like to choose?"

Owen was not sure of the verb 'to choose' but he followed the sales assistant outside. There were three different sizes, and as she pointed at each size, she quoted the price, which Owen did understand, because he could count to one hundred in Dutch. He was estimating whether the middle-sized windmill would be large enough. He thought it might.

"That one, please," indicated Owen, pointing.

"Very good. I will wrap it for you."

Owen was not sure that he wanted it wrapped, because he would probably tear the paper, trying to conceal the cannabis. He watched as the sales assistant carefully unclipped the sails, and rolled up the model in some tissue paper, slotting it into a cardboard box, taken from beneath the counter, with a label of a wooden windmill. Obviously, mass-produced, rather than crafted locally. The sales assistant put the box into a plastic bag and Owen handed over his money.

"Thank you. Goodbye."

"Goodbye," replied Owen.

"I'm impressed," Anton encouraged him.

"I didn't understand everything, but just enough to make the purchase."

They entered a café and were ushered to a vacant table.

"Three coffees please," Owen requested, in Dutch.

The waiter brought over the coffees and the three friends sat in silence, their hands cupped round the mugs.

"It's cold outside," commented Kristina, after a few moments.

"Is it true, the canals freeze?"

"Sometimes. They didn't freeze this winter."

"Do you ice-skate?" asked Owen.

"Once," replied Anton.

Kristina shook her head.

"Hopefully, the weather will get warmer very soon," added Anton.

"It's not just the British who talk about the weather," laughed Owen.

Anton and Kristina joined in the laughter.

"We should go back. I have to go to work."

"Thank you for bringing me here," said Owen, attracting the waiter's attention.

Owen paid for the coffees, left a tip, and the three of them went back to the car.

Back in Amsterdam, they ate bread and cold meat, for lunch. Anton went to work, and Owen went to find somewhere to hire a bicycle. He could not see any locks. Did no one steal bikes in Amsterdam? Having found someone to pay money too, he cycled off to his favourite café, and leaned the bike against the wall, just outside the door.

"Hello," he said, in Dutch.

The waiter from before recognized him.

"Welcome back to Amsterdam. What can I get you?" came the question, in fluent English.

"I would like a coffee please," came Owen's Dutch request.

"You speak Dutch?" asked the waiter, in Dutch.

"A little."

"Would you like some cake?"

"Not this time, thank you," replied Owen, in English again. "I was wondering about what I asked you before. Can you tell me where I can buy some cannabis? A lot of cannabis."

"Hold on."

The waiter went back to the counter, prepared Owen's coffee, got a piece of paper and a pen, and wrote down the name of a dealer, with the house number and street. When he brought Owen's coffee over to the table, he placed the piece of paper under the mug.

"Thank you," responded Owen, in Dutch again.

"You're welcome," said the waiter, in Dutch.

As he drank his coffee, Owen checked the map he had bought on his last visit. When he finished his coffee he paid, left a generous tip, and cycled off to the contact's address. It took about ten minutes to reach the house. He rang the doorbell and waited, holding the handlebars of the bike. The door opened a few inches.

"Hello. Can I help you?"

"Do you speak English?"

"Yes."

"I was given your address. I would like to buy some cannabis, if it's possible."

"How much?"

"I have two hundred guilders. How much will that buy?"

The man gestured with his hands.

"That is good."

"Wait here."

The man disappeared back into the house and came out with a package. It was a little larger than he had anticipated. He figured he would probably be able to sell it for around four hundred in sterling, which was a decent profit. Opening the package, he smelt it, closed the package again, and handed the man two hundred guilders.

"Thank you," responded the man.

"Thank you."

Owen stuffed the package in his inside jacket pocket and sped off on the bicycle. He did not stop peddling until he was beyond the end of the street and halfway along the next, whereupon he free-wheeled round into a side-street and felt like he was not being followed. After consulting the map again, he took a slight detour back to the centre and returned the bicycle to the stand where he had hired it.

"You had a good ride?" asked the attendant, in fractured English.

"Thank you. Yes," replied Owen in equally fractured Dutch.

He walked back to Anton and Kristina's and decided not to say anything about his purchase. Anton was at work and Kristina was ironing.

"May I take a shower?"

"Of course."

Owen put the package in his holdall under some clothes and went into the bathroom. When he came out, he got dry and dressed, unwrapped the windmill, stuffed the cannabis inside, re-wrapped it and returned it to his holdall. Unfortunately, there would not be enough room for both Delft tea service and windmill in the holdall, so he would have to carry the windmill in the plastic carrier bag. He went into the sitting room.

"Coffee or beer?"

"Beer please."

Kristina got a beer from the fridge and removed the top.

"Are you OK. This is the second trip."

"I can't say 'No' to them. That said, they treat me well."

"I know, but I wish we could get away from here, especially now the baby is on its way."

"Why don't you?"

"Anton is scared. He doesn't show it, but he is."

"What will you do?"

"I don't know. I expect we will see you again, in three months, Owen."

"Quite possibly."

Ten minutes later, Anton arrived home. After greeting Kristina with an affectionate kiss, he acknowledged Owen.

"Hello, my friend. Pleasant afternoon?"

"Yes. I hired a bicycle, like you suggested and went for a ride. I don't cycle much in England because I have a motorcycle."

"I would love to own a motorcycle. A big, powerful one. Then I would ride far away with Kristina."

That was the closest Anton had come to admitting he wanted to leave Amsterdam. It felt strange, Anton and Kristina wanting to leave and Owen wanting to move there.

There was a roast chicken and potatoes for the evening meal, and of course, more beer, for Anton and Owen.

"Do you want to play cards again?" asked Anton, after the meal.

"Yes."

They played until around eleven.

"I really need to go to bed. Early start. Very early."

"Then, you will need this," laughed Anton, getting another Delft Tea Service out of the cupboard and passing it to Owen.

"OK. I will see you at breakfast. Seven o'clock."

"Maybe if I am not feeling sick, I will get up as well. If not, goodbye, be safe, until next time you visit us."

"Thank you. Goodnight."

Once the tea service was packed in the holdall, Owen lay in bed, waiting to fall asleep. He felt confident that Anton and Kristina were not on the same side as Nikolai. If he were able to move to Amsterdam, it was likely that he could spend time with them. Or were they playing him? Were the questions to test his loyalty? He'd always been insecure, but now he was caught up in drugs, he found he trusted no one.

In the morning, Anton made him coffee, but Kristina did not appear.

"Kristina had a rough night. She's sleeping."

"Say 'goodbye' from me."

"I will, my friend."

Owen went to shake Anton's hand, who refused the hand and gave him another bear hug. He grabbed his holdall and plastic bag and left for the train station.

"Thank you, again, bye."

"Goodbye, my friend."

Once aboard the train, Owen put the plastic carrier bag between his legs and the holdall on his lap. He removed his jacket, folded it and lay it across the top, leant back into the corner between seat and window and closed his eyes. Just before Antwerp, he heard a voice.

"Passport please."

He must have drifted off to sleep because he was momentarily disorientated.

"Passport," repeated the official.

Owen lifted his jacket, took his passport out of the inside pocket and handed it to the guard.

"British?"

"Yes."

"Is that your bag?"

"Yes."

"Not left your sight?"

"No."

The guard handed him back his passport and moved on.

Owen felt fortunate to have been woken and therefore disorientated, because otherwise, he might have come across as nervous.

The train reached Ostend, and Owen boarded the ship. There was still the UK border to pass through at Dover, but he was nearly home. If he slung the strap to the holdall over his shoulder, and carried the plastic bag, it might help him to relax. He was almost wishing he had worn jeans and T-shirt, not his suit, although it was perfectly possible for a returning businessman to buy a model of a windmill for his mother or sister or friend.

As the passengers moved towards customs, Owen swung the bag over his shoulder, narrowly missing the woman behind. He turned to apologize and caught sight of the punk-rocker. Was the punk-rocker doing the same thing as he was? Owen managed to stroll nonchalantly through customs and reached the platform at Dover train station. As the train pulled out of the station, he relaxed, free to anticipate an affectionate reunion with Kochai. Watching the Kent countryside rush past the window, he began to imagine what it might be like to travel on the Orient Express, to take an iconic steam train across Europe, from London, via Paris, through Switzerland, all the way to Istanbul. Which led into an even more ridiculous idea. What if he went from Istanbul to Afghanistan, right to the poppy fields, and bought his own supply, at source?

It was the end of term, and so far, none of the tutors had asked Owen where he had been, when he missed classes. Although he had stopped going to Old Russian Literature lectures, he still went to the fortnightly tutorials and bluffed his way through them. He made the decision to stay on until the end of the year, not so much because of the summer term grant cheque, although that was always welcome, but because he wanted to carry on using the language laboratory, for his Dutch. The problem facing Owen was that although there were no lectures in the summer term, there were exams to take.

He had always been the kind of student who gets away with the minimum study required. Every exam, throughout his school life, he had winged it. It there were three questions in a paper, he would revise five topics, sometimes even four. On his next trip into the university, he went to the library to look at some past exam papers, to find out how many questions there were. The matter may well have been addressed in one of the lectures or tutorials he missed, when he was in Amsterdam. So, even though he fully expected to drop out at the end of his first year, he figured it was sensible to do some revision, and at least sit the exams. And that is what he did.

To his great surprise, he did better than expected. For his two language papers, he gained a two-one and a two-two. For three of his literature modules, he achieved a two-two, but for Old Russian Literature, even though he had revised, and felt he had made reasonable attempts at his exam questions, he was not even awarded a pass. Only then did Owen consider his absence might have been noted, and the lecturer failed him through lack of attendance, not lack of essay content. The bottom line, Owen felt, was that the grant-awarding body were unlikely, now, to ask him to repay any money, and if by some strange quirk of fate, he ever wanted to attempt a Batchelors degree, at some point in the future, he had evidence of his capability. What he did, on receiving his results, was draft a letter to the head of the department, explaining his decision to leave the course, and thanking the lecturers for their excellent input.

Just after receiving his results, Nikolai asked Owen to make a third trip to Amsterdam, which Owen welcomed, largely because he was running short of his own supply of cannabis, again. Besides, it would be great to catch up with Anton and Kristina, and the £100 he received for his troubles, was an added bonus.

And for the next eighteen months, Owen's life consisted of shifts at The Prince Albert, trafficking drugs, dealing cannabis out of Caterham railway station, and visiting the 'banya'.

The local council still had not noticed he was living rent-free in one of their flats. Kochai was still his loyal companion, enjoying his three-monthly breaks at Wendy's, who was still pressuring Owen to find out who his imaginary girlfriend was. Anton and Kristina had a gorgeous baby boy, named Ivan, but they insisted Owen still come to stay at their house. Owen's heroin addiction was being fed weekly, through his regular trips to the 'banya', where he had become something of a celebrity, although he only even injected into his legs, now. His own network, in Caterham, had expanded and he was earning a reasonable income. He had increased the amount of cannabis he sourced in Amsterdam. It was all going rather well, given his situation, when he first landed at Francis' house, at the end of his 'A' level exams. That was until personal tragedy struck.

Owen was out walking Kochai, on 12th January 1982. It was bitterly cold, and there had been a frost overnight, with temperatures below zero. As they came out of the park gate, onto Plough Road, a car skidded on some black ice, mounted the pavement, missing Owen, but catching Kochai's rear end. The dog shrieked in pain, collapsing on the floor, as the driver sped off. Owen cupped Kochai's face in his hands.

"Hang in there, mate. I'm going to get you to a vet. Good boy."

Owen took off his jacket and lay it on top of Kochai. He had no idea where the nearest vet practice was, as he had only ever been to the dogs' home, and he started to panic. A driver, who came along a few minutes after the incident, had seen them on the pavement, pulled in, got out of her car and walked over to them.

"Can I help? Can I take you to a vet?"

"I don't know where the nearest one is. You couldn't take us to the dogs' home, could you? That's where he came from and where he last saw a vet."

"No problem at all. Just tell me when and where to turn."

She helped Owen lift Kochai into the car, but the pain was so great, Kochai yelped, and then fell unconscious. They carried him into the dogs' home and were ushered straight into a side room, where the duty vet attended them.

"Thank you," Owen said to the driver. "He would surely have died right there, without your help. Thank you."

"I hope he's OK," replied the woman, leaving Owen and Kochai with the vet.

After an initial examination, the vet turned to Owen.

"I am really sorry, but his pelvis is shattered. I don't think we can fix it. His heartbeat is weakening. I think there must be some internal bleeding. We need to get him x-rayed, but you must prepare for the worst. Owen went numb. We can take him to the vet practice we use, where they have the technology. Please come with us."

The vet stuck his head out of the door, and an animal nurse came in. They loaded Kochai into a car and beckoned Owen to sit next to him. Kochai did not make it to the vet practice. He died next to Owen in the back of the car.

"What happens now?" Owen asked the vet.

He did not have a garden to bury Kochai and had no idea what he was meant to do with a dead Afghan Hound.

"We can cremate him, if you wish. Then you can scatter the ashes in a special place. It's not free, though, but when dogs have been rescued, we usually share the fee with the dogs' home."

"Whatever. Just tell me how much and when."

"We will. Are you still living where you were when you adopted Kochai?"

"Yes."

"Then don't worry. We'll contact you through them. They'll have your address."

"Wendy. Don't tell Wendy. I'll tell her myself."

"Wendy who volunteers there?"

"Yes. She has looked after Kochai when I have had to go on a business trip. She'll be devastated. She introduced me to Kochai."

"Would you like to say your goodbyes?"

Owen cupped Kochai's lifeless face in his hands, one last time, bent down to kiss his forehead, and whispered in his ear.

"Goodbye, my best ever friend."

Back at the empty flat, Owen poured himself a large vodka and downed it in one. He sat on the settee, staring at Kochai's basket. Going into the kitchen he saw the empty food and water bowls, and having held it in for so long, he allowed himself to cry. The hot tears flowed, and his body convulsed with grief. He had never felt so completely and utterly alone.

Telling Wendy was difficult. He left it until the next day, when his tears had stopped flowing, even though he looked like the morning after the night before. She knew something was wrong when Owen rang her doorbell at ten o'clock in the morning.

"What's wrong, Owen? Do you want to come in?"

He followed her into the house, not saying a word, and sat down on the sofa.

"I think you probably need to sit down too."

"What is it?"

"Kochai. He got hit by a car yesterday morning. He died from his injuries on the way to the vet."

"Oh, Owen. I'm so sorry."

Invading Owen's personal space with a pinch to the cheek was second nature to Wendy, but now, she sat next to him and held him in her arms. He started crying again.

"It's OK, Owen. Let it all out. I won't tell a soul."

After what felt like an eternity, Owen stopped sobbing, wiped his eyes, and pulled away from Wendy's matronly embrace.

"Cup of tea or coffee?"

"Thanks. Tea. One sugar."

Wendy went into the kitchen and boiled the kettle. She had been crying herself, and now took the opportunity to blow her nose, energetically. She carried two mugs of tea into the living room and sat back down on the sofa, leaving a cushion's width between them.

"What happened?"

"It was bizarre, like in slow motion. We had just come out of the park when a vehicle skidded on some ice and came flying towards us. It missed me but caught Kochai's back end. The driver drove off. A really nice lady pulled up just afterwards and took us to the dogs' home, but even though the duty vet checked Kochai over, he said we needed to get x-rays done and to prepare for the worst. It was in the car that he died. The vet said his pelvis was shattered and probably internal bleeding because his heartbeat was getting weaker. He really screamed when the car hit him and yelped when we moved him into the back of the car to go to the vet practice. But he was unconscious when he died. I just feel so empty, Wendy. He was everything to me."

"I know, I know. He was a lovely dog. He was special. It's going to ache for ages. And you know where I am if you need anything."

"I'm getting him cremated. Will you come with me when I scatter his ashes?"

"Of course, I will. When are you next on shift?"

"Not until tomorrow lunchtime."

"Will you be alright?"

"I hope so."

"Let me know if you need me to cover for you. Oh, wait a minute. Silly me. I'm already working then. If you need me to do the shift on my own, I'm sure Mr Longstaff will understand."

"Thanks. If I'm there, you'll know I'm there."

Owen went home. The lead and collar were still at the vets, but he parcelled up Kochai's basket, bowls and toys, in a bin liner. He thought about taking the things to a charity shop, but the bedding was well-used, and the bowls had seen better days, so he put everything in the dustbin. The flat was quiet, too quiet, and Owen grabbed his helmet and keys and went for a motorcycle ride. He knew he would still have to go home and sleep in the empty flat, but he just had to get out for a while. He was in Caterham, before he'd given any thought to direction or destination, but decided not to call in on Francis.

Over the next few weeks, Owen came to the decision that he would leave Battersea and go and live in Amsterdam. He had to let his customers know and he would have to hand in his notice at the pub, but he was not short of money. The most opportune moment to leave would be when he was running out of cannabis. It surely could not be that hard to find a squat in Amsterdam. Like when he arrived in London, he could find temporary work, until he established a network of customers. He also resolved not to tell Nikolai that he was leaving. Maybe, it would be uncomfortably difficult until he could find a Dutch supplier of heroin, and he was certain to experience some withdrawal symptoms, but it seemed like the lesser of two evils.

He had no idea when, or even if, he would return, but the simplest solution seemed to be to leave the little furniture he had, in the flat, along with the kitchenware. The addition to his luggage of a small suitcase would be sufficient for his belongings. What to do with his motorcycle, though? He decided to advertise it, and if it sold before his final trip to Caterham Station, he could always take the train. After all, it was on the same line as Clapham Junction. As for transport, in Amsterdam, there was a pedal cycle for short distances, and if he wanted to go any further afield, he could probably afford a small car, by now.

The winding down process took Owen until the end of February, and he was just finalising his plans, having sold the Honda, and using public transport, for his last couple of trips to the 'banya', when Nikolai asked him to make another trip to Amsterdam. This was a major predicament for Owen to find himself in. He dared not refuse. On the other hand, Nikolai was not going to be very happy when he found out Owen had used the already-paid-for ticket to travel to the Netherlands, and not returned with the shipment. Would he be able to disappear? A deliciously dangerous idea occurred to Owen, that he could stay with Anton and Kristina as usual, take custody of the Delft tea service, and not return to the UK. He might even be able to sell the heroin, keeping some back, for his own personal use. Would Nikolai come looking for him or did he have enough connections in Amsterdam to find Owen, at arm's length? If he did, Owen knew he was facing certain death.

Whilst imagining what certain execution might feel like, he was overcome by a sudden rush of responsibility for Anton, Kristina and baby Ivan. If Nikolai knew Owen had stayed at their house and been given the shipment, the repercussions for them might be very ugly indeed. There was only one thing for it. Owen would wait to receive the brown envelope, address it to Nikolai at the building where the 'banya' were housed, and buy his own ticket. He would post the envelope, on the morning he left for the Netherlands, and he would not stay with Anton and Kristina. By the time Nikolai realised he was no longer acting as a mule, Owen would have disappeared into the alternative, Amsterdam drop-out scene, and Anton would be able to report, hand on heart, that the shipment remained uncollected. Owen was just going to have to find his own, new supply of heroin.

And so it was, that on the second Tuesday in March, Owen took a meter reading, checked the water and electricity were turned off, locked the door to his flat and walked to Clapham Junction, where he boarded a train to Waterloo, which was a short walk from Charing Cross Station. After posting the large brown envelope to the 'banya' and the meter reading to the electricity company, Owen got on the train bound for Dover and the new life which awaited him, in Amsterdam.

Arriving at Amsterdam Central Station and knowing that he could not go and stay at Anton and Kristina's house was frustrating. Apart from the practical challenge of needing to find somewhere to live, he genuinely liked their company. Owen left his holdall and suitcase in a large luggage locker, using some of his guilders left over from the previous trip, and went to hire a bike. His plan was to cycle round the residential areas until he saw a building which might have potential as a squat, even though he was unsure of the Dutch legal system.

Still nervous about Nikolai's connections in the city, Owen had not shaved for two days, with the intention of growing a beard and letting his hair grow. He even considered wearing glasses. The three places he was known, excluding the houseboat where Floyd and Sally ran their mission, were Anton and Kristina's, the café where he asked the waiter for a dealer, and the dealer himself. All these people could have been part of Nikolai's empire, but the least likely one was the waiter. It had never been obvious to Owen, whether Nikolai was interested in supplying and dealing cannabis, as well as heroin, and he was really in need of a fix.

After identifying a couple of potential squats, he called at the dealer's house.

"Do you sell heroin or only cannabis?" asked Owen, with his basic Dutch.

"I can sell you cannabis. If you want heroin, there is a Russian on the other side of town. I also have a friend in Utrecht. Two hours by bicycle and thirty minutes on the train. He is Turkish."

Owen understood what had just been conveyed to him and wondered if Anton was, in fact, the Russian.

"Give me the name and address of the Turkish man in Utrecht, please. Also, please can I have one hundred guilders worth of cannabis?"

"Wait here."

The man closed the door on Owen. Two minutes later he re-opened it and handed Owen a slip of paper. Owen handed the man some banknotes, and the man brought out his other hand from behind the door, passing Owen a package.

"Thank you."

Like his previous visit, Owen cycled back to the city centre via a circuitous route. He was not intending to establish himself as a cannabis dealer, not in Amsterdam anyway, but he wanted to try and win friends and influence people on the alternative scene.

Owen's next stop was his favourite café. The waiter greeted him.

"You back again? You must like it here."

"I do. I've just moved here. Do you know anywhere that is looking for new staff," asked Owen, in his best Dutch. "I speak English, Russian, French, and now a little Dutch."

"Have you worked in a café before?"

"No. I have worked two years in a pub."

"It would be good to have someone else here. I can't remember the last time I had a day off."

"Seriously?"

"Yes. Can you start tomorrow? On a trial basis. We'll pay you cash. Unless you prefer cake!"

"Great. What time?"

"Nine in the morning."

"Thank you. I would like a coffee. No cake!"

"Coming up. I'm Kees, by the way."

"Owen."

Owen sat waiting for his coffee and noticed a newspaper on the adjacent empty table. It looked like a local, city paper. Owen had no idea how much he would understand, but he figured he could work out where the houseboat adverts were. It had occurred to him, that he might be able to afford an old houseboat. Probably not in the best condition, but as long as it was watertight, and had a wood-burning stove, he could make it liveable. He browsed the classifieds and then remembered Floyd and Sally. They might even know someone who wanted to sell a houseboat. He still did not have anywhere to live, tonight, and they might also be able to help him on that front. At least, they could point him in the direction of a cheap hostel. He would happily pay two or three days, even a week's board.

After paying for his coffee, he walked to the houseboat. He had to go that way in order to pick up his luggage from the station. Walking down the gangplank he entered a cloud of freshly baked bread aromas.

"It's Owen, isn't it?" Sally greeted him.

"You remembered my name. And you even recognised me through the stubble."

"We try our best to remember people. How are you?"

"Great. I've moved to Amsterdam. I really liked it before. My dog died, and I wanted a fresh start. I don't suppose you know a good cheap place to stay tonight. Or two or three nights. Also, how much does a houseboat cost and are they easy to find?"

"Sorry to hear about your dog. I can definitely recommend a hostel. The houseboat thing is almost 'How long is a piece of string?' because it depends on size, quality, age etcetera."

"Do you know anyone who might be selling a basic, watertight, old, cheap houseboat?" laughed Owen.

"I'll ask Floyd, when he gets back. In the meantime, would you like some soup and freshly made bread?"

"I'd love some. Thank you."

Sally ladled some soup into a bowl and put a homemade bread roll on a plate.

"There you go."

"Thank you."

The bread tasted as good as it smelled, and the soup was full of flavour. It was tomatoey and garlicky and there seemed to be lentils in it.

"When you've finished, there's cake. Chocolate."

Owen nodded because his mouth was full. He probably was not the first drop-out they had welcomed onto their houseboat, and he probably would not be the last, but the fact that Sally remembered his name made him feel special.

Owen was halfway through his slice of chocolate cake when Floyd walked in.

"Owen! How've you been?"

"I landed in Amsterdam, today. My Afghan Hound got hit by a car and died. I needed a fresh start. I like the city."

"Wow. Sorry for your loss. Do you have somewhere to stay?"

Sally said there's a hostel nearby, whilst I look for something more permanent."

"Owen wanted to know how much it would cost to buy a houseboat," added Sally.

"I know where there is an empty one. I could try and find who owns it."

"Cool. Thanks. I've got a part time job. Well, I'm on a work trial at one of the cafés, starting tomorrow. I've been learning Dutch."

"I'm impressed. I take it you gave up your university course?"

"Yes. I took the exams. Failed one of the papers. Maybe one day, I'll consider going back."

"Never say never," responded Floyd, cutting himself a slice of chocolate cake. "Would you like another slice?"

"No, thank you. That was great."

"Let me take you to the hostel," offered Floyd.

"Thanks. How far is it from here? I have luggage in a locker at the station."

"Suitcase? Holdall?"

"Small suitcase and a holdall."

"I would suggest that you get the holdall, with whatever you need for a night or two, and leave the suitcase in the locker."

"I'll do that then."

"Good. We'll call in at the station first, then."

Ten minutes later, Owen was crouching by the locker, sorting some clothes from the suitcase into the holdall. He locked the locker again, and Floyd took him the short distance to a hostel. It was a back-packers hostel, although Floyd had an arrangement with the staff, that if he found a homeless person or an addict who was in trouble, there was a small room that he could use. Floyd then stayed with the addict until they had gone cold turkey, or visited the homeless person daily, to make sure they got back on their feet. A few words were exchanged in Dutch, most of which Owen did not understand, but he got the gist of the price and the number of days he would be staying.

"I'll leave you in Jan's good hands, then. Drop by the houseboat at the weekend and, hopefully, I'll have an update on the houseboat, or at least some possible longer-term living options."

"Thank you."

Floyd left and Jan spoke to Owen.

"Dutch or English?"

"Try Dutch, but slowly," replied Owen.

"These are the rules," said Jan, holding a sheet of paper in front of Owen. "It's very simple. You have a room with two bunks, so possibly four people. Shared toilet and bathroom at the end of the corridor. Leave it as you would want to find it. Lock-up at eleven o'clock. No smoking on the premises. Definitely, no drugs on the premises. No food in your room. Except chocolate bars or sweets. No pets. Eight o'clock in the morning, come to reception, and tell us if you are staying another night. Floyd booked you in for a week. He's a good guy. He will do everything he can to find you somewhere to live. Did you understand?"

"I think so. Thank you."

"Here is your locker key. We don't lock the room, but you can have a personal locker."

"Thank you."

Jan showed Owen to his room and pointed out his locker.

"Perhaps you will go and see some of the city, after dark. It is very pretty."

"I won't stay out late. I have work in the morning."

Jan left Owen to sort himself out. Owen lay on the bottom bunk nearest his locker. It was firm but comfortable, and he drifted off to sleep, tired out by the stress and the travelling.

In the morning, he went to reception at eight o'clock, just to confirm that he was still booked in, and left for the café. On the way, he called in at a different café, in order to buy a coffee with some bread and jam for breakfast. The place had opened at seven, and since Owen was not able to take food to his room, this would be where he would have to stop for breakfast, on his way to work, until he moved out of the hostel. It was cheap and cheerful, and the food simple but good quality.

Owen's favourite café was called 'The Coffee Room'. Close to one of the canals, it had a lot of tourist footfall. At ten to nine, Owen tried the door, but it was locked, so he knocked and caught Kees' attention.

"Good morning."

"Hi. I'm a bit early, sorry."

"That's good. No worries. Grab an apron from behind the counter. Wash your hands, thoroughly, in the sink. I'll be with you as soon as I've finished putting the menus on the tables."

Owen did as Kees requested and watched him setting out the day's menus in little wooden holders on each table. Kees approached the counter, holding three menus.

"We open at nine and close at six, so you work eight-thirty to six-thirty, with a half hour lunch break, before or after the lunchtime rush. Every day, we change the lunchtime special, which is written here, on the chalkboard. The cakes can vary every day, but they are labelled. There are usually two types of cannabis cake, which we keep at the opposite end of the counter, so we don't make a mistake. But first things first. Come into the kitchen and I'll introduce you to Ruud."

Owen followed Kees into the kitchen, where a man of about forty, was sorting out the fridge.

"Ruud. Meet Owen. He's trialling today as a waiter."

"Hello. I won't shake your hand."

He was wearing the kind of gloves which suggested he was clearing up a spillage.

"Hi. Nice to meet you."

"Have you used a coffee steamer before?" asked Kees, turning to Owen and walking back out of the kitchen.

"No."

"Right. I'll show you. The really important thing is to clean off the nozzle every time you use it. Now watch."

Kees scooped out some coffee, pressing it into the filter which he slotted into the coffee machine. Whilst it was running, he poured some milk into a jug and held it so that the steamer nozzle rested in the milk. Switching on the steamer, the milk started to splutter and whoosh. He turned the knob to off, removed the jug, and wiped down the nozzle.

After pouring the coffee into a mug, he filled it with the milk, generously topping it off with the froth.

"Easy as that. The boiling water is here. Teas, coffees, syrups, all here. Milk and cream in the fridge. You'll get the hang of it soon enough. You've worked in a pub, so you know how and when to clear away tables. Watch me use the till and tell me if it's any different to the pub."

Owen watched. It was similar enough to the till in The Prince Albert for him to feel confident in using it.

"All good."

"And finally, for now anyway, how to take orders. We happily speak Dutch and English, as you know. Take a look at the menu and familiarise yourself with it. Again, tell me if there is anything you don't recognise or can't pronounce. We keep all the order tickets for the day in this basket. Customers pay when they have eaten, so keep one eye on who has come in, if they're still eating or drinking, and make sure they don't leave without paying. It'll be a blast!"

"All seems fairly straightforward. Impatient to start."

"I will pay you for today. You can keep any tips."

"Thanks."

Kees put the pavement sign outside.

"In the summer, we also have tables outside. It's a bit more difficult to keep an eye on customers. But that's not until May. Now we wait for our first customer."

It was not long until an American couple came through the door.

"Do you want to deal with them?" Kees encouraged Owen.

Owen was not sure if he was relieved or frustrated that his first customers spoke English. At least, he could translate the menu if required. He went over to the table with his order pad.

"Good morning. What can I get you?"

"Howdy. Two coffees with cream and two eggs over easy on toast, if you have it."

Owen wondered if he needed his own English translation of 'eggs over easy' as he'd not come across it before. He was embarrassed.

"'Eggs over easy'? Forgive me. I'm new today."

"Fried egg, flipped until the white sets."

"Thank you. Coming right up."

Owen went to the kitchen door and passed the order onto Ruud, in Dutch.

"Fried eggs on toast. Turn the egg on both sides. Americans," he smiled.

Owen went to make the coffees and carried them to the table. There were individual portions of cream, so he put two for each coffee, along with sachets of sugar. Having served the coffees, he returned to the kitchen where Ruud was just plating the 'eggs over easy'.

"Thanks!"

When Owen put the plates in front of the American customers, the man stared intently at his egg.

"Not bad!"

"Enjoy your breakfast."

Meanwhile, an elderly lady had come in and Kees was serving her. Owen went behind the counter and carried on checking out the various varieties of tea, coffee and syrup. The next customer who came in was Dutch, and Owen felt chuffed to complete an order in Dutch. He was just serving the man, when the American couple stood up to leave.

"Where do we pay?"

"I'll bring you the bill."

"The check?"

"Yes."

Owen fetched the bill and placed it on the table, on a small plate. The American man looked at it, took two notes from his wallet and put them on the plate.

"Keep the change."

"Thank you. Have a nice day."

"You speak good English," said Owen's first Dutch customer, as the Americans were heading out of the door.

"I am English," laughed Owen, sensing the irony of the situation.

At the end of the day, Owen fetched in the pavement sign, and helped Kees clean the tables and chairs, sweep up, and make sure the counters were clean. All the crockery and cutlery were taken into the kitchen, to a dishwasher.

"First job in the morning is to stack the shelves with the clean things. Now, million-dollar question. Well, not million, but you know what I mean. More like two hundred and twenty-five guilders for twenty-eight and a half hours, eight-thirty to eighteen-thirty Thursdays and Fridays and alternate Saturdays and Sundays. How does that sound?"

Owen did a quick calculation in his head. He had made just under thirty guilders in tips in only one day, so compared to his wages at The Prince Albert, this was a good deal.

"Brilliant."

"Fantastic. I'll see you tomorrow, Friday and Saturday, this week, then. I'm so looking forward to taking a couple of days off, as soon as you are up to speed."

"My pleasure. See you."

Owen poked his head into the kitchen.

"Bye Ruud."

"Bye."

"Bye. Thanks for the job."

"You're welcome."

Owen went to the nearest supermarket and bought some bread, cheese and a bottle of Coke. He wandered along the canal, crossed over and found a bench to sit and eat his evening picnic. Having crossed back, he found a bar and bought a beer, making it last an hour. When he got back to the hostel, there was another man in the shared room. He was Danish.

"Hello. My name is Aksel. I'm from Denmark."

"I'm Owen, from the UK, although I've moved to Amsterdam."

"This is a nice place."

"Yes. How long are you in Amsterdam for?"

"Maybe one week, maybe two. Then, I will go to Brussels, and then Paris."

Aksel spoke better English than Owen spoke Dutch, which was hardly surprising.

"I'll see you later. I'm off out to find somewhere to eat."

"I've been working all day. I'll probably be asleep," laughed Owen.

Aksel left and Owen went to the bathroom. As predicted, hardly had he laid down on his bunk, he was fast asleep, still fully clothed. When Aksel returned, at shortly after ten, he tried to be quiet, but somehow managed to kick the leg of Owen's bunk, tripped and crashed into one of the lockers. Owen woke with a start.

"I'm so sorry," mumbled Aksel.

Owen could smell that he had been smoking cannabis but said nothing. After removing his jeans and folding them under his pillow, Owen went back to bed, under his duvet, this time. Aksel was soon snoring, but Owen lay awake. He started to ponder a break from dealing. With his job at the café, as long as he had enough money to pay for food and accommodation, although he would still try to find out the Dutch laws on squatting, and enough to get a weekly heroin fix, he had money in the bank. Now he had the job, he would not be able to take any holiday, just yet, but maybe in September, he would ask for a week off. Unfortunately, that would not be long enough to take the Orient Express all the way from Paris to Istanbul and back again. It was still his hope, one day, to experience the luxury journey, with a steam locomotive, but his immediate plan was to try and get to and from Afghanistan. He only needed a day or two there, to purchase heroin at source, but he would probably have to hire a car and drive there. The whole adventure needed more time and thought, but he had all summer to finalise his plans.

Owen thoroughly enjoyed his next three days working in 'The Coffee Room' and he earned one hundred and eight guilders in tips, to add to his two hundred and twenty-five guilders in wages. Aksel did not wake Owen in the night again, but a third guest joined them on the Friday evening, staying until the Sunday morning. Owen could hardly believe his eyes, when Jody walked in. It was the punk-rocker from Owen's first trip to Amsterdam.

"What are you doing here?" asked Jody. "My name's Jody, by the way."

"I'm Owen. I left the UK and moved here at the start of the week. Not sure where I'm going to live yet."

"Were you on a business trip, before?"

"You could say that."

"I've got a contact in the city. I come here every so often to stock up. Personal use, of course. Sometimes I bring my gran with me. She's a wild one!"

Owen wondered if the contact was the same man, he had bought cannabis from.

"Is that the lady I saw you with the first time?"

"Yes. She brought me up. My mum was in prison and my dad had pissed off when I was three."

"Where are you from, in the UK?"

"Ashford."

"I used to live near Maidstone, until I moved to London."

"Really. My sister lives in Maidstone. Small world."

"I think my sister still lives there, but has gone off to university somewhere, no doubt."

"My sister was at the Girls' Grammar."

"So was mine. They probably knew or knew of each other."

"Unfortunately, my sister was kicked out in fifth form for getting pregnant."

"So, you're an uncle. That's kind of cool."

"I don't see much of my nephew. Maybe I should make more of an effort?"

"Tell me. Do you just smoke your cannabis, or do you eat it?"

"Here, I mostly eat it, and in the UK, I just smoke it."

"I work in a café. I went in there on my first journey to Amsterdam and bought a slice. It was crazy!"

"Is that 'The Coffee Room'?"

"Yes. I've been there a few times, but only ate the cake once."

"I'll maybe see you when I'm in there, tomorrow, then? Do you want to come out for a beer, now?"

"Just the one. Sure."

They left the hostel and walked to the bar where Owen had been earlier in the week.

"We should go Dutch," laughed Jody. "I buy mine and you buy yours."

"Very funny," conceded Owen.

They sat at a vacant table.

"Don't mind if they stare at me," apologised Jody. "So, why Amsterdam?"

"I had a dog. It died. I needed a fresh start. I was at university, but I've dropped out."

"What did you study?"

"Russian."

"Wow! Have you picked up any Dutch?"

"I spent a few sessions in the language laboratory, before I quit university, and I pick it up here. I try to read a Dutch newspaper once a week. You?"

"A few words. Enough to get by. You're obviously a linguist. Whereabouts in London were you?"

"Battersea. I lived in a squat for two years. An empty council flat. I want to find out what the law is here. Whether squatters have the same rights."

"Can't help you there, I'm afraid. Do you want me to get you some stuff tomorrow?"

"No, I'm good thanks."

"So, why did you choose Amsterdam? Not Paris? Or Moscow, even?"

"Well Moscow didn't seem a very good idea because we're in the middle of the Cold War, and the Soviet Union isn't exactly the freest county in the world. Paris is a great place to visit, but I'm not sure I would want to live there. I love the lifestyle here, and as I'd been on several business trips, I thought I'd make it more permanent."

"What business are you in?"

"Well, I was working for someone who collected and distributed Delft pottery. I would come and pick up the merchandise and take it to the UK. They paid me well."

"Are you sure it was only pottery?"

"What difference did it make, knowing or not knowing?"

"So, you did know, then?"

Owen grinned.

"Is that why you used Harwich and Dover?"

"Probably, although I didn't buy the tickets."

"And you never got stopped?"

"No. Have you? Ever been stopped?"

"Once, but it really is only for personal use, and I was able to convince them it was three months' supply. They probably had bigger fish to fry, though. Like you, for instance!"

Owen finished his beer.

"Right. That's me done. I'll see you back at the hostel."

"Are you sure I can't tempt you with another?"

"No. Thanks, but no thanks. I want to make sure I keep this job. I can always eat cake on Sunday!"

He got up.

"Bye."

"Laters."

Owen walked back to the hostel, reflecting on the conversation. Jody was probably right. There must be hundreds of passengers passing through the Dutch borders, with cannabis for personal use. Customs want the hard drugs and the smuggling cartels. He got into bed and fell asleep thinking about what Helen was doing now. Had she gone to university? It was not often he thought about any of the family, these days.

Jody and Aksel were both sleeping when Owen left for work in the morning. He called in at reception to book his place and wondered if they remembered. Jody was leaving today, so it would not matter, but Aksel was not planning to go to Brussels just yet, or so Owen thought. The day at work was busier than any of the other days he had worked. It was not yet the height of the tourist season, so Saturdays still brought more customers than midweek. Lo and behold, halfway through the afternoon, Jody showed up to buy some cannabis cake. It so happened that Owen was busy with another customer, so Kees dealt with him. Owen acknowledged him, in passing.

Later that evening, when Owen returned to the hostel, neither Aksel nor Jody were anywhere to be seen, and someone had broken into Owen's locker. His stash of cannabis was gone. To Owen's relief, he still had the heroin for personal use in his knapsack, which he carried with him, at all times, along with his money and passport. Who was the thief? Jody? Aksel? Or someone completely different? Owen went to reception and explained to Jan, that someone had broken into his locker.

"I'm really sorry. Anything missing? It happens sometimes."

"Nothing of any importance."

Jan accepted his response. Owen was telling the truth, in as much as the cannabis was just for making friends and influencing people, if necessary. He was not trafficking it for someone who might cause him significant harm. That said, since he had resolved to try and avoid dealing, whilst living in Amsterdam, it was just an expensive inconvenience, rather than a major dilemma, although he did question the wisdom in having been so open with Jody about the tea service shipments.

On Sunday morning, Owen went to tell reception he would like to stay another night and paid for his bunk, again. Even if Floyd had come up trumps, Owen could not see himself sleeping any place else, tonight. He thought about going to see Floyd and Sally, on their houseboat, until he remembered it was Sunday, and they were likely to be doing something churchy. Instead, he hired a bicycle and rode out of the city, with no particular destination in mind, along the River Amstel. There was something mesmerizingly peaceful about the place. St Petersburg, Venice, Stockholm, even Birmingham, were all cities with canal networks and waterways. Owen had only been fortunate enough to visit St Petersburg, and that was more rivers than canals, but he had felt a similar peacefulness there. Realising the route was mostly flat, he made a spur of the moments decision to cycle to Utrecht. If he was too exhausted, when he got there, he could always take the train back.

Two and a half hours later, he arrived at the house on the slip of paper the cannabis dealer had given him. Nervously, he knocked on the door. A short man with black hair and glasses peered out through the window and mouthed something at Owen that he could not lip-read in Dutch. Owen pointed at the door, which opened on a chain, a few seconds later.

"I was given your name by a man in Amsterdam. He said you can sell me some heroin."

"Yes. How much do you want?"

"I have one hundred guilders."

"Wait there."

The man closed the door and came back five minutes later with a small package. Owen could not make up his mind whether to ask to check it, or just hand over the money. He opted for the latter and reached for his wallet.

"There you go," he said, counting out the notes.

Taking the notes, the man relinquished the package and closed the door. Owen stuffed the package in his knapsack and rode off, in the general direction of the city centre, in search of the train station. He bought a ticket, wheeled the bike onto the platform, where another man stood waiting with his bicycle, and watched for the train.

Back in Amsterdam, he rode out to a park, leant the bicycle against a tree and sat down at the foot of the trunk. His gear was in his knapsack, so he made up a solution and, having glanced around to see if anyone was nearby, injected himself through his jeans, into his leg. As the effects intensified, he watched a man walk across the park at about a hundred paces, followed by a large, lolloping dog. A gut-wrenching ache ambushed his rush, as he recognised how much he still missed Kochai. Closing his eyes, he rested until he felt able to cycle back to the bike stands.

Finding a local bar-restaurant he scoured the menu and went through the door.

"Is it too early for meatballs and beer?" he asked, in Dutch.

"Please, sit down. We can always cook meatballs."

The waitress indicated where Owen should sit. The meatballs were prepared quickly. All they had to do was take them from the freezer and deep-fry them. He ate them with mustard. The snack gave him a burst of energy and removed any remaining effects from his recent fix. He did not want to arouse Floyd or Sally's suspicions. It was probably past whatever time they did churchy things, so Owen walked to the houseboat.

"Greetings, Owen," smiled Sally. "Will you have some soup and cake?"

"I just ate meatballs, but I wouldn't say 'no' to your cake."

"Hi, Owen," Floyd greeted him, coming through a doorway near the front of the houseboat.

"Are you well?"

"Yes, thank you," replied Sally.

"I have some amazing news for you, Owen," added Floyd, beaming from ear to ear, "but first, tell me about your new job. How's it gone?"

"Great thanks. I did the trial on Wednesday, and they took me on. I worked Thursday, Friday and Saturday, and in the future, I'll work Thursday and Friday and alternate between Saturdays and Sundays. Average wage, but I get to keep the tips, and I made just over one hundred guilders.

Which reminds me, is there somewhere I can make a contribution for all the soup and cake?"

"Absolutely not. Just try and stay safe and healthy."

Owen did not argue.

"Now then. I was speaking to a friend, who lives on a houseboat, moored on one of the canals over that way, somewhere," explained Floyd pointing. "That friend is moving to America, for a year, at some point in the next month, and they asked if you might look after the boat for them. No rent. Just pay for the electricity and Calor gas. No wild parties, and no smoking on board."

"That is unbelievable!"

"I thought you'd like that."

"Like it? I love it. When do they go to America?"

"Well, how about I take you to meet them this afternoon? There's half a chance you can lodge with them until they go."

"This afternoon it is, then. Thanks."

"I need to pop out for an hour, but then, we can go. I was wondering if you could do me a favour, while you're waiting, assuming you weren't going off anywhere else, in the meantime."

"Name it."

"We've just had a delivery of leaflets. It would be helpful if you could count them into bundles of twenty and put an elastic band round each bundle."

"No problem. Where's the box?"

"I'll fetch it back out from the other room."

He disappeared back through the door he had just come from and returned with a large, heavy cardboard box.

"There's two thousand of them. Do what you can. It will be much appreciated."

"Will do."

Owen pulled the tape from the box and opened it to find piles of threefold flyers advertising the houseboat mission. He started reading one of them.

"Who are the flyers for? I mean, where do they get put?"

"Mostly churches, public agencies, any places where you find information leaflets, hostels, hotels, doctors' surgeries. You name it," replied Sally, as Floyd left the houseboat. "Anywhere there are people or people who know people who might need a place to chill and talk things over."

"Shall I take some to 'The Coffee Room'?"

"Please. Take a bundle."

Owen nodded and started counting. He started out by counting out a bundle of twenty and putting a rubber band on. This did not feel like the most efficient method, so he started to count out the bundles and lay them criss-cross on the table. When he had ten or so bundles, he put the rubber bands on, and counted out some more. Five minutes before Floyd returned, Owen put the last rubber band on and piled all the bundles back in the box. They took up more space, now, and he was unable to close the box, which he left open and sitting on the table, retaining one bundle which was on the table in front of him. Floyd walked through the door.

"My, my! You have been speedy!"

"I simply got into a method and went at it like a machine."

"Well, thank you."

"My pleasure. Sally says I can take these to work, with me."

"Thank you. Are you ready?"

"May I use the bathroom?"

"Of course."

Floyd waited while Owen used the bathroom, counting out five bundles.

"I can drop these off on the way," he remarked when Owen came out.

They set off, walking along several streets and crossing several bridges. Floyd put some of the bundles through letterboxes and the remaining two he took into cafés they passed by. Eventually, when Owen had lost his bearings, somewhat, they arrived at a beautiful houseboat. Floyd led them on board and knocked at the door, which was opened by a woman in her sixties.

"Hello, Floyd. This must be Owen?" she greeted them. "Come in."

They went in and a man, also in his sixties, stood up, holding out his hand.

"I'm Ike and this, here, is Thelma."

"I'm Owen," he said, shaking Ike's hand and offering his hand to Thelma, which she squeezed, warmly.

"Tea? Coffee?" she asked, looking at Owen, who looked across at Floyd, who nodded.

"Coffee would be great. Thank you."

"Sit yourselves down. Cake?"

"Yes please," Floyd jumped in, before Owen had a chance to respond.

"So, Owen," started Ike, "Floyd, here, tells me you've just moved to Amsterdam and are looking for a houseboat."

"Something like that," laughed Owen. "I have just arrived in Amsterdam, and already started a job. I asked Floyd and Sally about accommodation, although, yes, I did mention it would be nice to know what it would cost to live on a houseboat and if they knew of any cheap, watertight vacant boats."

"We have spent the last few months trying to decide what to do with our houseboat, when we go to the States, so you are an answer to prayer for us, Owen. If you can look after the place, not throw any wild parties, and not smoke on the premises, you are more than welcome to stay here, rent-free, and look after it. Just pay for electricity and the gas cylinder when it gets empty. It would be a huge wait off our minds, really, as we'll be gone a year."

"I don't know much about prayer, but I guess you must be my answer to an unvoiced prayer. This is very kind of you."

Owen was not paying lip-service or mocking. He was genuinely curious about the way Ike and Thelma saw the timing and provision as an answer to something they had asked God for. He was already impressed with Floyd and Sally's welcome and hospitality. He did not pray, ever, but he could quite see how, if he had asked this God-person for a place to live, being introduced to Ike and Thelma might be construed as an affirmative answer. Whatever it was, he was more than happy to accept their invitation.

"Well then, if you are going to look after our houseboat while we're away," added Thelma, "would you like to move out of the hostel and into the spare room, aft, there, until we leave?"

"As long as I won't be getting under your feet, I accept. Thank you, again."

"You'd better go and get your things. I'll write down the address for you and draw a little map. How much luggage do you have?"

"A holdall and a small suitcase."

"Ah. Ike will give you both a lift, in the car, and bring you back. Any other time, there's a bicycle you can use."

"Amazing. I've been hiring a bicycle this last week. Thanks."

"Now. Let's eat our cake and drink our coffee."

Owen had never eaten anything like it before, but what Thelma placed in front of him was mouth-watering. It was crumbly, nutty, fudgy, biscuity and cakey, all at the same time.

"This is incredible!" announced Owen, after his third mouthful.

When the last crumbs had been picked off their plates, and their coffee mugs were empty, Ike stood up.

"Right. Let's go get your luggage."

"I have no idea where I am. Floyd will have to direct you."

"Got a pretty good idea where I'm going."

"My holdall is at the hostel, but my suitcase is in a locker at the station."

"Not a problem. I might well call in on Sally, while you fetch your belongings. You can meet us at Floyd and Sally's houseboat. I'll park at the station."

"Perfect."

"Do you like Amsterdam, then, Owen?"

"I love it. It's chilled and peaceful and pretty. And up to now, I've received a warm welcome everywhere."

"That's what we like to hear, isn't it, Floyd."

"It is, indeed."

Ike parked at the station and went with Floyd, whilst Owen went to the hostel to pick up his holdall and tell them he no longer required the room.

"The policy is that you still have to pay, I'm afraid, as there's no guarantee we can now fill the vacancy."

"Absolutely not a problem."

He unlocked his new locker, took out the holdall, checked under the duvet and under the bunk, and went to reception to hand in his key.

"Goodbye and good luck!"

"Thank you."

Owen slung the holdall over his shoulder and walked the short distance to the station, to retrieve his suitcase from the locker. The suitcase was quite light, although he did swap hands several times between the locker and the houseboat.

"Hi Sally," he greeted her, as he entered.

"Hi, Owen. Come by anytime for soup or coffee and cake. You know where we are."

"I will."

"We'll say our proper goodbyes when you leave," Sally informed Ike.

"Absolutely. See you next Sunday."

"Yes. Love to Thelma."

"Come on, then, Owen. Let's go."

"Thank you, so much, Floyd, Sally. Really appreciate it."

"Take care, Owen," responded Sally.

Floyd nodded.

"Here, let me carry the case," insisted Ike.

Owen handed it to him. They got into the car and Ike set off.

"I'm afraid we can't leave the car with you. That's going to be taken care of by some friends who live in Leiden. They will meet us at the airport and take the car away, when we eventually go.

"No problem. First, you've been more than generous. Second, I can't drive. I had a motorbike, but I can't drive a car. Not yet, anyway."

"Can't drive a car?"

"No. My parents didn't have one, so I got the motorbike, and then didn't need a car."

"What do your parents do? Where do they live?" Do you have sisters and brothers?"

"I'm not going to lie. It all went wrong. I left home at eighteen and I haven't been back in touch. And, yes, I have a younger sister."

"I see. Maybe, one day, eh?"

There was a brief uncomfortable silence. Uncomfortable for Owen, not Ike, who came across many troubled young people in Amsterdam, as did Floyd and Sally.

"What sort of motorbike?"

"A 250cc Honda."

"Nice. Our eldest has a Honda Goldwing. He rode all the way across the old Route 66 last summer."

"That's something I'd love to do. Where do you live, in the states?"

"The family home is in Vermont, but we've lived all over the place. Our eldest, Henry, lives in Chicago, with his wife and two grandchildren. Our next eldest, Susan, lives in Pittsburgh, with her husband. Our youngest, Georgia, is divorced and lives in Santa Monica, with our other two grandchildren, half of the time, when they're not with their father."

They pulled up outside the houseboat and got out. Ike took the holdall and suitcase from the boot of the car and carried them both into the houseboat.

"Beer?" offered Thelma.

"Thank you. Yes."

"I'll show you to your room, Owen," added Ike, before he had even let go of Owen's luggage.

Owen followed him.

"There's an en-suite. It's tiny, but it's yours. Join us when you've sorted yourself out."

"Thanks."

Ike went back into the main living area and Owen used the en-suite. Fifteen minutes later, he came out of his room, to find Ike holding a bottle of beer in each hand. Thelma was laying the table.

"I hope you eat brisket?" she announced.

"Definitely. Can I do anything to help?"

Owen knew it was unlikely, but he asked anyway, to try and be polite and appreciative.

"No thank you. The meal will take another twenty minutes or so. Now, relax and tell me about yourself."

"There's not a lot to tell. I'm trying to escape the past and make a fresh start."

"And what was so bad about the past that you need to escape it."

"I left home because I got expelled. I went to university but dropped out. I had a dog that died. He was my best friend," Owen summarised his past, and paused, "And I got involved with a bad bunch of people who might hurt me if they ever found me."

"Parents have a lot of room in their hearts, Owen. Whatever you did, I'm sure it wasn't so bad that your mum and dad couldn't put it behind you."

"It's complicated. They made a lot of sacrifices for me to get a good education and I ruined it. I was ashamed. But it wasn't just that. I just felt that my whole life had been about living their dreams. No one ever asked me what I wanted to do."

"What do you want to do?"

"That's just it. I have no idea. I don't really know who I am and what I'm passionate about because I've always been filling my time with the things I was expected to do. During the time I lived in London, I discovered I loved a dog. A rescue dog. I worked in a pub because it was a job, the first opportunity I had. In the end, the shifts worked around university and owning a dog. At university, I discovered I don't like old literature and history, that I enjoyed literature that spoke up for the disadvantaged in society, and also, that I might have a knack for picking up languages. Before I quit university, I started to learn Dutch. And here I am. Working in a café, because I asked if the waiter knew anywhere that was looking for staff and he gave me a job."

"We have three children. They're all grown up now. Parents hope for the best for their children. They don't always see beyond their own world, beyond their own values and priorities. I'm sure your mum and dad just wanted you to achieve your potential, and they did what they thought would make that possible."

"I guess. I just want to find my own path in life before I go back."

"Don't leave it too long, Owen, believe me," commented Ike, after sitting quietly while Thelma was speaking. "Sometimes, we wonder whether our decisions had a negative impact on our children."

"How do you mean?"

"Well, I'm a pastor. Thelma and I have lived in several different states and also two different countries. Sometimes we moved when our children had built friendships or settled in a school. It was hard for them. We felt the call of God was a priority. Hindsight can be a stick to beat ourselves up with, or a springboard to growth as a human being."

After a short silence, Owen asked, "Which countries have you lived in?"

"Paraguay and here."

"What did you do in Paraguay?"

"As a pastor, I went to teach and develop local church leaders."

"And is that what you do here?"

"No. We have different role here. We actually came here to support Floyd and Sally's work. Our eldest, Henry, reacted badly to the rootlessness of being moved around the world. He got hooked on drugs, and we supported him through rehab. When we heard about Floyd and Sally's work with drug addicts we asked if there was anything we could do, and they invited us to come and be 'houseparents' to young adults who want to go through withdrawal."

"Houseparents, like the tutors in a house at school?"

"Maybe. Is that what it was like at your school?"

"Not as a couple. It was an all-boys school and there was a head of house who looked out for the pupils in his house. But it wasn't like being invited into a home, like this. Like Floyd and Sally's houseboat. There was a lady I worked with in London, old enough to be my mum. She invited me round for meals with her husband and son and looked out for me."

"I think Floyd told you about the room at the hostel. No?" asked Ike.

"Yes."

"We have spent many hours in that room with people going through 'cold turkey'. It's not just the physical pain.

It's helping them to deal with the emotional pain. With the reasons they started to take the drugs in the first place. And then providing practical support, so they can start out again, breaking from the drugs scene."

Owen nodded but said nothing.

"When did you start taking drugs, Owen?" asked Thelma.

The question threw Owen. Firstly, how did they know? But more importantly, if they knew, why had they asked him to look after their houseboat for the year? He did not want to lie but he was embarrassed.

"It started out as cannabis. I tried mushrooms but didn't like it. In fact, I know someone who broke their back, thinking they could fly off the stairs. When I moved to London and got Kochai, my Afghan Hound, I never wanted to use drugs at all. Not even cannabis. But then I met a girl on my course. She was Russian. She invited me to a secret club with a steam bath and somehow, she got me using heroin, first through a pipe, and then through injecting it. By the time I realised what was happening, it was too late. The people had a hold over me. To be honest, I feared for my life. I didn't know what to do. I didn't want to leave my dog. I didn't know if they were watching me. They knew where I lived. Then there was the car incident, when I lost Kochai, and I just decided to leave the country. It wasn't the first time I'd been here. I like it here. So, one day, I just left."

"And you're still using," confirmed Ike.

"Yes. Just like when I was in London, if I keep the dose regular and low, I can live a normal life, with a job."

"Owen, we are still going to let you live here," responded Ike. "In fact, we suspected you might be using. You get to know these things, when you spend as much time as we have, with drug addicts. We will be here for the next three weeks. If you want to take this opportunity to come off the drugs, we will be happy to support you."

"Seriously?"

"Yes. We can time the initial withdrawal with the days when you aren't at work, so hopefully, you won't have to miss a shift," Ike encouraged him.

"You'll have to be completely straight with us. You'll have to give us your gear. All your heroin," stated Thelma.

"Part of me wants to say I'll think about it. The other part knows it would be easy to talk myself out of it," responded Owen, after a brief pause.

"When is your next fix due?" asked Thelma.

"Tuesday."

"And when are you working this week?" she continued.

"Thursday, Friday and Sunday."

"If you go ahead with this," interrupted Ike, "the first few days may feel like hell. Nausea, vomiting, diarrhoea, cramps, sweating, aches, anxiety. It'll be like a bad case of the flu. Day three is often the worst. On the other hand, it's also quite possible, from what you have told us about your pattern of heroin use that you are non-dependent. We won't really know how dependent you are, until you stop taking it. One of us will stay with you at all times, whilst you're going through withdrawal."

"So, if my body, or my brain, thinks it needs heroin on Tuesday, that means that if I don't have a fix, my body will then go into withdrawal, and I need to be at work on Thursday. This is going to sound really stupid, but should I inject today and next Sunday, for the last time, so that by the time the following Sunday comes around, and my body and brain need the drug, if I don't feed the addiction, I've got Monday, Tuesday and Wednesday to go through withdrawal?"

"That's not stupid at all," responded Ike, "although I would suggest you still give us your gear, and we can control the timing and use."

"Think about it over dinner," suggested Thelma. "You have to want to do it."

"I will."

"Excellent. Now let's eat."

"I know you'll make the right decision, Owen," added Ike.

He gestured to Owen, to sit down, while Thelma switched off the cooker. She drained the water from some carrots into a gravy-jug and stirred it rapidly for a few seconds. The brisket had been sitting on the counter while they chatted. It was in a casserole dish, along with some potatoes. She removed the meat and carved some slices, plating up the meat potatoes and carrots.

"Would you like sauce?"

"Please."

She poured some sauce over each plate and carried Ike's and Owen's to the table, before going back for her own. Owen sensed he should wait.

"Loving Father. Thank you for bringing Owen to us and thank you for this food. Amen."

Thelma repeated the Amen and Owen found himself agreeing, also.

"Tuck in, then," Thelma invited Owen.

It was a delicious meal. Simple, but prepared with care and eaten with welcoming hearts. Owen felt at home, which was something that did not come easily to him. Sometimes, he knew he was too trusting. His recent experiences, in London and at the hostel, demonstrated as much. Floyd and Sally, Ike and Thelma, seemed different. He could not quite put his finger on why, but their hospitality and vulnerability made him feel like he could trust them. True, he had thought he could trust Katya and the hospitality afforded him at the 'banya' but in hindsight, they wanted him to do things which were not any good for him. Ike and Thelma seemed to want what was best for him.

"We have banoffee pie, for dessert. Thelma makes awesome desserts."

"The brisket was awesome too," added Owen.

"Thank you," answered Thelma, piling the plates up and taking them to the sink.

She took the banoffee pie from the fridge and put it on the table, going back for the dishes and spoons. The one serving spoon had been used for the first course, so she served each person with the dessert spoon they would use. Owen savoured his first mouthful. Of all the cakes he had been treated to in Amsterdam, this was the best dessert he had tasted. There were a million and one rational arguments he could have used, to make his decision, but the moment he swallowed the first mouthful of banoffee pie, he knew he wanted to stop being a heroin addict.

"Can I help with the washing up?" asked Owen, at the end of the meal.

"Thank you. I'll wash, you dry," replied Ike.

They got up and Ike filled the tiny sink with hot water. Everything in the houseboat was slightly diminutive, a bit like the caravan he stayed in near Dartmoor, with Mason Somersby and his family. The cooker functioned like a normal cooker but had only two rings and a tiny oven. It was powered by a large Calor gas cylinder. There was only a small amount of cupboard space. He was glad only to be five feet nine inches tall, because he did not have to duck. The bed was full length but narrow. The settee was built into the side of the boat. The chairs were full-size, but the table was only three feet by two feet. Owen thought it would be interesting living here.

"That's the last of it," announced Ike, fishing around in the bottom of the sink, in case there was a teaspoon lurking.

He let out the water and Owen folded the tea-towel.

"Coffee?" asked Thelma.

"No thank you. It'll keep me awake," replied Owen. "I want you to know, I've made my decision."

There was a brief pause.

"I'm going to inject today, here, in front of you and give you my gear. I'll do the same next Sunday, and that's it."

"Good lad," Ike encouraged him. "You've made a good decision, Owen."

Owen went into his room and came out with his last two syringes, a bottle of water, the citric acid and a small plastic bag containing heroin.

"I no longer use a tourniquet. Also, I inject into my leg because I had to roll my sleeves up at work."

He made up a syringe, rolled up his trouser-leg and injected in front of Ike and Thelma.

"I'll leave the rest of this stuff with you," said Owen, drinking the water, covering the needle with its cap and putting the syringe into the empty bottle to dispose of it.

"Thank you. Sleep well."

"I will. Goodnight."

"Goodnight, Owen," replied Thelma.

Owen went to bed to experience the remainder of his rush and fell asleep when he came down. When he woke, he was momentarily disorientated, until he collected his thoughts and realised where he was. No longer in a hostel, an elderly couple, who hardly knew him, had invited him into their home, and trusted him to look after it. They were also completely open about drug addiction and understood it from a parent's perspective. Had he really injected himself in front of them? Had he actually handed over his gear? Was he about to take up the opportunity of getting clean? He got dressed and went into the living area where Thelma was making coffee and scrambled eggs.

"Good morning. How did you sleep?"

"Good morning. Well, thank you."

"Eggs and coffee?"

"Thank you."

"What are your plans for today?"

"I'm not sure. Is there anything I can do to help? I'm not at work until Thursday. I could go and be a tourist, but it's nice to know I can chill, maybe read. That said, if there's anything useful I can do, please tell me."

"I don't think there is today. We don't tend to lock the boat during the day. There's not a lot here worth stealing, anyway, but if you would feel happier, we can lock up when we go out, if you're not here, and let you have a key, in case you come home while we're out."

"I'm good, thank you. I keep my money and passport with me, at all times," replied Owen and added, with a smile, "And you now have custody of the only other stuff of any value."

"Yes, we do. That was very brave of you, Owen."

"Thank you for being there for me. I think I might just chill this morning."

Owen was washing up the breakfast things, when Ike arrived back at the boat carrying a newspaper.

"Good morning, Owen. How did you sleep?"

"Hi Ike. I was very comfortable, thank you."

"What are your plans for today?"

"I just asked Thelma if there was anything I could do to help. I might just chill here this morning. It's kind of nice to be able to."

"Well, OK, then. When I go out again, you're welcome to read the paper. I've got a copy of the local paper and a Washington Post."

"Thank you."

Owen went back into his room and lay on the bed. It occurred to him that he would be considerably better off, once he was not paying for accommodation or needing to buy drugs. He wondered about opening a Dutch bank account, so that his wages were kept safe. He would investigate, one day this week. Also, although there was nothing he particularly wanted to buy, he thought he would take a stroll round the non-tourist part of the city and do some window-shopping in the stores. What he did not have access to, was any music, because he had left his cassette player in the flat in Battersea. He would go in search of a Walkman and also find a music store, to buy some cassettes.

By the time Owen came to 'W' day, he had walked round the city centre several times, opened a Dutch bank account and bought a Walkman and earphones. He also treated himself to Led Zeppelin, *The Song Remains the Same*, Pink Floyd, *Wish you were Here*, Yes, *Close to the Edge*, Barclay James Harvest, *Octoberon* and Mike Oldfield, *Tubular Bells*. He figured having music to listen to might be a distraction whilst he was going through withdrawal. He knew it would not exactly be 'Withdrawal' Day, as the process would last a few days, but the significant moment was not having a fix when he was due to have one.

He sat in the living area with Thelma and Ike.

"Right. This is it. Do you want to ceremonially get rid of the last of the heroin, Owen? Flush it down the toilet. There's hardly any left, to be fair. I'll dispose of the syringes where we always do, when we're working with addicts."

"I've made a cake, to celebrate," added Thelma. "It's a carrot cake."

"Wow. You're so kind. Yes. Watch me do it."

He took the last of his heroin and opened the package over the open toilet.

"Here's to freedom!" he announced, as he flushed it away.

Ike and Thelma applauded, and they ate carrot cake.

"It probably won't kick in for a day or so. One of us will be here, at all times. I suggest staying in, until you're over the worst. We can go for a drive if you feel up to it. Away from the city. We just won't know how bad it is until you go through it."

"I'll keep you posted. I bought a Walkman and some cassettes, to keep me occupied."

"What kind of music do you like?" asked Ike.

"Mostly rock. A few other things."

"Our youngest, Georgia, was married to a drummer. She didn't want to be on the road, with the children, and he didn't want to give up the band. It was all really rather sad. We've learnt, you just can't live your children's lives for them. But I guess you already knew that, Owen."

"I do. You and Thelma seem like really great parents."

"Bless you. We pretty much made it up as we went along, with the help of a couple who took us under their wing, and our faith, of course. Faith doesn't make you a better parent, it just gives you an opportunity to find forgiveness when you mess up," admitted Thelma. "Being grandparents is like a second chance at parenting, with the wisdom you've picked up over the years. We don't get to see anywhere near as much of our grandchildren as we'd like. That's what I'm most looking forward to, when we go back stateside."

"So again, thank you for looking after our houseboat," chipped in Ike. "One less thing to worry about."

Ike and Thelma had a way of affirming Owen, for things he never even considered something he was doing for them. They seemed to turn everything around, away from themselves, for the good of others. He was almost envious.

"What music do you listen to?" asked Owen.

"Johnny Cash, Leonard Cohen, country music. Thelma likes musicals."

"What's your favourite musical?"

"That is a hard question to answer. *Fiddler on the Roof, The King and I, Evita, West Side Story*. Please, don't ask me to choose between them."

"Have you seen them live?"

"I have seen all of them at the theatre, yes."

"My school did a performance of *West Side Story*. I was one of the Jets."

"I bet that was fun."

"It was."

On day two, Owen began to feel stomach cramps and started to sweat. He was shivery and felt like he had the flu. The best place to be, was under the duvet, and Thelma brought him herbal tea, orange juice and water on a regular basis. He drank all of it to keep his fluids up. The last thing Owen felt like was eating, but Thelma also brought him a thin slice of carrot cake. It was to spoil him rather than feed him, although she reminded him, it was good to eat something if he could. By the end of day three he had stopped sweating and feeling like the flu, but still had stomach cramps. It was possible these were hunger pangs rather than withdrawal symptoms.

"Do you feel up to some dinner tonight? We're eating chicken and fries," Thelma informed Owen. "Maybe a little bit of chicken? Nothing rich."

"I think I would like to try something. Perhaps I could have a slice of bread instead of fries, with it?"

"No problem. How are you feeling?"

"Mostly like I got hit by a train. Very tired."

"You're over the worst, I think," reflected Ike. "You may have got away with it, given that you had a controlled weekly dose."

"I'm just hoping I'll be fit for work. I don't want to call in sick. I don't want to lie. And I definitely don't want to tell them I'm withdrawing from heroin."

"You can only do what you can do. Sleep tonight and see how you feel in the morning."

It was a joy to eat the chicken and bread, and the stomach pains disappeared. Owen drank camomile tea before going to bed. It tasted like he remembered the chaff smelling, from the combine harvester on Osea Island. Quite frankly, it was disgusting, but it was the only non-addictive substance available to help him relax. He slept ten hours, and when his alarm went off, in the morning, he felt he might be able to work his shift.

"Do you want me to run you to work, to save on energy?" asked Ike, at the breakfast table.

"That might be a good idea. Thank you."

"We all have our addictions," laughed Ike, downing the remainder of his cup of coffee. "This is mine! I've heard it said that withdrawal from caffeine can be as bad as withdrawal from an opioid. I'm not sure I want to test out the theory. You've done brilliantly, Owen."

"Thanks. It wasn't as bad as I feared, but I still felt like death warmed up."

"Better death warmed up than dead," replied Thelma, her tone serious.

"I know. I can't thank you enough."

"The hardest part is what comes next. You've stopped taking heroin, but what caused you to take it in the first place? Happy to listen when you're ready to talk. If there are any strategies, we can help you put in place before we leave for the US, we can talk it through. I don't want you to start feeling alone and sad."

"To be honest, I don't think I am alone. Of course, I miss Kochai, but it's a new life here. The houseboat will feel empty without you guys here. The thing is, I ended up taking heroin, because a girl I fancied lured me into taking it. That's not passing the buck, but it just happened that way. If I hadn't been besotted, I might have said no."

"We live and learn. Maybe one day you'll meet a really nice girl. No need to rush these things."

"True. I'm just going to brush my teeth," announced Owen, "and then, I'm ready when you are."

Owen worked three long days, and by the end of the third shift, he was able to cycle and not feel exhausted. Three days later, he stood on the side of the canal, waving Ike and Thelma off on their trip to the States. As soon as they disappeared from view, he locked the houseboat and cycled out of the city, along the River Amstel. He felt more alive than he had in ages. That evening, he made himself some cheese on toast, decided to pay Floyd and Sally a visit, and fell asleep listening to Led Zeppelin.

For the next nine months, Owen's life fell into a routine. In between his three shifts on and four days off, or two days on, a Saturday off and a Sunday on, Owen went for cycle rides, listened to music, visited galleries and museums, and dropped in, once a month at Floyd and Sally's. He felt healthier than he had ever felt. Even on the occasions when he drank a beer too many, almost falling into the canal one time, his body recovered quickly, and he had bundles of energy. The summer had brought out the glory of Amsterdam and the surrounding countryside. Kees had been correct. It was harder to keep an eye on the customers, once they starting to serve at tables outside, but as far as he was aware, no one had escaped without paying, on his watch. His Dutch was improving, and he had, so far, not bumped into Anton, Kristina and baby Ivan, which was both a disappointment and a relief.

One chilly morning in early February, Owen was out walking, when he decided to pop into a café for a coffee.

Having ordered at the counter, he picked up a Dutch newspaper and sat at a vacant table. Reading the newspaper was one way of practising his Dutch, even if the content of the articles interested him somewhat less. The waitress brought Owen's coffee across on the same tray as a coffee for the man who had followed Owen into the cafe. After about ten minutes, the man got up and came over to Owen's table.

"Excuse me," he apologised, in English. "Aren't you Owen Linton-House?"

"Dominic Andrews. No way! Is that you?"

"One and the same."

"What are you doing in Amsterdam? Come to think of it, what have you been doing for the last few years?"

"Well, as you know, I went off to Oxford. I graduated in the summer of 1982 and since then I've been working with MI6."

"Gosh. That sounds exciting."

"It can be exciting, scary, boring, complicated. All these things. What about you?"

"I went off to SSEES, dropped out at the end of the first year. Worked in a pub. Lived in a squat in Battersea. Had a gorgeous Afghan Hound rescue. Tragically, he died, and I moved out here to start afresh."

"To be honest, Owen, I was being disingenuous, when I asked what you had been doing."

"How so?"

"The thing is, we, that is MI6, have been watching you. Sorry about the dog. We know all about your cannabis dealing in Caterham and your trips to Amsterdam for the 'banya'. What's more, we probably owe you a few ounces of cannabis, which Jody nicked from your locker at the hostel.

Yes, he's one of ours too. We've been watching you, since you first hooked up with Katya, mainly because we were watching her."

"I'm not sure I fully understand."

Owen was feeling uncomfortable to the point of paranoia.

"Obviously, our relationship with the Soviet Union is permanently on a knife-edge. We picked up chatter about drugs at the 'banya' and so we have been monitoring the situation. Since the start of the Soviet-Afghan war, we know that the drugs have been coming into London and going out again, we think to Canada. The Soviets are using income from the poppy fields in Afghanistan to fund their political and military activities. Now, we would really, rather prefer it, if the drugs income from Afghanistan were to line British coffers, so that we can fund the Mujahideen to fight back against the Soviets."

"That is very interesting, but it doesn't explain why you have been watching me."

"Allow me to continue. We aren't entirely sure where the drugs are coming from, at source, or the precise details of the supply chain into the UK. We know that there are regular shipments of heroin coming from Amsterdam, of which you have transported several, in the Delft tea services. What we don't know, also, is where they are being trafficked to."

"So, wait a minute. Why did you never arrest me? If you knew what I was doing, that is."

"Because, if we had arrested you, we would be no further forward in tracing the supply chain, from start to finish. And that, Owen, is where you come into the equation."

"Apologies if I'm being a bit slow here, but where do I fit in?"

"I'm so glad you asked. We want you, with your language skills, of Russian, Dutch and French, to do two things. One is going to Afghanistan and buying some heroin at source."

"You do realise I came to Amsterdam to escape from what Nikolai might to do me, if I stopped transporting his shipments for him? Is that the two things, by the way?"

"We understand your situation, believe me, we do. Amsterdam is only the middle of the chain. In addition to Afghanistan, at our expense, of course, and reporting back to MI6, we also want you to go to Canada, and identify the distribution network. Our intelligence tells us, that there is a lady in Ottawa, who goes by the name of Caroline Dupont. We want you to go to Ottawa, to befriend her, seduce her, get into a relationship with her, and send us back information about who, where and how, the drugs are being distributed. Our friends in the CIA, would also very much like to know if any of the drugs are making their way across the border into the States. We will pay your expenses, of course. We will set you up in a job with a publishing company and provide you with a decent-looking flat. The rest is up to you, but we will expect regular contact from you to our contact in Toronto."

"What if I decline your exciting offer?"

"You can't decline it. At least, not if you don't want arresting for dealing cannabis or trafficking heroin. That would be worth at least ten years in prison."

"So, what you're saying is, you are making me a job offer I can't refuse?"

"In a nutshell."

"Can I name one condition?"

"Try me."

"I am currently houseboat-sitting for a rather wonderful American couple, who helped me kick my heroin habit. They have been in the States since the end of April last year and are due back at the end of March. If I am to do what you ask, can I have until they return, before I go."

"I think we can manage that. So, we have a deal?"

"We have a deal. Oh, and tell Jody to keep the cannabis!"

"Good man," responded Dominic, holding out his hand for Owen to shake.

"I'll be back in touch at the end of March, then. Watch how you go."

"Apparently, I don't need to, because MI6 is watching for me," laughed Owen.

Dominic went to the counter, paid for both coffees, acknowledged Owen, with a nod, and left the café. Owen walked back to the houseboat, trying to get his head round what had just happened. He was not sure whether to laugh or cry. All this time, when he had been looking over one shoulder for Russians, it was MI6 who were watching his every move. On the other hand, what he was being offered was terrifyingly exciting. Were they going to offer him any training? Would he be given a gun? Was he going to have a legend?

On 25th March, Owen was on shift at 'The Coffee Room', when in walked Jody. He winked at Owen and sat down at a vacant table. Putting down the plate he was about to stack, Owen picked up his order pad and went over to the table.

"Good afternoon, Jody."

"Good afternoon, Owen. I'd like a cappuccino, please."

"Anything else?"

"Maybe a slice of chocolate cake."

"Coming right up."

Owen prepared a portion of ground coffee and started the coffee machine. By the time he had steamed some milk, the coffee nozzle was dropping its final drip. He made up the cappuccino and took it over to Jody with the slice of cake.

"Would you like chocolate sprinkled on top of the cappuccino? I forgot to ask, before."

"No, thanks. I'm good," replied Jody, handing Owen a folded twenty-five guilder note.

When Owen took hold of the note, he realised there was a key within a folded piece of paper, which had something written on the inside, although he could not see what. As he went behind the counter, he slipped the folded paper and key into his back pocket and went to the till to get Jody's change. Just as he handed Jody his change, another customer came in, taking him away from Jody, not that there was anything left to say. Jody downed his cappuccino and left, while Owen's attention was on the new customer.

"Interesting hair," commented the customer, referring to Jody's Mohican.

Owen smiled, knowing he had been completely fooled by Jody's appearance.

The next time Owen had occasion to use the toilet, he sneaked a look at the key and folded paper. The only word written on it was 'STATION', which was helpful, since there were at least three places with lockers, which Owen knew about, and possibly others. This must be Dominic's promised communication, some instructions perhaps. His curiosity was well and truly piqued, and he was impatient to reach the end of his shift.

After work, he left the café and cycled to the station, where he located the locker, a small one, at eye-level. Opening up the door, he found an envelope addressed to him. Although impatient to know what it contained, and there was something inside, more substantial than a letter, he knew the sensible thing to do was take it home to read. He put it in his knapsack and cycled back to the houseboat.

Hardly through the door, he peeled open the flap. There was a ferry ticket from Ostend to Dover, dated 7th April, along with train tickets from Amsterdam to Ostend and Dover to Charing Cross. There was also a sheet of paper with a typed message, 'Go to the statue in front of the station. You will be met by a man asking if it's a nice day for a river trip. Tell him you've always wanted to go to Greenwich and go with him to the hotel.' It was really happening.

Two days later, Ike and Thelma arrived back at the houseboat, greeting Owen as if he were their second son.

"You look well," commented Ike.

"I am well. How was your time in America?"

"Let's go eat at a restaurant. We'll pay, of course, and we can tell you all about it."

"You've kept the place beautifully, Owen. Thank you," said Thelma.

"I hope so."

"And we want to hear all about your year, too," she continued.

"Aren't you tired from the journey?" inquired Owen.

"Not as tired as we might have been. Our friends from Leiden met us at the airport. We actually arrived back yesterday, so we had a bit of a lie-in, this morning," responded Thelma. "We knew we didn't have to rush back to check on the houseboat."

"What do you fancy eating, Owen," asked Ike.

"I don't know. Anything, really, although I'd prefer not to have seafood."

"Then we'll go and get us a steak."

"Haven't you eaten enough steaks, this last year," laughed Thelma.

"I'm suffering from steak withdrawal," joked Ike, looking at Owen.

"It's alright. I haven't touched drugs since you left."

"Good lad."

"Well done, Owen," added Thelma.

Ike led them to a local restaurant, where he ordered steak and fries for all of them.

"Wine or beer?"

"Beer, thank you. So, tell me about America."

"Vermont was relaxing. Lots of horse-riding and fishing. We stayed there three months. The next three months were spent touring different churches talking about Floyd and Sally's mission."

"Ten different cities," interjected Thelma.

"Yes. That's the part that wasn't rest. Then, we spent two months in Pittsburgh, with Susan. After several years of trying to have a baby, she's finally expecting. Thelma spent most of the time running around pampering her."

"No, I didn't. I just wanted to make sure she rested enough."

They all laughed.

"After Pittsburg, we flew to Chicago. The children have grown so tall."

"How old are they?"

"William is seven and Jessica turned ten while we were there. It was a special birthday party."

"We've missed all but one of William's and two of Jessica's," added Thelma, her voice giving away her disappointment.

"Then, we flew to California, to see Georgia and our other two grandchildren."

"And how old are they?"

"Michael is sixteen and Barbara is fourteen. Georgia got married a few years before Henry settled down. We have asked ourselves whether she was too young. The good news is that Jason came over several times while we were there. His band split up and we're holding out hope that he and Georgia might patch things up, but it's early days."

"As you can see, we caught the sun, while we were in Santa Monica," laughed Thelma, holding out her arm, which was a deep, golden-brown. "But enough of us. What's your news, Owen?"

The food arrived.

"I've pretty much got into a very boring routine of work, tourism, cycle rides, sleeping and eating. That's until I bumped into an old school friend who has offered me a job."

"A job? Where? When?"

"That's just it. It was a couple of months ago that he made contact, but I asked if it could wait until you came back. I go next week. Of course, I'm happy to move back into the hostel, if you need the space."

"Don't be ridiculous!" exclaimed Thelma. "What is the job? Where is the job?"

Just as he was about to enthuse about the assignment, Owen reflected he should perhaps be a little circumspect, not because he lacked trust in Ike and Thelma, but because MI6 meant official secrets.

"It's with a publishing company," answered Owen, followed by a dramatic pause, "in Canada."

"Canada!" replied Ike, surprised.

"Where in Canada?" asked Thelma.

"Ottawa."

"That's only a couple of hundred miles from Vermont."

Owen thought how two hundred miles was probably nextdoor for Americans.

"Father, thank you for keeping Owen safe and for this food," prayed Ike.

The three of them said "Amen."

"So, when do you leave?" inquired Ike after a couple of mouthfuls.

"I have tickets for 7th April. I go to London to meet up with my friend and then, fly to Canada."

"You must keep in touch," insisted Thelma.

"I'll not forget you," responded Owen.

The steaks were finished in silence, whilst Ike and Thelma processed Owen's news.

"Dessert?" asked Ike. "I fancy some ice cream."

"Thank you. That would be great."

"Thelma?"

"Yes. Ice cream's good."

The menu indicated a choice between vanilla, pistachio and chocolate.

"I don't think I've tried pistachio ice cream," reflected Owen.

"It's my favourite," responded Thelma. "I'll order pistachio and you order whichever you prefer, between vanilla and chocolate, and you can have a taste. If you like it, I'll swap one scoop with you."

"Thank you. I'll go for vanilla."

When the ice cream was brought to them, Thelma grabbed Owen's spoon and scraped a tiny morsel from one of her scoops of pistachio ice cream.

"That's really nice."

"Here," replied Thelma, using her unused spoon to dump a scoop in Owen's bowl and picking up one of his scoops of vanilla."

"Thank you," responded Owen.

Ike had ordered chocolate.

Early on 7th April, Owen had his final breakfast in the houseboat. Thelma was slightly subdued. Even though she and Ike had spent the last year in America, she felt attached to Owen. He had packed the night before and was hoping for a short goodbye.

"We'll run you to the station, of course," insisted Ike, coming into the living area.

"Here's a packet of Stroopwafels, to remember us by," laughed Thelma, reaching over to the counter.

"Thank you. I love them."

"And here's a Bible," added Ike, "in case you're ever looking for answers."

"Thank you."

It was the first time, Ike or Thelma had done something so unsubtle, but Owen was not complaining. He had felt genuine warmth from them, as well as from Floyd and Sally. He was not yet ready to explore the faith they professed, but he could see they were not hypocrites, unlike his mother, who paid lip-service to church, or his father, who never mentioned Christianity, at all, which was, possibly, less hypocritical than his mother.

Owen went back into his room and packed the Bible in his suitcase and the Stroopwaffels in his knapsack, which was inside his holdall, for ease of carrying. When he came out, just as when they had fetched his suitcase from the station, Ike grabbed the luggage and put it in the boot of the car. Owen climbed in the back. Once parked at the station, Ike and Thelma followed Owen into the concourse. Owen checked the side pocket of the holdall, where he had put his tickets and passport. The train was due to leave in fifteen minutes. Thelma held out her arms, inviting a hug. Owen obliged. Ike also gave him a hug.

"We're here if you need us. Write."

"Words are not enough. I am so grateful to you."

"Stay strong, Owen. Stay clean," replied Ike.

Owen picked up his holdall and suitcase.

"Bye then."

"Be seeing you," responded Ike and Thelma, simultaneously.

Hardly had they turned and left than Owen made his way onto the platform, destination new chapter. It was the first time he had made the journey from Amsterdam to London and not felt guilty crossing the border, which is why Owen felt the irony of being stopped at customs, in Dover. It occurred to him that Dominic might well be either making a point or having a laugh, at Owen's expense. He was still smiling to himself when he boarded the train to London.

When the train arrived at Charing Cross, he gathered his belongings, got off the train, passed through the ticket barrier and went out to the forecourt to the statue to honour Queen Eleanor. After five minutes or so, a man, possibly in his forties, approached Owen.

"It's a nice day for a trip on the river, isn't it?" he asked.

"Yes. I've always wanted to go to Greenwich," replied Owen.

"Come with me."

The man led Owen to the taxi rank and got into the next available cab.

"Hyde Park Hotel, if you don't mind."

"Certainly, sir."

The taxi weaved in and out of the traffic, bringing back memories for Owen of his motorcycle trips into Central London, and came to a halt outside the Hyde Park Hotel. The man paid and he and Owen got out of the taxi, whereupon he took hold of Owen's suitcase. Owen followed him through the unstaffed hotel reception and into the lift. They got out on the second floor and walked along the corridor to where the man opened a door and ushered Owen in. Dominic Andrews was sitting waiting.

"Thank you, Brian, that'll be all for now."

Brian nodded and left.

"Owen. Good to see you again," Dominic greeted him, standing to shake his hand. "I trust you appreciated your reception at Dover."

"Very funny, yes. Making a point or having a laugh?"

"Both, I think. You will spend the next two weeks at this hotel. Breakfast and evening meals are included, from the hotel dining room. Brian will pick you up each morning and take you to headquarters where you will receive briefings and minimum operational training. At the end of the second week, you will be given your new passport and your air ticket to Canada. We've decided to focus on the Canadian end first, before sending you to Afghanistan. When you arrive in Ottawa, you will be met by your MI6 contact and given further information, along with your flat and employment details. Any questions, so far?"

"What about expenses, here, for lunchtime? I mean, am I being paid for these two weeks. Am I employed by MI6?"

"Here is two hundred pounds for this week and next. You buy your own lunches. Next week, we will sort out a couple of suits for you, shirts, ties and shoes. Underwear you can buy for yourself. Are you employed?"

"Not in so many words. No contract, and no tax."

"From your first week in Ottawa, you will be employed by Ontario Publishing Inc. A Canadian bank account has already been opened in your new name, which you will receive during training."

"How long will I be living and working in Canada?"

"The short answer is, I don't know. I don't know how long it will take to achieve our objectives. One year, three years? Who knows? You're employed by the company, for the duration. More information will be made available at the briefings."

"Final question. Will I have a gun?"

"Yes. Part of the operational training is around safe handling of a weapon, but firstly, you're not an assassin, the gun is only for self-defence, and secondly, it will be given to you when you arrive in Canada. Right. I shall bid you a good evening. You are permitted to leave the hotel, should you wish to, to buy necessities, but please stay out of bars and other social or leisure venues. I look forward to seeing you in the morning."

Dominic stood up, handed Owen the door key which he had been toying with, put on his jacket and left. Owen browsed the hotel information folder. He was hungry and it was later than he'd realised. After using the bathroom, he went downstairs to the dining room, and caught the last hour of the dinner window.

"Good evening, sir," the waiter greeted him. "Breakfast is a self-serve buffet. Evening meal is served at the table. Please choose your table. I'm afraid we've run out of the fish, but I can recommend the roast chicken."

"Looks like it's roast chicken, then. Thank you."

"What would sir like to drink?"

"Wine. House red. And a glass of water, please."

"And it's the chicken?"

"Thank you, yes."

The waiter went to get Owen's drink. He brought back a glass of wine in one hand and a jug of water in the other, turned and went to get the chicken. Owen tasted the wine. It was not bad for house red, not that he was any kind of wine expert. The waiter returned with the chicken dinner.

"Enjoy your meal, sir."

Owen wolfed down the main course. He decided not to bother with dessert. He would eat some of the Stroopwaffels, up in his room. The waiter noticed he had finished and came over.

"Would sir like dessert?"

"No thanks."

"Coffee?"

"I'm very tired from travelling. I think I'd prefer to have coffee in my room, thanks."

"I'll have someone bring you up some fresh coffee and cream."

"Thank you."

Owen got up to leave.

He was back in his room, before he realised, he had not told the waiter which room he was in. He needn't have worried, because five minutes later, there was a knock at the door. Opening the door, he found himself facing the hotel manager, holding a tray.

"I just wanted to convey our welcome to you, and hope you have a pleasant stay with us. Mr Andrews has indicated that your expenses are covered, so don't worry about room service or the mini-bar."

"Thank you," responded Owen, holding out his hands to take the tray.

"If you don't mind, I'd prefer to ensure it's placed in your room."

"Of course. Come in."

The hotel manager placed the tray on the table and left.

"Call reception, if you need anything, sir, otherwise, I bid you goodnight."

"Goodnight."

Owen poured himself a coffee and hunted for the Stroopwaffel packet in his knapsack in his holdall. Even though he counted out two of them, it was impossible not to eat four. Did he simply have an addictive personality? Before going to bed, he showered. Another question to ask was whether he should keep the beard or not and get a haircut. To unpack or not to unpack, for the two weeks he would be in the hotel? Definitely, not tonight. The next thing he knew, he was woken by his alarm clock, still inside his suitcase. It took him five rings to work out where the buzz was coming from and another five rings to retrieve the clock from his suitcase and switch it off.

After a satisfying continental breakfast, Owen made his way to reception, where Brian was already waiting, his car parked just outside the entrance.

"Good morning," the chauffeur greeted him.

"Good morning."

There was an awkward silence. Owen did not know what he could or could not, should or should not ask, and Brian was an introvert, who liked to do his job with as little conversation as possible. The silence continued for the entire journey, until they arrived at Century House.

"I will pick you up again, here, at six o'clock. You can go in by yourself. They are expecting you."

"Oh, right. Thank you. See you at six. Bye."

The sentence almost caught Owen out, as he had long since given up hearing Brian say anything. He got out and went into the building. Dominic was waiting for him.

"Good morning. I trust you slept well."

"Thank you, yes. And good morning."

Dominic led him to a room, set out like a university exam, where eight other recruits were sitting. They were all ages, one was African Caribbean, one Indian, and there were three women. Owen sat at the last remaining vacant desk.

"Good morning, everyone," Dominic greeted them, as he took up a position at the front of the room. "Now that Owen is with us, we can begin. I would ask you to introduce yourselves, but there's little point. Two weeks from now, you will all go your separate ways, with new identities, sworn to secrecy, and with no prospect of communicating with each other again. Sorry to sound so brutal."

He paused dramatically.

"Now, I want you to set aside any images you may have in your heads of James Bond. For a start, there is always a guarantee that he will survive to the end of the film. Am I being too brutal again? You have been recruited to go into dangerous situations which may cost some of you your lives. We don't want this to happen, so pay close attention to the training and briefings you are about to take part in. The skills and knowledge you acquire may turn out to be the difference between life and death."

He paused again, looking round the room at people's faces, searching for reactions, hoping to spot the poker faces from the ones who wore their hearts on their sleeves.

"Over the next few days, we will test your fitness and your reflexes. We will teach you how to defend yourselves in a range of different scenarios and how to handle a weapon safely. Each of you will have a specific mission in a specific context and you will have to absorb, in a very short space of time, knowledge about the context, its history, your adversary and your allies. We will also test your language skills, and if necessary, put you through intensive language training. If you survive until the end of this fortnight, we will send you out into the four corners of the globe. There is a global intelligence support network out there, in case you need it, but my advice to you is to be independent, self-reliant, to trust no one, except the MI6 contact we put you in touch with, and to carry out your mission as if you are on your own. The more chatter, the more risk. The more people in the know, the more you can be known. Secrecy is both our motto and our modus operandi. You will be invisible, because you blend in. You will change the story, but you will not be the news. You will make a difference, because the alternative is unacceptable. Your country will be forever grateful, although will not be able to show you our gratitude. Any questions?"

No one dared ask a thing.

"In that case, please open the envelope in front of you. It contains your security pass for the building, to get in and to use within the walls. You will also find a personalised timetable and a map of the building. At certain points, throughout the fortnight, you may find yourselves in the same place as one or two others, but that is no indication of your future proximity. There is a cafeteria for your lunchtime or comfort break refreshments. Toilets can be found on each floor. I will catch up with you all at regular points throughout your training. Thank you and good luck."

Owen's next activity was weapons training. Having been a member of the Tonbridge School Combined Cadet Force, he was not unfamiliar with guns, and was not, in fact, a bad shot, with a rifle. After several rounds of firing practice, monitored and scored, he was shown into a room with a dismantled pistol, scattered across a table.

"Put it together will you, please."

It was an order, not a question, given by a man in military attire. Owen sat at the table and reassembled the pistol, fairly quickly.

"Can you demonstrate the safety to me now?" requested the soldier, with an element of respect.

Owen demonstrated.

"Jolly good. I'm now going to show you how to stop yourself being disarmed and how to disarm someone else."

"OK, I'm ready when you are."

Owen had hardly got the words out when his pistol was in the hand of the soldier and pointing at him.

"I think we may have a way to go," laughed the soldier, ironically.

An hour or so later, Owen was able to defend himself against an adversary wanting to remove his gun. It took another hour for him to successfully disarm the soldier.

It was lunchtime, and he was grateful for a chance to have a drink and recharge his concentration batteries. Hopefully, his next session would be less physical, although potentially no less draining on his powers of concentration. He was about to go and have his reactions tested, but first, some steak and chips. The steak was better than his meal with Ike and Thelma, but he preferred fries to chips. There were stodgy chips which you smothered in salt and vinegar, from a fish and chip shop, and thoroughly enjoyed as a meal in themselves. Then, there were crispy chips which went well with steak. The cafeteria had not quite managed to enhance the crispiness enough for Owen's taste. Either way, he was hungry. No sooner had he cleared his plate, than he regretted eating such a satisfying meal, because its effects were soporific.

In the reactions test, Owen's various senses were bombarded with stimuli. Thankfully, most of his reactions were above average. His reactions test was followed by a full medical. He had to undress to his underpants and was self-conscious about the puncture scars in his thighs.

Even though he had been clean for a year, there was still evidence of his drug abuse. Curiously, the doctor said nothing about it. Either it was not relevant, or more likely, they already knew everything there was to know about him.

"I think you might need to work on your physical fitness," reflected the doctor, looking at the data on Owen's print-out. "It says you have been cycling regularly, but I suspect, in Amsterdam, there were very few hills. Try the gym. The treadmill and the bench. We will test you again next week."

"When am I supposed to fit in using the gym, if my transport is booked for six, each day?"

"Firstly, it's only booked for six o'clock, today, and can be changed. Secondly, don't eat such a big meal just before you pay me another visit. Thirdly, if you refer more closely to your timetable, you do in fact have an hour between five and six."

"Thank you," responded Owen, feeling small.

In his final time-tabled session, he discovered his new identity. For the next however many years, Owen Linton-House would become Ian Elton-Craig. For so much of his adolescence, Owen had wanted to be someone other than Owen Linton-House. He had longed to be his own man, not living in the shadow of his parents' pagoda. Finally, he had a chance to be someone else, except, he had just as little control over his new identity as he had had over his present one. Ian Elton-Craig shared a number of similarities with Owen Linton-House, notably a double-barrelled surname, which was explained as an auditory consideration. If Owen had been used to responding to a two-part appellation, he would react better, if his new surname also had two parts.

Educated at a second-tier public school, Ian had achieved 'A' levels in French, Geography and History. He also enjoyed drama and creative writing, which was why working for a publishing company seemed like a good fit. On the other hand, he had lost his parents in a housefire and had been brought up by an aunt and uncle, who owned a dog and two cats.

His dossier caused him more emotional pain than he might have anticipated, when reading about his new family background. They had also included the loss of the dog, a beloved family pet. The psychologist who was over-seeing the session, approached Owen.

"I would apologise, but it has to be this way, Ian. The more natural your responses, the more in character you can be. We know you enjoy drama, so you will be familiar with method acting. These are not emotions that you need to feign. They come straight from the heart. The key thing, right now, is that we address any inappropriate responses to the emotional pressure and stress triggers you might experience in the field. Is there anything you would like to tell me?"

"Other than I think the whole thing seems remarkably unfair."

"I concede, you may well be right. However, you may find yourself in a situation where your adversary will use your weaknesses against you, so this too, can be preparation for future scenarios."

"Do I get to take the dossier home with me?"

"Unfortunately, no. For the next two weeks, you will have time each day, to get to know yourself. It is up to you to find your best method of remembering your story. The one thing you don't have to worry about is your public identity. What does not exist in the dossier, feel free to make up. What is in the dossier does not just exist for you. Ian Elton-Craig exists in school archives, medical records, utilities company customer bases, bank accounts, etcetera. From tomorrow, you will be quizzed about your life. You will no longer be called Owen by anyone here."

"I'd better become Ian, then," responded Owen.

After another twenty minutes of reading, Owen-Ian went to the gym and ran five miles on a treadmill, in borrowed shorts and running shoes. Even in the gym, someone was on hand to monitor his time and record the data. No doubt, they expected significant improvement, by the end of the fortnight. There was no time left to shower and, in any case, he had neither towel nor clean clothes to change into. It was time to go home, and Owen-Ian was shattered. He had to wait outside the building for ten minutes, until Brian pulled up.

"Good evening."

"Good evening," responded Owen-Ian.

It was another silent journey.

At the evening meal, Owen-Ian had no potatoes, just meat and vegetables. He was feeling guilty about the steak and his poor aerobic performance, although the guilt did not prevent him from consuming four more Stroopwaffels, back in his room. His reflection on the day was one of quiet exhilaration. He did not bother with vodka and was asleep by nine-thirty.

In the morning his muscles were stiff, but he had noticed that today included a session on self-defence. That was going to be uncomfortable, if not painful. Having eaten bacon and eggs, he went down to reception. Brian was not there, so he went outside to wait. Brian pulled up and Owen-Ian got in.

"Good morning," Brian greeted him.

"Good morning, my reticent friend."

"We aren't friends."

"My apologies."

Owen-Ian endured another silent journey and let himself into Century House with his security pass. This morning, he went straight to a room next to the gym, where he was given a tracksuit to change into. As anticipated, the self-defence activity involved using muscles he had already awakened from a lengthy slumber, the day before. He was perhaps not as speedy with his reactions as he should have been.

"You're behaving like an octogenarian," mocked the instructor.

"Yes. I am discovering muscles I didn't know I had. I'm sure things will improve."

"You can always take a sauna here, before you go home."

"But I already have to use that last hour to get fit."

"Can't you stay an extra half hour?"

"I'm not sure. I'll have to ask the driver, when I see him again."

At the end of the session, he was handed a towel and directed to the showers. When he was refreshed and clothed again, he went to the cafeteria where he ate a cheese toastie. One of the other recruits came over and sat down next to him.

"Hi. I'm Maurice."

"Is that who you were or who you are now?"

"Who I am now, although, to be honest, I'm not quite sure if it's pronounced 'Morris' or 'Morees'."

"I'm Ian. How are you finding the training?"

"Hard. You?"

"Tough but exhilarating."

The psychologist came into the room and saw them chatting. Walking over to them he sat down opposite.

"I trust you are quizzing each other on your new identities."

"That's a really good idea," responded Owen-Ian. "Far more useful than trying to find out about who we were."

"It's confusing," commented Maurice.

"Not if you decide to forget your former identity and just become who you are now. Focus on one story only," replied the psychologist.

His wisdom imparted, he got up and walked away.

"So, Maurice. Tell me about your family."

"I'm an only child. My dad died when I was thirteen, from lung cancer. I was a very angry adolescent. My mum had a mental breakdown and I had to spend eighteen months in foster care. I got a job in a Balti house. That's where I learnt Punjabi."

"Wow. Are they sending you to Pakistan?"

"I'm not at liberty to say."

"Good man."

"What about you?"

"Ian Elton-Craig. Went to public school. Studied French, Geography and History 'A' levels. Enjoy drama and creative writing. Parents died in a house fire. Brought up by my aunt and uncle."

It was time to go to their next sessions. Owen-Ian spent an hour reading about Ottawa. His story was that he had been in the area for the last twelve months, so he needed to be familiar with Ottawa and the local area. He had to hit the ground running, and be aware of any potential difficulties, geographical or historical. It was beginning to feel like being back at school, especially as he also had to cover enough of the geography 'A' level syllabus, to make a grade 'C' believable, in two weeks, and learn a new language.

After a short comfort break, he went to a language laboratory to begin intensive Pashto lessons. He would be expected to continue with the Pashto throughout his time in Canada, using language cassettes. At some point, he was to expect a trip to Afghanistan. The whole experience was emotionally difficult for Owen-Ian. All he could think about was Kochai. Did not Floyd say he was in Afghanistan and spoke Pashto? Maybe one day, he would go and have a conversation with him. He encouraged himself that he picked up languages quickly. Russian had been a whole new alphabet, but Pashto was something else entirely. Getting used to reading in the opposite direction was challenging.

Owen-Ian finished off the day in the gym, back on the treadmill. He felt like he had run even slower, because his muscles were aching, but according to the trainer, he was running at the same speed. He was permitted to take the shorts, running shoes and tracksuit home with him. Having stuffed everything in his knapsack, so that the zip was straining, he decided to bring his holdall, tomorrow. He went and waited on the street, and on the dot of six, Brian pulled up. Owen-Ian amused himself by wondering if Brian was inside the building and knew exactly when he was going to leave. The car was probably parked at Century House.

"Good evening."

"Good evening. I was wondering if it might be possible to change my pick-up time from six to half-past, only they have suggested I finish the day with a sauna, as I'm unfit and doing a lot of physical training. Please."

"Of course."

It was the last thing Brian said for the rest of the journey.

Owen-Ian was becoming more and more confident with his story, and his body was getting fitter. The days passed in much the same way, reading, exercise, language studies, monitoring, chats with the psychologist, and so on. On the Friday, a session was set aside for clothes measuring and fitting. Owen-Ian was given two suits, one grey, one navy, two shirts, two ties and two pairs of leather shoes, one black, the other brown. Up to that point, since leaving home, most of his clothes had come from a charity shop. It was not Saville Row, by any stretch of the imagination, but it felt good to have new, fitting clothes. He was certain he had lost weight, too.

The last session on the Friday, was a de-briefing, with Dominic.

"I am about to hand out a sketch of your new images. If you do not look like the person in the image, you need to spend some time on your appearance, over the weekend. By all means, make a brief trip to the barbers or hairdressers, do some shopping for necessities, but please, keep your trips short and stay away from bars and restaurants, or other social and leisure venues. It's not that we don't have confidence in your ability to conduct yourselves appropriately, but we can't have you getting caught up in any drunken incidents. For those of you who used to live in London, neither can we risk you being apprehended by nefarious individuals."

Owen-Ian realised why Brian's driving was so fast and along convoluted routes. He was probably avoiding being tailed. They would have known all about the 'banya' and Nikolai.

He looked at his sketch and saw that not only did he have short hair and was clean shaven, but he was also sporting metal rimmed glasses. His primary task for the weekend would be a trip to the barbers. The flowing curls had to be trimmed and the birds' nest had to be removed. It was a while since he had shaved. He thought it would be best to have the beard removed at the barbers, as they would have suitable clippers. Dominic came over to Owen-Ian and handed him a pair of glasses.

"Try them on."

Owen-Ian put on the glasses and was surprised to be able to see clearly.

"There's no prescription. Your passport photo will have no glasses, but you wear them at all times, apart from passing through border control."

Owen-Ian was curious to see what he looked like.

"I would like the glasses back, until your transformation is complete. I trust you will go to the barbers, tomorrow."

"Absolutely."

Dominic returned to the front of the room.

"You have all done phenomenally well, this week. Try and rest at the weekend when you're not working on your appearance. I will see you all back here, on Monday morning."

Owen-Ian had an hour and a half before Brian was due to pick him up. He went to the gym and ran for half an hour. It felt much easier than at the start of the week. He took his holdall and went to the sauna. As he sat in the steam, he fully expected Vasily to walk in. More memories came flooding back. This work with MI6 would be his opportunity for pay-back. Owen-Ian felt sure Nikolai was the kingpin in the drugs supply chain, from Afghanistan to Canada.

When the recruits assembled in the main room, on Monday morning, there was general hilarity, as some of them had had haircuts, dyed their hair, or shaved. Apart from one of the women who had changed long dark hair to a blonde bob-cut, Ian-Owen was the greatest transformation, especially once he put his glasses on again. They all had their photographs taken so their new passports could be prepared. After the photographs, there was another day of tests and a long chat with Dominic.

"How are you feeling?" asked Dominic, as Ian-Owen closed the door to his office and sat on the opposite side of his desk.

"I'm good, thank you. The psychologist has been helpful. Some of it has been a bit challenging emotionally. I feel like I'm making progress."

"You are making good progress. Your Pashto is coming along nicely."

"Thanks. I was going to ask you about that. If I'm off to Canada next week, when do I go to Afghanistan?"

"We think the drugs are entering Canada in books. That's part of the reason for your job with a publishing company. That and your general set of skills and background. We wanted to find a job you would pick up quickly. Ontario Publishing Inc. is a company with a global network. When the time is right, you will be sent on a business trip to Pakistan. From there, you can go into Afghanistan and 'holiday' your way back across Europe, having purchased some drugs, at the source, somewhere in the poppy fields of Helmand. For now, we need you to gather intelligence on a competitor, Ottawa Books, and befriend Caroline Dupont."

"I get it now."

"Anything else?"

"Yes. What if Caroline Dupont isn't interested in me?"

"We're not asking you to sleep with her on day one. Be creative. Use your imagination. There's a file on her for you to read, this week. Manufacture 'chance' meetings. Build on your common interests. Charm her. I'm sure you'll think of something. You're not a bad looking guy and you're in a lot better shape than you were a week ago. I hope you'll keep up the gym work, in Ottawa."

"OK. Thanks."

"A piece of advice. Don't let on that you speak Russian, while you are in Canada. We are certain there is a strong Russian connection there, and we need you to be able to get close enough to eavesdrop on conversations and report back."

"Understood."

Ian-Owen got up to leave for his next session in the language laboratory.

In the afternoon, he started to read the file on Caroline Dupont. She liked cats and jazz music, lived across the river from Ottawa, in Gatineau, Quebec, on Rue Jeanne-d'Arc, and her job was in international book sales. Her photo showed her to be blonde with blue eyes. Ian-Owen found her attractive. He loved cats, but unfortunately, he had little or no knowledge of jazz music and even less of French-Canadian jazz music. He took himself off to the resources room.

"Good afternoon. Would it be possible for you to research some French-Canadian jazz music for me and get hold of some cassettes?"

"Any particular period?"

"No idea. Fifties, sixties and seventies, maybe."

"Come back tomorrow afternoon and we'll have something for you."

"Thank you."

Ian-Owen had no idea what to expect, although he was impressed with the reach of the resources department.

On the final Friday afternoon, the recruits received their passports, their air tickets and their final instructions, including contact details. In Ian-Owen's case, he would be met at the airport by a man called Grant Waterstone, who would make the observation, 'Lake Ontario is so beautiful, at this time of year', to which Owen was meant to respond, 'Yes, I hope to visit it, soon'. His passport photo resembled how he looked when he started sixth form, although the glasses made him look about ten years older.

Ian-Owen had his final UK run on the treadmill and spent twenty minutes in the sauna. He felt physically in good condition, but mentally, he was feeling increasingly apprehensive about what lay ahead. He told himself it should be easier than settling in Amsterdam. For a start, his accommodation was all sorted, his job lined up and they spoke English. The problem was his niggling lack of confidence with women. For the final time, he waited outside Century House, and Brian pulled up in the car.

"Good evening, Brian," Ian-Owen greeted him cheerily, getting in.

"Good evening. I will be picking you up from the hotel at seven-thirty on Monday morning and taking you to Heathrow."

"Thank you."

Just like every other journey, nothing more was said, until they reached the hotel.

"Goodnight," said Ian-Owen.

"Goodnight."

That weekend, Ian-Owen introduced himself to French-Canadian jazz music. Even if it did not grow on him much, he could, at least, appear knowledgeable and interested. No doubt he would end up having to attend a jazz festival or a jazz club, with Caroline Dupont. Buying tickets might even turn out to be a pretext to get together with her. Ian-Owen really wanted to drop by his former flat and call in at The Prince Albert, but he knew Battersea was off limits. He wondered if the council had moved a new tenant into his flat yet. When he was not listening to jazz music, and the resources department had thrown in a couple of internationally famous jazz musicians, Herb Ellis and Bob Brookmeyer, Ian-Owen listened to one of the Pashto language cassettes.

Halfway through the Saturday afternoon, it occurred to Ian-Owen that he should buy a book for the flight. Also, it made sense to buy a larger suitcase. Then he realised he had no home to go to, so there would be nowhere to leave the small suitcase. He tried to pack his suits, shirts, tracksuit, running shoes and leather shoes, in the small suitcase, along with his existing wardrobe. There was not enough room, even with the holdall. A solution popped into his head. He would buy a large suitcase and ask Brian to dispose of the empty small suitcase. On the edge of Knightsbridge, Ian-Owen could not resist the temptation of buying his suitcase in Harrods. It was not cheap, but he had spent very little of his two hundred pounds in expenses. He also bought two leather luggage labels, some toiletries and a new sponge bag. As for his book selection, he was torn between John le Carre's *Smiley's People* and *Zen and the Art of Motorcycle Maintenance* by Robert Pirsig. He came down on the side of Pirsig, reflecting that a spy thriller was perhaps not so helpful, given the very real prospect he was currently facing, wavered and bought both.

By Sunday evening, Ian-Owen was packed and ready. He hardly slept a wink, through nerves, but told himself there was plenty of time to sleep on the plane. At seven-thirty in the morning, Brian pulled up and got out of the car, to put Ian-Owen's luggage in the boot.

"Good morning."

"Good morning. I have a favour to ask. This small case is empty and needs to be disposed of."

"Not a problem."

"Thank you."

The journey to Heathrow was as quiet as all the previous journeys, with Brian. He pulled up in the dropping-off zone outside departures and got out to unload Ian-Owen's luggage. Having stood the suitcase on the pavement, he held out his hand, to shake Ian-Owen's.

"It's been a pleasure, Ian. Good luck."

"Thank you. Goodbye, Brian," he responded, taking Brian's hand and shaking it, firmly.

Brian got back in the car and drove off, while Ian-Owen stood watching, his life in a moment of suspended animation. Presently, Ian Elton-Craig checked in at the Air Canada desk and passed through security to the departure lounge, where he bought a cup of coffee and waited for the gate-number to be displayed for the ten o'clock flight to Ottawa.

Between buying a coffee and boarding the flight, Ian went to the toilet twice. When he came out of the toilet for the second time, the gate-number had appeared. Sensibly, he had purchased a suitcase with integral wheels, so he was able to wheel it the considerable distance to the gate, where more time was spent sitting around, waiting. Outside, it had started to rain heavily. Eventually, boarding was announced, and he joined the queue of passengers filing past the air stewardess who was checking boarding cards.

Ian's was a window seat, and as he settled himself in, he watched the raindrops splashing in the expanding puddles on the concrete below. Up to now, Ian's only previous flights were on the school trip to the Soviet Union, which were much shorter. Seatbelt on and novel resting on his lap, until he was permitted to lower the table, he sat glancing sideways at the middle-aged woman who had squeezed into the adjacent seat and claimed the armrest between them.

Not usually competitive, but seeking amusement, Ian thought he might claim the space when she next moved her elbow, which she did, a few minutes later, to manipulate the air conditioning. Ian soon wished he had not as her unusually sharp elbow reclaimed the armrest, assertively, when she lowered her arm.

"Oh. Sorry. I wasn't expecting your arm to be there," she apologised, insincerely.

Ian understood her implication and relinquished any opportunity of resting his left arm, for the duration of the journey. The plane taxied to the runway, the engines roared, and the plane gathered speed. Any hope Ian had of watching the patchwork of rural England scroll by was soon thwarted by the cloud cover. The seatbelt sign remained illuminated for what felt like an eternity, and the plane started to experience turbulence. Outside his window, Ian caught sight of flashes of lightening, in the murky darkness. They must have been flying into a severe weather front. An hour passed before the atmosphere calmed down and light broke in through the window. They were somewhere over the Atlantic Ocean, but all that Ian could see was an ocean of cloud.

Ian had almost forgotten the novel, resting in his lap. He started to read and was soon enthralled by the narrative. The arrival of lunch forced him to put the book down. He was completely put off eating by the noises which the middle-aged woman, less than a foot away from him, was making as she chewed her food. As subtly as he could, he got his Walkman out from the knapsack between his feet, inserted a Led Zeppelin cassette, put on the earphones, turned up the volume and resumed eating. By the time he started his dessert, a miniature strawberry cheesecake, the woman was stacking her plastic pots. She shut her eyes and leant back, which made it somewhat inconvenient for Ian to escape to the toilet, when he had finished eating.

"Excuse me, but I need to go to the bathroom."

She glared at him. Her table was still in the lowered position, with the empty lunch packaging resting on it, and she could not work out how to get out of her seat.

"I think you'll have to wait until they clear away the lunch things," she hissed.

Ian stood up and waved at the air stewardess, beckoning her over.

"Please could you remove this lady's rubbish, so I can go to the bathroom?"

"Madam, I'll take these items for you," responded the stewardess, kindly, picking up the little tray.

Ian escaped, and after using the bathroom, decided to walk round the plane a few times, before returning to his seat. When he did return, the middle-aged woman was sitting with her head back and eyes closed.

"Excuse me, again, but I need to return to my seat."

No response.

"Madam. Hello. Excuse me."

Still no response.

"Excuse me," repeated Ian.

He did not want to shake her shoulder, in case she accused him of assault, so he went and found the stewardess.

"Hi. I have a slight problem. The lady next to me is sleeping and I need to return to my seat. She won't wake up when I speak to her, and I don't want to touch her."

"Would you like to move seats?"

"I would love to move seats, but my book, knapsack and Walkman are by my window seat."

"Ah. I see."

The stewardess approached the woman and put a hand on her shoulder. Ian stood just behind her.

"Madam," she said firmly, nudging the shoulder gently.

"Leave me alone. Stop. He's attacking me!" she shouted as her sleep was disturbed.

Realising the situation, the woman turned beetroot-red with embarrassment.

"Excuse me, Madam. I would like to access this gentleman's belongings. Would you stand up, please?"

The middle-aged woman hauled her corpulent bottom from the seat and stood aside. The stewardess gestured to Ian to rescue his belongings.

"Thank you, Madam," she said, politely. "Now, sir. Come with me."

Ian followed her to the opposite side of the plane, where there was a vacant aisle seat.

"Is this suitable, sir?"

"Thank you."

Ian sat down next to a man, probably in his sixties, who was reading a copy of The Times. The man acknowledged Ian and turned back to his newspaper. Ian took out his novel and resumed reading.

"Good read?" commented the older man.

"It is good, yes," replied Ian, hoping the man would not attempt to engage in further conversation.

"Have you ever ridden a motorcycle?" asked the man, thirty seconds later.

"Yes. Have you?" replied Ian, making a spontaneous decision to be polite.

"Yes. I once owned a Triumph, but I'm a little old now."

"Is someone ever too old to ride a motorcycle?"

"Yes. When you no longer have the strength to put it on its stand," laughed the older man. "I once rode all the way to Italy. Have you ever been to Italy?"

Ian was just about to respond that he had not been to Italy but had been to Russia, when he remembered who he was, now.

"No."

"During the second world war. I had to go and observe what Mussolini was up to, and report back to my superiors in London."

"Sounds dangerous."

"It was. I nearly got caught escaping from the back window of a woman's house, when her husband came home early."

Ian smiled.

"Seriously, the Resistance risked their lives on a daily basis. The man was quite clearly unhinged."

"Most Fascist dictators are."

"And Communist dictators. Some animals being more equal than others."

Ian picked up on the reference to Orwell's *Animal Farm*.

"I read *Animal Farm*."

"You know, I've been to Russia, too. In the sixties."

Ian knew he must avoid any admission of his ability to speak Russian.

"Where abouts did you go?"

"Moscow. We were in the middle of the Cold War. I was a correspondent, reporting on the Soviet space programme. It was such a huge relief when the Americans reached the moon first."

"I'd love to experience the view of earth from space."

"I've seen a lot of technological change in my lifetime but watching the moon landing was the greatest triumph. Talking of Triumph, what was your motorcycle?"

"Honda 250."

"There's nothing like speeding along the open road on a warm summer's evening, wind in your hair."

"I've always had to wear a helmet," laughed Ian, "but yes, I get the speed thing."

"Will you excuse me, only I need to go to the toilet."

"No problem."

Ian stood to let the older man out and sat back down to his book, thinking how interesting his interlocutor's life must have been, and wanting to ask more. The older man returned, and Ian was about to ask him about the changes he had lived through, when the older man spoke first.

"For a man who has never travelled, how come you're flying to Canada?"

"I was invited to go and stay at my cousin's house. You're only young, free and single once, so I thought, why not."

"Where will you travel, as a tourist, I mean?"

"I don't know. I would love to see the Rockies, but my cousin lives in Ottawa. I guess, I will go where they take me."

"Well, if you get a chance to travel to Toronto, take it. The CN Tower is the tallest free-standing structure in the world. The so-called Space Deck is well worth a visit."

"I'll bear that in mind."

"Now, if you'll excuse me, I must finish doing my crossword."

"Nice talking."

Ian picked up his book, again, and resumed reading. After three quarters of an hour, his eyes started to grow heavy, so he put the book in his knapsack and took out his Walkman again, changed the cassette to Pink Floyd *Wish You Were Here*, and put the earphones on. Somewhere in 'Shine on you crazy diamond,' he fell asleep. He slept for just over three hours. When eventually, he did wake up, the older man was desperate to escape to the toilet. As soon as he returned, Ian went to the toilet, himself.

"Tell me about the changes you've lived through," Ian invited the older man, sitting back in his seat.

"Where to start? Television, electric razor, cats-eyes in the road. The helicopter, nuclear reactors and microwave ovens. Personal computer. Space travel. Lots of medical things, like the first heart transplant. And that's only the tip of the iceberg."

"Were you a trend-setter or a follower?"

"Most of the technologies available to the ordinary person were hugely expensive when they first came out. I couldn't have afforded to be a trend-setter even if I'd wanted to be."

"Which invention would you say was most important to you?"

"To me personally?"

"Yes."

"I would have to say cats-eyes, because during the war they were so important to travel around the country, especially during the black-out and when car headlights had to be shuttered. I would have had to slow down, otherwise!" the older man joked. "Are you any good at crosswords?"

"Sorry."

"I'm determined to finish this, before we land, and I'm stuck on one last clue."

"Try me."

"Jolly good. Two parts to this. Nineteen across and twenty-three down. Five and eight. Here's the clue. 'Cyclist brings small change.' I must be missing something."

"Five letters and eight letters, you say?"

"Yes."

"Penny farthing."

"Of course. The man's a genius!"

Ian laughed.

"Listen. I know we've only just met, on an aeroplane, but here is my card, if you would like to come and have a beer with me."

Ian looked at the card and read aloud, "Adrian Zorkin. Real Estate?"

"At your service."

"Ian Elton-Craig. I don't have a business card."

The older man laughed.

The seatbelt sign was illuminated, and the captain's voice came over the loudspeaker, "Ladies and gentlemen. We are beginning our descent into Ottawa."

Half an hour later, as Ian peered through the window, across the older man, the plane passed through the clouds and banked. Ian could just begin to make out a cityscape, before the plane levelled off again.

"It looks like we are approaching the airport from the south, today," observed the older man.

"Do you fly often?"

"Oh yes. Every couple of months."

"The real estate business must be thriving," joked Ian.

"Business is good."

The cabin crew were now strapping themselves in, ready for landing. Ian wished he were sitting by the window, because he could not really see anything from where he was. Suddenly, there was a bump, the wheels connected with the runway and the engines went into reverse thrust. Five minutes later, the plane came to a standstill, by the terminal, and there was a rush of activity, with people undoing their seatbelts and reaching into the overhead lockers. The older man needed Ian to step back.

"Tell me which your case is, and I'll lift it down," offered Ian.

"The grey metal one. Thank you."

Ian reached up and dislodged the case from the tightly packed locker. When he lowered it to the seat, he was glad he had been working out in the gym.

"That's heavy."

"Yes, I try only to travel with one small case, but I have a weakness for buying books," chuckled the older man.

They joined the mass of people, pushing to get off the plane and walked together to immigration.

"This is where we go our separate ways, my friend. I have a Canadian passport."

"It was nice chatting."

"Don't forget the open invitation."

"Thank you. I won't," replied Ian, extending his hand.

The older man shook it warmly and went to his passport queue. Ian waited nervously in his, hoping MI6 had done their job properly. He was waiting by the baggage carousel, inside ten minutes, glad that he had chosen bright red leather luggage labels.

He cleared customs, without a hitch, and stood looking around for Grant Waterstone to appear. A tall slim man with grey hair, maybe forties, maybe early fifties, approached him.

"Lake Ontario is so beautiful, at this time of year," he commented.

"Yes, I hope to visit it, soon," responded Ian.

"Welcome to Ottawa, Ian. Shall I take your case. The car's outside."

"Yes. Thanks."

"Did you have a pleasant flight?"

"Yes. Very interesting," he replied, almost sarcastically.

Waterstone did not ask why. They walked to where his car was parked.

"Get in," he said, putting Ian's case in the boot.

Ian went to the wrong side of the car, felt embarrassed, continued round the front of the car to the passenger door and got in. Waterstone got into the driving seat.

"I'll drive you to your flat. You'll find all the details you need for your job and how to contact me, when you get there. We've even stocked your cupboards for you. I'm going to stick around for a couple of days, in a downtown hotel, in case you need me for anything, and then, I shall go back to Toronto."

"The man I sat next to on the plane said I should visit the CN Tower."

"One day, you should, but all in good time. Right now, you have a new job to get stuck into and, from all accounts, a rather desirable mission. If I were twenty years younger, I might have volunteered myself."

Waterstone looked across at Ian and winked.

Twenty minutes later, they pulled up in front of an apartment block on St. Patrick Street. Waterstone retrieved Ian's suitcase from the boot and led him to the first floor. He reached into his pocket and pulled out a bunch of keys which he handed to Ian.

"You can let us in. It's your new home."

Ian unlocked the door and walked in. Compared to his flat in Battersea, it was luxurious.

"Sorry the government budget doesn't run to the penthouse," Waterstone laughed. "Having just said it's your home, I know there are beers in the fridge."

"Would you like one?"

"Please. Was I that unsubtle?"

Ian looked in the fridge and smiled at what he saw. There was enough food for a week, including a steak. He took out two bottles and hunted in the drawer by the sink for a bottle-opener.

"There you go," he said, handing one to Waterstone.

"Cheers! Perhaps you should open the envelope, while I'm here."

"Good idea."

Ian took the envelope that was lying on the coffee table, replacing it with his bottle and tore open the flap. He pulled out a brochure, a smaller envelope and some papers. On closer inspection, he could see that the papers were his resume, a job offer letter, and the utilities contracts. He opened the brochure to find a business card inside a cellophane pouch on the inside of the front cover. The smaller envelope contained his bank card and a statement.

"Right. The name on the business card is your boss. The address is there, but I'll drive you around the city for a bit, shortly. You won't need to pay any bills. They are paid for you. The utilities contracts are really only there, in case there's a fault. The bank statement tells you who and where your branch is. You will receive a monthly statement. Ontario Publishing Inc pays your salary, but MI6 transfers an expenses budget. It'll be in the name of Brunswick Holdings. You should have plenty to live on, comfortably, and to wine and dine Caroline Dupont."

"Brilliant. I think I'd quite like to buy a bicycle, and Dominic Andrews says I should join a gym."

"If you check your bank balance, I believe you'll find you have been paid for your time over the last couple of weeks. That should be plenty to buy a bike and take out a gym membership."

"Excellent."

"Let's go for a ride," suggested Waterstone, finishing off his beer.

Ian gulped down the rest of his own bottle, went to the toilet and grabbed his jacket. Waterstone drove Ian via the shortest route to his new employment.

"That's where you will be working."

As they continued their tour, Waterstone started to point out places of interest.

"That's your main bank branch. This is the commercial centre. We're going to drive down Parliament Hill, past the national government building and over the river into the province of Quebec, to the city of Gatineau. It's all so close, you can cycle over there easily. I'm going to drive past Caroline Dupont's house. It's on Rue Jeanne-d'Arc. It'll be on my left, so it shouldn't be obvious to anyone who might happen to look out of the window, that you are looking, and neither should they be able to see you. We don't want her to think she has a stalker, when finally, you come to meet her!"

After a brief silence, Waterstone added, "I expect you're tired, after your flight. You don't start work until Monday next week. That should give you plenty of time to get over any jetlag."

"And time to do some exploring. Get my bearings."

"There you go. It's the white one," announced Waterstone, as they drove along Rue Jeanne-d'Arc.

Ian looked across.

"Nice house!"

"Don't forget, we suspect her of being involved somewhere in the drugs distribution. She can probably afford a house like that."

"I wonder if she's got a swimming pool."

"She has."

"What other surveillance is there. If I do manage to get intimate with her, you're not going to be watching, surely."

"No. No internal surveillance. One of the reasons you are here, and your mission to befriend her is so we can have ears on the ground. We don't believe she is the head of the cartel. We need to find out who is and where they are operating. They have so far outwitted us."

"Just out of interest, do you know anything about French-Canadian jazz?"

"Not a lot. I know there's a jazz weekend or festival, whatever they call it. Started in 1980, has become an annual event, in June. You'll have to ask around. Why?"

"Caroline's file says she likes jazz music."

"There you go. That's your way in. Seek her out at the festival, next month. In fact, just over Alexandra Bridge, I'm pretty sure that's where the first jazz weekend took place, in Major's Hill Park. There'll be posters and flyers everywhere."

They pulled up outside Ian's flat.

"I almost forgot," confessed Waterstone, reaching into the glove compartment. "Here's your gun and a hundred rounds of ammunition. I hope you won't ever need one, let alone one hundred."

"Thanks. I hope I won't ever need to use it."

"Call me if you need anything," Waterstone instructed Ian, handing him a business card.

"Grant Waterstone. Lawyer?"

"It's my day job. That number is only for more personal issues, in the next few days. Every week, you will receive a letter with the latest contact details, so you can submit a report. It changes every week. You have a home telephone, but please never use it for anything relating to your assignment. If you should find yourself under siege, call the police. Not that I'm trying to scare you in any way."

"OK. Thanks."

"You're welcome. Final thing. When you contact me with your weekly update, I will say a word in one of the four languages you speak. Dutch, French, Pashto and Russian. DFPR. Translate it back to me in the next language, alphabetically. Dutch comes after Russian. If no word is spoken for you to translate, you'll know we have been compromised. If you translate into the wrong language, I will know we've been compromised. Good luck."

"Bye."

"Bye, Ian. Take care."

Ian got out and went into his apartment building as Waterstone drove off. He started to cook the steak. It all seemed rather surreal.

Ian slept well through his first night in Ottawa. Having eaten toast for breakfast, he listened to a Pashto cassette for an hour. As with most languages, learning what you want to say is the easy part. The challenge comes when a native speaker reels off their answer at break-neck speed. After a shower, Ian realised he had two smart suits, his charity shop suit, some T-shirts and shirts, but not a lot that could be considered smart casual. He would check his bank balance and do some clothes shopping.

Walking to the recently built Rideau Centre took no time at all. He nearly fainted when he saw his bank balance. There were four thousand three hundred Canadian dollars in his account. Ian had no idea which part was salary and which part expenses, but even on the assumption that they paid him five hundred pounds for each of the two weeks, with the exchange rate of just under two dollars to the pound, that meant he could expect around a thousand pounds each month in expenses, on top of his salary at the publishing company. Just how dangerous was this assignment? How essential was he to the national fight against drugs? There was a darker, political objective, at stake, of how to cut off funds for the Soviet cause in Afghanistan. He had been cherry-picked for the assignment.

By the time Ian arrived back at his flat, he had bought three lots of chinos, shirts, ties and jackets, and a pair of less formal, brown leather shoes. Not usually vain, Ian was pleasantly surprised by his reflection in the changing room mirror, and the glasses were a definite winner. He felt slightly more confident about the challenge of attracting Caroline Dupont but was immediately plunged into despair at the thought of someone so gorgeous not already having a boyfriend, which meant competition.

After a quick snack, he went back out to go and join a gym and buy a bicycle. The gym membership was reasonably priced. Gyms were starting to become popular with the general public, not just bodybuilders, so there was an element of competition between the various gyms and fitness centres. The bike Ian bought was considerably sportier than the one he had grown accustomed to riding in Amsterdam, but then Ottawa was hillier than Amsterdam. He cycled back to his flat.

Over the next few days, he cycled all over the city, especially in the parks. Waterstone had been correct about the promotion for the jazz festival, and Ian sat perusing a flyer, over a beer, at his kitchen table. He also reread the brochure about Ontario Publishing Inc. As yet, there was no indication of what his job role would be. All he knew was to arrive at nine o'clock on Monday morning.

In spite of cycling all over the city, Ian resolved to visit the gym twice a week, partly to run on the treadmill, and the rest of the time, to do bench work and lift weights. He was there, ready in his sports gear, at eight o'clock on Saturday morning. Only three other early birds were in the gym, so there was no competition to use the equipment. Ian ran for thirty minutes on the treadmill and then lifted weights on the bench. Comfortable with ten repetitions with one hundred and forty pounds, Ian could not decide whether to increase the number of repetitions or increase the weight. He watched two other men. One was clearly not a novice and was lifting what Ian estimated to be two hundred and sixty to two hundred and eighty pounds. He did twenty repetitions. The other man was less muscular and was lifting what looked like two hundred pounds. He did thirty repetitions. That settled it. Ian would carry on until lifting his present weight twenty-five times became too easy, and then, he would increase the weight. He went home for a hot shower. It was then, that he realised he had forgotten to finish *Zen and the Art of Motorcycle Maintenance*. Reading for pleasure, rather than reading in order to write an essay or discuss in a tutorial, was still quite a new experience for Ian, but one which he resolved to build on, although it occurred to him that he was about to become a whole lot busier. Nevertheless, next time he was downtown, he would buy a couple of novels to read after *Smiley's People*.

On Monday morning, he put on a smart suit, to make a good first impression, but intended to check out his colleagues, to see if they wore smart-smart or smart-casual. Until he knew if there were showers at work, he also thought it would be preferable to walk, rather than cycle. Folding the job offer letter and placing it in his inside jacket pocket, he set off, arriving in reception at five minutes to nine.

"Good morning. I have an appointment with a Mr Thomas Sydney."

"Good morning. What is your name?"

"Ian Elton-Craig."

"Ah, yes," responded the receptionist slowly, as she checked in the diary. "Yes, you do have an appointment with Mr Sydney. I'll call him for you."

"Thank you."

A few minutes later, a balding man, in his fifties, with glasses, wearing smart-casual, exited the lift and approached Ian.

"Welcome to Ontario Publishing, Ian," he said, holding out his hand.

Ian shook it.

"Have you settled in?"

"Yes, thank you. I have been cycling all over, getting to know the city. My apartment is really great."

"Did you cycle here, today?"

"No. I wasn't sure if there were any showers."

"We try to encourage cycling. There are showers and lockers here. Come, I'll give you a tour of the building."

Sydney led the way.

The company covered the whole of a three-floor building. The ground floor consisted of the reception area, with the stairwell and lifts, and some toilets, and extensive warehousing. Behind the building was a twin bay for loading and unloading delivery vehicles. The first floor was mostly open plan offices and was also where the showers were located, behind the lifts, along a corridor. That was also where the storage rooms were situated. The second floor was divided up into several smaller rooms, was where Sydney had his office, and also where the boardroom could be found. As they walked past the mostly plate glass front, Ian could see a meeting taking place.

"That's the weekly Monday catch-up. Obviously, I have been excused midway through it to welcome you. Come on in," he gestured, opening the door to his office. "Sit down, please. Can I get you a coffee?"

"Coffee would be great, thank you."

"Cream and sugar?"

"No sugar, thank you."

Sydney picked up his phone and rang through to reception.

"Please bring me up two coffees. Cream no sugar. Thank you."

"I expect you're wondering what your job role will be."

"I am."

"Any minute now, I am hoping Jeanette Laroche will walk through that door. She is our new International Marketing Manager and you, Ian, will be working with her, to expand our market to any country where French or English is spoken as the official language. I believe the job role we have created for you is International Negotiator. Within the next three years, we want to be selling as many Canadian books across the globe as we sell at home. Do you think you're up for that?"

"I hope so."

"Good. There'll be a whole team of people around you and Jeanette will guide you. You will be making the connections with booksellers and distributors in those different countries.

So, we can make good use of your English and your French."

The door opened and in walked a smartly dressed lady, maybe mid-thirties, carrying three cups of coffee.

"I hijacked the receptionist. You must be Ian. Welcome," Laroche greeted Ian, putting the coffees down on the desk and extending her hand towards him.

He shook it.

"Have you worked in publishing before?"

"No, but I have worked in a pub and a café, so I communicate well with customers. I also studied a lot of literature, so bookshops are familiar to me."

"Jolly good. We will need you to hit the ground running, but mostly, you will be making international phone calls and building up a picture of where the best markets are likely to be."

"Will I be based on the first floor. In the open plan office?"

"Yes. The section at the far end has been set up and equipped for the international department. I will take you and introduce you to your two immediate colleagues when we have drunk our coffee."

"How confident are you with technical French?" asked Sydney.

"I'm sure I will pick it up quickly. I don't suppose there is a publishing glossary with French translation, is there?"

"As a matter of fact, there is," responded Laroche, warmly. "I completed it, only last week."

"Excellent," Sydney encouraged her.

Ian was already feeling like the company was ambitious but was not too large. It appeared personal in the way it related to its employees. Of course, it could simply be that he was new. The moment their coffees were finished, Laroche led Ian out of the door.

"I'll come and find you later, with your contract, Ian. Have a catch up with you," Sydney called after them as they disappeared along the corridor.

"We won't bother with the lift, just to go down one floor. To be honest, I rarely use the lift at all."

"Mr Sydney just told me about the showers. Tomorrow, I will cycle into work."

"Excellent. How much do you know about what Ontario Publishing does?"

"I read the brochure. It appears that most of the books we sell are non-fiction."

"That is correct. The board feels that there is more money to be made with glossy hardbacks. Personally, I would like to see us supporting new fiction writers and breaking into the global market, before our competitors do, but it is what it is."

"What is the non-fiction about?"

"Culture. Tourism. Promoting this beautiful country of ours. Biographies and autobiographies of famous Canadians. Unfortunately, most of our famous sons and daughters are not recognised as Canadians. The world out there thinks they are American. For example, did you know William Shatner is Canadian?"

"I confess, I thought he was American."

"Case in point."

In the international end of the open plan office, there was a man, similar in age to Ian, and a woman who looked like she was straight out of college.

"This is Brad Kalowski. He's the other one of you. You're both international negotiators. And this is Rachel Stein. She is our admin support."

"Hi," Ian greeted them both, noticing that Brad was wearing smart-casual.

"This is your desk and telephone. That is our customer filing cabinet. The company is just getting to grips with IBM compatible computers. Rachel is ahead of the game."

Ian noticed that only Rachel had a computer on her desk.

"At some point, we will all have computers, but for now, you work with pen and paper and Rachel processes it all. The best thing for you to do today, is shadow Brad. Tomorrow, Rachel can give you the low-down on how she likes information presented. Here is a product brochure and a catalogue. Bedtime reading for you. At least, please familiarise yourself with it during this first week. Next week, you can start making phone calls to potential customers. Any questions?"

"No. Not yet, anyway. Thank you."

"Good. I'll leave you in Brad's capable hands."

Laroche turned and walked off.

"Do you enjoy working here?" asked Ian when she was out of earshot.

"Love it," responded Brad.

"It's my first job. I've nothing to compare it to. The managers are really supportive," added Rachel.

"Great. That's what I hoped you'd both say. Ready when you are, Brad."

"Pull your chair over here, watch and listen. I'm working on Belgium, at present."

Ian grabbed the back of his chair and pulled it over to Brad's desk. Brad dialled a number, waited, spoke in French, wrote down a name and an address, along with a number, wished the interlocutor a pleasant day, all in fluent French, and put the phone down.

"Did you get the gist of that?"

"Well, yes, in as much as I only heard your side of the conversation and deduced the rest. I presume the number you quoted is potential sales this year, or was it just first order?"

"In the case of the company I just phoned, the number represents both. They only require one shipment and asked for a year to offload it. They are local to Namur. I write the details on this form. The large box is for any comments or special circumstances. I might write, 'Really keen,' or 'Sample required first, but hope to expand sales,' or whatever. When I have completed the form, with date and time of conversation, I pass it over to Rachel. There you go Rach."

"I add the details to the database and file the form in the filing cabinet."

"Then, what happens?"

"Finance pick up the order," replied Brad. "At the moment it's early days, so there aren't really orders, in the way you'd understand orders to be. These are mostly samples, or our best estimate, in negotiation with the customer, of what we think these booksellers and distributors can shift. When the orders are sent out, information will be sent to the customers about re-ordering, but to be honest, it's all going to be push, push, push, from our side, until the local markets are created. Once the global booksellers and distributors realise they can make money selling our books, we will start to receive orders that we haven't had to chase."

"Once the orders are processed, the finance department invoices the customer," added Rachel, "and when the payment comes through, warehousing ships the books."

"And what often happens, is we have to phone up and encourage the customer to pay the invoice. Some of them change their minds and don't go through with the order. We can't afford to send out two hundred free samples across the globe," explained Brad.

"Why not?" responded Ian. "A book is really cheap. It only costs twenty dollars because we want a wide profit margin. The book itself probably only cost a couple of dollars to produce. Wouldn't it be more effective to send a sample? They could mark it up at a ridiculous profit, gauging what they think a good local price is. Then they would add up the dollar signs and order more books from us. Apologies. What do I know? I've been here two hours."

"No. I think you have a point. Maybe you should leave it a while before you question the bosses though!" laughed Brad.

Owen sat watching and listening in silence, until lunchtime.

"What do you guys do about lunch?"

"I go home," replied Rachel. "I live five minutes away."

"Mostly go to a café, somewhere close, and get coffee and a sandwich. Sometimes I go for a run. We get an hour, and they like us to take it. I think it's so we are in the office for a longer period of time, to catch the various international time zones. Mme Laroche has already spoken to me about working some late shifts, so I can speak to people in different time zones. Melbourne is sixteen hours ahead of us, Bombay ten. Thankfully, London is only five hours ahead and Paris six. We can start as early as eight and finish as late as six, unless it's a specific late shift to call the other side of the world."

"I go home because firstly, I have a dog, and secondly, because the food is cheaper," explained Rachel. "Do you have a dog?"

Ian winced and had to stop himself from talking about Kochai.

"Had a family dog, when I was growing up, but it died.

"You can join me today, if you want," Brad offered.

Up to this point, Ian was not sure if Brad and Rachel were aware he had arrived in Canada, the week before, but he did have an English accent. A plausible reason for moving continents had not been included in his dossier, just that he would work for the publishing company. Rather, it was included in the part of his story which he was supposed to make up. Ian was thinking on his feet, because he knew that if he accepted Brad's invitation, he was bound to be asked to fill in some of the blanks. They say that to be a good liar, you need to have a good memory. The same applied to living as someone else, so whatever he decided, he would have to remember it and refer to it, as time went by.

"Great, thanks."

He followed Brad out of the building to his favourite café. Once they were sat at a table eating smoked meat sandwiches and drinking coffee, conversation resumed.

"Whereabouts are you from?"

"London," replied Ian because it was the simplest option.

"What brings you to Ottawa?"

"Cousin," Ian answered, remembering he had told Adrian Zorkin about his cousin, on the plane, not that Brad was ever likely to meet Adrian Zorkin. "He wanted to go travelling for a while, so invited me to come and look after his apartment.

He told me about jobs I could apply for, and here I am. Did you grow up here?"

"Yes. Born and raised in Ottawa."

"What's the best thing about living here?"

"Healthy environment. Open space. Freedom. Life is uncluttered. That's until you watch a hockey game. A hockey game is more important than life and death."

Ian laughed.

"And what's the worst thing?"

"People thinking we're American."

"You're not the first person to mention that to me. Are you into jazz? I heard there's a jazz festival in Ottawa."

"Personally, jazz isn't my kind of music, but something flips a switch in the city, when the festival takes place. There's a great vibe."

"I'm looking forward to it. Jazz isn't really my thing either, but I heard it's good."

"Are you into sport?"

"I've joined a gym, and I bought a bicycle, last week."

"You didn't waste any time!"

"Just wanted to carry on where I left off, before I got unfit, again. You?"

"I skate. Not well enough to play in a hockey team. Hey, you know, everyone skates when the Rideau Canal freezes over. You've got to try it. Just like you've got to go to a hockey game. Trouble is, we don't really have a top team, here in Ottawa, at the moment. For that you need the Toronto Maple Leafs of the Montreal Canadiens."

"I'll remember that. Does the canal freeze every year?"

"Pretty much. January and February. Sometimes late December until early March."

They returned to the office and Ian carried on listening and watching.

"Come over here, Ian, and I'll talk you through my processing," Rachel said, encouragingly.

Ian rolled his chair nearer to Rachel's computer.

"See here? We can see at a glance when the conversations are held, with whom, what books are ordered and how many, and any special instructions. I print off a daily list, so that you know which companies need to be chased. You spend half your time breaking new ground and the other half chasing up the companies who said, 'Yes please' but meant 'Not interested.' As you can see, Brad has mainly been focusing on French speaking companies in Europe. Once you get started, you'll probably be focusing on English-speaking countries or French-speaking countries in the rest of the world."

"Which is where, exactly?"

"French Guiana, Ivory Coast, Chad, Zaire. I'm not sure. There'll be a list somewhere."

"There is a list," said Brad, finishing his phone call.

At the end of his first day employed by Ontario Publishing Inc. Ian walked home and cooked some chicken. Brad and Rachel seemed friendly enough. Mr Sydney was welcoming, and Mme Laroche was helpful and supportive, at least on his first day. He began to wonder whether Brad would become competitive once he started negotiating with companies for himself. When would that be? There did not seem to be much to the job, other than getting to know the product catalogue and being confident with the customers. Having poured himself a vodka and orange, he picked up the product catalogue and started to read.

At the end of Ian's first week in his new job, a letter arrived on Brunswick Holdings headed notepaper, alerting Ian to call a certain number to update his details, signed by Grant Waterstone. This was how he was to know where to make contact this week. He got on his bike and rode to the train station where he found the booths and made his call.

"Hello."

"Hello. Paard."

"Cheval."

"Do you have anything to report this week? I doubt it."

"No, nothing to report. First week on job went well and I've got the information I need about the jazz festival."

"Destroy the letter. Further instructions next week."

"Bye."

"Goodbye."

After two weeks on the job, Ian concluded that this was, by far, the most boring job he had so far undertaken, although he conceded it was only his third job. Any interest and stimulation came through interaction with the team. The entire set-up prioritized quality of life, with hour long lunch breaks designed to build relationships with colleagues or so you could use the time positively, outside work, instead of rushing back to the office or trying to eat a sandwich whilst still at your desk. The managers with whom he had contact were caring and supportive, and Ian discovered that there was an employee profit-sharing scheme in place.

Were it not for his mission and the jazz festival, Ian's existence in Ottawa could have turned into a monotonous routine of unchallenging job, weekly letters from Brunswick Holdings and reporting to Grant Waterstone, even when there was nothing to report, his trips to the gym and his regular cycle rides. By the time he attended the first event, some of the jazz music he had been familiarizing himself with started to grow on him. He wandered down to the Major's Hill Park and sat on his jacket in the sun, in one of the few remaining vacant patches of grass.

A few yards away, he caught sight of a woman with long blonde hair, talking to an older man. Ian could only see the backs of their heads, and looking around, there were several women with long blonde hair. He was distracted by the arrival on stage of some musicians. The crowd erupted into cheering. When the noise died down, the musicians started to play and some people in the crowd got up to dance. That was when Ian recognised the older man as Adrian Zorkin. Taking out his wallet, Ian pulled out the photo of Caroline Dupont, hoping that the woman would turn in his direction. At the end of the song, whilst she was applauding, with her arms above her head, the woman turned around. Ian was certain she was Caroline Dupont, but what on earth was she doing talking to Adrian Zorkin? It was a perfect opportunity to meet Caroline Dupont, by going over and reintroducing himself to Zorkin.

Picking up his jacket and brushing of the cut grass, annoyed with himself for causing a grass stain, Ian made his way, weaving between several other spectators, over to Zorkin and Caroline Dupont.

"Hello. Remember me?"

"Ian, isn't it? How is your cousin?"

"He went off on his travels, leaving me to look after his apartment, for the next twelve months."

"Caroline. May I present to you, Ian … gosh, my memory isn't what it used to be, something double-barrelled."

"Ian Elton-Craig."

"Pleased to meet you," responded Caroline, holding out her hand.

"I met Ian on the plane coming over," explained Zorkin, as Ian shook Caroline's hand.

"What are you doing in Ottawa."

"Well, my cousin invited me to come and stay. It wasn't until I got here that I discovered he didn't plan on sticking around. So, I got myself a job."

"Where do you work?"

"Ontario Publishing."

"No way. I work for Ottawa Books."

"How do you two know each other?" asked Ian, as it seemed a natural thing to ask.

"I don't work for a publishing company, but I love books. We met at a book fair."

"What's your job at Ontario Publishing?" asked Caroline.

"International Negotiator. You?"

"Quality Manager."

"Would you like to go for a drink, sometime? We could try not to talk shop?"

"That would be great. Stay over here, with us, now."

Ian could not believe his good fortune.

After the next artist finished performing, their conversation continued.

"What do you like doing when you're not at work, Ian?"

"I go to the gym and go on cycle rides."

"Really. I love cycling."

Caroline looked Ian up and down, trying to glean from his clothing, what his physical form was like underneath. He was fit and not bad looking. For his part, Ian had to stop his gaze fixing on Caroline's chest and force himself to look into her eyes. It occurred to Ian that Caroline looked very similar to Katya. It was probably just the long blonde hair and blue eyes, although they might even have passed for sisters. If Ian had a type, it must surely be women with long blonde hair and blue eyes, because he was as attracted to Caroline as he had been to Katya, definitely. There was also hope that she did not have a boyfriend, given her readiness to go for a drink with him, and her attendance at the festival with Zorkin.

Two more artists came on stage before the session ended.

"Do you like jazz music, then?" Caroline quizzed Ian.

"Some. I like lots of different music. You?"

"I love it. Are you coming back this evening?"

"Yes."

"Meet me here, at eight, then," she invited him.

"Great. See you later," replied Ian. "Nice to catch up with you Mr Zorkin."

"Adrian, please."

Ian walked off and Caroline gave Zorkin a knowing look. Zorkin nodded.

Later that day, Ian made his way back to Major's Hill Park. It was more crowded than the afternoon session, and he was worried he might not find Caroline again. He need not have worried. Five minutes after his arrival, someone tapped him on the shoulder.

"Bonsoir."

Of course, she was French-Canadian, so why would she not greet Ian in French.

"Bonsoir," responded Ian.

"Do you speak French, Ian?"

"Badly. Enough to do my job. I have to phone companies around the world where French or English are spoken, or both."

"Would you prefer we speak in English or French, Ian?" she asked, in French.

"I don't mind, Caroline," replied Ian, in French.

"We will speak in English, when we are in Ottawa, and in French, when we are in Gatineau," Caroline insisted.

"Is that where you are from?"

"From, no. I was born in Quebec City. Live, yes. Do you want to have our drink in Gatineau? It's only over the river. You have a cycle, yes?"

"Definitely. That said, I don't know Gatineau. I'm only just getting to know my way around Ottawa."

"If you come over the Alexandra Bridge and find the Rue de l'Hotel-de-Ville, we can meet in the Brasserie du Chien Noir, if you like. What about next Friday evening?"

"Great. Yes. At the Brasserie du Chien Noir. Eight o'clock?"

"Eight o'clock."

There was an international jazz star due on stage this evening, Milt Jackson. Caroline appeared to love every minute of it, but Ian was not so sure. He made every effort to pretend to enjoy it and hoped Caroline would not notice he was not a fan.

"I found a cassette by Jean Derome, in my cousin's apartment. As well as Bob Brookmeyer and Herb Ellis," commented Ian, lying about the provenance of his cassettes.

"Jean Derome is too avant-garde for me," replied Caroline.

"He also had some music by Leonard Cohen. I never realised he was Canadian, until I read the blurb on the cassette."

"The blurb?"

"The bio, the writing, on the cardboard insert in the cassette."

"I like this word 'blurb'."

"Do you prefer the soloists or the bands?" asked Ian.

"I quite like piano and clarinet. What I really enjoy is female jazz singers, more so than pure band music. There should be some singers on stage tomorrow."

Ian kicked himself for not thinking more about jazz singers and going down the instrumental route, when trying to prepare for an encounter with Caroline Dupont.

"Shall we meet up again, tomorrow?" he suggested, hopefully.

"Pourquoi pas."

"Same time, same place?"

"Bien sûr. Of course."

"Tell me about Ottawa Books. What sort of publishing is it?"

"Up and coming Canadian writers, mostly first novels."

"What would you recommend?"

"All of them, of course," laughed Caroline. "Seriously, W P Kinsella, *Shoeless Joe* and Joy Kagawa, *Obasan*. We didn't publish either of them, but I think you'll like them. They both won Best First Novel awards."

"Great. I will seek them out."

At the end of the performance, they went their separate ways. Ian was amazed at how well things were going. Queen of her own little cartel in the French-speaking part of Canada, Caroline was already wondering how she might engage Ian in her drugs empire. Her romantic interest in Ian was as clinical as his was in her. Unfortunately for Ian, he was living in glorious ignorance of the turf war, he was about to get mixed up in.

Ian was excited, when his weekly letter from Brunswick Holdings came through, and he made the call to Waterstone.

"Hello."

"Hello. Paisant."

"Bazgar."

"What is your update?"

"Have made contact with Caroline. Promising start. Date arranged."

"Jolly good. I look forward to your next update. Goodbye."

"Bye."

"What are your plans for the weekend?" asked Rachel on the Friday afternoon.

"Nothing much," replied Ian, not yet prepared to reveal his romantic adventures to his colleagues, in spite of the regular banter and bonding.

"I'm visiting family," continued Rachel, immediately realising what she had said and adding, "It must be hard being so far from home."

"Not really. We weren't that close."

"Well, I'm going to see a local band. Fancy joining me, Ian?"

"I can't but thank you."

"What? The housework getting on top of you?" Brad ribbed Ian, "Wait. You've got a date, haven't you?"

"OK. So, I've got a date."

Brad whistled. The three of them laughed.

"I want to hear all about it, on Monday," insisted Brad.

"A gentleman never shares such things," responded Ian.

"A gentleman isn't likely to have anything to share!"

"See you on Monday," Ian deflected the conversation.

"Yeah. Enjoy yourself," said Rachel.

"If you can't be good, be safe," Brad continued to rib Ian.

When Ian got home, he showered, shaved, and ironed a clean pair of chinos and a shirt. Cheese on toast was innocuous enough as a meal. No onions or garlic. He hoped his deodorant would mask the effects of cycling. After brushing his teeth, he set off to find the Rue de l'Hotel-de-Ville and the Brasserie du Chien Noir, realising after he had crossed the Alexandra Bridge that he had no lock for his bicycle. There was nothing to be done about it, for the immediate future. All he could do was hope that no one stole it from outside the brasserie.

Caroline was sitting at a table when Ian arrived.

"Hi. How are you?"

"I'm well thank you. How are you?" she replied, in French. "Remember, we are this side of the river, so we should speak in French.

"I'll do my best," responded Ian, in French.

He was able to hold a conversation about everyday matters, as well as discuss philosophy and literature, but he was still lacking some of the more technical, industry-based vocabulary, if the conversation turned to publishing.

"What would you like to drink?" offered Ian.

"Wine. White. Thank you."

Ian went to the bar and came back to the table with a bottle of white wine and two glasses.

"Tell me more about Adrian Zorkin. He seems really interesting."

"He likes books. He's well educated and even more travelled. He brings me books from Europe. He's a friend."

"Yes. On the plane I sat next to him. He was doing a Times crossword and got stuck on the final clue. I was able to give him the answer."

"Are you well-educated, Ian?"

"I don't know. I have a reasonable general knowledge, I suppose. I haven't got a degree, if that's what you're asking. I read."

"I read, but mostly fiction. I love a good romantic novel."

"And does your reality match up to the novels you read?"

"I don't have a boyfriend, if that's what you are asking," laughed Caroline.

"What's your favourite animal?" asked Ian, immediately realising the question was as random as it was childish.

"I love cats. I have three."

"I love cats, too. What colours?"

"Black, black and white, and ginger. They are all rescues. The black one is called Smitty. The black and white one is called Arthur. He's quite old. Nine or ten, probably. The ginger one is named Chingachgook, Chin, for short."

"Last of the Mohicans," responded Ian, in English.

"I'm impressed. Have you read the novel?"

"Yes. It was a very old, tatty hardback on the bottom shelf of my aunt and uncle's bookcase."

"Did you spend a lot of time at your aunt and uncle's house?"

"They raised me. I lost my parents in a house fire."

"I'm sorry."

There was an awkward silence, whilst both of them took a drink of wine.

"Would you …"

"I'd love to …"

They both picked up the conversation simultaneously.

"You first," conceded Ian.

"Would you like to meet them? My cats?"

"I would love to meet them."

"What were you going to say?"

"That I would love to meet your cats."

They both laughed. Ian replenished their glasses.

"Do you have family?" he asked.

"Yes. I have a brother in Vancouver. We see each other a couple of times a year. My parents are divorced. My father met someone else, so I don't see him, ever. My mum lives a few streets away. I see her every week."

"Families. You can choose your friends, but not your family. I know. Bit of a cliché."

"But true."

"Have you travelled much?"

"Venezuela. Haiti. The US. France."

"What are they like? Is South America like carnival? Is Haiti poor?"

"Venezuela is a beautiful country. Tropical islands and snow-covered mountains. That said, it is a developing country, with lots of social and economic challenges. Its official wealth comes a lot from oil, but it has just fallen into an economic crisis. Its unofficial wealth comes from drugs. Both rely heavily on the American market. Haiti is also a beautiful country of coast and mountains. And yes, it is very poor."

"And whereabouts in France did you go?"

"Marseilles, Bordeaux, Toulouse, Paris, Dijon. Sometimes I think if you've seen one French city you've seen them all, especially cities in the south, but Paris, well, Paris is something else. If I didn't live in Gatineau, I think I would choose to live in Paris. And you Ian?"

"To be honest, I never had the resources to go travelling. I've mostly worked in bars and cafés, since I left school, and it took me a while to save enough even for my air ticket here. One day I would love to travel."

"And where would you go?"

"South America. Spain. France. Italy. Australia. Japan. Israel. The States. Pretty much everywhere."

"Maybe one day, you will go to some of these places," Caroline encouraged him, thinking about how he could go to France, Venezuela or the US for her.

Caroline's interest was importing cocaine out of Venezuela or, via Haiti, up through the United States to Canada. She had a distribution network in Ontario and Quebec, and a growing export market to Europe. Ian, in his naivety, did not make a connection between the countries that Caroline had visited. She had nothing to do with the Afghan connection, about which he had learnt and prepared. They finished their bottle of wine.

"I think we shouldn't buy any more drinks here. I think you should come back to my place, meet my cats, and we can work out what to consume next."

"I think I like this idea very much."

They got up to leave.

"I need the bathroom," declared Caroline.

They both went to the toilet.

"Did you cycle?" asked Caroline when they met up again by the door.

"Yes. I hope my bike is still outside. I haven't bought a lock for it, yet."

"I drove. Maybe we can put your bike in the trunk."

They walked out of the brasserie, and to Ian's relief, his bicycle was still where he had left it.

"My car is just over there," indicated Caroline.

Ian wheeled his bicycle across the road and Caroline unlocked her car.

"Plenty of room," she confirmed, lifting the tailgate.

Ian picked up the bicycle and placed it in Caroline's car. Ian did not let on that he had driven past her house. It seemed nearer than when he had been in Waterstone's car, but they had been driving all around the city, and Caroline only had to drive from the Brasserie du Chien Noir to her house on Rue Jeanne-d'Arc. She pulled into her driveway. Ian removed his bicycle from the boot of Caroline's car.

"Stick it behind the gate," suggested Caroline.

The gate was not locked, but the bicycle would be out of sight from the road. Ian wheeled it through the gate and leant it on the side of the house. Caroline had unlocked the front door and was crouched down to prevent a feline escape. Ian followed her in.

"Chin! Smitty. Arthur!"

A black and white cat appeared in the hallway.

Hello, Arthur. I've brought a friend to meet you. They went into the kitchen. A ginger cat ran in, meowing for food.

"Hey Chin."

Caroline poured some dried cat food into three bowls and put two of them on the floor, for Arthur and Chingachgook.

"Smitty! He's the shy one."

Eventually, a black cat hovered at the kitchen door and Caroline put his bowl on the floor.

"Whiskey?"

"Do you have any vodka?"

"Erm, no. Cognac?"

"Cognac it is, then. Thanks."

"So, you are a vodka drinker? How do you take your vodka?"

"With orange juice."

Ian arrived at a conclusion, in his head, that if Caroline had had any Russian connection, surely, she would have had vodka, in the house. It was possible that she had run out, or that she never invited her drugs associates into her house. He would report this lack of vodka to Waterstone, along with the list of countries Caroline had travelled to. Caroline poured two glasses of cognac.

"This way," she beckoned Ian into the sitting room.

There were two large First Nation drawings framed on the walls.

"They are really pretty."

"Yes. I got them from a contact on the Manawan Reserve."

"Do you go to reserves often?"

"Sometimes. We have First Nation writers, some of whom are new to publishing."

Ian was uncertain of the intended outcome of his invitation to Caroline's house. He thought about how Brad had ribbed him for being a gentleman. Was Caroline anticipating sex? This was a first date, but it was gone nine o'clock and she had asked Ian back to her house, for a drink. He did not know what to do. He did not want to blow his chances and there were no signals, as yet. Caroline was meant to be a long-term project, and he had to keep his eye on the intended intelligence gathering outcome.

"Can I see you again?" he asked, finishing off his cognac.

"Yes," replied Caroline, wondering herself, how best to keep Ian on board.

She thought he must be shy.

"How about that cycle ride?" suggested Ian.

"Absolutely. Sunday afternoon. Meet me here, at two-thirty."

"Excellent," responded Ian, getting up.

He took his glass into the kitchen and washed it out under the tap, not wanting to leave any fingerprints. He tried to remember if he had touched anything else.

"You didn't have to do that," remarked Caroline, as he returned to the sitting room.

"I know. Force of habit," he laughed, knowing full well, his actions had been deliberate.

Caroline held the door ajar, preventing Ian from leaving, until she had given him a kiss on each cheek, seductively more than socially. Ian wheeled his bike out from behind the gate and rode home, as fast as he could. Caroline's scent remained in his nostrils for some time before the rushing air dispersed it.

"Well?" inquired Brad, first thing on Monday morning. "How did it go?"

"I told you. A gentleman doesn't tell."

"So, you were a gentleman, then?"

"I have a second date. How was the band?"

"Not as good as I hoped. You made the right choice!" joked Brad, as Rachel arrived at her desk, carrying three coffees, in take-out cups.

"Morning. I thought we'd start a coffee rota. First cup of the day. I chose vanilla, today. Thought it might be nice to get something a bit more interesting than the filter coffee machine. I know you probably get coffees at lunch."

"That's a great idea, Rachel," Ian encouraged her. "How about we just make it Monday mornings? Get rid of the Monday morning blues. How was your meal with the family?"

"Good thanks."

"What Ian said," added Brad. "I think just on a Monday. I'll get the coffees next week."

"I'll run up a rota and stick it on the board, then, shall I?"

"Thanks, Rachel," responded Ian.

"You're welcome," she replied.

"Yeah. Thanks Rach," added Brad.

"Good date, Ian?" asked Rachel.

"I have a second date."

"Well done, you! How was the band, Brad?"

"Let me put it this way. I wouldn't buy any of their stuff."

"Oh dear."

Rachel switched on her computer and printed off the week's list for each of Brad and Ian.

"Thanks. Nice coffee," said Ian, picking up the receiver to make his first call of the day.

The week passed with its routine repetitiveness, during which Ian, now fully responsible for his own list of potential customers, secured some new business in the Ivory Coast and Lebanon. He was feeling chuffed, and his head nearly exploded, when Sydney came into the office and praised him in front of the others. Interestingly, neither Brad nor Rachel showed any inkling of jealousy. Ian soon learnt that they too had received public praise. There was a brilliant sense of team, of family, at Ontario Publishing, to the point at which Ian wondered how Sydney or Laroche or any of the other managers, received their praise.

Ian's letter from Brunswick Holdings arrived, and he searched out a new public phone kiosk.

"Hello."

"Hello. Butylka."

"Fles."

"Please let me have your weekly update."

"Second contact with Caroline including visit to house. Has travelled to Venezuela, Haiti, the USA, France. Cities in France include Marseilles, Bordeaux, Toulouse, Paris and Dijon. Has contact who transports books to and from London. No vodka in the house. Visits First Nation reserves."

"Goodbye."

"Bye."

Ian was excited for Sunday. He put toothbrush, deodorant, and clean underwear in his knapsack. He was just about to set off for Caroline's house, when he thought about a drink. Up to that point, he had no empty plastic screw-top bottle and no bespoke drinks bottle. The only option was a can of Coca-Cola, which meant he would have to drink it all in one go once it was opened. The weather was pleasantly warm, so that was not likely to be an issue.

When he arrived at Caroline's house, he rang the doorbell, with his knuckle, and she came out of the side gate, wheeling her bike.

"I asked to meet here, because I thought we could put both bikes in the car and drive out to one of the local nature trails."

"Sounds good to me," replied Ian.

Once Caroline had pushed her bicycle as far into the back of the vehicle as she could, Ian rested his on top. There was just room to close the tailgate.

"That's a relief," commented Caroline. "Let's go."

They drove for about half an hour and pulled up at a car park on the edge of some woodland. Ian could see a family cycling along the trail. He got out his bicycle and stood waiting for Caroline to get hers out. She was wearing bright turquoise leggings and a cerise-coloured vest top. Ian noticed she had a great figure. They set off along the trail, with Ian watching Caroline's bottom moving from side to side, a few feet in front. If there was opportunity, he decided tonight, he would not be a gentleman.

For the first hour, they were mostly in dappled shade, riding through pine trees, but then the trail opened out onto the edge of a lake.

"We're going to ride about two thirds of the way round the lake. Everything OK?"

"Yes," responded Owen, although he could feel the ride, in his knees, having already cycled from home to Caroline's.

"Let me know if you need to stop."

"I will," responded Ian, breathing in a fly.

He tried to cough it out.

"You OK?" asked Caroline.

"Just a fly. It'll be out in a second or two."

Ian coughed up a little more phlegm and spat out the fly.

"That's better."

They passed very few people on the trail.

"There are loads of possible routes," reflected Caroline, as they came to a crossroads, "We're doing a ten-mile ride. We could have done a shorter one, or ridden twice as far, with any number of paths criss-crossing through the trees."

"How far have we come?"

"About six miles."

They continued on their way and eventually arrived back at the car park. Ian sat astride his bicycle and took his can of drink out of his knapsack. Caroline had a drinks bottle on her bike frame. Ian downed his entire can and felt a massive burp forming. Turning away from Caroline, he tried to hide it in his shoulder, and failed.

"Pardon me!"

"What did you expect?"

"I will get myself a proper bottle, like yours, I think. I didn't have a screw-top bottle to put water in, and this was all I had in the fridge."

"Shall we get the bikes back in the car and go back to mine. Would you like to eat with me? I'll order a pizza. Go on."

"Thank you. That would be great."

"You can use my shower, if you want."

"Thanks."

They put the bicycles in the back of the car and drove back to Rue Jeanne-d'Arc, where Ian wiped the door handles, inside and out, with the bottom of his T-shirt, hoping Caroline had not seen from the other side of the car.

"What do you like on your pizza?" asked Caroline as soon as they were inside.

"Ham. Pineapple. Pepperoni. Peppers, mushrooms, and onion. I guess they all come with tomato and mozzarella."

"OK. I'll order a spicy one and a Hawaiian one."

Arthur was hovering by the kitchen door. Ian lowered himself to the floor, gently, so as not to frighten Arthur, who trotted over and sniffed. Caroline sorted out three bowls of cat food, and Smitty and Chingachgook came running, until Smitty saw Ian, whereupon he skidded to a standstill. The pull of food was stronger than the presence of a stranger in the house, and even he tucked in. Ian stayed seated and Caroline got two bottles of beer out of the fridge. By the time the cats had emptied their bowls, Ian was about halfway through his beer.

"Would you like to go and shower? You'll probably be done when the pizzas arrive."

"What about you?"

"I can always shower after we've eaten. Just use one of the towels on the shelves. Help yourself to shampoo and soap. It's unscented!"

"Cheers."

Ian went along the corridor to the bathroom. There was no lock on the door, but then, why would there be? Caroline lived on her own. He used the toilet, wiping the flush with some toilet paper, and turned on the shower, rubbing his hand round the tap, to destroy any prints. He knew from his training how important it was to be as anonymous as possible, wherever he went, but he had to concentrate and remember what he had touched all the time. Having selected a bath towel, he got undressed, held his arm under the extremely hot deluge, and stepped in. As the water rained down on his head, and the steam filled the room, he did not hear the doorbell, signalling the pizza delivery. Nor did he hear the bathroom door open. Caroline dropped her bath robe on the floor and stepped into the shower, causing Ian to drop the soap. He stood looking at her, uncertain about reaching down to pick up the soap, in such a small space. She was naked, and he tried desperately to keep his eyes on her face.

If he had been looking for signals, this was like the ranks of green lights at the start of a grand prix race. Caroline crouched down and picked up the soap and started to soap his chest, turning him round by the shoulders and soaping his back. She pressed her firm breasts into his back and folded her arms under his, around his chest. By now, Ian had an erection. He turned towards her and started kissing her, but he could not work out how to make love to her, standing in the shower, when they were both so soapy. In the end he put both arms under hers, lifted her out of the shower, laid her on top of her bath robe and made love to her on the bathroom floor.

As with Katya, he was not sure if Caroline faked an orgasm, but after both of them had let out a groan of satisfaction, he moved from on top of her to beside her.

"Thank you," he whispered, breathing in the steam which now filled the room.

"We should go back in the shower, now," laughed Caroline, standing up.

Ian chose to wait for her to come out from under the shower.

"I'll go and heat the pizza through in the oven," said Caroline, as Ian went back into the shower.

They sat eating pizza and drinking beer, at the kitchen table. Arthur had come in and was meowing for titbits.

"Wait until I've finished," insisted Caroline.

Owen wondered if cats spoke French.

"There you are," she said, giving Arthur the last piece of ham from her Hawaiian pizza.

Ian gathered the plates and now empty bottles and took them to the sink. He filled the washing up bowl and left them to soak.

"Would you like some coke?"

Ian was pretty sure Caroline did not mean Coca-Cola. Having got himself clean in Amsterdam, he did not want to start taking drugs again, but he was faced with a dilemma. Was snorting some cocaine going to be necessary to keep Caroline on board?

"I'd rather not, but don't mind me."

"Sure?"

"Absolutely. I'll be honest. I used to take drugs, but not anymore," he added, realising that a drug user, especially one who might be mixed up in trafficking, would have recognised the scars on his legs. His arm had mostly healed, and any remaining marks could have been explained away as giving blood regularly, but the marks on his thighs were harder to lie about.

"Really?"

"Yes. Really."

"Where did you get them from?"

"Friend of a friend, in London. I just paid him the money. I never knew exactly where he got them," Ian lied. "Anyway, I should be going. Can we meet up again?"

"I really enjoyed today, Ian. Why don't you come for a meal, next Saturday evening? I'll invite Adrian Zorkin. The two of you have a lot to chat about. You can stay overnight."

"Great. See you next Saturday. Seven-thirty?"

"Make it eight."

"OK. Bye. Thank you for pizza. Wait! What do I owe you?"

"Now you're being ridiculous. You can get them next time. Bye."

Caroline leant forward and kissed Ian on the lips.

"Bye," repeated Ian, letting Caroline close the door behind him.

He cycled home resolving not to share what had just happened with Brad. His confidence had grown exponentially, now he believed Caroline wanted to be with him. The signs of being involved with her, long enough to gather information, were also promising.

Brad arrived at work with caramel lattes for Ian and Rachel.

"Good weekend? Hot date, Ian?"

"It's on a good trajectory. How was your weekend."

"Uneventful," replied Brad.

"Rachel?" Ian looked at her.

"I had to take my dog to the vet. I think he ate something, when I let him off the lead in the park. He spent ages in the bushes. Anyway, he had bad diarrhoea and was panting lots. The vet checked him over and gave him an injection and said to monitor his behaviour."

"Is he OK now?" asked a concerned Ian, remembering painfully, his last trip to the vet.

"Seems to be."

"That's a relief," Ian reassured Rachel.

He only just had time to drink his coffee before he was due in Laroche's office for a probationary appraisal.

"Good morning, Ian," Laroche greeted him. "Coffee?"

"Er, no thanks. Just had one. Rachel has instigated a Monday Morning Speciality Coffee Rota. She, Brad and I take it in turns to come in with a flavoured coffee. I really like the team atmosphere here."

"I'm glad to hear it. We put lots of effort into team building. What else have you enjoyed during your first few weeks?"

"Well, I've got into a routine now. It's all making much more sense than it did."

"Excellent. I am delighted with the business you've been winning. We may have to think about planning some follow-up visits, to go and meet the customers."

"As in, going to the Ivory Coast or the Lebanon?"

"I'm thinking of sending you to a book fair, in Paris."

"Wow. That'd be awesome."

"Business not tourism, obviously, but I'm sure you'll be able to find a couple of hours to visit the Eiffel Tower or wherever you fancy."

"Thank you."

"Is there anything you want to ask me? Any issues you've uncovered?"

"No. All good."

"Well, that was short and sweet. Thank you, Ian. It's great having you on board."

"Thanks. It's great being on board," replied Ian, leaving the room.

"How did it go?" asked Brad when Ian returned to his seat.

"Fine."

Ian did not feel it was appropriate to talk about the book fair, firstly, because it was not definite, and secondly, because it might have come across as gloating. He started calling the numbers on his list and was distracted by Brad's strained conversation at the adjacent desk. Ian realised soundproofing in an open plan office was a bit of a problem. He waved at Brad, put his hand to his ear. Making a phone sign, and pointed at his ear, then covered both his ears. Brad understood what Ian was trying to say and took his call to the stairwell.

"Sorry about that," apologised Brad when he returned to his desk.

"It's a bit of a problem, now there are two of us on the phone, all the time. Even a less strained call can still be overheard. Confidentiality and all that. Anyway, have you sorted the problem?"

"I just get really tired of customers who say they want hundreds of books, and when you call them again, they've changed their minds."

"I know. Pain in the butt. Do you think we should approach Mme Laroche with the idea of sending samples?"

"As in, together? You want to share your pitch with me?"

"Why not? I don't gain or lose anything personally, but the team gains something, if it's adopted."

"Cheers."

"How do we go about it? Making the pitch, I mean."

"The monthly team meeting, I guess. It's on Thursday."

"Right. We'll do it then."

Thursday came round quickly, and Brad, Rachel and Ian found themselves sitting with Sydney and Laroche, in what was jokingly referred to as 'the goldfish bowl', the boardroom with the plate glass front. The agenda began with sharing one success each, after which, they went into a staff suggestions section.

"Any suggestions this month?" asked Sydney.

"Actually, yes. Brad and I have an idea. We've been monitoring the number of new customers who agree to large orders, don't pay the invoice, and when we call to follow up, they say they've changed their mind. We figured that a book is sold at say, fifteen dollars, but it only costs maybe a couple of dollars to produce. Why don't we send samples? Sure, it's a bit of a loss leader, but if the distributer or bookseller makes a load of profit on the sample, and then knows our books can make them money, they are more likely to go through with an order. Perhaps. We just wondered what you thought."

"That makes a lot of sense. We'll take it away and discuss it. Thank you, Ian. Thank you, Brad."

Brad glowed inside. He caught Ian's eye and nodded in appreciation.

"I have a suggestion," added Rachel, nervously.

"Yes, Rachel," responded Sydney.

"Now there are two negotiators talking on the phone, it's noisy and not very private. I was wondering if we could turn the desks round ninety degrees, so we're still a team, but put a low barrier between the two desks, to soften the volume."

Ian and Brad looked at each other in surprise.

"We can certainly trial the idea, Rachel. Excellent. Well, thank you, team. Next up, it's finance report."

Brad, Ian, and Rachel let the figures wash over their heads. Although their work contributed to the overall picture, finance was one step removed from the frontline. All three of them perked up when the next item on the agenda was discussed.

"We are at a point, where our business is expanding nicely. It doesn't seem fair, if Jeanette and I have all the fun, so we'd like to send Brad to a book fair in London, and Ian to one in Paris. Rachel, we can't send you to Europe, but there's a national publishing event in Vancouver in the autumn and I would like you to come with me."

"Thank you, Mr Sydney," responded Rachel.

"That's brilliant," added Brad.

"Really looking forward to going," replied Ian, realising that he was sensible not to mention it.

On reflection, Brad might already have known about London and was not telling him either in case it was seen as gloating. The next day, Ian arrived home from work to find his letter from Brunswick Holdings. He went to the Rideau Centre and made his call.

"Hello."

"Hello. L'aigle."

"Sarbaz."

"I'm impressed!" came the reply. "What is your update?"

"Relationship with Caroline progressing. No business talk as yet. Was invited to try coke but declined."

"It wouldn't be the end of the world to accept."

"Bye."

"Goodbye."

Ian was frustrated. He had come to accept his lack of choice in this assignment, but the lack of concern that he should become addicted, again, piqued him. He resolved to put off partaking as long as possible. Caroline might not ask him again, accepting his excuse. If the relationship progressed, all well and good. If it started to falter, accepting coke might be a way of prolonging it. He had gone cold turkey once and if needs be, he could go cold turkey again. It had been unpleasant, but not impossible.

Ian filled his Saturday with household chores, shopping, and a short cycle ride. After showering and putting on clean clothes, he packed his knapsack with toothbrush, deodorant, and a clean T-shirt and underwear, and set off for Caroline's. He arrived shortly before eight, so rode past, to the end of Rue Jeanne-d'Arc, turned, and rode back again. A black sedan was pulling into the driveway, as he arrived back at the house. Zorkin waved at him. Ian put his bicycle through the side gate, rubbing the heel of his hand across the latch. Zorkin got out of his car.

"Hello, Ian. How are you?"

"Very well. How are you?"

"All good here. Just got back from London, again. Retirement is fun," he laughed, going to the boot and removing a small suitcase.

The two men approached the door together and Ian gestured to Zorkin to ring the bell. Caroline opened it to them and gave Zorkin a kiss on each cheek and Ian a peck on the lips. Zorkin placed the suitcase on the floor and followed Ian and Caroline into the sitting room, where Caroline poured each of them a Cinzano.

"Cheers. How was London, Adrian?"

"As dreary as ever. It's always raining or overcast, when I'm there."

"I know what you mean," laughed Ian.

"I have some great new titles for you, Caroline," Zorkin informed her.

"Excellent," she replied.

They both knew exactly what they were talking about, and it was not books.

"What are we eating?" asked Ian.

"Brisket."

"Mmmmmmm," went Zorkin. "You never disappoint."

"I love beef," added Ian. "Anything I can do to help?"

"No thank you. The table is laid. I just need to bring the food in from the kitchen. If you'd like to make your way to the dining room."

Ian was trying to work out how to remove any fingerprints from the Cinzano glass without Zorkin seeing him do it.

"After you," he gestured, "Placing his glass on the coffee table and rubbing the sides between his palms, the second Zorkin turned away.

The meal was delicious. At the end of the first course, Ian excused himself.

"I just need to use the bathroom. I'll take the plates into the kitchen on my way," he offered.

He placed his knife, fork, and plate on top of the pile and as soon as he was in the kitchen, rubbed his fingers round the rim of the plates, top and bottom, and along the handle of the knife and fork, just removing his hand before Caroline came into the kitchen after him.

"That really was delicious," he announced, kissing Caroline on the cheek as he walked past to the bathroom.

He was sitting on the toilet, looking around for some air freshener, when he heard the doorbell. A man's voice, spoke in Russian.

"This is a message from the boss."

"Give me a second chance," replied Zorkin, also in Russian.

The next thing Ian heard was what sounded like two gunshots, muffled with a silencer. Caroline screamed. If he had not already been sitting on the toilet, Ian might have needed to. He thought he heard the front door closing, so wiped himself and washed his hands. Placing his ear to the door, he could hear Caroline sobbing, but no other activity.

He pulled the door ajar and peered out. The coast appeared to be clear, so Ian exited the bathroom and walked slowly into the dining room. Zorkin was slumped in his chair, with a gunshot wound to his forehead. Caroline was sitting on the floor, cradling a lifeless Chingachgook.

"What on earth just happened?" he asked, crouching down next to Caroline. "Who were those men?"

"Russians. Drug dealers."

"Why were they here? And why have they shot Zorkin and your cat?"

"Do you remember last time you were here, I offered you some coke? Adrian had an argument with the man who sold it. This is payback."

It was a beautiful story, but somehow, Ian could not square it with what he overheard. Yes, they were Russians. That much was obvious, not that he was about to let on that he spoke Russian. Who was the boss? Ian did not believe for one moment that Zorkin had bought the cocaine for Caroline, at least not as some local customer. He might have bought the cocaine on Caroline's behalf as part of a much larger shipment. Ian was not sure where Haiti or France fitted in, but Venezuela plus cocaine could mean only one thing. Caroline must be selling cocaine from South America. Questions started to bounce around Ian's head. Where were their drugs coming from? What was the Russian connection? Did it really have to be Russians, again? Up to now, Ian had left his gun in the bottom drawer of his chest of drawers. From tomorrow, he decided to take it with him, wherever he went.

"I'm really sorry about Chingachgook."

"We have to get rid of the body."

"Can we bury him in the garden?"

"I don't mean the cat. We have to get rid of Adrian's body. We can't have the police coming round here. I can't be connected to him. Will you help me?"

"Of course," replied Ian, thinking he could do with not being connected himself, even if MI6 would get him out of any scrape that he found himself in. "What are we going to do?"

"Get him into the back of my car and drive him out to the woods, near where we cycled. Take a back road and bury him."

"When? After dark?"

"Yes. We should leave it until really late, though. Eleven o'clock. Make sure no one else is likely to drive by."

"If we put a hat on him, and we put our arms round him, on either side, we can probably sit him in the back seat, as if he were drunk. If anyone sees, they'll just think we're taking him home late," suggested Ian.

"What about his car?"

"Don't look at me. I can't drive."

"OK. Stay here with Adrian. I will put my bike in the back of his car, drive his car to his house and ride back here. He lives about ten minutes away, by car."

"Won't it look odd if we then carry him out to your car, drunk?"

"Not if he's drunk. I just did him a favour of driving his car home for him.

"Alright, then. See you in a bit. Would you like me to bury Chingachgook in the garden?"

"Would you do that?"

"Of course. Just tell me where to lay him."

Caroline led Ian out into the garden.

"You have a swimming pool," declared Ian, feigning surprise.

"Yes. Come and swim next time," she invited him.

"Thanks."

"Here," added Caroline, pointing at a spot between two shrubs. "There's a spade in the shed. It's not locked."

They went back indoors.

"Do you want to say goodbye to Chingachgook?"

Caroline went and knelt down by the dead cat and gave him a kiss.

"Bye, my little warrior."

She was crying as she stood up and extricated the keys from Zorkin's jacket pocket.

"Better take his wallet, too," suggested Ian.

"Yes. We can get rid of it in the lake," she replied, feeling in his pockets.

Caroline went out to get her bicycle, put it in the back of Zorkin's car and drove off. Ian went out to the garden, found a spade and started digging. After lifting off a two-feet-by-one-foot layer of turf, he found there was little resistance from the earth, so dug down three feet. He went back indoors, found a pillowcase, that did not appear to match any of the others, and wrapped the cat in it. After placing the bundle carefully in the bottom of the hole, Ian said a short prayer, which surprised even him, and backfilled the hole treading down the soil and replacing the turf. In time, he was certain the grass would grow back and knit the edges together, so it was no longer obvious. It was up to Caroline, whether or not, she marked the grave.

He did not put the spade back in the shed but went and rested it against the fence by the side-gate. Even though he would probably be the one digging Zorkin's grave, he wiped down the handle, and remembering he had opened the shed, also went and wiped off the latch. He started to do the washing up and became curious to know what would have been for dessert, had the gunmen not crashed the dinner party. In the fridge, he found a lemon cheesecake, and although tempted, knew he ought not to help himself.

The front door opened, and he froze, hoping it was just Caroline and not the gunmen returning. Why would they?

"Sorted," came Caroline's voice from the hallway.

"Would you like to see where I buried Chingachgook?"

"Let's just have a drink. I need a whiskey. I bought vodka if you're interested. And orange juice."

"Thanks."

When they had sat for a while, drinking, Caroline looked at Ian.

"I'm ready now."

They went out to the garden.

"I replaced the turf, so it can grow over, and no one will know he's there, unless you put a marker down."

"I think you're right. Leave it unmarked. I know he's there. Have you seen Arthur and Smitty since the commotion?"

"No."

Caroline went and looked under her bed and found the two frightened cats. She poured some food into their bowls and Ian sat at the table.

"Smitty. Arthur. Food," called Caroline.

The two cats came out from their hiding place.

"They're going to know something is wrong. That Chin is missing."

"I know."

"I don't suppose you want some lemon cheesecake. I'm not that hungry, but it seems a shame not to eat it, if you want some."

"I confess to seeing it, in the fridge, and being tempted. Shall I help myself? Are you sure you don't want some?"

"Yes, and yes."

Ian cut himself a slice of cheesecake and put the knife in the washing up bowl, which he had not got round to emptying. The cheesecake was melt-in-the-mouth. He washed up the spoon and bowl and used the tea towel to remove any fingerprints.

Zorkin was still slumped in his chair. Apart from the red hole in his forehead, he looked just like he had looked the afternoon Ian saw him, sitting on the plane. Ian would have enjoyed getting to know him better.

"I am going to miss Adrian. Not just as a friend. I depended on him to find and deliver books for me in France and the United Kingdom."

Ian now surmised the delivery of books had something to do with the delivery of drugs.

"That's a pain."

"It is. How would you like to go on an all-expenses-paid weekend to Europe, every so often?" asked Caroline, passing her fingers through Ian's hair.

Ian immediately thought that he should say yes, but knew he needed to talk to Waterstone about it. This was, clearly, a drugs network, but not the one he was originally assigned to uncover, the one which was funding the Soviet occupation in Afghanistan, that is.

"That sounds like a great opportunity. It will have to be weekends only, because of my day job. I haven't been there long enough to get any holidays."

"I think we could make it work."

Caroline leant towards Ian and kissed him.

"We can't go for our drive yet. I can think of a good way of passing the time," she coaxed Ian, undoing his top button."

"There's a dead man in the next room," he whispered.

Caroline jumped up and closed the dining room door and the sitting room door.

"He won't notice," she added, drawing the sitting room curtains.

Sitting astride Ian's legs, she pulled her short, yellow, cotton dress off over her head, threw it on the floor, put her arms round his neck and carried on kissing him. He undid her bra as she undid his shirt buttons and chinos. She got off his lap, pulled his chinos and underpants to the ground and sat astride him again. She did all the work and moaned and groaned until she had brought them both to a climax, at which point, she got off him and went and took a shower. Ian thought how detached she could be from the present circumstances. He found it slightly unnerving, notwithstanding the pleasure he had just experienced. When she came out from her shower, he went in for his. After he came out, she made them each a coffee. It was ten to eleven.

"We'll go for our drive as soon as we've drunk our coffee," stated Caroline.

Getting Zorkin into the car was easier than Ian had anticipated, because he was quite slight of stature. He wondered at the cunning of Caroline's trafficking strategy. No one would ever have thought of stopping an unassuming man of retirement age, travelling with some books in his suitcase.

"I'll get the spade. Have you got a torch?" asked Ian.

"Good idea."

"What about the wallet?"

"Don't worry. I can get rid of it, tomorrow. Probably better, not doing it on the same trip. I doubt anyone will notice Adrian is missing until later on, tomorrow."

Ian fetched the spade and slid it behind the seats, at Zorkin's feet, whilst Caroline found a torch in the garage. They got into the car and drove off. After driving for about half an hour and taking a turning off the main road, they did not meet any other cars. Caroline pulled into a siding on what was now a dirt logging track. It suddenly occurred to Ian that Caroline might double-cross him and kill him at the same time as burying Zorkin. He knew too much. Then he remembered her offer. Surely, he was valuable to her, now. They took Zorkin out of the car.

"You take the spade. I'll carry him over my shoulder," suggested Ian.

"OK."

They walked about fifty yards into the trees, with Caroline holding the spade in one hand and the torch in the other.

"Let me have the spade. It might be worth attempting to work with the torch switched off, letting our eyes become accustomed to the light. There's a bit of moonlight."

Caroline switched off the torch, plunging them into deep blackness, which little by little revealed shadowy forms, the trees, each other, the crumpled body of Zorkin. Ian started to dig. The ground was friable, like compost, from many years of needles falling to the floor of the forest. The challenge was the roots, which were quite shallow. Every few spadefuls, Ian caught a root. None of the roots was so broad as to be impenetrable, but it made the work harder than it might have been.

"How deep should we go?" he asked, when he had managed to open up an eighteen-inch-deep trench. "We don't want some wild animal digging him up."

"We should try and go another foot, at least. Possibly another eighteen inches. Let me have a go."

Ian was glad to hand Caroline the spade and she started digging at one end of the trench. She dug down about eighteen inches and started to work her way backwards, slicing down at the edge of the shelf she had created. Halfway along the trench she handed the spade back to Ian.

"I'm pooped!"

He finished levelling the bottom of the trench and between them they lay Zorkin's body in his grave.

"We could do with getting all of this earth back in the hole, which means we will have to trample it down on top of him."

"I know. It seems disrespectful but needs must."

Ian shovelled and Caroline trampled.

"We should also gather a load of needles from further away and cover the surface," suggested Caroline.

"That might be a challenge without the light. I think we're far enough into the forest for nature to take its course. The likelihood of someone coming to this spot is remarkably slim, don't you think?"

"You're probably right. Let's go home."

They walked back to the car without the torch and drove back to the main road, where a car drove past, as they waited at the junction.

"That's unfortunate."

"I doubt they even clocked us, let alone saw how many people were in the car or what the registration plate says," Ian reassured her.

When they got back to the house, at five past one, Ian opened the back door to retrieve the spade.

"Leave it until tomorrow," whispered Caroline.

"It's no trouble."

"The gate creaks. Leave it."

"OK," replied Ian, removing any fingerprints from the handle and closing the car door as quietly as he could.

They went indoors, whereupon Caroline flopped down on the sofa.

"Thank you. And thank you for burying Chin, earlier. The last thing I need to do is make sure there is no blood anywhere, or Adrian's fingerprints."

"Best get it over and done with before bed. I'll do a fingerprint wipe if you check for any blood spatter."

"Deal."

Ian used the opportunity to make doubly certain his own fingerprints were removed whilst wiping away any possibility of Zorkin's remaining intact. Caroline got a bucket of water and added carpet cleaning fluid. She rubbed it into the carpet along the length of the table and across to the wall, on the side where Zorkin had been sitting. Having satisfied herself that the carpet was clean, she wiped the wall, the sideboard, and the chair, and also removed the tablecloth which she pushed down into the bucket. Having washed through the tablecloth, rinsed it, and hung it in the bathroom, she emptied the carpet cleaner solution from the bucket. Before returning to the sofa, she picked up Zorkin's wallet and looked inside.

It contained two hundred dollars in notes, his driving licence, and several business cards. She pocketed the notes and removed the cards and licence to the sink, where she set them alight with a match, and ran the ashes down the plughole. It was a quality leather wallet, and it seemed a shame to throw it away, but throw it away she must.

"This evening has not panned out quite as I expected. At least we made love earlier. All I want to do now, is sleep. Are you coming to bed?"

Ian nodded, went to the toilet, and joined Caroline in her bed. They both fell asleep within five minutes. In the morning, Ian was not sure when to leave. He felt the relationship had progressed, but they were a long way off his moving in with her.

"I probably need to get back home. I have things to do before work tomorrow. Shall I come over with my swimming shorts next weekend?"

"Yes. Come on the Saturday afternoon. You can stay over again. You can get the takeaway. Do you have a phone number, by the way?"

"Yes."

Ian got out of bed and went to the kitchen to find a pen and notepad. He put the kettle on while he was there. Back in bed, he wrote down his home phone number.

"What's yours?" he asked, handed his to Caroline.

"Give me the pen and notepad."

She wrote her number down.

"There you go."

Ian got dressed and made coffee while Caroline showered. When she came into the kitchen, Ian had wiped down anything he had touched apart from his mug. It was so hard to remember, all the time.

"Hungry?"

"No thanks."

Caroline poured some breakfast cereal into a bowl. Ian finished his coffee, kissed her on the cheek and left, while she was still eating.

When Ian next reported to Waterstone, on the Friday evening, it was a week since the incident. He half wondered if he should have called sooner, using the mobile number Waterstone had given him.

"Hello."

"Hello. Le prince."

"Mehtar."

"What is your update?"

"I now know there is a cocaine connection with Caroline. But Caroline is not the only operator here. A man has been executed at Caroline's house. Last Saturday. He was Caroline's trafficker to Europe, I believe. Caroline has asked me to transport books for her. The other operator is Russian, I think. The gunmen spoke Russian. Zorkin replied in Russian. I wasn't seen because fortunately, I was in the bathroom."

"What has happened to the body?"

"Caroline and I buried him in the forest. His car was returned to his home. His ID destroyed."

"We will have to meet. Review how to contact the Russian connection. I need to know where the body is buried. I have to contact local law enforcement. We will talk about next steps and plans for book distribution in London and France. I'll pick you up from the apartment. Six o'clock on Tuesday evening. Good work."

"Thanks. Should I have called sooner?"

"We will re-evaluate protocols."

"OK. Bye."

"Goodbye."

Ian could not wait to be picked up on the Tuesday evening. Six o'clock did not give him a lot of time to get home from work and eat. He got changed out of his work clothes and grabbed a can of Coke and a couple of slices of cheese on toast, which he had just about finished when his doorbell rang. He opened the door to be greeted by Waterstone's grin.

"Come in. Can you give me two minutes?"

Waterstone stepped inside whilst Ian went to fetch his gun which he put in his knapsack, and went to the toilet.

"Ready," Ian declared.

"Let's go."

Ian locked the door, and they got in the car.

"I made contact with the police. As yet, the only missing person's reports, in the last week, were a teenage girl and an elderly woman. What is the name of the victim?"

"Adrian Zorkin. He is, was, a retired man who lived alone. Unless he has a cleaner, or an appointment, his absence may not have been noticed yet."

"That is helpful. Please tell me you didn't remove the bullet."

"As far as I know, we didn't. Unfortunately, the gunmen also shot Caroline Dupont's cat. I buried it for her, in the garden."

"That's sad. I don't like that one bit."

"They were sending a very clear message to Caroline. I heard 'from the boss' but there was no mention of a name. If it was just Zorkin who was the issue, I don't think they would have killed Caroline's cat, but why kill her cat and not her?"

"Good point. Where did you bury Mr Zorkin?"

"Forgive me if I'm a bit hazy. It was dark and I don't know the area. I think it was out along the road towards Chelsea. Then we took a right turn and drove for about twenty minutes more, taking a right turn onto a back road, that soon became a logging track."

"That narrows it down to about fifty. Let's see how we get on."

"I remember there was an old building on the left and then almost immediately we turned right."

"Let's just keep going this way, and shout if something looks familiar."

Ian sat watching the road ahead. It was so different in the daylight. At night, all the trees and colours looked the same, in the headlights, and you could not see more than five yards back from the road.

"Maybe there," he announced. "Turn right here."

Waterstone turned up the road and the tarmac quickly disappeared.

"We stopped in a layby. There was fallen branch at the edge, which I nearly tripped over."

Waterstone slowed as they approached the next layby they came to. Ian shook his head. Waterstone drove a little further.

"There."

Waterstone pulled into the layby and stopped the car.

"We walked about fifty yards through the trees," indicated Ian, pointing straight ahead. "We used a torch to walk there but dug the grave in the dark, once our eyes had got used to the lack of light."

They walked through the trees and came to the grave. Ian was glad he and Caroline had not covered it in fresh pine needles.

"Our main priority is recovering the bullet. If it didn't go through him. My hope is that it will lead us to the organisation or person responsible. We need a way to make contact with the Russians."

"We cleaned up the blood spatter. I didn't see a bullet hole in the wall. If Caroline keeps doing what she's doing, it won't take long before the Russians come back again?"

"That puts you at enormous risk. There is no guarantee you will be in the bathroom, the next time they come for Caroline Dupont."

"Have you got a better idea?"

"Tell me more about the trips to London and Paris, or wherever, in France."

"All I know is that Zorkin, and in future me, brought a small number of specific books, into and out of the country. I think the drugs must be concealed in the books which go to Europe. Don't ask me how the drugs get from Venezuela to Canada."

"I suspect they come via Haiti and the US, although that isn't really our concern. Your assignment is to identify the distribution network funding the Soviet occupation of Afghanistan. We have been chasing a red herring in Caroline Dupont."

"So, do I stay in the relationship? What if she won't let me break it off?"

"It's to your advantage that she doesn't know you suspect her of drugs trafficking. Just bookselling. I think we have limited options. We recover the bullet and dispose of Zorkin's body in such a way that it can never be found. We leave you in the relationship with Caroline, either until we have connected the bullet to previous murders, and so have a new lead, or the Russians make contact again and provide you with new information to act on. Agreed?"

"Do we have a choice?"

"Just make sure you have your gun with you, at all times. And if you are at Caroline's house, when the doorbell rings, hide and take evasive action. If we have to take Caroline out of the game, in order to protect you and whatever progress we have made, rest assured we will not hesitate."

"I am not sure whether that helps, but it is what it is. Do I still take her books to Europe?"

"In theory, yes. Although, it depends on how quickly we make contact with the Russians. Let me know when your first trip is planned. We can get the suitcase checked. To confirm it really is drugs."

"So, are we going to retrieve the bullet now?"

"No. I'll send a team to do it, as soon as."

Waterstone dropped Ian back at his flat.

"Bye. Watch yourself."

"Will do."

As soon as he was inside his flat, Ian poured himself a vodka. What had he got himself into? As he lay back on his sofa, a thought popped into his head. What if Caroline knew that Zorkin was going to be killed? Just for argument's sake, what if Caroline were cold enough and calculating enough to have her own cat shot, in order to make Ian believe she was a victim, as much as Zorkin? Perhaps it was Caroline who had ordered the hit. It still did not identify who 'the boss' was, or what Zorkin had done to deserve being killed, but it would be perfectly possible for Caroline to be working with 'the boss', and that meant Ian was in real danger.

Then there was the problem of his gun, which he would find hard to conceal from Caroline. If he wore it in a holster or in his belt, her spontaneous sexual invitations would give him no chance to hide it. If he kept it in his knapsack or inside jacket pocket, apart from her being able to search his belongings, when he was in the toilet or asleep, not to mention swimming, he needed the gun close to hand, if it were to be any use as protection. This was a conundrum.

Approximately three weeks after Ian's meeting with Laroche, she informed him that he would be going to France, the following weekend. She wanted him to go to the book fair in Paris, and then, on to Bordeaux to meet a customer, who could become one of their largest, in person, to wine and dine the CEO. All his tickets were purchased, and hotel reservations made. The samples and promotional materials would be shipped out, ahead of him, to arrive at the venue. All that was required was for Ian to turn up and work his charm. That Laroche considered him to have charm to work, amused Ian. He was really looking forward to the trip.

Two things were necessary, prior to the trip. Firstly, Ian needed to report to Waterstone. Secondly, he had to tell Caroline he would not be able to go to a jazz concert with her. They had got into a routine of cycle rides, jazz events and meals at her house. They always made love, and Ian was growing in confidence. Concerning his gun, Zorkin's errands had given him an idea. He had cut out the inside of a Bible and concealed his gun inside. The first few pages were left uncut, should anyone try reading it. The Bible was packed at the bottom of his knapsack, and his hope was that Caroline would be uninterested in a Bible so not look any closer.

Friday evening arrived and Ian made his weekly call to Waterstone.

"Hello."

"Hello. Boek."

"Le livre."

"What is your update?

"Off to Paris and Bordeaux, next Friday, with work. What do I do if Caroline asks me to take any books?"

"I will call your home phone on Sunday evening. If yes, you will be stopped in departures and led to a room, long enough for x-rays to be taken."

"OK. Was the bullet recovered.?

"Yes. Listen for the name Krukov."

"Krukov?"

"Yes. Krukov is a known associate of a man linked to a previous shooting with the same gun that fired the bullet we removed from Zorkin."

"OK. Bye."

"Goodbye."

The following day, Ian and Caroline went on a cycle ride. They put their bicycles in the boot of her car and headed out to the forest, again.

"Do you think anyone's discovered Adrian yet?"

"I doubt it," replied Ian. "We buried him really deep. Too deep for an animal to pick up the smell, I think."

"I hope so."

"Listen. I have something really exciting to tell you," Ian announced, changing the subject.

"Tell me, tell me."

"I'm being sent to a book fair in Paris at the weekend. It means I can't go to the concert. Sorry."

"That's a shame," replied Caroline, putting on a slightly disappointed look. "I mean, it's exciting for you."

"Yes. And after the book fair, I have to go to Bordeaux to meet a customer. I get to take them to a posh restaurant, all-expenses-paid."

"Will you have much luggage? I mean, I don't suppose you could drop off half a dozen books for me, and bring the same amount back again?"

"To Paris?"

"No. Bordeaux. I can have someone meet you at the train station."

"How heavy are they?"

"Normal, paperback size. They'll be in cellophane wrappers to keep the corners from curling."

"No problem."

"You are a star. Thank you."

"I know."

"And modest," she laughed.

The request was not unexpected. Ian was almost excited to find out what really was contained in Caroline's book shipments. They rode along the forest trails for an hour, stopped for a drink, and rode for another hour. At the end of the ride, when the bicycles were packed into the boot, Caroline put her arms round Ian's neck, kissed him and whispered in his ear.

"How can I reward you for being so cute and kind?"

"I think I'll have a chocolate cake," Ian ribbed her, adding, "I think you know exactly how to reward me. You're so sexy. You know that, don't you?"

"Would you like me to give you a massage first?"

"That would be great."

Ian had a sudden flashback to the time he massaged Katya, and for a brief moment, reflected on how similar, Katya and Caroline looked. What if they knew each other? Was Katya still in Canada, or had they redeployed her father again? Ian really did not want to bump into her. As the federal capital, it was possible that Ottawa was where her father had been sent, although Katya had mentioned her mother was French-Canadian, so she could be in Quebec or Montreal. Apart from the fact he would not know what to say to her, he was pretty sure she would know he had left Nikolai in the lurch. It had hurt Ian, when he realised Katya was just using him to draw him into the drugs underworld. At least with Caroline, he had gone in eyes wide open, and whilst she turned him on, he was under no illusion that the relationship was as functional as it was temporary. He just was not sure how long it would take for their relationship to outlive its usefulness.

When they got back to Caroline's place, they each showered, and Caroline told him to lie on the bed, whereupon she massaged him. They were both naked and oily, and after she had massaged his back, she rolled him over and massaged his front. Sitting astride him, she aroused him, and slid down onto his manhood. He rolled her over onto her back and thrust back and forth until they both exhaled in gasps of pleasure. Caroline pulled the sheet over them, and they lay in each other's arms for almost an hour before Ian's stomach started to grumble.

"What would you like to eat?"

"You," he replied, gnawing at her shoulder in jest. "I'll order pizza."

"OK. I'm going back for a quick shower."

"I'll go after you. In the meantime. I'll go make that phone call. Spicy and Hawaiian, as usual?"

"Sure."

Ian slept at Caroline's. In the morning, when they were eating breakfast, she returned to the subject of the books.

"If I give you the books now, will they fit in your knapsack?"

"I think so."

Caroline disappeared into her spare room and came back with six, individually wrapped, paperback books. The titles were all in French."

"New authors?"

"No. These have all been around a few years. The titles are always specific requests. They could be new. They could have been published years ago. They are not available in France, though, and have to be ordered in."

"I see," replied Ian, playing along with Caroline's explanation.

He packed them into his knapsack, which now weighed a considerable amount more than it had when he came. He was slightly worried that the stitching might give.

Shall I come and see you the following Saturday?"

"But of course. Come here," she beckoned him.

They shared a long embrace, and Ian rode home.

Later that evening his phone rang.

"Hi, Ian. Did you get the books?"

"Yes. I did."

"Jolly good. Have a great trip. Remind me. When do you leave?"

"Friday morning."

"I'll look forward to hearing all about it, the following week."

"Understood. Thanks. Bye."

"Goodbye."

Ian arrived at the airport in good time to check in and get through security. The assistant checked his passport and ticket.

"Just the hand luggage, Sir?"

"Yes."

"There appears to be an issue with your ticket. Would you follow me please?"

To the annoyance of the passengers who were waiting in line, she leant towards her colleague, said something, stood up and placed a closed sign at her position. Having come out from behind the check-in counter, she led Ian through an unassuming looking door to a room where Waterstone was waiting and returned to her position.

"Hi. Take the books out of your case, so we can x-ray them."

Ian obliged, and Waterstone exited the room through a different door. When he returned, ten minutes later, he handed the books back to Ian.

"Just as we suspected. They are hollowed out and contain what look to be like packages. Are they going to Paris?"

"Bordeaux. I have to meet someone at the train station, on Sunday. My train gets in around one o'clock."

"We will have someone watching. They will tail the person who collects the books from you. You don't need to worry about them after that."

"I am swapping books. I have to bring some back, on Monday."

"Then, we will x-ray them when you arrive back in the country. Good luck."

"Thanks."

"You're doing great work, Ian."

"If you say so."

"I do."

"Thanks. Bye."

The books packed neatly back in his case, Ian left the room and found his gate number had been called, so he made his way there, frustrated not to have bought a coffee. It was not until they started boarding, that Ian realised his ticket was first class. He had never travelled first class on a plane, before now. It was amazing. There was space to stretch, a seat he could recline in and feel comfortable, and no unpleasant women to dig their elbows into him.

The journey passed uneventfully, with Ian reading, listening to cassettes and sleeping. He was excited to go to Paris, even if most of his time would be taken up with the book fair. His hotel was near the Jardin du Luxembourg, and he had been permitted to take a taxi from the airport to the hotel, where he arrived just before eight o'clock in the evening. It was four-star, the Hôtel Trianon Rive Gauche. Ian walked into reception and spoke in French.

"Good evening. I am from Ontario Publishing Inc. I believe you have a reservation for me in the name of Ian Elton-Craig. Also, there should be some equipment and books delivered here, for the book fair tomorrow."

"Good evening, Sir. Welcome to Hôtel Trianon. We do have a room booked for you. All of your equipment is in the conference suite. Do you wish to see it now?"

"No. In the morning, please. I'll come down here at eight o'clock. There is nothing I can do about it now, even if something was missing. I'll just go to my room, thank you. Then, I'll probably go for a short walk. I've been sitting down for most of the day, in an aeroplane."

"Here is your key, Sir. Let us know if you need anything."

"Thank you," responded Ian, taking the key and going to the lift.

His room was similar in standard to when he stayed at the Hyde Park Hotel, for his MI6 training, in London. Ian was hungry and tired. Having used the bathroom and freshened up, he went for a walk, in the direction of the Seine and went along the river, past Notre Dame, keeping one eye open for a suitable restaurant. He fell into a characterful little auberge just off the Boulevard Saint-Michel and ordered steak and fries, with a glass of house red. A sense of freedom and anonymity came over Ian, until he came to his senses, realising that even here, MI6 were probably watching his every move. However, being apprehended by a Russian drug dealer was unlikely, and that served as a relief, for Ian. It was ten o'clock, by the time he got back to his hotel room. He slept soundly until awoken by his alarm at half-past six.

Today was an important day. It was the first time he was solely responsible for the commercial reputation of Ontario Publishing. He had never actually run a stand at a book fair, before now, but his work in The Prince Albert pub and The Coffee Room café had given him a sound grounding in connecting with customers. He knew his product well, from weeks of making phone calls, and by now, he was also confident with his technical vocabulary.

After showering and dressing, smart-casual, he went to the hotel restaurant for a breakfast of two pains au chocolat and coffee, before going to reception for directions to the conference suite.

"Good morning, Sir."

"Good morning. Would it be possible to show me where the book fair is being held, and where my equipment, which was delivered here, can be found?"

"Certainly, Sir. Wait one moment, please."

The man on reception made an internal phone call.

"There is a gentleman in reception who needs to be shown the conference suite. He has equipment stored in the room. Thank you," he concluded, replacing the receiver. "Someone will be with you immediately."

"Thank you," replied Ian, moving away from the counter and staring around the room.

A young man with a hotel uniform appeared through the lift door and came over to Ian, who being the only person currently in the foyer, was most certainly, the resident requiring assistance.

"Good morning, Sir. You wish to go to the conference suite?"

"Yes. Thank you."

"Follow me."

They got in the lift and the man led Ian to the conference suite where his equipment was piled in a corner, next to an empty table. Half a dozen other companies had already set up their stalls.

"Let me know if you need anything."

"Thank you," replied Ian, wondering what each large black crate contained.

He pulled off the plastic tape and opened the lids. Two crates contained books. A display board was in pieces in another, and a fourth contained paperwork, business cards, merchandise pens and brochures. Getting out the pieces of the display board he slotted them together to reveal a picture of Ottawa, and the company logo. That, presumably, was his backdrop. There was a folded tablecloth, in blue and grey, the company colours, in the bottom of the crate, which he spread over the table. Now, it was just a matter of arranging the books, and making sure that the necessary paperwork was available. He positioned some brochures and business cards and scattered the pens in the gaps. Thinking the pens looked messy, he gathered them up and arranged them in a neat pile, instead.

By nine o'clock, there were a total of twenty stalls at the book fair, amongst which Ian could identify several European countries represented, apart from British ones, along with some American companies. The other stalls were from Israel, India and Australia. Ian was glad to have been sited away from the American companies. A quick glance at each stall, as Ian circulated the room, suggested that the books were written in English, French, Russian or Spanish, which seemed illogical to Ian. The book fair was in Paris, so surely, the customers would be French. Unless companies were sending delegates from across Europe. The public started to filter through the doors.

Throughout the morning, Ian held conversations with curious members of the public, literary buffs, book club members and wannabee authors, in French and English. None of these would add significantly to his company's business, unless they were all referred to a book seller or distributor, who bought from Ontario Publishing. The real reason Ian was at the book fair, was to identify new book sellers and distributors, only five of his conversations were with the likes of these. However, the most bizarre exchange Ian had was at lunchtime.

The event closed its doors between twelve-thirty and one-thirty, and the hotel provided a buffet for the stall holders. Ian found himself sitting next to a publisher from Nottingham, a man in his thirties, who introduced himself as Christopher McGuirk. Their conversation turned to the value of competitions, as a method of discovering new authors, and McGuirk showed Ian a collection of short stories, written by university students, the finalists from a competition he had organised the year before.

"There are lots of opportunities for children to write, competitively, but very few for adults, I think. I find university students, especially those who study literature, an inspiring bunch."

"I would probably agree, that when you have studied literature, you expose yourself to a broad range of techniques and styles. Not that you can't experience a similar literary diversity from reading widely and not having gone to university."

"True. But for me, it's about general knowledge, about history and geography, science and the arts," responded McGuirk.

"Wouldn't we rather limit our market, if we only published books for academics to read, or people who didn't have a wide general knowledge? And surely, there's enormous skill in writing a novel which appeals to many different people at many different levels. I think a lot of what has been published in the last thirty years is experimental, or at least, the authors play games with the text. When you turn a book into a film, you lose those levels which are purely about textual and linguistic play. Apart from anything else, the film is just one reading, that off the director."

"Ah! Cinema. We are moving from a reading world to a watching world. Soon, the only texts will be film scripts."

"Doesn't watching a film based on a book ever make you want to go and read the book?" asked Ian.

"I have done, but I am always disappointed, because I can't get the director's imagination out of my head, long enough to exercise my own imagination. I will happily go and watch a film after I've read the book, though."

"Coming back to the competition and your collection of short stories. Were any of the writers promising enough to encourage further writing, or is that not how it works? Forgive me, only my work is mostly about non-fiction."

"The bottom line is it's very difficult to get a novel published. All my published collection will do is flag up the names of writers who, if, and it's a big if, get a novel published, the customer might buy it because they recognise the name. At Major Oak Publishers we can't guarantee to publish a novel, even written by a short story competition finalist."

"Wouldn't that be a more useful prize. A first novel publishing contract?"

"You might well be right. Anyway, please take this collection. It's yours to read and enjoy."

"Thank you very much."

"Tell me to mind my own business, but you sound like you're from England, not from Canada."

"Yes, I am. I went to stay with a friend, liked it, and stayed, which meant I needed to get a job."

What Ian omitted to say, was that he enjoyed creative writing and amateur dramatics. He did not want to appear to be fishing for a publishing contract, not that he had written much more than poetry. Definitely no short stories or novels as yet. Ian put the collection of short stories in his knapsack. He would read it on the train to Bordeaux. They finished eating and returned to the conference suite.

Ian's afternoon passed much the same as his morning, except he took the opportunity, immediately after lunch, when all the stalls were staffed, again, to take a pen and a brochure to each of the representatives. Late in the afternoon, just before the event closed, an agent came over to speak with Ian. He was carrying a travel book, about the rail journey through the Rockies.

"My name is Rupert Derbyshire. One of my contacts was so inspired by this book that she went to Canada and followed the journey. However, she did the whole thing as a stowaway, living on a shoestring, and has written an alternative guide to the rail journey through the Rockies. I was wondering if you might take a look at the manuscript. I can't get a British publisher to touch it."

"Well, I don't really make the decisions, but I am more than happy to read it, and take it to the person who does make the decisions, with an enthusiastic endorsement, if I enjoy it."

"Would you do that?"

"Of course. I think it's a brilliant concept. It appeals to the rebel in me. Your contact should write other stowaway guides. Ultimately, they're likely to be quite unique, because once in the public domain, the travel companies are bound to tighten up on their security."

"Thank you for your enthusiasm and understanding. Here is my card."

"You're welcome."

The doors closed, and Ian had to pack everything up. His instructions contained the necessary packaging, labelling, customs paperwork to return the equipment to Ottawa. All he had to do, was leave it at the hotel ready to go, and they would take care of the transaction. He had thoroughly enjoyed himself, and there was still the trip to Bordeaux, tomorrow, to look forward to. For all the boredom of an average week on the job, these opportunities were well worth the monotony. It was seven o'clock, and there was still time to do some sightseeing. He had no idea if it would still be open to ascend, but he really wanted to go to the Eiffel Tower. Having returned to his room to use the bathroom, he walked to the nearest Metro station and hopped on a train.

The Eiffel Tower was one of those iconic structures that simply had to be experienced, in reality. Pictures in a book or photos in an album failed to impress upon someone, the true scale of this imposing triumph of engineering. Standing beneath it, Ian imagined the weight of the girders. And there were so many of them. As for the bolts and rivets, Ian imagined they had been brought along by Gulliver, to inspire a Lillputian world exhibition. He bought a ticket and took the lift to the second stage, which was where he came to the conclusion that it was not going up the Eiffel Tower, or even the view that mattered. After all, you could have experienced a similar view from the Tour Montparnasse. What was most striking, was that the Eiffel Tower existed at all, that it had been constructed by men, towards the end of the nineteenth century.

Once back on the ground, Ian decided to walk back to the hotel, past the French parliament building and the Invalides, across the Jardin du Luxembourg. When he got nearer to the hotel, he would find a restaurant. It was quarter to ten when Ian exited the Jardin du Luxembourg. He could see a restaurant opposite, and it looked like they were still serving. Everything inside him wanted to order steak, again, but he knew it would weigh heavy on his stomach, and quite possibly, prevent him from sleeping. Instead, he ordered chicken escalope, fries and a glass of wine. This house red was lighter in texture than last night, and from the shape of the bottles, he deduced it was from the Burgundy region, as opposed to the Bordeaux region.

On his return to the hotel, he fell onto the bed and slept with his clothes still on. At four-thirty, he woke up, realised what had happened, and after using the bathroom, undressed and got beneath the quilt. He managed another hour and twenty minutes of sleep, before his alarm went off. He showered, dressed, and went to the dining room for croissants and coffee. His train was at six minutes past eight, from the Gare d'Austerlitz. It would be a very long day, because after lunch, he had to return to Paris. The flight home was early, so staying overnight in Bordeaux was not an option. He was just about to leave the hotel room when he remembered the paperback books. Forgetting the shipment would have been a complete disaster. They made his knapsack annoyingly heavy, and he would have others to bring back. One of the stall holders had been giving away branded plastic bags. Ian placed the books in the plastic carrier and set off.

Once on the train, he took out the collection of short stories and scanned the contents page. To his great consternation, one of the names was Helen Linton-House. No way! Apart from not knowing she dabbled in creative writing, the information alerted Ian to the that fact that his real sister, his 'Owen' sister, must have gone to Nottingham University. For a moment, he wondered what she was studying, what she looked like now, whether Gail and Ben were proud of her. Would they be proud of him if they knew what he was doing now? Did it matter any longer, what they thought? Although he tried to argue with himself, he could not prevent the sick feeling in the pit of his stomach, or the sense of shame, which engulfed him. 'Sundial at teatime' was the title of Helen's entry in the collection. He flicked through the pages, to her story. The other stories could wait until later.

« "Pretty extortionate, if you ask me, even with the membership card," scoffed Colonel Oswald Mayes retired, through the wisps of his colonial moustache.

"I know, Dear, but the brochure does promise a hundred and one things to do, and after all, we do get a free tea, in the Lady's Garden."

"I suppose we will just have to make the most of it, then. I suggest we visit the building first, have tea, and visit the maze later. Isn't there supposed to be an ancient sundial in the centre?"

Mrs Gwendoline Mayes flicked through the glossy brochure, the pages falling open along the staples, which traversed a plan of the house and grounds. To the front of the building was an ornamental pond.

Although the waters were murky, in the dusty heat of summer, it was possible to discern the orange backs of goldfish, or Koi, as they chased and searched amongst the tangled weeds in their watery labyrinth. On the surface, midges darted back and forth, breaking the tension on the surface with their wings, as they played in the late afternoon sun. Where they touched the water, a ripple, in a perfect circle, spread outwards and raced towards the stone edge. The colonel picked up a tiny pebble and cast it into the middle of the ring. Immediately, another ring appeared, following the first towards the edge. Meanwhile, the splash caused by the pebble set off a chain reaction of other ripples, all spreading out and colliding with each other.

The colonel and his wife stood watching the fish and the ripples in the pond for a short while, before turning their gaze to the clock tower.

"I'm really rather thirsty, Oswald. It's gone four o'clock, already. I really feel we should take a cup of tea and tackle the maze when it's a little cooler. We'll still have plenty of time for the house, afterwards."

"Jolly good idea," the colonel agreed.

Another brief scan of the brochure indicated that the Lady's Garden lay to the rear of the house, reached by crossing a small ironwork bridge over a stream.

They followed the path and soon arrived at a door, leading into the walled Lady's Garden. The colonel pushed open the door, and the elderly pair stepped into a timeless world of fragrant roses, with honeysuckle hanging from a network of wires. From wall to wall, the garden was laid out with ornate symmetrical flower beds, planted in the form of a compass, with the sculpture of Apollo, where the paths converged. Beyond the flower beds, was the maze. In front of the flower beds, just inside the entrance, half under the honeysuckle trellis, was an area of crazy paving, decked with white iron tables and chairs, and adjacent, a small pavilion where cream teas were being served.

Taking a seat, the colonel signalled to a waiter who immediately brought over to them a tray, with a pot of tea for two, milk, sugar, cups, saucers and teaspoons, and having removed the items from the tray, returned to the pavilion for scones, jam, cream, plates, knives and paper serviettes. After half an hour of leisurely sipping and savouring, the colonel and his wife had another glance at the clock tower.

"Follow me, dear," he commanded Gwendoline.

They stood and wandered down to the maze. It all seemed quite straightforward. Having located the entrance, the colonel read, and they proceeded along a path. Progress was slow, since on several occasions, he dropped the guide, and when he picked it up again, he held it the wrong way up. Instead of bearing west and turning south, they found themselves turning east and coming to a dead end, where the *Buxus sempervirens* towered over them, casting geometric shadows.

Time passed by and the shadows became elongated. The two tourists continued on their way, turning right, and left, and left, and right. Or was it right and right and left and left? He read aloud to her, from the brochure.

"'If directions are followed keenly, the traverse of the maze should require approximately three quarters of an hour. The middle is reached when a small clearing is entered. There are four small flower beds, in the form of a compass, dissected by paths. A sundial (see chapter one for the history) can be found where the paths converge. A more simplified exit can be achieved by taking the opening directly in line with six o'clock.'"

The sun was still fairly hot, and they were both feeling quite flushed, when after two more corners to the left, the two tourists entered a clearing. There were four small flower beds with a sundial in the centre. She gave a gasp, as they approached. Instead of finding a superbly restored timepiece, of Greco-Roman genius, as the description of the restoration of the garden indicated, they found only a lichen-covered plinth, adorned with a warped piece of rusty metal, that cast a circular shadow on the stone. At the foot of the sundial two skeletons were slumped, one draped in tattered silks and sporting a withered straw hat, the other dressed in khaki. »

That was a twist in the tale which Ian had not anticipated. He was proud of Helen, for what it was worth. Flicking back through the pages, he found the first short story, the winner of the competition, and continued to read. His enjoyment was interrupted by the guard, requiring him to present his ticket.

As the train pulled into Bordeaux train station, Ian packed the short story collection into his knapsack, made a point of remembering the plastic carrier bag with Caroline's books in and moved towards the door. He had no code or cryptic introduction to the contact who was meeting him at the station. How would they know each other? The train stopped and another passenger opened the door. Ian followed him to the main concourse, where he stood waiting. Once most of the other passengers had exited the concourse, a man who looked not dissimilar to Zorkin, approached Ian.

"Do you know Caroline?" asked the man, in French, with a Russian accent.

"Yes," replied Ian. "Do you have some books for me?"

"Yes. Do you have some books for me, too?"

"I do. Shall we exchange?"

"Yes."

The Russian held up a bag to Ian and he held up his plastic carrier bag to the man. Ian peeked inside the Russian's bag and saw similar plastic covered books to the ones in his own bag. Handing his own carrier bag over, he took hold of the Russian's bag.

"Thank you. Caroline will be very pleased."

"So too will my boss."

Ian wondered who the Russian's boss was. Surely not Nikolai. He was sure he had never seen this Russian before, either in the 'banya' or in Amsterdam. Ian did not really care what happened to the books he had handed over, but he needed to return to Canada with the return shipment, otherwise he was in danger of the same response Zorkin had received. He stood watching the Russian walk away, and as he exited the station, another man stood up from his seat and walked briskly to the door. Ian felt sure that must have been the tail Waterstone spoke to him about.

Outside the main entrance were bus stops, and Ian needed to get into the city centre. He purchased a book of tickets from the nearby tobacco kiosk and joined a queue. Ten minutes later he was on a bus, heading for the Place des Quinconces. He did not really know the centre at all, but several of the buses stopped there, so he figured it could not be far from the theatre, where he was meeting the Ontario Publishing customer. He alighted and asked someone to point him in the direction of the theatre, which turned out to be a stone's throw away.

Standing on the corner of the steps, leaning against the end column, was a man in his forties, smoking a Gauloise. He held a book in his other hand. Ian approached.

"Excuse me. Are you Monsieur Bernard?"

"Yes, I am. Ian? Forgive me, I have forgotten your family name. My head is telling me it's Elton-John, but it can't be that."

"No worries. It's an easy error to make," replied Ian graciously, extending his hand. "Ian Elton-Craig at your service. Can you recommend a nice restaurant for us?"

"Yes, of course. François Bernard," he replied, taking Ian's hand and shaking it warmly. "There is a nice place just up the Cours de l'Intendance, over there. Would you like a cigarette, by the way?"

"No, thank you. I am in between smoking, if that makes sense," joked Ian.

"Ah, you are resigning yourself to starting, again, no?"

"That's about right."

They both laughed.

Crossing over the road, they walked about fifty yards along the pavement, until they came to a terrace.

"I think it is better to eat indoors," suggested Bernard, "Even though I smoke."

"Have you eaten here before?"

"Once, a long time ago, but I have colleagues who eat here. It comes highly recommended."

Then let's follow the recommendation."

They went in.

"Bonjour, messieurs."

"Bonjour," replied Bernard.

"Bonjour," added Ian.

The waiter showed them to a table, against the wall.

"Just to be clear, this is Ontario Publishing's bill," insisted Ian, as they sat down.

The waiter had gone off to get a menu and a basket with bread.

"Gentlemen. What can I get you to drink?"

Ian looked at Bernard.

"Shall we have a bottle of red?" suggested M. Bernard.

"Of course. A St Emilion?"

"One bottle of St Emilion, please."

The waiter left them to peruse the menu whilst he went to get a bottle. He returned to the table and uncorked it in front of them, offering Bernard a taste. He tasted and nodded, and the waiter half-filled their glasses.

"What would you like for your starter?" asked the waiter.

"Mushroom soup, please," replied Ian.

"Lobster mousse."

"And your main course?" added the waiter.

"Salmon, please."

"Trout for me."

The waiter left them to their wine.

"Santé!" said Ian.

"Santé!" responded Bernard, raising his glass.

"Ontario Publishing is delighted at the number of books you are selling."

"Thank you."

"I have been working with the city hall, to identify local businesses, and I think there are around twenty outlets I can distribute them to, all across the city and surrounding towns, like Libourne. I think we can start to double the turnover, from January, with a special gift-type promotion at Christmas. Gift books for your coffee table!"

"That is excellent news."

The soup and lobster arrived.

"Bon appetit!" said Ian.

"Bon appetit!"

They paused from their conversation, to eat. The soup was made with wild mushrooms. It was quite the nicest mushroom soup Ian remembered eating. Bernard's lobster mousse was tiny, but he confirmed it was top quality. Seeing they had finished their starters the waiter came over to collect their plates. He returned five minutes later with the salmon, the trout and some vegetables. As he had predicted, silently, in his head, the trout still had a head. Ian was relieved to have ordered a fillet, instead. He gestured to Bernard to serve himself vegetables. There was no holding back, and he took half of them. It pleased Ian, that Bernard was not one to hold back or stand on ceremony. He served himself the remaining half. If the soup had been good, the salmon was even more excellent.

"I will talk to my manager about a discount. If you are doubling your order, I am sure we can look at ten percent."

"That would be much appreciated."

"Dare I ask what sort of a mark-up you are getting?"

"Probably not, but I can assure you, I am making a satisfactory middle-man's cut."

"I'm sure you are, chuckled Ian, reassuringly.

The waiter came over to check if everything was satisfactory.

"Delicious," responded Ian.

Bernard nodded, and the waiter walked away again. Bernard topped up their glasses.

"You speak good French. With a strong accent."

"Thank you. It's easy to speak it in Ottawa. Or should I say, Gatineau, over the river in Quebec."

"How long have you worked in publishing?"

"Not that long. I started earlier this year. I just love books and my previous jobs were with customers. And you?"

"I have only ever worked with books. I used to have a book shop and then I found it was easier to distribute books. One day, I would love to write my own book."

"What would you write about?"

"Medieval Bordeaux."

"Medieval Bordeaux? Has no one written about it, yet?"

"I want to write an illustrated story guide, that turns the history into legends and ghost stories."

"Interesting. Have you started it yet?"

"As a matter of fact, I have."

"I would be really interested to read it."

"Thank you. I would ask if Ontario Publishing could publish it."

"I cannot say, but I think it would sell well, and so the board of directors might consider it. You have my support and enthusiasm. Even though I haven't read it yet," he added, laughing.

"Ian, you have to try canelés for dessert. They are sweet and sugary, with rum and vanilla flavours."

"Sounds like heaven."

Bernard attracted the waiter's attention.

"Can I get you some dessert, or a coffee, perhaps?"

"We would both like canelés, please. That meal was first class, by the way."

"Thank you, Sir. Coffee, too?"

Ian nodded.

"Coffee, too. Thank you."

"I have just been at a book fair, in Paris, and there is one other book recommendation I shall be following up. If it was up to me, I'd say yes to both."

"You are very kind. How long are you in France?"

"Arrived on Friday, returning tomorrow. I did manage to go up the Eiffel Tower and walk along the river, though. It was business, not pleasure. Although the business has given me much pleasure. Present company, included."

"Flattery, indeed!"

"Sincerity."

The canelés and coffee arrived. Ian took his first mouthful. He had never tasted anything quite like them, but they melted in his mouth and left him with so many flavours to continue savouring.

"Good, yes?"

"Amazing!"

They finished their dessert in silence.

"That was a really great meal."

"Yes, it was. Thank you, Ontario Publishing."

They sipped on their coffees. Ian was beginning to succumb to his postprandial lethargy. He would be able to sleep on the train, going back to Paris. He attracted the waiter's attention.

"Might I have the bill, please?"

"Certainly, Sir."

He went to the counter and returned with the bill. It was more expensive than even Ian had anticipated, but he was not paying. Looking in his wallet, he took out some notes, enough to leave a generous tip, and placed them on the plate, keeping the receipt for his expenses. They stood to put on their jackets and the waiter came to collect the money. Ian picked up his knapsack and carrier bag.

"Please, keep the change," insisted Ian.

"Thank you, Sir. I trust you enjoyed your meal."

"It was excellent."

"Au revoir, messieurs."

"Au revoir."

"Au revoir. I shall come again," promised Bernard. "He's only visiting."

"Very good, Sir."

They left the restaurant.

"Now I must go back to the train station."

"The bus goes from the cathedral, or you can go back to the Place des Quinconces. Or I can walk you down to the river and show you some of the medieval history before you catch your bus."

"That would be excellent. Thank you."

The two men walked down the Cours du Chapeau-Rouge to the banks of the Garonne, where they turned right onto the Quai Richelieu and went as far as the Cailhau Gate with its diminutive turrets.

"There, you see. Built to commemorate Charles VIII's victory at Fornovo. This gate takes us into medieval Bordeaux. Did you know that Bordeaux spent some time under the rule of the English?"

"No, I didn't."

"Same Queen Eleanor of your Charing Cross, I believe. She divorced our king, Louis VII, who, incidentally, she had married in Bordeaux Cathedral, and married yours, Henry II. Mother of Richard the Lionheart and John. I've read Shakespeare! Then, there were the years under the

Black Prince. Three centuries we were English. Can you believe that? Our victorious King Charles VII ended the Hundred Years War and Bordeaux became French again. There are so many stories to tell of intrigue and betrayal and of resistance against the English."

"I look forward to reading the book! Thank you."

"If you walk in that direction, you will come to the cathedral, where you can get your bus. It was lovely to meet you."

"Likewise. And again, thank you from Ontario Publishing."

They shook hands, and Bernard walked off up Rue Sainte-Catherine. Ian made his way to the cathedral and waited for a bus. He was soon back at the station, checking the departures for the next train to Paris. He had half an hour to wait. Realising he was desperate for the toilet, he went in search of the public conveniences, and found he had no change to pay the attendant. Leaving, embarrassed, he went across the road to a café, where he bought another coffee and used the facilities.

Back on the platform, he stood watching the train approaching further down the line, thinking how sinister the engines always looked. There was a very un-British melee for the door when it opened, but there were plenty of seats to choose from, once he had boarded. He fell asleep ten minutes out of Bordeaux and slept as far as Orleans.

Curious about the books the Russian had given him, he peered into the bag. They were written in French. One was set in wartime, another in the sixties. One looked like it had an Algerian connection. Ian thought of Camus' *The Outsider*, but he had not heard of any of these authors. He took out the collection of stories he had begun in the morning. The more he read, the more he found himself agreeing with Christopher McGuirk. Writing a short story was a whole different ball game to writing a novel.

Ian looked up from his reading. There was a brief commotion as a mother and small girl, who had recently joined the train, walked along the aisle looking for a seat without any reservation. Now they sat themselves down across from Ian. Immigrants? At least, they appeared to be Algerian, or Moroccan, or Tunisian, possibly, as the woman wore a head scarf. He smiled. The woman looked away, but the child, who was giggling, offered Ian a beaming grin, with a gap where her upper front incisors would grow.

"Would you like a sweet, Mister?" she said in French.

"No, thank you," replied Ian.

"Don't disturb the gentleman," whispered the mother to her daughter, in French.

Ian noted that she spoke French, not Arabic. He assumed that they must have been living in France, reflecting that they were more likely to have spoken Arabic to each other if they were still connected in some way to any rebellion against the former colonial oppressors. Those wars had long since been fought, and there were many immigrants now living in France, first or second generation.

"But, Mummy, he looks so sad. Perhaps he wants to play a game," continued the determined child, in French.

"I'm sorry. She is too young to have learned etiquette," apologised the mother, a little embarrassed.

"It's fine, really. What game did she want to play? I can play 'I spy with my little eye', if that is of any help?"

The woman looked at him blankly.

"What is 'I spy with my little eye'?"

"Is this not a game, French children play? Oh dear."

"You are very kind. Perhaps you are familiar with the imagination game," she suggested, helpfully. "You say, for example, 'I see something with ears', and the other person has to ask questions."

"Please, please, please, Mummy."

The woman looked at Ian inquiringly.

"OK. I see something with ears. What do you think it is?"

"Is it a rabbit?"

"No."

"Is it big or small?"

"That depends. It's small."

"Is it a mouse?"

"No, it's not a mouse."

"Is it a baby elephant?"

"No, it isn't."

The little girl looked around the carriage, racking her brain.

"Shall I give you a clue?"

She nodded.

"He's peeping at us."

"Bear!!!!!" she announced, giggling.

Her teddy bear was poking out of the corner of her bag.

"Yes. Now it's your turn."

"I am thinking of something with a long neck."

"That's easy! A giraffe."

"No. It's not a giraffe."

"Not a giraffe? It must be a llama, then."

"It's not a llama."

"Not a llama. Hmm. It must be a snake."

"Snakes don't have necks."

"Snakes are all neck!!!"

The little girl giggled, and her mother smiled.

"I know," declared Ian. "A swan."

The little girl shook her head.

"I give up."

"Ask me a question."

"Alright. Is it big or small?"

"It's big."

"Something big, with a long neck, that isn't a giraffe. Does it live in France?"

"It doesn't live in France?"

"Where does it live?"

"It's not alive anymore."

"It's a dinosaur. Like a Diplodocus."

"Yesssss"

"You're very kind," responded the mother.

"Maybe we could have one more turn each," laughed Ian.

"Just one more each, then," she replied, smiling.

"Now I'm thinking of something shaped like a rectangle."

"A book?"

"My, my! You got that one right, first time. Well done!"

"My turn. I am thinking of something soft."

"It's not your bear again, is it?"

"Yes, it is," replied the girl, dissolving into more giggles.

"That's enough, now, darling," whispered the mother, lovingly but firmly.

"Thank you, Mister. Would you like a sweet, now?"

"Yes, please. I would like a sweet very much."

She reached in her bag and pulled out an open packet, which she held out to Ian. He picked a red one.

"Strawberry!" announced the girl.

"I like strawberry. Thank you very much."

Ian put the sweet in his mouth and the girl picked out a red one as well, copying him. She offered the packet to her mother, who searched out her own red one.

"We all like strawberry," announced the girl, giggling again.

Ian was not sure he would now be able to concentrate on his reading, but he opened the book, nonetheless. It was not long before the train started to decelerate, and the Paris suburbs came into view. The walls alongside the tracks were covered in graffiti and there was lots of litter. Ian could see the blocks of flats, the French equivalent of high-rise council estates. It was all very similar to living in Battersea. As the train pulled alongside the platform and came to a standstill, the little girl offered Ian another sweet.

"Thank you for playing a game with me."

"You're very welcome. Thank you for the sweets."

"Thank you. Goodbye, Monsieur," added the mother. "You really are very kind."

"Take care," responded Ian, waiting to let them out of their seats first.

They were met by an Arab looking man who scooped up the little girl. Ian could see her pointing in his direction. The man was planting kisses on each of her cheeks. The woman leant across and kissed the man on the lips. They turned and walked over to the exit, leaving Ian wondering how hard it must be, living caught between two cultures, like that. He had found living in Amsterdam and Ottawa interesting, in that the brands were often different, and what people ate was a little bit strange, sometimes, but it cannot have been as hard as moving from North Africa to France. Were they first generation or second-generation immigrants? Ian remembered how hard Pashto was to learn when he started. Should he travel to Pakistan or Afghanistan, any time soon, he knew that it would be quite strange, and he was sure the customs would be more conservative, more religious, less accepting of women's freedoms. He set off for his hotel, about thirty minutes away, walking. It was getting late and although he had eaten a substantial meal, earlier in the day, he was starting to feel hungry. Passing a late-opening grocery store, he went in and bought a packet of biscuits, with chocolate filling, and a wedge of Port Salut cheese, along with a litre of water. His intention was not to eat the cheese and biscuits together. He simply fancied both items, and they could be readily consumed in his hotel room, without cutlery and without making a mess. Ian would have loved to have done a little more sightseeing, but he was exhausted.

Back in his room, he started on the cheese and opened the packet of biscuits. A ridiculous idea dropped into his head as to what eating cheese and chocolate biscuits at the same time might taste like. Taking a mouthful of each, he chewed them together and concluded that, whilst the flavour was an interesting sweet and sour mix, it did justice to neither the cheese nor the chocolate biscuit. He took a swig of water and washed his mouth around, before finishing the cheese. Six chocolate biscuits later, he thought that was probably sufficient. He showered and went to bed.

On Ian's final morning in France, he had pain aux raisins and coffee. Before returning to his room, he asked reception to call a taxi. He packed his return shipment of books into his suitcase, along with the manuscript of the stowaway rail journey through the Rockies, and checked the bathroom, under the bed and in the wardrobe and drawers, to make sure he had left nothing behind. The rest of the chocolate biscuits were in his knapsack, with the short story collection.

At reception, he handed in his key and signed a form. The taxi was waiting outside, and an hour later he was checking in. Ian was unsure whether he would be detained by MI6 in Paris or Ottawa. No one took him aside in at the check-in desk in Paris, so he assumed it would be Ottawa. He passed through security, bought coffee, and sat waiting in departures until his gate number was called. He was looking forward to travelling first class, again.

As he settled back into his seat, he heard the men in the two seats in front talking in Russian. Unfortunately, it was no longer possible for Ian to avoid an adrenalin rush, any time he heard Russian, since Nikolai made him the offer he could not refuse. He tried to hear what they were saying. Amongst a discussion of the shops on the Champs Elysées, Ian was convinced he heard one of them say, 'I would love to take Katya to bed.' The other man replied, 'But Krukov would probably have you shot.' 'Fathers and daughters, my friend. I take it, you don't have children.' 'Not yet, no.'

So, Krukov was Katya's father, the man who worked for the Russian Diplomatic Service. The information was highly significant, although it did not tell Ian how they operated or if there was any connection to Caroline. Ian continued to listen, but nothing else was said relating to the family business. It went silent, and he assumed one or both men must have fallen asleep or were engaged in reading or had headphones on. Ian was unsure if the men were the assassins, responsible for Zorkin's death. Those men had not seen him, but he did not really want to be seen now. He was toying with the idea of removing his glasses, so that he would look different, from how he looked out and about in Ottawa. They had not seen him get on the plane, but they may have seen him in departures. Without seeing them he could not know if he recognised them from the 'banya'. Glasses on or glasses off? In the end, he took out the eye-cover, put on his Walkman earphones, pulled the blanket up over his chin, removed the glasses to cover his eyes, and reclined his seat. Somewhere over the Atlantic, he fell asleep.

When Ian did eventually wake up, he had missed lunch. Reaching into his knapsack, he took out the biscuits and polished them off. The next time a stewardess passed, she saw he was awake.

"Do you need anything, Sir? I didn't want to wake you, earlier."

"A glass of red wine and a coffee, please," he replied, in French, even though an awake Russian might know from his accent, that he was British.

"Anything to eat?"

"I can bring you some snacks. Or maybe a sandwich. I think we have some sandwiches in the fridge."

"A sandwich and some snacks, thank you."

"What flavour sandwich?"

"Any."

"I'll be right back," confirmed the stewardess, disappearing through the curtain.

She returned five minutes later with a ham sandwich, some crisps and peanuts, and a small bottle of wine, which she placed on Ian's table.

"Thank you."

"I'll just go and get your coffee."

She disappeared again.

Ian had already consumed half the packet of crisps when she reappeared with his coffee, two sachets of sugar and a little plastic container of cream.

"I don't need the sugar, thank you," he indicated, before she handed them to him, so she could use them again.

She checked the two men in front, but said nothing, so Ian assumed they must be asleep. Ian took the opportunity of going to the toilet.

After the crisps, Ian ate the sandwich, but decided to keep the nuts for later. He drank the coffee and the wine, and returned to his music, beneath the eye-cover. When the time came to change the cassette over, and the music stopped, even before he removed the eye-cover, he could hear muffled Russian voices. Pulling the eye-cover down, he peeped over the top. They were talking but not standing, so he quickly changed the cassette and put the eye-cover back on. Finally, when the captain's voice announced they were beginning their descent, Ian kept the eye-cover on, feigning sleep, but removed his earphones.

"Are we being met, at the airport?" one of them asked.

"I think Katya will be there."

Ian panicked, momentarily. What to do? He kept the eye-cover on, until the last possible moment, and then buried his head, practically between his knees, searching in his knapsack, until the two Russians had left the first-class cabin. He hung back, as long as he could.

"Everything alright, Sir?" asked the stewardess, finding Ian, still in his seat.

"Yes. I don't really like crowds, so I thought I'd let the rush go first."

She peered beyond the curtain.

"I think the rush will be gone in a couple of minutes," she reassured Ian.

"Thank you.

Ian had to pass through security first. He could see the Russians, at the head of the line. He was about to put his glasses back on, as the Russians passed through the passport control, when he remembered, he would have to remove them anyway. He decided just to keep them off, until he too had cleared passport control. Once the other side, he hovered at a distance, to see if the Russians were in the baggage hall.

He could not see them, so put his glasses back on. Ian, himself, had nothing to retrieve from the carousel, but he wanted to allow as little opportunity as possible, of bumping into Katya.

As he was standing watching, a man in a suit came over and asked Ian to follow him. The man led Ian to a room, where again, he found Waterstone waiting.

"Good to see you, Ian. How was your trip?"

"I really enjoyed it from both a work and a tourist perspective. I went up the Eiffel Tower and walked loads."

He did not mention Helen's short story.

"We followed the man you gave the books to. He is now being kept under surveillance."

"The really exciting thing is there were Russians, on the plane, who, incidentally, I think I managed to avoid being seen by."

"Tell me, please."

"They work for Krukov and Krukov is Katya's father."

"And Katya is the woman who lured you into heroin in the 'banya' and got you into trafficking?"

"Yes. But the important bit, if what Katya said was true, is that her father works for the Russian Diplomatic Service. I think it may well be true, and they use being moved around, as a state-sponsored drugs network. Surely, it's worth checking it out?"

"That's great, Ian."

While they were talking, a man had removed the books from Ian's case and passed them through a portable scanner.

"Interesting. It doesn't look like there is anything in these books. Not even hollowed out spaces."

"It must be a front, a decoy. They want to give a pretence of normality," reflected Waterstone. "That, or the books contain something else. Coded messages. But we cannot see that without breaking the seals. Never mind, for now. Each time you travel, we will monitor your luggage, to see if this is the normal pattern. Now, hopefully, Katya will have cleared the terminal, by the time you get out into arrivals."

"I'm pretty sure they'll be travelling under false papers, but won't it also be worth finding out who the two Russians are? It'll be in the system, and you can compare names and images, perhaps?"

"Absolutely. When do you see Caroline again?"

"As far as I'm aware, Saturday."

"I'll speak to you on Sunday. Let's change the updates to Sundays, so it's immediately after your meetings with Caroline."

"Makes sense."

"Good work, Ian. Bye for now."

"Bye."

Waterstone shook Ian's hand, warmly, and Ian went through customs to the concourse.

Caroline was standing waiting.

"What kept you?" she asked, as she kissed Ian on the lips.

"Hello, lovely to see you. What are you doing here? I was asked at check-in to put my suitcase in the hold. It was over cabin limit, in weight. Sorry. I had to wait at the carousel. I don't think there's a problem. Anyway, I thought we weren't meeting up until Saturday."

"I thought I would surprise you."

"And a lovely surprise it is, too," replied Ian.

He was immensely relieved that there was no reunion in arrivals, with Katya and the Russians. Caroline had decided it was not yet time for Katya to meet Ian, otherwise there might have been. Caroline had seen Katya enter the building and hidden from her. Apart from anything, she hated it, when Katya, as the senior cousin, made decisions about her life. It suited Caroline to use Ian as her gofer and the sex was good. If she was being honest, she was no longer even sure that she might not be developing feelings for him, which was against the rules.

"Would you like to lighten your load? Let me take the books now. So, you don't have to cycle over to mine, with the weight in your knapsack."

"Good idea," replied Ian, playing along. "Shall we have a coffee?"

"Here? Or in town? I can drop you off, if you like."

The last thing Ian wanted, for now, was for Caroline to know where he lived. He was thinking on his feet.

"I know a great little place, just around the corner from work. We can go there. Then, I need to buy some things."

"Excellent. My car is in short-stay."

She led Ian to her car. They drove into the centre of Ottawa, and Ian directed her to the café, where she parked on the street, outside.

"They do the most amazing caramel flavoured coffees here. Do you want to try one?"

"Please."

Ian went to the counter and ordered two caramel flavoured coffees and two slices of cake, while Caroline sat at a vacant table. He joined her, crouching on the floor, opening the case, and removing the bag containing her books.

"There you are."

"Thanks. Did you enjoy Bordeaux?"

"I did. I had an amazing meal with a guy who is passionate about the medieval history of Bordeaux. I never knew that it was English for three hundred years."

"I'm saying nothing," laughed Caroline.

The coffee and cake arrived.

"I hope you like cake. You choose."

"I'll cut them both in half," she suggested, getting her knife and performing the operation with symmetrical precision.

"I slept on the plane and missed the meal. The stewardess brought me some snacks and a sandwich."

"The cake is excellent. I shall need to go jogging!"

"Shall we cycle, on Saturday?"

"Excellent idea."

Ian finished his cake and coffee.

"See you at two o'clock, then?"

"Yes. Now go and get over your jetlag."

He kissed her, watched as she drove off, and went round the corner to Ontario Publishing.

Another four months passed, until Caroline asked Ian to take some books to London for her. Now that Ian was aware of the Russian connection, he was reluctant to take a shipment to London, as he might be recognised by the person sent to pick up the books. He agreed, of course, but how could he get out of making the exchange in person? Ian was impatient for his weekly conversation with Waterstone to happen.

"Hello."

"Hello. Le soleil."

"Lmar."

"Very good! Now, what is your update?"

"Problem. Caroline has asked me to take some books to London. Now we know the exchange is made with Russians, I can't risk being recognised. What do you suggest?"

"How much time do we have?"

"Next Friday evening, overnight flight."

"I think we need to get you a disguise and a new passport."

"But won't the ticket have been bought in my name?"

"That's not a problem. The contact in London will be expecting Ian Elton-Craig, not Owen Linton-House. We will give you a blond wig and a moustache, and a passport with a new photo, for Ian Elton-Craig. You won't look anything like yourself!"

"What if the contact is one of the Russians from the plane, or the man in Bordeaux? They will think the blond bandit is an imposter."

"There will be someone watching you at the meeting point. If needs be, we will take out the courier."

"Sorry, but what if they ask me to go to the 'banya', to deliver the books?"

"Tell Caroline that you want to make the exchange at Paddington station, because you want to meet up with friends, for a drink. See what she says. If there is a problem, call me using my business card. I will call round, in any case, on Wednesday evening, six o'clock, with the disguise and passport."

"OK. Thanks. Bye."

"Goodbye."

Ian was still a little apprehensive about returning to London, but he trusted Waterstone.

Saturday arrived and Ian cycled over to Caroline's house. He was going to cook a meal for them both. Why he had suggested it was beyond him because he lived on steak or toast. He would cook steak in a cream and peppercorn sauce and serve it with fries and salad. That was simple enough. Dessert would be fruit salad. He showered and cycled to the local supermarket, filling his knapsack with produce. There was not enough room for everything, and he had to go back and get two plastic carrier bags, one for each handlebar. His knapsack weighed almost as much as when filled with books. Perhaps he needed to buy a slightly larger backpack. He had purchased one orange, one banana, one tin of pineapple, one peach, one apple and a small punnet of strawberries. Also, a large carton of cream, enough for the steak sauce and to pour on dessert, some frozen fries, a jar of black peppercorns, a lettuce, some tomatoes and a half-cucumber.

Relieved to have arrived at Caroline's, with shopping intact, he removed the bags from the handlebars, opened the gate and wheeled in the bike. Closing the gate, he picked up the bags and rang the front doorbell. She opened the door and gave him a lingering kiss.

"How has your week been?" he asked when the kiss came to an end.

"Good. Yours?"

"Good."

"That's a lot of shopping. What are you cooking?"

"Steak in cream and peppercorn sauce with fries and salad. Fruit salad."

"I'll open a bottle of wine."

Ian made his way into the kitchen, washed his hands, and began cooking. He put the fries in the oven, seasoned the meat with salt and started to fry off the steak. While it was cooking, he sliced and chopped, salad vegetables in one bowl, fruit in another. By the time the chips were almost ready, the steak was medium rare, and it was time to prepare the sauce. He removed the steak and cracked some peppercorns over the heat, poured in the cream and stirred until it bubbled, at which point he turned off the oven and ring. Caroline had already laid the table. Ian served and they tucked in.

"This is excellent," she encouraged Ian.

"I don't know that it involved much culinary complexity!"

They finished their steaks, and Ian went to bring out the fruit salad and cream. Caroline followed him, to carry the bowls.

"You've only got two hands," she laughed.

Ian served the fruit salad and they each poured their own cream. Caroline topped up their glasses.

"Do we have a long-term future?" she asked, out of the blue.

"I hope so," replied Ian, knowing that this was just a job, in spite of his physical attraction to Caroline.

Did he really want to be in a long-term relationship with someone as ruthless as her? She smiled back at him.

"Shall we watch a film? I can offer you some videos, in English. I have *Ghandi*, *ET*, *Pink Floyd - The Wall* and *An Officer and a Gentleman*."

"Now I'm torn between *ET* and *The Wall*, not that I've seen any of them at the cinema. Let's watch *ET*."

They cleared away the meal things from the table, Ian washed up, and Caroline turned up the fire, poured glasses of cognac and set up the video. It invited snuggling up together on the sofa, under a blanket.

"Are you crying?" asking Ian, at the end of the film.

"Might be."

He put his arm round her. The last time he had seen Caroline cry, was when Chingachgook got shot, and he was never sure if the tears were fake or real. This, at least, showed Ian that Caroline had emotions.

"Spielberg is brilliant, isn't he?"

"Certainly is," agreed Caroline. "Are you looking forward to going to London?"

"Yes. I would very much like to do the exchange at Paddington, so I can take the train off to meet up with friends I haven't seen in a while. Would that be possible?"

"I'm sure that can be arranged. Your flight gets in around six-thirty, in the morning. Say another hour and a half, to get through security and take the train into Central London, Paddington terminus?"

"Sounds about right, to me."

"I'll let the contact know to meet you by the main entrance to Paddington Station at eight-thirty. That should allow for delays."

"Excellent. Shall you give me the books, when I leave in the morning?"

"Yes," replied Caroline, somewhat distractedly, as she started to undress Ian.

Ian was hoping she did not describe him to the contact as he undid her shirt. She was not wearing a bra.

"It's cold. Your hands are freezing!" laughed Caroline, reaching for the blanket, on the floor.

Ian had started kissing her breasts as she reached over him for the blanket and was now caressing her abdomen. They made love under the blanket, and by the time they reached their peak, they were all sweaty, in their woollen cocoon.

"We should have turned the fire down, a little," laughed Caroline.

They remained in each other's arms, until Caroline could not bear the heat any longer. She stepped out from under the blanket, altered the knob on the fire and slid back under the blanket. They both fell asleep.

At about two in the morning, Ian woke with a dead right arm, where Caroline had been lying on it. He was also desperate for the toilet. He tried to slide out from beneath her, without waking her up. His efforts were successful, but then he had to negotiate getting back on the sofa, under the blanket, without waking her, and that was nigh on impossible. In the end, he went into her bedroom, pulled the quilt from the bed, dragged it into the sitting room, and wrapped himself in it at the side of the sofa. Caroline managed to disturb Ian at six-forty-five, when she got off the sofa to go to the bathroom. She was half asleep, did not expect him to be there, and almost fell headlong over him. Ian got up and put the kettle on.

As they sat eating eggs and drinking coffee, it started to snow outside.

"Do you know what I'd really like to do?"

"What would you really like to do?"

"Go skating on the canal."

"I have to visit my mother, this afternoon. How about the weekend after your trip to London?"

Sounds perfect."

Caroline got up to go and fetch the books. Six, again.

"Your tickets are in the bag.

"I thought a couple of the last lot I brought back looked interesting. I really should find more time to read. Maybe as it gets colder, I'll stay in more, but I still like to cycle and go to the gym."

"I'm pretty sure you'll soon have no choice, once the snow sets in. You'll just about be able to walk to work.

Hopefully, there will be some sort of transport from here to there."

"Right. Midday, a week on Saturday?"

"With your skates."

"I'm looking forward to it. Now, give me a kiss, and I'll be on my way."

They kissed, and Ian set off home, feeling more confident, now that Caroline had confirmed he could hand the books over in Paddington Station.

Ottawa to London and back in a weekend was a slog. He would arrive on Saturday morning and fly back on Sunday morning. That left Saturday afternoon to catch up with friends. It would be brilliant to go and see the Caterham crowd, but Ian suddenly remembered he would have a disguise. Maybe, he would visit a gallery or a museum, again, instead. The disguise gave Ian confidence to return to London, after the uneasiness he felt throughout his MI6 induction. If his assignment was successful, it might bring down the whole Russian drugs empire in western Europe, whether it was Nicolai or Krukov or one of their allies who was at the top of the food chain.

When Waterstone came round on Wednesday evening, he brought Ian's disguise and new passport.

"You should be able to remove and replace the moustache, if you have a shower. There are several of them in the box. My advice is to remain in disguise throughout the trip."

"I will. I have the books. My hotel is near the station. Here's the address," he added, passing Waterstone a piece of paper. "I will go and visit a museum or a gallery, but I won't visit anyone I know."

"I think we might well keep someone in the background, just to make sure you aren't followed."

"That would be comforting to know."

"So, I think we're done. You'll be pulled from departures again. No doubt I will see you on Friday evening."

Waterstone got up to leave.

"Thanks. Bye."

"Bye," responded Ian, closing the door behind Waterstone.

On the Friday evening, after work, Ian went home and transformed himself into a blond-haired, blond-moustached legend, who did not wear glasses. He ate, packed, and caught a bus to the airport. Just as Waterstone had predicted, he was detained. However, this time, it was not the lady behind the counter who led him to a room, but an officer, beyond security. Waterstone was waiting and the books were scanned. To everyone's surprise, the books were empty.

"That is interesting," reflected Waterstone.

"It's going to be one of two things if you ask me. Either, the flow of traffic is from London to Ottawa, not the other way round. Or, and this would be very concerning, they're onto us, and nothing is going to be trafficked this time."

"Did the books have cavities inside?" asked Waterstone.

"Yes."

"Well, it looks like we'll just have to wait until Sunday evening, then. On your way, Ian. Have a good trip," Waterstone wished him, shaking his hand.

"Thanks."

Ian replaced the books in his case and left the room.

This flight was second class. He had to sit next to a teenage boy, whose mother and younger brother were in the seats behind.

"Why can't we sit together?" whinged the younger one.

"Because you always end up fighting."

"But how will we ever learn not to fight?" reasoned the elder.

"Alright. If you are as good as gold, all trip, I'll think about it for the return journey."

Ian remembered how he and Helen used to drive their mother mad with their squabbling. He watched the inflight movie, *48 hours*, and fell asleep, remarkably, until four-forty in the morning. The teenager was sleeping soundly, next to him, as was the younger brother, behind. When Ian stood up to go to the toilet, glad he was in the aisle seat, he saw that the mother was reading and smiled at her when she looked up from her book.

On his way back from the toilet, he asked the flight attendant if he might have a coffee, and was brought one, a few minutes later. He had no idea, that the man, three rows back on the opposite side of the plane, was a member of Krukov's network. The Russians had become nervous after whatever Zorkin had done to get himself executed, on his final trip between London and Ottawa. This Russian did not know Ian, but he knew that an exchange was to be made, and what was confusing him, was there was no person fitting Ian's description, Ian with dark hair and glasses that is, who boarded the plane, in Ottawa.

The plane landed, and Ian proceeded through border control and customs. He had just under two hours, before the exchange was due to be made, which gave him plenty of time to catch the train to Paddington. Still unaware of who Ian was, the Russian caught the same train. At Paddington, Ian went and bought a coffee from the station buffet and sat watching out of the window. He could see the Russian pacing up and down, watching the passers-by, and wondered who this person was. Was he the contact? If he was, he had been hanging around the station a long time, and the rendez-vous was meant to be by the main door. The man passing up and down looked Russian to Ian, although he fully acknowledged that the USSR contained any number of types from several ethnic groups. When he finished his coffee, he did not know whether to approach the Russian-looking man or whether just to go to the main entrance. In the brief window of opportunity, where the Russian was pacing away from the buffet, Ian sneaked out and stood out of his line of sight, by the main doors.

At eight-thirty, exactly, a man approached him carrying a plastic carrier bag.

"Do you have any books, from Caroline?" he asked.

"I do."

The man held up his own carrier bag, which Ian took as a prompt to exchange, and without checking in the bag he had just been handed, walked out of the station and went to find his hotel. Meanwhile, an MI6 agent had been watching the whole scenario. He had clocked the pacing Russian and watched the bag exchange. He followed the man with the books out of the station and saw him get into a silver car on the other side of the road. Noting the registration number, he quickly hailed a cab, and asked the driver to please take him along Praed Street, watching which direction the car turned.

"Please just follow that silver car."

"Where to. Mate?"

"Wherever it goes. I am trying to catch up with a man who dropped his wallet, in the station."

"No problem. This is like in the movies!"

The silver car drove along Praed Street, crossed over the Edgware Road onto Chapel Street, joined the Marylebone Road, and carried on until it became the Euston Road, finally stopping outside Euston station, where the man got out, and the car sped off.

"Stop here, at the station," commanded the MI6 agent, who, having been watching the monitor, handed the driver a ten-pound note. "Keep the change."

He got out of the taxi, as the man from the silver car was crossing the road, and followed him, at a discreet distance, until the man disappeared into the building where the 'banya' were. The MI6 agent carried on, walking by the building, noting the address. After making his way to Euston Station, he joined the queue for taxis.

Waterstone had booked a room for the agent on the same corridor as Ian's room, and he went to the hotel to check in. The agent already knew which room Ian was booked into, and he left his own door slightly ajar, to listen for doors opening, checking for when Ian might walk past. It was an educational day for the agent, who tailed Ian on the Underground, to the Tate Gallery, followed by a walk to the British Museum. Eventually, after taking the Underground from Tottenham Court Road back to Paddington and eating a meal in an inexpensive restaurant, they both made it back to the hotel, the agent delaying his entrance by five minutes. Ian did not leave the hotel again, on the Saturday. In the morning, the agent followed him to the station to catch a train to Heathrow. Once Ian had cleared security, the agent went back to headquarters.

When Ian arrived back at Ottawa, he was detained in baggage retrieval, and went into a room where Waterstone was waiting.

"Hi. How was your trip?"

"I'm not sure, but the exchange went off without a hitch. The odd thing was a man I'm pretty sure was Russian was hanging around the station. I gave him the slip, I think, just before I made the exchange."

"Well, we know the exchange was made, because we had an agent watching you and following you. He enjoyed his day visiting the Tate and the museum!" laughed Waterstone. "He stayed in the same hotel as you."

By now, the books had been scanned.

"Empty," said the man doing the scanning. "Not even any cavities."

"If I was a betting man, from what Ian has just told us, I think they may suspect something. I'm pretty sure they don't know who Ian is, though."

"They may be thinking about Zorkin and not necessarily connect me to his demise," responded Ian, removing the wig and moustache. "Shall I keep these?"

"No. I'll take them, until we need them for something else."

"OK. Is that all?"

"Yes. Good work, Ian. Speak to you next Sunday."

"Thanks. Bye."

As he left the baggage hall, Ian half expected to be met by Caroline, but he was not. He caught the bus back into the city and walked to his flat. Tired out from the journey, he poured himself a vodka and went to bed.

The following Saturday, he bought some ice skates and thick socks and made his way to the Rideau Canal skating rink, the skates hanging round his neck, the books in his knapsack. He could see Caroline leaning against the barrier, her long blonde hair flowing in the breeze beneath her bobble-hat. She did not appear to have any skates, either on her feet or round her neck.

"Hello," he greeted her when he was a few paces away.

She turned about. Ian froze in his shoes. He was standing face to face with Katya.

"Hello, Owen. What are you doing in Ottawa?"

"Katya! I live here now."

"And you didn't call me up?"

"Come on, Katya. You and I both know you weren't really interested in me, just in getting me hooked on heroin. I'm clean, now, by the way. In any case, how would I even know you were in Ottawa?"

"Are you meeting someone, here?"

"As a matter of fact, I am. My girlfriend. I thought you were her. She has long blonde hair too, and you were standing where we had agreed to meet," he replied, not putting two and two together.

"Actually, I know you were meeting someone. Caroline is my cousin. She had an accident. She couldn't reach you on the phone, so she asked me to come and tell you."

"Caroline is your cousin?"

"Yes. Our mothers are twins. The difference is that her mother married a Canadian and mine married a Russian."

"Yes, you told me your mother was French-Canadian. I remember."

"You left London very suddenly, I hear."

"That is true. I did, but as far as I am aware, I never took anything that wasn't mine. Kochai died and I wanted a fresh start. If I had gone to Nikolai and said I wanted to leave, I am pretty sure he would not have let me. So, I gave him back the tickets and bought my own. If anything, he still owed me for my services. But I am not interested in collecting on the debt."

"How do you know my cousin?"

"I went to the jazz weekend and bumped into her. We started dating."

"But you are not telling her the truth, are you? You go by the name of Ian, now."

"I do. When my friend asked me to come and stay, I changed my identity and got a new passport."

"Just like that?"

"Well, it was someone who knew someone, and it wasn't cheap."

"And you weren't asked questions at passport control?"

"Not when I came to Canada the first time. Funnily enough, when Caroline asked me to take some books to France, the check-in desk questioned my passport, and I had to go and answer questions. It turns out my face is similar to someone the police were looking for, but after interviewing me, they were happy I was not their man."

"Well, Owen, I mean Ian, I hope we can meet up for a drink sometime. No hard feelings. Caroline will know how to contact me. Goodbye."

Ian stood there bemused, watching Katya walk off down the street. He was worried about Caroline. What kind of accident had she had? Katya did not mention the hospital, so it cannot have been serious. He went to find a public telephone and called her number. It was engaged. He waited five minutes and tried again. Still engaged. Ian was still carrying his skates. Skating without Caroline was not much fun, but having invested in the skates, he decided to go and experience the rink. He would try Caroline's number again, later.

Ian's only previous experience on ice had been a birthday party at Streatham. He had not taken to it, and his feet hurt for having to tie the laces so tightly. This time would be different. He had bought hockey skates, not figure skates, and he was determined to become proficient, by the time the ice thawed. There were five-year olds rushing past him, which was all very embarrassing, but after gingerly making his way across, he started to glide his feet more freely. After half an hour or so, he felt like his speed was improving, even if he had not yet perfected the ability to stop without crashing into the side.

Ian skated for an hour, before going to phone Caroline again. Her phone was still engaged. Either she was having a long conversation with her mother, or everyone was phoning up to check on how she was, after her accident, and Ian kept missing the gaps. If he did not get through by the end of the day, he resolved to pay her a surprise visit, tomorrow morning. The next time Ian phoned was from his home phone, and Caroline's number was still engaged. It occurred to him that she might not have replaced the receiver properly and was not actually on the phone with anyone. She would not know, until she went to make another call. There was nothing he could do, so he cooked some chicken and boiled some rice. Although most of the time, he lived on toast, he did try to make a bit of an effort at the weekends, with at least one meal, and you cannot always eat steak.

Before going to bed, Ian tried once more to reach Caroline. The phone was still engaged. His thoughts turned to Katya. No wonder the two women looked so similar. They had mothers who were twins. This was important news to relay to Waterstone tomorrow evening. The link between Caroline and Krukov was clear. He was her uncle. He wondered how much Katya had shared with Caroline. Did Caroline know he had been in a relationship with Katya, that he had trafficked drugs, that she had got him hooked on heroin and that he had changed his identity? If Katya had told Caroline, he not only had a lot of explaining to do, but he was also in more danger than he had previously been. He drifted off to sleep, fuelled by the two bottles of beer and three vodkas he had consumed.

When he got up, the following morning, he tried Caroline's number yet again, and again, it was engaged. Even though the books were empty, he still needed to give them to her. Would she be expecting them to be empty? What if she accused him of stealing the drugs she assumed were concealed within the books? Something in his guts told him to carry his gun where he had easy access to it, so he removed it from the Bible and stuck it in his belt, in the small of his back.

On arriving at Caroline's house, he opened the side gate, as usual, and wheeled his bicycle in, returning to the front door and ringing the bell. There was no reply, but he could here Arthur or Smitty meowing vociferously. He rang again. Still no reply, so he went to the back door. It was not locked. Certain that Caroline would forgive him his audacity, he opened it and went inside, into the kitchen, to be met by a strong aroma of cat-poop.

"Caroline! Are you there?" he called.

Arthur and Smitty came running into the kitchen, meowing.

"Hi guys. Where's your mum?"

He went into the sitting room, but Caroline was not there, so he went into the bedroom, in case she was having a lie-in, with earplugs and eye-cover. The bed was made. He went into the bathroom. There was Caroline, lying on the floor, a bullet wound in her forehead. Ian went cold. That was what Katya had meant by 'accident', but who had carried out the shooting? Katya or one of her henchmen? He had no idea how long she had been dead, but the cats were obviously hungry. He went back into the kitchen and poured some food into their bowls. They rushed at it and wolfed it down. Ian went through into the utility room, where the litter tray was kept. It was full of poop. The cat flap was locked and in Ian's estimation, the cats had been using the litter tray for two to three days, unable to do their business in the garden. He checked the phone and found the receiver lying at the side. That explained why it was engaged each time he had tried to reach Caroline. His head was all over the place. His phone call to Waterstone was not due until five o'clock.

Ian's main concern, now, was the welfare of Arthur and Smitty. He could not stay there or even come back to the house, but he dare not call the police yet, either. He needed Waterstone's advice. In the end, he cleared out the litter tray and replaced it with clean litter, filled several bowls with water and all of the remaining food, turned the dial on the cat flap to incoming only, just in case the cats escaped when anyone else entered the house, wrote a note with his right hand, 'Please make sure the two cats are looked after' and wiped off his prints from everything he remembered touching. Having given each of the cats a cuddle, he left the bag of books on the kitchen table and headed for the door. Just before he shut it behind him, he remembered his phone number. He knew Caroline kept a phonebook in the small bedroom she used as an office. His number was not written in the book, not under 'I' nor 'E' nor 'C', but what had she done with the page of notepad he had written it on? He looked in the drawers and in a pile of papers. Giving up on the office, he went to her bedroom and checked the drawers in the bedside table. Perhaps she kept it on her, in her jeans pocket. Reluctantly, he moved her lifeless body and felt in the pockets. Nothing. He gave up and left.

Five o'clock could not come along quickly enough for him. He went to the call box he had used to phone Caroline, near the canal, and dialled the latest number in his weekly letter from Brunswick Holdings.

"Hello."

"Hello. Ziekenhuis."

"L'hôpital."

"What is your update."

"Caroline is dead."

"Caroline is dead! What happened?"

"Executed, like Zorkin."

"When and where?"

"In her bathroom, at least that is where I found the body. Don't know when, but by the amount of cat poop in the litter tray I would say late Thursday, Friday or Saturday. I found the body on Sunday morning."

"OK. Did you leave things as they were?"

"Yes. But there's more. I was due to meet Caroline at the Rideau Canal on Saturday, lunchtime, to go skating. She wasn't there, but Katya was. They look very similar from behind. Long blonde hair. Slim figure. She was facing away when I greeted her. When she turned round it was Katya. Our brief conversation began with her telling me that Caroline had had an accident and asked Katya to tell me because she couldn't reach me on the phone. Katya and Caroline are cousins. Mothers are twin sisters. So Krukov is Caroline's uncle. Katya told me Nikolai wasn't happy about my leaving London and the 'banya'. She asked me why and how I no longer went by the name of Owen Linton-House and if I had any problems at the airport. I replied I got the passport to start a new life and was stopped when I went to France with work, because I looked similar to someone the police were looking for, but that they realised I wasn't him. I was thinking on my feet. She said we should meet up for a drink sometime and that she would get in touch via Caroline. Well, that isn't going to happen now."

"It is highly likely that they were watching you when you went to France, and saw you taken into a side room. That may be why they made the London exchange blanks. We are faced with two immediate questions. What do we do about the body and recovering the bullet? What do we do about Katya and your continued assignment?"

"And what will happen to Arthur and Smitty?"

"Arthur and Smitty?"

"Yes. Caroline's remaining two cats. They were starving when I went into the house. I gave them lots of food and water and cleaned the litter tray. I also left a handwritten note, asking whoever discovered the body to take care of the cats. Don't worry. I'm left-handed, but I wrote it right-handed, like a spider on speed."

"OK. We need to send in a team to recover the bullet, remove the body and clean the crime scene. We should also drive her car to some remote location. I'll make sure someone sends an anonymous message to an animal welfare charity, about two cats being shut inside a house, with the owner gone away. I will have to think about your next move."

"Right."

There was a brief pause in the conversation.

"No, we need to leave the body for the police to discover it. You are probably being watched, now."

"What about the bullet? What about the cats?"

"OK. Here's what we're going to do. I will send someone to recover the bullet and the bag of books. We will carry out a thorough search of the house for drugs. Someone will drive the cats in Caroline's car, to a remote location, leave the car and take the cats to an animal shelter, saying they heard the cats meowing in the car, and didn't know what to do when the owner didn't return for several hours. At some point, someone will report Caroline missing, and the police will discover the body. I will have someone watching you, at all times. Be on your guard. Wait to see if Katya contacts you. We can't close in on Krukov yet, because we still need you to follow the network to Afghanistan. We also need a stronger link this end, to the drugs distribution. This is bigger than we first thought. It looks like both Venezuela and Afghanistan are the source of Russian drugs. Anyway, when they discover the body, the police will likely question Katya, as they are cousins, but I doubt Katya pulled the trigger, and nor do I think the police will take the drugs angle. As far as I am aware, they have no idea what is going on with regards drug distribution and the Russian network. If there's a problem, we'll talk to our friends in the CIA."

"OK. I'll wait for Katya to contact me."

"Yes. You're doing great work, Ian."

"Thanks. Bye."

"Goodbye."

When Ian went to work on Monday, he could not help watching over his shoulder, all the time. Once safely at work, he tried hard to concentrate but kept thinking about Smitty and Arthur. He hoped they would be found good homes. He would have taken them himself, if he were not supposed to be going to Europe or Afghanistan every so often. In any case, it would not be fair on the cats, because he might have to flee for his life at the drop of a hat. He was also feeling slightly more reassured that Caroline had killed neither Zorkin nor Chingachgook. The 'message from the boss', when they were killed, must have come from Katya or Krukov. Unless, that is, Caroline had been more senior to Katya, and now, Katya was staging a coup.

Did Katya know where he lived or worked? Had they been watching him since Zorkin was killed? Somewhere in the shadows, Waterstone's man was watching Ian's back, just as the MI6 agent had done, in London, and whilst knowing as much, gave Ian some comfort, he started to ponder whether, if push came to shove, he could pull the trigger and take out Katya or one of her henchmen, in self-defence. Would it come to that?

To his surprise, on the Wednesday evening, his home phone rang.

"Hello."

"Hello, Ian. It's Katya. How about we go for that drink?"

"When? Surely you don't mean now?"

"Why not now. I am in the city centre. Why don't you join me in The Royal Oak? Shall we say half past eight?"

Ian did not feel he could refuse. He was also pretty certain that Katya was in possession of the page from the note pad on which he had written his phone number.

"Half-past eight it is, then."

"Bye, Ian."

"Bye."

Ian felt sure that Waterstone's man would be watching him and would follow him to the bar. He changed into a clean shirt and left for The Royal Oak on his bicycle, his gun in his belt. Katya was sitting at a table drinking white wine when he walked in. He acknowledged her, went to the bar, ordered a vodka and orange, and joined her at the table. A few minutes later, Waterstone's man also walked in and went to the bar. He sat at a table, within earshot of Katya.

"Good evening, Katya. I take it you know that Caroline is dead."

"Aren't you supposed to say something along the lines of 'Sorry for your loss' Ian?"

"Why? You were the one who told me about the accident. I doubt she would have had an accident, told you to meet me and then been shot. I went round to see her, on the Sunday, when she did not answer her phone. I found her there, bullet in the head, just like Zorkin. I fed the cats by the way, and then made sure they went to a rescue. So, why are we meeting?"

"I told you. For old time's sake. You said you got clean. Where and how did you manage to do that?"

"If you must know, I went to Amsterdam, where I got involved with a church. Cold turkey was uncomfortable, but not as bad as it might have been, because my habit was weekly and manageable, no thanks to your friends at the 'banya', I hasten to add."

"So angry, so hostile, Ian. And there I was, wanting to ask you if you would carry on delivering books for me, now that Caroline is out of the picture."

"So, you did have Caroline taken out of the game."

"Tell me, Ian. Who was better in bed? Caroline or me?"

"I can't believe you just asked me that!"

"Do you want to deliver books for me, or not?"

"What do I get in return?"

"Your life, Ian. You get to live."

"Then, I will tell you exactly what I told Caroline. Friday evening, overnight flight, return Sunday morning, arrive afternoon, Sunday. That way I don't have to take any time off work."

"No problem. We will meet here on the Friday evening, before your flight, and here, again, on the Sunday evening, when you return. A purely business relationship. You can always buy me a drink if you so wish."

"We'll have to see about that. Perhaps you should buy me a drink, for delivering your books. It's the least you can do."

"Oh, Ian. The least I can do, is to let you celebrate your next birthday."

She got up to leave.

"Caroline was," he added, realising he had nothing to lose.

"Caroline was what?"

"Better in bed. You asked who, between you, was better in bed."

"I'd be careful what you do with your manhood, if I were you'" she sneered, in Russian, as she went through the door.

Ian refrained from asking why but went to the bar and ordered another vodka and orange. He made it a double.

Cycling back to his flat, the vodka started to turn his mind a little fuzzy. He had drunk three shots of vodka in quick succession. Waterstone's man had followed him, at a distance, and now parked along the street. There was no way of seeing if someone climbed over the back wall, but he could watch for Ian to leave his flat in the morning, and throughout his journey to work. As soon as Ian's lights went out, Waterstone's man allowed himself to sleep, in the back seat, an alarm set for six thirty. He did not have to watch Ian when he was at work, Thomas Sydney was there to do that, not that Ian had any inkling. The whole company had been set up as a front, as a way of legitimising the lives of agents and of giving them reasons to travel. Currently, Ian was the only person on assignment. Only Sydney knew of the reason for being of Ontario Publishing Inc. even though, to all intents and purposes, it was run as a proper business.

At just before seven o'clock, a black sedan car pulled up at the side of the road, about fifty yards beyond Ian's apartment block. It looked to contain two men. When Ian left for work, and Waterstone's man followed him, the other vehicle stayed put. As soon as Ian had entered Ontario Publishing, Waterstone's man circled back and drove back down the street where Ian lived. The other vehicle was parked where he had seen it pull up, but now it was empty. What he did not know, but suspected, was that the two men were inside Ian's flat, installing bugs. Waterstone's man went home, showered, shaved, ate breakfast, and returned to Ontario Publishing.

As was his usual custom, Ian came out of the building at around twelve o'clock, with Brad, and they walked round to Brad's favourite café. Waterstone's man got out of his car and went to look in the windows just along the street and moved to a doorway opposite, where he stood smoking a cigarette. When Brad and Ian exited the café, he returned to his car, until it was time to follow Ian home, again. Waterstone's man did the same thing, or variations on a theme, in the vicinity of Ontario Publishing, for the rest of the week. At the weekend, another agent watched over Ian.

On the Sunday evening, Ian went and found a phone kiosk.

"Hello."

"Hello. Velosiped."

"Fiets."

"What is your update?"

"We're back in. Actually, Katya has pretty much told me, either I deliver books for her, or I die."

"Try not to worry. We are watching. In fact, check your jacket, trousers, knapsack, and shoes, as we speak. I think you have been bugged."

Ian felt under his collar and in his pockets. He also ran his finger and thumb along the hem and collar of his jacket.

Nothing. He checked his trouser pockets and ran his finger and thumb along his belt and trouser waistband. Removing his shoes, he checked the insoles and heels.

"Everything seems fine."

"Expect wasp control to pay you a visit."

"Katya says that when I deliver books, we will meet in the Royal Oak on the Friday evening and again on the Sunday evening when I return. No doubt she will phone me at home when she needs me."

"How did she get your number?"

"Caroline had it written down. Stupid, I know."

"No. I think you probably had to give her your number."

"So, I look forward to our next update and whenever your next book delivery will be."

"Yes, we can't have me seen to be pulled aside though. We don't know if I will be tailed. We have to find another way of scanning the books."

"I'll give it some thought. Thank you."

"Bye."

"Goodbye."

The following morning, when he was just waking up, his doorbell rang. He peered through the spyhole to see two men in grey boiler suits, holding some equipment. He opened his door, and one of the men held up an identification badge. 'Wasp-out'.

"Good morning, Sir. We understand you have a problem with a wasp nest."

"I do. It's on the balcony, but they get in when the door is open."

"We'll get right onto it."

He let them in, and they began to systematically search his flat for listening devices or hidden cameras, including checking all Ian's clothing and the contents of his drawers, shelves, and cupboards. There were bugs in the kitchen vent, the telephone, one in his Walkman and another in the bedroom, under the bed. They did not find any cameras. One of the men took out a pen and a piece of paper and wrote, 'We can't remove them, because it will alert the Russians. Do not talk about anything relating to your assignment inside the flat. Buy a new Walkman!'

"That should do the trick," said one of the wasp controllers, taking out a bag from his toolkit, which already contained a broken wasp nest. "Leave the windows open, to let the wasp-killer spray out."

They packed up their tools and left. Ian, feeling mischievous, put a cassette into his Walkman and turned up the volume, and immediately felt stupid, because the sound only came out through the earphones.

Two weeks after his drink with Katya, Ian received another phone call from her.

"Meet me at seven o'clock, this Friday, in The Royal Oak. You are going to Paris."

Ian realised this gave him no chance of confirming with Waterstone, when his flight was, or where he was flying from, if it was not Ottawa, which with Katya, was a possibility. His next update was not due until Sunday evening. The only way to contact Waterstone was using the number on the business card.

He went to work, and before going into the building, made a call to Waterstone's business number, from a public kiosk.

"Really sorry. No notice given. Friday trip to Paris. Seven o'clock in The Royal Oak."

"Use the toilet before leaving the pub. We've got your back. Use your new suitcase."

"Thanks. Bye."

"Goodbye."

As he returned the receiver to its cradle, Ian wondered what Waterstone had meant by his new suitcase, but he trusted him to have everything in hand.

At the end of the day, before cycling home, he went and bought a new Walkman. He did not want to be without music on his trip to Paris. Perhaps on the Saturday afternoon, he would get a chance to do some more sight-seeing. It was not all bad, having to deliver books, at least not to Paris. He was not looking forward to being sent to London, because Katya was the sort of person who would send Nikolai to make the exchange. When he arrived back at his flat, there was a box, outside his door. Hopeful it did not contain a bomb, he took it inside and opened it to find a new suitcase. What was the plan?

Ian was partly apprehensive and partly excited throughout the week. On the Friday after work, he went home, ate eggs on toast, packed his new suitcase and knapsack, and walked to The Royal Oak. Katya was seated at the same table as before, without a drink. Ian nodded at her and went to the bar, where he bought two glasses of white wine. As he sat down, she slid an envelope across to him. He opened it to find air tickets from Montreal to Paris.

"How do I get to Montreal?"

"I will drive you. Someone, probably not me, will meet you at Montreal when you return and bring you back here. The books are in my car."

"Thanks. And the hotel?"

"You'll be met at the airport and taken to a hotel. Leave your books in the car. Same thing on your return.

You will be picked up from the hotel at seven in the morning. There will be some books in the car for you to bring back."

"Right," responded Ian, slipping the cardboard ticket wallet in his inside jacket pocket.

"We need to leave in, ten minutes."

Waterstone's man had been sitting at the adjacent table and heard everything. After eight minutes, he got up and went to the toilet.

"Drink up," Katya urged Ian.

He downed the last mouthful of wine and stood up.

"I need to use the toilet," he insisted, picking up his knapsack, but leaving his suitcase.

When he entered the toilets, Waterstone's man was standing by the basins.

"Let me see the tickets. Waterstone sent me."

Ian took out the ticket wallet and let Waterstone's man look inside.

"Thanks," he said, handing the ticket wallet back to Ian and leaving the room.

Ian used the toilet, washed his hands, and went back out to Katya, who stood up. He grabbed his suitcase and followed her to her car. Waterstone's man drove after them, at a suitable distance. Halfway to Montreal, a second car joined the road and took over the role. The driver was a second agent, and he had an identical suitcase to Ian's.

At the airport, Ian got out of the car, opened the rear door, opened his case, and packed the bag of books that had been lying on the seat.

"Goodbye. Have a pleasant trip, Ian."

"Bye."

Ian watched Katya drive off, before going to check in. The second agent also checked in, just behind Ian, and when Ian sat down on the other side of security, the man sat next to him. The agent started up a conversation.

"I haven't been to Paris before. Have you?"

"Yes. I went last year. I love it there."

"What do you recommend?"

"The Eiffel Tower, of course."

It was at this point that Ian noticed the man's suitcase, which he had placed on the floor, right next to Ian's. The agent stood up.

"I think I'm going to stretch my legs. Wait here. See you in a bit."

He picked up Ian's suitcase and walked off. Fifteen minutes later, he returned and put Ian's suitcase back where he had picked it up from. When the gate number was called, he picked up his original suitcase.

"I doubt we'll be sitting together."

"Probably not. Enjoy your trip to Paris," replied Ian, impressed by Waterstone's ingenuity.

The second agent boarded the plane and sat on the opposite side to Ian. As with his trip to London, Ian watched the movie, this time *Sophie's Choice*, and fell asleep. Not only was the second agent the means to testing the books, but he was also the protection for Ian. Ian could not take a weapon on the plane, but as an agent, the man with the identical suitcase could. Once they had cleared Parisian security, the man came up to Ian again.

"Here's a box of biscuits for you."

"Thanks," replied Ian, taking the biscuits, and putting them in his knapsack.

Out in arrivals, a tall man with a blond crew-cut was waiting at the barrier, holding a card on which was written, 'Ian from Ottawa'.

Ian approached him.

"Bonjour," he greeted Ian, with a Russian accent.

"Bonjour."

"I will take you to your hotel."

Ian followed him out to his car and got into the rear seat. The man drove off, at speed, and they were soon at a three-star hotel near the Moulin Rouge. Ian undid his suitcase and took out the bag of books from Katya.

"I will pick you up at seven o'clock, tomorrow morning."

"Bye."

"Bye. Enjoy your sightseeing."

Ian got out and went into the hotel.

"Good morning, Sir."

"Good morning. I believe I have a reservation."

"Your name, Sir?"

"Elton-Craig."

"Yes. You have a reservation. May I take your passport, please?"

"My passport?"

"Yes, we hold your passport for security, in case you don't pay."

"But isn't the room already paid for?"

"Let me check for you," replied the assistant, looking in her file. "No, it isn't. So, please may I have your passport."

"Of course," responded Ian, getting out his passport, and feeling a little confused. "How much is the room?"

"Two hundred and thirty francs. Here is your key."

"Cash or credit card?"

"It's your choice."

"Thank you."

Ian took his key and went to his room. Why was Katya being so mean? Was it because he told her Caroline was better in bed? He was going to have to get a credit card if this was going to be a regular occurrence. He had brought three hundred francs, which was a relief, although he did have a hundred Canadian dollars in his wallet, which he could exchange, if needed. Having used the bathroom and freshened up, he opened the tin of biscuits, took out the gun concealed there, and stuck it in his belt. He was just about to close the tin when he spotted a note. 'Pack in suitcase' was all it said. He screwed up the message and put it in his pocket, to throw in a waste bin. Leaving the hotel, he went in search of the Moulin Rouge. His understanding was that this area was the Paris red light district. Katya really was having a laugh at his expense. He came to a bin and threw away the paper on which the message was written.

Having viewed the famous windmill, Ian set off for the nearest metro station, to go to the Arc de Triomphe, where he wove his way through the traffic to the middle of the roundabout, before realising he could have used an underpass to reach the monument. From the Arc de Triomphe, he walked all the way down the Champs Elysées to the Jardin des Tuileries. As he was walking towards the Louvre, he saw a couple with a pushchair approaching. They looked familiar.

"Is that you Owen?" asked the woman, in Russian.

"Kristina? Anton? And is this Ivan?"

Ian's first thought was that it was a massive coincidence that he should bump into Anton and Kristina in Paris.

Were they there because they worked for Krukov? He was guarded in his responses.

"What are you doing in Paris?" asked Anton.

"And why did you disappear so suddenly?" added Kristina.

"I think you know the answer to the second question. As for the first. My job sends me to Paris and London every so often. Look I'm really sorry I didn't get in touch, but I didn't want to cause you any more grief, given the need to transport the Delft tea service shipments."

"Are you not living in London anymore, then?" inquired Kristina.

"No. I went to visit a friend in Ottawa and ended up staying."

"That's in Canada," responded Kristina, surprised.

"Yes, it is. What are you three doing in Paris?"

"We left soon after you stopped visiting," explained Anton. "Nikolai paid us a personal visit. He told us we were moving to Paris. At least Ivan will grow up speaking French and Russian."

"We wanted to escape from it all, but here we are meeting the Orient Express every month," reflected Kristina.

"Kristina, secrecy," insisted Anton.

Ian did not want to cause Anton, Kristina and Ivan any more difficulties than he might already have. For certain, he was being followed by the Russians.

"Where's the nearest metro station to here?" he asked.

"Tuileries, probably," replied Anton, pointing.

"Over there," confirmed Ian, also pointing. "Great to see you. Sorry I can't talk longer. Take care."

Ian headed for the Tuileries metro station in the hope that anyone watching him, would deduce he was simply asking for directions. He would have loved to stand chatting and ask more about the Orient Express.

Having arrived back at the Moulin Rouge, Ian decided it was not too far to climb up to the Sacré-Coeur, which he did. As he neared the basilica, he was approached by several Africans selling souvenirs. He smiled each time and shook his head. Entering the door, he was somewhat overwhelmed by the decorations. He found the fresco on the ceiling over the high altar interesting. It was not the usual crucifix you might expect in a Roman Catholic church, but showed a golden heart, exposed in Jesus' chest. He thought about Ike and Thelma, Floyd and Sally, and how unostentatious their lives were. Their faith seemed to demonstrate Jesus' golden heart. He was not quite as sure about the basilica. When he passed the Africans on the way back to his hotel, he bought something small from each of them.

At first, he thought about giving his keyrings to Brad and Rachel, but immediately realised he would have to explain how he got them. Ian returned to his hotel room, showered, and went out again to find a restaurant. Quite tired from all his walking, he did not want to stray far, but nor did he want to eat in the red-light district. He walked south for about ten minutes, and went into the first, inviting-looking restaurant he came to, where he ordered steak and fries. When he got back to his hotel room, Ian packed his clothes and the empty biscuit tin in his suitcase and went to bed. He had an early start in the morning.

Ian took his case and knapsack down to the reception and paid for his room. His passport was duly returned to him, and he went to stand outside the entrance. As promised, the driver arrived on the dot of seven, and Ian got into the back of the car.

"Bonjour, Monsieur."

"Bonjour."

Nothing else was said. There was a carrier bag lying on the seat next to Ian, containing six plastic-covered books. Ian undid his case, flattened the carrier as best he could, on top of his clothes, and closed the lid. He was dropped in front of departures.

"Merci, au revoir."

"Au revoir, Monsieur."

Ian was not sure what to do about the gun, still stuck in his belt. He could not take it through security. Looking around the departure hall he spotted a man with an identical suitcase and hoped he might be the agent. Moving to a slightly secluded position against the side of a kiosk, Ian knelt down and surreptitiously removed the gun from his back to the biscuit tin and went and stood back in full view. The man with the matching suitcase strolled over and placed it on the floor next to Ian's. Ian recognised him as one of the recruits on the training course.

"What's the time please.?"

Ian checked his watch.

"Twenty-past eight."

"Thank you. I'll probably bump into you on the other side of border control, in Canada," added the agent, stooping to pick up Ian's suitcase.

Ian went to check in, passed through security with no idea what was in the case, and bought a coffee. As he sat drinking his coffee, he wondered what the agent's assignment currently was, apart from supporting 'Operation Cold Turkey'. Actually, Ian had no idea what official name MI6 had given this project, but it entertained him to come up with a suitable descriptor for getting heroin out of the Russians and the Russians out of heroin.

They did bump into each other in Montreal. Quite literally. The manoeuvre allowed the agent to pick up his own case again and return Ian's to him, no longer containing the biscuit tin and with the books x-rayed. As Ian walked out into the main concourse, in arrivals, a man was waiting for him with a sign that said, 'Welcome home, Ian', another subtle attempt by Katya, to make Ian feel about as not-at-home as he could possibly feel. Ian approached the man and followed him to his car. He was dropped at The Royal Oak.

"How lovely to see you again, Ian. Did you have a pleasant trip?"

"Actually, I would like to be reimbursed the two hundred and thirty francs I had to pay for my hotel room. What if I hadn't taken that much money with me?"

"Do you have my books?" replied Katya, ignoring Ian's request.

Ian opened his case and took out the carrier bag which he placed on the table, between them.

"There is your payment," said Katya, sliding an envelope towards Ian and taking hold of the carrier bag. "I can't stop, but we'll be having a drink together very soon, I'm sure."

She stood up, put on her jacket, and left. Ian looked inside the envelope and counted three hundred dollars. He went to the bar and bought a double vodka and orange. Frustratingly, he had to go home to find the latest communication from Brunswick Holdings, before going back out to find a public phone.

As he walked home, he realised that drinking a double vodka on an empty stomach was a bad idea. As soon as he got back to his flat, he drank a pint of water and made some cheese on toast, which he ate whilst opening his post. Feeling like the snack had soaked up the vodka, he used the bathroom and went back out on his bike to find a telephone. It occurred to Ian, that if he was being watched, by people who knew he had a home phone, would they not be slightly suspicious of his weekly Sunday evening calls from different public telephones around the city?

He was riding at speed and was not paying much attention to the road. He cycled straight over at a red light and two minutes later, a police car pulled in front of him. He screeched to a halt, nearly going over the handlebars.

"Good evening. Did you know you had just ridden through a red light?"

"I'm sorry. Are bicycles meant to stop, even when there are no cars around?"

"Are you from England?"

"Yes. Really sorry. It won't happen again."

"I'll let it go, this time. By the way, speed limits apply to bicycles too!" laughed the officer.

"Thanks. Sorry."

The police officer got back in his car and drove off. Ian continued on his bike, paying more attention to the junctions. There was no danger of him speeding again this evening as he had lost momentum, and it would be mostly uphill on the way back. He stopped at a phone near the Parliament Building.

"Hello."

"Hello. Daryab."

"Reka," replied Ian, in Russian.

"What is your update?"

"I think the trip to Paris was successful. The suitcases were brilliant."

"Here's the good news. Books were empty going out and full coming back."

"So, they were onto us."

"I think we already knew that," laughed Waterstone.

"I bumped into Anton and Kristina. I was their guest in Amsterdam. They have been moved to Paris. Nikolai visited them in person. I'm pretty sure the drugs from Afghanistan enter Paris on the Orient Express. Kristina said they met the Orient Express every month, before Anton reminded her it was secret. She had confided in me in Amsterdam about her own fears, and advised me to get out, even back then."

"Well done. I think it's time we sent you to Afghanistan."

"Does that mean I get to ride on the Orient Express?"

"If it was anyone else, I might ignore that attempt at fishing, but I am so impressed with you, I think you deserve it. I'll be in touch."

"Thanks. Bye."

"Goodbye."

Four weeks after Ian's trip to Paris, he was working at his desk, when and internal call came through to him, from Sydney's secretary, that he wanted to see Ian. He put down the customer file he was working on and went up to Sydney's office, feeling slightly nervous that he had done something wrong. He knocked on the door. Sydney opened it and ushered him in. The secretary was nowhere to be seen, but Waterstone was sitting there. He stood up and shook Ian's hand.

"I expect you're somewhat confused, right now," observed Sydney.

"I am, a little."

"We think it's time for you to be brought up to speed with something that is on a need-to-know basis. Thomas here is one of us. I am here under the pretext that I have come to talk about books, today, but we have always tried to keep the practicalities of the operation away from the day to day running of the company."

"I see," replied Ian.

"Thanks to your tremendous aptitude for the role to which you have been recruited, Operation Beluga has built up a head of steam. We have reached a critical point. Based on the information you have been acquiring, we are in a position to arrest, Katya, Nikolai and several members of their network, including shutting down the 'banya' in London, although our goal is to take out the entire network. What we don't currently have, is anything that directly implicates Krukov. A smart lawyer would soon point out that being Katya's father is not enough to indict him for drugs trafficking, or any of the murders which have recently been committed, although there is a tenuous ballistic link. Not only that, but we still don't have any actual evidence that the Soviets are behind all this, even though Krukov works for the diplomatic service. The death of Zorkin, the empty books in and out of London, the handling of your trip to Paris, flying out of Montreal, leaving you no time to plan, being driven from airport to hotel, etcetera, etcetera, not to mention the bugging of your flat, all suggest that Katya, and probably Krukov, are suspicious of you, and concerned that they, themselves, may be under suspicion."

"Is that good or bad?" Ian interrupted.

"As I said, your work has been phenomenal. We are not sure, how expendable you are to Katya, and to Krukov, though. Couriers tend to have a fairly short shelf-life. At the moment, Katya is toying with you. I half believe that's out of jealousy, because you had a relationship with Caroline. Don't forget, Caroline didn't know you were using her, and as far as we are aware, Katya does not know you work for MI6. We very much hope to make the necessary arrests, as soon as the right moment comes along. However, we recruited you in order to benefit from your many language skills, including Pashto, and we think the time has come for you to go to the source of the supply chain. We are hopeful that your skills in Russian and Pashto will enable you to speak to the people who will give us the proof that Krukov is working for the Soviet government. And we can't close down Krukov's network before we can have him arrested."

"I understand," responded Ian, thoughtfully.

"And that's where I come in," remarked Sydney. "You haven't been working for us long enough to take the holiday time you would need, and if we were to send you on an extended work trip, Brad and Rachel might start asking questions. We also believe, and please hear me, when I say we are currently deploying as many agents as required to ensure your safety and the success of Operation Beluga, that the time has come for you to leave your job here and to move house. Over the next week, start bringing whatever of your belongings you can fit in your backpack to work. You can have a store cupboard here, for the short term. You can stay at my house until you go to Pakistan and Afghanistan. If you go abroad for two or three months, and Katya tries to contact you, apart from whoever is watching you letting her know you've not been in your flat, she might become suspicious enough to have you killed, and we can't have that. There is half a chance she will just think you disappeared once before, after being trapped in the service of the Russian drugs network, so you might have done it again. We will tell your colleagues that you lied about your resume and have been dismissed. When you do return from your trip, you can stay at my house until we work out the next steps."

"How does that sound?" asked Waterstone, encouragingly.

"It is what it is. To be honest, I'm really quite looking forward to going to Afghanistan. I thought about going several times, in my former life."

"I can imagine," smiled Sydney. "I'm a little disappointed that we have had to make this decision so soon, because you're very good at your negotiator job, Ian. I shall be sorry to lose you from the business."

"Thank you."

"Any questions?" asked Waterstone.

"No."

It was a lot to take in. He returned to his desk, a little stunned.

"Everything alright?" asked Rachel.

"Yes, just a complaint from a customer."

"Happens all the time, mate," Brad encouraged him. "I really wouldn't worry."

"Thanks, guys."

Ian went back to the customer file he had been dealing with when he was called up to Sydney's office.

"You need a drink. Let's all three of us have a drink, after work," suggested Rachel.

"Great idea," responded Brad.

"Yes. Good idea. Thank you."

At the end of the day, Brad, Ian, and Rachel went to a bar and successfully managed to get Ian drunk, and Brad did the decent thing of walking him home. He was in no fit state to ride his bicycle.

"Now don't forget you left your bike at work," laughed Brad, when they reached Ian's apartment building. "See you tomorrow."

"Cheers, Brad. You're a diamond."

Ian fumbled his key in the lock and flopped onto his bed, in the recovery position.

For the next few days, he took to work his personal belongings, cassettes, books, official correspondence, passport, and some clothes, and left them in the store cupboard he was allocated. He was due to fly to Pakistan on the Saturday, and when he went to the cupboard on the Thursday morning, he discovered a new suitcase and holdall. It was much appreciated as he could not work out how he was supposed to get his own suitcase to work. On the Friday morning, he filled his backpack with as many clothes as he could, ones that he thought he would need in Pakistan and Afghanistan, along with his full spongebag, and rode to work, feeling like a camel.

For the second time, he was called up to Sydney's office.

"You're coming home with me tonight. We'll put all your things from the store cupboard in my car. We'll leave by the rear of the building. I'll call you up here again, at three-thirty."

"Thank you. See you later."

"You're welcome."

At three-thirty, just as Sydney had indicated, Ian received an internal phone call. He picked up his jacket and knapsack.

"Got an appointment. Have a good weekend."

"You too," replied Brad.

"Thanks. And you," added Rachel.

Sydney met Ian at the rear door.

"I took the liberty of loading the car."

"Thanks."

"Get in the back and lie down, until I give you the all-clear."

They got in the car, Ian lay down on the back seat, and Sydney drove off.

"Do you live in the city?"

"Me? No, about half an hour out. Do you mind if I put some music on?"

"It's your car. What music do you like to listen to?"

"Would it surprise you if I told you that I'm a huge fan of Pink Floyd?"

"Really! I love *Wish You Were Here*, *Dark Side of the Moon* and *Animals*. I used to live just down the road from the Battersea Power Station."

Sydney pushed in the cassette and 'Us and Them' started to come out of the speakers.

"You can sit up now," said Sydney, after about ten minutes.

Ian sat up and looked out of the window. They were driving through countryside, with only the occasional building along the side of the road.

After a while, they entered the village of Munster and pulled up in front of Sydney's house. It looked like the sort of house a man in his position ought to live in. Ian had no idea whether Sydney had a wife or children. There was a second car in the driveway. They got out.

"Leave your things for a bit. We can unload when we've had a beer," he insisted, unlocking the front door. "By the way. I've got a couple of cats. You're OK with cats?"

"Love them."

As Sydney opened the door and gestured to Ian to walk in, two cats scurried along the hallway.

"They look just like Arthur and Smitty. Caroline had two cats just like these. Wow!"

"They are Arthur and Smitty."

"No way!"

Ian crouched down and made a huge fuss of both cats. His eyes watered up. He hoped Sydney did not notice.

"Make yourself at home."

"Cheers," said Sydney, raising his beer bottle.

"Cheers," replied Ian chinking his bottle against Sydney's.

"I know that MI6 didn't give you a lot of choice, but you seem to be really cut out for this job. I read your file. Have you considered a career with us?"

"To be honest, I don't know what I want. As you know, Owen left home to find his own path in life. Ian seems to be realising his potential. I'm not sure I'll ever get used to never really being able to relax. I know I was always looking over my shoulder when I was into dealing drugs, but this is different. It would be really nice, one day, to meet a girl who wasn't using me, or who I wasn't using, to settle down and have a family. And I always told myself that when I was thirty, I would go back to my family. How does a career with MI6 fit with any of that?"

"I think I understand. Believe you me, though. You will never stop looking over your shoulder, for the rest of your life. Even if you went and found an office job somewhere, or trained as a teacher, or some other worthwhile job. You would always be wondering if someone was coming for you. I've simply learnt to live with it."

There was a pause in the conversation.

"Shouldn't we unload the car?"

"Relax. I haven't even shown you to your room yet. Let's open another couple of beers. It might be the only opportunity you get to relax for a while."

Arthur came and jumped on Ian's lap. For a few moments Ian did feel safe enough to relax.

"From today, you need to stop shaving. You fly to Islamabad, where you will be met by one of our agents and driven to your hotel. He will meet you at the airport and will be carrying a mango and a box of dates. He will ask you if you have missed eating mangoes and you will say you have, as well as dates. He will give you the mango and the box of dates. You will be driven to your hotel, where you need to stay in your room. The agent will provide you with a gun, a new passport and some traditional clothing, including a turban. You will have some instructions about different ways to tie it. Practise well. The agent will come each day to bring you food. After a week, when hopefully your beard has grown, he will drive you to Kabul. From Kabul, a different agent will drive you to Lashkar Gah, where you have a house that you share with two friendly locals. They run a bookstore, and that will be your cover. You will probably end up making several trips to Kandahar, Musa Qala and various other towns. The situation in Afghanistan is complicated. The cities are still mostly controlled by the Soviets and the puppet Afghan government. The smaller towns and villages are under the control of the Mujahideen. Pakistan, the British and the Americans are supporting the Mujahideen. You will have to work out who you are speaking to and when. You will mostly be speaking Pashto, but in the cities, you may find yourself speaking Russian, and of course, you are trying to locate the Krukov network. There is a western supported drugs network out of Musa Qala, run by a man called Nasim Akhundzada. The drugs come out via Pakistan, to support the rebels with arms and expertise. He will have contacts who may know about the competition, that is, the Soviet backed drugs network. What we need from you is to identify how the competition get their drugs as far as the Orient Express and to find something that connects Krukov to Afghanistan."

"I will do my best."

"I know you will. Right, let's get your stuff into the house. There's a chicken casserole in the oven, when we're done."

"Excellent."

Sydney showed Ian his room and the two men went out to the car for the luggage. Once installed in his room, Ian re-joined Sydney who was laying the table. Sydney went back out into the kitchen and returned with the chicken casserole.

"This is good," observed Ian, after a few mouthfuls.

"Thank you. I am a lazy cook. I have never wanted to spend more time preparing a meal than it takes me to eat it, but I decided, a long time ago, that I wasn't going to live on junk food or snacks."

"I mostly eat toast with a weekly portion of steak or chicken," laughed Ian.

"Tomorrow, I will drive you to the airport. You've got a long journey ahead of you. Ottawa to London and staying overnight at the Post House Hotel. The following day you fly to Pakistan stopping in Doha. The journey from Islamabad to Kabul, the following week will take between ten and twelve hours, depending on roadblocks. By the way, drink bottled soft drinks or bottled water. Always boil your tap water. I'm pretty sure you received your cultural awareness training when you were in London."

"I did."

"Now, would you like some ice cream?"

"Thank you, yes."

Sydney removed the plates to the kitchen and came back with a carton of ice cream in one hand, two bowls in the other, and a bottle of chocolate sauce stuffed precariously under his arm. He divided the whole carton into the bowls and smothered the ice cream in chocolate sauce.

"You'll not get this for a while," he reflected.

"Can I help with anything?" asked Ian when they finished their meal.

"Yes. You wash and I'll dry."

They did the washing up between them.

"Vodka?" asked Sydney, as he was drying the last plate.

"Yes, please. With orange juice if you have it."

"Coming right up. Go and give those cats some love."

Ian went into the sitting room and knelt down beside Smitty, rubbing his head. Sydney came in with a glass of vodka and orange and a glass of bourbon.

"Cheers," he said, handing Ian his vodka and orange.

"Cheers. What time do we need to leave, in the morning?"

"Half seven, I should think. Coffee and eggs at seven."

Sydney turned on the television and they watched a comedy show. Ian did not find it as funny as Sydney did, but it took his mind off the dangerous road that lay ahead, for a while. Afterwards, he went to bed.

"Good morning. As we can't be sure that the airport isn't being watched, we're bypassing security," explained Sydney, when Ian appeared in the kitchen. "At least, we're going in through the freight terminal, and taking you across to the passenger terminal. Your passport will be checked in the freight terminal, and you won't need to check-in your baggage in departures. It will be added to the luggage transporter on the tarmac. We'll also take you up a side entrance onto the corridor between the gate and the plane before the other passengers start to board. You'll be in first class. Just in case you're wondering, by the way, your monthly expenses will increase to replace your Ontario Publishing salary. Here's your ticket, your boarding pass, and a credit card. And this is the number to call Waterstone on when you get to your hotel. He will issue you with further instructions. Now, get some eggs and coffee down you."

"Thanks."

Ian forced himself to eat. He was feeling nervous.

At the airport, Sydney accompanied Ian as far as the side entrance to the corridor between gate and plane.

"Good luck. I'm sure you'll make us proud. No doubt, I'll see you in a few weeks, when you land back in Canada."

He extended his hand, and Ian shook it warmly.

"Thanks."

"Goodbye, then."

"Thank you for your hospitality. And everything else. I'm so glad you took on Arthur and Smitty. Bye."

Ian turned and went through the door and Sydney disappeared through another door into the hidden maze of staff passageways.

When Ian stepped off the plane in Islamabad, the heat hit him like a runaway steam train. The passenger boarding bridge had no air-conditioning. He passed through border control and collected his suitcase from the baggage carousel. On the other side of customs, a small crowd of individuals were milling around, looking out for loved ones and business associates. On scanning the crowd, Ian spotted a man holding a mango and a box. He could not see if the box contained dates, at such a distance, but he approached the man, nevertheless.

"Have you missed these?" asked the man, holding up the mango and dates.

"Yes, and I haven't eaten a decent date since I left."

"Welcome to Pakistan, Ian. Come with me."

"Do you have a first name?"

"Sorry, yes. I'm James."

"Pleased to meet you, James."

They walked out of the terminal and went to where James had parked his car. The air was hot and dusty, and the place seemed to be filled with impatient drivers and hapless pedestrians. The journey took around twenty minutes, and they came to a stop in front of an unobtrusive hotel. Ian had no idea how close any amenities were, but it would not make any difference as he was confined to his room for the week. James accompanied him into the reception and spoke with the attendant, who handed Ian his key.

"I will be back to see you later today. Here's some water and bread, to eat with your mango and dates!"

"Thanks. See you later."

"Don't forget. No shaving!"

Ian nodded and gave a wry smile. He went up in the lift and found his room at the end of a corridor. There was a balcony, at least, which helped him feel less caged in. The bed was firm but wide and there was air conditioning. The bathroom was adequate. Ian lay down on the bed and contemplated the next three months. At some point he must have drifted off because he was woken by a loud knock at the door. Taking a few seconds to collect his wits, he opened the door to see James standing there.

"Hi. Come in."

James stepped inside and put the holdall and carrier bag he was carrying on the floor.

"First things first," he stated, removing two cans of Coca-Cola, a cooked chicken and some naan bread from the carrier bag.

Rummaging around again, he brought out some tissues and plates.

"I'm afraid it's got to be tearing it limb from limb."

"Smells good."

"When we've eaten, I'll show you what else I've got for you."

For the next few minutes, the two men tore at their naan bread and chicken and ate in silence.

"You'd better not forget to leave your left hand out of it, when you're eating with others."

"Of course. I was too hungry to think. That'll be tough because I'm naturally left-handed."

"Tomorrow I'll bring some dahl or similar. It'll be easier to eat with one hand."

"Great."

They finished their meal and James produced a small box of sweets, coconut ice and barfi.

"Whatever you don't eat now, you can have for breakfast. I think you can make tea in your room, yes?"

Ian nodded and pointed at the kettle.

"I don't think there is any milk or sugar."

"I'll bring you some tomorrow."

They both washed their greasy fingers in the bathroom, and James opened the holdall.

"Your name, while you're in Afghanistan, is Ewan Chandler-Brown. I will come two days before we leave to take a photograph for your new passport. Here's your gun and some rounds of ammunition. I think this is the same as you had before?"

Ian-Ewan looked more closely and nodded.

"Then, there are your clothes and a couple of turbans," added James, pulling out a length of cloth. "Let me show you how to tie it one way."

Ian-Ewan sat and watched while James made one of the turbans on his own head.

"There's a diagram in the bag."

"Thanks."

"Is there anything else you need?"

"Any chance of some more batteries for my Walkman. I would like to practise my Pashto and listen to some music, whilst I can't go out."

"I'll see what I can do."

"Cheers."

"Right. I'll leave you in peace."

"See you tomorrow."

"Yes. See you tomorrow. I'll also bring you some papers and a map to familiarise yourself with."

"Thanks."

"Bye," said James, going out of the door.

"Bye."

Ian-Ewan was left alone again. He locked the door and went out on his balcony. It was almost too warm, so he went back inside, closed the door and switched on an electric fan. Curious to see what the clothes were like, he unpacked the holdall, changed into a traditional shirt-suit and sat practising tying his turban. When he was satisfied with his efforts, he got out of the clothes and lay on his bed listening to a Pashto cassette.

When James returned the following day, around lunchtime, he brought a packet of eight batteries. The Walkman needed two of them, so Ian-Ewan was confident they would last at least the week. James also handed him a box which contained a cassette player with an electric cable.

"I thought while you were here, you could save on batteries. You should be able to use your existing earphones, if you don't want to listen without."

"Brilliant. Thanks."

Ian-Ewan was now fairly certain the batteries would be enough to see him through three months in Alghanistan.

"Now then, lunch is pakora and kebabs. And I've got you a couple of litres of water and some orange juice."

"Thanks. I practised tying my turban yesterday. It's getting there."

"Excellent. I'll be back later with dinner."

"You're not stopping to eat?"

"Can't. Not today, anyway. Got to be somewhere else. Enjoy. Bye."

"Bye."

Ian-Ewan's stubble was beginning to irritate him. It was not quite long enough yet to not itch. Having washed his hands, he washed his face and then decided to take his second shower of the day. He was sure he would get used to the heat, eventually. When he had dried himself, he returned to the box that the cassette player came in, where he had noticed a pile of papers. Ian-Ewan started to leaf through them. There were maps of Kandahar, Lashkar Gah, and various other towns in Helmand Province, including one which showed where the poppy fields were found, and some of the farms. Just like his first experience of Amsterdam, Ian-Ewan would have to find a way of connecting with people who sold drugs. Hopefully, the friendly booksellers would be able to point him in the right direction, based on their local knowledge.

By the Thursday evening, Ian-Ewan was experiencing cabin fever. His beard had grown, and he was dressed in T-shirt and shorts when James knocked at six-thirty, holding a camera.

"Hi. You have no idea how much I'm looking forward to being out of here, even if the first thing freedom affords me is a ten-hour road-trip."

"I can imagine. Would you like to put on one of your shirt-suits for the photo?"

Ian-Ewan grabbed the items and disappeared into the bathroom for a couple of minutes.

"I think there's every chance you will blend in. Look at me and don't smile."

Ian-Ewan turned to the camera and heard the shutter click.

"Let me take another three, just in case."

Ian-Ewan held his expression and heard three clicks of the shutter.

"That should do it. Thank you. Hopefully, I'll bring your new passport tomorrow."

It was six o'clock in the morning when James returned to Ewan-Ian's room.

"The transformation is complete," laughed James, handing Ewan-Ian his new passport. "Have you got all your things?"

"Yes," replied Ewan-Ian, glancing inside the passport and chuckling. "Could you carry the cassette player box for me, please?"

"Certainly."

When they got down to reception, James checked Ewan-Ian out of the hotel, and they walked a few yards down the road to where his car was parked. No one stared at Ewan-Ian, so he started feeling a little more confident that he would be able to blend in.

"I have no idea if or how many times we'll get stopped but let me do the talking. It's a long journey, but I think you'll enjoy the scenery," added James, as they drove off.

They stopped in Peshawar and Jalalabad, crossing the border near Torkham. The border control officers were armed, which made Ian feel nervous, although having taken a look in the boot of the car, nothing else was done to hinder their progress. Whatever James had said to them, it caused a few smiles. They pulled up at the hotel in Kabul, just over ten hours after they had left Islamabad.

"I'll come into reception with you, but I thought you might like to check us in. Practise your Pashto in the field. I'm staying here overnight to introduce you to your Kandahar chauffeur."

Having unloaded the luggage, they approached the desk.

"Good afternoon," started Ewan-Ian, in his best Pashto. "We have a room booked."

"Good afternoon, Sir. What name?"

"Ewan Chandler-Brown and James …."

"James Marlborough," interjected James.

The man looked down his list of guests.

"Yes. A twin room. One night?"

"One night."

"Thank you. Here is your key. Please ring down if you need anything."

"I will ring if necessary. Thank you," responded Ewan-Ian, taking the key.

"How did that feel? You did alright with your Pashto."

"OK, I think. It's always OK until the person you're talking to reels something off at break-neck speed," laughed Ewan-Ian.

"You'll be fluent, I'm sure, by the time you leave Afghanistan."

"But I'm only supposed to be here, for three months."

"You'll see."

Ewan-Ian opened the window and looked out, standing back almost immediately, when he heard Russian voices down below. He peered back over the windowsill to see a couple of Soviet soldiers on the pavement below.

"Are you OK?" asked James.

"Just heard Russian. Of course, I'm going to hear Russian in the cities. It just took me by surprise, that's all."

"I don't know about you, but as soon as we've had something to eat, I think I'm going to have an early night. I was up at five and been driving all day."

"Where are we eating?"

"There's a restaurant attached to the hotel. Coming?"

Ewan-Ian nodded, and the two of them headed out for a meal.

They ate their breakfast in the same restaurant, the following morning, and hardly had they returned to the hotel room, when there was a knock at the door. James opened it and beckoned the man to come in.

"This is Tofan," James introduced him in Pashto. "He's an agent, like us. He is your driver to Kandahar and your local contact. Based in Kandahar."

Ewan-Ian shook Tofan's hand.

"My work here is done. Good luck, Ian, or should I say, Ewan?" continued James, in English.

"Thank you. Drive safely back to wherever you're going," responded Ewan.

"I will."

"Let's go," said Tofan, in Pashto.

Ewan got his luggage and followed Tofan to the car.

"We have another long journey ahead of us," remarked Tofan.

"How long is the journey?" asked Ewan, in Pashto.

"Hopefully we will arrive in Kandahar by eight o'clock this evening. Get in."

Ewan obliged and Tofan set off.

"Is it your first time in Afghanistan?"

"Yes. And Pakistan. But I have been to France, the Netherlands, Russia and Canada."

"Your Pashto is encouraging. How long have you been learning?"

"A few months. From a cassette."

"Can you read Pashto, also?"

"I know the alphabet. I recognise some words. Sometimes it's difficult. When the letters connect."

"Yes. My English is like your Pashto."

"You speak English?" replied Ewan, in English.

"I speak English, but we must speak Pashto here," laughed Tofan.

"You are MI6. The men in the bookshop. Are they agents?"

"No, but they are friendly. They are Mujahideen. Although they hide this from the government officials, in Lashkar Gah. Do you understand?"

"Yes. I will work in the bookstore, no?"

"You will do whatever they require. Serving customers, Delivering books. Stock-taking."

"How do I know where the drugs are? Where can I buy heroin?"

"They will introduce you to people and places."

"How long will we stay in Kandahar?"

"That depends. I've heard a report I need to verify, before we drive to Lashkar Gah. Maybe one day. Maybe three."

"Do you mind if I sleep, for a while?"

"Be my guest."

Ewan rolled up his jacket and rested his head against the jacket and the frame. He was woken two hours later by the car pulling off the road and into a village. Tofan needed the toilet. Ewan took advantage of the same opportunity. They continued on their way.

"How many stops?" asked Ewan.

"Four or five. We'll stop in Ghazni, for lunch. There is a family I always visit. They are friends of the resistance."

After almost three more hours, they arrived in Ghazni, where Tofan wove his way through the streets and pulled up in front of a square, flat-roofed two storey house. There were two small boys, five and six, sitting on the steps, who ran over to the car when they realised it was Tofan. He scooped them both up in his arms and carried them back over to the steps.

"Uncle Tofan. Have you come to visit?"

"Who is the man, Uncle Tofan?"

"This is my friend Ewan."

"Do you play football, Mr Uvan?"

"Do you have a ball?" he asked.

The older boy ran into the house and came back out with a football, followed by his mother.

"You are welcome," she greeted Tofan.

Ewan had already gone to stand near the car and was kicking the football back to the younger boy. Tofan and the woman went indoors, and a few minutes later, she reappeared in the doorway.

"Time to eat," she called.

Ewan followed the boys into the house to be greeted by a meal of lamb and rice, spread out on the floor, with some dried fruits.

"Peace be upon you," he greeted the woman, sitting on a cushion, like Tofan.

He reminded himself not to use his left hand to eat, which made him a little cack-handed. The advantage was that using his right hand slowed him down, and he always ate too fast.

"What are your names?" Ewan asked the boys.

"This is Zaram and this is little Mehtar," she replied.

"Bazir and Gulnar have been friends for just over three years," explained Tofan. "Bazir is a mechanic, and I met him when my car broke down."

Mehtar made a crunching-donking sound and banged one hand into the other. They all laughed.

"Thank you for your welcome," said Ewan to Gulnar, helping himself to a dried apricot.

"Tofan's friends are our friends," she smiled.

Gulnar stood up and made some tea.

"Can we go and play, Mummy?" asked Mehtar.

"Yes, but please wash your hands first."

"When will you reach Kandahar?" Gulnar asked Tofan.

"Hopefully, by eight o'clock."

"I have heard there is a roadblock near Gelan. Please be careful."

"I heard the same."

"Time to go Ewan. The bathroom is outside at the back of the house."

Ewan went out into the backyard to find the small outhouse where he relieved himself. He went and kicked the ball while he waited for Tofan.

"Thank you. Goodbye," said Tofan, getting into the car.

"Yes. Thank you. Goodbye," repeated Ewan, jumping into the passenger seat.

They re-joined the main road and continued south until just before Gelan, where, just as Gulnar had suggested, they were stopped.

"You see that road," explained Tofan, "It goes up into the mountains. They might be searching for insurgents."

A Soviet soldier approached the car.

"Where are you going and where have you come from?"

"We have been visiting family in Ghazni and we are going to Kandahar," replied Tofan, in Russian.

This pleased the soldier, and he waved them through without asking to see their papers.

"Is it that easy? To get through a checkpoint, I mean?" asked Ewan, when they had passed the roadblock.

"The Soviets have taken a pasting on the international stage. Anyone who behaves like they appreciate the Soviets, like by speaking Russian, is welcomed with open arms."

"That is useful to know."

"It's easy enough to see who the Soviet sympathisers are, if they wear a uniform. It's a bit more difficult when they dress like us. Of course, another clue is when they're holding a Kalashnikov," laughed Tofan. "That said, some of the soldiers have been relieved of their weapons by the insurgents."

"So, if a Soviet soldier stops me, I should speak in Russian?"

"Yes. There may be more roadblocks. We can test my theory."

After another couple of hours, they stopped in another village, bought some bottled fizzy soft drinks, and used a toilet. Machine gun fire crackled in the distance, towards the mountains.

"Come on. Best to keep going."

They arrived at a second roadblock, near Qalat-e Gilzay. This time it was an Afghan flaunting a Kalashnikov.

"Where are you going? Papers please."

Ewan handed his passport to Tofan who held them up to the man. Ewan was slightly nervous, because he had blue eyes, not brown.

"I asked where you are going."

"Kandahar."

"What for?"

"We live there. We have been visiting family in Ghazni."

The man handed the passports back to Tofan.

"Long live the Communist government."

The man smiled and raised the barrier to let them through.

They made one more toilet stop, about ten miles beyond the roadblock, at the side of the road. Just as they were getting back in the car a Soviet armoured vehicle rumbled past, in the direction of Ghazni. Tofan waved. The soldier standing in the open hatch waved back.

"I really hate having to bow to the Soviets, but it's the best way to see another sunrise."

It was not the only military vehicle to pass them. There were two more armoured cars a few minutes after the first one.

"Probably has something to do with the machine gun fire and the reason for the roadblocks. I'm glad we are heading south to Kandahar. We're nearly there."

The outskirts of Kandahar came into view. Tofan turned off the main road as soon as possible and wove his way through the back streets. He stopped by a house, with a walled garden.

"We don't stay in a hotel?"

"No, my friend. We have a safe-house."

Tofan got out and opened the gate and got back in to drive through into the enclosure. Ewan jumped out and closed the gate behind them. They carried their things in from the car.

"Make yourself at home. I have to make a phone call."

Ewan used the bathroom and went into the kitchen. He could hear Tofan speaking on the phone but could not really make out what he was saying. He understood 'See you next week' and 'Goodbye'.

"Tonight, I will make us flat bread. In the garden. But first, please go and fill this with water, from the well."

Ewan went out into the garden to look for the well and drew up a bucket of water. Meanwhile, Tofan had come out of the house with the ingredients for flat bread in a bowl. He took a cup of water from the bucket Ewan had filled, and mixed, kneaded, and covered the dough with a cloth. There was a clay oven, and he started to stack some kindling inside it. The dry wood caught light immediately, and he added thicker lumps of wood.

"We must wait until the wood turns to hot ashes, before we can cook the bread. It's OK to drink the water you have taken from the well. It is clean."

"Thank you. I'm thirsty."

Ewan disappeared into the kitchen and came back outside with two cups. He filled both of them.

"I love this house and garden. Can you smell the flowers?"

Ewan breathed in deeply.

"Yes. Beautiful."

"I was talking to our field office. It appears that someone was stopped at the border with Iran, trafficking drugs. Unfortunately, they tried to escape and were shot and killed.

I don't know what this means, but it may be useful for you to be aware of it."

"Noted."

Tofan tested the embers.

"I think they're ready."

He took some of the dough and flattened it into a disc, placing it on a flat iron skillet, which he sat on top of the ashes. While it was cooking, he flattened out another one. After turning over the flat bread which was cooking, he went indoors and came out with some fruit and something which looked a little like curd cheese. He wrapped the cooked flat bread in a clean towel and cooked the second one, which he gave to Ewan, reserving the first one for himself.

"Tonight, we eat like kings," he laughed.

"It's very good," responded Ewan, after a few mouthfuls.

The curd cheese had an acquired taste, but he masked it with slices of mango and some other star-shaped fruit which he did not recognise.

"If you wish, we can sleep in hammocks, in the garden," suggested Tofan, pointing at a hammock, sensing Ewan didn't quite understand the word. "It is not too cold, with a blanket."

"Yes. It's a long time when I slept under the stars."

"I'm really impressed with your Pashto."

"Thanks."

Tofan put some water to boil in a small iron pan. He went indoors to get some tea leaves and a bowl. When the water boiled, he made two cups of tea and poured the rest of the boiling water into the bowl, adding some of the cold water from the bucket, until he could safely immerse his hands. He washed up.

"Perhaps tomorrow, we'll find out what the roadblocks were for."

"Perhaps we will. Thank you for a tasty meal."

"You're welcome. Now I will fetch a second hammock and some blankets. You won't need an alarm clock. There's a local cockerel to wake us up at five o'clock."

"Better to sleep, now. Goodnight."

"Goodnight."

Ewan clambered into his hammock and covered himself with a blanket. He was asleep in a matter of minutes. He woke at about three in the morning with a stiff shoulder. The pain prevented him from going back to sleep, but he was not too disappointed, because the starry sky was phenomenal, and he spent a long time trying to pick out constellations and work out which of the lights were stars and which were planets. He was awake when, just as Tofan had suggested, the cockerel crowed at five o'clock. Ewan got up and went to the bathroom. When he came back outside, Tofan was lighting the fire again, to make some tea.

"How did you sleep?"

"Well until about three. Then I lay awake and watched the stars. Do you have any paracetamol? My shoulder hurts me."

"I have something much better."

Tofan went indoors and came back out with a small glass bottle.

"Rub some of that in."

"What is it?"

"Cannabis oil. I picked it up last time I was in India. Works like a dream."

Ewan undid the bottle, poured a small amount into his palm, and rubbed it into his shoulder. After a few minutes, he realised he could not feel the pain anymore.

"Miracle medicine!"

"Has it worked?"

"Yes."

"I often use some on aches and pains after a fight."

"Do you fight often?"

"I try not to. Occupational hazard."

"What would you like for breakfast. I can make some bread."

"Yes please."

The fire was about ready for the water, and while the pan boiled, Tofan made up some dough. He added some honey to the mix and some raisins and pulverised a piece of cinnamon stick, rolling the dough into small buns. When the water boiled, he made tea, and put the buns on the embers to bake.

"Where did you learn to cook?" inquired Ewan.

"At home," replied Tofan, his face changing to a sad expression. "My wife was killed when the Soviets invaded. I looked after our children. They liked buns."

"I'm sorry. Where are your children?"

"With their grandparents. I had to work, and this job is unpredictable and dangerous."

"Is this your home?"

"It was. It is. Now it's not so much a home as a safehouse. There's no laughter. No children's toys."

"Do you see your children?"

"Every three to four months, for a weekend."

There was a short silence.

"Today, I will show you some places in Kandahar. I know you will focus on Lashkar Gah, but I want you to see the houses and farms we have been watching, here."

They got in the car, and Tofan drove them to several different locations. One such place was a farm, on the outskirts of the city.

"I have heard Russian spoken here. I cannot tell you if it's drugs or soldiers."

"Or both," responded Ewan, with an element of sarcasm.

They drove to another farm.

"I have seen armoured cars here, as well as trucks coming and going in the middle of the night. I believe this is part of the weapons distribution that is funded by drugs. That is our problem. Your problem is the drugs distribution."

"What was the report you spoke about?"

"Ah, yes. It is worrying. Some of the poppy farms were raided earlier this week and farmers were killed. Our reports suggest it was either Soviet troops or Russian drug barons. Mujahideen are more than likely to retaliate and then it will probably escalate."

"The reason for the roadblocks?"

"Wrong area. Helmand is too far south. Look at this map. The Mujahideen are more active in the north of Helmand. Your area of interest will be south of Lashkar Gah, all around here, I think. Here is the road from Kandahar to Herat. The Iran border is here. Helmand Province goes all the way down here, to the border."

"What will you do?"

"Well, if you are happy to look after yourself, today, I will go and see what I can find out."

"It is better to stay here?"

"I think so, for now."

Later that afternoon, while Ewan was catching up on his sleep, Tofan went to the field office.

"What have you been doing?" asked Ewan when he returned to the house.

"I have discovered that a farm near Marjah was burned. You might want to investigate further. And, I found out that the drug trafficker who was killed at the border, near Herat, was Dutch."

"I met a man in Amsterdam who sold drugs, and I bought drugs from a man in Utrecht. I wonder if they were connected."

Tofan had come home with meat, and he now prepared some chicken to cook with rice. Ewan lit the fire and fetched water from the well.

"How's your shoulder?"

"I don't feel it."

"Tomorrow, I will drive you to Lashkar Gah and introduce you to the booksellers," declared Tofan, as he crushed some garlic.

"Thank you."

Tofan mixed the garlic and spices together in yoghurt, and marinated the chicken in it, whilst he boiled some rice. When the rice was ready, he skewered the pieces of chicken and placed them in the oven. He chopped various herbs from the garden and mixed them with some oil and lemon juice, stirring it into the rice. It was not long before the chicken skewers were ready. He served up the rice on two plates and stripped the skewers of the pieces of chicken, on top the rice.

"There. Enjoy."

"Thank you. It smells good."

Before tucking into his own plate, Tofan put a pan of water to boil. The food was excellent.

"It tastes very good," confirmed Ewan.

When they finished their chicken, Tofan made tea and offered Ewan a plate of cookies. At least, that was what he would have described them as. They were pistachio flavoured.

"I didn't make these," confessed Tofan. "I bought them."

"Thank you."

"Now listen. Seriously. I will visit you once a week in the bookstore to buy a book. Here is the field office phone number if you have an emergency. Wear your gun at all times. You are a student, learning Pashto, living in Lashkar Gah for a few months, working in a bookstore."

"I understand."

Ewan did the washing up and they played a game of chess. They slept in the hammocks for a second night, with Ewan sleeping a lot better than the previous night. Predictably, they were rudely awoken at five o'clock by the cockerel. Tofan lowered himself from his hammock and went to light the fire. Ewan drew some water from the well.

"Bread and fruit for breakfast, if you're hungry."

"Can I make the bread?"

"If you want. Need any instructions?"

"Don't think so. Just measures."

"Measures! I guess. Whatever feels right."

"Please guess for me."

Tofan put the ingredients in a bowl and handed it to Ewan, who mixed it together and kneaded it, while Tofan made the tea. When the tea was ready, Ewan rolled out some flat breads and cooked them in the skillet.

"It hasn't had time to prove. Hope it's OK."

"Not bad, my friend, not bad," Tofan encouraged him.

At the end of their meal, Ewan did the washing up and went to pack his belongings, while Tofan checked the fuel, oil and water in the car.

"Today is a much shorter journey, but the one where we are most likely to be stopped."

Ewan put his belongings in the car and went to open the gate. Tofan drove out of the enclosure, Ewan closed the gate, and they headed out of the city. It was not long before they saw a Soviet tank, at the side of the road. Tofan smiled as they drove past, and the tank commander raised a hand in response.

"Every smile is in the hope of revenge for my wife's death. I hate the Soviets. I want to live in a free Afghanistan. Not a conservative religious republic and not a Communist Party controlled state. The western allies are supporting the Mujahideen to rise up against the Soviets, but I fear the consequences, when the Soviets eventually leave."

Ewan nodded. He thought he understood what Tofan had just said.

They came to a roadblock which Tofan talked them through.

"Did you understand the conversation?"

"They were asking if we had seen any Mujahideen, yes?"

"Yes. They told us to keep our eyes open. Like I would report it to the authorities!"

They could see Lashkar Gah in the distance.

"Lashkar Gah is a beautiful city. It's on the River Helmand."

Driving into the city, they were passed by two more Soviet tanks and some soldiers.

"I think they have nothing better to do than drive round all day," reflected Tofan, sarcastically.

The car turned into a street and slowed to avoid running over a group of boys who were playing football. Tofan crawled along, smiling at them, until one of the boys picked the ball up and stood aside to let the car through.

"Thank you," called Tofan through the open window, as they passed.

He pulled up at the end of the street, next to a bookshop.

"Bring your belongings in with you. I never trust leaving things in my car."

Ewan grabbed his things and Tofan led them into the shop. The two men inside hugged him.

"This is Salar and Faridun. I present Ewan to you."

"Peace be upon you," said Ewan.

To Ewan's surprise both men hugged him, also.

"Welcome to the cause," Salar greeted him.

"Shall we eat and drink before you leave, Tofan?" asked Faridun.

"Yes, my brothers. We shall eat."

Salar led them out of the back of the shop into the living area, where they and Ewan, would be residing. It was cramped but clean. There was a backyard with a fire for cooking, and their lunch was steaming away in a cauldron.

"Please. Sit down," Faridun gestured to Ewan and Tofan.

They sat on the floor. Salar brought over some drinks and Faridun tended the cauldron.

"It is nearly ready," he commented, placing some bread and dried fruit on the floor in front of the guests. "Five minutes more."

"You speak Pashto, yes?" Salar asked Ewan.

"A little."

"He speaks Pashto well, for an English man," interjected Tofan, laughing.

"Do you like books?" inquired Faridun.

"To sell books was my job. But not in a shop."

"Where did you sell books?" Faridun pressed him.

"International. I made phone calls. We sent the books by mail. Mostly English and French."

"You speak French, as well?" responded Salar.

"And Russian."

"We will become an international bookshop," laughed Faridun. "I will serve our food, now."

He spooned the casserole onto a large dish.

"Enjoy!" he added, setting it on the floor in the middle of the men.

Ewan broke off some bread with his right hand and scooped up some of the meat and sauce. It was a little chewy. He thought it must be lamb. Between them, they polished off the entire dish and finished their meal with some dates. Tofan got up to leave. He stood with his arms stretched out, inviting a hug from Ewan. Ewan stepped towards him.

"Be safe, my brother."

"You too," replied Ewan.

"I will see you next week."

"Of course."

Tofan hugged Salar and Faridun and left.

"Come," gestured Salar, "I will show you how we sell books, here."

Ewan followed him back out to the shop, leaving Faridun to clear away the lunch things.

"The shop sells new and second-hand books. The new books are all at the front. Fiction on this side. Non-fiction on that side. Alphabetical. Don't forget we read from right to left," explained Salar.

"Do you sell a lot of books?"

"Business is OK. We have to sell certain newer books that, how shall I say, support the Soviet Union."

"That must be hard."

"You do what you have to do. The second-hand books are just lined up in crates, in no particular order."

Ewan started to browse the spines of the books in one of the crates and stopped at one that was entitled 'The History of Bost.'

"Bost?"

"That's what the city used to be called, many years ago."

Ewan took hold of the book and started to flick through it. The pages were filled with photographs.

"Are all these things in the city?"

"I imagine so."

"I will explore on my days off."

"Are we giving you days off?" laughed Salar.

Ewan joined in the amusement.

"We understand. We know you have other work to do. Special work. We trust Tofan."

Just then, Faridun joined them.

"How familiar are you with Afghan currency?" he asked, taking a note from the till.

"Not a lot. I haven't spent any money since I arrived."

"Come with me. We have an errand to run."

Faridun led Ewan to the market, where they bought some food for the evening meal. Ewan listened to the voices around him, trying to make out what was being said. When Faridun had made the purchases in the market, they walked to where many of the shops were.

"There is a bank here if you need it. That is a good tailor, there. This is an interesting shop. They fix things."

"Fix things?"

"Radios, bicycles, tools. If it's broken, usually, they can fix it. They fix things and sell them."

"Perhaps I shall buy a bicycle."

"Can you drive?"

"Maybe."

"You can borrow our car. Practise?"

"Thank you."

"I love this shop," declared Faridun.

Ewan looked up to see a line of kites fluttering in the breeze.

"I first came here when I was five years old. My first kite was my birthday present."

"Lots of people fly kites here, don't they?"

"Yes. There are competitions. Can you fly a kite?"

"I don't know. When I was a child, I tried."

"I will teach you. You must buy a kite, if you are good at flying my kite."

"Thanks."

"There is a competition, here, in the city, soon. We must attend."

"Yes, please."

"Do you have sunglasses? So, you can look up to the sky."

"No."

They returned to the bookshop and Ewan browsed amongst the books until a customer came in. He watched the transaction. The bookshop was his cover, not a proper job, but he needed to know the basic processes, in case he was on his own, when a customer came in. Otherwise, he would be given books to deliver, and the use of Salar and Faridun's car, which would allow him to travel around the local area.

"I have a question," proffered Ewan, when the customer left.

"What do you want to know?" replied Faridun.

"Do you know where I can buy heroin, locally? It's not for me to use! Where is it sold?"

"There is a man in the cafe we passed, just close to the bank, who sells something. I think he speaks Pashto and Russian. There is a farm, not far from here. The friend of a friend buys heroin there. Maybe they can help."

"Thank you."

Three weeks went by, with Ewan learning the ropes at the bookshop, and familiarising himself with the city, whilst running errands. He was asked to take a parcel of books to a house on the outskirts of the city. The delivery address was in the direction of the farm where he thought he could buy drugs, so having delivered his parcel, Ewan drove to the farm. He had his gun, and he was very nervous. When he arrived at the gates, it was obviously not a place where you bought drugs. No guards. No locked gate. He parked by the gate and got out. As he stepped up to the gate, a large dog came towards him, running and barking. That was why there were no guards. A man, in traditional clothing but carrying a Kalashnikov, came out of the door and walked down the garden.

"What do you want?" he asked, as he arrived at the gate.

"Is this where I can buy heroin?"

"This is a farm."

"Yes. A poppy farm. I would like to buy some heroin."

"Go away," responded the man abruptly, removing the Kalashnikov from his shoulder.

"It's OK. I'm going," said Ewan, holding up his hands, and backing away.

He got back in the car and accelerated away. Ewan was sure, from the man's reaction, that the farm did sell heroin. He just was not sure how to be able to gain access and buy some. As he drove back into the city, he weighed up the pros and cons of returning on another occasion. Maybe he would have better luck with the man in the café, although how he was supposed to recognise the man who sold drugs was beyond him. He could not very well walk up to someone and ask them if they sold heroin. That was when he remembered the man in The Prince Albert, who used to sit at a table and sell drugs to other customers, right under the landlord's nose.

The following week, Ewan went each day, and drank tea in the café. He took along *The History of Bost*, to disguise his purpose for being there, and positioned himself in such a way that he could read and keep one eye on the comings and goings. To his surprise, by the end of the third day, he was sure that one of the customers was exchanging something under the table where he sat, with different customers who sat opposite. Ewan decided to return the following day, in the hope that the exchanges continued to be made. He was disappointed and resolved to return to the café the following Wednesday, since it was on a Wednesday that he had first seen the transactions being made. He returned to the bookshop, where Tofan was drinking tea, with Salar and Faridun.

"My brother. Peace be upon you," he said, hugging Ewan.

"And on you. Good week?"

"You know me. Here, there and everywhere. Shall we go into the back room, so we can talk, in case a customer comes in?"

Salar nodded, and Tofan and Ewan took their tea into the living room.

"So?"

"I asked the brothers where I can buy heroin. They told me about a farm and a café. I visited the farm, and a man threatened me with an AK-47. I left. Pretty sure they have drugs. This week I saw a man in the café change something under the table. I will return next Wednesday and ask him for drugs."

"Good. Anything else? Do you have everything you need?"

"Yes. Thank you."

"Then let us go back out to the brothers."

They got up from the settee and went back into the shop. Tofan and the others started chattering away in Pashto, far too fast for Ewan to follow all of it. He listened and smiled. This was three months of his life, six at worst. These guys had to live in this place. They needed each other's encouragement, not to entertain him. Twenty minutes later, the conversation slowed to a halt and Tofan said his goodbyes.

"See you next week, Ewan."

"Take care."

He left the shop.

"Time to shut, I think," reflected Salar.

"I'll go and start the cooking. Do you want to light the fire, Ewan?"

"Of course."

The following Wednesday, Ewan was not disappointed. The same man was sitting there. Ewan found it difficult to distinguish between the bearded faces, but this man had a particularly aquiline nose, so he was sure it was the same person. He sat down opposite the man.

"Hello. I wish to buy heroin. Can you help?"

The man looked uneasy. Perhaps it was because he did not recognise Ewan.

"Not here. Come to back of this building in one hour."

"How much?"

"One hundred afghani."

"What will I get?"

"You ask too many questions. One hour."

The man got up and left. Ewan ordered some tea and remained at the table for the next fifty minutes, whereupon he used the toilet and went for a short stroll, arriving behind the café at the appointed time. He stood by the rear entrance looking up the street. Suddenly, he froze, as he felt the muzzle of a rifle in his back.

"Who are you?"

"My name is Ewan. I am a student. I am studying Pashto and Arabic at university. I am working in a bookshop for six months, to speak Pashto better."

"Turn around. Slowly."

Ewan turned slowly to face the man with the rifle and smiled.

"I just need some drugs. It's lonely here."

He was not quite sure why he gave that explanation, but it just came out.

"Do you have the money?"

Ewan reached into his pocket and brought out the cash. The man took it from him, reached into his own pocket, and handed Ewan a small package.

"If you are lonely, you can spend time with me and my friends. Come to the café in the evening. Seven o'clock, any day except Fridays."

"Thanks."

The man went back into the café, leaving Ewan slightly shaky, standing in the street. He walked back to the bookshop, checked he had been sold what he thought he had paid for, and stuck it in his holdall, beneath his clothes.

The offer of spending time with the man and his friends was something Ewan knew he had to explore. Unlike the 'banya', he knew what he might be letting himself in for, this time, so the following evening, having told Salar where he was going, in case he did not make it home, he headed back to the café. The man with the aquiline nose was playing some sort of card game with two others.

"Ewan. Peace be upon you. Welcome. Sit down and we'll deal you in. I am Atal. This is Gharzan and this is Rokhan."

"Peace be upon you," responded Ewan, sitting down. "What is the game?"

"Teka. It's for four players, but sometimes, we adapt it to three. Now you are here, we can play properly. You can partner with Gharzan. We deal the cards and then we have an auction. The winner chooses trumps. We play. You'll see."

He dealt the cards and Gharzan bid five. Rokhan bid six.

"How many more can you win, added to Gharzan's five?"

"Ace is the top, yes?"

"Yes."

Ewan pondered a moment.

"Maybe two more. Seven."

"Nine," responded Atal.

"Pass," said Gharzan.

They started to play. Ewan thought it was similar to Solo and after a few rounds, he felt he understood the game better. He and Gharzan kept winning. After six rounds, Atal ordered some tea.

"Where are you studying?" asked Atal.

"London."

Ewan knew he was now making up his life-story. It would be too complicated to factor in Canada.

"I would love to go to London," declared Rokhan. "You are the second man I know who is from London."

"Really?"

"Yes. He came here last year."

"I want to go to Moscow," stated Atal, somewhat categorically.

"Why Moscow?" asked Ewan.

"Why Moscow? Isn't it obvious? I want to go to where the soldiers come from."

"Do you speak Russian?"

"Yes. A little. Well. Not very much at all, but I have a Russian friend."

Ewan was now curious.

"Is your friend a soldier?"

"No. He sells paintings. I met him about eighteen months ago. He visits every month."

"Paintings? Are they famous paintings?"

"No. Modern paintings. He came in here asking if I knew someone who makes the frames. I told him, the only place I knew was the shop behind the market, where they fix things."

"And he teaches you Russian? Wow. Russian too difficult for me."

"We talk. Mostly in Pashto. Then he tells me what the words are in Russian. And simple phrases. 'What is this?' or 'How are you?' It's hard to speak, but it's enjoyable. If he comes when you are here, I'll introduce you to him."

When Ewan left the café, he believed he had stumbled on a Russian drug-smuggling connexion. It would be easy to hide heroin in picture frames. Surely, someone who visited every month was up to no good. Modern art covered a multitude of styles and examples, and was unlikely to draw attention to itself, not like old masters. Of course, it could be no more than innocuous transporting of modern art, but Ewan had grown suspicious of any toing and froing that involved Russians. He resolved to find an excuse to spend some time in the shop where things got fixed and see what he could hear. Perhaps they would teach him how to fix something. A radio. Or a bicycle, maybe. He was not too sure he wanted to be introduced to Atal's Russian friend, just in case he recognised him from somewhere, but he would talk to Tofan about it, when he saw him.

The next time Tofan came to the shop, Ewan shared his thoughts.

"I think I have discovered something. I bought drugs from the man at the café. I told him I take drugs because I am lonely. He invited me to join his friends in the café. We played cards. He told me a Russian man teaches him Russian. The friend visits regularly and he sells paintings. The frames are made in the shop where they fix things. I want to spend time there. Maybe they teach me to fix a bike or a radio or something?"

"It's possible. They make money from selling the things they fix. If you fix something yourself, they don't make any money. Try telling them you are a student. You work in the bookshop, but you would like to help them and learn more Pashto. Tell them you will let them keep the bike or the radio, to sell."

"Good idea. Do you know where I can find a broken radio or a broken bike?"

"I will see what I can do."

To Ewan's surprise, Tofan returned to the bookshop, later the same day. He brought with him a cardboard box, which he presented to Ewan, grinning from ear to ear. Ewan looked inside to find a radio.

"Wow. Thank you. Is it broken?"

"Not yet. But it soon will be," joked Tofan, taking a screwdriver from his bag and opening the back of the radio.

Ewan watched him unscrew one of the screws which held the speaker in place and break off a few of the tiny components. Not enjoying physics at school, Ewan did not remember what the components were. Tofan also broke the connection on one of the wires attached to the speaker.

"These are not expensive to replace. Hopefully this will give you a couple of sessions with the men in the shop. I will try to find you a broken bike, now."

"Thank you."

Tofan left him with the radio and the following day, Ewan took it to the shop where they fixed things.

"Hello. Peace be upon you."

"Peace be upon you also."

"My name is Ewan and I study Pashto. I would like to spend some time with you. I would like to learn to fix this radio. You can keep it, afterwards. I only want to learn and chat."

"Let me see the radio."

Ewan handed the man the box containing the broken radio and a couple of the components which Tofan had broken.

"Well, Ewan. Sit down and we will fix your radio."

"Thank you. What is your name?"

"My name is Bahrawar. How long will you stay in Lashkar Gah?"

"Six months."

"Don't you miss your family?"

"Yes, but I write to them. Do you have a family?"

"I have a wife and two sons."

"How old are your sons?"

"Fifteen and thirteen. Do you know how a radio works?"

"No."

"I will try to explain. This is the power supply. We need to fix this connection. That is the oscillator. It makes a wave. This is the modulator. It adds the words and music to the wave. This is the transmitter, here. This one is the amplifier. That is the antenna. Can you solder?"

"I'm sorry. I don't understand."

Bahrawar pointed at the soldering iron.

"Show me how, please."

Bahrawar demonstrated how to make a soldered joint.

"Now you try."

Ewan soldered the next joint along.

"Good. Here are the new components. I will not show you anymore. Let's see if you can do it by yourself."

Bahrawar was grinning at Ewan. For the next few minutes, Ian soldered the various components in place. When he had finished, Bahrawar checked over the connections but said nothing. He handed Ewan two batteries.

"Now let's see if it will work."

Ewan slotted in the batteries and switched on the radio. Nothing. He looked at Bahrawar, who stood up and reached for another radio that was on a high shelf.

"Open this radio and see if you can identify what is wrong with your radio," he instructed Ewan, encouragingly.

It took another two attempts on Ewan's part before he switched on his radio and a crackling sound came out.

"Try tuning it," suggested Bahrawar, moving his fingers like he was turning a knob.

Ewan turned the tuner knob slowly to the right and picked up some words.

"That is our local radio station. If you listen, it will help you to learn Pashto."

"You are very kind. Thank you for showing me how to fix the radio," responded Ewan, holding it out for Bahrawar to take.

"No, no, no," he insisted. "You must take it to listen to the radio. You can come here on Tuesdays and Thursdays to help me fix things."

"Really! Thank you so much."

"You are welcome, Ewan."

Ewan noted how the shop was laid out. All the electrical items were at one side, next to small household items. Opposite were bicycles and small garden or farm machinery. At the back of the shop, on the same side as the electrical items, were piles of wood and sheets of cardboard. Ewan could see some framed paintings, sitting on the floor by the work bench. He knew better than to ask about the picture framing part of the business.

After Ewan's third session fixing things in the shop, Tofan found him a decrepit old bicycle. Ewan carried it to the shop.

"My landlord gave me this. Can we fix it? Then it's your bicycle."

Bahrawar looked over it and smiled.

"My eldest son needs a bicycle. When it is ready you must come and eat with my family. You can meet my sons. They will want to know who fixed the bicycle."

"It will be my pleasure."

He busied himself with the bicycle, something he knew more about than a radio or record player, while Bahrawar worked on a picture frame. Ewan was watching out of the corner of his eye, and he saw Bahrawar empty some powder all over a piece of cardboard, squeeze glue round the edge and cover it with another piece of cardboard, the same dimensions. Bahrawar positioned the picture on the top piece and fixed the frame to the back piece of cardboard. He lent it against some others, against the leg of the work bench.

No one would suspect that the backboard was double thickness, just from looking at the finished article. Ewan was sure that the powder was heroin. Once Bahrawar had made up two more framed paintings, he wrapped them individually in brown paper, along with the ones stacked on the floor. Finally, he put them into three lots of four and bound them together in cellophane, ready to be collected, presumably by the friend who spoke Russian.

As well as putting bits of machinery back together, Ewan was trying to piece together a figurative puzzle. He was not in the shop on the days when the framed paintings were removed. But on Thursdays, there were never any cellophane-wrapped packages leaning on the work bench. The shop was closed on Fridays. On Tuesdays and Thursdays, Bahrawar probably made up twenty-five picture frames. If he did the same on Mondays and Wednesdays, that was fifty paintings. Based on the size of the books he used to deliver for Caroline and Katya, six at a time, Ewan calculated that the amount of heroin being sprinkled across each painting was probably double the amount concealed in each book. That was a lot of heroin.

It did not appear that Bahrawar lived at the shop, in the same way Salar and Faridun lived at the bookshop. That would leave a reasonable amount of storage space. Ewan had gone to the toilet, at the back of the shop, but the door he passed along the corridor was always shut and padlocked. He was afraid to ask what was in the room, because if Bahrawar was hiding things, he would be both suspicious and angry that Ewan had looked, and probably stop Ewan from going to the shop. Of course, it could simply be where Bahrawar kept the takings of the business. Somehow, Ewan needed to find out where the paintings went and when. Being able to find out what the powder was, for definite, would be useful, as well. He wondered if Tofan might be able to organise a nocturnal break-in. That said, Tofan would have to gain entrance to the premises, pick the padlock, unwrap, cut open, re-glue and re-wrap one of the paintings, and exit the premises without being discovered and without leaving any sign of the operation. It was a lot to ask.

He was still pondering the situation when he went to the café that evening, to play cards with Atal and his friends. Gharzan and Rokhan were at their usual table, but there was no sign of Atal. Ewan walked over to the table and sat down with them.

"Peace be upon you. How are you?"

"Hello. Peace be upon you also. Life is good," replied Gharzan.

"Good to see you again," added Rokhan. "Atal will be late. He is meeting his Russian friend."

Ewan could not believe his good fortune, although there was no guarantee, this Russian would not be someone he knew or who might recognise him. He had his gun in a leg holster.

"Deal the cards," he said.

Rokhan had just dealt the cards when Atal walked in with a taller man, in traditional clothes, and with blond hair under his turban.

"This is Dimitri. Dimitri, please meet Ewan and Rokhan and Gharzan. They are my friends."

"I am pleased to meet you," replied Dimitri, in Pashto. "May I buy everyone tea?"

He went to the counter and ordered tea. Atal grabbed a chair from a nearby table and dragged it over to where they were playing cards.

"Do you come here often?" asked Ewan, trying to make conversation which would give him clues about the operation.

"I come here to buy paintings. Every month."

"What do you do with the paintings? Is your house full of art?"

"Haha. I take them to Paris," replied Dimitri, and added, rubbing his fingers together, "And I sell them. Big profit."

The men laughed. The tea was brought over to them.

"Do you like to fly?"

"I don't fly. I drive to Istanbul. I take the train to Paris."

"Is that a long journey?"

"Three days. Do you like Lashkar Gah?"

"Yes. It is a beautiful city. I am here for six months. Maybe I travel with you to Paris, when I return to London?"

"It is a good idea."

"Thank you."

"Now, we must play cards."

Atal dealt four hands.

"Rokhan, you can watch. Next game, I watch. And so on."

"Agreed," replied Rokhan.

That evening, when Ewan returned to the bookshop, he was impatient to see Tofan again. Could it be that he had just discovered the route to Paris? He was so pumped with adrenaline he could not sleep. He would have loved a glass of vodka, but there was no alcohol in the house, and he did not want to offend his hosts.

Tofan arrived at lunchtime on Wednesday.

"Peace be upon you, my brothers," he greeted Ewan, Salar and Faridun.

"And upon you," replied Ewan, securing the first hug.

Tofan hugged them all.

"I've brought lunch," he announced, holding up a bag. "Roast chicken and some of my homemade bread."

"Sounds great," responded Ewan.

"I'll get things ready for us," added Salar, disappearing out of the back of the shop.

They feasted on the chicken and bread, followed by some tea.

"We'll leave you to talk," suggested Salar, gesturing to Faridun that they should return to the shop.

"I have so much to tell you."

"Tell me, then."

"I have met the Russian who transports the paintings. His name is Dimitri. He takes them to Paris on the train. He drives to Istanbul. I asked can I travel with him when I will return to London. He said yes. I have seen Bahrawar put the frames on paintings in the shop where we fix things. He puts powder between two backs. The paintings are wrapped in brown paper. Three or four paintings are wrapped together in plastic. I think they are put in a room. The door has a padlock."

"That is amazing. You have been busy!"

"I've been lucky."

"Is the shop locked? Does someone live there?"

"No one lives there. Yes. It is locked at night."

"I think I will carry out surveillance."

"So, I continue doing what I am doing? Playing cards with Atal. Fixing things in the shop?"

"Yes. But see if you can discover where Bahrawar gets the heroin from. It could be at the shop on the days you aren't there, or he goes to a farm. Also, try and find out if Atal and Bahrawar know each other. After all, it was Atal who sold you the drugs. Maybe he delivers to the shop where they fix things. He is keen to learn Russian."

"I can follow Atal, perhaps? Bahrawar has invited me to his house to meet his sons."

"He may not take the drugs home. That part of his life may be just at the shop. It is also going to be hard to follow Atal. Even if you were to be invisible in the city, it would be obvious if you followed him to a farm. Find out what car he drives, if you can."

"I am going to the café this evening."

"Then, be safe. Until next time my brother."

Tofan stood and hugged Ewan. Ewan went out to the café.

After the evening's second game of Teka, Ewan started a conversation about driving.

"You know, here in Laskar Gah, I miss my car," he reflected, randomly.

"Your car?"

"Yes. I have an old Morgan."

"You have a sports car?" asked a surprised Gharzan.

"I thought you said you were a student," laughed Rokhan.

"I am a student. The Morgan was broken. Rusty. It was the car of the grandfather of a friend. He asked me to fix it. My friend doesn't drive. When he will have his licence, the car will be his."

"It's true. You do like to fix things," added Atal.

"Yes. That is why I help Bahrawar at the shop where they fix things."

"You know Bahrawar?" asked Atal, his curiosity piqued.

"Yes. He teaches me to fix electrical things. And I fix tools and metal things."

"Do you help him with fixing wooden things?" Atal pressed him.

"The picture frames? No. Do you know Bahrawar?"

"He is my brother-in-law."

"So, you are an uncle?" smiled Ewan.

"Yes. Has he told you about his sons?"

"I fixed a bike. He gave it to his sons. He has invited me to meet his sons."

"They are good young men."

"So, what cars do you all drive?"

"A lorry. I don't have a car," answered Rokhan.

"I have a Lada," replied Atal.

"I don't drive," added Gharzan, a little sheepishly.

"Is your Lada a good car? Does it break down?"

"Could you fix it, if it did break down?"

"I don't know. I only fixed a Morgan, and someone helped me with the engine. I repaired the outside and painted it. Red. What colour is your Lada?"

"Grey."

"And your lorry, Rokhan. How big or old is your lorry?"

"It is a small lorry. It is very old."

"Do cars have tests here? Every year, to say they are safe? Like in my country?"

"You must be joking!" laughed Gharzan.

"I would really like to drive a tank," declared Ewan, laughing.

"A tank?" replied Atal.

"Yes. I have seen tanks on the road. I think they are fun to drive, yes?"

"Soviet tanks? You are dreaming," Rokhan ribbed him.

"I must go, my friends. Peace be upon you," Ewan said, getting up to leave.

"Hey Ewan," said Atal, just as he turned to walk out. "Do you want to come to a poppy farm with me?"

"Yes please. When?"

"I will tell you next week."

Ewan left, happy in the knowledge that Atal and Bahrawar were brothers-in-law, that Atal drove a grey Lada, and that he seemed slightly nervous about Ewan's involvement with the picture frames. The invitation to see a poppy farm was a bonus.

The following week was a busy one for Ewan, in as much as his usual routine was added to by a meal with Bahrawar's family and a trip to a poppy farm with Atal. Tofan would come on Wednesday and Saturday. Atal turned up at the shop where they fix things on the Tuesday afternoon.

"Peace be upon you," he greeted his brother-in-law and Ewan. "Tomorrow, I will pick you up here, at nine o'clock in the morning, and take you to see a poppy farm."

"I look forward to it."

"Now I have somewhere I need to be."

Atal left the shop.

"And after work on Thursday, you must come and eat at my home," announced Bahrawar.

"Thank you. I look forward to that, also."

"My sons will be so happy."

"What are your sons' names?"

"Baseer and Khialay."

"Are they in school?"

"Yes. Baseer wants to be a mechanic. Khialay wants to be a doctor."

"One fixes cars. The other fixes people," chuckled Ewan.

"And what do you want to do, Ewan? When you finish your studies."

"I don't know. I like to work with people. I like to sell things. Perhaps I will be a diplomat, in this region."

"A diplomat? What use are diplomats, when we are always at war?"

"A good question. I will try to stop war."

Ewan fixed a hand-powered sewing machine. Bahrawar made some more picture frames. After lunch, he took the car keys from the shelf.

"I have to drive to Kandahar. Please look after the shop for me. I will be back after closing time. Please lock up the shop and take the keys with you."

"Certainly."

Bahrawar left Ewan to his own devices.

As the afternoon wore on, Ewan was sorely tempted to take a peek in the storeroom, but worried Bahrawar might find out. Instead, he came up with a better idea. After locking up and going back to the bookshop, Ewan took one of his spare bars of soap, and made an imprint of the front door key, the rear door key and two other smaller keys, which looked like padlock keys. He wrapped the bar of soap in brown paper and placed it in a plastic bag. Having scribbled a short note, 'I am eating at Bahrawar's tomorrow evening', he dropped it in the bag and tied the handles together.

"Tomorrow, please will you give this to Tofan. I must go to a farm with Atal."

"Certainly," replied Salar. "Put it next to the kettle, when you leave in the morning."

"I will."

In the morning, Ewan not only put the package by the kettle, but also wrote a small note, 'Please remember the parcel', which he stuck on the counter, next to the order book. He took the keys over to the shop where they fix things and greeted Bahrawar.

"Peace be upon you."

"And you. Thank you for looking after the shop."

"You are welcome."

"I had to go to Kandahar to buy more paintings, to fill the frames I make. It is a good business for me. The wood comes from old furniture and the paintings are painted by a cousin. I make a decent profit from Dimitri."

"I see."

Ewan wondered how much profit Dimitri made, or Krukov, but he was not about to pass comment. Bahrawar unlocked the shop and Ewan waited outside. It was not long before Atal pulled up in his grey Lada.

"Peace be upon you."

"And on you," replied Ewan, getting into the car.

"Is petrol expensive here?"

"We have oil in Afghanistan. But prices are going up. And in England?"

"Prices are rising."

Atal drove them across the river, on the road towards Marjah. They drove past the farm where Ewan had been threatened with a Kalashnikov. He could see Atal's Kalashnikov sticking out from under a blanket, on the back seat. Ewan had his gun in his leg holster, well hidden under his baggy trousers. After driving for about three quarters of an hour, Atal turned off the main road onto a track. They were driving into the sun, and Ewan put his sunglasses on, so he could see the landscape. Halfway between the track and the farm, a dark vehicle was speeding towards them. Atal pulled off the side of the track to let it past. The driver hardly slowed down, but Ewan could tell it was a Mercedes. He was also quite certain that the driver bore an uncanny resemblance to Nikolai. Ewan was so glad he had put his sunglasses on.

Atal pulled up in front of a dilapidated looking farmhouse, with a newer, more robust-looking concrete-block-built barn to the side. They got out of the car. Ewan could see poppies growing in abundance, in a field beyond the farmhouse and barn.

"Come," gestured Atal.

He walked beyond the farmhouse and barn, like he belonged there, and led Ewan to the brow of a low hill. As they reached the top, the land opened up beyond, and all Ewan could see were opium poppies. The closer flowers were fluttering in the breeze. The flowers that were further away, created a pastel shaded palette.

"Wow! That is beautiful," he remarked.

"Yes, it is. It is my family business. Come. I will show you the best part."

He turned back down the hill and took Ewan into the barn where machinery was whirring, and three men were wearing clean white clothing.

"This is where the flowers turn into profit."

"The heroin that you sold me comes from here?"

"Yes. Do you need to buy some more?"

"Yes. But I don't have enough money with me."

"Tonight, when we play cards."

"Yes. Thank you."

As Ewan stood looking at the operation, Atal approached one of the men in white clothing. They spoke in Russian. Ewan could not hear properly, but he definitely heard the name, 'Krukov'. He was pretty sure that the man in white clothing said, 'Krukov wants to double production and distribution', and Atal replied, 'It is a good year'. Ewan was trying not to look like he was listening, because he had not let on that he understood or spoke Russian. He watched Atal enter a room, towards the rear of the barn and came out carrying a small package, which he put in his pocket. Ewan surmised it was the heroin that he would purchase in the evening, and several other people's too. The man in white clothing who had spoken Russian looked at Ewan and nodded at him. Ewan raised his hand in greeting.

"We must go home, now."

The two men got into Atal's Lada, and headed back to Lashkar Gah. Atal dropped Ewan off at the shop where they fix things.

"See you later."

"Yes. Thank you. Interesting farm."

The shop was closed, so Ewan went back to the bookshop. He went into the back room and rummaged around in the bottom of his holdall, where he retrieved a bundle of money. He took out one hundred afghani, wrapped the remaining notes back up, and squashed them back down into the depths of the holdall. The evening meal was ready, out in the back yard. He went out to join Salar and Faridun, neither of whom had noticed his arrival.

"Peace be upon you. Was today a good day?" he asked them.

"Tofan came. We gave him your parcel. What have you been doing?"

"I saw a poppy farm."

As soon as they had finished eating, Ewan did the washing up and went to the café to play cards. Atal arrived and indicated with his head that Ewan should join him outside. They went out of the front door, into the street, where Atal exchanged some heroin for Ewan's afghani, and returned to the café using the rear entrance. The four men played their usual round of Keta, and Ewan went home.

The following day, in the shop where they fix things, Bahrawar showed Ewan the paintings he had bought in Kandahar. Ewan saw the irony. Each painting was a landscape of poppy fields. Flowers on the front, heroin in the back. At least, that was what he hoped Tofan would confirm tonight, whilst Ewan was at Bahrawar's house, using keys made from the soap-casts.

Bahrawar spent most of the day stock-taking and sorting out lots of broken items which had been delivered to the shop. Ewan worked on two transistor radios.

"Does Khialay have a bike like Baseer?"

"Not yet. Perhaps you can find him one."

"I will try. I am excited to meet your family."

"And they are excited to meet you."

They went straight to Bahrawar's house, at closing time, without Ewan going home first. It was a short walk from the shop, two streets away.

"Welcome to my home," said Bahrawar, opening the door and ushering Ewan inside.

The two sons stood up.

"This is Baseer and this is Khialay. Sons, meet my good friend Ewan."

"Thank you for fixing my bike," blurted out Baseer.

He seemed nervous, uncomfortable, in the presence of a stranger.

"My pleasure. When we find a bike, you and me, we must fix it together. Your dad says you want to become a mechanic. And you want to become a doctor, I hear."

Just then, a beautiful lady came into the room.

"And this is my wife, Apana."

"Hello," said Ewan, uncertain how he should greet another man's wife, especially one so beautiful.

Baseer had a look of his mother. Khialay looked more like Bahrawar. Apana went back into the kitchen and returned with orange juice.

"Please. Sit down," she gestured to Ewan.

He sat down on a carpet and was joined by Baseer and Khialay. Bahrawar was about to sit down when the telephone rang.

"Hello ….. Next week ….. About twenty."

Each time, Ewan could only hear this end of the conversation, but it was the next sentence which most interested him.

"Nikolai is here, in Lashkar Gah."

Over the last twenty-four hours, Ian had talked himself out of believing the driver of the Mercedes was Nikolai. Now he realised he was very much not mistaken with his first reaction. This could prove tricky. Dimitri came to the café and knew Atal. Atal's family owned a poppy farm and produced heroin. Nikolai had been at the farm. What if Nikolai came to the café when Ewan was playing cards with Atal, Rokhan and Gharzan? He told himself that he looked quite different to when he was in London, especially wearing Afghan clothing, but he was not really winning the argument with himself. At least he would see Tofan, prior to his next visit to the café. But if Bahrawar knew Nikolai, what was to stop Nikolai coming to the shop where they fix things? Maybe, Nikolai had come this month, instead of Dimitri. Ewan's hope was that, if Nikolai visited the shop, he would do so on a Wednesday, not a Tuesday or Thursday. Ewan felt he needed to ask for Tofan to watch the shop where they fix things, this week and next week at least, until the coast was clear.

Bahrawar came and joined them on the carpet, and Apana served their stew and rice. Ewan enjoyed it. The flavour had a touch of pomegranate and spices, which he had not tasted up to now. The dessert was fruity, sweet, and contained nuts.

"What is this?" asked Ewan, pointing at a berry.

"It's a mulberry," replied Apana.

Ewan realised he now knew the Pashto for this berry, but as he did not understand the word, he was no nearer knowing what he had just eaten. It tasted good. Apana went and made tea. The boys switched on an old black and white television. Obviously, one of the perks of running a business where you fix things, was having a telephone and a television. Ewan wondered which other gadgets Bahrawar owned.

"They are allowed to watch a comedy, if they watch the news first," laughed Bahrawar.

"Good idea."

After half an hour, Ewan realised that he did not grasp a lot of Afghan humour, apart from the slapstick. Slapstick works in any culture. He got up to leave.

"Thank you so much. I promise I will look for a bike."

"I'll walk you out," insisted Bahrawar.

He accompanied Ewan to the front door.

"There is someone I want you to meet next week. Nikolai."

"Yes. Thank you. See you on Tuesday."

"Goodbye, my friend."

Ewan felt sick. He had until Tuesday to work out how to avoid having to meet Nikolai. He would have to feign illness and send Salar or Faridun to the shop where they fix things to tell Bahrawar he was sick.

Ewan woke up in the early hours of Tuesday morning realising that he could not face going to the shop where they fix things. Nikolai would surely recognise him, and then, he was as good as dead. He drank some water and took himself out to the toilet, where he made himself sick, by sticking his fingers down the back of his throat. At seven o'clock, when Salar and Faridun, were making bread for breakfast, with coffee, Ewan joined them.

"I don't feel well. Vomiting in the night. I can't eat breakfast. I will drink water from the well."

"Poor you. My cooking?" smiled Salar.

"I don't think it's food poisoning. Please, can you go to the shop and tell Bahrawar I can't work today? Possibly not this week."

"I will go," Faridun reassured him. "I can go to the market at the same time.

"Thank you," replied Ewan, rushing out to the toilet and making himself sick, again.

He went back to bed with an empty bucket by his side. If he had genuinely been ill, he would have struggled with being in Afghanistan, and would have longed for proper plumbing, but this was a pretence. He slept for a while, woke, drank, made himself sick again and lay in bed listening to his Walkman. Ewan succeeded in keeping the charade going all day, until his stomach ached from being empty and from being sick. Salar and Faridun looked in on him every so often and made him cups of tea, which he started to drink in the afternoon. By the evening, he ate some bread and stopped making himself sick.

On Wednesday morning, Tofan came to the shop. Ewan could hear the conversation from his bed.

"Ewan is ill. He has been vomiting. He thinks it's illness not my cooking," said Salar.

"I told the shop where they fix things," added Faridun. "Do you think you should avoid him?"

"I'm willing to take the chance," responded Tofan.

He appeared in the living area and placed a chair about four feet away from Ewan's bed.

"Peace be upon you. The brothers say you are ill."

Ewan smiled.

"I can't go to the shop where they fix things, this week. Nikolai is here and Bahrawar wants me to meet him."

"I see."

"Did you go to the storeroom?"

"Yes."

"And?"

"It's heroin."

"Last week, Atal took me to his farm. About forty-five minutes along the road towards Marjah, turn right up a dirt road. Family business growing poppies. Also, there is a barn for heroin production. He spoke in Russian with one of the workers. I heard the Russian say, 'Krukov wants to double production and distribution'. Atal was very happy. Atal is Bahrawar's brother-in-law. I think the heroin in the shop where they fix things comes from Atal's farm. Also, I was sure I saw Nikolai. He was driving a car. He was leaving. We were arriving. I had sunglasses on."

"I understand."

"There's more. I ate a meal at Bahrawar's house. He took a phone call, and I heard him say, 'Nikolai is here in Lashkar Gah'. Then, he told me I must meet Nikolai."

"No wonder you're ill," laughed Tofan.

"Can you watch the shop that fixes things until it's safe. Maybe Nikolai is here only a few days."

"What does this Nikolai look like?"

"About fifty years old. Tall. Grey hair cut very short. Square chin. Not thin and not fat. Piercing blue-grey eyes. Drives a black Mercedes."

"We may have to send you home. For a family bereavement. Via Istanbul and Paris. Let's see how it goes."

"On the Orient Express?"

"Hey, don't get too excited. I will pick you up on Saturday and we will go to the kite flying competition."

"Will you fly your kite?"

"If I do, you will have to be my runner."

"What does a runner do?"

"Follows the kite and retrieves it from where it lands."

"Let's hope I'm well," replied Ewan, winking.

"Now I must go," declared Tofan, standing up and replacing his chair. "Stay here until the end of the week. I will come back later with some medicine for you."

"Bye. Stay safe."

"And you."

Later that day, Tofan returned to the book shop with a bottle of orange liquid. Ewan could have sworn it tasted just like Lucozade. Tofan had been watching the shop where they fix things. He had seen a man he assumed was Nikolai, based on Ewan's description, loading plastic-wrapped paintings into the boot of a black Mercedes car.

"Nikolai collected the paintings today."

"Interesting."

"I will see you at eight o'clock on Saturday morning."

"Bye."

Ewan stayed in the back of the bookshop, as Tofan had advised.

"Please could you go to the café, this evening, and tell Atal that I am ill. It is important," Ewan requested of Salar and Faridun when they closed the shop.

"Yes, of course," replied Salar. "Will you be eating, this evening?"

"I think I will have some bread, please."

"And tea?"

"And tea, thank you. I will stay at home tomorrow. I am weak."

At eight o'clock, on the Saturday morning, Tofan came to the shop. He was carrying his kite.

"Peace be upon you," Ewan greeted him.

"And on you. Are you feeling better?"

"Thank you."

"Will you be my kite runner?"

"Sorry. I don't think I am able to run! I'm still weak."

"Then I will put my kite back in the boot of my car. It will be fun to watch the competition."

"Yes. I am looking forward to it."

"Come," said Tofan, as he closed the boot.

"Wait. I need my sunglasses."

Ewan popped back to his bed and grabbed the sunglasses which were lying on his pillow.

They drove into the city centre and parked as close to the stadium as they could, on a street next to a park. From there, they walked to the stadium, which was about half full of spectators. The competitors were at one end of the field, preparing their kites, checking knots, coating the strings with ground glass. Tofan led them to two vacant seats, on the front row, on the far side of the field from the entrance. They sat down.

"It is very competitive. One kite will chase another kite and try to cut the string. That is why they coat the string with ground glass."

"Wow!"

A group of runners gathered near the entrance to the stadium. Around twenty minutes later, as the stadium filled up, an official looking man stood up to the microphone, which was positioned on a podium, in the middle of the field.

"Fellow Afghans and citizens of this, our beautiful city. Welcome to this annual competition. As you know, champions here have gone on to conquer the nation. Just like our champion two years ago."

His voice was drowned out by the cheering of the crowd.

"We hope it will be the same for this year's champion."

More cheering.

"So, it is my pleasure to count us down to the start. ..... Five ..... four ..... three ..... two ..... one ......"

There was a loud crack as he fired his gun in the air. The crowd cheered some more, as multi-coloured kites started to rise above the stadium. Ewan could see that some of the kites were chasing other kites. He watched one particular pair circle round each other, when suddenly, one of the kites started to plummet to the ground. A cheer went up.

"There, you see," stated Tofan, "That is the first kite to be eliminated."

It came down somewhere outside the stadium. One of the runners had already disappeared in pursuit.

"I'll go and buy us some drinks," suggested Tofan, pointing at a stand, about fifty yards away, at the side of the field.

"Thank you," responded Ewan.

Tofan walked off. Ewan was just getting into the competition when he felt the presence of some spectators in close proximity. He looked up to see Nikolai to his right and Bahrawar to his left. Atal was standing a couple of paces behind, his Kalashnikov over his shoulder.

"Hello, Ewan. Are you feeling better?"

"Yes, thank you. Nasty vomiting."

"May I introduce you to Nikolai Krukov."

"A pleasure," said Ewan, in his best Pashto, holding out his hand, which Nikolai shook.

He was wearing his sunglasses and hoped Nikolai did not recognise him, unable to see his eyes and with his clothing and beard. His brain was rebounding from the introduction. Nikolai was Krukov. Krukov and Nikolai were one and the same person. Was he living in Canada or was he still in London? He knew that Nikolai Krukov had made a personal visit to Paris, to Anton and Kristina. The connection was complete. Nikolai Krukov was the mastermind behind the entire drugs network from Atal's farm to Paris, London, probably still Amsterdam, and however many other European capitals. And at the Canadian end, was Katya, his daughter. Ewan remembered when she left London. Presumably, Katya and her father were not transferred to Ottawa, because Nikolai stayed in London. Was she sent there because Caroline was becoming too powerful?

Tofan had purchased their drinks and was walking back towards his seat when he saw the three men approach Ewan. He stopped in his tracks and watched. As he stood, he was passed by a woman carrying a tray of drinks. She wore a head scarf, with a dress over baggy trousers. When she reached Ewan and the three men, she stopped.

"And this is Nikolai's daughter Katya."

The blood drained from Ewan's face.

"Peace be upon you," Ewan forced himself to greet her in Pashto.

"This is Ewan," Atal introduced him. "He is a very good card player."

"Ewan? This is not a Pashtun name," reflected Nikolai, in Russian.

"Ewan is English," explained Bahrawar. "He is a student. He is learning Pashto. He helps me fix things in the shop."

"Where are you from?" Nikolai asked Ewan, in English.

"London."

"I also knew a student from London. His name was Owen. Perhaps you know this man, Ewan. Such a similar-sounding name, don't you think? Or are you Ian, from Ottawa? Take off your sunglasses, please."

Ewan removed his sunglasses, pondering the odds. It was four against one, although he could see Tofan watching. Four against almost two, if Tofan could cover the distance at speed.

"The beard suits you, Ian, and the Pashto is impressive," observed Katya, in French, with some irony. "You could almost be Afghan, although I would recognise those blue eyes, anywhere. I am so disappointed that you just disappeared like that. And not for the first time."

"How was I supposed to contact you when I had no address and no telephone number? I had no time. One day, my boss at Ontario Publishing called me into his office, and the next day I was on a plane to Pakistan," he replied in French.

"So, what are you doing in Lashkar Gah?" asked Nikolai, in Russian.

"Taking some holiday and buying my own heroin," replied Ewan, in Russian.

"I would believe you if I wasn't wondering how you managed to get another new passport so quickly."

"That's easy to explain," replied Ewan, still in Russian, thinking on his feet. "After my experience in Amsterdam, I had two new passports made, in case I needed to disappear again."

"It is possible," agreed Nikolai, in Russian, again.

"I understand you aren't happy, Nikolai, but please remember, I never stole from you. I returned the tickets, and in fairness, you owed me at least one hundred pounds for the previous shipment of Delft tea services."

"That is very true. And that is why I might be lenient with you and not torture you before I have you drowned in the river."

"Tell me, Katya. Did you get sent to Ottawa to keep an eye on Caroline? Because your father didn't go with you, did he?" asked Ewan, in Russian.

"You are very perceptive, Ian. Our French-Canadian connection was becoming a problem. Caroline didn't know where to draw the line. And yes, my father visits often, but he is still based in London."

"Be careful, Katya," Nikolai chided her. "We don't know who Owen will tell."

"But he isn't going to have the chance, is he?"

"Now, it's a shame the kite-flying competition is reaching its climax because you need to come with us. Right now, Owen," insisted Nicolai.

It had been a brief two weeks of induction and training, but it was for precisely this scenario that Ewan had been prepared. He always hoped he would not find himself in a life and death situation, but he felt certain, the only way to survive this situation was to use his gun. He stood up and replaced his sunglasses.

"Wait," asserted Katya.

She placed her hands provocatively on Ewan's chest and moved them to feel under his arms and into the small of his back, checking for weapons.

"Carry on," she said.

They walked along in front of the seats, Katya and Nikolai flanking him, Atal, and Bahrawar behind him. They passed by Tofan, who had taken everything in, and made their way to the entrance. Tofan followed at a distance, as the group crossed over the road and went into the nearby park. Ewan could see the Mercedes parked just along the street, with Atal's Lada behind it. He wondered why they were not getting into either of the cars. It was unlikely they would do anything in the open, surely.

Tofan concealed himself behind the trunk of a tree and watched as the group came to a stop in the middle of a grassed area. There was no one else to be seen. No doubt, everyone was at the kite-flying competition. The four of them spread out a little, one at each point of the compass, with Ewan in the middle. "Did I say I wouldn't torture you, Owen? I think Katya would be very disappointed if we threw you straight in the River Helmand."

Beyond the park, was the River Helmand. Nikolai nodded at Atal who took his Kalashnikov from his shoulder and rammed the butt into Ewan's stomach. He sank to his knees. Katya moved over to him and slapped him in the face.

"That's for screwing my cousin."

She slapped him on the other cheek.

"And that is for lying."

Atal hit him in the face with the butt of his Kalashnikov.

"That's for pretending you didn't speak Russian."

Bahrawar stood watching, silently.

Tofan was unsure how much of a beating Ewan could take. He could not leave it too long in case Ewan was not able to draw and fire his weapon. He was sure that if he took out two of them, Ewan could take out the other two. The priority was the man with the Kalashnikov, followed by one of the others who had not drawn their weapon. He stepped out from behind his tree and walked over to the group, shouting.

"Hey! Does it take three men and one woman to beat up one man? Leave him alone."

"I suggest you mind your own business," Atal shouted back.

"What has he done that you want to hurt him?"

"I'll give you one final warning. Leave now," insisted Atal.

"I can't stand by and watch you and this woman beating up this man," retorted Tofan, hoping that Ewan would catch on. Bahrawar and Nikolai stood to Ewan's left. Tofan intended them to be Ewan's targets.

Drawing his gun from beneath his waistcoat, Tofan fired one shot into Atal's chest and another into Katya's forehead. Even though he was feeling nauseous and dazed, Ewan had enough presence of mind, as soon as Tofan fired, to draw his own gun from the leg holster and shoot Nikolai in the chest before he had a chance to draw a weapon. Bahrawar, stunned by what was going on around him, was rooted to the spot, which gave Tofan a window of opportunity to fire a third shot. Bahrawar crumpled to the ground.

"Can you walk, my brother?" Tofan asked Ewan, holding out his hand to pull him up from the ground.

"I think so. They didn't touch me legs."

"Come then. As fast as you can. Let's get to the car."

"What about them?"

"No time," responded Tofan.

He could see that Atal and Katya were dead and quickly felt for a pulse on Nikolai's neck.

"Dead," he declared, moving over to Bahrawar. "Also, dead. Now, let's go. Our priority is to get you safe. The local police will do what the local police will do."

They reached the car and Tofan sped off down the next side street.

"We will swing by the bookshop. You can grab your belongings and then we must go."

"Go where?"

"Kandahar. The field office and then the safehouse. I must contact MI6 as soon as I can. It is vital that Operation Beluga is brought to completion before the end of the night. Hopefully, we will make it to Kandahar before local police discover the bodies and make any response."

"Thank you. I probably owe you my life."

"Think nothing of it, my brother."

"By the way, the woman was Katya. I knew her in London and more recently, in Canada. The man was Nikolai Krukov. I knew him in London, as Nikolai. I never knew he was Nikolai Krukov. We thought Krukov was a different person. Katya is his daughter. Now we have linked Krukov to the drugs network."

They arrived at the bookshop and went inside. Neither Salar nor Faridun had gone to the kite-flying competition.

"Peace be upon you my brothers," Tofan greeted Salar and Faridun, with a hug. "I am sorry, but Ewan has to leave."

Ewan had already gone to his bed and was gathering his belongings. He nipped to the toilet.

"What happened to you?" asked Salar when Ewan came back into the front of the shop.

"Long story. The special work hit a problem," offered Tofan, by way of limited explanation. "We have to get Ewan to safety. Right now."

"Thank you for your hospitality and friendship," said Ewan. "I don't think I will be coming back."

"You are always welcome," affirmed Salar, "If things change."

"Yes. Perhaps one day, you will visit us," added Faridun.

Ewan hugged each of them, which caused pain to shoot through his body. He winced.

"Come. We have no time to waste."

Ewan left with Tofan, who had taken hold of the holdall. They took the back streets out of the city and drove at speed to Kandahar. To both their relief, there were no roadblocks along the way. Tofan drove them straight to the field office, where he made a secure phone call. Ewan sat listening to Tofan's words, as he spoke in English.

"Time to wrap up Operation Beluga. Canada, London, Paris and Amsterdam, plus all known operatives. Nikolai Krukov and Katya Krukov are both dead. It was them or us. Atal and Bahrawar are dead, but the farm needs shutting down. Do you want to speak to Ewan? ..... OK. Debrief in London, Wednesday. Go to HQ on arrival. Catch up soon. ..... He's done an amazing job. He's been pretty badly beaten up. ..... Yes. Bye."

"That was Grant Waterstone. He doesn't want to speak to you on the phone, but he said you've done incredibly well. He'll see you in London, on Wednesday. All we have to do now, is get you there in one piece. Right now, let's get you to the safe house and cleaned up."

"It's starting to hurt a lot. I need some more of your miracle medicine," laughed Ewan.

"Glad you can laugh about it."

"But not too much."

They left the field office in a different car and drove to the safehouse.

"Here's the cannabis oil."

"Thanks."

Ewan started to apply some to his face and stomach. Reflecting on the incident, he thought of Houdini, who died from a punch in the stomach he was not ready for, and he was so glad he had tensed his six-pack as he saw Atal swing the Kalashnikov back, otherwise it might have been far worse. He lay down on a bed and closed his eyes. The cannabis oil started to sooth his pain. Tofan came into the bedroom.

"You will need to use your Ian Elton-Craig passport again, as soon as we get you across the border. I want to try and take you to Quetta, leaving right now. I am worried about being stopped by the Soviets, though. If Krukov had state-backing, and the bodies have been identified, it is very possible the authorities here won't be happy."

"What happens if we are stopped?"

"I'm not sure I want to find that out. If we leave now, we might make it before they find out. If not, we can try the longer route through the mountains. Ready?"

"Ready."

They left for Quetta. Tofan drove at the speed limit out of the city and then added a few miles per hour on the open road.

"Once we get across the border, we'll stay overnight, in Quetta. In the morning, we'll change into suits, back to your Ian Elton-Craig passport, and I'll drive you to Karachi. From there, you can fly to Heathrow. The Pakistanis are our allies, remember, in the fight against the Soviets."

"What will you do?"

"Hopefully, make my way safely back to Kandahar. Although I may have to hang out in Pakistan for a while, until the dust settles."

The drive was hot and dusty. As they approached the border crossing, a queue of traffic had formed.

"I don't drive through here that often," remarked Tofan, "so I don't know if this is normal."

"Well, we don't have a choice."

"I don't know. Better to turn around now, than when they check our passports. Here, we might just be avoiding the traffic. Later, we could be seen as trying to hide something."

"Stay in the queue," insisted Ewan-Ian. "We can say we have a friend in hospital in Quetta. He drives fruit and vegetables across the border and fell from his lorry."

"Very good."

The queue edged forward until Tofan and Ewan-Ian were at the barrier.

"Passports, please."

Tofan handed over their passports.

"Where are you going?"

"Quetta."

"Where have you come from?"

"Kandahar."

"Please get out of the car.

They both got out.

"Now open the boot, please."

Ewan-Ian suddenly remembered he had two small packets of heroin in the bottom of his holdall. He started to panic, as Tofan opened the boot. The border guard looked at the luggage.

"Please open this bag," he instructed Tofan.

"It's his," replied Tofan.

Ewan-Ian stepped forward and unzipped the bag. The border guard looked inside and ran his hand round the sides of the clothes, feeling for items considerably larger than Ewan-Ian's two tiny plastic packets.

"All OK. Thank you."

The two men got back in the car and the border guard raised the barrier.

"That was close," reflected Ian-Ewan.

"How so?"

"I have two small packets of heroin at the bottom of my holdall, evidence from Atal's farm. I was sweating."

As soon as they were beyond the immediate vicinity of the crossing, Tofan accelerated away.

"I guess that's the hardest part, getting across the border," surmised Ian-Ewan.

"I'm just happy that we're in Pakistan. Are you hungry?"

"Very."

"Let's check in at the hotel and find somewhere to eat."

"Good plan."

They checked into a three-star hotel. The room was clean, the sheets crisp, and there was a fan. The shower and toilet were also more modern than Ian-Ewan's experience from the last few weeks, and he spent far longer in the shower than he would normally have spent.

"Sorry," apologised Ian-Ewan when he came out of the bathroom. "It wasn't just that I am stiff all over. I haven't had the opportunity of a shower like that for a while."

"No matter," responded Tofan heading into the bathroom.

Once showered and changed into their clean clothes, they left the hotel in search of a place to eat.

Ian-Ewan was a simple guy who generally fed himself, at home, on something and toast, with the occasional steak, but the monotony of his diet, over the last few weeks, left him hankering after something more interesting. Not that he was ungrateful for any of the hospitality he had experienced. They wandered into a restaurant and ordered a Balochi dish made from lamb and okra. It was spicier and richer than the stews he had eaten in Afghanistan, and it went straight through him. Thankfully, by morning, and the long journey to Karachi, he had washed it all through his system.

They left at six-thirty in the morning and drove for two hours before stopping for coffee, breakfast, and use of a toilet. It was nice not to wonder if there would be a roadblock or feel the need to look over his shoulder all the time. Back in the car, they continued on the long drive south.

"You will be flying on a private jet from Karachi to Dubai. From there you fly to London."

"Wow. Who owns the private jet?"

"The CIA."

"The CIA?"

"Yes. They have been working alongside the British and the Pakistanis to ensure the Mujahideen are trained and supplied with arms. The head of the agency has been here for a couple of days."

"I don't know what to say."

"I know you wanted a trip on the Orient Express, but this has to be second best."

"Great."

Tofan remembered there was a radio in the car. He switched it on, and a man's voice came on. He turned the tuning button a little and caught some bursts of music, looked at Ian-Ewan and shook his head.

"Wait you have cassettes, don't you?"

"They're in the boot."

"Well, next time we stop, we'll play some music. Assuming the cassette player isn't broken."

"Do you like rock music?"

"I don't know."

"What music do you like?"

"Pop music."

"Seventies?"

"Motown! Currently, I like A-ha 'Take on Me'. George Michael 'Careless Whisper'. Billy Joel 'Uptown Girl'."

"Do you like to dance?"

"I used to. Since my wife died, I haven't been anywhere to dance. I don't think I want to dance without her."

"I'm sorry."

They drove on for a while, in silence, until they reached Khuzdar, where Tofan filled up with petrol, and Ian-Ewan sorted out two of his cassettes. They got back in the car and Ian-Ewan put his *Wish You Were Here* cassette into the player.

"It's broken," observed Tofan.

"No. The first part is a bit quiet. It will get louder soon."

The intro got louder.

"Does it have any words?" asked Tofan.

"Wait!"

"Remember when you were young, you shone like the sun. Shine on you crazy diamond."

Ian-Ewan lost himself mouthing the words and moving his head in time with the music. After a bit, the lyrics gave way to instrumentals, again. Ian-Ewan was in his element. Eventually the album came to an end.

"What do you think?"

"I think I'd like to listen to it again before I decide. But not immediately."

Ian-Ewan replaced the cassette with *Dark Side of the Moon*.

"I've been mad, I know I've been mad, like the most of us ...."

It was difficult to hear the first part of the lyrics, but Ian-Ewan knew them by heart. The music got louder and then came the opening line to 'Breathe.' When 'Time' came on, Tofan jumped at the clocks chiming.

"So, what do you think the dark side of the moon is like?" asked Tofan, at the end of the album.

"There's no dark side of the moon. As a matter of fact, it's all dark," laughed Ian-Ewan.

"That was in the song."

"Yes."

"It's true. The moon has no light of its own."

"I would love to go to the moon," mused Ian-Ewan. "Actually, no. Not necessarily to the moon. I would love to see the earth from space."

"I watched the moon landing."

"Me too. My dad woke us up. We had to go next door. Me and my sister, with my mum and dad. We didn't have a television."

"I was in America, learning the language, when it happened."

"Amazing. I love the film footage of the Apollo rocket taking off."

"Yes. It moves so slowly, at first. Then it goes ridiculously fast. More than twenty thousand miles per hour."

"I know."

There was a town coming up, Bela.

"We should stop," proposed Tofan.

"Agreed."

"We need to eat something," suggested Tofan. "I need energy. I'll drive round until we find a café."

He turned off the main road and entered the town where they soon came upon somewhere that looked like it sold food.

"Is that roast chicken I can smell?" wondered Tofan out loud.

There was a spit, over a fire, with a chicken on it.

"Peace be upon you," said the proprietor.

"And upon you. Are you serving food?" inquired Tofan.

"We have roast chicken."

"Perfect."

"Take a seat, please."

He brought them over two bottles of Pakola and a plate of naan bread, and returned to the counter, where he removed the chicken from the spit and took it over to Tofan and Ian-Ewan. He replaced the chicken with an uncooked one and pushed the spit back over the fire. Tofan cut the chicken in half and placed one half in front of Ian-Ewan. When he had pulled every last piece from the carcass, Tofan lent back and sighed.

"That was just what was needed."

"Yes, it was good," replied Ian-Ewan, licking his fingers, and wiping them on a towel.

Tofan paid and they each used the toilet.

"Let's see if we can make it to Karachi without stopping," remarked Tofan.

"Are you feeling full of energy, again?"

"I am. Tonight we are guests of the CIA. I'm sure they will have heard what you did, by now."

"What we did. I would be dead, without you."

"True, but you put yourself on the line and uncovered the supply chain. Don't forget, it's because of the work you did in Ottawa, that we were able to take out both Nikolai and Katya Krukov. The CIA might offer you a job."

"MI6 offered me a job. I don't want it. I want to live to see my grandchildren. I don't have children yet, of course. I want to meet someone. Someone who doesn't lie to me or use me."

Somewhere between Bela and Karachi, Ian-Ewan fell asleep. He was woken abruptly, by Tofan doing an emergency stop, to let a chicken cross the road, and realised he had been dribbling. Wiping away the saliva with his sleeve, he looked at the chicken and thought better of cracking a joke. Jokes never translate well across cultures. The chicken reached the other side of the road and Tofan set off, again. The roads became increasingly busy, the further into the city they drove. At several points, Tofan had to bring the car to a complete standstill, as market traders and impatient taxi drivers criss-crossed the road. Eventually, they pulled up in front of a building guarded by soldiers.

Tofan wound down the window, held out his passport and spoke to one of them, who approached the car. The soldier made a phone call and allowed Tofan to proceed. He parked the car, and the two men went inside. A man in a suit met them.

"Come this way, gentlemen."

He led them up to the first floor where they were directed to wait in a room. A few minutes later, the door opened, and in walked William Casey, Director of the CIA.

"Gentlemen," he greeted them, holding out his hand.

Tofan and Ian-Ewan each shook his hand.

"I don't mind telling you, we've been trying to nail that Russian S.O.B. for years. You're celebrities."

"It was Ewan, not me," deferred Tofan, now showing off his English. "Or should I say Ian?"

"I think it's always a team effort," responded Casey. "That said, you were in the frontline. I hear you took out Katya Krukov as well as Caroline Dupont, over in Ottawa."

"Well, technically, I think it was Katya who took out Caroline," responded Ian, "but yes, all part of the same distribution network."

"I understand you're flying with me?"

"Just me. Not Tofan."

"And then back to our friends in MI6? You know, we'd love you to come and work for us."

Ian caught Tofan's eye and smiled.

"I appreciate that, but I think I've probably had enough of being in the line of fire, so to speak."

"Well, if you change your mind."

"Thank you."

"Now, Ian. Let's go catch ourselves a plane. Are you staying overnight in Karachi, Tofan?"

"I thought we both were. Are you flying out tonight?"

"Change of plan. Yes, we are. In fact, we're going all the way to London. I want to meet up with my counterpart in MI6. Your hotel is booked, and your meal is on expenses. I can't thank you enough."

"Much appreciated," replied Tofan.

"Better get my belongings," remembered Ian.

"Meet me in the foyer, in ten minutes," directed Casey.

Ian and Tofan descended to the ground floor and went out to Tofan's car. Ian ejected the 'Dark Side of the Moon' cassette and lifted his luggage from the boot of the car.

"Thank you for everything. Maybe catch up one day. Stay safe."

"Thank you," answered Tofan. "Ian, it's been an absolute pleasure."

Tofan stepped forward to hug Ian.

"Peace be upon you, my brother," whispered Ian, as his face passed Tofan's ear.

"And upon you, my brother."

"Bye."

Tofan got into his car and drove to his hotel. Ian went and stood in the foyer. Fifty minutes later, he was on a private jet, being served vodka and orange, somewhere in the air space over the Gulf of Oman.

"We should be in London in time for some brunch!" laughed Casey.

"Tell me about your real family, Ian. The person you were before MI6 gave you this assignment," inquired Casey, about an hour into the flight.

"When I was Owen, you mean. I have a sister, Helen. Two years younger than me. My dad is ill much of the time. My mum looks after him. She used to be a nurse, before I was born. We lived in a council house, but I won a scholarship and ended up at a fee-paying school. I got expelled, left home, went to university in London, to study Russian, fell in love with Katya and got sucked into Krukov's empire, although I only knew him as Nikolai. Became a heroin addict, quit university, ran away to Amsterdam, got clean, lived on a houseboat and worked in a café, and somehow ended up being recruited by Dominic Andrews, who I knew from school. He kind of made me a Hobson's choice. Either I worked for MI6 or I went to prison, for smuggling Krukov's drugs."

"That is a unique combination of language skills, experiences and connections. No wonder you enabled us to take down Krukov's empire. Are you sure you don't want a job with the CIA?"

"Honestly, I was offered a job by MI6. I'm hoping my recent success will buy me my freedom from MI6. No more threat of prison."

"What will you do?"

"No idea. Maybe do a bit of travelling. I always hoped I would get to make that journey on the Orient Express."

"You won't go back to your family?"

"One day, When I'm thirty. In the meantime, I'm still trying to make it on my own."

"If there's one piece of advice, years of working in this shadow world has taught me, it's you can never truly make it on your own. There's always someone watching your back or opening doors for you."

"You're probably right, Mr Casey. If it's OK with you, I think I'll get some sleep. I'm still feeling a bit fragile from the last time I saw Krukov."

"Be my guest."

The private jet was like travelling first class in a commercial aeroplane. Ian reclined his seat and laid his head on a pillow. He slept for three hours. A stewardess served him coffee and orange juice when he woke up. Picking up a copy of a weekend newspaper, Ian browsed the articles. Earlier in June, there had been a military operation to capture the leader of the Sikhs, Jarnail Singh Bhindranwale, who was hiding out in the Golden Temple at Amritsar. It had caused a certain amount of both domestic and international fall-out. The Soviet Union was planning to boycott the

Los Angeles Olympics, in a few weeks, by way of retaliation for the United States having boycotted the Moscow games in 1980, after the Soviet Union invaded Afghanistan. Floyd had been right, during Ian's first trip to Amsterdam, that the United States should boycott the Moscow Olympics. And there was a miners' strike crippling the United Kingdom. Ian gave up on the news and decided to try the crossword. He was getting nowhere fast when he heard Casey's voice.

"Good morning. How long have you been awake?"

"An hour or so."

"You slept better than I did. Anyway, I think they'll maybe give us breakfast now."

The stewardess, having heard them talking, came into the cabin and served them pancakes and coffee.

"No doubt they'll want a full debrief when you get to HQ. I expect they'll find a hotel for us for tonight. Beyond tonight, do you have a place to stay?"

"I doubt my old flat is still vacant. I was squatting. The council probably have a tenant in there, by now. I can afford a hotel for a few days, wherever I decide to go. I quite fancy Spain. Don't ask me why."

The pilot's voice came over the intercom.

"We are beginning our decent into London Gatwick. Please return to your seats and fasten your seatbelts."

"Gatwick?" remarked Ian, with surprise.

"Yes. Not possible to land at Heathrow, this time. Too short notice."

"Will we take the train or is someone meeting us?"

"I hope someone is meeting us."

Ian got up and quickly went to the toilet before sitting back in his seat and fastening his seatbelt. The plane passed through the clouds into rain. Ian remembered how his June birthday parties were always a washout. In all the nervous excitement of last week, feigning illness to avoid Bahrawar and Atal, Ian had completely forgotten his birthday on 20th June. Today was 25th June, and he was about to pass within a stone's throw of his former flat in Battersea, in a car, in the rain.

As the plane taxied to a standstill by the terminal, Ian wondered what name he would go by from now on. Once he was, officially, stood down from his assignment, could he go back to being Owen Linton-House? Or would he be given another new identity, a bit like if he were part of a witness protection programme? With Nikolai and Katya Krukov dead, and many others in the network arrested and prosecuted, perhaps he would be called on to testify. Casey and Ian stepped off the plane into the pouring rain. There was only one umbrella, and they were unable to share it efficiently on the steps. Even on the ground, it was hard for Ian to juggle his luggage whilst remaining dry.

"You take it. I'll make a dash for the building," he insisted, trotting the twenty-five yards to the door into the terminal. He stepped half inside and waited for Casey to reach the entrance.

There was no emotional reaction within Ian to setting foot on the tarmac in the United Kingdom, but he did feel safer than the last time he had visited London. To his great pleasure, Waterstone was there to meet them, on the other side of customs. He gave Ian a man-hug and shook Casey's hand.

"Good to see you again. Alive and well and victorious," he greeted Ian, adding, "Welcome to the UK," in Casey's direction.

"What happened to you?" he asked, noticing the bruise on Ian's face.

"That would be the butt of a Kalashnikov, courtesy of Krukov's poppy farmer."

"Poor you. It doesn't look like the cheek is broken. I think you should get it checked out, while you're here."

"It is very painful, still."

"We can probably find you some painkillers, too."

"The Kandahar contact gave me some cannabis oil to rub on it. That worked like a dream."

"I think the best we can do is Co-codamol. Sorry."

"Whatever you have. Thanks."

"Why does it always rain, here?" laughed Casey, changing the subject.

"I don't know. Don't forget I'm not from here, either. It was hellish, getting here, with the spray on the road. I hope I can find my way back into Central London."

"I might be able to help with that. I used to go to Caterham, regularly," replied Ian, hopefully.

They followed Waterstone to where the car was parked, and Casey had to correct himself from going to the passenger door.

"I don't think I'll ever get the hand of right-hand drive," he laughed.

"I have to concentrate a lot more," answered Waterstone.

They got in and set off for Westminster.

"What are you most looking forward to, Ian?" inquired Casey, jovially.

"Fish and chips."

"Ah, yes. Chips, not fries. Crisps, not chips," Waterstone ribbed him.

"Very funny, but it's the chips themselves. There's nothing like a good chip-shop chip. Let's face it, even though I'm looking forward to some mod-cons, I had those in Ottawa. And yes, not having to think twice before crossing a road."

There was a lot of traffic, and it took longer than anticipated to arrive at Century House. Waterstone swiped his temporary card and ushered Ian and Casey into the building.

"I think this is where I leave you. I have a meeting to attend. With C. Ian, it's been a pleasure to meet you."

He extended his hand, and after a warm handshake, disappeared into the lift.

"Right, then. You and I are due at a meeting with Andrews in half an hour. What say you we go and get some brunch, in the cafeteria? I'm paying, of course."

"The pancakes on the plane didn't really satisfy my morning hunger. To be honest, my stomach doesn't know what time it is. Thank you."

As they stood in front of the counter, Ian remembered when he ate too much before his physical tests.

"Do you think they'll want to do any physical tests, this time? Only, I fancy a full English breakfast."

"I'm pretty sure you can eat a full English breakfast. Remember, we've now only got twenty-five minutes."

"OK. I'll have a bacon roll, thank you. And a coffee."

"That'll be two bacon rolls and two coffees, please," Waterstone directed the assistant.

"I'll bring it over in a couple of minutes."

"Thank you," responded Ian.

"I'm not going to ask you what happened," explained Waterstone, as they sat at a vacant table, "because you're going to have to start at the beginning, with Andrews, but I am curious about your shooting Krukov. Are you OK with it? Do you need counselling? Your gun was only ever for self-defence, but we always hoped you wouldn't ever have to use it."

"I know. I really didn't have a choice. Tofan was brilliant. He managed to alert me that he was going to shoot Katya and Atal, the poppy farmer. Luckily, Bahrawar, the distributor, was stunned by it all, and so in the time it took for me to shoot Krukov, Tofan was firing a third time, killing Bahrawar. Killing Krukov was self-defence, but I tell myself he deserved it, for what he made me do. Bahrawar has two teenage sons. I met them. I went to his house, for a meal. I met his wife. I keep thinking about them."

"I know, the families don't get to choose the way of life. It's hard. We'll book you in for a psych-evaluation. They can decide if you need more help."

"Thanks. That's why I didn't accept your job offer. I want a family, one day."

"I understand."

They finished their brunch and went up to the meeting room, where Dominic Andrews was waiting. He shook Ian's hand.

"Owen, what can I say? Wait, do you want to be called 'Owen' or 'Ian' now?"

"Ian is fine. I'm pretty sure I'm about to get another new identity."

"Quite probably. Well Ian, you have surpassed all expectations. We rounded up so many network members, across Afghanistan, Canada, France, the Netherlands and here in London. Operation Beluga has been a total triumph.

I believe Casey is currently talking to the boss about the Venezuelan connection."

"Forgive me for asking but does that mean I've upheld my side of the bargain. Am I allowed to walk away, without any further threat of prison?"

"I'm sure you have, but I'm still hoping we can offer you a proper job."

"I really do just want to find a girl, who isn't going to try and get me hooked on drugs, settle down and start a family. Getting beaten up or shot were never part of the plan. I have no idea what I will do, but I don't think I'm cut out for MI6. Even if I can do the thinking on my feet and communication side of things, I just don't want to die young."

"I respect that," responded Andrews. "Just remember, that once you walk away, if you should be tempted to return to your former lifestyle, of addiction and dealing, you will no longer be under the protection of MI6. That said, I promise we will not give you special attention either and you will have the same rights to privacy as anyone else."

"So, will I be given another new identity? Will I be a witness at subsequent prosecutions?"

"In answer to the first question, yes. That is, if you want it. In answer to the second question, possibly. In fact, what I'd like to do next, is a short interview, recorded, in which you talk me through your time in Canada and in Afghanistan. Likewise, a full description of the contacts you had with the Krukov network in London and Amsterdam. Depending on which individuals who you've encountered are still alive, the need for witness testimony will become clearer."

"OK. Ready when you are."

Andrews placed a cassette in the recorder and pressed 'record'.

"Fire away," he invited Ian-Owen.

"On the flight over from London to Ottawa, last May, I sat next to Adrian Zorkin. I met him again as a friend of Caroline Dupont. He transported the books containing drugs. He was later executed by someone. I was in the bathroom and heard two men speaking in Russian. One of them fired the gun that killed Zorkin. Caroline Dupont asked me to replace Zorkin in transporting the books. When I went to Paris with work, and to Bordeaux, meet a customer, I exchanged a shipment of books, usually only six, with a man in Bordeaux station. There were two Russians on the plane flying back. I hid from them, but I overheard their conversation. They knew Katya. Not long after, Caroline asked me to go to London. I avoided the 'banya' because I requested the exchange took place at Paddington Station. Grant, here, had given me a disguise. However, someone had grown suspicious. Katya caught up with me and told me Caroline Dupont had had an accident. Actually, she was killed, just as Zorkin was. I was watched by two men in a vehicle outside my flat who planted bugs. Katya must have been suspicious because when she forced me to go to London, she gave me no time at all to do anything, and the itinerary was much stricter. She gave me the books on the Friday evening, I was picked up at the airport. The books were left in the taxi, and the return books were in the taxi when I was driven back to the airport. I had to fly from Montreal, as well, and was taken to the airport and picked up from the airport. But for Grant's genius, we wouldn't have known there were drugs, but we did the suitcase exchange manoeuvre. After I returned from Paris, that time, it was decided I should go to Afghanistan."

"I will be able to talk you through the details of the drugs and the timings of the activities, as well as telling you about the agents who shadowed Ian, based on their debriefs," interjected Waterstone.

"Great," replied Andrews. "Tell me about Afghanistan."

"I was told by the bookshop owners that I could buy drugs from a man at a local café or from a farm. I didn't get very far with the farm because of a guard with a Kalashnikov. I watched from a table in the café and saw a man exchanging small packages, so I asked for drugs. He was very suspicious and told me to meet him outside, where he stuck the muzzle of a Kalashnikov in my back. He then invited me to play cards with him and his friends, probably because I had said I needed drugs because I was lonely. His name was Atal and he was shot and killed in Kandahar. He had two friends, but I don't know if they knew about the drugs. Those card games led to my becoming aware of the shop where they fix things, which is where the drugs were concealed in paintings. I got a job helping fix things and watched the framing process. The shop was owned by Bahrawar, who made up the painting packages. I saw how he hid the drugs between double backboards. I met a man named Dimitri, who taught Atal to speak Russian, and who took the paintings to Paris, via Istanbul, on a train. Bahrawar was also killed, at the same time as Atal. Atal took me to his family-owned poppy farm and showed me where the drugs were processed. That was where I saw Nikolai, speeding past in a car, leaving the farm. It was also where I heard another Russian say that Krukov wanted to double production. Not sure I would recognise the worker again. Bahrawar told me he wanted me to meet Nikolai, and I had to pretend I was off sick, to avoid it. That was when the MI6 contact in Kandahar took me to a kite flying competition and I was approached by Atal, with his Kalashnikov, Bahrawar, Krukov and Katya. It was in that moment, that I realised Nikolai, the Nikolai I knew from the 'banya', was Nikolai Krukov. They were leading me away to kill me, drown me in the river, but decided to beat me up on the way. The MI6 contact rescued me and shot Atal, Katya and Bahrawar. I shot and killed Krukov."

"How did that feel?"

"He deserved it. I haven't really thought too much about the fact that I have taken a human life. It was him or me."

"Tell me about the parts we don't know about in London and Amsterdam."

"Well, I met Katya as a student and fell for her. She introduced me to the 'banya' and got me hooked on heroin. Really thought she was into me, but now I know better. There was a man called Vasily and a woman and her daughter who worked there, can't remember their names. That was where I met Krukov, although I didn't know Nikolai was Krukov, at that time. Katya told me she and her family were being moved to Canada, and that her father worked for the diplomatic service. In hindsight, we now know her father stayed in London, unless he was only visiting when I met him. Anyway, he basically forced me to run the Delft shipments between Amsterdam and London. I stayed with a couple, Anton, and Kristina. Kristina definitely wanted to help me and wanted them to be able to get out. I think they felt as trapped as I did. I met them, by chance, in Paris, the last time I went there, and Kristina let slip they met the Orient

Express every month. Anton told her to be quiet. I also bought cannabis from a man in Amsterdam and heroin from a man in Utrecht. I could show you where, but I don't remember the addresses. I think that's about it. Oh, and I still have two samples of heroin. Not for me, I hasten to add."

"Thank you," responded Andrews, switching off the tape recorder. "Unless we can trace the various operatives back to the KGB, we still can't really prove the Soviet government is behind this, but at least, for now, we have taken down a network. Can I show you some photos?"

"Yes."

"They're dead people, just to forewarn you."

"It's OK."

Andrews opened up a folder.

"Tell me if you recognise any of these people," instructed Andrews, laying the photos on the table. "These two are London. These five are France. This one is Canada. He's Dutch."

"That one is the man from Bordeaux station. That is the man from Paddington station, who was watching and waiting for me. That man, I'm sure I met in the 'banya'. That's the French driver. Noooo! That's Anton."

"Thank you. Now you need a medical and a psych-evaluation. When you're finished, we can talk about the future and your new identity. Just get reception to call through to me. Meanwhile, Grant and I have things to discuss. Dr Prescott will be expecting you."

"Cheers. See you in a bit."

"Thank you, Owen."

Ian-Owen left the room and went to find Dr Prescott. The set-up was the same as when he did his training. Hearing his proper name again felt odd. He had grown accustomed to answering to and introducing himself as 'Ian', for the last year and a bit.

"Welcome back, Owen. Long time, no see. You're looking fit and well, although your face is looking a little worse for wear."

"Yes. My stomach isn't looking much better. I got rather beaten up at the weekend."

"Let me take a look at the damage."

He moved his thumbs gently across Ian-Owen's cheek, applying very slight pressure, watching for Ian-Owen's reaction.

"That's good. I don't think it's broken. Lift your shirt will you."

Ian-Owen lifted his shirt to reveal his six-pack and the bruising.

"You have been keeping fit, since I last saw you."

"Yes. I attended a gym, when I was living in Canada, and I cycled everywhere."

"This bruising is nasty, but just a flesh-wound. It should heal quicker than the cheek, and I think they missed your ribs."

He took his stethoscope and listened to Ian-Owen's chest and back.

"Change into these shorts and hop onto the treadmill, will you?"

Ian-Owen went behind the curtain and changed into the shorts. Dr Prescott attached some sensors to his torso and turned on the treadmill. He slowly increased the speed, until Ian-Owen was running. After two minutes of making him run, he reduced the speed again.

"Now rest."

Dr Prescott printed out the data.

"This is amazing. You were so unfit when you came to us. Now look at you. Have you gone back on the drugs, at all?"

"No. Funnily enough, I nearly came a cropper at the Afghaistan-Pakistan border, because I completely forgot I had two hits in the bottom of my holdall, from where I bought heroin to identify the supply chain. Never felt the need to take it, though."

"Mr Walton, the psychiatrist, is going to walk through those doors, any minute now, so you'd better get dressed again."

Ian-Owen changed back out of the shorts and was just tying his second shoelace, when Walton walked in.

"I'll leave you to it," announced Dr Prescott, exiting the room.

"Owen Linton-House. Good to meet you. Your celebrity precedes you."

"I don't feel much like a celebrity."

"And what do you feel like?"

"Like I'm not quite in the real world."

"How so?"

"Well, for a start, I've been Ian Elton-Craig and Ewan Chandler-Brown for the last year, but now, people are calling me Owen, again. In the last two years, I've been in Amsterdam, Paris, Bordeaux, Ottawa, Islamabad, Kabul, Lashkar Gah, Kandahar and Karachi, and although I made a trip to London, during my stay in Canada, it feels weird to be back in the United Kingdom. I've had to live a lie and pretend to be and do a whole load of things I'm not. I've been high and I've been clean, and I went cold turkey. I have no permanent home and no idea of what the immediate future holds. I've been threatened twice with a Kalashnikov. I've been up close with several dead bodies, and I've taken someone's life. It is true that when I left home, I was searching for who I was, trying to make my own way in life, but I never anticipated any of this. So, yes, it all feels slightly surreal."

"How do you deal with all these surreal experiences?"

"Bury them. Learn from them. Pretend they didn't happen. Question them. Escape from them. Wonder if I'll ever step back into reality, whatever that is."

"And which of those is your response to taking a life?"

"I think I've rationalised it. If I hadn't shot Krukov, for sure, he would have killed me. So, I tell myself it had to be done, and that he deserved it."

"And the other deaths?"

"Again, it was them or me. Except for the fact that I met Bahrawar's wife and two teenage sons. That leaves a bad taste in the mouth. And I've just seen a photo of Anton. He had a wife and a very young son. They told me they wanted to escape. They were trapped in Krukov's network, pretty much as I was. Anton was a friend."

"I cannot tell you how you should feel. Nor can I tell you how you can deal with the feelings you presently have. If you should start to experience flashbacks, or you cannot sleep at night, you must get in touch and we will work with you, through counselling."

"So, everyone keeps reassuring me."

"As for reality. You will probably never stop looking over your shoulder, even when we give you another whole new identity. What you do with that identity, is entirely up to you. People change their names all the time, for any number of reasons. What matters is that you begin to identify with your new circumstances. If you bring integrity into these circumstances, you will become more comfortable in your new reality. Life will start to feel less surreal."

"I hope so."

"Where do you want to live?"

"I'm thinking Spain."

"Not here in the UK?"

"Nothing here for me. As long as I can communicate in the language and I have a bed, a cooker, a proper toilet and clean water, I'll be fine."

"I was not aware that Spanish was one of the languages you have mastered."

"It isn't, but I think I will pick it up quickly, especially if I am living there. And just think about what sort of job I might secure, being able to speak English, Russian, French, Dutch, Pashto and Spanish. Surely, there are European countries crying out for those language skills."

"And what thoughts do you have about a name?"

Ian-Owen paused for a moment.

"Well, I've been Owen, Ian and Ewan. Perhaps I should become Evan. Evan Stoner-Ward."

"Any particular reason for the Stoner-Ward?"

"Not really. I quite like having a double-barrelled surname."

"I think that's all I need from you. I wish you luck."

"Thank you."

Mr Walton shook Ian-Owen's hand.

In reception, they rang through to Dominic Andrews.

"Go on up."

"Thanks."

Ian-Owen went back to where he had left Waterstone and Andrews.

"All good?" asked Waterstone, who had become fond of Ian-Owen, in a fatherly way.

"All good. The psychiatrist asked me where I wanted to live and what name I want to go by. I told him Spain. As for another new name, I said Evan Stoner-Ward."

"Certain?"

"As I'll ever be."

"Right. We'll get you a new passport, and a new history."

"Can I have my real back story up until university, and my nomadic, international curriculum vitae. Then I can just talk about travelling and other cultures. After all, how else did I learn so many languages. I just won't mention the MI6 stuff."

"If that's what you want."

"It is. I talked about wanting to live in reality, with Mr Walton. Talking of living, where will I be living for the next few days?"

"You can come and stay at my place, for a few days. Just while we get your Spanish accommodation sorted. Any thoughts on where in Spain you'd like to go?"

"How about Barcelona?"

"You do realise they speak Catalan there," laughed Waterstone.

"That's true. Maybe I could learn both. I just thought it would be easy to get some sort of job in tourism."

"Far be it from me to tell you what you should do, but have you considered starting out in Madrid, and maybe, getting a job teaching English, whilst you learn Spanish, and then move to Barcelona, after a couple of years?"

"That makes a whole lot of sense," conceded Ian-Owen. "Actually, do you know what I really want to do first?"

"What's that?" responded Waterstone, warmly.

"Take a vacation. I can end up in Madrid."

"Yes, and when you arrive in Madrid, you can go to the British Embassy, and one of our contacts will meet you. They will help you open a bank account, for the rent, sort the paperwork for the rental agreement, and get you settled in your new flat. After that, you're on your own."

"Works for me."

"I'll get onto it, tomorrow. Gentlemen. Shall we? I forgot to mention, Grant is staying with me too."

Ian-Owen-Evan grinned.

Three days later, Evan Stoner-Ward boarded the Orient Express in London, to travel the first leg of his journey to Venice, in a luxury pullman carriage, pulled by a steam engine. As the train puffed its way through the Kentish countryside, Evan could not help thinking about Helen, and her love of Turner's painting, *Rain, Steam and Speed*. He could smell the sulphur and hear the distinctive rhythm of the engine. What was she doing now? What Evan could not have known, was that Helen had just finished her third year of a university degree in French with Spanish and had just returned from her year abroad in Luxeuil-les-Bains. She would shortly be travelling to Salamanca, in order to try and resurrect her Spanish, after ten months of speaking French and being immersed in French language and culture, and would be in Spain, at the same time as her brother.

The steam train option cost rather more than anticipated, but it was something he wanted to do, and in Calais, he would pick up the journey in a train pulled by a regular electric-powered locomotive. The greater part of this European odyssey would take place at night, through Switzerland and the Simplon tunnel, to Venice. Maybe, one day, he would do the journey in style, staying at hotels, sight-seeing along the way, all the way to Istanbul. This time, his journey was a little more functional, travelling as far as Venice, which he would follow up by spending a couple of days in Rome and on to Naples, taking in Pompei.

Catching the ferry to France, was not something Evan had yet experienced, his previous regular crossings being Hook of Holland and Ostend. It seemed like such a short crossing, by comparison. Contemplating how many hapless drug-traffickers were about their business, unaware of MI6 surveillance, amused Evan. He smiled to himself, fully expecting to catch sight of Jody's spiky hair amongst the passengers. Even when he was not consciously watching over his own shoulder, Evan realised he had now grown suspicious of just about everyone he met, apart from Waterstone, Ike and Thelma, Floyd, and Sally, and possibly Andrews. Why was he going to Italy, when he could pay his American friends in Amsterdam a visit? Maybe he would not go to Naples, after all. Did he really want to see the tortured figures of people who died under a shower of molten rock and ash, their lives cut short, in the blink of an eye? He did, because ancient history fascinated him, but on this occasion, not as much as he felt the strong pull in the direction of the Netherlands. He would fly from Rome to Amsterdam, unannounced, and surprise his friends.

On the train journey from Calais to Paris, Evan thought how boring the landscape rushing past appeared. Not that it mattered. He was just happy to be on holiday. There was no sinister objective to his travel, no secret mission, no implementation of someone else's bidding. As the train made its journey round the periphery of Paris, Evan wondered what had become of Kristina and little Ivan. How was she coping, both with the loss, and practically? How would Ivan turn out, growing up without his father?

As soon as the train had left Paris, Evan went to the restaurant car and ate the set menu, which offered lobster as a starter, beef tornado with piped mashed potato in a rich sauce, for the main, and gateau for dessert. He washed it all down with two glasses of St Emilion. Having booked a sleeping cabin, Evan took himself to his quarters, lay on his bed listening to music, and fell asleep.

He woke briefly to see the train pull into Lausanne, but somewhere before the Simplon Tunnel he dropped off again. The next time he woke he could see mountains but was not sure if he was in Switzerland or Italy, perhaps the Ticino, the Italian-speaking part of Switzerland. Having unsuccessfully tried to read the station names as they flew past, he looked at the buildings and decided he was in Italy. He must have missed the border. Not wanting to miss out on a pre-paid breakfast, he went along to the dining car for coffee and croissants.

Eventually, the train crossed the causeway and pulled into Venice Santa Lucia station. His hotel was beyond the Piazza San Marco, somewhere on the waterfront. Evan threw his rucksack over his shoulders and set off, following the arrows along the narrow, paved streets, over the Rialto Bridge to the Piazza San Marco, and continuing past the Doge's Palace to the water's edge. The empty gondolas were bouncing on their moorings and the waves lapped against the concrete. The splashes were mesmerising. Evan's hotel was about a hundred and fifty yards along, over two bridges, one of which gave a view of the Bridge of Sighs, with tourist-filled gondolas jostling for space beneath it.

After relinquishing his passport at the hotel reception, he found his room, freshened up, and left the hotel again, in search of food. Evan fancied lasagne, only to discover it was served as a starter, not a main course. He ended up with a pizza. Somewhere along one of the streets, he bought an ice cream, by way of dessert. He walked until his feet ached and sat on a terrace to drink beer. It struck Evan, that Venice was about atmosphere. He was not that interested in visiting the Doge's Palace or the Basilica. The problem with not visiting the museums, was that you ended up doing a lot of walking, and he was exhausted, when he returned to the hotel.

The following day, Evan bought a phrasebook and took a water taxi to the island of Murano where he watched a glass-blowing exhibition. As he wandered around the island, he thought about the film, *Death in Venice*. He began to reflect on all the places he had been and seen, recently, and how bad he was at relaxing on vacation. Most of his travels had involved making the acquaintance of various individuals, driven by ulterior motives. He suddenly felt alone and wished there was someone in his life he could share the experience with. As he watched a young couple, holding hands as they walked across the square, he questioned how he was even supposed to meet someone, when he was never in one place long enough to settle? Perhaps all that was about to change, now he neither had to run away, nor be sent on an assignment.

He caught a water taxi back to Piazza San Marco, and now he had no burdensome rucksack to carry, walked back to the Rialto Bridge and looked at the market stalls. There was so much cheap looking but over-priced merchandise on offer, typical of any tourist trap. Instead, he went and found a proper men's outfitters and bought a shirt, just to say he had an item of clothing that was made in Italy. After taking it back to his hotel room, he flopped onto the bed and fell asleep, waking up an hour or so later feeling distinctly disorientated and completely unrested. He went for another walk and satisfied his hunger with street food, finding a quaint little bar, off the beaten track, where he drank two beers, before returning to his hotel.

In the morning, he paid, retrieved his passport, walked back to the station, and caught an express train to Rome, arriving mid-afternoon. Consulting the map, he decided to take the Metro to the Vatican Museum. His hotel was nearby. Again, although a four-star hotel, he had to let them keep his passport. As soon as he had dumped his rucksack in his room, and used the bathroom, he set off to buy a bottle of water and to visit the Museum. The pavement was crowded all the way up the hill. He meandered to the entrance, only to realise that the crowded pavement was, in fact, the queue. Undeterred, he sidled into a group of American tourists and pretended he did not speak English. Once inside, he was on a mission to reach the Sistine Chapel.

When he had seen the *Mona Lisa*, in Paris, he had felt a little cheated, due to its small size. Although taken as a whole, the artwork surrounding him was impressive, he was surprised by how small *The Creation of Adam* appeared to be. Admittedly, it was a long way up. All Evan could think of was

Melvyn Bragg, the South Bank Show, and Paganini's 24th *Caprice*, or at least, Andrew Lloyd Webber's variation. He made his way to the exit and went in search of a restaurant, where he sat listening to the flowing Italian and watching the enthusiastic gestures of the people around him. Every so often, he caught some German. For one brief moment he considered changing his mind and moving to Italy.

Having eaten, he wandered through the streets to find the Trevi Fountain. The place was crowded with Interrailers. Evan was not at all superstitious, but when he made it to the edge of the fountain, he threw in a coin and made a wish. Perhaps it was the trauma of the last few weeks and months, or even the years of both distance and absence, but he surprised himself by wishing to find a way back home, at some point, by the time he turned thirty.

While he was standing next to the fountain, thinking about his life, a woman moved into the space next to him. Her long dark hair was held behind in a scrunch band, and she had the most piercing blue eyes. Was this déjà vu?

"Sometimes, it is difficult to choose your wish," she said, in English, with a Spanish accent and diction.

Evan looked at her.

"Yes, it is. How did you know I'm English?"

"I didn't, but everyone speaks English."

"Not everyone, but yes, you are right. English is an international language. I'm Evan, by the way."

"My name is Mariana. Do you speak Spanish?"

"No."

"Then I must speak English."

Evan sensed he was being chatted up. This caused a certain amount of confusion for him. Firstly, he was not used to this. Secondly, he was deeply suspicious, now, of any woman who approached him. His guard was well and truly raised. Under normal circumstance, meeting a girl by the Trevi Fountain would be the stuff that romantic novels are made of. The trouble for Evan was that nothing about his circumstances was normal.

"How long do you stay in Rome?" Mariana pressed him.

"Until tomorrow."

"Then we have tonight. Come. Let us have a drink."

Evan was torn. For a few seconds, he looked into her eyes, trying to make up his mind. Unfortunately, the gaze suggested to Mariana that he was attracted to her. He was attracted to her. He just was not sure if she was unattached to any drug network or secret agency.

"No, it's OK. Thank you, really," he waffled, nervously. "I've had a long day. I have an early start tomorrow. I think I'll just go back to my hotel."

"Which hotel do you stay in?" inquired Mariana.

Mariana came across to Evan as unusually forward, which made him even more suspicious. He realised, in that instant, that his efforts to one day find a decent girl and settle down would never be straightforward.

"Somewhere near the Vatican Museum," he stuttered. "Bye, then. Enjoy Rome, and wherever else you travel."

He walked away, wondering if he was safe, and quickened his pace. Just over half an hour later, he arrived back at his hotel.

After breakfast, the following morning, he packed his rucksack, paid for his stay, recovered his passport, and set off to look at the Colosseum, which was about a forty-five-minute walk. Halfway there, he popped into a travel agent and bought a one-way ticket to Amsterdam, for late in the afternoon. Further on, he found a café and sat down on the terrace, in the morning sun. A waiter approached.

"Buongiorno, signore."

"Buongiorno. Café espresso per favore."

The waiter disappeared, and returned, a couple of minutes later, with Evan's coffee and a saucer with the bill.

"Grazie."

"Prego."

Taking his last swallow of coffee, Evan sorted the money which he left on the saucer and walked the short distance to the Colosseum. A human statue was standing on the pavement. The man was dressed as a gladiator, covered in silvery green paint, and standing quite motionless. There was a bucket in front of him, into which kind tourists dropped coins. Evan reached into his pocket and drew out all his small change, which he dropped into the bucket. The gladiator made no reaction whatsoever. Evan mischievously considered how the gladiator might react if someone were to attempt theft. He was still smiling to himself when he joined the end of the queue into the Colosseum. Although his early learning at school presented history as a series of potted dates, to be learnt by heart, his 'A' Level had been inspiring. Evan enjoyed Ancient History, so this kind of opportunity to see and touch it, excited him.

The queue ground its way forward, and after about half an hour, he walked out into the amphitheatre. As he sat looking down on the arena, thinking of Kirk Douglas in *Spartacus*, he looked up to see Mariana walking towards him. In his head, Evan wanted to ask her if she was following him, but she spoke first.

"I think we like the same things."

"I guess there are a few things everyone wants to see, in Rome."

"I can sit down?"

"Please," gestured Evan.

Mariana sat a couple of feet away from him.

"Where are you from, in Spain?" asked Evan, not letting on that he was going to Madrid, in the not-too-distant future.

"Gijon."

"Where is that?"

"The Atlantic coast. In the north. In the region of Asturias."

Evan had heard, somewhere, that the north of Spain was historically close to Breton and Celtic cultures. That explained the fairer skin, dark hair, and blue eyes.

"Is that where you live, now?"

"I am a student in Madrid."

Evan felt trapped in some kind of grotesque state of déjà-vu. This was SSEES and Katya, all over again. He was now engaging in mental gymnastics. If there was a mole in MI6, it was possible, Mariana could have tracked him from London to Rome. If there was no mole, she would have no idea about his new identity, his journey to Venice and Rome, and absolutely nothing of his long-term plans to re-settle in Madrid. In that case, their meeting was coincidental. How could there be a mole when they took down the Krukov drugs network? Surely, a mole would have prevented it from happening.

"What are you studying?"

"I am studying to become a teacher. In my free time, I teach Spanish to people who come to Spain and don't speak our language. What do you do?"

"I am travelling the world. Before that, I used to sell books. And before that, I worked in a pub."

"How long will you travel?"

"I'm not sure."

"You should come to Spain. I will give you my phone number. You can call me, if you come to Madrid."

"Thank you."

She reached into her bag, took out a pen and some paper and wrote down her phone number.

"Thanks," responded Evan, taking the paper from her. "Now I have to leave."

"Goodbye, Evan."

He exited the amphitheatre and started to walk in the direction of the train station, where he intended to catch a bus to the airport. Still slightly sceptical about the randomness of his encounter with Mariana, he went into a department store, got immediately into the lift, pressed the first floor and the third floor, got out at the first, went back down to the ground floor by the stairs and left through the exit at the rear of the building. He ran along the street, took the first side street he came to, ran again, took a left, and walked along the parallel street to his original route, arriving at the station to find a bus for the airport already at the stop. He got on, sat down, and caught his breath.

Three quarters of an hour later, he checked in and went straight through security to departures, where he went into the toilets and changed his shirt, for one of a different colour. He found a bar and ordered a beer. A skilled agent would not have lost him in the department store, but having eluded the agent in Paddington Station, he felt confident that he had shaken Mariana from his tail, had she been following him. He had not told her of his intention to travel to Amsterdam, and if he were to contact her in Madrid, it would be his choice. This was no way to live, but what was done was done, even if that meant spending the rest of his life looking over his shoulder and fearful of starting a relationship. Another glass of beer later, and his gate number was displayed. After using the toilet, he made his way to the gate, and twenty minutes later, was settling into his seat for the two-and-a-half-hour flight to Amsterdam. Evan was excited to see Ike and Thelma, Floyd and Sally. He even considered dropping by to see Kees, at The Coffee Room.

When the plane touched down in Amsterdam, it was nearly eight o'clock in the evening. The bus dropped him outside the station, and he walked round to the hostel. He was just about to go in, when he suddenly remembered he had a new identity, and the chances were, he might be recognised, so he continued walking and booked into a hotel just off the Dam. Although it was four times as expensive, Evan considered it a safer option. After he had checked in, he found a restaurant and ate steak and fries. He was back in his room by ten o'clock.

In the morning, after a much-needed shower, he strolled round to The Coffee Room to get some breakfast. Kees was nowhere to be seen, and there was a woman behind the counter who Evan did not recognise. He ate eggs and drank coffee, paid, and left. His memories were flooding back, as he walked to Floyd and Sally's houseboat. As he approached, he picked up aromas of soup mixed with bread baking, in preparation for lunch, and inexplicably felt nervous crossing the gangplank. Sally looked up from her cooking.

"Owen!"

Of course, she knew him as Owen. There was no point in mentioning his new identity. No one else was on the boat.

"Hello. How are you?"

"Floyd!" she called.

Floyd appeared and before Evan could say a word, hugged him.

"You look well. Come. Sit down. Coffee?"

Sally poured three coffees, but stayed next to the cooker, stirring the soup.

"What brings you back to Amsterdam?" inquired Floyd, obviously pleased to see Evan.

"You guys. I was taking some holiday, and I thought, why not come to Amsterdam, and catch up with you and Sally, Ike, and Thelma.

"Oh, Owen," responded Sally, her expression changing to reflect her sense of loss. "Ike had a heart attack earlier this year. The Lord took him. I'm so sorry."

"Is Thelma still on their houseboat?"

"No," replied Floyd. "She went back to the States to be closer to family. Tell us about what you've been doing."

"I went to Afghanistan."

"Really," responded Floyd, "Where?"

"Kabul, followed by Kandahar, but mostly Lashkar Gah. I was there for three months."

"Wow," said Floyd.

"And before that, I was in Ottawa, working at a publishing company. It was all temporary. I'm now taking a short holiday before going to Spain, hopefully, to teach."

"What happened to your face?" asked Sally.

"Long story. Short version is some Russians took a disliking to me."

"Are you still clean?" inquired Floyd.

"Definitely."

"Where are you staying?"

"Hotel on the Dam. I'm only here for a couple of days."

"Will you stay and eat lunch with us?" Sally invited him.

"Is grass green?" replied Evan, laughing. "How is the project going?"

"Good, thank you. Obviously, we miss Ike and Thelma," responded Floyd. "They were so good with addicts who wanted to break free."

"They were, indeed," smiled Evan.

"What did you do in Afghanistan?" asked Sally.

"I helped out in a bookshop and also in a shop that fixed things," replied Evan, in Pashto.

"Your Pashto is very good, for such a short time," Floyd encouraged him.

"Thank you."

"Did you see the poppy fields?" added Floyd.

"Yes. And a kite flying competition. The place is full of Soviets. I stayed with a man whose wife was killed by them. The politics is complicated, isn't it?"

"Yes. And it's not helped by the drugs, which fund the conflict."

Evan desperately wanted to tell them about the true purpose of his time in Afghanistan. He trusted them one hundred percent. He just knew that to tell them probably laid him wide open to accusations of contravening the Official Secrets Act.

"Well, I'm pleased to tell you that I wasn't tempted," laughed Evan.

A student-aged girl came on board, looking lost.

"Hello," Sally greeted her. "Would you like some soup and bread?"

"I was told to come here and ask for a man called Floyd. Is one of you Floyd?"

"I am. And this is my wife Sally. Owen is a friend of ours."

Evan winced on the inside. He was no longer Owen, in the world's eyes. It was different, behind the locked doors of MI6, but this was public.

"I'm Lisa. I ..... I, ummm ..... I've been raped."

"Please, sit down," gestured Sally.

"I think I need to leave you to be with Lisa," reflected Evan, standing up. "It was great catching up with you."

He left before Floyd or Sally had time to plan how to continue their conversation, as they were pre-occupied with Lisa. Evan did not mind. He made an instant decision to hire a bike and go and attempt to purchase cannabis in Amsterdam and heroin in Utrecht, purely out of curiosity. His rationale was to settle his mind by making sure Krukov's network really had been taken down.

Having hired a bicycle, he set off on his former route and knocked on the door of the house where he had bought cannabis. A man Evan did not recognise peered round the door.

"What do you want?"

"I heard I can buy cannabis here."

"You heard wrong. Now go away."

Evan cycled away, his heart racing. After returning his bicycle to a hire point, he went to the station and caught a train to Utrecht. When he reached the place where he had previously bought heroin, the door was boarded up. Perhaps the network really had been taken down and he was free to look up Mariana when he got to Madrid. Before catching the train back to Amsterdam, Evan did some sight-seeing amongst the canals and medieval buildings.

Evan's flight to Madrid was a morning one, which meant he arrived in Madrid in time for lunch. He sat in the Plaza Mayor, drinking a beer and watching the world go by. When he thought the extended lunchtime might be at an end, siestas and evening opening hours being part of the local culture, he set off on foot for the Calle de Fernando el Santo. The embassy was in a fascinating building. It was circular in construction, and to Evan, it looked like a giant revolving filing carousel. He went to the reception desk.

"Hello. I'm sorry, I don't speak Spanish, yet."

"That's perfectly alright, sir. We do speak English within these walls, as well as Spanish, when necessary. How can we be of assistance?" asked a woman in her forties, with a received pronunciation English accent.

"My name is Evan Stoner-Ward, and I was told that someone would meet me here. I don't have an appointment, as such. I was just asked to turn up, on arrival in Madrid."

"Wait a minute, please, and I will find out who to contact."

She opened a drawer and took out a file, ran her gaze down the front page, smiled and made a phone call. Evan could only hear her side of the conversation.

"Do you know anything about an Evan Stoner-Ward? He's here in reception. ….. You do? Oh, good ….. yes, I will."

She put the receiver back in its cradle.

"Juan Johnson-Ramirez will be down to see you shortly."

"Thank you."

Evan moved away from the desk and stood looking around at the décor. A few minutes later, he was approached by a man he might have considered Spanish-looking, olive-skinned, dark hair. He was not much older than Evan and was carrying a briefcase.

"Hello. I am Juan Johnson-Ramirez," he introduced himself, holding out his hand.

His English was impeccable. Evan took his hand and shook it warmly.

"I believe you know where I shall be living."

"Yes, I do. Would you like to come with me?"

The two men left the building and headed south.

"It's a fifteen-minute walk. No need to take the car. Happy to help carry anything."

"I'm all good, thank you."

"Do you speak Spanish?"

"Not yet. I plan to enrol on some classes as soon as I'm settled. I enjoy learning languages."

"I will do my best to translate the rental agreement for you."

"Thanks."

"Which languages do you speak?"

"Russian, Dutch, Pashto, French. And English, of course. Your family name is Spanish and English. Are you fluently bilingual?"

"Pretty much. I can get you a list of Spanish classes if you like. I mean, after I've got you settled in, there is no intention of MI6 contacting you again. So, I'm just offering, out of personally wanting to help. In any case, the embassy has this kind of information. Just ask at reception."

"Thank you. I'll see how I get on, and if I'm struggling, I'll drop by the embassy. I imagine there are lots of leaflets and posters around at the library, the city hall, the university, tourism office. It will be all part of settling in, to find my way around these things."

"As you wish. The apartment is just along here, on Calle de Gravina," indicated Juan, as they reached a junction.

Juan unlocked the door and started up the stairs. Evan's flat was on the first floor. The first key, Juan selected did not unlock the door to the flat. He tried another.

"After you," he gestured, standing back to let Evan in.

They entered, and Juan closed the door behind them.

"As you can see, it's a furnished apartment. MI6 has paid the deposit, and the first three months of your rent. We have also paid fifty percent of the next three months. Our hope, and to be honest, our requirement, is that you find yourself a job, during the first three months. The contract is for a year. After that, it's your choice. Would you like me to read and translate before you sign the agreement?"

"Just the gist of it. The important stuff."

"OK. This tells you who, what, when and how long. This is when the rent is due. This bit tells you how to be a good tenant and this bit a good neighbour. If you've rented an apartment before, it's fairly standard. This bit is about damages and the deposit. This is who to contact if the heating breaks down or the place floods, or if any of the fixtures and fittings break. Happy to sign?"

"Yes," replied Evan, reaching into his rucksack to find a pen.

"We have opened an account for you with Banco Santander. There is already a standing order in place for the rent. You will discover that your Canadian account has been closed, and the balance transferred to this account. Oh, and you have a telephone. When the bill arrives, pay at the bank. It's not that expensive for the line rental, and if you keep your calls to a minimum, you should be able to afford it. Again, we've paid the line rental for the first six months. Now, let me show you where the fuse box and heating switches are, and the hot water tank."

Juan gave Evan a guided tour of the flat and handed him the keys.

"Good luck. If you need anything, just come to the embassy and ask for me by name. And to be honest, I'd love to hear your story. If you'd like to meet up for a beer, sometime, get in touch."

"Thank you."

"Bye then," said Juan, as he walked towards the door. "I'll see myself out."

"Bye."

Evan was on his own. The flat was clean, even if the fixtures and fittings were not entirely to his taste. The location was excellent, and the rent did not seem unreasonable. What was missing was bedding, and he could probably do with getting some more towels. His plan, for the rest of the afternoon, would be shopping for essentials, bedding, and cleaning materials. All of his French francs, Dutch guilders, and Italian lira could be exchanged into pesetas, along with additional sterling, before going shopping. If he had time, he would find the library and identify some Spanish courses. Tomorrow, he would visit the bank. After using his new bathroom, he emptied the contents of his rucksack out onto the settee and went out to find a bureau de change.

Once all Evan's notes had been exchanged for pesetas, he felt he needed to exchange a further fifty pounds in sterling. He was embarrassed to have to have them speak English to him and resolved not to ask for any further directions in English. This meant his search for a grocery store, supermarket or department store would be more challenging than anticipated. He felt that it was the only way to learn, and by immersing himself in Spanish, he would start to pick it up. Already, he could begin to identify certain words by looking at the descriptions and names of shops and connecting the word with the window display. He also had a phrasebook to fall back on.

As he walked, he found himself in front of the library, so he went into look for information about Spanish courses. He picked up two flyers. One of them had a telephone number and an address. The other just showed a telephone number. Evan figured he would just turn up at the address at the displayed start time and see what happened. He discovered a grocery store and bought some essentials, along with some non-essentials, like vodka and orange juice. His rucksack was quite heavy, and he still needed to buy some bedding.

He walked back along a different street and came upon a shop that looked like it sold soft furnishings. Intrepidly, he entered and made a quick scan of the shelves. The lady behind the counter greeted him.

"Buenas tardes, señor."

"Buenas tardes," Evan repeated.

He made a beeline for the shelves which looked to be displaying sheets. Below the sheets and pillowcases were quilts and pillows. He had no idea what the descriptions meant, but he picked up two medium-priced pillows and what looked to be a low-tog quilt. Thankfully, the measurements were in centimetres. Unfortunately, Evan had forgotten to measure the bed, so ended up with the widest quilt and two equivalent sheets. As he carried his selection to the counter, he spied some towels, so grabbed a bath towel and a couple of tea towels. Evan had already worked out roughly what the cost would be. Trying to do the arithmetic in his head, of what the pesetas equated to in sterling, was complicated. The purchases seemed good value for money. It was only when he got back to his flat and redid the calculation, that he realised he had left a naught off and everything was more expensive than he had first thought. He kicked himself, thinking that he should have noticed that the shop was an upmarket boutique. What did it matter, in the greater scheme of things?

Back at the flat, he squirted bleach into the toilet and made the bed, poured himself a vodka and orange, filled another glass with water from a bottle and settled down on the settee to eat bread and chorizo. As he ate, he pondered how he might get a job. It was likely to be a lot of legwork, just asking in cafes and restaurants. After taking the plate and glass to the kitchen, he washed his hands and topped up the vodka and orange. He took his Walkman and drink and laid down on the bed. The next thing he knew, it was eleven-thirty at night, and he had just been abruptly awoken by a loud crash outside the window. He stumbled over and looked out to see two vehicles which had collided at the junction. Evan closed the window, went to the bathroom, and got into his bed. He fell asleep thinking about Mariana.

When Evan woke up at just after seven o'clock, his plans for the day included visiting the bank, spending a couple of hours trying to find employment, and turning up at the Spanish language classes. The venue was about a twenty-five-minute walk from his flat, and the classes started at six o'clock.

He showered, made coffee, and having worked out how to use the grill, toasted a couple of slices of bread, which he ate with butter and apricot jam. Looking at his clothes, he came to the conclusion that chinos, his Italian shirt and a tie, with smart shoes, were appropriate to the kind of job he was after. Had he been going to an interview, he would have worn a suit, but here, he was turning up on spec, in the hope that someone would give him a trial shift. In Amsterdam, pretty much everyone spoke English, so not speaking a lot of Dutch, was no barrier to working in a café. Madrid was a little different. English was still not spoken widely. Even as the Madrid Scene, or Movida Madrileña as the Spanish called it, was taking off, with a new openness to American and British music, he knew he needed to learn Spanish, and fast.

The cultural upheaval, of the post Franco years, began in the mid-seventies, but really exploded in the eighties. The conservative values of a nation which had been restricted in every way possible under the thirty-five years of dictatorship, had given way to new freedoms. A generation of young adults were now experimenting with anything from recreational drugs to counter-cultural music to alternative expressions of sexuality. It was into this context, that an Irish couple, in their twenties, had embarked on an adventure in the Spanish capital. Their dream was to open and Irish pub. Its realisation came about, six months prior to Evan's arrival, in the form of The Shamrock.

After two failed attempts, and already growing despondent, Evan stumbled upon The Shamrock. Curious to know how a traditional Irish pub could be profitable in Spain, and partial to a pint of Guinness, Evan went through the open door. He was met by the electric voice of a female lead singer, supported by fiddle, bodhran, flute, accordion, and guitar. By the time he reached the bar, Evan's foot was tapping.

"Excuse me. I am new to Madrid. I was wondering if you need any bar staff."

Connor O'Donnell looked Evan up and down.

"Have you worked in a pub, before?" came the soft Irish brogue.

"As a matter of fact, yes. I worked in The Prince Albert, in Battersea, for eighteen months."

"And what brings you to Madrid?"

"I travelled a fair bit and decided to settle in Madrid. I have a flat, not so far from here. Within walking distance, anyway."

"How's your Spanish?"

"I'll be honest. It's almost non-existent. However, I speak Russian, Dutch, French and Pashto. I pick up languages quickly, and I'm enrolling on Spanish classes this evening."

"That'll be Thursday evenings when you're not available. Any other commitments?"

"None. I really am new here."

"It's true I could use some help. My wife, Ellie, is about six months pregnant with our second, so she's finding serving behind the bar more and more difficult. Would you come tomorrow lunchtime for a trial shift?"

"My pleasure. Thank you. What time would you like me here?"

"Eleven o'clock."

"Brilliant. I'll have a pint of Guinness, please."

Connor poured the pint and left the bubbles to settle while he served another customer. Having topped up Evan's pint, he placed it on the bar in front of him.

"It's on the house."

"That's very generous of you. Thank you."

Evan took the pint and moved to a vacant table where he sat soaking in the music. The lead singer really did have the most extraordinary voice. He made his pint of Guinness last half an hour, while he enjoyed the music, returning the empty glass to the bar and acknowledging Connor before he used the facilities and left. Evan was not aware he was feeling hungry, until the smell of churros infiltrated his nostrils. He turned a corner to see a mobile churro seller. Street-food appealed to him, so he bought some and wandered along eating them. He came to a small square and sat down on some steps. When the churros were finished, he decided to do some more exploring before going to the bank.

In the bank, they humoured him with speaking fractured English, but it was better than his Spanish, and he was grateful. He left the building with the promise of a cash machine card, an understanding of how to pay in any wages he might earn and how he could transfer money from his English account, if needed. Outside, the temperature was rising, and Evan thought it made sense to return to his flat, rest and shower, before going to the Spanish class. He was relieved to be back indoors, the closed shutters having kept the air cool, and drank an entire bottle of water. He lay on the settee, listening to music, and resolved to find a radio and a Spanish language course on cassette. Listening to music was not going to improve his Spanish, and if he was successful in his work trial at The Shamrock, he would be speaking and listening to a lot of English.

The time came to eat some toast, shower, get changed and go to the Spanish class. He was feeling nervous, as he entered the building. Having taken the flyer with him, he held it up to a student-aged man and pointed at the wording.

"Follow me. I'm going there myself," came the reply.

"Are you Australian?"

"No. New Zealand."

"I haven't enrolled. I just thought I would turn up."

"I think most of us did. There's seven of us. The teacher is good," he reassured Evan. "And she's hot!" he added laughing.

"My name's Evan, by the way."

"Pleased to meet you, Evan. I'm Paul."

They arrived at the classroom.

As he walked into the room, Evan was overtaken by surprise. The teacher was Mariana.

"Hello. What are you doing here?"

"I saw the class advertised and I'd like to join, if possible."

"Are you staying in Madrid, now?"

"As a matter of fact, I've settled here."

"You didn't say anything, before."

"I wasn't a hundred percent sure I would be. I was torn between settling or travelling some more. And here I am."

"Well, find a seat and fill in this form," she said, handing him a form.

He sat on an empty chair and completed the enrolment form, by which time, all the other learners had arrived. Evan realised he may have committed the error of sitting in someone else's seat, because a French lady, old enough to be his mother, was hovering at his shoulder.

"Siéntate aquí, Nicole, por favor."

The lady looked a little miffed but moved away to an empty chair opposite.

"Buenas tardes. Hoy nos vamos a presentar. Me llamo Mariana," she instructed the class pointing at Paul.

"Me llamo Paul."

The students took it in turn to introduce themselves. Evan guessed from the accents, that four of them were English speakers. He was not sure about the others, maybe French, or Belgian, and some sort of Scandinavian, and possibly Dutch, or Flemish Belgian. No doubt, all would become clearer.

"Me llamo Evan," he said, when it was his turn.

"Muy bien."

By the end of the class, Evan had realised that whilst the good thing about learning Spanish is that it is pretty much spelt as it is spoken, there are two verbs for 'to be', and it would take a while for him to master the difference between 'ser' and 'estar'. Mariana indicated he should hang on until the others had left. Paul noticed, and as he went by, said, "Maybe get a drink, after class next week?"

"That would be great," replied Evan.

"Shall we go for a drink, now, to catch up?" suggested Mariana once Paul had left the room.

"Yes. Let's."

Evan was far more decisive than he had been in Rome, simply because the coincidence reassured him that there was no way Mariana could have known he would be in Spain or that he would choose her Spanish language class. They found a nearby bar, where Mariana insisted on buying Evan a beer.

"Why did you choose to live in Spain?"

"It's warm. It's a new language for me. I met a girl in Rome who invited me to visit."

Mariana looked Evan in the eyes when he said the last part.

"Where do you live?"

"My apartment is on the Calle de Gravina. I have a job trial tomorrow. In The Shamrock pub."

"That's exciting."

"When I lived in London, I worked in a pub. I will probably speak more English than Spanish. The owners are Irish, and a lot of the customers are English-speaking."

"Then you must remain in my class and learn Spanish."

"Is one of your students allowed to take the teacher on a date?" laughed Evan.

"It depends. Only when the student is handsome."

Evan took a drink.

"So, shall we go to a disco at the weekend?" suggested Mariana.

"Yes. OK. Where and when?"

"The Sala El Sol. Meet me at the Puerta del Sol at eight o'clock tomorrow. We can eat and drink and go to the club to dance."

"That's settled, then."

They left the bar and went in opposite directions. Evan kicked himself for not kissing her, but he walked on air, back to his flat.

As Evan was making his way to The Shamrock for his trial shift, it occurred to him that, if he was successful, he might be working in the evening. He had just told Connor that he did not have any commitments. In his pocket was the Spanish phrasebook, which included a section on eating out with a list of various drinks. Connor had unlocked the door, so Evan could go straight in.

"Good morning," Evan greeted him.

"Good morning to you too."

"How is Mrs O'Donnell?"

"Happy to know I might be getting some help. To be honest with you, I don't think we anticipated how much work was involved in setting up a new business with a young family and none of the usual family support around."

"We had three staff plus the landlord, when I was at The Prince Albert. Once he took me on, he spent less time behind the bar and more time focusing on the business, although he still liked to connect with the customers through a few shifts, especially if one of us was on holiday."

"Holiday. What's one of those?" laughed Connor, with some irony. "That's probably what's needed, here. You've already told me you can't do Thursday evenings. I should probably get an advert out there."

"What would you like me to do first?"

"We'll start in the cellar. Tell me if anything looks any different to The Prince Albert."

He led Evan down to the cellar.

"I'm about to change a barrel. Do you want to do it?"

"Let's see if it's the same as I'm used to."

Evan started to go through the procedure and changed the barrel easily.

"Great. Grab one of those crates will you," requested Connor, pointing at a stack.

Evan picked up the top crate of soft drinks bottles and Connor took hold of a crate from another stack. They lugged them up to the bar.

"This is where these need to go. Half on the shelf, half in the fridge. I'll show you the till, before you sort them all out."

He opened the till and pulled two rolls of coins from his pocket, which he proceeded to unwrap and drop into the compartments.

"You put in the actual prices, but I'm afraid you have to work out the change in your head. There's a lot of noughts, so be careful. Write it down if you have to."

Evan decided against confessing to his bedding purchase error.

"Ask, if you need anything explaining."

"I will."

"By the way, we're open until three and then again from six-thirty to eleven."

"Is there any music today?"

"Later on. We try to have music at lunchtimes in the week and evenings Friday, Saturday, and Sunday."

Evan nodded and started to arrange the bottles while Connor distributed some beer mats around the tables. It felt like being back in The Prince Albert. The only thing Evan was unsure about was communicating with the Spanish-speaking customers. Connor opened the doors wide and put an A-frame chalkboard outside. The first customers of the day, an English couple, came in. In fact, by the end of the shift, Evan only counted three Spanish-speaking customers. It had been busy, with holidaymakers finding this little oasis, this little piece of the Emerald Isle. Connor locked the doors.

"How was that, for you?"

"Great!"

"Well then, let's talk about wages and shifts."

"Thanks."

"I'll pay you three hundred and ninety pesetas an hour. Until someone else comes along to share the load, you can have as many shifts as you want. I could use you here, on Friday evenings and alternate Saturday and Sunday evenings as a minimum, and then it's up to you, which evenings and lunchtimes. Evenings are six till midnight. Lunchtimes are eleven till three-thirty."

"How about I do Monday, Wednesday and Friday evenings, plus Saturday or Sunday, and then Monday to Friday lunchtimes?"

Connor got out a calculator and totted up the hours and cost.

"That's fine by me. Cash in hand until I can work out how the tax works."

"Stupidly, I arranged to go out tonight with someone from my Spanish class. Can I work Saturday and Sunday evening instead this week? In future, I'll plan around my shifts."

"Be my guest. You need to have some friends here."

"Thank you. Really. Much appreciated. Now, let's get cleared away. Where do the empties go? Is there some sort of glass bin outside?"

"There is. I'll start wiping down tables. When you're done, you can start on the glasses."

It was nearer four than three-thirty, when Evan left The Shamrock, but he was not bothered. Happy to have secured a job so soon, and not having to change his date with Mariana, more than made up for it. He went home, showered, and set his alarm for seven o'clock, to allow himself a chance to take a nap. Woken at seven, he was glad to have set the alarm, otherwise, he might have been late for his date. Having spruced himself up, Evan set off for the Puerta del Sol. Arriving before Mariana, he sat down to wait on the edge of the flower bed surrounding one of the fountains, in some way replicating his first encounter with her at the Trevi Fountain. His stomach was rumbling, and he regretted not having a slice of toast before he left the flat. Looking up, he saw a young woman with short, boyish dark hair, standing halfway between the two fountains, looking up at the statue of a man on horseback. She looked strangely familiar, but he was not sure how. Not knowing which direction Mariana would appear from, he looked the other way. When Evan looked back, the young woman was nowhere to be seen. It could not possibly have been, but Evan realised she resembled Helen, his sister. Looking back the other way again, he saw Mariana approaching, but stayed seated until she was only a few paces away, at which point he got up, moved towards her and kissed her on the cheek, watching closely for her reaction. She did not flinch.

"Hello."

"Ola, Evan. From today, we speak in Spanish. You can ask me to translate a word, but we speak in Spanish."

"How was your day?"

Mariana said the sentence back in Spanish, and Evan repeated it. She replied, in Spanish, that she had had a good day.

"You've had a good day," repeated Evan, translating it back into English.

"Muy bien."

Evan realised he was really going to struggle to convey any information at all. He opened his phrasebook.

"I work in a pub," he read, in Spanish.

"You've started a new job? Where?"

"I start a new job. Where? The Shamrock."

"Muy bien. Are you hungry?"

"Yes," responded Evan, in Spanish, but reverting to English? "Where shall we eat?"

Mariana repeated the question in Spanish and pointed down a street.

"In a restaurant just down that street. It's not expensive."

Evan guessed at the translation and repeated back what he thought Mariana had said. They started walking towards the street, across the square, and he took hold of her hand. She did not seem to mind.

As soon as they were seated at a table, he opened his phrasebook at food and drink, and consulted the menu.

"I would like steak and chips. And a beer," he said in Spanish when he had worked out what he wanted.

The waiter came over and Mariana gestured at Evan that he should make his own order. He repeated the phrases in Spanish and Mariana confirmed that she would have the same. The waiter disappeared into the kitchen.

"I know I have to learn Spanish, but I feel like I can't ask you normal things, to get to know you."

Mariana looked deep into Evan's eyes and repeated what he had said in Spanish, adding, "How will you learn?"

"OK. But it's going to make progress slow."

"Are you in a hurry to get anywhere?" she challenged him affectionately, in Spanish.

"I don't understand."

"Are you in a hurry to get anywhere?" she repeated in English.

Evan realised he was stressing too much. He shook his head and laughed. The waiter came over with their beers. Evan looked into Mariana's eyes and said nothing. His gaze was interrupted by their food arriving.

"Buen provecho," said Evan.

"Buen provecho," replied Mariana, smiling.

They ate in silence, with Evan trying to eat as slowly as he could, to make not having to say anything last longer. It was only five to nine, when they did finally finish, and Mariana spoke first.

"That was delicious."

"Yes, that was delicious," Evan repeated back.

"Do you want another beer?"

"Yes, please."

Mariana called the waiter over and nodded at Evan.

"Two beers please," he ordered.

"Two more beers," Mariana corrected him, as the waiter walked away.

"Two more beers," repeated Evan.

"Do you want dessert?"

"No. You?"

"I'm good. Just the beers."

"What is the club like?" asked Evan after another brief pause in the conversation.

"Colourful. Loud. Fun. Hot. Very hot."

"Can we buy drinks there? Alcohol and water?"

"Yes. We can buy alcoholic drinks and bottled water."

Evan repeated what Mariana had said, feeling more confident that he could make whatever conversation he needed to, and simply have Mariana repeat it back in Spanish. She was right, of course, it was the best way to learn, and no different to the Spanish language cassette he was going to buy.

"Did you teach today?"

"No. I didn't teach. I studied at the university."

"How many years will you study?"

"I will study for two more years."

"Have you always wanted to be a teacher?"

"I have wanted to be a teacher since I was twelve years old."

"What subject will you teach?"

"History and politics."

"I studied history at school, to 'A' level. I like Ancient History. I know very little about politics."

"Politics in Spain is fascinating. Surely, you know we are less than ten years since Franco."

"That is European history, for me, not politics," replied Evan, laughing.

"This night club was not possible during the dictatorship. Now people dance and take drugs and enjoy free sex."

"Do you take drugs?"

"Sometimes, but only when I am at a nightclub. And you?"

"I haven't taken drugs for a long time."

Evan thought he might not mind taking recreational drugs, or even the occasional speed pill, but there was no way he was going anywhere near heroin or cocaine. He was convinced that Mariana was no drug dealer, just a young adult in Spain, enjoying her new-found freedoms.

When they reached the bottom of their second bottle of beer, Evan attracted the waiter's attention and consulted his phrasebook.

"I would like the bill, please," he said, when the waiter came over.

"Yes, sir."

He went away and came back two minutes later with the bill.

"Shall we go halves?" asked Mariana.

Evan was not sure whether agreeing would count against him. Mariana seemed fairly independent to him.

"Yes. Halves."

He had left his wallet at the flat, only going out with enough money for the evening, as notes folded in his back pocket. Taking out the notes, he counted out his half, rounding up the numbers. Mariana counted them again, in Spanish, leaving Evan space to repeat the words. Then she counted out her half, also rounding it up, so between them, they left a generous tip. They left the restaurant and Mariana led them to the nightclub. A short queue was forming outside, which they joined. On the way in, they paid their entrance fee and had their hands stamped.

In the main room, the dance music was reverberating round the walls, with lights flashing. Evan really was not a fan of this kind of music scene, but he was a fan of Mariana. She took hold of his hand and dragged him to the dance floor. Evan was terrified of making a fool of himself and tried to copy what some other men were doing a few feet away. In his head, he was having an argument with himself about not concentrating on his moves, because the harder he concentrated, the more likely he was to make a mistake. Mariana was in her element, and the way she swayed her body was turning Evan on. He wanted to make love to her and started to wonder what chance he had, tonight. He had no protection in his pocket, and no change, even if there was a vending machine in the gents. He did not know if she was on the pill, but he had been reading about HIV/AIDS, globally, not just as a consequence of the new-found freedoms embodied by the Madrid Scene. He was concerned for his own future wellbeing.

The music was mostly in Spanish, with the occasional American or British song. When they had danced for almost an hour, Mariana made a drinking gesture with her hand, and Evan was relieved to leave the dance floor. They found the bar, and Evan bought two bottles of beer, which gave him some coins. He had no idea how many pesetas condoms cost in Spain.

"I need to use the facilities," said Evan, in her ear, not waiting for a translation before heading for the gents.

He genuinely needed the bathroom. It was not just a pretext to buy protection for later. In the gents, he relieved himself in a cubicle. Two men came in, and Evan assumed they used the urinals. When he came out of the cubicle, one man had left, and the other was getting a tablet from a small plastic bag which contained several.

"You want one?" the man addressed him, as he washed his hands.

Evan thought he understood, and shook his head, smiling. The man left, and Evan took a closer look at the vending machine. He reached in his pocket and checked the coins, which were enough to buy some protection. He put in his coins, hoping no one would come in. No sooner had he pocketed the packet when a man came in. Evan re-joined Mariana.

"I thought you were lost."

"A man just offered me drugs."

"It is common, here. Did you say yes?"

"No."

"Another time, perhaps?"

"Another time."

Evan did not tell her what he had purchased.

They drank the water and took the open beer bottles back onto the dance floor as there was nowhere to sit down. Evan looked at his watch. He did not want to stay beyond midnight, and hoped for earlier, if there was an excuse to leave. A slower track came on.

"Do you want to dance with me?"

"Yes. I want to dance with you."

They moved closer and he put his arms round her back. She put hers round his neck. He could feel her breasts against his chest. To Evan it felt like only two layers, his shirt and hers, with no bra. Her hair smelt of some sort of herbal shampoo. He kissed her neck and continued to kiss her until his kisses had reached her lips. He kissed her on the mouth and hesitated to see if she responded. Within seconds, their tongues were entwined. Another slow track followed the first, and they continued to sway gently, all the while kissing.

"Shall we go?" he asked, as the track came to an end.

"Where to?" asked Mariana.

"You can come to mine, if you want to."

"OK, but I think my apartment might be closer."

"Where is your apartment?"

"Two streets from here."

"Then yes, let's go to yours."

As they left the night club, he put his arm round her waist, and she did the same. The fresh air was helpful. The last thing Evan wanted was to be too tired to perform. They arrived outside Mariana's apartment block.

"It's on the second floor," she informed him. "There's no lift."

They walked up the stairs, holding hands, but had to release them for Mariana to get her key and unlock the door.

"The bathroom is that door," she indicated, whilst chaining and bolting the front door.

Evan went to the bathroom, used the toilet, and washed his hands and face. When he returned to the living area,

Mariana was standing there holding a bottle of whiskey and a bottle of vodka.

"Do you have any orange juice?"

"I have orange juice."

"Then, I'll have a vodka and orange, please."

He followed her into the kitchen and distracted her from pouring the drinks, by placing his arms round her from behind and kissing her neck and shoulder. She succeeded nonetheless, so he allowed her to escape long enough to carry the two glasses over to the sofa, where she handed one of them to him, and sat down. Evan sat next to her, took a swallow of his vodka and orange, waited for her to do the same, and took her glass from her, placing it on the coffee table. He took her in his arms and started to kiss her shoulders and the part of her collar bone which was uncovered. He was moving his hands across her back and sides, confirming her lack of bra, and brought his left hand to the front, tracing the form of her nipple, through her shirt.

He pulled her shirt up over her head and continued to kiss her whilst unbuttoning the waistband of her skirt. He could have left the skirt on, but he wanted to undress her completely. When all that she was wearing was her briefs, he pulled off his shirt and unzipped his chinos. As he pulled them off, he pulled out the condom from the rear pocket. With the condom still in his hand, he lifted Mariana up and carried her through the only other door, which he assumed was the bedroom. Laying her on top of the bed, her pulled down he briefs and started kissing her abdomen. He lay on top of her so that she could feel his manhood through his underwear and continued to kiss her on the lips and breasts. In one skilful movement, he pulled down his underwear, tour open the wrapper, rolled on the protection, and penetrated her. She moaned as he moved slowly back and forth. He could feel her body tensing and increased the speed and strength of his thrusting, until, to his huge relief, she let out a massive groan and he was able to bring on his own climax. He withdrew, his right hand ensuring the condom remained in place and slid sideways off her. They both lay there breathing heavily, for a couple of minutes, until she sat up and pulled the quilt, which had been folded across the bottom of the bed, up over them. When she lay back on the pillow, he put his left arm over her tummy and kissed her shoulder. They were both asleep within minutes.

It was Mariana who woke first, around six-thirty. She got up and made coffee, leaving Evan to wake up by himself. He woke with a start when she dropped a cup on the floor.

"Good morning," she greeted him, in Spanish. "Did you sleep well?"

"Good morning. What did you ask me?"

"Sleep. Did you sleep well?" she repeated, gesturing a sleeping person with her hands by her cheek and closing her eyes.

"Yes. Good. Thank you. Thank you for yesterday and last night."

"Breakfast?"

"Just a coffee. Then, I need to go sort myself out for work. I will be working Monday, Wednesday, Friday evenings and weekday lunchtimes as well as alternate Saturday and Sunday evenings. I would like to go on another date with you. I have a phone in my apartment. I will call you or we can speak after the class."

Mariana repeated what he had said in Spanish and then slowly went through the days of the week, making Evan repeat them in Spanish.

"You will learn quickly, with all of this extra tuition," she added, laughing.

They drank their coffees, and Evan gave her a kiss and left. As he walked back to his flat, he started to doubt how she felt. The 'extra tuition' seemed to suggest she wanted to continue to meet up outside of class. It was just so hard to be himself when he could not communicate. But then, Mariana seemed happy to make the effort of teaching him, and maybe her English was not good enough for deep, meaningful discussions. Why were relationships so complicated?

Evans' first proper evening shift at The Shamrock went well. The female lead singer with the awesome voice was back, this time, solo, with just her acoustic guitar. When she had finished performing, she came over to the bar and introduced herself to Evan. She was not wearing a wedding ring, or an engagement ring, which Evan noticed.

"You're new here."

"I am. First proper shift. Yesterday was a trial. I'm Evan."

"I'm Colleen."

"Well, Colleen, you have the most amazing voice."

"Thank you, Evan. You have the most amazing smile."

Was she chatting him up or just being kind?

"How long have you been in Madrid?" he asked.

"Since Connor and Ellie opened The Shamrock."

"Did you know them before they came to Spain?"

"I was Ellie's Maid of Honour and I'm godmother to Brendan. What about you?"

"What? Did I know Ellie and Connor?"

"No, silly! How long have you been in Spain?"

They both laughed.

Less than a week. I have a flat, and now, I have a job too. I started my first Spanish class on Thursday evening. Do you speak Spanish?"

"A little bit. I studied Spanish at school and the rest, I've picked up here."

"Have you been in the band a long time?"

"Since I left school."

"So, a couple of years then," bantered Evan.

"More like five years. We were all at university in Cork. We all came out here together. Live in a shared flat with the two guys who play flute and accordion. Not dating them, though."

Why did she add, 'Not dating them', as if it mattered to him? Was she hoping to date him?

"Would you like a drink?" inquired Evan.

"Are you offering or just serving?"

"That depends."

"On?"

"On whether you'll go on a date with me."

There was a pause, while Colleen looked into Evan's eyes.

"Don't mind if I do. I'll have a Martini. Thank you."

"That's settled then. Have a think about where and when. One Martini coming up," responded Evan, winking at her.

She giggled and pulled over a bar stool to sit on. It was about twenty minutes to closing, but then Evan had to clear up and close the bar. He served a couple of customers and moved back to near where Colleen was sitting.

"Does being in a band pay? Or do you have to have another job?"

"I do have another job. I clean here."

"So, have you decided where you want to go on our date?"

"Have you been to the Prado?"

"As in the art gallery?"

"Yes."

"Not yet, but I'd love to go."

"Do you like art?"

"When I was living in London, I used to go to the National Gallery. I've been to the Van Gogh Museum in Amsterdam, the Louvre in Paris, and the Sistine Chapel in Rome. Always wanted to go to the Prado. What about you? Do you like art?"

"A lot of art, but not all art."

"So, which painters do you enjoy?"

"The Pre-Raphaelites. Turner….."

"Turner! My sister's favourite painter is Turner. She loves *Rain, Steam and Speed*. I'm inclined to agree. I like Turner, Van Gogh, and other Impressionists. In fact, Monet's *Gare St-Lazare* makes a great pair with *Rain, Steam and Speed*."

"*Rain, Steam and Speed* is in the National Gallery, isn't it?"

"Yes. So too, is a version of the *Gare St-Lazare*. Monet painted several canvasses in and around the station."

"Maybe I'll go to the National Gallery, one day. I also love illuminated manuscripts."

"Really. Like the *Book of Kells*?"

"Yeah, but that's in Dublin. Well, some of the volumes are, amongst other places. I've seen the ones in Dublin."

"When shall we go to the Prado, then? I'm working every lunchtime, here."

"How about Tuesday, when you've finished up here?"

"I'm looking forward to it, already."

"Great. Now I have to go. See you on Tuesday, if not before."

"Bye, Colleen."

She swallowed the last of her Martini and left The Shamrock.

As Evan washed up the glasses, he wondered at himself. He had been worrying about how he might meet someone he could trust was not using him or trying to get him addicted to drugs, and here he was, on the verge of two-timing Colleen and Mariana. On first impressions, he could not make up his mind. It was certainly easier to communicate with Colleen. She and Mariana were not dissimilar to look at. Both had blue eyes and brown hair. Colleen's was about five inches shorter, shoulder-length, and she was more petite. He could not wait for Tuesday to come around.

Halfway through Evan's Tuesday shift, Colleen walked through the door. There was a different band playing. Evan had been present for three different bands, all playing variations on Irish folk music. So far, Colleen was the only female lead singer. She pulled up a bar stool and sat at the bar.

"Checking out the competition," she laughed, nodding in the direction of the band. "I'll have a Guinness, please. How are you?"

"All the better for seeing you. It's been quiet in here, today."

"I'm going to nip through to the back, to go and check on how Ellie is. See you in a bit."

"Yes. See you in a bit."

Colleen went behind the bar, carrying her glass, and disappeared out the back. A stag-do fell in through the front door, singing *Swing Low, Sweet Chariot*.

"Good afternoon, gentlemen. What can I get you?"

"Five pints of Guinness, please. Do you do food, here?"

"Five pints of Guinness coming up. Sorry, we don't do food. Who's the groom-to-be?"

"The one with the black eye. He's got four days for it to heal, otherwise his bride will kill him!"

"There's always stage make-up!" laughed Evan, pouring the pints, and placing them one by one on the bar to settle, before topping them up.

"Are you here for the rest of the week?"

"Yes."

"Well, tomorrow, there's a fantastic lead singer performing with her band."

"Cheers."

The friend of the groom carried two pints to the table and came back for the other three, and to pay. Evan started to hope they would be gone, by the time Colleen came back into the bar. He was already jealous and did not want rowdy single blokes chatting her up. Clearly, Evan underestimated her, because she did come back into the bar, and the groom-to-be did come over and try to chat her up, and Colleen looked him up and down and said, "Have you ever seen the *Book of Kells*?"

"What's that?"

"I'll take that as a 'No', then. Sorry, I can't allow myself to be chatted up by a man who doesn't know what the *Book of Kells* is."

The groom-to-be skulked back to his friends and downed the rest of his pint of Guinness.

"I'm really rather glad I've heard of the *Book of Kells*. That was impressive."

"I could understand if it had been one of the others, but I hate it when a groom-to-be starts trying it on with the ladies. It doesn't sit well with me."

Evan silently figured that two-timing probably did not sit well with her either.

The band finished and packed their equipment away. The pub emptied, with two friends propping up the groom-to-be between them.

"I'll give you a hand," offered Colleen.

"Thanks, but you really don't have to," responded Evan, locking the front door.

"Quicker we get it cleared up in here, the quicker we can go on our date. Connor won't mind. It's not like I don't clean here. Ellie said he'd gone off to some suppliers. She's feeling exhausted. I played snakes and ladders with Brendan when I went to see her, just to give her a moment to herself. Brendan doesn't know how to play, but he likes rolling the dice and the pictures of snakes. I'm teaching him to count. He's a cool kid, but he's in the 'nightmare in Toddlersville' phase, at the moment. It always strikes me as slightly bonkers that the second one usually comes along just when the first one is at the worst stage they can be. It's enough to put you off parenting!"

"And does it?"

"Notice I said 'almost'. I'd love to settle down and have kids."

"Me too. One day. When I've lost the nomadic urge."

He hung up the cloths, checked the taps were off and took off his apron, with 'The Shamrock' and a shamrock emblazoned across the front.

"Ready?"

"Just need the bathroom."

They both used the facilities and left for the Prado, which was within easy walking distance.

"Do you paint?" asked Evan, as they were walking.

"Partly. I like to practise calligraphy and do my own watercolour illumination. Do you paint?"

"Sadly, no. I'd love to see some or your manuscripts."

"Maybe."

"If they're any good, I could commission you to do something for my flat."

"What would you have me write?"

"Hmmm. Not sure. I'll get back to you on that."

Once inside the building, they stopped talking, and focused their energies on taking in the art.

"Goya is disturbing, don't you think?" reflected Evan.

"Yes. We absolutely have to go and see Picasso's *Guernica*, in the annexe."

"What's special about that painting?"

"What do you know about the Spanish Civil War?"

"I know it's what brought Franco to power. I know he was in a similar camp to Hitler and Mussolini."

"Well, Guernica is a city in the Basque region, which was bombed by the Nazis, at Franco's invitation. The whole city was razed to the ground, to tear the hearts out of the Spanish people."

"And the painting shows this?"

"Yes, with Picasso's take on it, of course."

They made their way to the painting.

"Wow! It's in black and white."

"Yes. All adds to the effect. Picasso painted it in Paris. It's toured the world. He said it would never come home to

Spain, until the country was once again a republic. And here we are!"

"What did you study at university?" asked Evan, after they has spent a few moments in silence, listening to the painting speak to each of them.

"Irish history. Have you been to university?"

"I lasted a year. Then, I dropped out and went travelling."

"What did you study?"

"Russian."

"That sounds complicated. I mean, the alphabet is weird."

"I suppose it's easy once you know what you're doing. The course was language and literature."

"I've read some Russian literature. In translation, of course."

"What have you read?"

"*The Brothers Karamazov* and *War and Peace*."

"I'm impressed. Some of the best Russian literature I read hasn't yet been translated into English."

"You should translate it."

"I'm not that good at Russian."

"Why did you study it at university?"

"Long story. I think I was just doing what my parents wanted. Russian was unusual. I suppose it offered career options. I never really wanted to go to university. That's why I dropped out."

"What did your parents say?"

"I don't know. I left home. I haven't been back. Do you have parents back in Ireland?"

"Yes. I write to them. They miss me. They're proud of me. If I had children, I'd try not to make them live my dreams."

"Me too. My flat's not far from here. Do you want to come back with me? I can cook something for us."

"OK. I'm a vegetarian."

"Do you eat cheese?"

"Yes."

"Then it looks like it's cheese on toast."

"Works for me."

They reached the Calle de Gravina and Evan led them up to his flat. He opened the door and ushered Colleen in ahead of him.

"Wow. This is nicer than our flat."

"It's OK. Convenient. It's only got one bedroom."

"How did you find it so quickly?"

"I went and asked at the embassy. There was a man there who knew about it. I don't think they normally have a list of accommodation. Sometimes, it's just about being in the right place at the right time."

"Well, I like it."

"Vodka and orange? I'm afraid it's that or a bottle of beer."

"Vodka and orange, then. Thank you."

Colleen followed Evan into the kitchen. He poured them each a vodka and orange.

"Now, let's get to work on the cheese on toast."

"Do you have eggs?"

"Yes. I think there's a couple left in the box. Why?"

"How about we make cheese-egg on toast."

Evan remembered the snack his mother used to make when he and Helen were children. He felt a tiny bit defensive, as he had wanted to impress Colleen. On reflection, cheese on toast was hardly a culinary triumph. It was good to take on board her suggestion.

"OK. I have some Tetilla. Hopefully that will work?"

"Let's try it. You put the bread under the grill and start to scramble the eggs. I'll grate the cheese."

Evan took the grater from the cupboard and handed it to Colleen with a plate. He went into the fridge and took out some butter, the eggs, and the cheese. As they carried out their simple tasks, Evan thought how nice it was to be cooking together. Perhaps that was what Colleen was striving for all along, with a snack they could both contribute to.

"I quite like this cooking a meal together idea."

"Me too," responded Colleen. "Now, tell me when the scrambled eggs are half-done."

She checked the toast whilst Evan stirred.

"Ready."

Colleen tipped the grated cheese into the eggs. Evan kept stirring until it was all mixed in together and the cheese had melted. Colleen found two plates and buttered the toast. Evan spooned on the cheese-egg, and they carried their plates to the table, with Evan grabbing knives and forks from a drawer. He cut a mouthful and savoured it.

"Cheese-egg. Not bad, even if I say so myself."

They ate in silence, not because there was nothing to say, but because the cheese-egg on toast was so morish. When it was all gone, Evan reached out and placed his hand on Colleen's.

"An artist and musician, a historian and a gourmet cook."

"I don't know about gourmet. Don't forget, I was a student for three years, and there's a limit to the amount of cheese or beans on toast you can eat. Variations on a theme."

She did not move her hand.

"Would you like some chocolate. I have chocolate in the fridge. And I can put some coffee on."

"Chocolate would be great. What about another vodka and orange?"

"Vodka and orange, it is."

Evan took the plates and cutlery and placed them in the washing up bowl. He covered them in water and poured another drink. The already-opened bar of chocolate was nearly finished, so he grabbed the unopened one from the fridge and returned to the living room to find Colleen on the settee.

"There you go," he said, handing over her vodka and orange.

He sat beside her and snapped off some squares.

"I am always interested to taste chocolate in different countries. Some is tasty, some not so."

"Which countries have you travelled to?"

"The Netherlands, Russia, France, Italy, Canada, Pakistan and Afghanistan."

"Oh my! To be honest, that is a strange selection. Most people do the USA and Canada, or they go interrailing round Europe."

"That is very true. I had a friend in Canada who invited me. Amsterdam has a lot of freedoms. Russia was a school trip. France is France. Everyone has to go to Paris once in their life. And Afghanistan, well, I had a rescue Afghan Hound and I just got curious about the place. Thankfully, I speak Russian, because it's occupied by the Soviets, and I learnt a bit of Pashto while I was there. Venice is another must, and I am interested in Ancient History, at least, since I did 'A' Level."

"Where is your dog, now?"

"He died. Hit by a car. I called him Kochai. It means 'nomad' and I became a nomad in Afghanistan for a few weeks."

"I'm sorry."

"Thanks. Now, where have you travelled?"

"Spain. Madrid. And I went from Cork to Dublin."

"So, this is a first for you?"

"Absolutely."

"Do you have a boyfriend? You mentioned you weren't dating any of your flat mates."

"No boyfriend."

"Can I kiss you?"

"I'm all chocolaty."

"So am I. We won't notice. I really want to kiss you. You're lovely, and clever, and interesting."

"OK."

Colleen came across as shy, or perhaps, inexperienced with men. Evan took her face in his hands and leant towards her. He kissed her gently, until she joined in, and a few seconds later, they were French-kissing. Evan had no idea how far she wanted to go. He already knew how far he wanted to go.

"Can we, er … will you stay over tonight and share the one bed with me. I really want to make love to you. It's your choice."

Colleen looked deep into Evan's eyes.

"Let me go and freshen up. Do you have any protection?"

"Yes."

Colleen went to the bathroom and Evan went into the bedroom, sprayed some deodorant under his armpits and went back into the living room.

"I just need the bathroom myself."

He took her in his arms, as they passed each other, and kissed her longingly.

"Did you borrow some toothpaste?" he laughed.

"Well, I'm probably not going to give it back," she joked.

Evan went into the bathroom, peed, washed his hands, and brushed his teeth. Colleen was reading the names on his pile of cassettes when he came back out.

"Shall I put some music on?"

"Yes. What is the French jazz like?"

"Ah. That's a French-Canadian artist. It's perfect mood music."

He had bought a small stereo radio-cassette player so he could listen to Spanish and his cassettes. Evan inserted the cassette and pressed play, turned up the volume a little and picked Colleen up in his arms. When he lay her on the bed, they could still hear the music. He pulled off his shirt and lay on the bed, next to her. Immediately, she climbed on top and sat astride his loins, pulling off her dress, up over her head. If Evan had thought Colleen was inexperienced, he was mistaken. He held his hands against the sides of her rib cage and slid them behind to undo her bra.

"Where's the protection?" she inquired, undoing his belt and chinos.

"Pocket. My left."

She lowered his chinos and underwear, removing the condom from his pocket, tearing off the top and unrolling it onto his manhood. Slipping off her own briefs, she eased herself onto him, and controlling the entire experience, she brought both of them to a state of ecstasy. Evan did not mind one bit. He reached out and grabbing the edge of the quilt, flung it over them both like a cocoon, where they lay until they slept. Colleen crept out at six o'clock in the morning to go and clean The Shamrock.

For the next six months, Evan worked his shifts at the pub, made progress in his Spanish classes, and dated both Mariana and Colleen. He would go dancing and clubbing with Mariana, on a Saturday or Sunday evening off, always staying over at her flat. Tuesday afternoons after work and evenings, he would go to a place of cultural interest with Colleen, and she would sleep over at his flat. Evan had not planned it this way. He just did not want to have to choose between them. For someone who had longed to set aside his double life and step into reality, Evan felt deeply, the irony of his complicated love-life.

Christmas at The Shamrock was the source of more fun than Evan had enjoyed in a while. He was invited for Christmas dinner with the O'Donnell household, which now included two-month-old Tabitha, who was just about the cutest baby Evan had come across. Around the table sat Ellie, Brendan, in his highchair, Connor, Evan, Duncan and Louis, the other bar tenders who had responded to Connor's advert and interviewed successfully, and Colleen, the cleaner. She had been abandoned by her flatmates, who had both chosen to fly home to their families.

"What's going on between you two?" asked Ellie, in the kitchen, as Evan was helping carry in the dirty plates.

"What do you mean?"

"Colleen's definitely looking at you in a 'That's my man' way."

"I'd be lying if I denied we were going out."

"So, there is something going on?"

"She's smart, kind, and lovely. We share an interest in art and history. What's not to like about her?"

"Really, pleased for you, Evan. But how come I saw you holding hands with some other woman on Saturday evening?" she whispered.

"Err. Long story. Please don't say anything."

"Just don't you go breaking Colleen's heart. We need her here."

"I'll try not to. Promise. Trying to sort my heart out. I know I've got to choose one of them."

He remained in the kitchen, a few seconds longer than Ellie, who had carried out the pudding. He brought out the brandy butter.

At the end of the meal, when everyone was stuffed, Connor went into the bar and came back with a bottle of whiskey and a bottle of vodka.

"Time to play 'Truth or dare'," he announced.

The others groaned.

"Count me out. I need to go and feed Tabitha," insisted Ellie, getting up to leave.

Brendan followed her out.

"The rules are as follows. Spin the bottle. Whoever it points to asks a question of the person on their left. You can choose to answer truthfully or take a dare. The person who asks the question decides the dare. The person who's answered spins the bottle next. Simple."

Connor poured everyone shots and spun the bottle. It stopped, pointing at Colleen who was next to him on his right.

"So, Evan. Have you ever been in love?"

"Yes."

Colleen spun the bottle and it pointed at herself.

"You have to spin again," declared Connor.

This time, the bottle came to rest pointing at Duncan. Connor was on his left.

"Have you ever broken the law?"

"No. Not as far as I know."

"Sure?"

"It's the truth," Connor defended himself, spinning the bottle. It stopped pointing at Colleen again.

"This bottle's biased," pleaded Evan.

"Have you ever taken drugs?"

"Yes."

There was a lot in Evan's life he would prefer not to reveal, but so far, his answers were not unexpected or shocking. They were all on their second shot, having emptied two bottles of wine with the meal, and the walls were coming down, as was the tone of the questions. He spun the bottle and it pointed at Connor.

"How old were you when you first slept with someone?" he asked Colleen.

"I'll take a dare," she replied, her face belying her uneasiness.

"I dare you to snog Evan."

Always slow to grasp the obvious, Connor had not spotted what Ellie had seen. Evan turned to Colleen, and they kissed to the whistles of the other three. They spun the bottle a few more times, and only Louis took a dare, to drink a shot without touching the glass with his hands. The others were in stitches. Ellie came back into the room.

"Keep the noise down a little, will you. Brendan and Tabitha are both asleep."

"Would you like a hand with the dishes?" offered Evan.

"Thank you, but it's probably time for you all to go home and sleep off your alcohol."

After lots of hugs and handshakes, Louis, Duncan, Evan, and Colleen left. Evan and Colleen set off together, in the direction of Evan's flat, much to Louis' frustration, as he had been hoping to walk Colleen home. He was too drunk to compete, which was a relief to Evan and Colleen. Duncan had disappeared.

Back at Evan's flat, they lay together on the bed.

"I'm a bit too drunk to make love, this evening," confessed Colleen.

"Me too, probably. Can I ask you something?"

"You can ask. Can't promise to answer."

"Why did you take a dare? You can tell me to mind my own. I won't mind."

Colleen said nothing, for a few moments.

"Because I was twelve. My uncle abused me."

"I'm so sorry," responded Evan, folding her into his arms and kissing her head.

They fell asleep.

When he woke, at just after three o'clock in the morning, Evan lay there feeling guilty for two-timing her. She deserved better than that. But now, he was in a dilemma. He did not want to hurt either Colleen or Mariana. Nor did he want to lose his job or lose his Spanish classes and ending the relationship with either of them would result in a change of routine. He would not be able to carry on working alongside Colleen or continue to learn Spanish in Mariana's classes.

The following Saturday, he went clubbing, as usual, with Mariana. Evan had gone to the toilet, when he noticed the lid of the cistern was wedged open. Curiosity got the better of him, so he lifted it, to see why, and possibly even replace it. Whilst the toilet bowl is dirty water, the water in the cistern is clean. In any case, he would wash his hands. As he lifted the lid, he saw a plastic bag, tied at the top, sitting in the water. Reaching in, he pulled it up enough to see it contained pills. On closer inspection, he surmised they might be amphetamines. The whole, slightly surreal experience was reminiscent of his cannabis find in Battersea. Figuring that the wonky cistern may have been a signal, he wrapped the pills in his handkerchief and pocketed them. Wrapping the bag in some toilet paper, he flushed it down the toilet and replaced the lid on the cistern snuggly, so as not to indicate the presence of any drugs. He resolved to try one, when he was alone in his flat, and not due at The Shamrock in the evening.

Once back on the dance floor, he whispered in Mariana's ear.

"Let's go. I'm tired, and I still want to make love to you tonight."

"OK," she responded, kissing him.

They left for her flat.

"Would you like an alcoholic drink or a coffee?" Mariana invited him, as they walked in through the door.

"Just some water, thank you. To put beside the bed."

He was grinning as he said it. Mariana used the bathroom first, and when Evan came out, he joined her in the bedroom, where he carefully removed and folded his chinos, taking out the protection from the opposite pocket to the pills, before getting into bed with her. He dived under the quilt, nibbling at her, and arousing her, before putting on the condom and surfacing from the covers to lie on top of her. They helped each other reach fulfilment and fell asleep.

Evan woke in the small hours and did not want to disturb Mariana by getting out of bed. He lay staring at the ceiling, contemplating his options. The responsibility of paying the rent had crept up on him, and his wages were not that great. It was in that moment that Evan arrived at his decision. If the pills were amphetamines, he would break up with Mariana and stop attending Spanish classes, but would continue to date Colleen, and supply speed to nightclub users, in the places he and Mariana had frequented. The supplement to his income from the pub would more than cover the rent. There were several clubs and discos around the city, as well as bars hosting live music. What would be stupid, would be to sell them in the Sala Del Sol. Evan also felt sure there was a market at the university. He and Mariana had visited the student bar one Saturday.

It was the weekend, and Evan had spent the last few days working out how he should break up with Mariana. In the end, he did not, and decided to spend a few weeks observing the behaviour of nightclubbers and disco-goers, to see if he could work out how dealers introduced themselves and where trades were made. Obviously, he had witnessed, through the closed door of the toilet cubicle in the Sala Del Sol, a drugs deal, and been offered drugs himself, but what he was curious to know, was how individuals knew to go into the toilet, or where they were first asked if they were interested. It occurred to him that he still knew very few people in Madrid, and when he had wanted to sell cannabis in Caterham, he had simply asked a friend to put the word out on the street. Maybe he would begin with his fellow Spanish students, as well as Duncan and Louis, not that he would ever consider dealing at The Shamrock.

So, that Saturday evening, when Mariana and Evan went clubbing, he made a point of observing the others on the dance floor, as they danced opposite each other. After a while he came up with the excuse of being tired, to allow for some time to sit and watch the way people were interacting around the room. Just when he was about to give up, he spotted a man lean in towards another man, say something, and then follow the other man towards the toilets. Evan followed and walked in just one of them put something in his pocket.

"Do you know where to buy amphetamines?" he surprised himself by asking.

"I have a friend near the airport. I have a new drug if you are interested, from the United States of America. It's a dance drug. I'm sure it is going to come to Spain, too. Do you want some?"

"I just need amphetamines."

"Go to the bar and buy a drink. I will come to you and give you the address."

"Thanks."

The dealer left and Evan used the facilities.

"Would you like another drink?" he asked Mariana when he came out of the toilet.

"I'd like a beer, please."

"Keep the seats."

Evan went over to the bar to order the drinks, and as he stood waiting, the dealer sidled up beside him, leant on the bar, and slid a folded slither of paper in front of him. The bartender approached.

"Three beers, please."

"Sorry. I hope you like beer."

"Thank you. Is that your girlfriend?"

"Yes. Shall I introduce you?"

"She is very pretty. If you break up, let me know."

Evan hoped the dealer was not a mind-reader. Whether Mariana would be interested when he ended things with her, was a whole different matter.

"Come. What is your name?"

"Javier."

"I'm Evan."

Evan handed Javier one of the beers and walked back to where Mariana was sitting. Javier followed.

"Mariana, this is Javier. He thinks you are pretty and asked me for an introduction. I told him you are my girlfriend, but he insisted."

"Hello, Mariana," Javier greeted her, taking her hand and kissing it, before winking at Evan and walking away.

"Where did you meet him?"

"He just offered me drugs in the toilet. He says there is a new dance drug, from the US, and he is establishing a market here."

"He's cute. But not as cute as you."

That evening, when they went to bed, for the first time since meeting her, Evan made his excuses and went straight to sleep. Mariana said nothing, but he could tell she was surprised.

"Do you still like me?" she asked, at the breakfast table.

"Of course. I think I need a holiday. I'm tired, that's all," he lied, wondering whether he should be decisive or let her down gently.

"Let's go to the university bar, next weekend?" he suggested, keeping her hanging on, when really, he just wanted to observe the sub-culture. "I should go. See you on Thursday."

Evan made a point of pulling her towards him and kissing her like he meant it. She seemed convinced.

"See you at classes."

When Evan and Mariana went to the university students' bar the following Saturday, Evan took a small number of amphetamines in his pocket. He watched the interactions as best he could, whilst trying to give Mariana the attention she needed, and soon realised it was impossible to pay as much attention to his observations as was required. He gave up, and resolved to go back by himself, one evening in the week. It also occurred to him that he would make little progress in his new business venture if he continued to date Mariana and go to the various venues with her. He would be forever making excuses to her.

"Your Spanish is improving," she encouraged him, as they sat at the table.

"Thank you. I have a good teacher."

"You're welcome."

"The thing is, Mariana, I'm not going to be able to keep coming to classes."

"Why not?"

"Because we need to break up. I'm sorry, but I've met someone else."

There was a stunned silence, before Mariana stood up, turned, and left. In fairness, she had handled the situation quite well. Evan told himself that the reason of having met someone else was harsh, but not something he could be persuaded out of. Not that Mariana needed to persuade him of anything. That would have come across as needy. He finished both his drink and hers and went to the bar for another. Now alone, he was able to focus on the task of identifying potential customers or business competitors. Deep down inside, he knew he preferred Colleen. He felt bad, though.

After another hour of watching and waiting, he went to the toilet. As he was washing his hands, a man came in.

"Do you want speed?"

"Are you selling?"

"Yes, but this one, I will give you this for free. Tell your friends. I will be in the bar next Saturday between twenty and twenty-two hundred hours, to sell."

"That's all? I just have to tell my friends?"

"Well, if next Saturday, six friends come to me, I will give you another one for free. Every six I sell, you get one."

"OK. Deal."

Evan reached into his pocket and took out a pill and handed it to the student.

"Thank you."

Evan exited the toilets, leaving the student to relieve himself in peace. He was chuffed that he had just carried out a drugs deal in Spanish. Only time would tell, however, if his small loss-leader would bring in new custom. To find that out, he would have to return next Saturday.

After buying another bottle of beer, he leant against the bar and listened to the conversations, to see what he could understand. A couple of female students approached him and introduced themselves.

"Hello. Are you on your own? My name is Natalia, and this is Paulina."

"Hello ladies. Can I buy you a drink?"

"Thank you. You are not Spanish, I think. No?" responded Paulina.

"English. Would you like a beer?"

"Yes. We would each like a beer," replied Natalia. "What is your name?"

Evan was in playful mood and had no intentions of hooking up with either Natalia or Paulina, whatever their plans were. For a split second he forgot who he was.

"I'm Ivor. It's a Welsh name."

"You just said you were English." Natalia reflected back.

"What's in a name?" replied Evan, nonchalantly. "They're all translations."

"So, where are you from?" asked Paulina.

"Everywhere."

"How can you be from everywhere?"

"It's not where you're from that counts. It's how the places you have been to influence your soul. And I have been to many places."

"You are crazy," laughed Paulina.

"Where have you been?" asked Natalia.

"Russia, France, Canada, Pakistan, Afghanistan, the Netherlands, Italy, and now, Spain."

"How many languages do you speak?" Paulina pressed him.

"Is this an interrogation?" responded Evan, frowning.

"Don't you like to impress the ladies?" retorted Paulina.

"Five."

"What do you do?" asked Natalia.

"I sell pleasure. Are you interested?"

"You're a gigolo?" queried Natalia.

"No. I have pills that give you a high. Would you like some?"

"What pills? Speed or the new dance drug someone's been selling across the city?"

"Speed. Two thousand pesetas a pill."

To Evan's surprise, Paulina opened her handbag, took out four thousand-peseta notes and slipped them into Evan's hand. He reached into his pocket and fumbled in the bag, pulling out two pills, which he slipped into her hand, leaning across to kiss her on the cheek as he did.

"Now I have to go, ladies. It's been lovely chatting. I'll be here next week."

Evan finished his beer, in one gulp, and left.

For the next few weeks, through charm or guile, he succeeded in establishing a customer base in five different bars and clubs. He continued to date Colleen, on Tuesdays, and was growing fonder of her by the week. She knew nothing of his second income stream, and he did feel a little guilty that he was concealing it from her.

One Saturday evening, towards the end of April, he was walking home from the student bar, when he found himself being approached by two men wearing dark suits. Several paces from them, Evan realised they were not going to give way. He stepped off the pavement, to avoid a collision, but as he passed them, one of them grabbed hold of his arm. Before he realised what was happening, the man had pulled him off balance and taken hold of his other arm and was now standing behind him. The other man punched him in the stomach and the face. Thankfully, Evan was still doing sit-ups, and was able to tense his abdomen to receive the blow. He felt the blood run from his nose as a left hook came in.

"That is for trespassing on someone else's turf. If we find out where you got your pills, you're a dead man."

The man who was holding him, threw him to the floor, and kicked him in the stomach, for good measure. As they walked off, Evan was certain he heard them speaking Russian. He was in a bad way. The last time he had been hurt this badly was in Lashkar Gah, the day he shot Krukov. Of course, the Krukov empire might have been taken down, but that was never going to stop the Soviets. Evan was trembling, partly from pain, partly from fear. He stumbled back to his flat and went to bed.

He woke to find he could hardly move for stiffness and aches. When he went into the bathroom, he surveyed the damage. One shining, puffy, purply-pink eye, extending over the now somewhat enlarged bridge of his nose, and a swollen jaw. As for his stomach, there was a wide tender, bruised area, and he was unsure whether the bottom rib, where the final kick had landed, was broken. He was due at The Shamrock for the evening shift. Evan was half-tempted to take one of the pills, but instead, he took two paracetamol tablets, drank a glass of water, and crawled back to bed, where he slept on and off all day.

Come five o'clock, he took two more paracetamol, forced himself through the pain barrier to shower and dress, and hobbled to the pub.

"What on earth has happened?" asked a bemused Connor.

"I got beaten up on my way home late last night."

"Should you be here?"

"Didn't want to let you down. I can't lift barrels or crates, but I can still work a bottle opener and a beer pump. Probably."

"I won't lie, I could use the help, but honestly mate, you need to rest. Let me give Louis a call and see if he can come in. Have you been to the police?"

"What's the point. I couldn't tell them what they looked like."

"What motive could they have?"

"Theft?" lied Evan.

"Did they take your wallet?"

"I didn't have it. I only ever go out with a few notes in my pocket."

"Wise move."

Connor went through the bar to the back room and made a phone call. He came out smiling.

"Louis says he'll be here in half an hour. Take yourself home and rest. Don't come in until Tuesday. I'll ask Louis to do your shift tomorrow as well. Does Colleen know?"

"Not yet. I'll see her on Tuesday. She'll only worry if she sees me like this."

"OK. Look after yourself."

"Thanks. I'll try to. Bye."

"Bye."

Evan left and returned to his flat where he made scrambled eggs on toast and went back to bed. As he lay there trying not to hurt, he realised he had to leave Madrid. He only had May and June to pay on the flat rental before the end of the twelve-month contract. One place he had always wanted to go was Barcelona. He would find another job and try to establish a new customer base for his amphetamines, of which he had only sold about half of the stash from the cistern. Evan hated the idea of letting Connor down, but at least he had Louis and Duncan. It was not like he was leaving him completely in the lurch. As for Colleen, he would ask her to go with him, and settle down together.

The following day, he was due to meet her to go to a concert of the *Aranjuez Concerto*, dropping into a tapas bar beforehand. First, he had to get through a shift. The swelling had gone down, and his bruises were now a duller shade of purple with yellowy tinged edges. His ribs were still sore. Nevertheless, he arrived at The Shamrock, willing to work.

"How are you feeling?"

"Still not sure I can lift a crate, but I'm good to go."

"Pleased to hear it. Your face looks a little better. Less swollen."

"It's not quite as delicate," laughed Evan.

"I'll fetch the crates, if you stack the shelves."

"No problem."

The first couple of customers were regulars and commented on Evan's face. There was no way he was going to tell them why he got beaten up but felt guilty for all the sympathy he was receiving. Especially, when Colleen appeared, showing him genuine, heartfelt concern.

"What on earth happened to you?"

"Be gentle with me," laughed Evan. "I got beaten up on Saturday night."

"You poor thing. I won't attempt to kiss it better."

"You can kiss the unbruised parts of me better, later," responded Evan, winking at her. "What are you drinking?"

"Orange juice, please."

Evan reached for a bottle of orange juice, and winced, as he stretched the intercostal muscles.

At the end of his shift, Evan and Colleen went to her favourite tapas bar. As they nibbled and drank, Evan plucked up the courage to be honest with her.

"Colleen. I'm about to tell you three very important things. Please can you let me finish before you respond?"

"OK," she mumbled, looking at him with dread in her eyes.

"I didn't get these injuries because I was robbed. I was beaten up, but it was because I have been supplementing my income by selling amphetamines. I found them in a nightclub toilet and decided to sell them. It isn't the first time in my life that I've sold drugs. The problem here was that I've been selling them on someone else's turf, and they didn't like it. That's the first thing. The second is that I was threatened and as I know from experience that such threats need to be taken seriously, I've decided I am going to have to move away. I'm going to go to Barcelona. The third thing is that I really, really like you, Colleen, and I'm asking you to come with me, and settle down with me, in Barcelona."

"You idiot," she chided him, after a short silence, looking into his eyes. "I really like you too, Evan, but the band is here. I can't just drop everything and move to Barcelona."

"Can't you go solo?"

"I probably could, but I don't want to let the band down. We've been through a lot. Not to mention the role we have here, supporting Connor and Ellie with the business. I'm sorry."

"Shall we still go to the concert?"

"Yes, but I don't think I'll stay over tonight. The news has really hit me.

Evan could see it was hurting her. It was hurting him, too.

"To be honest, I have spent several years looking over my shoulder. I thought settling here would be a fresh start, but when I heard the men who laid into me speaking Russian, I feared for my life. It was Russians who tried to kill me before."

Nothing else was said. They sat silently, sipping at their drinks until it was time to go to the concert. Evan went to hold Colleen's hand, but she pulled it away.

"I wish there was another way, but there isn't. At least, not one that I can see."

"I know. I wish there was too."

"Please don't tell Connor and the others. I'll tell him tomorrow."

"I won't."

"Thanks."

"Come on. Let's go to the concert."

They drank up and left the tapas bar. There was an awkward distance between them as they walked. At least in the concert, the auditorium was dark, and no conversation was necessary, or desired. At the end of the event, they went their separate ways.

Evan felt empty, as he made his way, nervously, back to his flat, constantly looking over his shoulder. Once safely indoors, he wrote a letter to Juan Johnson-Ramirez at the embassy. In it, he mentioned the need to move on, and asked if Juan could pass a message onto Dominic Andrews, that they speak Russian in the clubs and bars in Madrid, where amphetamines and a new dance drug are readily available. His plan was to hand the keys back in the envelope, the day he caught a train to Barcelona. Evan was not looking forward to the conversation he would have with Connor, in person.

The following day, before going to work his shift, Evan packed his belongings into a large suitcase and his holdall. He was not bothered about leaving the household items he had accumulated, but he wanted to take his quilt, bedding and stereo. The suitcase could be left in a luggage locker, until he sorted out where to stay. Figuring he could afford a week in a cheap hotel, he would look at the newspaper and find a shared house, until he settled into something more permanent. It had not occurred to him to share, until Colleen had mentioned the members of her band.

At the end of his shift, he went up to Connor, feeling bad.

"Hey, Connor. Have you got a moment?"

"Of course. What's up?"

"I'm really sorry, but today is my last shift. I didn't want to leave, but I can't stay in Madrid any longer. When I got beaten up it was by Russians, and the reason I settled in Madrid was because where I was before, Russians were trying to kill me. I'm terrified they won't stop at a beating next time if they find out my name. I really want to thank you. It's been amazing. And I'm really sorry to go. Especially like this. At least you've got Louis and Duncan for now. Sorry."

"You've got to do what you've got to do. I'm sorry to lose you. Where will you go?"

"Maybe the Costa del Sol. There's lots of English and Irish bars out there."

"Good luck. Here, let me get your pay for yesterday and today."

He went to the till and took out some notes.

"There you go. Send us a post card!"

"Thank you. Please give my regards to Ellie and the kids."

Evan held out his hand and Connor shook it warmly.

"Bye, then."

"Bye, Evan."

Evan walked out of The Shamrock for the last time. He went back to the flat, grabbed his luggage, locked up, took the letter and keys to the embassy, and went to catch the train for Barcelona. It was the evening when he arrived. To his relief, there were large lockers at the station, so he parked his suitcase and went in search of a cheap hotel, carrying only his holdall. He found a hostel not far from Las Ramblas and booked in for two nights. The room was basic, but single and lockable. The facilities were shared. Having dumped his luggage, Evan went for a stroll, to find somewhere to eat and to get his bearings.

As he wandered along the boulevard, he came upon a human statue, similar to the gladiator he had seen in Rome.

This artist was dressed as a multi-coloured lizard. Or was it a chameleon? It took a few moments of staring, for Evan to realise it was actually two artists, entwined with each other. The make-up and paint which covered them was so realistic. Evan put some change in their bucket and walked away smiling to himself. He went into a restaurant and ordered a paella, which he washed down with a glass of red wine. Back at the hostel, he went straight to bed.

Unlike the hostel in Amsterdam, where he had to share his quarters, Evan was able to keep himself to himself. More importantly, he felt his belongings were safe. He had stashed the speed in his holdall. When he left the hostel in search of breakfast, he left them locked in his room. He was halfway along Las Ramblas, when the thought suddenly hit him that there might be a cleaner who could not be trusted, so he returned to the hostel and packed the drugs in the bottom of his knapsack.

After a latte and a donut, he bought a local newspaper and looked in the classifieds, where he found two suitable shared accommodation adverts to check out. One was to the north of the city centre, the other not far from the hostel. He rang the number.

"Ola."

"Ola. I'm a student and I'm looking for a shared house or apartment. I saw your advert."

"American?"

"No. English."

"Smoker?"

"No."

"Can you come and see the apartment now?"

"Yes."

By lunchtime, Evan had paid a month's share of the rent, and moved into a flat with two women and a man. They were a similar age to Evan, but not students. Technically, nor was he, although he fully intended to resume language classes. The flat mates were all street entertainers and knew the lizard statue artists. Apparently, they were forming the famous salamander from the Parc Güell. The man, Julio, threw a diabolo to entertain the tourists, in a small square. Evan went to watch. Julio was incredible, with the heights to which he launched the diabolo, and catching it again.

"I'll teach you," he offered, whist he took a short break.

During his break, Gabriella ignited her flame-throwing batons and began to juggle them. Evan was impressed, and a little attracted to her.

"Are you dating Gabriella?" he asked Julio.

"No. Angelina is my girlfriend."

"Where is Angelina?"

Just then, a very tall clown appeared round the corner of a building.

"That is Angelina."

Evan stared up at the figure on stilts and just recognised Angelina behind the make-up. She started to throw sweets into the small crowd which had gathered.

"Is Gabriella dating anyone else?"

"I don't think so. You can't date her, though."

"Why not?"

"She's not attracted to men."

"Oh. I see. That's a shame."

"We'll introduce you to women you can date. There are lots of parties we can take you to."

"Great."

"Now I must get back to my diabolo."

Julio got up and walked to the opposite end of the square. Evan started to contemplate being invited to parties and was hopeful that he might be able to develop a new customer base.

That evening, the three street entertainers went back out to the square. Evan went with them, stopping off at a fast-food outlet for some fries, and sat munching them as he watched his new friends perform. The evening crowd which gathered was much larger than the daytime one. Evan could not believe that Julio was still throwing his diabolo high into the night sky and catching it. For a short while, he stopped throwing and walked around the spectators, gathered at the perimeter of the square, holding out an upturned cowboy hat for people to put money in, and indicating by a sweeping movement of his outstretched arm, that the collection was for all three of them. People were happy to oblige, both applauding and giving. He pocketed the money, replaced the hat on his head and gestured to five individuals to come forward. He took five diabolo sets from his bag and handed them to the somewhat embarrassed and reluctant victims, whereupon he started to demonstrate how to get the diabolo spinning. Ten minutes later, all five were throwing their diabolo about three feet into the air, with a fifty percent success rate catching them again. Eventually, the performers decided it was time to go home.

"That was just amazing. How can you see the diabolo to catch it?"

"Concentration. I see it later than in the day, though. And practice. Lots of practice."

"Is that how you live? Earning money from performing?"

"In the summer, yes. In the winter, there are not so many tourists, and I give diabolo classes."

Back at the flat, Julio took out a diabolo set and handed it to Evan.

"Now it's your turn. Come on."

He started to make his diabolo spin. Evan tried to do the same, failing miserably.

"I don't think I'm cut out for this."

"Anyone can do it. You just need to practise," laughed Julio, encouragingly.

The first party Evan got invited to, was a few days later. It was in a flat about thirty minutes' walk away. Gabriella introduced Evan to a friend, Sofia, in whose flat the party was. He was unsure, at first, if she was straight or not. As he looked around, Evan could tell there were several gay and lesbian friends. Julio and Angelina were kissing in the corner and Evan identified three other heterosexual pairings. He sidled over to Julio and Angelina.

"Excuse me guys, but can you introduce me to the girls who I can date?"

"No, my friend," laughed Julio. "You will have to discover this for yourself."

He returned his attention to Angelina, leaving Evan helplessly surveying the partygoers.

Evan had placed twenty pills in his pocket. He decided to occupy his time developing a customer base, rather than finding a girlfriend. Slowly, he made his way round the room, interrupting the carousing couples to offer them amphetamines. By the end of the evening, he had sold all twenty pills, and relaxed into a beanbag, with a bottle of beer. That was when Sofia approached him.

"Do you have any more pills?"

"Sorry. No. But I can make you just as high!" added Evan, in the hope she was straight.

"What is your name?"

"Evan."

"Well, Mr Evan, how do you intend to make me high?"

"Come with me and I'll show you."

Evan stood up, grabbed Sofia's hand, and pulled her out into the corridor. He tried two of the three doors, but one was locked, and the other revealed passionate activity in the shadows, when he peered in. Figuring the third door was the bathroom, he made an instant decision.

"Come with me. I live not far from here."

"OK, Mr Evan."

They left the flat together. Before heading off along the street, Evan took Sofia in his arms and kissed her, passionately, just to emphasise his intentions. She seemed completely in agreement, which reassured him. The flat appeared to be empty when they arrived.

"Anyone home?" he called.

No reply. He opened his bedroom door and pulled Sofia into the room, pushing the door shut with his foot. Sofia was a couple of inches taller than Evan, until she removed her heels. She was wearing pink jeans and a loose white, broderie anglaise blouse, which rested on fuller breasts than Mariana or Colleen possessed. Evan started to undo her belt and jeans, and following his lead, she did the same with his. As their kissing became more frenzied, he fumbled with the buttons to her blouse, so much so that she completed the task herself. After removing his own, he gently pushed her backwards towards the bed, where she lost her balance and fell back onto the quilt, giggling all the while. He tugged down her briefs and lowered his own, only just remembering the need for protection. No longer ever unprepared, he had a condom in the back pocket of his jeans and had to break off their passionate embrace long enough to take hold of the protection. Once covered, he entered her, and between them, they ended up satisfied. As they lay there, coming down from the hormone-fuelled high, Evan reached into the drawer of the bedside table and took out an amphetamine. Taking the bottle of water from the top of the bedside table, her handed both to Sofia.

"This one is free!"

"What about you?" she asked, swallowing the pill.

"I'll stay alert, in case you have a bad reaction."

He poured himself a vodka and orange and lay back on the bed, next to her.

"So, tell me all about you, Sofia."

"I am twenty years old. I live in Barcelona. I have a Catalan father and a French mother. I like cats."

"Are you bilingual?"

"My Catalan is better than my French. My mother lives in Perpignan. Do you know where Perpignan is?"

"A bit over the border, near the coast. And where does your father live?"

"He is in jail. He is a political prisoner, but the authorities argued he assaulted a police officer. The police officer was holding his neck, and he couldn't breathe, so he lashed out. He fights for an independent Cataluña."

"How long is his sentence?"

"Eight years. He has served eighteen months."

"What do you do for a job or are you a student?"

"I am a student of politics. I also fight for an independent Cataluña."

"Wow! Have you had trouble from the police, like your father?"

"No. But my mother couldn't handle it. She went back to her roots. I am scared to cause her even more trouble."

Outside the room, Evan could hear the others come into the flat. There was lots of giggling and the bedroom doors opened and closed, muffling the giggles. Evan and Sofia stayed awake most of the night, chatting, only falling asleep at around five in the morning. This meant that when they did surface from Evan's room, Julio and Angelina were having breakfast in the kitchen.

"Oh yes! A very good morning to you. Nice to see you Sofia," Julio greeted them, winking at Evan.

"You two know each other?" she replied, not having been in Julio and Angelina's flat, before now.

"I was going to ask the same questions," added Evan.

"We were all in school together," replied Julio. "Coffee?"

"Please," responded Evan and Sofia, in unison.

"Are you really studying politics?" asked Evan, as they sat sipping their coffees. "Or did you mean following in your father's footsteps?"

"Really. I am a student of politics and history. I choose to research local politics and apply any assignment I do, to the injustices of the Catalan people."

"I see."

"In fact, I must finish an assignment today, so I have to leave you Mr Evan."

"You don't have to call me Mr Evan," he laughed. "Can I see you next weekend?"

"I am visiting my mother and going to a reunion in Perpignan."

"Oh."

Evan could not hide his disappointment, and Sofia picked up on it.

"Why don't you come with me? If I drive it will take us maybe two and a half hours."

"Great."

"I will pick you up on Saturday at ten o'clock. We will have lunch at my mother's. I promise it won't be awkward. The party is in the evening. We can stay at my mother's house. She will give us separate bedrooms, though!"

"See you on Saturday."

He went up to her and kissed her. She left the flat with a spring in her step.

"I think she likes you," suggested Julio.

"I think I quite like her," responded Evan, smiling.

Evan still had around fifty pills in the stash from the toilet and was starting to wonder how he could get hold of some more. One idea he had was to return to Madrid and go to the house near the airport. What if they were Russian? Evan resolved to take all the remaining pills to Perpignan and see how many he could shift at the party. Was he really going to have to find a proper job? It occurred to him, that the only regular, salaried job he had ever had, was at the publishing company, in Ottawa, and he only secured that role, because it was all part of his cover. All his other jobs were cash in hand or paid-by-the-hour hospitality jobs, serving customers. The shifts were both a blessing and a bind. It gave him his mornings or afternoons free to do something else, but it restricted any kind of social life. Unfortunately, he had no career plan and no real training. If he applied for jobs in publishing, he would have to account for not only the job in Ottawa, but also the reason he quit.

On the Monday, he went to buy a newspaper, and started flicking through the job adverts. Baristas and waiters were needed in several places. He decided to visit the named establishments, in person. One of Evan's strengths, given the touristic nature of the city, was the number of languages he spoke, and he always thought he presented himself well. In short, he hated using the telephone.

The first venue was an ice cream parlour. They sold around twenty flavours of ice cream in a variety of forms, both over the counter and in the parlour.

"Hello. I saw your advert and I'm interested in the job."

"Have you worked in a café before?"

"Yes. I was in Amsterdam for a while."

"So, you speak Dutch?"

"Dutch, French, English, obviously, Russian and Pashto."

"What's Pashto?"

"They speak it in Afghanistan. I have travelled quite a lot, working in bars and cafes along the way."

"Have you sold ice cream before?"

"No. But I'm sure you can train me up."

"Do you have a phone number?"

"Yes, but I don't know what it is. I only moved in recently, and I haven't learnt it yet."

Evan felt he was beginning to look hapless, even for a job at an ice cream parlour.

"Come back tomorrow and you can do a trial."

"OK. Great. Thank you. What time?"

"Ten o'clock."

"See you tomorrow. Thanks.

"Bye."

Evan decided to visit the other two venues as well, on the off chance that they might be more exciting. The second job was in a restaurant. Evan stopped at the door to read the set tourist menu. It was in English, Spanish, French, German and possibly Japanese. Evan was not quite sure of the difference in characters between Chinese and Japanese. He went in. A man with a waistcoat was arranging glassed behind the bar.

"Hello. I saw your advert. I speak English, French, Dutch, Russian and Spanish."

"Have you served as a waiter before?"

"I worked in a café and two pubs."

"How many plates can you carry in one go?"

"I don't know. I don't think I've ever carried more than one in each hand or used a tray."

"We don't use trays. There is skill in carrying five plates."

The man set five plates on the bar, picked two up in his left hand and placed a third lodged between his bicep and the other two, picked up two more and carried them to the table.

"That is impressive."

"You try. Take the plates back to the bar."

Evan managed to pile the third plate onto his right arm, being left-handed, and picked up the remaining two plates. Two steps from the table, there was an almighty crash, as the balanced plate on his right forearm slipped onto the floor. Evan winced and looked at the man, sheepishly.

"Imagine if they had been full. I'm sorry, but I need someone who can carry several plates at once."

"OK. Thank you. Sorry for taking up your time. Bye."

Evan left and walked to the third venue.

As he reached the club, he could hear two men having a heated argument inside. Reluctant to interrupt, he edged his way quietly into the room and stood waiting. One man left abruptly, pushing past Evan, grunting an apology.

"Excuse me. You know what it's like."

Evan wondered what 'it' was and what 'it' was meant to be like.

"I saw your job advert. I thought coming to see you was better than phoning. Perhaps I should have phoned."

"I need a doorman. I don't mean I need muscle. I just need someone who can keep an eye open, spot when drugs are being sold or used on the premises."

Evan hoped he did not go red.

"What do they do if they see something?"

"Report it to me. I am always somewhere on the premises when we are open."

"And when are you open?"

"Friday and Saturday from ten until two in the morning. Those are the shifts."

"Thank you. I don't think the job will be enough, and then it's a lot harder to find somewhere else. Sorry."

"Good luck."

"Thanks."

Evan was grateful for the opportunity to turn the job down. He fully intended to try and sell drugs here. The ice cream parlour had just become the favourite.

The following day, Evan turned up at five to ten. They gave him a cap and an apron. The woman he had spoken to before showed Evan how to scoop the ice cream and stick it in a cone, firmly enough that it did not become detached when you inverted it to bury it in the sprinkles.

"Always use a clean scoop for each flavour," she explained, dropping the scoop into a jug of water, and taking a clean one for her second cone.

She handed the finished cone to Evan.

"Really? For me? Thank you."

"You'll soon get sick of ice cream!"

It was strawberry.

"The sauces are here. The cones and shells are here. Sometimes people just want the scoops in one of these tubs. Till's here. That's the easy part of the job. We swap around quite a bit. An hour at the counter, an hour in the café. The only difference here, is that it's all in dishes with spoons.

No cones or throwaway tubs in here. Coffee, tea, hot chocolate and soft drinks served as well. Have you used a steamer before?"

"In Amsterdam."

"Great. Have a bit of a practice, with this tub of vanilla."

"What do I do with the finished cones?"

"Do ten of them and take them outside to give to passers-by. The serviettes have our logo on. It's good publicity. I always give away ten cones at the start of the day. Some people would say I'm mad. But business is thriving. That's why I need a new member of staff."

Evan scooped up ten balls of ice cream, making up ten vanilla single cones, which he placed in one of the stands on the counter. As soon as the tenth was made up, he went out onto the street with the stand and a bunch of serviettes.

"Good morning, Señora. Would you like a free ice cream?"

The woman did not know what to say.

"Please. It's good publicity, to make customers happy," replied Evan, laughing.

"Well, alright. Thank you," she responded, taking the cone which Evan was holding out to her wrapped in a serviette.

"Good morning, Señor. Can I interest you in a free ice cream? We would love you to tell everyone how tasty our ice creams are."

The man took the ice cream from Evan, looking a little confused. Two students trotted over.

"Are you giving away free ice cream?"

"Yes. We want you to come back another time and buy ice cream from us," replied Evan, knowing there was unlikely to be a second time.

He handed each of them a cone. It felt just like selling his amphetamines.

Ten o'clock on Saturday arrived, and Evan was ready and waiting with his fifty pills in his pocket, his knapsack containing clean underwear and toothbrush, and his passport, to get into France. Just in case the chance of sneaking into Sofia's room came about, he checked he had a condom in his wallet. The intercom buzzed, and, assuming it was Sofia, he answered.

"Down immediately."

He quietly closed the flat door, although if Julio and Angelina were still sleeping, the chances were, the intercom would already have woken them. He reached the car, only just stopped himself from going to the driver's side, even after all this time living out of the UK, got in and leant across to kiss Sofia.

"How's your week been?"

"Good. Yours?"

"I got a job at an ice cream seller and café. Did you finish your assignment?"

"Finished and graded."

"That's fast. What did you get?"

"Sixty-four percent."

"Are you pleased with that?"

"Well, I feel like I would have got more if I hadn't used the historical rights of Catalans as my example."

"That's tough."

"That's why we need change!"

"So, what have you told your mother about me?"

"I told her not to mention weddings and children."

"What! Does she make a habit of that?"

"She kind of thinks I should be married and settled down, not fighting for Cataluña. Don't forget, she hasn't really forgiven my father for ending up in prison."

They drove for a little over two hours and came to the border commune of Le Perthus, where they had to go through passport control. Sofia stopped and wound down the window.

"Good day. Passports, please," grunted the border guard. Do you have anything to declare?"

Evan passed his passport to Sofia who gave them both to the officer.

"Please pull over and get out of the vehicle. We're doing spot-checks. You can have these back in a minute."

Sofia pulled into the designated bay and they both got out of the car. Two customs officials started doing a thorough search of the inside.

"Come this way."

The guard with the passports led them into a room. As they were standing there, another officer came in with a dog which started pawing frantically at Evan's trouser pocket.

"Empty your pockets, please."

Evan took out the bag of speed and handed it to the guard.

"Oh dear. This looks like rather more than personal consumption. Were you planning to supply others?"

"Yes. But please believe me. Sofia knew nothing and doesn't have anything to do with this. She invited me to a party, and I thought I'd make some money."

Sofia was looking at Evan in a quizzically bemused way. The guard with the dog left the room and in came a female officer.

"I have to search your body if you don't mind. Lift your arms."

The female officer ran her hands up and down both legs, arms, tummy and back.

"As you admitted to what you were doing, we will spare you the strip search and internal examination."

"Thank you," responded Evan.

"You can go on your way, miss," said the guard, handing her back her passport. You, sir, have to come with us."

"I'm so sorry," whispered Evan, as Sofia walked past.

"I'll bring you your bag," she whispered back, and added, at full volume, "May I bring him his bag?"

"I'll come and get it, with you."

The guard accompanied her out and returned shortly with Evan's knapsack. Evan was arrested, taken back to Barcelona, and placed in a holding cell. Twenty-four hours later, he had pleaded guilty to transporting amphetamines across the border and was beginning a six-year stretch in Barcelona prison. It all happened as if in a trance. Evan was aware of what was going on around him, but he was terrified and had switched off his emotions. The prison loomed oppressively over him as the van entered the gates, and he feared for his life. There was no telling how many Russian inmates there were, with connections who may know him, not to mention the brutal prison gangs operating on the wings.

After being processed quickly, he was led to a cell. To his relief, it did not look like anyone else would be sharing it, at least not for now. He could hear shouts and bangs along with the constant slamming of doors. Evan remembered how lonely he felt on his first night in the squat in Battersea. This was a thousand times worse, because he had no idea of the routines or expectations, he understood little of prison slang and culture, and he was not free to protect himself from harm. It was twelve hours since he had eaten, and his stomach was rumbling. Without a watch, and no obvious presence of a clock, he had no inkling of the time. Dinner was at seven o'clock, but how near was seven o'clock? He lay on the bed, staring at the ceiling.

An hour or so later, his cell door was unlocked, and he joined the exodus from the wing to the refectory. The prisoners marched in silence, a few feet from each other, some with their heads down, others curious to see what their fellow inmates were like. Evan looked across and saw old and young men alike. He tried not to stare and returned his gaze to the heels of the man in front. They collected their food from the counter, rice, beans, and meat. It did not look appetizing, but neither did it look unappetizing, and Evan was hungry. Scanning the room for an empty table, he sat right at the end, hoping to be ignored. Several mouthfuls into the surprisingly tasty meal, a man in his late forties came and sat opposite him.

"Are you Señor Evan?"

"Evan nodded, because his mouth was full."

"My name is Gabriel Brugué. I believe you know my daughter, Sofia."

"Señor Brugué," replied Evan, nodding in acknowledgement.

"She telephoned me and asked me to look out for you."

"I am very grateful to her. And to you."

"I will look after you. Until you can stand on your own two feet. Even then, I will be watching. Have you been assigned a job?"

Evan shook his head.

"I help in the laundry. Everyone does something. Maybe they will tell you tomorrow. I understand. You are scared, yes? It's OK to admit it. I was terrified. Lucky for me, there are many of us here who are political prisoners."

Just then, they were joined by three other men.

"For example, here are Bernat, Maxim and Xavier. All of us fighting for an independent Cataluña. Gentlemen. This is Evan. He is sweet on my daughter. He got caught trafficking speed. I promised my daughter we would take of him."

"Hi," replied Evan, finding his voice, at last. "Nice to meet you."

"He is a polite Englishman, don't you think?" laughed Bernat.

"We will have to keep him away from El Capità," joked Maxim.

"Who is El Capità?" asked Evan, struggling to understand the Catalan which all four men spoke.

"You never want to find out," replied Xavier. "Hopefully, he will ignore you, when he sees you with us."

"Thanks," responded Evan, partly wishing he had not heard of El Capità, and partly grateful the political prisoners were keen to protect him.

At the end of the meal, they were allowed an hour of recreation. Gabriel pulled a pamphlet from his pocket and unfolded it in front of Evan. The folds were stained, and the edges were somewhat the worse for wear.

"This is our manifesto. You should read it."

Nothing was further from Evans' mind than becoming a Catalan separatist, but he knew his safety lay in becoming one of them. The four men played cards whilst Evan read. When he reached the end, he looked at Gabriel.

"Did you understand? Do you see why we must fight?" asked the avuncular freedom-fighter.

"I understood a lot. Catalan is difficult for me. I only learned Spanish in the last year."

"We forgive you. What's a few wrong words if your heart is in the right place?" laughed Xavier.

The bell rang, and they returned to their cells. Evan watched where his new friends went. It turned out that Maxim was two cells away and Gabriel was at the end of the corridor. Evan's cell door was locked behind him, and he lay on his bed, reflecting on his new circumstances.

Evan slept sporadically and woke up with a blinding headache, caused either by stress or dehydration or both. Not only had he gone hours without eating, the day before, but also without water. There was no chance of any paracetamol. At breakfast, he drank as much as he could. His new friends beckoned him to the table where they had saved him a space.

"How did you sleep?" asked Maxim.

"On and off."

"You'll get used to it," Xavier encouraged him.

"Do you think there is anyone here who might want to learn English?" asked Evan.

"I would," replied Gabriel, "If Cataluña is to be on the world stage, one day."

"Me too," added Xavier. "Bernat already speaks a little English, don't you, my friend?"

"A little," responded Bernat, in English.

"Then I will find out what my job is, and when I am not doing that, I will teach English."

"That is your plan for survival?" smiled Maxim.

"He makes a good point," reflected Gabriel. "The way forward is to speak English, or American. Some people trade tobacco. Evan can trade English skills."

A prison guard appeared, carrying a clipboard.

"Prisoners who have jobs assigned, go to them now. Everyone else, remain seated."

"That'll be us," responded Maxim. "See you later Evan."

"Until later," replied Evan.

Bernat and Gabriel both placed a hand on one of Evan's shoulders, by way of reassurance. The refectory emptied in an orderly manner, leaving nine inmates sitting at the tables.

"Evan Stoner-Ward," announced the guard, struggling to pronounce the 'w' in his name.

"Yes, sir," replied Evan, standing up.

"Library."

"Where is the library, please?"

"Wait."

The guard rattled off the other eight names and duties, one of whom was also assigned library duties. The two who had been assigned kitchen duties, went behind the counter into the kitchen. The guard proceeded to lead the four remaining inmates first to the laundry and then to the library.

"Good morning," grunted the librarian. "Please tell me you have some interest in books."

"I used to sell them, sir," responded Evan, politely.

"Yes, but do you read them?"

"Yes, of course."

"What about you?"

The other prisoner, a man in his fifties, even sixties, shook his head.

"I can't read."

"Why have they sent you to me? How can I get you to even catalogue the books if you can't read?"

The librarian was exasperated.

"I'm sorry. I didn't ask for this job. They sent me here."

"Excuse me, but I am happy to help this man by showing him where to put things, and in between sorting out the books, maybe one hour a day, I can teach him to read."

The librarian was somewhat taken aback.

"Why?"

"Because I can't think of many ways of turning this negative experience of being in prison into a positive experience."

The librarian looked at the older man, questioningly, waiting for a response.

"I would like that," he responded, quietly, after a few seconds.

"Then the two of you had better get to work. You can organise yourselves. Three hours until lunch. Three hours after lunch. Toilet breaks when you need them. I'll only interfere if you start taking advantage of my good nature. Understood?"

"Yes sir," replied Evan.

"Very good, sir."

The librarian walked away to his desk and buried himself in a book.

"I'm Evan, by the way."

"My name is Antonio. Can you really teach me to read? You aren't Catalan, or even Spanish, are you?"

I learnt to speak and read, so I am sure I can teach you the basics. After that, it's up to you."

"That's very true."

"Now, I think if we are to catalogue the entire library, we should work out a system where you can be useful, without being able to read. How about we begin by putting the tables in a line. You can count, yes?"

"Of course, I can count."

"Apologies. I didn't mean to offend."

"No offence taken."

"There are twenty-six letters in the alphabet. We can begin by placing the books on the tables. We catalogue by author's name. A-B-C-D-E we place on table one. Have you learnt the alphabet?"

"Many years ago. I just never learnt to put the letters together."

"OK. A-B-C-D-E goes on table one. F-G-H-I-J goes on table two. K-L-M-N-O goes on table three. P-Q-R-S-T goes on table four. U-V-W-X-Y-Z goes on table five. I'm going to say the name of the author, hand you a book, and tell you which number table. Read back to me, the name of the author, paying attention to the way it's written. Once we're on a roll, I'll say the author's name and you can read it and tell me which table."

"Very good."

Evan took a pile of books from the shelf.

"Cervantes. C. Table one."

"Cervantes," repeated Antonio.

"Pla. P. Table four."

"Pla."

"Guimerá. G. Table two."

"Guimerá."

"Espriu. E. Table one."

"Espriu."

"Borges. B. Table one."

"Borges."

And so the morning passed. By lunchtime, there were empty shelves and books piled high on the tables. The librarian came to inspect their work.

"I heard what you were doing. I'm impressed. Let's go for lunch."

When they arrived in the refectory, Evan could see his four friends. Bernat was looking out for him. Evan signalled to save two seats. Antonio and Evan collected their food, which appeared remarkably similar to yesterday's meal, and joined the others.

"My friends, this is Antonio. We're working in the library. Antonio, this is Gabriel, Bernat, Xavier and Maxim."

"This boy is amazing. He is teaching me to read! I've been in here for twenty-five years and I never experienced such kindness."

Evan went red but did not mind being referred to as a boy. He noted the twenty-five years. In the circumstances, it did not necessarily mean Antonio had done something serious. He resolved not to ask but wait until Antonio should choose to offer an explanation. At the end of their meal, Antonio and Evan waited by the door until the librarian came to lead them back to their books.

"I have a plan for this afternoon. We now need to place the books in order. All the authors beginning with 'A' need to be put in order, according to the second and even third letters, so we're going to write the alphabet down."

Antonio nodded, and Evan went to ask the librarian for some paper and pencils.

"Do you want to write?" he asked Antonio.

"You do it."

"Perhaps we will work on writing as well as reading."

Antonio nodded again. Evan wrote out the alphabet using lower case.

"Read the letters back to me," he encouraged Antonio.

"A ... b... c... d... e... f... g... h... i... j... k... l... ll... m... n... o... p... q... r...s... t... u... v... w... x... y... z."

"Well done. So, I'm going to start on table five. You start on table one and place the books with authors whose surnames begin with 'A' in alphabetical order. I'll come and check, and then, you can do B-C-D-E and move on to table two."

After Evan had explained what they were doing, not a lot was said, for both men were concentrating. After about a quarter of an hour Evan went to check.

"Perfect. You are doing really well."

Antonio glowed and carried on. The librarian brought them both a drink of water when they had been working for another hour and a half. They stopped long enough to drink and carried on until all the books were in order.

"Now all we have to do is put them on the shelves. Starting on the left, move across to the divider, and go back to the left on the next shelf down. We can do this together. Just take the next pile of books on the table. By the end of their working day, all the books were back on the shelves in some semblance of alphabetical order. Evan went along the shelves checking. He had to swap six books around.

"Brilliant. Well done. We don't have time for a lesson, but I would say that the whole day has been a lesson."

"Me too. Thank you, Evan."

"You're welcome."

"I'm well impressed," the librarian congratulated them. "What are your plans for tomorrow?"

"A catalogue," responded Evan, beaming. "How well-used is the library?"

"Not much."

"As well as teaching Antonio, I was wondering if I might be able to run a weekly English class. It will be a good skill for the men when they leave prison. All it would need is lots of paper and pencils. We have plenty of books to read and talk about."

"I suppose there's no harm in trying."

"In my life outside, when I worked for a publisher, we sold more books that were non-fiction. As we were sorting them, I noticed there are very few books about places and skills and experiences. It's mostly fiction. Is there any way we could get some books about sport or cars or animals and so on?"

"Let's take it one step at a time, shall we?" responded the librarian. "I'm not saying never. I think it's a good idea, but this place has a bad history, and the culture isn't going to change overnight."

"Thank you. So, you'll get the paper and pencils?" reiterated Evan, smiling.

"I will do my best."

"Can't ask for more than that, interjected Antonio, who had become Evan's number one fan.

"No, we can't. Thank you, sir," added Evan.

Eighteen months into Evan's stretch, Antonio was making great progress with his reading and writing, there was a group of ten inmates learning English, and the library loans had more than quadrupled. The librarian also managed to secure some donations of non-fiction books. It was all going well, until one morning, Antonio and Evan were sorting a box of donated fiction books and stumbled on half a dozen hollowed out paperbacks containing cocaine.

"My God!" exclaimed Antonio. "What are we going to do?"

"I've seen this before," responded Evan, realising too late what he had said, and correcting himself. "At the airport, a man got stopped at customs."

What Evan did not say, was how involved he had been in the whole trafficking business for MI6. He was gravely concerned though. Having already come across Russians in Madrid, he now wondered if this was an accident, a coincidence, or whether the drugs had been sent into prison deliberately.

"We have to tell the librarian," whispered Evan.

"What if he's involved?"

"We can't go to the governor without telling the librarian. He'll feel betrayed and we'll lose our privileges."

"You're right. We could do nothing."

"Or we could monitor the situation and see who borrows these books and how quickly they ask for them. We know the drugs are here. If the librarian is involved, the books, or the contents, will disappear from the shelves, either because he has lent them without our being involved, or because he's taken them."

"Write down the titles of the books."

"You write down the titles of the books!" laughed Evan, encouragingly.

That evening, in the refectory, Evan asked Gabriel, Bernat, Xavier and Maxim if they knew of any drugs or Russians in the prison.

"Is there a drug problem here?"

"Officially or unofficially," laughed Maxim.

"Either."

"Yes, there is," confirmed Gabriel.

"How does it work? I don't want any. Is there a cartel here?"

"You remember on your fist day we told you about El Capità?" inquired Bernat.

Evan nodded.

"How do you think he got his name, other than as the head of a cartel. I don't know if it's outside as well as inside," continued Bernat.

"He's Spanish, yes? Or Catalan?"

"As far as we know," replied Maxim.

"Are there any Russians in here?"

"There are three that I know of," replied Xavier. "When we're next on exercise, you'll see them standing at one end of the yard chatting."

"And do they run a rival cartel?"

"Why all these questions, my friend?" asked Gabriel. "Isn't it better to not know these things?"

"We were unloading some books today," explained Evan, lowering his voice several decibels, to the extent that the friends could hardly hear him. "And we found some hollowed out books containing cocaine. I got beaten up in Madrid, by Russians, because I was dealing on their turf, so to speak."

"You found cocaine?" mouthed Xavier.

"Yes. And we're not sure what to do about it," added Antonio.

"What's your advice, Gabriel?" asked Evan.

"My advice is to do nothing."

"Seriously?" whispered Evan.

"Deadly serious."

"OK. I respect that. Thanks."

The next day, when Antonio and Evan were expecting to be led off to the library, they were instructed to go and help out in the kitchen. Antonio raised his eyebrows to Evan when the guard was not looking. Evan shrugged. They peeled potatoes and mopped the floor without so much as a word of conversation. Evan was extremely frustrated and disappointed. By the evening meal, a rumour was circulating that the librarian had been stabbed. What Evan, Antonio and the friends could not work out was whether he had been killed. The library was closed with immediate effect.

"Looks like we'll have to have our classes in here. If they'll let us, that is," declared Evan.

"I have three books in my cell. When I've finished reading them, I expect I'll have to start to re-read them. I want to keep practising."

"You have done brilliantly, Antonio. Really you have. I don't think you need me as a teacher anymore. I have a couple of books you can borrow."

"Thank you."

"Hey, guys! Can you see El Capità anywhere?" asked Xavier.

"No. Do you think he's been arrested or something?"

It was not until a few days later that the official report trickled through to the prisoners. El Capità had gone to the library to collect his books, something he was accustomed to doing, every two months, but never when Evan and Antonio had been there. The librarian had been taken by surprise and caught in the situation. One of the three Russians had been killed and the other two moved to solitary confinement. Evan's suspicions and fears seemed to be confirmed. What he did not know was whether the remaining two Russians had any inkling of who he was. If he had felt unsafe from the start, he now felt even more in danger, especially as he had been working in the library. Perhaps they thought he had tipped off the authorities?

Evan approached some of the students of English, while they were seated in the refectory, to let them know the class would continue during recreation, if they were interested. They did not have any paper or pencils, so until such time as they did, it would have to be entirely conversational. The downside of being with all the others was noise and interruptions, but a few days into trying, Gabriel came up with his own plan for classes, which he shared with his small band of compatriots.

"Since no one seems to care what's going on, and there's too much noise to hear what is being said, why don't I start a history class. The history of Cataluña. We can discuss what we have learned and how we want to develop it."

"Do you think that's wise?" asked, Bernat.

"When did wisdom ever bring about independence!" snorted Gabriel. "I have some books, which they didn't take from me, probably because the guards had never read anything, about our history. We could read a chapter together each week and discuss it. We won't be political, we'll be historical!"

"I'd come, if I wasn't teaching English," Evan encouraged his mentor.

"Thank you, Evan. We can do the class on a different day to your English classes."

And so, Evan became a student of Catalan history and of the movement for independence. As the weeks passed, he found his sympathies aligning with the separatists, just as he had identified with Vladimir Vladimirovich Mayakovsky, in his days at SSEES, which all seemed like an eternity ago. The group contained fourteen inmates, including his friends. Although always a revolutionary at heart, Gabriel contained his political urges, leading imaginative and creative discussion around lessons learned and what the future of Cataluña might one day look like, all the while quashing negative, political criticism of the powers that be and the status quo. Given that Sofia had described her father as a political prisoner, the guards paid surprisingly little attention to what he was doing. Evan convinced himself that his newfound interest in Catalan history and politics had nothing to do with his attraction to Gabriel's daughter.

For the first two years of Evan's sentence, Sofia had visited her father on three weekends out of every four, and on the fourth, Gabriel gave up his time with her so that she could visit Evan, instead. It was hard not being allowed any physical contact with her, but he valued their conversation, and now, they had a growing shared passion.

"My father speaks very highly of you," she confirmed one weekend.

"I see him as my mentor. He has looked out for me and taught me a lot."

"You should see it as an honour that he treats you this way. I think it's his way of saying he approves. Fathers and daughters and all that. It's not like we had even been dating properly before you ended up in here."

"Six years is a long time not to be able to make love to you. I hope we can pick up where we left off. I'm really grateful that you visit me. I'm sorry I got caught."

"Don't be. If you hadn't got caught, it would have been many years before you met my father, if ever."

It was a total shock, two days after their conversation, when Gabriel had his heart attack at breakfast. At first, he thought it was indigestion, that he had eaten his bread too quickly, but the pain shot from his chest to his arm. He had stood up and was about to call for help when he just keeled over. He grabbed Evan's arm and died. First Ike, now Gabriel. Evan had not anticipated the losses which life would inflict on him. Gabriel was carried out on a stretcher, a blanket draped over the full length of his body. Needless to say, Evan was not permitted to attend the funeral.

Evan felt down for the rest of the week. He had lost his mentor and his protector. What he did not realise was that he was losing his girlfriend as well. On the Saturday afternoon, he filed into the visiting room and waited in his chair. It was not the weekend he was due a visit, but he somehow assumed Sofia would visit him every week, now she was not coming to see her father. All the other prisoners received their visitors, but Sofia failed to make an appearance. Evan felt stupid.

The next day, he received a letter from her. It was short and to the point. Honest but not brutal so much as disappointing. 'Dear Evan. I am so sorry, but I will not be visiting you anymore. Six years is a long time to wait when we hardly know each other. I have met someone else. Stay safe. Goodbye. Sofia.' Evan felt choked. First it was drugs, now it was politics. A recruiting tactic for the struggle for an independent Cataluña, no doubt. Mariana and Colleen, at least, were genuine. Evan realised he genuinely missed Colleen. Of all his girlfriends, she was the one with whom he shared most in common. He regretted his move to Barcelona, not that he could have stayed in Madrid, and even though he knew he had asked the impossible of her, he so wished she could have come with him.

Right now, he had more pressing matters to worry about, like staying alive. The two Russians had come to the end of their period in solitary confinement. Bernat, Xavier, and Maxim would still look out for him, he was certain, but it was clear that Gabriel had carried some weight amongst the prison population. Evan started to wonder how he might manufacture a route away from the wings and into the hospital. He was still working in the kitchen, since the library was closed, and considered eating something that would make him violently sick. It probably needed to be more convincing than his performance in Lashkar Gah.

There were several options open to him. Salt water, if gulped down in sufficient quantity would make him sick, and if it did not, he could make himself sick with his fingers anyway. However, the bulk salt container sat in full sight in the middle of the kitchen. Diluted disinfectant would make him sick but might damage his insides. At that point, Evan remembered what his mother used to give him when he or Helen said they felt sick. She would dissolve a small amount of sodium bicarbonate in water and ask them to drink it. It would either make them vomit, and so end the discomfort, or it would calm everything down. The challenge would be opening the cupboards without anyone else noticing.

Evan half-filled a bucket with diluted disinfectant and got a clean cloth. He opened the storage cupboard and started to clean down the inside of the door, followed by removing the contents from the shelves to wipe the surfaces clean.

"Hey, what are you doing?" called the guard.

"Cleaning the insides of the cupboard, sir. More hygienic that way."

"OK. Carry on."

Pleased with his ruse, Evan continued until he discovered the sodium bicarbonate, in a small cardboard drum. He made sure there was tissue in his pocket and accidentally dropped the drum on the floor, so it burst open. The guard appeared at the cupboard door.

"Watch what you're doing!" he grunted.

"Sorry. I'll clear it up, sir."

Evan collected most of the spilt powder in the tissue and put it in his pocket, replacing the lid and the now near-empty drum on the shelf. He mopped the floor and finished cleaning the cupboard. When he had completed the task, he moved onto the cupboards containing the saucepans, but before he could empty the first one, the guard announced the end of work.

That evening, Evan took a mug of water back to his cell.

"What are you doing with that?" asked an observant guard.

"I'm sorry, sir, but I have a splitting headache. I don't feel well."

"Well, if it gets any worse, tell me. We may have to take you to the infirmary."

The guard had unwittingly played right into Evan's hands. Once the cells were locked, Evan poured the sodium bicarbonate from the tissue into the water and stirred it with a pencil. He gulped it all down, the vile aftertaste reminding him of his childhood. Not many minutes later, he started to feel increasingly green round the edges, and volcanic rumblings bubbled in his stomach. The contents of his stomach erupted into the toilet bucket. Evan retched a few times and convulsed a second time, the throes causing him acute pain. Removing his watch, he stuck the prong of the buckle into his gum, between two molars, sucked out the blood and spat into the bucket. He banged the mug on the door of his cell.

"Guard!" he shouted.

The guard approached and opened the peephole.

"Everything alright?" he asked, not intending to come across as sarcastic.

Evan picked up the bucket and tilted it so the guard could see.

"I've just been violently sick. I think the headache is getting worse."

"Hmmm," responded the guard, unlocking the door, "You'd better come with me."

Evan stepped forward, and the guard locked the cell door behind him. They walked through several doors and along corridors to the hospital wing.

"Good evening, doctor. I have a blinding headache and I was violently sick."

"We'd better examine you, then. Remove your shirt, please."

The doctor proceeded to take Evan's temperature, listen to his heart, test his reflexes, and look into his eyes and ears.

"Better keep you in under observation. I'll give you something to help you sleep."

He showed Evan to his new bed and went to the medicine cabinet, returning with two pills. There was a jug of water on the bedside cabinet. Evan swallowed the pills and lay on his bed, his back propped up on two pillows. Three of the beds were occupied. As the pills started to take effect, Evan manoeuvred himself lower into the bed and closed his eyes. They left him sleeping for ten hours, before the doctor came to check him over again.

"How are you feeling?"

"I had a good night's sleep. The thing is, I'm ashamed to admit it, but since I entered the prison, I have feared for my life, and the tension has built up over time. I'm depressed and scared and exhausted. I don't think I'm physically ill. It's the physical impact of stress, but you're the doctor."

"Why do you fear for your life?"

"Initially, it was because I've heard so many horror stories about prison. Then, I saw the Russians, and there was that whole incident with the library. My mentor and protector had a heart attack. Now I'm terrified."

"Yes, but why are you afraid of the Russians?"

"They run drug cartels across Europe, and I reported them to the police before I came to Spain," was Evan's partially truthful reply. "I saw drugs hidden in the books when I was working in the library, but I was too afraid to say anything. In my head, the Russians came for their drugs and the librarian got caught up in it. If the Russians think I told the librarian about the drugs, they will kill me."

"I see. You're English, aren't you?"

"Yes."

"Your Spanish is good, mixed up with some Catalan."

"Thank you."

"I trained in London."

"No way! I lived in London for a while. Do you speak English?"

"Not as well as I'd like to. If you will give me private English lessons, I'll see to it that you get to stay here. Not in a bed, mind. You'll have to sleep in solitary, but you can work here, as an orderly."

"Seriously?"

"Of course."

"When do you want your lessons?"

"Every morning as soon as I have done my rounds. You can come along and wheel the trolley for me. Then we'll go to my office."

"Brilliant. Thank you."

For the next eighteen months, Evan slept in solitary confinement and worked as an orderly in the hospital. He did not mind the solitary nights, in fact, he quite enjoyed them. There were never more than five inmates in the hospital at any given time, so his duties were easy. He learnt hospital corners on the beds. The job had its downside, like cleaning bedpans, but as jobs in prison go, it was nicer than the kitchen, less sweaty than Evan believed the laundry to be, but not as much fun as the library. Evan and the doctor shared many pleasant chats about the United Kingdom and his time in London, and the doctor's fluency had multiplied tenfold over the course of the eighteen months, until the day he was offered a transfer.

"I'll be sorry to see you go," admitted Evan.

"I'll miss our conversations. Thank you. But I won't miss this place. I'll put in a good word for you with my successor. Have to hope for the best."

"Thank you."

By now, the prison governor had been made aware of Evan's situation and was surprisingly sympathetic. The new doctor did not arrive for a week, and although there were no prisoners in the hospital, Evan was allowed to carry on his duties and continue to sleep in solitary confinement. Dr Emilio was younger than his predecessor, and having not long completed his training, saw the move to Barcelona as beneficial to his career. It was not that he did not care, he simply had no plans to stay any longer than he had to. He quickly worked out that Evan was useful, in as much as he could teach him English, enhancing the possibility of transferring to the States. Evan was happy to oblige.

Since Sofia's letter, Evan had not received a single visitor. About six months into Dr Emilio's stint as prison doctor, he passed on a message to Evan to expect a visitor the following Saturday. Evan wondered who on earth it could be. His curiosity caused him to count down the days until the weekend. So, as he sat in his chair in the visiting room, he could never have guessed in a million years that Grant Waterstone would walk through the door. Evan felt joy, shame, and embarrassment in equal measure, as he stood to shake Grant's hand.

"No contact," called the guard.

Evan held up his hand in acknowledgement.

"What? How? Why? It's great to see you, but what brings you to Barcelona to visit me?"

"I'd say I was passing and wanted to reminisce, but that would be impossible. We both know I'd have no idea you were even here if it wasn't official."

"So, this is an official visit. I was under the impression when I left that if I went back to my old ways, I would be excluded from any official help."

"That is very true, but when Dominic Andrews got your message, we started to refocus on Spain and the Latin American connection. It is absolutely true that thanks to you we took down the Krukov empire. However, not long afterwards, it appears a new Russian empire sprang into being. We're not making huge headway, which is when I decided to use my connections to try and trace you."

"And here I am. Not going anywhere until 1991."

"How are you?"

"Living in fear. There's a Russian connection in the prison. I've been fortunate enough to be allowed to work in the hospital and sleep in solitary confinement. I tend to get by offering English conversation classes, to curry favour."

"Tell me more about the Russian connection, would you?"

"It must be about eighteen months ago, now. I lose track of time. I was working in the library with another prisoner. Anyway, one day, we were sorting out a crate of donated books and discovered some paperbacks, hollowed out like the Krukov books, filled with cocaine. At least I think it was cocaine. I left well alone and told no one. Shortly afterwards, there was some kind of altercation between Russians and the librarian, and the librarian was stabbed. Since then, I've been more fearful than before, in case they thought I had snitched."

"We think the network is in the clubs and music venues of the big cities, as the country has opened up in the post-Franco years, and also across the prisons. We're going to send an agent in as a prisoner to protect you and monitor what's going on. I can't get you out of here, but I'm happy to make the rest of your time safer."

"That's some comfort. Thanks."

"You're welcome. Now, tell me, how did you end up here?"

"My luck ran out. I was transporting amphetamines into France, and they did a spot-check. I found them in a cistern at a club in Madrid. Then I got beaten up by some Russians, for selling them on their turf, so I moved to Barcelona. If they had known who I was, they probably wouldn't have stopped at a beating."

"I guess they wouldn't. The new prisoner is bound to talk about the Parc Güell. Right, it's time for me to go. When you eventually get out of here, get in touch. No strings."

Waterstone stood up to leave and was about to shake Evan's hand when he remembered the no-contact rule. He winked at Evan, turned, and walked out.

A week later, Evan was changing sheets on the hospital beds when a prisoner was brought in. After his initial examination in the treatment room, he was shown to his bed. As soon as he was tucked up under his sheet and blanket, he called Evan over.

"Tell me. Have you ever been to the Parc Güell?"

"Not yet. I wanted to, but I never got the chance."

Nothing else was said. Whatever his imaginary condition, the Gaudi fan made regular short stays in the hospital, which was reassuring for Evan.

The weeks turned to months and the last two years of Evan's sentence passed without incident. About two months before he was due to be released, he was taken to the governor's office, where he was introduced to a man from the British Consulate. The governor left them on their own.

"I'm Barrington Haynes. I have been asked to handle your return to the United Kingdom."

"Hi. I'm Evan Stoner-Ward, but I guess you know that. Who says I'm returning to the United Kingdom? I'm not saying I don't want to. In fact, over the last six years I've had lots of opportunity to reflect on my life. I think it's time I went home. I mean. Home to my parents."

"I'm very glad to hear that. What you may not realise is that you cannot stay in Spain. How shall I put it? You are now persona non grata. Your passport will be returned to you, but you're no longer welcome here."

"I see."

"How would you feel about having your original passport back? It's been a long time. It's unlikely that you'll bump into any Russians in Maidstone. Owen Linton-House, I believe."

"That would be me. But there's still no guarantee that my parents will have me back."

"Then we'd better call them. No time like the present."

"I don't remember the number."

"I already took the liberty of using government networks. Here it is," he said, removing a small square of paper from his wallet and setting it down on the desk, in front of Evan-Owen. "The governor has given permission to make the call from here. Are you up for it, or shall I speak to them first?"

"Can you test the waters?" asked Evan-Owen, hesitantly.

Haynes dialled the number, which rang for a long time.

"Hello. Is that Benjamin Linton-House? …. My name is Barrington Haynes, from the British Consulate in Barcelona,

Spain. I have your son Owen here with me. He'd like to come home. ………………………….. Yes, I'll pass him the receiver."

Haynes passed Evan-Owen the phone, who cleared his throat.

"Hello. Daddy. It's a very long story. I'm sorry for everything. Can I come home?"

"Of course, you can. Do you need Mummy and me to send the fare?"

"Probably. I think the Spanish authorities cleared out my bank account. I've been in prison for the last six years."

"It doesn't matter. Phone us when you know. Can you pass me back to Barrington Haynes?"

"Yes. Thank you. See you soon."

Evan-Owen handed back the receiver to Haynes.

"He wants to speak to you again."

"Hello. …. It might take three or four weeks to sort this all out. You should receive a letter in the next few days with bank details and the price of the ticket from Barcelona to Heathrow and train journey to Maidstone. Once the money is received, we'll purchase the tickets, and your son can travel. …. You're welcome. It'll be nice to have a happy ending after all this time. …. Yes. Bye."

Haynes replaced the receiver.

"Well, well, well! That went better than we could have hoped. As you can gather from what I said. It's going to take three or four weeks to sort, but you'll be home soon, all being well."

"Thank you so much."

"I'll be back in touch when the tickets have been purchased and will take you to the airport myself. By the way, your parents have moved from Yalding to Leeds Village, near the castle. You'll have to get a bus from Maidstone. Oh, and there's the small matter of a replacement passport. Can you fill in and sign this form, please?"

He handed Evan-Owen a pen and the form.

"I really am very grateful."

"You're welcome. Now, I have to dial an extension. I think this is it. Yes ….. We're done here. Thank you."

A few minutes later, the governor returned.

"Can you sign and stamp this form please, to say that Evan has been here for the last six years."

The governor signed without remarking on the name. Haynes shook the governor's hand and left, and Evan-Owen was escorted back to the hospital. He could hardly think straight, he was so surprised, confused, and excited.

Four weeks later, Owen Linton-House stepped onto an aeroplane bound for London, just shy of twelve years since he left home the day before his eighteenth birthday. He had long considered returning when he was thirty, but it was more by luck than judgement that his sentence ended when it did. He tried to picture his parents. Doubtless, they had not aged a bit. Helen was a different story. Would he even recognise her?

From his window seat, Owen paid no attention to the safety demonstrations, preferring to watch the activities on the tarmac below. The plane reversed away from the terminal and taxied to the end of the runway. Although he had experienced take-off many times before, on this occasion, he felt a deep sense of freedom. Owen genuinely believed prison had changed him, and he was curious to discover his new life. There would definitely be no more drug dealing, and he hoped his many languages would help him find a decent job with a monthly salary.

The plane surfaced from the clouds, and for a few minutes, the sun shone in through Owen's window, until the plane banked and set a northerly course. At this point, Owen realised he had nothing to entertain himself with, for the journey. Closing his eyes, he thought through what he might do and say, when he reached home. Not wanting to arrive empty-handed, he decided to buy a bottle of something when he landed. When on his release, his belongings were returned to him, he discovered two ten-pound notes in the back compartment of his wallet, but he still had no idea if there was any money left in his English bank account. Halfway through the flight, the cabin crew distributed sandwiches, but Owen was not hungry and just accepted the offer of coffee.

The descent into Heathrow began. All Owen had to his name was the knapsack he was carrying when he was arrested, which contained little more than clean underwear and a toothbrush. He was wearing the same clothes he had swapped for his prison outfit. It occurred to him that the weather in London might be considerably colder. Hopefully, he could buy a sweatshirt and a cagoule at the airport. The plane wheels bumped onto the tarmac and the engines went into reverse thrust. Fifteen minutes later, Owen stepped foot in the United Kingdom, for the first time in seven years. It was five o'clock.

The passengers had to get on a bus, to be transferred to the terminal building. Owen shivered, his arms developing goosebumps, even on the short hop from plane to bus. In spite of his previous activities, the new passport number meant nothing was flagged as he passed through security. With just a knapsack, and wearing T-shirt and jeans, Owen was certain he would be stopped in customs, which he thought would be somewhat ironic, but no one was on duty. He bought a bottle of Courvoisier cognac. However, there was nowhere to buy clothes in arrivals. As he was going from Heathrow to Paddington and Paddington to Victoria, he knew there would be opportunities to shop in Central London.

As soon as he exited the Underground at Victoria, he nipped out and found a cash machine. To his surprise, there was forty-eight pounds in his bank account. He withdrew forty-five and went and bought a cheap jacket, which made him feel quite dapper with his jeans and T-shirt. Returning to Victoria Station, he boarded the train for Ashford. This was not a journey he had taken previously, as he had always gone from Charing Cross.

Owen had the address written on a piece of paper in his pocket. He alighted at Maidstone East and walked through the town to the bus station. So many memories came flooding back. It was not until he asked at the bus station that he discovered the buses for Leeds left from King Street. He walked back up Gabriel's Hill and found the bus stop. Unfortunately, rural transport being fairly infrequent, he had missed the last bus to Leeds. When he had left home all those years ago, Ben and Gail did not own a car, both preferring to ride mopeds, so phoning for a lift was not an option. A taxi was the only real solution, but looking around, Owen could not see any.

"Excuse me," he approached a couple of lads, out on the town. "Can you tell me where the taxi rank is, please?"

One of the lads pointed in an imprecise rolling movement with his arm. They were both drunk.

"Thanks," responded Owen, not wishing to offend, and walked in the direction of the High St, where he saw some taxis.

As if the universe were responding with irony, the heavens opened. He had left home in the rain, and he would now return home in the rain. It quickly became heavy. Owen got into a taxi.

"I need to go to Farmer Close in Leeds Village, please."

"That won't be cheap."

"I know but needs must. I missed the last bus."

They set off.

The taxi pulled into Farmer Close and stopped in the cul-de-sac where cars were parked by back gates. Owen paid and got out. A few residents, including Gail and Ben, had stuck numbers on their back gates. Owen wondered whether he should go round to the front and ring the doorbell or to go in through the back gate. He needn't have worried, because when he opened the back gate, Gail looked up and saw him through the window. What followed felt somewhat surreal, but then parents with unconditional love have the ability to make everything seem perfectly normal. She opened the door to him and hugged him. Ben was in one of his poorly phases, so he did not get up from his chair.

"Let me have a look at you," he insisted, surveying the man he had last seen as a teenager.

"I bought you some cognac," remarked Owen.

"Then we'd better drink some to celebrate," responded Ben.

Gail went to the kitchen and came back with some glasses.

"Are you hungry? I can make some sandwiches."

"That would be great, thank you, but not just yet. So many questions. So much to tell."

He poured them each a drink.

"Cheers!"

"To hope fulfilled," responded Ben, raising his glass. "Before we get into your story, we need to make a phone call to Helen. She got married last year to some lowlife called Finn. Nasty piece of work. She lives in Nottingham."

The phone was next to his chair. He had to look up the number in the address book, sitting on the shelf next to the phone. Having dialled, he waited. Helen answered.

"Hello."

"It's Daddy. There's someone here who wants to speak to you," Ben informed his daughter, handing Owen the receiver.

The deep, ex-patriot voice Helen heard next was unfamiliar to her.

"Hello, Sweetheart. How are you?" Owen greeted her.

For a split second, she did not know what to think or say, which caused her to ask a somewhat daft question.

"Are you in the UK?"

"Yes, I'm at Mummy and Daddy's. We've already started the bottle of cognac I bought."

"Stay up. I'm leaving now. I should get to you by one-thirty, two o'clock."

"See you soon."

When Helen did arrive, Owen, Ben, and Gail had already polished off most of the bottle of cognac. Helen was not the slightest bit offended as she did not much care for cognac, other than as flavouring in brandy sauce, or flaming a Christmas pudding. She hugged Owen, hardly able to believe her eyes.

"Cup of tea?" asked Gail. "There are a couple of cheese sandwiches left in the fridge. I'll go and make the bed up. You can have your old room and Owen can have the settee for now."

"Yes please to tea and sandwiches. Now tell me, where have you been, all this time?"

"I'll save most of the story for tomorrow, as we're all really tired, but in a nutshell, London, Amsterdam, Ottawa, Afghanistan, Spain."

"Wow. I speak Spanish, after a fashion. I studied French with Spanish at Nottingham. Did you go to SSEES?"

"Yes, but I dropped out at the end of the first year. Tell me, have you ever been to Madrid?" inquired Owen, as it dawned on him why the girl in Madrid had looked so familiar.

"As a matter of fact, yes. I was there briefly in the summer of 1984, on my way to Salamanca."

"No way! You were in the Puerta del Sol, weren't you?"
"Yes."

"I saw you. I just didn't recognise you."

Gail brought in the cup of tea and sandwiches.

"Thank you," said Helen.

"Helen and I have just discovered we were a few yards apart in Madrid but didn't recognise each other."

"How many languages do you speak?" asked Helen.

"French, Russian, Dutch, Spanish, Catalan, Pashto."

Ben and Gail went up to bed, leaving the siblings to catch up.

"Listen, I can only stay until tomorrow and then I'm back on shift."

"Where to you work?"

"At a drop-in centre for homeless, rootless and unemployed people."

"So why is Daddy singularly unimpressed with Finn?"

"Because he's divorced twice, and I met him at the night shelter. To be honest, it's not great. He gets drunk every time he gets his giro."

"Can I ask a stupid question."

"What?"

"Why did you marry him?"

"I guess because he asked me. Haven't had a lot of joy with guys. Are you in a relationship?"

"To be honest, I haven't had a lot of joy with relationships either. I think you missed the part where I've just done six years in prison in Barcelona."

"Oh, my goodness! What for?"

"I was taking speed from Spain to France and got stopped at the border."

"What was it like in prison?"

"I made some friends. I taught English. I worked mostly in the hospital. I was pretty scared most of the time."

"Did you do drugs?"

"Gosh! Is this an interrogation?"

"No. I'm just curious."

"After I went to university I got hooked on heroin. I was a functioning addict. I had a job in a pub, and I dealt cannabis. When I went to Amsterdam, I went cold turkey."

"Was that as bad as they say?"

"Not so bad, but then I was only on a weekly hit."

"Look, I really need to go to bed. Will you visit?"

"Will Finn mind?"

"He doesn't have a lot of choice. It'll be fine, I'm sure."

"OK. Let me get settled in and I'll hitch a lift up there."

"If you get to junction 25 of the M1 I'll come and pick you up."

"Brilliant."

"Good night."

"Night."

Helen went upstairs to her room that was not her room. Ben and Gail had moved when she was a student, and so the room was hers, but not decorated to her taste or personalised as her room in Yalding had been. Now, presumably, it would be Owen's room, until he got a place of his own. Owen bedded down on the sofa, with Misty, the lilac point Burmese who had succeeded Cadbury and Joey, for company.

In the morning, Helen was up early. She made Owen, Gail, Ben, and herself a cup of tea. She took Owen's into the sitting room not knowing if he even drank tea.

"Morning. I didn't think, until I'd made it. Do you even drink tea?"

"Well, I haven't in a while, but I'm making up for lost time. Thanks."

Helen took Gail's and Ben's upstairs leaving Owen to put some clothes on. He was dressed when she came back down.

"Now then," exclaimed Owen. "Let's see if Mummy has the where-with-all to make pancakes."

Gail came into the kitchen as he was rummaging through the cupboards.

"Do we have enough eggs, flour and milk to make American style pancakes."

"We do, but I'm not sure we have anything other than bacon or lemon juice and sugar. No maple syrup, I'm afraid."

"OK. Let's give pancakes a miss this time. I promise I'll cook you some when I visit you, Helen."

"Thanks."

"There's toast or cornflakes or muesli. I didn't know either of you were arriving yesterday."

"Of course."

Owen grilled several slices of toast which they ate with marmalade and butter, a simple pleasure that he had not savoured in years.

"I'm going to need to go into Maidstone and get some clothes, especially if I'm job-hunting. I'm guessing there are a fair few charity shops. When I lived in Battersea, I got well kitted out from charity shops."

"Yes, lots of charity shops. I use them all the time to get items for the pantomime costumes."

"You do panto?"

"Village Players. Yes. I paint the scenery and make costumes. I usually end up with a bit part."

"I'm impressed," Owen affirmed his mother. "Come to think of it, you always did do us proud for school plays."

"Thanks. Would you like to borrow one of the mopeds?"

"That would be brilliant. When I have a job, and some money, I'll get a motorbike. Only a small one."

"What happened to your Honda?" asked Helen.

"I sold it when I went to Amsterdam. It served me well in London. When I was in Amsterdam, and then in Ottawa, I rode a bicycle. I was quite fit."

They finished their toast.

"I need to be getting back. How soon do you think you can come to Nottingham?"

"Next week if that's OK? Do you have a computer?"

"Yes."

"Would you help me with a résumé and then print it off."

"A what?"

"A curriculum vitae. I'm heavily influenced by American English, these days," laughed Owen.

"Of course. I help the guys at the drop-in centre do that kind of thing all the time."

"Thank you. I'll phone you to let you know which day."

"Brilliant."

Helen got up to go and Owen stood to hug her. She hugged Gail and went upstairs to see if Ben was awake, which he was not.

"Say goodbye to Daddy for me," she added as she went through the back door.

"What do you drive?" asked Owen.

"A mini. I got it cheap when I came back from Switzerland. It was a rust bucket, but my friend put new bodywork on it and taught me to drive in it. I had to take my test in a BSM car though."

"Did you pass first time?"

"Of course. Bye."

She closed the gate behind her.

Gail got her moped out of the garden shed.

"Have you ridden a moped before? It doesn't have any gears. It's two-stroke. The oil is in the top-box if you fill up. Use the measure to a gallon. Hopefully, my helmet will fit you."

"Thanks."

"If you go to the top of the hill, past the Ten Bells and keep going for about half a mile, take Horseshoes Lane which cuts across to the Sutton Road. Turn right along the Sutton Road and keep going until it merges with Loose Road. Carry on until it becomes Upper Stone Street and Lower Stone Street and then you're in the town centre."

"I think I got that. It'll be coming home that I'll get lost!"

Owen tried on the helmet, which fitted snuggly.

"Right. All good. See you later."

"Bye."

Owen set off up the hill and found Horseshoes Lane. The rest of the journey was easy. He parked up in Palace Avenue and walked up Gabriel's Hill, crossing King Street and continuing along Week Street. By lunchtime, He had bought two T-shirts and a pair of jeans, some cream chinos, a blue shirt with a red and blue silk tie, some smart brown shoes, and a navy blazer, all for five pounds. From the final charity shop he walked back along Week Street and went into Marks and Spencer to buy new underwear and socks. Surprised by his cheap haul, he walked back down Gabriel's Hill, stopping in The Ship for a half of cider. Heading home, he missed Horseshoes Lane and had to turn left at the Five Wents.

"Did you get what you needed?" asked Gail

"Yes. I did amazingly well. Look. What do you think of these for a job interview?" he asked, taking the chinos, shirt, tie and blazer from the plastic bag.

"Really smart."

"I got these, some shoes, some jeans and two T-shirts for a fiver. Then I got pants and socks in M&S."

"How are you off for money. You could sign on until you get a job."

"That's a good idea. Can I borrow the moped again tomorrow, to go and sign on. If I'd thought, I'd have done it today."

"Of course. Actually, you're probably best phoning for an appointment. It's not too late to do that today."

"I will."

When Owen phoned the Job Centre, he was given an appointment for the following Tuesday, which gave him plenty of opportunity to hitch up to Helen's. He rang her to tell her of his plans.

Early on the Friday, Owen walked to the A20 and stuck out his thumb.

"Where do you want to go?" asked a middle-aged man who stopped and wound down his window, after Owen had been waiting all of ten minutes.

"I want to visit my sister in Nottingham, so anywhere you can take me on the journey with a good option for my next lift, if you could."

"Well, it's your lucky day, because I'm heading for Luton. I'll take you to Toddington Services, though."

"That is brilliant, thanks."

Owen got in.

"Do you always hitch?"

"I only just got back to the UK. Until I get a job, I'm pretty much reliant on others. I haven't seen my sister in a while."

"Do you travel a lot? Abroad, I mean."

"I was out of the country for twelve years. Spain, Holland, France, Afghanistan. Canada."

"Never been out of the country, me."

"Not even for a holiday?"

"No. Got a caravan in Cornwall. Can't beat Cornwall, if it doesn't rain."

"I've been to Bodmin. Many years ago. Not been to the coast."

"Beautiful."

There were about thirty miles of silence until they reached the Dartford Tunnel.

"When I was a kid, we visited my grandparents in Essex. There was just the one tunnel, back then. Traffic jams were horrendous."

"It's not much better now, at certain times. You can see they've nearly finished the bridge. That should make a huge difference. Opening sometime this year, I hope."

"What sort of job are you looking for?"

"To tell you the truth, I don't know. I've mostly worked in pubs and cafes since I left school. In Canada I worked for a publishing company and sold books. Now I speak several languages, I'm hoping I'll find a job where I can use them."

"Which languages do you speak?"

"Russian, French, Spanish, Catalan, Pashto."

"What's Pashto?"

"They speak it in Afghanistan."

"I'm impressed! Listen, I've got a mate in Tonbridge. He runs a company in West Malling. They're looking to expand into Europe. I'll give you his phone number when we stop. His name is Brian Millington. Tell him Jim Warner gave it to you."

"Thanks. I'm Owen, by the way."

As they were heading round the M25 towards the M1, the traffic slowed to a standstill.

"Accident, no doubt."

Warner switched the radio on and tried to pick up a local radio station, to find the traffic news. He failed miserably and settled on Radio Two.

"What music do you like?"

"Mostly rock, progressive rock. You?"

"Jazz. I play the saxophone."

"Wow! When I was in Canada, I lived in Ottawa. They have a cool jazz festival there. Do you play in a band?"

"I do. We don't get a lot of gigs, but then, I work full time, so it would be difficult. Do you play anything?"

"Never learnt."

The traffic started to move again, and they were soon doing seventy miles an hour. *House of the Rising Sun* started playing on the radio.

"Oh boy. This takes me back. I was sixteen and in love."

Owen worked out that Jim was not as old as he had thought. He was forty-four but looked older due to his bald head.

"I was three. That said, I've heard the song many times and I quite like it."

"Now, New Orleans is somewhere I'd like to go."

"Is that because of the jazz music?"

"Yes."

"What's stopping you?"

"Family. Paying for two kids at university."

"Where are they?"

"Well, Sarah, she's my eldest, is at Bristol doing medicine and Jack, he's at Manchester doing engineering of some sort. I never had the chance. Went to night school and ended up with a Masters in Business Studies."

Owen decided not to mention he had dropped out of SSEES. They reached the M1.

"No more than half an hour, now, if there are no more hold-ups."

"Thank you so much for taking me to Toddington Services."

"You're welcome. Is your sister older or younger?"

"Younger. She's married. My dad can't stand his son-in-law. I'm nervous to meet him!"

"Well, your sister must have seen something in him."

"To be honest, she says it's difficult. I think she regrets it."

"That's not good."

"Now I'm back in the UK, all I can do is be there for my sister, if she needs me."

"Good man. I don't know how I'd react if my daughter married a jerk. Well, I do know. At least, I'd have to have a lot of self-control."

Owen was thinking it was not just men who were bastards. Some women just use you and abuse you, getting you addicted and then forcing you to traffic drugs, but he said nothing. They pulled into Toddington Services.

"Hopefully, you'll get your next lift as quickly as mine. Best to wait on the exit road, just after the fuel station. Here's the contact details for my mate in West Malling."

"Thanks. Can I get you a coffee, or something?"

"No. Thank you. Save your money. Take care."

"You, too."

Owen got out of the car, went inside to use the facilities, and went and positioned himself where Jim had suggested.

This time, it took about twenty minutes for a vehicle to stop. It was a lorry, with a foreign number plate, and Owen had to run round the back to the passenger side. That was when he noticed it was Russian. Filled with a sudden panic, he went back round to the driver's side and shook his head, shrugged his shoulders, and held up one hand in acknowledgement. The driver shook his head and drove off, not knowing Owen's back story. His heart was racing, and it had just about calmed down when a car pulled up.

"Where are you going?" asked a young woman, whose partner was driving, winding down the passenger window.

"Junction 25, if you're going that far, otherwise as far as you're going."

"We can do that. Hop in the back."

"Thanks."

Owen got into the back seat.

"We're on our way to Leeds so we can certainly drop you at junction 25."

"Much appreciated. I'm going to Nottingham to see my sister. She'll pick me up from junction 25. I have to ring from the hotel there."

"I went to university in Nottingham," said the woman.

"Really. So did my sister. When she graduated, she stayed in the city."

"A lot of people do. I would have, probably, if I hadn't met Joe, here."

"What did you study?"

"French."

"No way. So did my sister. When were you there?"

"1981 to 1985."

"Then you must know Helen Linton-House."

"'Helen vox maxima'? There was this ridiculous old lecturer who called her 'Helen vox maxima' and me 'Helen vox minima'. I don't think he liked her. What's she doing now?"

"Married and working at a drop-in centre for homeless and unemployed people."

"Tell her 'Helen vox minima' says, 'Hello'. She'll know who I am."

"I will."

"That's amazing. What a coincidence. To be honest, I didn't know her that well. I certainly didn't know she had a brother."

"Guilty as charged. Where did you do your year abroad?"

"Bordeaux. It was an amazing year."

"I was in Bordeaux for a weekend with my job in August 1983."

"That's just before I went there, in the September. What job were you doing?"

"Selling books. I also went to a book fair in Paris and while I was there, I met a man who had an anthology of short stories written by Nottingham University students. Helen had one included."

"Yes, I remember that competition. I didn't write a short story though. One thing I did know from talking to her, was that Helen enjoyed writing. Maybe one day she'll become a published author."

"Who knows. What do you do now?"

"I'm a translator for a chemicals company."

"I'm hoping to use my languages. I've been out of the country for twelve years, but now I'm looking for a job."

"Which languages do you speak?"

"Russian, French, Spanish, Catalan, Dutch and Pashto."

"Did you learn those at university or from travelling?"

"Well Russian and French I learnt at school. Then, I lived in Holland and Ottawa, where I dated a French Canadian and travelled to France. Pashto, I learnt from a tape and then I lived in Afghanistan. Spanish and Catalan, I learnt from living in the country."

"I'm sure you'll get a job really easily. Are you based in London?"

"Currently living in Kent, near Maidstone. I don't really fancy going back to London. I lived there for a couple of years."

"I went to Barcelona, the summer I graduated. I saw some amazing circus artists."

"Really. What did they do?"

"There was a diabolo thrower, someone who juggled flaming batons and a clown on stilts."

"I shared a flat with them."

"No way! Small world. Can you juggle?"

"No."

"Joe can juggle, can't you. love?"

"Sure can."

"What do you do for a living. Joe?"

"Test water samples."

"As in rivers?"

"As in any water samples that come into the lab. And I can tell you that you wouldn't want to know what's in your drinking water sometimes."

"I probably wouldn't. It's quite hard where I live, but when I was a kid, we visited my grandparents, who lived on an island in the Blackwater Estuary, in Essex, and the water there tasted vile."

"Needless to say, we use a filter," commented Helen.

The motorway sign indicated that junction 25 was one mile ahead.

"We've made good time. Shall we drop you at the hotel?"

"Thank you."

Joe pulled off the motorway onto the slip road and turned onto the A50, immediately indicating to turn into the hotel.

"Thank you so much. Helen will be blown away. Safe journey to Leeds."

"You're welcome. Bye."

"Bye," added Joe.

"Bye," said Owen.

The car drove off and Owen went into the hotel to find a payphone.

"Excuse me, but do you have a public phone?" asked Owen, walking over to the reception desk.

"Just round the corner, beyond the lift."

"Thank you."

"Owen found the phone and dialled Helen's number.

"Hello.

"Hi, Sis, it's me. Can you come and fetch me from the hotel at junction 25, please?"

"Sure. I'll be there in about half an hour."

"Great. See you."

"Bye."

Owen went back round to the reception.

"Is there a bar here, where I can have a drink while I wait for my lift?"

"Yes. Through those doors."

"Thanks."

He went through the doors, bought half a pint of cider, and sat at a table by the window. Two men, sitting at an adjacent table were nattering away in Russian. One of them was the lorry driver, but Owen was not sure if he had seen him, or recognised him. Unfortunately for Owen, when the driver stood up to go to the bar, he saw Owen.

"You don't like my lorry?"

"Sorry. Saw the number plate and did not know if you spoke English."

It was the best excuse he could come up with, thinking on his feet.

"I do speak English. I am happy for you that you have come here."

"Thank you."

The driver went to the bar and returned with two halves of lager. As he sipped his cider, Owen listened to the conversation, because he understood Russian. He could hear words like 'Derby' and 'ecstasy' and 'Dover'. Owen was fairly sure that those three words alone added up to the ecstasy coming in through the port of Dover and being supplied to Derby. He decided to go out to the front and wait for Helen, but not before he had gone to the car park and noted down the registration of the lorry. Waterstone's business card was still in his wallet, so he would phone him once he got to Helen's. Having swallowed the last of his cider, Owen walked out of the bar, acknowledging the two Russians, went to the toilet, carried on down the corridor, exiting the hotel via the rear door onto the carpark and jotted down the registration number on a beer mat he had filched from the table where he was sitting. Having accomplished his investigation work, he followed the path round the side of the hotel and stood at the entrance to the driveway. Five minutes later, Helen arrived. He felt sure that they would drive off without the number plate ever being visible to the Russians, and they would have no idea he was heading for Nottingham.

"Hi. You're never going to believe this, but 'Helen vox minima' says, 'Hello'. She and her partner gave me a lift from Toddington. She said you'll know who it is."

"I do. I often wonder what my course colleagues are doing now. Did she also mention no one liked the lecturer who called us 'vox minima' and 'vox maxima'?"

"She did."

"How many lifts did it take you to get here?"

"I was so lucky. The first guy picked me up on the A20 just up from the village. He took me all the way to Toddington Services. He also gave me a contact in West Malling about a job. The second lift, Helen and Joe, picked me up at the services and dropped me here."

"Brilliant. I expect you'll be wanting some lunch when we get in. I know I will."

"Don't mind admitting to being a bit hungry. Is Finn at home?"

"I expect so. I mean, he doesn't have any money, so unless he's gone round to the local pub in the hope of charming someone into buying him a pint, he'll be home. There's someone I want you to meet more, though. Fudge. He's six months old. The colour of vanilla fudge."

"You have a kitten?"

"Yes."

The journey along the A453 was traffic free and they soon arrived in Radford.

"Mummy worries that I live in Radford, because Hyson Green is just down the road and there were serious riots there."

"Do you feel safe?"

"Yes. Mind you, I wouldn't wander the streets alone late at night, but that's because I'm a woman."

"I got beaten up walking through the centre of Madrid late at night, but that's because I was selling drugs on someone else's turf."

"Oh dear," responded Helen, unlocking the door. "Welcome."

Finn came out of the kitchen.

"Hello. I'm Finn. Pleased to meet you. I'm just on my way out."

"No doubt, see you later, then."

"Bye."

He left. Helen did not ask where he was going, and he did not say. No sooner had he left than Fudge came running down the stairs.

"He's gorgeous."

"He is a bit. He also has very sharp claws. He likes to run up my legs and back, when I'm at the kitchen work surface or the sink. Right. Let's get some lunch. Scrambled eggs on toast?"

"Yes. But have you got any cheese to make cheese-egg?"

"Great idea!"

"Shall I sort the toast?"

"Thanks."

Between them they made their snack lunch and, predictably, Fudge scrambled up Helen's back and jumped onto the top of the cupboards.

"Can he get down?"

"Usually. I'm afraid there's no table. We eat on our laps."

"No problem."

"After lunch," reflected Helen, having eaten half her cheese-egg on toast, "we'll get on with your CV."

"Thanks."

Nothing more was said until they finished.

"Cup of tea or coffee?"

"Coffee, please."

Owen did the washing up whilst Helen made hot drinks, which they took into the living room. She switched on her computer, an Amstrad.

"So, our job is to turn the last twelve years of your life into something that will send you to the top of the pile. Let's begin with the work history. You went to London and worked in a pub, yes?"

"The Prince Albert. 1979 to 1982."

"Skills used or gained?"

"Customer service. Dealing with challenging situations. Practical skills in the hospitality sector."

Helen could not touch type, so the typing took a lot longer than the dictation.

"Then I worked in a café in Amsterdam. Similar skills, fewer challenging situations, learnt Dutch."

"How long were you there?"

"1982 to 1983. Then I went to Ottawa and worked for a publishing company. Ontario Publishing Inc. International negotiations in book sales and distribution. Travelled. Book fairs and responsibility to meet individual customers, representing the company. Listen, you can't put this in my CV, and you must promise never to tell anyone, at least not whilst I'm alive. When I went to Canada, I was working for MI6, trying to take down an international drugs network led by Russians."

"Oh, my goodness! Seriously? Did you have a gun?"

"Yes, but I wasn't licensed to kill. Only in self-defence. I wasn't a proper agent and I only had two weeks intensive training. That's why I went to Afghanistan, to find the source of the network which was funding the Soviet occupation."

"You've got to tell Mummy and Daddy. They would be so proud of you. Did you succeed?"

"Yes. And I ended up having to shoot dead the head of the network."

"Why didn't you stay working for MI6?"

"I wanted to settle down. I didn't want to be looking over my shoulder for the rest of my life. So far, I've been wrong on both counts. I get nervous every time I hear Russian. There were two Russians in the hotel, by the way. May I make a very quick international phone call, to tell the guy in Canada about Russian drugs in Derby, please?"

"Be my guest. So, what did you do in Afghanistan?"

"Well, I was a year in Ottawa, 1983 to 1984. The Russians caught up with me, so I got sent to Afghanistan. I worked in a book shop. I was there from April 1984 to June 1984. I did some travelling, holidays for two weeks and went to Madrid, where I worked in a pub from July 1984 to April-May 1985. That's when I moved to Barcelona and got caught transporting amphetamines. I was in prison from June 1985 to last week."

"OK, go and make that phone call, whilst I try and work out how to be creative with your prison sentence. What jobs did you do?"

"Library work, teaching English and kitchen work."

"Leave it with me."

Owen went and phoned Waterstone.

"Hello."

"Ian?"

"Well, yes, although I'm back to plain Owen, now."

"How's home-life?"

"Getting to know them again. Just spending the weekend with my sister. That's why I'm making a quick call. In the hotel at junction 25 of the M1, I heard two Russians, one was a lorry driver, talking about Dover, ecstasy, and Derby. Thought you might want to follow it up."

"Thank you. Take care, won't you?"

"I'll try. Bye."

"Bye."

Owen returned to Helen and the CV.

"All done. How are you getting on?"

"Well, unless someone asks you, I think we can just say you travelled to Spain, spent some time in Madrid and Barcelona, worked in kitchens and a library and taught English. I've added in a load of skills. And I've put all your languages in. Now we need to do education. We don't need to say you were expelled and neither do we need to mention university, so we don't have to say you dropped out. I need your 'O' Levels and 'A' Levels."

"I can't remember my 'O' Level grades, it's been so long. Not without my certificate. There were eleven of them, grades A-C including Maths and English Language. 'A' Levels were French, Russian, History and General Studies. I think I got B, B, B, A, in that order."

Ten minutes later, the draft CV was complete.

"Do you want to have a read, before I print off a copy?"

Owen read through each section.

"I'm impressed. Thank you."

"I'll proof-read it and print it off, then. Do you want to take your things to the spare room, whilst I check it?"

"Sure."

"Top of the stairs, turn right, bathroom straight ahead, bedroom on the right."

Owen went upstairs and Helen re-read the CV. When she was happy with the quality, she printed off three copies. Owen came back downstairs.

"I've printed off three copies. You can get more photocopied."

"Thanks, Sis. You're a lifesaver."

"You're welcome."

Finn turned up wreaking of beer, about half an hour after the CV was completed. He had obviously managed to get someone to buy him drinks.

"My wife is a good woman, you know," he announced in his slightly inebriated state, before disappearing upstairs to bed.

"He's like that often," whispered Helen. "He pretends to be all nice, but if you weren't here, he would probably say something derogatory. He hasn't yet hit me, but he likes to tell me I'm useless in bed and make me feel bad, at the same time, making out he could get another woman any time he wanted."

"I'm sorry."

"Do you want to go for a walk?"

"Good plan."

They walked along Gregory Boulevard to the Forest Recreation Ground.

"There are a lot of Asian people here, aren't there? It makes me feel like I'm back in Afghanistan."

"I believe that outside of London, this area has the highest ethnic diversity in the country. I love it here."

"I could get used to it here. Maidstone is quite monochrome, I think."

Owen thought back to his journey from Bordeaux to Paris, playing imagination games with the little girl who offered him a sweet. It seemed a lifetime ago. They wandered back to the house.

"I'll cook us a bolognaise."

"Great."

"Finn can heat his up later if he's not up."

On the Sunday morning, to Owen's surprise, Helen asked him if he was OK with going to church.

"I didn't know you went to church."

"Since 1985, when I became a Christian. I belong to a Baptist church. It's across the city, where I used to live. I'm so looking forward to introducing you to a couple who have looked out for me since I joined the church. Rita and Alex. They have been praying for you since I first told them I had a brother, but I didn't know where he was."

"Always happy to be someone's answer to prayer. I met some amazing Christians in Amsterdam. One couple even let me live on their houseboat for a year, whilst they went back to the States. They supported me when I went cold turkey before they left for home. It wasn't even a condition of staying in the houseboat. I was blown away that they trusted me. Still am, although sadly, when I went back to visit, just before I moved to Spain, they weren't there.

Ike had died of a heart attack and Thelma had returned home to family. I caught up with Floyd and Sally though."

"You met the McClungs? I love *The Father Heart of God*. Floyd's book."

"Do you have a copy?"

"Yes."

"Can I borrow it?"

"Of course."

"Thanks."

When they walked into the church, Rita came and greeted them.

"This is Owen. He came home!"

"I am delighted to meet you. Alex is around somewhere. Will you sit with us?"

"Of course."

"See my cardigan, over the back of the pew?"

"Owen and Helen went and sat down.

"You know, I do believe in God. It's not like with Mummy paying lip service. I'm just not ready to give up the things I would need to give up."

"I'm not sure you have to give up anything."

The pastor stood up to welcome everyone, and Helen and Owen stopped chatting.

"Will you come for lunch?" asked Rita, at the end of the service.

"That would be nice. Can I call Finn, when we get to your house, and tell him he needs to fend for himself?"

"No problem."

Rita went with Helen and Owen, leaving Alex to do whatever he needed to do and then return in their car.

"You're OK with dogs, Owen?"

"Yes, I used to have an Afghan Hound, when I lived in Battersea, but sadly he got hit by a car and died."

"That's so sad," responded Helen.

"What dog do you have?"

"Dogs. Two Labradors. Clover and Archie."

Helen was not a huge fan because they were prone to drooling.

"I'll go in and let them into the back garden, before you come in."

"It's no bother. Honestly."

"Well, as long as you're sure?"

Rita opened the front door, and as they walked in, a boisterous Labrador almost knocked Owen off his feet. She managed to restrain Clover by her collar, but Archie darted back and forth along the hallway, beside himself with excitement, so Rita went into the kitchen and opened the back door anyway. Both dogs ran out into the garden, barking. They were barking because Alex had just pulled up outside the back gate. Helen made her phone call to Finn.

"Can we do anything to help?" asked Owen.

"Yes. Thank you. Can you lay the table, for me, please?"

Helen and Owen took the cutlery and glasses into the dining room. Rita filled a jug with water and made some gravy.

"We're about ready. Do you need to use the bathroom?"

Owen went and washed his hands, followed by Helen who used the facilities. When she came out, there was a joint of beef and vegetables on the dining table. Alex was carving.

"So, Owen. Where have you been?"

"Gosh. Long story. I left home the day before my eighteenth and went to Caterham. From there I moved into a squat, an unused council flat, in Battersea. I started working in The Prince Albert pub and began my course at SSEES. I met a girl, Russian dad, French-Canadian mum. She introduced me to the 'banya' near Euston, and that's where she got me hooked on heroin. I found a stash of cannabis, so I dealt to support my habit. Then, I got made an offer I couldn't refuse, by the Russian drug boss who owned the 'banya'' and started going to Amsterdam every three months to smuggle drugs in a Delft tea service. I met Floyd and Sally McClung on their houseboat. I got a dog and life ticked over until Kochai died and I realised that I didn't want to smuggle drugs, so I moved to Amsterdam. I worked in a café and thanks to Floyd and Sally, and some friends of theirs, Ike and Thelma, I got off heroin and lived on their houseboat for a year. Just when everything was becoming an enjoyable routine, I was made another offer I couldn't refuse, by the British Secret Service, who it turns out, had been watching my every move, which is why I was never stopped in customs, because they had bigger fish to fry. They trained me for two weeks and sent me to Ottawa, where I worked for a publishing company, whilst getting to know a woman call Caroline, who was involved with drugs. I was reacquainted with the girl from the 'banya' who we later discovered was the daughter of the head of the network, which ran from Afghanistan to Canada, with distribution across Europe. When my identity was blown, the Secret Service moved me to Afghanistan to seek out the source of the drugs, which I did. That all came to a head with the girl and her father catching up with me in Lashkhar Gah and them ending up dead. I shot the head of the drug network. I had no choice. Well, I did. His death or mine. The Secret

Service made me a job offer, but I wanted to settle down. I went to Madrid and stumbled on a supply of amphetamines, so I started dealing again. A different lot of Russians caught up with me and I moved to Barcelona, which was painful as I finally met a great girl while I was working in an Irish pub. I got apprehended transporting speed into France and served six years. The British Consulate got in touch with our parents and my dad sent the fare home. And here we are."

"Well, you have been more than honest," reflected Alex.

"Now it's no more drugs and hopefully a job with a future. I speak French, Russian, Dutch, Spanish, Catalan and Pashto. I'll live with my parents until I get sorted. It's really great getting to know Helen, again."

"What was it like in prison?" asked Alex after a short pause in the conversation, mostly whilst Owen got a chance to eat.

"To be honest I was terrified, but I met some Catalan Independence political prisoners who looked out for me. My first job was in the library and I was teaching English, until some drugs got smuggled into prison and some Russians killed the librarian. After that, I got a job in the hospital and slept in solitary confinement, for my own protection."

"What were the McClungs like?" asked Rita.

"I was really impressed by them and their friends Ike and Thelma. They were generous, trusting, saw the best in me, and they were just open and vulnerable to young people, especially on the alternative scene, who needed help. They hardly mentioned God. They just lived his love. They were a good advert for Christianity."

Usually, when Helen went round to Rita and Alex's, the time ended with her listening to Alex teaching something of the faith, but not on this occasion. They did the washing up, had coffee and cake, and Helen and Owen went home. Finn made a few sarcastic remarks and went out.

"It'll be worse when you've gone. How long can you stay?"

"I'm sorry, but I need to get back tomorrow. I'll leave early if you can give me a lift to junction 25, again. That'll give me a chance to catch traffic heading for Dover."

"No problem."

"I can visit in a few weeks, or you could come down to Kent. I promise to visit when I can. I need to get a job, first and foremost."

"I know. Hopefully, the contact from your first lift will be fruitful."

On the Tuesday morning, Owen rang the number Jim Warner had given him.

"Hello. Is it possible to speak to Brian Millington?"

"Speaking."

"Hi. Jim Warner gave me a lift on Friday, and he said you might have an opening for me. I speak Dutch, French, Russian, Spanish, Catalan and Pashto, and I've worked in publishing and book sales as well as in pubs and cafes."

"Well, it's true we will be looking to expand into Europe. How about you come for an interview. We'll call it an informal chat. Nothing promised, but we can see what might be possible."

"Thank you. When?"

"Can you make this afternoon at three. Do you know where West Malling is?"

"Yes. I grew up round here. I am currently living in Leeds, near the castle. I have a moped."

"I'll see you at three, then. What's your name?"

"Owen Linton-House. I look forward to meeting you. Thanks."

"Bye."

"Bye."

"Hey, Mummy. Can I borrow your moped again, this afternoon? I've got a chance at a job. The man who gave me a lift on Friday has a contact who runs a company in West Malling and he's invited me for an informal chat to see if there's any potential for me."

"Well, that's a start. Of course, you can."

"Thanks. Where's the iron? I need to iron my interview shirt. It's informal, but I'll go with tie and blazer."

"Cupboard under the stairs, along with the ironing board."

"And shoe polish?"

"Also, under the stairs. Brown tin on the shelf to the left."

Owen ironed his shirt and cream trousers and polished his shoes. He went out to the shed and checked the petrol. The tank was almost empty.

"Where's the nearest garage? I'll go and fill up, before I get into my glad rags."

"Probably the Five Wents, or Sutton Valence or Parkwood. I tend to fill up on the way to or from Maidstone."

"I'll head over there now."

"Do you have money? You can borrow it and pay us back when you get a job."

"That would be helpful. Thanks"

"Here's five pounds. The tank is only small."

"See you in a bit."

"Don't forget the two-stroke oil in the top-box."

"Ratio? I know, I've forgotten already."

"On the back of the container. Use the measure to one gallon of petrol."

He was back inside the hour, smelling of petrol.

"I trod in a spillage. I'm glad I went now."

"Take your shoes off outside, please!"

Owen sat on the back doorstep and removed his shoes. He went into the kitchen for detergent, a bucket, and an old cloth, which he found in the cupboard under the sink.

"I haven't had a chance to ask you, without Daddy around. He's pottering round the recreation ground. How were things with Helen and Finn?"

"Not great. She puts on a brave face, and he makes snide remarks. Then, he bigs her up, but when I'm not there, I know he'll be putting her down."

"Daddy would probably kill him, if he knew the whole of it."

"Hopefully, it won't last, and she'll find someone worthy of her."

"And what about you? Have you had any serious relationships?"

"Almost. I had two relationships based on deception and drugs. When I was in Spain, I met someone I really liked, but after six months, I had to move to Barcelona, and she wouldn't leave her band. The rest were short flings. I really do want to settle down, at some point in the not-too-distant future and start a family."

"These things happen when you least expect them."

"Thanks, Mummy."

At two o'clock, Owen set off for West Malling. He did not know where the company was situated, being unfamiliar with the local geography. He had Gail and Ben's Maidstone and district map. He could always ask someone. In the event, it was just south of West Malling, along the A228, but Owen arrived in good time, parked up, removed his CV from the top-box, replacing it with his helmet, and went into reception, ten minutes early.

"Hi. My name is Owen Linton-House. I'm ten minutes early, but I have a three o'clock appointment with Brian Millington."

"I'll let him know you're here."

Owen felt nervous, even though nothing was promised. The receptionist phoned through to Millington's office.

"Mr Millington. I have an Owen Linton-House in reception."

She replaced the handset.

"He'll be out in five minutes. Can I get you a coffee?"

"No, thanks. I'm good."

Owen still had no idea what products or services the company offered. He looked around at the walls. There were blown up photos. One was of West Malling airfield. He knew it well, from his parascending days at Tonbridge School. He thought a second might be Biggin Hill. The other two photos he did not recognise. Owen was wondering why there were photos of airfields on the wall, when a man appeared through the door.

"Owen. Great to meet you," came the greeting, with outstretched hand.

Owen shook Millington's hand.

"Good to meet you, too."

"Come this way."

Millington led Owen through to his office. Owen saw posters of flying suits on the walls.

"I don't think it's been mentioned yet, what the company sells," explained Millington. "Flying suits for the private market. Actually, we offer a range of flying suits, parachuting suits, and general aviation overalls. Bit of a niche market, I know, but we have eyes on Europe."

"I used to go parascending at West Malling airfield, when I was at school."

"And probably parascending suits, too," laughed Millington. "So, you'll be able to enthuse about the product. Which school?"

"Tonbridge."

"You speak a lot of languages."

"Yes. I learned French and Russian at school. Dutch I learnt living in Amsterdam. That's where I worked in a café. Then, I moved to Ottawa and worked for Ontario Publishing selling books, internationally. I had a French-Canadian girlfriend from across the river and I travelled to France for book fairs. I learnt Pashto when I went to Afghanistan. Then, I lived in Madrid for six months and Barcelona for six years. Here's my CV."

"Why did you go to Afghanistan?"

"This is going to sound daft, but I once had an Afghan Hound, and I was curious."

"Why have you come back home now?"

"I kind of left home at eighteen, wanting to find my way in the world. I always said I'd return when I was thirty and settle down."

Millington was perusing the CV.

"You have had various jobs where you have dealt with customers. Do you know what? I think we can give you a trial six months. During that time, you can learn the ropes and start prepping for selling in France, Spain and the Netherlands. If it works out, you can stay with us, and we'll move into the European market. We'll pay you minimum wage for six months and then put you up to something decent. Monday to Friday, nine to five-thirty. Half an hour for lunch. How does that sound?"

"Better than I could have hoped. When do you want me to start?"

"Monday? Nine o'clock. Do you have a National Insurance number?"

"I don't think so. Because I've been out of the country for so long. But I signed on last week, so I guess they'll have given me one. I'll find out."

"Great. See you on Monday. Smart casual, by the way. No jeans or trainers."

"Thank you so much."

Millington shook Owen's hand, warmly.

"See you Monday."

"Thanks. Yes. Bye," responded Owen, as he left.

He could not wait to get home and break the news.

By Christmas, Owen's new job had been going even better than he could have hoped. It was a cracking team. There were four of them in the office and six in production. One of the guys, Melvyn, lived in Maidstone, and Owen had got into the habit of joining Melvyn and his friends in The Ship on a Friday evening. Gail, of course, worried about Owen coming home on the moped, a few pints worse for wear. He started to get to know a young woman called Teresa, a trainee social worker, who lived in a flat, or rather a maisonette, up near Mote Park. She invited Owen round for a meal, the night before Christmas Eve.

"I might not be home tonight," Owen announced to his mother, somewhat apologetically. "I'll definitely be here tomorrow evening, and I'm really looking forward to spending Christmas with you. It's just that I've been getting to know someone these last few months. Her name's Teresa and she's invited me round for a meal, and well, you know how it is."

"I'm very happy for you. And even happier if you get to stay over, after you've had a lot to drink. I know. I worry, but it's in the job description. I'm your mother."

"Thanks Mummy."

Owen left at about quarter to eight, arriving just after eight, politely late. The maisonette smelt of wine and garlic.

"Hi. How are you? That smells good."

"Hello. We're eating beef bourguignon. I'll pour the remaining half bottle for us to drink."

"Here's some more, for when that's finished," responded Owen, handing Teresa a bottle. She poured two glasses of red, and they sat on the sofa.

"Have you been to France?" she asked.

"As a matter of fact, I have. I also lived in Ottawa for a while and spent time over the river in Gatineau. What about you?"

"I spent many a summer holiday in our holiday home in the Charente."

"How's your French?" asked Owen, in French.

"Not bad!" came the French reply. "So, tell me again. Which languages do you speak?"

"French, Dutch, Spanish, Catalan, Russian and Pashto. I can say 'You're lovely' in each of them."

Teresa blushed a little.

"Go on then."

Owen performed as asked.

"I'm impressed."

"Does that mean I get a reward?"

"What do you mean?"

"A kiss, maybe. For starters."

"You're hopeful."

"I am," laughed Owen, moving closer, so his mouth was a couple of inches from Teresa's.

They remained staring into each other's eyes for a while, until Owen moved forwards and started to kiss her. She responded, but then pulled back.

"We have to eat. There's plenty of time for intimacy later. I've put a lot of effort into this meal."

"And I will enjoy every morsel of it."

The table was already laid, and Teresa carried the casserole dish from the oven into the living room. Steam rose to the ceiling when she removed the lid.

"I thought we'd eat it with fresh bread. Would you cut some for us, please?"

"Certainly."

The meal tasted as good as it smelled. Owen mopped up every last drop of sauce with his bread.

"That was amazing!"

"Wait until you've had dessert. Mississippi Mud Pie."

"Mmmmm."

Teresa carried the casserole dish into the kitchen, followed by Owen with the plates. She handed him two dishes and went to the fridge to take out the mud pie. She served and they tucked in. Suddenly, in a very Proustian way, Owen was transported back to Osea Island, and the Albright family. He wondered if Jake had succeeded in becoming a doctor.

"The last time I ate this, I was ten years old. It was at my grandparents' house with a West Indian family. That was a bizarre summer. My sister fell in love, not that she really knew I knew. I was a bit of a gooseberry to her and Jake, a cricket-loving boy with a body I would have given my right arm for, even on an eleven-year-old. That was the year they discovered multiple bodies on the island. It turned out there was a serial killer on the loose."

"How horrid! Can we change the subject? Please!"

"Sorry. What's your earliest memory?"

"That would be when I was four and I was given a teddy bear for Christmas that was as tall as me. What about you?"

"My father not being around much. Wait! The meter man coming to count the coins."

"We had a meter too."

"This mud pie is delicious."

"Thanks. Coffee? Or something stronger?"

"Do you have any cognac?"

"Yes. Would you like some. You can have coffee as well, if you want?"

"That would be great, thanks."

They sat chatting on the settee, until Owen started to feel the effects of three glasses of wine and a glass of cognac.

"So, what about picking up where we left off before that excellent meal?"

"I need the bathroom. I am assuming you'll be sleeping over."

"Does that mean in the same bed?" he laughed, still not one hundred percent certain of the logistics.

"Come and find me, when you've used the bathroom, after me."

Owen was now intrigued. He waited his turn and went into the bathroom to freshen up, brush his teeth and pee. Double-checking he had some protection in his pocket, he made his way into the bedroom. Teresa was under the quilt. Owen stripped down to his underpants and slid in beside her, only then realising she was naked. He slipped his underwear off. Thoughts of Katya and Caroline, Mariana, and Colleen, and finally Sofia, flooded his mind. For a split second, he was uncertain where to start, which was stupid. He slid down under the quilt and starting to nibble at her nipples. He could hear Teresa's moans, muffled through the quilt.

It was at this point Owen could not believe his stupidity. The condom was in the pocket of his jeans which were on the floor at the side of the bed. He had to stop what he was doing, lean out from under the side of the quilt, and fumble in his pocket.

"Sorry. Just grabbing some protection."

He was back under the quilt, tearing off the wrapper and applying the condom before his absence had any real impact. With a few more nibbles of her nipples and kisses up her chest and neck, he surfaced from the quilt, resumed kissing her mouth, and entered her. Teresa moved her body in time with his. He could feel her starting to tense, ready for release, and he was regretting the cognac, which seemed to be having a detrimental effect on his ability to finish. She climaxed, but it was another twenty or so thrusts before he reached his own, falling onto her, panting. He had the presence of mind to withdraw, holding the condom, before he went limp, and lay beside her, his arm over her. They were both asleep in minutes.

The following morning, Owen woke at just gone seven. Teresa was still sleeping peacefully, so he slid out of bed and went to the bathroom. Not wanting to disturb her, he grabbed his clothes, got dressed in the living room and put the kettle on. There were three storage jars on the counter, one tea, one coffee and presumably, one sugar. He made himself a cup of strong black coffee and put two spoons of sugar in. As soon as it was cool enough to drink, he took a large swig and snorted much of it back out through his nose. Who keeps salt in the third storage jar next to coffee and tea? Perhaps, someone who does not take sugar in their drinks. A sleepy Teresa appeared at the kitchen door.

"What on earth have you done?" she inquired, laughing at the state of Owen's shirt.

"Why do you keep salt next to the tea and coffee?"

She laughed even more.

"Let me make you another coffee, whilst you get cleaned up. The sugar is in the cupboard. I hardly use it. Only for guests."

Owen went into the bathroom, soaked his shirt to try and remove the stain, rubbed in copious amounts of soap, and gave up. It was likely to need detergent and the washing machine.

"Listen, I really have to disappear. This is my first Christmas with my family in thirteen years. I'll ring you. Thank you for a great meal and a pleasurable night."

She approached him and they kissed.

"See you next weekend, hopefully," she suggested.

"I might be going to Nottingham to see my sister, while the office is shut. Do you have time off? We can make a plan, when I phone."

"Works for me. Have a good Christmas."

"Are you spending Christmas with family?"

"I'll go over to my parents on Christmas morning. They only live in Aylesford."

"Well, I hope it's a good Christmas."

"Bye."

"Bye. See you soon."

Owen rode home feeling happy.

Christmas Eve was spent wrapping presents and putting up the decorations. Once upon a time, Christmas and all the trimmings had lasted two weeks either side of the event, at their grandparents, with small, countdown presents for Owen and Helen under the tree. Now the tree seemed to go up later and later every year. It generally remained up until Twelfth Night, but that was more out of apathy to take it down, than any meaningful reason. Owen noticed there were two trees. One was a four-foot artificial one that stood in the space normally occupied by a large square pouffe, and a small, one-foot tall artificial one, in a little integral pot, which had been the family tree all through Owen and Helen's childhood. That one stood on the bookcase out of nostalgia. It felt good to be preparing for Christmas with his family. Only Helen was missing, but now she was married, there were the in-laws to consider, in Loughborough. In any case, Ben had banned Finn from the house, which made it difficult for Helen to visit at Christmas and Easter.

Come the evening, they poured glasses of Tarragona, the only alcoholic drink Ben drank these days, and played Scrabble. Gail won the first game and Owen the second. The house dictionary was a Chambers Twentieth Century volume, but the house rules seemed to accept various two letter words Owen had never heard of, along with some words which he would have considered proper nouns or Latin phrases. Gail liked to keep a really closed board, blocking in anything that stretched more than three letters in any direction. As for triple word score squares, you opened one of those up at your peril. Owen won by virtue of two bonus words. Ben played but he was not a huge fan. He did, however, enjoy compiling crosswords.

"I'm pretty tired. I think I'll call it a night. See you in the morning."

"Goodnight, Son," responded Ben.

"Goodnight," added Gail.

"Goodnight."

Owen went up to bed and was asleep in a matter of minutes. Ben went upstairs not long afterwards leaving Gail to potter in the kitchen.

On Christmas morning, Owen wandered down to the kitchen at about nine o'clock, after a lie-in which surprised even him. There was tinned grapefruit for breakfast, another family tradition dating back to time spent with their grandparents. During the morning, a considerable amount of cheese footballs and twiglets would be eaten, so a light breakfast was in order. At ten o'clock, sherry was poured and the three of them gathered in the living room to share gifts. It did not last long as there were three each for Gail and Ben, from Owen, Two each from Ben and Gail to each other, and four from Gail and Ben to Owen.

His main present was a full-face motorcycle helmet. This meant he no longer had to borrow Gail's. He was also about to purchase a small motorcycle, in the New Year. His other presents were a pair of motorcycle gauntlets, some waterproof over-trousers, and a box of chocolate-covered crystalised ginger, which he had liked since he was eight years old.

"We should phone Helen," he announced, having folded the discarded wrapping paper into a pile for re-use.

Owen had bought his mother a new copy of Verdi's *Requiem*, because she had played the 'Dies irae' section so often, it had started to crackle. He also gave her a 'Times' crossword book and a bottle of moisturiser. Ben was harder to buy for, but he was delighted with the scarf and gloves and new screwdrivers Owen gave him.

Owen dialled the number. Finn answered.

"Happy Christmas, Finn. Is Helen there?"

"Of course."

"Hello."

"Happy Christmas, Sis. It's me. Can I come and see you the day after Boxing Day?"

"Absolutely. Are Mummy and Daddy there?"

"Yes. I'll pass the receiver over. See you in a couple of days."

Ben took the phone.

"Happy Christmas. Owen will bring you your presents."

Ben passed the receiver to Gail.

"Happy Christmas, Darling. Will we see you in the New Year?"

Owen could not hear any of Helen's responses, so he was a little concerned when Gail sat down.

"Be careful. Bye."

She replaced the receiver.

"Helen's expecting!"

"When is it due?" asked Owen.

Ben said nothing.

"June. She left it three months to tell people."

"Wow!" exclaimed Owen. "Never imagined being an uncle."

"I'm going to start cooking dinner."

"Can I do anything?"

"Not until it's time to lay the table."

It was about four o'clock when they sat down to eat their Christmas dinner. The contents of the meal had not changed since the last time Owen had sat down for a Christmas dinner with his family, back in 1978: always two kinds of stuffing, sage and onion and something with lemon or apricot; never a starter; roast and mashed potatoes, roast parsnips, carrots, sprouts, and peas; bread sauce, made fresh, which always involved the search for an elusive fifth clove; pigs in blankets and gravy; and Cranberry sauce from a jar. There was always home-made brandy sauce with the pudding, which contained foil-wrapped one-pence pieces.

They pulled their crackers and read the ridiculous jokes. Although he hated the itchy paper crowns, Owen wore his. Unusually, his trinket was half useful, a miniature set of playing cards. Ben carved the turkey and they each helped themselves to vegetables. Owen had seconds of the roast potatoes and roast parsnips. A roast dinner was not something he had eaten that often in the last twelve years. He wondered how many days the turkey would last. Roast turkey, cold turkey, turkey curry, minced turkey burgers, turkey broth. He hated the smell of the carcass being boiled down.

After Owen had finished the washing up, insisting that Gail put her feet up, they watched the Batman film, on BBC, followed immediately, on ITV, by *Crocodile Dundee*. Owen wondered how Teresa had spent the day, at her parents' house. Was she watching the same films? Had she thought about him, at all? Should he have phoned her to wish her 'Happy Christmas' or were they not yet an item? They had slept together, and they were going to meet up again, but they had not labelled themselves yet. At this point, Owen realised he could not have phoned her, because he only had her home phone number, not that of her parents. He would phone her tomorrow, as agreed, to make plans. Right now, he could hardly keep his eyes open after three glasses of vodka and orange.

"Goodnight. Thank you for a lovely Christmas."

"Goodnight. See you in the morning. If you like, we can go for a walk around the castle grounds."

"That would be lovely."

"Goodnight, Son."

Just after ten o'clock on Boxing Day, Owen and his mother set off walking, down through the village and across to the castle along one of the lanes. As they neared the moat, a couple of peacocks were preening themselves.

"Such an amazing blue, isn't it?" remarked Gail.

"Yes. The reality, the sheen, is so much better than a paint chart. I always think of Cluedo and Mrs Peacock."

They continued walking, back round through Broomfield, along Burberry Lane and down into the village again.

"I can't remember the last time I walked that far," laughed Owen. "I have become very unfit, since my Canada days. In Amsterdam and in Ottawa, I cycled everywhere and went to a gym. Exercise was somewhat restricted in prison. Perhaps I should start going to a gym, again. I think there's one near the office."

"I do a similar walk, around the lanes, most days. It's a lot cheaper than a gym!"

"Fair point."

When they got back to the house, Owen rang Teresa.

"Hi. Did you have a good day, yesterday? Happy Belated Christmas!"

"It was great. Happy Belated Christmas to you, too. How was your Christmas?"

"Just lovely to spend it with the family. What's the plan, then? Fancy doing something on New Year's Eve?"

"Would you like to come here, again?"

"How about I bring some food and cook?"

"OK. See you about seven?"

"That should be plenty of time. Yes. See you then. I'm off to Nottingham tomorrow. Hey. Just heard my sister is expecting, in June."

"Nice. Uncle Owen!"

"Bye."

"Bye."

Owen sorted out his clothes.

"Can I do a wash load? Will it be dry by tomorrow morning?

"If you hang it outside, it can go in the airing cupboard overnight."

"Great."

Owen started the wash cycle and went upstairs to have a bath and a shave. By the time he came downstairs the cycle was complete and he hung out his washing. It was overcast, but there was a bit of a breeze, enough to aid the drying process.

"I'm going to go round to Teresa's on New Year's Eve," he announced to Gail, who was making turkey curry, in the kitchen.

"That's nice. Tonight, we have the cold gammon joint and cold turkey, with salad. And trifle."

"What can I have for lunch?"

"Turkey curry. It'll be ready in about twenty minutes. I'm just about to put the rice on."

"Thanks," responded Owen, realising that turkey curry was his second least favourite method of using up the turkey.

He went up to his room and packed Helen and Finn's presents. He had had no idea what to buy for Finn. In the end, he had purchased a scarf, like the one he had given his father. Helen had a framed print of Turner's *Rain, Steam and Speed*, about half the size of the original. He did not remember seeing any photos or paintings on the walls of her house and hoped she would want to display it. He already knew it was her favourite painting. It was wrapped in the recycled paper from the box his motorcycle helmet was wrapped in.

"Owen!" called Gail, from downstairs.

Ben appeared through the backdoor, after another one of his short strolls round the recreation ground, and Owen ran down the stairs. The turkey curry was much more palatable than Owen had feared. If you did not think you were eating chicken curry, you could convince yourself it was some non-descript meat. In the event, he was more concerned about splashing his clothes with the strongly turmeric-tinged curry sauce.

"How long will you be at Helen's?" asked Gail.

"Hopefully tomorrow until 30th December, if I get a lift coming back. I'm hoping there'll be traffic heading south. Some people will have returned to work. I'm sure some lorries will be out and about. If it gets late, I'll have to catch a coach and a train. I hope it won't come to that, though."

Owen wondered why he still hitchhiked when he had a paid job. Force of habit, partly. Train fares were expensive just for a couple of days, and the sheer complexity of living in a village and trying to get to a bus or train, meant it was almost easier to walk two miles down the road and stick his thumb out.

That evening, as they watched the news, Owen could hardly believe what he was seeing. Some footage from the day before showed the Soviet flag being lowered on the Kremlin and replaced with the Russian flag. The USSR was officially no more.

"Never thought that would happen in my lifetime. In any lifetime," commented Gail.

"Wind of change," responded Owen, thinking of his new favourite track from the Scorpions, released in 1990.

Owen arrived in Nottingham, by three o'clock in the afternoon. The journey had involved three lifts, with one man only being able to take him as far as Dartford. One of the toll booth operators had insisted Owen was breaking the law, waiting near the toll booths. Not wanting to argue, Owen had decided to move well away, standing on the non-tunnel side, just before cars decelerated to stop and pay. He had a cardboard sign with 'M1 NORTH PLEASE' written on it, which he held against Helen's wrapped, bin-liner covered, framed print of *Rain, Steam and Speed*. It took around three quarters of an hour for a driver to respond and pull in.

"Thank you so much. This wasn't a great place to be dropped off."

"No worries. Where are you heading?"

"Nottingham."

"I'm actually going up the A1 to Newark. Is that any use? You can get a lift cross-country to Nottingham. It's only about twenty-two, twenty-five something miles."

"My sister would have picked me up from junction 25. I'm pretty certain she'd pick me up from Newark if I can't get a lift."

"Hop in."

"Thanks. I think I need to put my rucksack and this parcel in the back," he remarked, pulling forward the front seat to put his things in the back.

He got in. The journey took them round the M25, up the M11 to the A14 and across to join the A1. Some of the place names near Huntingdon struck a chord in Owen's distant memory as places he associated with his grandfather's early years. The whole journey was spent listening to Elvis Presley. Owen did not appreciate the music, but he was grateful for the lift, and for not having to make conversation. As they passed Duxford aerodrome, Owen felt sure he had been to an air show there, once when they had stayed with their grandparents on Osea Island. Further north, once they hit the A1, they passed by various airfields. He had been fascinated with aeroplanes as a boy, making many Airfix kits, and at Tonbridge School, had joined the Combined Cadet Force. Owen's ambition was to become a pilot, but at the age of sixteen, he was told this could never happen, due to his hay fever. Whilst not one to blame his circumstances for some of the poor decisions he had made, once in a while, Owen still pondered how different his life might have been if he had become a pilot in the Royal Air Force.

"It's probably best if I drop you here, at the junction. That road takes you to Nottingham. Or I can take you into the town centre. I'm just thinking about where most cars will pass you."

"Can you take me into the town centre please. I can phone my sister from there, and I'm guessing there is a direct road from Newark to Nottingham."

"Absolutely. No problem."

He dropped Owen by the castle and went on his way. Owen stood looking round him for a few seconds and thought it best to ask a passer-by for directions.

"Excuse me. Is this the main road to Nottingham?" he asked an elderly lady.

"It's that way," she said, pointing, and wandered off.

On the back of Owen's sign, he had written, 'NOTTINGHAM PLEASE', so he placed it against Helen's parcel and held it out to one side as he started walking in the direction the elderly lady had just pointed. He continued walking, without any responses, until he reached a roundabout. He realised this was where the ring road that the driver had referred to, met the main road to Nottingham, so he positioned himself just along from the exit, on the main road, and waited for an approaching vehicle, to hold up his sign. The first six cars ignored him. The seventh pulled in just beyond him.

"I can take you to West Bridgford, mate."

"Brilliant," responded Owen, opening the rear door, putting his things on the back seat, closing the door, opening the front door and climbing in, not entirely sure where West Bridgford was, in relation to Radford.

"Used to do a lot of hitchhiking myself. Always try to stop."

"Much appreciated. Visiting my sister in Nottingham. I've come from a village near Maidstone, in Kent."

"There's buses into the city centre and buses out again."

"I can walk it, if it's less than three miles."

"Your choice, mate."

There was very little traffic about, even heading into the city for Christmas sales shopping, and they arrived at the Trent Bridge Cricket Ground forty minutes later.

"Head over the bridge, through the Meadows and into the city centre."

"Thanks for the lift. Have a great 1992."

"You too, mate."

Owen set off walking, over the river and along London Road, his rucksack on his back, the parcel under one arm. He did not cut through the Meadows because he did not know where he was going. When he reached the Canal Street roundabout, he turned left and walked along to the Broadmarsh Centre. He was determined not to phone Helen, so he kept walking round Maid Marion Way, up Derby Road to Canning Circus and down the Alfreton Road. The road seemed to go on forever, but at least it was downhill. Reaching the junction with Gregory Boulevard he turned left into Radford Boulevard and almost immediately right into Wordsworth Road, just as Finn was heading round the corner in the opposite direction.

"Hi Finn."

Finn looked at Owen blankly for a split second.

"Oh. It's you, Owen. Hello. See you later. Helen's in."

"Cheers."

One minute later, Owen was knocking on the door. Helen opened.

"What! How did you get here?"

Owen hugged her with one arm, handed her the parcel and walked through the door.

"I got a lift up the A1 to Newark followed by another lift to West Bridgford. I thought I might as well walk from there. I admit, it was a little further than I thought."

"I'd have come and fetched you from Newark!"

"I know, you would have. Thank you. That's for you. Happy Christmas."

Helen removed the present from the bin liner and tore off the gift-wrap.

"Wow! Wow! Wow!"

"I take it that's a good response," laughed Owen.

"You know it's my favourite painting?"

"Always have. I saw it in the National Gallery when I lived in London. I didn't see any pictures on your walls."

"I didn't have any. I do, now. Thank you so much."

"And these are from Mummy and Daddy," he added, handing her an envelope and three parcels ranging from tiny to about one foot square.

She opened them, one by one. Opening the envelope, she discovered a card with some banknotes inside. The largest parcel contained a Haynes Mini manual. The middle-sized present was from Misty to Fudge and rattled. It was a packet of feline treats. A trait of the Linton-House family was pets always sent and received birthday and Christmas gifts. The smallest gift was a new leather watchstrap, Helen having mentioned the week before Christmas that hers was about to snap along the frayed line of the buckle. Gail was always so attentive.

"Are you hungry?"

"Famished!"

"You'll be pleased to hear we had a Bernard Matthews turkey roast for Christmas dinner, so no leftovers! We do have bubble and squeak for our evening meal. Would you like a cheese sandwich, or cheese on toast to tide you over?"

"Cheese on toast would be great. Shall I stick the grill on?"

"Yes, please. I'm going to find a hammer and a nail. I don't think I have any picture-hooks as such. It'll have to hang on a nail."

Owen went to the kitchen and Helen banged a nail into the wall opposite the front door. She hung the picture and stood a couple of paces back, to see if it was level. Having put the hammer away, she joined Owen in the kitchen and made two mugs of coffee.

"I bumped into Finn as I turned into Wordsworth Road."

"Sadly, he still has some Christmas money, from his mother. He'll not be back until late, with a skinful."

"Sorry, Sis. I'm here, at least."

"Anyway, I almost forgot. Congratulations! How are you feeling?"

"OK. A little tired. I haven't really felt morning-sick."

"How does Finn react?"

"He's over the moon. It's all about 'his' baby. I can't imagine how many pints he's wangled out of people to celebrate. We only started telling people this week."

They took their coffee and Owen's toast into the living room.

"Looks good."

"And you see it when you walk in through the front door."

"I wonder whether Finn will notice it."

"I still have so many questions. What was Afghanistan like?"

"Like stepping back in time. The people I met were absolutely fantastic, welcoming, hospitable. At least the ones who weren't carrying Kalashnikovs. No, that's not completely true. The guy who stuck a rifle muzzle in my back proceeded to invite me to join him and his friends in playing cards. The facilities were old-fashioned. Cooking on a fire outside, or an outdoor oven. Toilets were primitive. The thing I had to concentrate on, all the time, was eat with my right hand, and as you know, I'm naturally left-handed."

"Was it scary?"

"The guy with the rifle, obviously. You were always worried about being stopped at road-blocks. Specifically, my role trying to identify a drugs supply chain put me in danger. I had an agent looking out for me. I feared for my life twice. Once, when I pretended to be off sick, in case I met the head of the network in the shop where I helped fix stuff. The second time, I was recognised, and they were leading me to the river to kill me. If it weren't for the agent watching my back, I'd be dead, for sure. That was when I had to kill the head of the network. Of course, then it was scary trying to get out of Afghanistan, again."

"How did you become a heroin addict?"

"I had just started at SSEES, when I met this gorgeous Russian girl. We started sleeping together. She introduced me to some friends at a spa. Part of the special treatment was a room for smoking drugs. I didn't realise she wasn't actually joining in, that it was all about getting me hooked. Then, I started injecting."

"Is that difficult?"

"Odd, but just a case of mind over matter and look forward to the rush."

"Doesn't it hurt?"

"No more than any other injection."

Owen finished his cheese on toast.

"And what about relationships? Was the Russian your only girlfriend?"

"When I went to Canada, my mission was to befriend, seduce, get close to a woman, who was not dissimilar to the Russian. It turns out they were cousins. When I stopped working for MI6, I went on holiday to Rome where I met a Spanish lady from Madrid who taught Spanish. I settled in Madrid, and by chance, turned up at one of her classes. We started dating. But alongside, I had started a job in a pub where I met a singer in a band who also cleaned at the pub. We also starting dating."

"You mean you were two-timing?"

"I didn't want to let either of them down. In the end, I did decide that I seriously wanted to be with the singer. I would have settled down with her. I think she felt the same way, but the experience of getting beaten up by Russians meant I had to leave. In Barcelona, I met a rather lovely Catalan Independence supporter. We were just starting to sleep together when I got arrested. The thing is, I've been wanting to tell you about Teresa for a while. I meet regularly with some mates in Maidstone at the weekend, in a pub. I've been getting to know a lady who is training to be a social worker. Anyway, things have moved to the next level. I'm really hopeful."

"I hope things work out for you."

"I'm so looking forward to being an uncle, but I really want to be a dad, too."

"All in good time."

"Hey. Does your cassette player work?"

"Yes."

"Can I play you a track?"

"Sure."

Owen reached into the pocket of his rucksack and pulled out a cassette. He stuck it in the music centre and turned up the volume as loud as he dared.

'Follow the Moskva down to Gorky Park listening to the wind of change…..' filled the air.

"What do you think?" he asked, as the whistling and music tailed off.

"Love it. I've been to Berlin, before the wall came down."

"Wow! What was that like?"

"Well, I spent the morning in the east. The cars were dull colours, the clothes were like factory clothes and the wall was pristine white. I spent the afternoon in the west, with its Mercedes Benz, neon lights, designer clothes and the wall, it was covered in graffiti."

"You've seen something I haven't."

"I have a small piece of the wall somewhere. A friend sent it to me."

Just then, Finn stumbled through the front door.

"What's that?"

"William Turner, *Rain, Steam and Speed*. It's my Christmas present from Owen."

"I like it. I'm going to bed."

"Goodnight," responded Owen, as Finn bumped his shoulder on the wall and the door frame, before his footprints clumped deliberately up the stairs. A few minutes later the toilet flushed, and the bedroom door slammed shut. Fudge appeared in the living room, having been expelled from the bedroom.

"Come here gorgeous," Owen beckoned him.

He mooched on over and rubbed his head on Owen's knee, making up his mind whether to jump up. Instead, he went and leaped onto Helen's lap, curled up and started purring. She held him whilst she kissed the top of his head.

"I'm sure he'll spend some time on your lap while you're here."

"Does Finn not like him?"

"It's not intentional. He's just loud and expansive with his movements, and Fudge tends to run for cover."

"One day I'll get a cat. I might even get another dog, but a lot depends on where I live and what sort of job I have."

"How did you end up with an Afghan Hound?"

"I worked with a woman at The Prince Albert who volunteered at Battersea Dogs' Home. She ambushed me. She took me there one day and I fell in love with Kochai. She looked after him for me when I had to go to Amsterdam every few months."

"How did that work?"

"They gave me a ticket. I went either Harwich to Hook of Holland or Dover to Ostend. I stayed with a Russian couple, who later had a baby. They would give me a box with a Delft tea service in it, and I would transport it back to London. I was then paid in drugs. When they couldn't pay me enough drugs, as in I would never use them all, they paid me money. I think the couple were scared. They ended up in Paris. I don't think they could escape the network. The man got killed during the international operation to take down the network."

"Do you sleep at night?"

"Sure. I just get nervous when I hear Russian spoken."

"Where have you been in France?"

"Paris and Bordeaux. I like Bordeaux. What's not to love about Paris. Where did you do you year abroad?"

"In a small town in the east of France called Luxeuil les Bains. I hated the year. After I graduated, I lived and worked in Lausanne, in Switzerland, for a year, well ten months. That was an amazing year. I learnt to ski. The mountains are awesome. I joined my first church. I made some wonderful friends."

"Why did you go to Lausanne?"

"I was all set to do a PhD in literature from French-speaking Switzerland. The main centre for research is in Lausanne."

"What happened with the PhD?"

"Life got in the way. I never completed it."

"Do you regret not finishing it?"

"Yes. One day I'll do a PhD, I'm sure. It just won't be irrelevant to everyday life, which that one was."

"I have no doubts, you will, one day. Speaking of writing, I was given a collection of short stories, when I was in France, by a book publisher. It turns out my sister is a published author. Loved the short story, by the way."

"No way! That was a piece of fun. I never expected to get published. I do want to be a writer. In fact, I have an idea for a novel which I started in 1985. I've just never got round to writing it."

"Don't give up on the idea."

"I read your book of poems when Mummy and Daddy cleared out your room. I still have it if you want it back."

"All that teenage angst. No thanks. Keep it."

"You weren't happy, were you? You felt put under pressure."

"True. Life can be strange. Look what has happened because of what I had to endure. You make of life what you can. Sometimes it's harder than at other times, to make something good from the raw materials."

"Like you did in prison?"

"Definitely."

The conversations they had over the next couple of days filled in a lot of the gaps. Helen began to understand the journey Owen had undertaken. When she considered their relationship as children, full of favouritism and jealousy, and compared it to now, where there was mutual respect and affection, she thought how much they had both grown up.

"I'm going to miss you," she declared on the Monday morning, when Owen was about to leave.

"I'm going to miss you too. I'll phone. Will you come down to Kent soon?"

"Hopefully. I shall look forward to seeing your new motorbike when you get it."

"Ah yes. I shall look in the paper next week and keep looking until I find the right one at the right price. Nothing too large. Happy with 100cc or 125cc for now."

"Did I tell you I had a motorbike? Yamaha RS100. Actually, I had a Honda SS50 from working on the farm, the summer you left. Then, the following year, I sold it, and after working on the farm again, I bought the Yamaha. It was great for riding to school and avoiding the buses. After I went to university, I didn't get a chance to ride it, and I sold it. Just like you are now, I then had to borrow Mummy's moped, which I always swore I wouldn't be seen dead on!"

"It's true, it doesn't pack much style, but it gets me from A to B."

"Anyway, you'd better be going. Do you want a lift into the city centre, to the Broadmarsh?"

"If you would, it would be much appreciated. Originally, I was thinking of hitching, but the coach is a better bet today."

Helen grabbed her keys, Owen threw his rucksack in the back of the Mini, and they drove into the city centre. Helen got out, just to hug Owen.

"Look after the two of you. I mean you and the bump!"

"I will. Bye."

"Bye."

Helen drove off and Owen went to get a National Express ticket.

All through the journey to London, Owen was thinking about Teresa, wondering if, maybe, he should get her a little post-Christmas present. He decided to buy something in Victoria, before catching the train to Maidstone. Halfway down the M1, the coach pulled into some services. Owen went to the toilet and popped into the shop. There were some keyrings hanging on a display stand, each one someone's name in the form of a tiny number plate. Of all the things he could buy for her, whether edible, or jewellery or a scented candle, he was not yet sure what her tastes were. He was not even sure if she used a keyring, but she had a maisonette and a car, so, presumably, she had some kind of keyring. He bought a 'TERESA' keyring for her. There was now no need to go shopping in Victoria. He made his way to the counter, paid, and returned to the coach. Ten minutes later, they were on their way, again.

There was a bit of a hike from the coach station to the train station, but it was a lot easier without carrying a framed print. His rucksack now contained Helen's presents for Gail and Ben, so weighed the same as his journey to Nottingham. At the station, he bought a ticket for Maidstone East and found he had about twenty-five minutes to wait for the train. Outgoing passengers were not allowed onto the platform until the incoming passengers were through the ticket barrier, and the incoming train had not yet pulled into the station. Owen went to a kiosk and bought a coffee and a Mars bar. As he stood snacking, he remembered how nervous he had felt, the last time he made this journey. There would be no need to take a taxi, either, as this time, there was no danger of missing the last bus to Leeds. Eventually, he saw signs of movement onto the platform, so he approached the ticket barrier.

The train was half empty, and Owen sat in a vacant double seat, facing the way the train was going. Just as the platform started to pass by the window, a man about Owen's age, claimed the seat opposite. He looked vaguely familiar, but Owen could not place him. Owen was not sure he had ever known more than half a dozen African-Caribbean males, so he reflected on the last twenty years. While Owen was trying to place him, in the recesses of his memory, the man spoke. Owen was struck by the lack of Caribbean lilt to his accent, and similar to Owen, there was little hint of any regional accent.

"Excuse me for asking, but did you ever visit Osea Island?"

"Jake Albright?"

"Owen Linton-House?"

"What are you doing on a train out of Victoria, heading for Ashford?"

"I graduated in medicine, from Cambridge University and now I am a doctor in Bromley Hospital. I've just been to see my parents."

"How are they? Well, I trust."

"My dad retired last year, and my mum is nearly retired. She still works part time."

"Is she still a nurse?"

"She is. How are you? How's Helen? And your parents?"

"Well, I've recently come back to the UK, after ten years travelling and working abroad. Helen is married and lives in Nottingham. She's expecting her first, in June. My parents are much the same as they were, just twenty years older. They live in Leeds, the village near Maidstone, not the city in Yorkshire. I'm living with them for the moment. Are you married?"

"Goodness me, no! Still paying the field. You?"

"I've met someone who could be the one."

"I'm glad Helen is happy."

"She's not. I mean, her marriage is difficult. Her husband gets drunk and puts her down. I worry about her. I've visited her twice since I got back. I'm on my way home from Nottingham, now."

"Tell her Jake says 'Hi', next time you speak to her. "I know I treated her badly, but my hormones got the better of me. She was still a child, and I was realising what girls were all about. She deserves someone who'll treat her right."

"I'll tell her you said that."

"Have you been back to Osea Island since our weird holiday?"

"No. We had several holidays in Snowdonia, until my grandfather died in 1977 and my grandmother moved down to Marden, to be near us. She died in 1988, I think. I wasn't around. Do you still have the Mirror dinghy?"

"No. I do have a sailing boat, but not the Mirror dinghy. That only lasted about four years."

"Do you still play cricket?"

"When I have time. I go to the Oval and Lords, when I can, if the West Indies are playing. My stop is just coming up."

"Small world. Really nice to catch up. Give my regards to your parents."

"I will," replied Jake, getting up. "Take care."

"You, too."

Owen could not believe how small the world was, after his lift up the M1 with Helen 'vox minima' and now meeting Jake. He made a mental note to ask his mother if he could look at some photos of his grandparents. Without a book to read or a crossword to attempt, there was little to do other than watch the landscape rushing past. Closing his eyes would be a bad idea, as he would probably fall asleep and miss his stop. A couple of teenage girls got on at Swanley and giggled their way to Otford, sitting opposite Owen. They were trying to apply nail varnish, but every so often, the carriage jolted. The seats opposite then remained empty as far as West Malling. Owen had forgotten the train passed by his workplace. A middle-aged man in a suit sat down and opened his newspaper. Owen skimmed the headlines on the front page and the sports news on the back page. It served to remind him that he needed to buy a copy of the Kent Messenger when he got off the train. He was pretty sure there was a newsagent not far along Week Street. Owen got his rucksack down from the luggage rack, wriggled the straps onto his shoulders and went and stood by the door as the train slowed to a halt.

Just as he had surmised, there was a newsagent in Week Street. He bought the newspaper along with a packet of cheese and onion crisps, as he was still feeling rather peckish. In King Street, he waited at the bus stop eating them and finished the entire packet before the bus arrived. Once in his seat, he opened the Kent Messenger at the classifieds and scanned down the adverts to see what motorbikes were for sale, and immediately regretted it, because reading on a moving bus was a recipe for nausea. It would just have to wait until he got home.

Owen got off at the Ten Bells and walked the short distance to Farmer Close. Gail was getting in the washing.

"Hello. Did you have a nice time?"

"I did thank you. Helen sends hugs and your presents. You'll never guess who I bumped into on the train from London."

"Then you'd better tell me."

"Jake Albright. He's a doctor, now. He says, 'Hello'. Raymond has retired and Fay works part time, still as a nurse."

"Well, I never!"

Gail started to fold the laundry, ready to go in the airing cupboard. Owen took his rucksack up to his room, took out the presents and ran back downstairs.

"Here you are. Where's Daddy?"

"He went into Maidstone, on his moped."

"I've bought a paper. I tried reading on the bus. Bad idea. Would you like a cup of coffee?"

"Thank you."

Owen made two cups of coffee and went and sat on the settee to look through the classifieds. Two of the adverts looked promising.

"Can I use the phone, please?"

"You don't have to ask."

"Thanks."

He dialled the first number.

Hello. Are you advertising a Suzuki 125cc?"

"Yes."

"Can I come and have a look?"

"Can you come this afternoon?"

"Probably. Where are you?"

"Sutton Valence. If you come now, you'll just get to see it before it gets dark."

"I'm only in Leeds. What address?"

"3, S Bank."

"I'll see you shortly. The name's Owen House."

Owen put the receiver back.

"I think I've found a bike. It's only in Sutton Valence. They said I can go and look at it now. Can I use your moped, please?"

"Again, you don't have to ask."

"Thanks."

He put on his jacket and boots, stuffed his cheque book in the inside pocket, grabbed his new helmet and went to the shed. Having checked there was fuel in the tank, he rode the short journey to S Bank and knocked on the door. A man answered.

"Hi. I've come about the bike. Owen House."

"Yes. That was quick. Come through to the back."

Owen followed the man through the house, into the back yard. There was a motorbike, disguised as an elephant. The man removed the grey plastic cover, shaped by the two wing-mirrors, so Owen could look at the motorbike. Owen inspected it.

"I can't see any rust. How old is it?"

"Five years. I've had it from new. Getting too old for this, in all weathers."

"Can you start her up?"

"I can do better than that. Do you want to ride her up and down the street? You can wheel it out of the back gate."

He handed Owen the key and watched whilst Owen put on his helmet and kick-started the Suzuki, at the third attempt. With his feet touching the ground, Owen manoeuvred the bike through the gate and accelerated up the street. After what he thought was about half a mile, he turned and rode back. It sounded fine. Putting it back on its stand, Owen handed the key back to the man.

"I'll have it. Shall I give you a cheque. You give me the logbook until the cheque clears and then I'll come back and fetch the bike?"

"Perfect. And I'll even throw in the cover."

Owen got out his cheque book and wrote the sum, concentrating as he put in the figures, and signed it.

"Who do I make it payable to?"

"Anthony Pyke."

"A-N-T-H-O-N-Y and Pyke with a 'Y'?"

"Yes."

"There you go," said Owen, tearing out the cheque and giving it to Pyke.

Pyke rummaged in one of the kitchen drawers and took out the logbook.

"I'll see you in three days."

"It's New Year. Better leave it four days, because the banks are closed."

"Good point. Why don't you call me before you come?"

"I will. Thanks," replied Owen, folding the logbook and putting it in his inside jacket pocket, with the cheque book.

Pyke let Owen out of the front door.

"Bye."

"Cheers."

As Owen rode back home, he was excited for his new purchase. However, he also knew that his mother would worry, like she worried when he had his Honda. He locked the moped in the shed and went into the house.

"How did it go?" asked Gail.

"I bought it. I have the logbook and the seller is waiting for the cheque to clear. In four days, because of New Year, I'll phone up and see if I can go and fetch it. It's in great condition."

"Well done."

"Where will you keep it. I'm afraid there isn't room in the shed for three bikes."

"It's OK. The man is letting me have the cover it's been sitting under in his back garden. I'll get a nice stout chain and padlock and it can sit in the corner, under the sitting room window. If anyone tries to steal it, I'll hear, because it's right under my window."

Ben walked into the living room.

"Did you buy it?"

"Yes. I should be able to pick it up after the New Year. I have the logbook. He has the cheque."

"What is it?"

"Suzuki 125cc. Five years old. Six thousand miles. Couldn't see any rust. he let me take it for a spin."

"How will you get there, to pick it up?"

"Well, I can walk. It's not that far to Sutton Valence. Or I can get a taxi or go into Maidstone and out again on the bus."

"Shame the mopeds don't have pillion seats."

On New Year's Eve, Owen wrapped the keyring, put clean underwear, a shirt, his deodorant, and his toothbrush in his knapsack and checked his wallet for some protection. Realising that he had forgotten to buy a bottle of wine he knew he would have to stop off in town first.

"I'll try and phone at midnight, always assuming I'm still awake."

"Always assuming we're still awake! Enjoy yourself."

"Thanks."

He borrowed Gail's moped, as usual, probably for the penultimate time as he would need it for his first day back at work. Hopefully, he would then be the proud owner of a Suzuki 125cc motorbike.

He parked the moped outside an off-licence and bought a bottle of wine. That was when Owen remembered he was meant to be doing the cooking. The off-licence did not sell groceries. He needed to find a convenience store that was open, or even a garage with a grocery section. He had about twenty minutes to solve his problem, before he would be embarrassingly late. Luckily, there was a garage just along the road from Teresa's house, with a mini supermarket attached. He bought steak, frozen peas and chips, and posh ice cream. Hopefully, she was not expecting a gourmet meal. With his purchases in hand, he arrived a polite five minutes late.

As he rang the doorbell and waited, he wondered, nervously, if he should kiss her. She opened the door.

"Happy New Year, almost," Teresa greeted him.

He leant forward and kissed her. She responded.

"Happy belated Christmas, again. I have a tiny little gift for you, which I hope you'll like, but first, let's get these things in the fridge and freezer."

"Ooooh. I'm intrigued. Both about the gift and what we have to eat."

"Well, the food is nothing out of the ordinary. Steak, chips and peas and posh ice-cream."

"Works for me. I'm hungry."

Owen put the chips, peas and ice cream in the freezer, and the steak in the fridge, along with the bottle of white wine, which probably should have been red.

"There you are. Just a little something that made me smile. I hope you like it."

Teresa unwrapped the keyring and started laughing.

"What's so funny?"

She went to her coat and pulled a bunch of keys out of the pocket. They were attached to a mini 'Teresa' number plate keyring.

"My grandma bought me the keyring for Christmas. I like your gift very much. Now I have two of them!"

Owen saw the funny side and started laughing too. He started on the meal. The chips would take about twenty minutes, so he put them in the oven and started to fry off the steak. When one side was done, he put the peas on to boil.

"Medium rare?"

"Medium not rare."

The peas boiled over, and Owen started to get flustered.

"It'll clean up. Shall I pour the wine?"

"Good plan. Do you have salt, pepper and ketchup on the table?"

"Yes."

The chips were ready, so Owen plated them up, along with the peas, leaving the steak until last. He carried both plates to the table.

"Bon appetit."

"Steak and chips is my go to meal when I eat out. You can't go wrong," declared Owen.

"I really like steak and chips, but I never think of cooking it for myself. This is lovely."

"Are we staying up to see the New Year in?"

"I hope so. Can I phone my parents and sister, at midnight?"

"As soon as I've called mine," laughed Teresa.

"Fair point."

They finished their steak and Owen served the ice cream.

"I could definitely handle seconds of this," remarked Teresa.

"I agree. I'll get the rest out of the freezer."

Owen went to the kitchen and Teresa topped up their glasses.

"Thank you. That was great," said Teresa, at the end of the meal. "Apart from the dishes, how would you like to spend the rest of the evening. We can watch a video, play a board game, make love or just chill and chat."

"I think you know how I'm programmed to respond to those choices," laughed Owen.

"I do, but I figured we might be too tired and too drunk if we wait until after midnight."

"How about we leave the dishes until afterwards," suggested Owen, hopefully. "Come and sit with me."

He plonked himself down on the settee and gestured to Teresa.

"Are we an item? Are we officially dating, now?" he asked.

"Like we couldn't do all this and not be official?"

The answer was a little disconcerting. Owen had not anticipated such independence, even after Sofia.

"Well, I suppose if you put it like that, no reason at all. That is, except I would quite like to be your boyfriend."

"As in, you'd quite like me to be your girlfriend. To own me."

Now Owen was even more confused.

"Don't you agree with exclusive relationships?" he asked.

"Of course, I do. Just not ones where one party feels it has ownership of the other."

"Well, I wouldn't own you. In truth, you've already taken custody of my heart."

"What if I don't want that burden of responsibility? What if I don't want to hold your heart prisoner?"

"I thought that's what women secretly longed for. To hold their man captive."

"Not this woman. Two people in a relationship should bring freedom to both parties. A freedom which confounds mathematical logic, building a new mutual partnership, where one plus one equals one. That may entail freedom to choose exclusivity. Freedom to say 'No' to others. But it's a free choice, not a confining label."

"So, would you like to be free to fail arithmetic with me?"

"Now you come to put it like that, I think I would."

"Phew!"

They both fell about laughing and ended up in a bout of tickle wrestling. When they were both too weak from laughing and being tickled, Owen started to kiss Teresa's face and neck, undoing her shirt buttons, and continuing the kissing odyssey south, all the way to her abdomen. He pulled off his own shirt and they spent a while in a fleshy embrace. It was Teresa who started to undo his belt and flies, first, feeling in his back pocket and pulling out the condom. She flipped him over onto his back, tore off the wrapper and applied the protection, and removing her own jeans and briefs together, sat astride him and took control of the encounter. Owen did not mind, but just lay there and enjoyed it, even allowing her to bring them both to a climax simultaneously. In that moment, he realised that if they were going to be together, he would have to get used to her self-confident ways. The more he thought about it, the more he felt comfortable with an emotional attachment that was not based on need, but on mutual development.

Having spent half an hour lying together, Teresa got up and went to the bathroom. Removing the protection, Owen got dressed, wrapped it in some kitchen roll and threw it in the bin. He was already washing up when a fully clothed Teresa resurfaced from the bathroom. She grabbed the tea towel.

"Thank you," he said, uncertain even now if that was the right thing to say.

"Thank you. We're going to be good together."

Finally, he regained a sense of confidence and certainty. There was still two hours and fifty minutes until New Year.

"What videos do you have?"

"*Dances with Wolves, Pretty Woman, The Hunt for Red October*."

"*Dances with Wolves* is too long, but I'd love to watch it another time. I'm thinking *The Hunt for Red October* has something to do with the Soviet Union?"

"Russian nuclear sub."

"Let's watch that."

"Not *Pretty Woman*," Teresa baited him.

"Surprised you even own it. Ownership and all that."

"What are you on about? It's precisely about him not treating her as a prostitute."

"Until he does."

"That's the problem with labels. *The Hunt for Red October* it is, then."

Teresa put the video in, and they snuggled up on the sofa.

"Wait. Do you want a vodka, before we start watching?"

"Please."

"She jumped up and poured two vodka and oranges and sat back on the sofa."

"I think Sean Connery has got better as an actor, since he played James Bond."

"I agree."

"That was great," reflected Owen, at the end of the film. "We've got about half an hour."

"Let's just sit and chill. I'll fill our glasses."

Teresa refilled their vodka and orange and came and sat back on the settee.

"I forgot to tell you. I bought a motorbike."

"What!"

"I have paid for a Suzuki 125cc and I have the logbook, but the cheque needs to clear before I can pick it up. It's been great borrowing my mother's moped, but the motorbike has more style. And a lot more speed."

"Well, watch out for the other idiots on the road, is all I can say."

"I will do my best."

"Have you considered having driving lessons and getting a car?"

"Yes, but I can't afford it at the moment."

"Fair point."

Teresa was fighting to stay awake.

"Come on, you. Don't fall asleep now."

Owen started kissing her and paused to add, "I'm just keeping you awake."

At two minutes to midnight. Teresa switched on the television to tune into Big Ben. They counted together.

"Ten, nine, eight, seven, six, five, four, three, two, one, Happy New Year!"

They kissed and Teresa got up to go to the phone. She quickly wished her parents and grandma 'Happy New Year' whilst Owen nipped to the toilet. When he came out, he phoned Ben and Gail, followed by Helen. It was all done and dusted by ten past midnight.

"Can we go to bed now?" asked a sleepy Teresa.

"Let's."

They fell asleep in each other's arms.

It was the middle of March and Teresa and Owen were spending most of their Saturday nights together now. They tended to stay in. On the Friday evenings they would both go along to The Ship to meet with colleagues and friends. They never actually got round to telling people they were together because Teresa did not feel it was necessary. Owen had his motorbike and generally went home on Sunday mornings to spend time with his parents and sort himself out for work on Monday mornings.

"I hear your wasp, pretty much as you come through Langley," announced Gail over Sunday lunch.

"My wasp? It's true, it has quite a high-pitched engine. I should get the tank sprayed yellow and black!"

It was Gail's way of coping with the worry. Once she heard the motorbike pull into the car park, behind the house, she could sleep.

"Have you met Teresa's parents yet? Are we going to meet her soon?"

"Soon enough. Teresa doesn't feel we need to be officially labelled. I'm sure you'll get to meet her in due course. Maybe I can persuade her to come round when Helen is here. She's coming next week, isn't she?"

"Yes."

"They've probably got a lot in common, with Helen's job and Teresa being a trainee social worker."

"It's probably the last time Helen will make it down here, before the baby is born."

"When's it due?"

"10th June, I think."

A few days later, on the Saturday evening, when Teresa and Owen were watching a video at her place, he broached the subject.

"I know you don't like the idea of labelling or being officially together, but my sister is staying next weekend, and I was wondering if you'd like to come and meet her, and my parents, at the same time."

"Of course."

Owen was surprised by the decisively positive response.

"Great. Come for Sunday lunch, before Helen heads back to Nottingham."

"Or we could forego our Saturday evening and I could come for a meal on the Saturday evening. We can skip spending the night together one time. It's not like you get to see that much of Helen."

"Deal. I'll mention to my mum that we need an extra place at the table."

So it was, the following weekend, that Helen met Teresa. They made an instant connection and spent the meal comparing case studies and ended by critiquing Tory politics, particularly Thatcherism, which had not disappeared even after the Iron Lady resigned.

"Like a lot or rural communities, even with a town the size of Maidstone, the constituency is never going to return a Labour MP, or a green one. The most we can hope for is a Liberal Democrat."

"They say that you should never talk about religion or politics," interjected Ben.

"Sorry," responded Helen. "We got a little carried away."

"Yes. Apologies," added Teresa.

"I can see that you are both passionate about your jobs and about social justice," contributed Gail, trying to be encouraging.

In reality, Gail was an educational snob, and Helen had never understood why her parents always voted Conservative, when they had no money, no assets, and no business potential. Her parents still had no idea of the pressure they put Owen under and why he left home. It was not that Helen was not grateful to have gone to university, albeit fully funded on a full maintenance grant. She had appreciated the impact of the compromise between local authority and central government, when she was at school, which allowed all pupils in state schools around Maidstone to be continually assessed over two years and move to the grammar or technical schools at thirteen, rather than have to face the pressure of taking an 11+ exam, which would shape a child's life and prospects forever. Owen had taken an entrance exam at the age of nine. Helen did not feel confident that she would have passed her 11+ exam. For Teresa, changing the life chances of children from disadvantaged backgrounds was her reason for going to work. With Helen, it was offering a second chance to adults whose circumstances and social backgrounds had had a negative influence over their education and employment.

Owen listened but remained silent on the subject. He could have ended up in a similar place to Dominic Andrews, Andrews through education and connections and Owen through taking his chances out in the field. It was true that he had learnt French and Russian at school, and it was unlikely he would have had the opportunity to learn Russian in a state school, but his other languages had been learnt from cassettes or from living in various countries. If he was being honest, most of his opportunities came more through luck than judgement. That said, he had no idea what he really wanted to do with his life. Unlike Teresa and Helen, he did not have a passion, a driving force. Maybe he was just more laid-back than Helen? His only ever ambition had been to fly jet planes, and that had been cruelly snatched from him. Now all he wanted was to settle down, have a family and be in a comfortable and challenging enough job to support them, not that Teresa would want to stay at home. Was Teresa the one he wanted to settle down with?

Owen was growing increasingly certain that he wanted to settle down with Teresa, but he was unclear in his head, how to broach the subject. He did not want her to feel tied down, labelled, owned, and her response to a proposal of marriage might be negative. He would happily have moved in with her on a permanent basis, but he did not want to have children and not be married. Her birthday was on 3rd June, and he resolved to ask her, when he took her for a meal.

The weekend before Teresa's birthday, as usual, they joined their friends in The Ship on the Friday evening. One of those friends, Jason, was celebrating his thirtieth, and lots of rounds were purchased. By the time Owen kissed Teresa goodnight and got on his Suzuki, he had probably had too much alcohol to ride home safely. In hindsight, the better option would have been to have ridden to Teresa's, left the motorbike there, walked to the pub and stayed over at hers, afterwards, even though it was a Friday. But he had not done the sensible thing. He was feeling in control, so he got on his motorbike and set off for home. As he rode along the Sutton Road, the alcohol in his system started to take effect. By the time he reached Langley Heath he was feeling a little fuzzy. That was when he mis-judged a bend in the lane and rode at thirty-five miles an hour into a gate post.

As was her regular custom on a Friday evening, Gail was lying in bed listening out for the wasp. Owen was probably about three miles from home, when she picked up the high-pitched buzz of his motorbike engine. A couple of minutes later, it all went silent, but she could not hear the gate open or the jangle of the chain, which no matter how careful he was, Owen never managed to keep quiet. She must have been mistaken. It was probably some other motorbike, with some other mother waiting at home worrying.

Forty minutes later the doorbell rang. Gail had fallen asleep, in the hope that Owen had stayed over at Teresa's house. She woke with a start, and her heart was racing as she threw on her dressing gown and descended the staircase. Through the crown-glass panes of the front door, she could make out the form of a policeman, and froze. She had to force herself to remove the chain and release the snib, opening the door to the officer.

"Mrs Linton-House? I'm really sorry to trouble you at this time. May I come in please?"

"Yes," she mumbled, opening the door wide enough for him to enter and pointing towards the living room.

"Is Mr Linton-House here? I'm afraid I have some bad news."

"Fearing the worst, Gail went upstairs and woke Ben.

"You need to come downstairs. There's a policeman here. I think it's the worst kind of news."

Ben grunted in acknowledgement, heaved himself out of bed, pulled his dressing-gown on over his pyjamas and followed Gail downstairs. They both sat on the settee. The policeman had sat himself down in the armchair.

"I am so, so sorry to have to tell you this, but we believe your son has had a fatal motorcycle accident in Langley Heath."

Stunned silence.

"The ambulance is still at the scene. Would you be able to come with me to identify the fatality? I wouldn't normally ask, but given the distance and the time, it seems to be appropriate. I can take you in my car."

"Can you give us a moment to put some clothes on?" asked a numb Gail.

"Of course."

Due to his health issues, Ben was used to wearing day-clothes over his pyjamas, so he pulled trousers and jumper on over the top and got his coat. Gail changed out of her pyjamas into trousers and jumper. They sat together on the settee, putting on socks and shoes. Nothing was said. Gail only just remembered to grab her keys before following the policeman out of the front door and along the pavement to where his car was parked.

After a short drive they pulled up in front of a mangled Suzuki and a brick gate post, the top half of which was leaning at an angle. The ambulance was a few yards along the road, with its blue light still flashing.

"He's in the ambulance."

The two paramedics were standing by the rear of the vehicle. One of them opened the door.

"This way, please."

Ben looked at Gail.

"I'll do it," insisted Gail.

Ben nodded. Gail stepped up into the ambulance where the paramedic lowered the blanket to reveal Owen's face. He looked completely at peace. Gail nodded.

"I am truly sorry, Mrs Linton-House," responded the paramedic.

Gail held onto the door as she climbed back down to the pavement, her legs jellified. Ben caught her eye and did something he had rarely done in over thirty years of marriage, which was to place his arms round Gail.

"It's him," stuttered Gail. "He looks so peaceful."

"My condolences," offered the second paramedic, who had remained outside the ambulance. "We are pretty sure that he died instantly. He wouldn't have known what was happening and he wouldn't have suffered."

"Thank you," replied Ben, leading Gail back to the car.

"We'll wait until morning to call Helen," proposed Gail.

"Agreed."

"There will be an inquest and we will keep you fully informed," explained the police officer. "Again, I am so, so sorry."

"If there is anything that it's not too late to donate, please will you use it," added Gail, looking over to the paramedics.

"Thank you," said the one who had been with Gail in the ambulance.

The paramedics got into the ambulance, and it sped off to the hospital. The policeman drove Gail and Ben back home.

"Is there anything I can do? Anything you need, right now?"

"No. Thank you. And please will you get rid of the motorbike," requested Ben.

"We will. Take care. I will speak with you again, soon."

"Goodnight," replied Gail.

After a few sleepless hours, Gail rang Helen, shortly after eight.

"Sit down."

Helen did not argue, but she knew, in her stomach, that something was wrong. She sat down.

"Owen crashed his motorcycle last night and died."

Helen was stunned.

"He was on his way home. He hit a gate post. The police came here and asked if we could go and identify him, at the scene, as it was only a mile up the road. The ambulanceman said he would have died instantly. There was no other vehicle involved."

"But he only came home a year ago."

"I know. There will have to be an inquest, so we won't be able to plan a funeral."

"Oh. OK."

"Please look after yourself. You are so close to giving birth. I'm worried about the impact of this news on your health and on the health of the baby."

"I'll be fine, Mummy."

"Bye."

And she was fine. After the initial shock and lots of crying, Helen set her focus on the birth of her child. When Emily was born, Helen was so in love with her, so taken up with being a new mother, that she never got round to processing her grief. Not, that is, until about six years later, at the funeral of a man she hardly knew, attending out of respect. That was when the flood gates opened, and the sight of the coffin brought out an entirely disproportionate response, because Helen imagined Owen, lying inside it.

Emily grew up never knowing her uncle. Helen had taken a photo of Owen, in the garden, the last weekend she saw him. He was amongst the framed family photos on the wall of Helen's home in Nottingham for twenty odd years, and she had introduced him to her daughter, when Emily was old enough to ask who the man in the photograph was. The framed print of *Rain, Steam and Speed* had been damaged by Finn, in a drunken rage.

As Helen sat in her house in Marrognac, having just written the last sentence in her novel about Owen, which turned out to be a wonderfully cathartic process of any latent residue of grief, she went to the cupboard and took out a jigsaw puzzle she had asked for, for this year's birthday. During the recent COVID pandemic, Helen had developed a taste for fine art jigsaws, of paintings by some of her favourite painters. She sat at the table and started to sort out the edge pieces for a jigsaw of Turner's famous painting, of her favourite painting, and Owen's too.